MW01616893

HUNTED

THE FERAL SOULS TRILOGY - BOOK 1

ERICA WOODS

Copyright © 2019 by Erica Woods

All rights reserved.

No part of this book may be reproduced in any form or by any electronic or mechanical means, including information storage and retrieval systems, without written permission from the author, except for the use of brief quotations in a book review.

This is a work of fiction. Names, characters, places, and incidents either are the products of the author's imagination or are used fictitiously. Any resemblance to actual persons, living or dead, businesses, companies, events, or locales is entirely coincidental.

Ebook ISBN: 978-82-93735-00-7

For all the lost souls out there, and for those brave enough, decent enough, and strong enough to find them.

HOPE

"Is she dead?" Gregory poked a finger through the hole in my aching side and waited for a reaction.

I gave none.

A familiar, sticky substance coated my skin in grimy layers of dark red, the puddles of blood on the floor barely distinguishable against the muted black.

I was weak. So very weak.

Blood loss and pain threatened to send me slinking into sweet oblivion, but if I wanted to escape this hellhole, I needed to stay awake.

Two fingers touched the base of my throat. Rather than flinch away in disgust, I remained still and hid behind the deep shadows in my mind.

"No pulse. She isn't breathing," Silva said. "Guess we finally did her in."

A beat of silence, then, "Let's just make sure, shall we?"

Something sharp and cold parted my skin and buried deep. If the monster sharing my body had not been shielding me, I would have screamed from the agony piercing my belly.

"Dead," Gregory pronounced. "You're lucky this didn't happen sooner or the boss would've had your hide."

Red spots danced behind my closed eyelids.

Silva snorted. "Luck had nothing to do with it. I've wanted to get rid of this bitch for years."

My lungs burned with the scream I refused to let loose, and my mind began to fracture with the agony I was forced to suppress.

They had to think I was dead. They had to. If Matthew had taught me anything, it was that only the dead left the Hunters' compound.

"When did you get permission to kill her?"

The burn in my stomach intensified. A thousand teeth were surely ripping me apart from the inside out.

"I didn't," Silva admitted. "Not exactly. Though they said to do whatever it took to—"

Just as I was about to lose my grip on the scream building in my throat, shadows danced across my mind and the monster that had once ruined my life came to my rescue.

The next minute passed in blissful peace. The cold seeping through my body stole the pain, and in the back of my mind I knew it was bad. Very bad. I hovered on the brink of unconsciousness, so near death I no longer needed the monster's help to shield my heartbeat or halt my breaths.

A small eternity passed while I drifted. Then, the sound of receding footsteps. When the heavy steel door grated against cement floors, the thought that I was alone whispered across my mind.

At first, I didn't react. The cold embrace of death seemed so sweet, so peaceful, I didn't dare leave it. But . . . I wasn't ready to die. Not yet. Not while there was still hope.

"If you are ever in trouble and I'm not around, go find your uncle Gavril. Gavril Sânrigla."

"But Daddy, I have you!"

My father tickled my five-year old ribs, making me giggle despite the sadness I saw shining in eyes so like my own. "I know, pumpkin. But someday I might not be here and you may need help. I know you've never met him, but he'll help you. He'll have to." The last part whispered beneath his breath, and when he tipped my face up, grief ravaged his expression. "He lives in Ontario, in Canada. Ask around for the family Sânrigla. They'll find you . . ."

The comforting voice of my father slipped away, and my eyes shot open.

That first breath was glass shredding my lungs. Though my eyes were no longer closed, I saw only darkness, the black pit of death hovering just out of reach. But then the flickering lights overhead came into focus and I became aware. Aware of pain.

I hurt. Dear god, how I hurt.

Lifting my neck took strength I didn't know I still had, and what I saw had me stifle a gasp. The ugly lamp hanging from the metal hook in the ceiling bathed my wounds in a grotesque light, giving the dark blood coating my skin a shiny quality I immediately hated.

Don't have long . . .

A groan rasped past my parched throat, my lips cracked and bleeding. Yet a swipe of my tongue was enough to close the most painful cuts, and I had to swallow back the hatred for the shadowed being in my soul as gratitude temporarily surfaced.

My monster may have put me in this predicament, but I would not be alive without it.

I clenched my fist and tested the bonds keeping me prisoner. Each movement was torture. Wounds reopened, bled, ached with the fiery inferno of hell. Air hissed through my clenched teeth, and I kept going. Who knew how long I'd have before the cleanup crew arrived?

The thought of being caught before I even made it off the

table had me thrashing against my restraints. No give, but the dull ache in my leg told me the bone in my shin had set sometime in the last few minutes and was nearly healed.

I heaved once more, used all my strength—

The bindings gave.

Shocked, it took me several precious seconds to lower my feet to the cold cement floor. A part of me couldn't believe my plan had worked. They'd never left me unsupervised before. Never.

I rose and choked on a sob. My stomach . . . it was being ripped apart. Ripped apart by fire. Only acid could burn like this.

I looked down, but there was no burning flesh, no withering skin eaten away by corrosive liquid. No, the reason for my pain was the knife still buried in my stomach.

Not giving myself time to think about it, I yanked the knife out and fell to my knees. A low, keening sound was stifled by the palm I pressed against my mouth. Despite the danger, it took me several breaths before I could quell the pained noise.

By then, the edges of the wound had begun knitting together and pain gave way to the staccato drum pounding in my ears. *Run*, its rhythm seemed to say. *Flee!*

I got to my feet and crept to the door, pressing my ear against the cold steel like the idiot I was. Soundproof—I'd forgotten. No self-respecting Hunter wanted to listen to the screams tearing through this room day after day.

I'd have to open the door without knowing if one of them waited on the other side.

I shuddered, my hand hovering over the handle.

A year ago, none of this would have been possible. The Hunters had never allowed me to get this close to death before. Torture, yes. Horrifying experiments, yes. But not death. Not until a few months ago.

Something had changed. There'd been a new desperation

in their quest to break me, to force the monster to the surface. Either my continued refusal had frayed their temper, or they'd simply decided I was no longer worth the effort. Whatever their reason, it had taken another death—Matthew's death—on my conscience before a plan took shape in my guilt-riddled brain. No prisoner left the compound alive, but no one cared about the dead.

With the image of Matthew's bloody and beaten face seared into my mind, I wrenched the door open before I could reconsider.

Empty.

I almost sagged to my knees in relief.

The unforgiving, rough stairs that had scraped the skin off my bones on more occasions than I could count, rose before me.

I took a step. And then another. Chills traveled up my spine, a cold hand squeezed my heart and whipped it into a gallop. Each step defied the Hunters. Each step increased the punishment I'd receive if I were caught.

A part of me, a small, shameful part, wanted to run back downstairs, strap myself to the table, and lie there until someone came back. If I was caught trying to escape again . . .

Ugly memories assaulted me. My skin crawled and my stomach threatened to heave.

But I didn't have time to be sick.

When I came to the top of the stairs, my whole body shook. Two doors separated me from freedom. The first—the one looming before me—opened up to a narrow hall that snaked down dim corridors and eventually led back to my cell. The second lay just beyond this one. It occupied the right wall just a few feet into the hall, and the prisoners knew it well.

We were marched past that door every time we were brought down to the torture room. Always unlocked, it led right outside, the path to freedom so close we could almost taste the wind. The Hunters used it as yet another form of cruel torment, taunting us with knowledge that if only we were brave enough, strong enough, we could get a few lung-fuls of fresh air before we were caught and punished—or killed—for our temerity.

The pounding of my heart seemed to echo off the concrete walls as the beat in my ears grew to unbearable levels. With a trembling hand, I opened the first door and prepared to run.

No voices rose in a cacophony of threats or commands to stop. No Hunters aimed weapons my way. The last door was right there—narrow and metallic, an unarmed, unlocked obstacle standing only a short sprint away.

I ran.

The first touch of the sun after eighteen years underground was not at all how I'd imagined. The rays were not soft and gentle on my face, nor did they disperse the chill in my bones. No peace flooded my system, no hope bloomed in my chest. Rather, it blinded me, the harsh glare forcing me to stop, to wait until my eyes adjusted to the relentless brightness.

The sun . . . the thing I'd dreamed of seeing all these years was jeopardizing everything. The escape almost within reach, the freedom I could feel in the breeze whipping my dirty, blood-streaked hair around my face, and the life I'd clung to with such quiet fervor I wondered if the Hunters hadn't managed to break me after all.

I lifted my hand to block the sharp rays burning my corneas and tried to control my growing terror.

Have to move. Have to run.

Despite the pain wracking my body and the fear souring

each breath until the very air itself tasted of poison, I had to take a second to appreciate the severe beauty of the outside world. Brighter than I remembered, the blue skies worked with the sun to create the harsh light that felt so unfamiliar to my sensitive eyes. The colors they created made little sense, overwhelming to someone who'd lived countless years in a sterile, mostly gray environment. The bright blue of the wide-open sky, the soft green of trees rustling in the wind, of grass swaying with each caress of the soft breeze, even the mottled browns of plants in their dying stages were a shock to my system.

I stood there, staring, unable to tear my gaze away from everything I'd been missing, everything I'd never thought to see again. Until the blaring screech of the Hunters' alarm rang through the air and terror once more flooded every cell of my exhausted being. The terrible noise kick-started my hazy brain and reminded me what was at stake.

This was it. My one shot at freedom. If I got caught, I'd either die, or they'd break me.

For the first time in years, I willingly reached inside myself to the monster lurking there and asked for its strength.

It came, but slowly, reluctantly. And it hurt. A punishing, angry hurt that screamed of disuse and tasted of sullen disappointment.

Gritting my teeth, I let the power fill me and vaulted over the rail that separated the little balcony on the second floor from the free-fall on the other side.

I landed easily, my knees bending to bear the brunt of the fall. Bare feet dug into cool dirt, the sensation so unfamiliar, so *alien* I had to force myself to get up, to not bury my hands deep in the earth and marvel at the connection. Then the alarm gave off another unholy screech, and bile rose in my throat.

Run! a voice screamed in my head. *Run!*

The adrenaline flooding my body should have propelled me forward, but I was frozen in place. A huge, towering forest stretched out to my right, only a barbed wire fence standing between me and the false sense of safety found beneath the canopy of green. And to my left—past the Hunters' small cabins, the outhouses, and the larger, free-standing buildings I knew down to my bones housed terrors I couldn't hope to withstand—lay a dirt access road.

A memory from when I was six flashed through my mind. The scent of my mother's perfume. Her angry voice as she yelled into the phone. Me sitting stock-still in the backseat, trying to become invisible as I watched that same road roll past.

To my relief, the memory faded when I closed my eyes. The pain and guilt I still carried with me wherever I went would choke me if I lingered too long in the past.

Move!

I looked from the forest to the road. My best chance of survival lay past the Hunters, down the worn, dirt road.

Unless they caught me first.

Indecision warred inside me. How could I make this choice? I hadn't been allowed to decide what to wear or what to eat for over eighteen years, and now I was supposed to make a life or death decision with the alarm screaming in my ears, the sound a blaring reminder that time was running out.

A stuttering, half step forward brought me no closer to a decision.

Once more, I looked between the forest and the dirt road that sparked memories of the last time I'd seen my mother. Her disgust as she looked at me, the knowledge of what I was, what I'd *done*—

I shook my head, sorrow squeezing my chest so hard I almost collapsed. Blinking back tears, I took another faltering step before spotting a car driving down the narrow road. One of theirs.

The decision had been made for me; I'd be going through the woods.

I took off at a run, the barbed wire fence looming impossibly far. The stretch between the compound and that fence was one unending, open space. If one of the Hunters looked outside, they'd spot me in a heartbeat. That knowledge acted both as a heavy rock in my stomach and as a whip against my back, urging me to push harder, to run faster.

But my broken body was tired. So very tired.

A roar began in my ears; my tongue felt thick in my dry mouth. Each breath felt like razors in my chest, and still . . . still the fence stood farther away than the distance I'd already run.

Faster! Faster!

With a moan, I reached down and stirred the darkness in my soul. This time it answered with a roar. Power coursed through my worn body and lent speed to my shaky legs. The shackles binding the bane of my existence shook as I tried to control that dark force. Whatever it was, whatever cursed *gifts* it saw fit to lend me weren't enough. Not with my mental leash hobbling it, the shackles I'd kept in place for so many years draining its strength.

The alarm stopped, and for one blessed moment, the emotion I was named after—*hope*—soared through me. But only for a moment.

My name was a lie. Despair was the only constant in my life.

When the alarm resumed, it sounded louder, closer than before. It was followed by the terrifying noise of raised, male voices and the whirring of motors starting.

Too late!

With a scream of pain, I did the one thing I swore never to do again. I let the monster out of its cage.

Just a little farther, I told myself as I dragged my worn body over a fallen log, hissing at the pain shooting up my mangled leg with every step. The metallic scent of blood permeated the air. It made me nervous, even knowing it was my own.

Stepping on that *thing* had been a big mistake. Leaves and dirt had hidden the sharp metal teeth from my sight, the trap concealed until it snapped closed around the lower part of my calf.

The pain had been . . . agonizing. But I was used to pain, knew how to deal with it, how to keep existing despite being torn to pieces by inflamed nerve endings and agony so great it threatened my very sanity.

I'd survived it more times than I could count.

What I was not used to was making decisions, finding solutions to a crisis as it was happening. And being rooted in place by an evil-looking contraption while being hunted by men who'd make this pain seem like nothing . . . that was definitely a crisis.

If not for my monster's strength, I'd have been stuck there still.

Moving was slow and painful. My injured leg protested each step, and I stumbled over various rocks and the uneven forest floor, constantly aware of the silence around me, how loud my labored breaths seemed in contrast.

The Hunters had yet to find me. Maybe they thought I was still inside? Or maybe they'd taken the treacherous road, assuming I—

Boom!

A tree exploded right next to my head. I threw myself to the ground, a pained whimper dragging up my parched throat while sharp splinters of wood rained down. With my ears ringing and shivers of dread shooting up my back, I looked at the massive, gnarled tree above me.

Ruined.

The intricate trunk had been destroyed by cracks and huge chunks of missing wood, leaving a gaping wound in the center close to where my head had been.

They were trying to kill me.

Run!

The roar of angry voices rose from somewhere behind me, and my breath froze in my lungs.

Too close. They were too close.

A cold, hideous terror whispered through my mind. It locked my limbs, captured my mind in a taloned grip, and drove the weapon of despair straight through my soul. I couldn't move. I couldn't think. I could only lay there, bound by the weighted chains of fear.

The forest shook with the thunder of running feet. They were almost here.

Get up!

Forcing my body to cooperate, I staggered to my feet and reached deep inside for my resting monster. The path felt paved with tar, resisting, slow, and when I tried calling the beast, begging for its strength, I felt its reluctance, its exhaustion. But it answered the call, and I didn't know if I should be grateful or terrified.

My vision sharpened; the darkness that had come with dusk seemed to disappear. My body, exhausted from hours of running and bursts of adrenaline, filled with dormant power. It tasted of darkness. Of untamed wildness. And again, I knew despair.

How can you use the very thing that ruined your life?

A moment of crushing guilt, then the monster's influence kicked in. I felt it there, assessing my broken body, calculating the best path forward.

With my enhanced hearing, it was easy to determine where the Hunters were coming from. I veered right and set off at a steady limp. The monster numbed the crippling pain in my calf, but it couldn't heal it, couldn't make it work right. I hoped the disregard it was showing my body wouldn't cause permanent damage. The Hunters would never stop. They'd hunt me to the ends of the Earth for the rest of my life. And if I couldn't run . . . well, the rest of my life probably wouldn't be that long.

2

RUARC

I slammed my fist into the dashboard, ignoring Jason's startled yelp and Ash's heavy sigh. "Enough!" I snarled. It was an effort to calm my breathing. Angry growls vibrated in my throat, and damned if I didn't give a shit. The Council had pissed me off for the last time.

Ash shot me a look out the corner of his eye, hands still relaxed on the wheel, not a god damned care in the world. "They will come around," was all he said in the same flat tone he used when talking about the weather.

Damned unflappable male. Ash's ability to make even the biggest problems appear manageable was an asset I didn't appreciate. Not right then, anyway.

"I just love how Ruarc's accent gets thicker and thicker the angrier he gets," Jason said, voice filled with such obnoxious glee it was a wonder—and a shame—he didn't choke on it. "He will be tellin' ye laddies tae pack up yer sheep and—"

"Shut yer mouth," I roared, forcing my body to turn to face the cackling idiot in the back seat.

Swear the car has shrunk.

Half an hour ago, I'd somehow managed to fold my considerable mass into the front seat—after having dragged a pissed off Jason out of *my* seat and thrown him into the back —and now my long legs were cramping from the lack of space while my neck threatened to snap. I'd had to keep it bent the whole ride. Was half tempted to rip off the roof to get some space. It'd also have the added benefit of pissing off Ash, whose tin box we were currently in.

"Please lower your voices," Lucien said in that cool, disdainful tone that never failed to make me want to deck him.

"He speaks!" Jason winked, ignoring the snap of my teeth, and elbowed Lucien in the side. "I thought you lost the ability to chat *aboot* the same time they put that stick up your ass."

Typical Jason, insulting the cold, deadly male at his side while simultaneously making me see red. "Pup," I warned, speaking through gritted teeth and casting Ash a furious glare when his lip twitched—never mind that he quickly schooled his face back into its neutral mask. When I continued, I made sure to suppress my Scottish brogue, hating it almost as much as I hated the reason for its existence, "Want to keep use of those legs?"

Jason ignored me, not so much as a flicker of fear crossing that smug face, but he stopped antagonizing me.

Would never kill him, but he knew I didn't have the same qualms about some light maiming.

Lucien sighed. "If the two of you could stop behaving like children then perhaps we could discuss the issue at hand?"

Jason snorted. "The issue at hand? Which issue, pray tell? The madness we'll face at the upcoming Assembly? The Strays lurking at the borders of our territory? Or do you mean that this one"—the insolent pup used his thumb to point my way, tempting me to snap it off at the joint—"can't keep his temper in check long enough for Lucien to do what he does best and sniff out the information we'll need to—"

The car screeched as Ash hit the brakes.

A flash of pale skin, the glistening darkness that could only mean blood, and huge, startled eyes was all I saw before my head smashed into the side window.

"What the fuck?" I snapped.

Ash said nothing, attention drawn to something outside. I followed his gaze and saw a pair of the biggest, most soulful brown eyes I'd ever seen. Huge, guileless, and rounded with such terrible despair my stomach dropped. I tore my gaze away to take in the rest of the girl standing frozen in the middle of the road.

I did *not* like what I saw.

She was pale. Skin almost translucent, like she'd never seen the sun before, and thin. Sickly thin. The threadbare gray clothes she wore hung off her tiny frame, so worn in places they were almost see-through. And what they revealed . . .

Bruises. Cuts. Scabs.

My jaw clenched, a growl built in my throat.

"Bloody hell."

3

HOPE

I broke through the tree line and stumbled onto hard asphalt. Air sawed in and out of my lungs in ragged gasps, each inhale like swallowing living flames.

How long had I been running?

The sun had disappeared over the horizon at least an hour ago, but the Hunters had not given up. Despite my monster's speed, two more shots had been fired too close for comfort.

I bent at the waist—too tired to stand upright—and glanced around.

The road looked like any other, but with no lights to brighten the area and the moon a weak half-circle, the darkness took on a sinister appearance.

I wasn't safe out here. Everything was too open, too exposed. If not for the Hunters, I would have turned back and sought refuge in the woods.

A prickle of dread traveled up my spine. How close were they? Were they watching, even now? I stumbled forward.

Picking a random direction—anywhere but back—I forced my body into another jog, dragging one leg behind me like the useless, limp limb it had become when the monster had grown weary and receded.

A car had to pass by soon. Though what I'd do when that happened was anyone's guess. The best I could hope for was a place to spend the night, far away from this place and the Hunters on my trail.

They can't be far.

I hesitated, small rocks biting into the raw soles of my feet.

I needed a place to sleep. Just for a little while. And when I woke up, maybe I could try to make my way north. But even if I somehow got all the way to Canada without money, identification, and the Hunters killing me, how would I find my uncle?

Suddenly parched, I licked my dry lips. What if Gavril had left Canada? What if he didn't want to help me? What if he saw what I was and turned me away, just like my mother—

A soft, pained cry crawled up my throat. My vision grew cloudy.

I was free. *Free.* Then why did I feel as though I was trapped in a coffin about to be buried?

They're gonna find you, a voice taunted. *You have no one. Nothing. You're hurt. How long can you run? How long—*

I squeezed my eyes shut. Stumbled. My calf ached. My lips tingled. My hands shook.

Choking on a sob, I pushed everything away and carried on as quickly as my lame leg allowed.

Can't stop.

Small sips of air pushed past my tight throat.

They'll find me!

My leg dragged along the rough asphalt and pain shot up the useless limb until black dots edged my vision.

Won't go back. I won't.

I'd rather die.

A deafening roar echoed in my ears.

I turned. Froze. Watched as two blinding lights barreled down the road straight at me. Moving was beyond me. Breathing proved impossible. Instead, I stood rooted to the spot as the car careened toward me.

Tires screamed across the pavement and filled the air with an acrid, burning scent. Metal groaned. Lights flashed. And still, I stood there, heartbeat thundering in my ears as the car came to a screeching halt only a few feet away.

Something moved inside the car, and the breath rushed back into my lungs.

RUN! my head screamed, but my feet weren't moving. They stayed locked in place while my knees shook and my teeth chattered so violently, I half expected them to jump out and flee in my place.

Thunder clapped in my ears and I jerked my gaze up to the sky, expecting a massive bolt of lightning to flash across the dark expanse at any moment. It took me a few seconds to realize the night air was still and clear, and that the awful noise was my heart trying to beat out of my chest.

Was this a normal reaction? Shouldn't I be happy? There was a car. A car that had stopped. With people in it. And people meant safety.

Right?

Not all people were evil. My father hadn't been. Even when I couldn't remember what he looked like, I still remembered the soothing baritone of his voice, the warm touch of a kind hand stroking my hair, the scent of cooling hot-chocolate—the drink he always made for me when I needed cheering up. Whoever was in the car could be good, kind people.

Or they could be evil. They could be Hunters.

I shivered and hunched my shoulders, wanting to disappear, to become invisible.

The driver's door creaked open. When no one immediately exited, fear overwhelmed my need to escape. Were they hurt? Had I . . . Was I responsible for . . . ?

I couldn't even think it.

Dear god, please not again! My fear was so great, the tenuous control I kept over my monster slipped, causing a spiral of terror to take root. I closed my eyes and concentrated on my breathing. In and out. Deep breath in. Long exhale.

"Are you all right?" A smooth voice broke my concentration.

I spun around, all my attention going to the man who'd spoken, and . . .

Those eyes.

Brilliant blue eyes framed by thick black lashes stared back at me with piercing intensity. Sharp intelligence tempered by endless patience; his eyes were oceans of unfathomable depth. It felt like he saw right through me, laid me bare to the soul. Those almost too-acute eyes radiated a controlled power that fascinated, drew me in against my will. They flayed me, peeled away layer after layer of skin, not stopping until my very essence was revealed, and yet there was something there that called to me, something dark and deadly. Something I wanted to recognize but couldn't.

He . . . he didn't look like a Hunter.

I forced myself to break his gaze before he could see too much, before he saw that part of me I never wanted anyone to notice, and quickly scanned the rest of his face.

His skin looked tanned, but with a copper hue no sun could produce, and though he wasn't truly handsome, his face held an odd sort of appeal that captured my attention and made me want to look closer.

Holding my breath, I tilted my head and tried to understand. His lips were a little too wide for his face. His jaw, though chiseled, a little too sharp. Skipping over those intense, blue eyes—afraid of what his shrewd gaze would uncover—I took in the harsh slashes of his black eyebrows, and the high, cutting cheekbones that gave him an almost severe look. In contrast, his nose was a little on the flat side, narrow at the top but with a broader bridge.

Taken individually, his features were all a little off, but together they blended seamlessly and gave him an air of quiet confidence.

"Are you hurt?" he asked, not moving closer.

No Hunter would be this patient.

My mouth was too dry to reply. Instead, I searched the rest of him, looking for answers, trying to find out if this were a man I could trust. Tall and lean, with broad shoulders and a tapered waist, he wore a pair of faded jeans that hugged his long legs perfectly, and a worn shirt that had seen better days.

An outfit made for work.

Tied back from his face with a brown, leather throng, his jet-black hair looked silky and longer than I'd ever seen on a man. From the top of his ponytail peeked a lonesome, defiant feather that bobbed in the wind.

For a brief moment, I forgot the fear that had ruled my every waking moment since I was six years old, another emotion taking its place.

Curiosity.

But then, with a lowered brow and a look of mild concern, he stepped forward.

My whole body locked down with renewed terror.

"D-don't come any closer." Each word scraped against my throat.

The man stopped right away, standing so still he almost disappeared into the night. His piercing gaze never wavered, never left my face, and slowly, excruciatingly slowly, he put his hands out—palms up—and hunched his shoulders.

"Do not be afraid," he said quietly. "We will not hurt you." His voice was smooth and reassuring, calm and controlled, like listening to the gentle ripples of a still ocean lapping at cliffs above.

I caught myself leaning toward him, wanting his soothing, almost monotone voice to take away my fear and do the impossible; make me feel safe. Contained power rolled off him in waves I could almost feel brush against my skin. Searching. Prodding. Assessing. And with it, a strange tranquility. It seeped from him, brushing against me until even my inner monster seemed calmer.

Movement to my left.

My head snapped around, breaking the eye-contact I wasn't aware I'd established, and whatever calm he'd wrapped around me broke against a tidal wave of panic.

A behemoth had moved out of the car and was edging his way closer. A strange feeling filled me. Something akin to betrayal.

He'd been distracting me so his friend could . . . so he could . . .

I didn't know, but I didn't intend to find out. They may not have looked like Hunters, but that didn't mean they weren't.

I bolted. Or, tried to bolt. But I'd forgotten about my bad leg, and instead of sprinting away, I stumbled and fell to the hard asphalt.

A scream lodged in my throat as a menacing figure loomed above me. He was by far the scariest looking man I'd ever seen. The sheer size of him overloaded my senses; his fierce scowl made my stomach dip and roll. I'd never seen a bigger, more vicious-looking example of masculine power in my life. He seemed like an escaped animal, all wild, furious strength.

He's like an untamed beast, I thought, unable to stop a shiver from working its way up my back.

The beast narrowed his luminous silver eyes at me, and . . .

Wow.

If I had been any less terrified, I may have taken a moment to admire those liquid, silver orbs. But the predatory way he eyed me made my heart shrivel in my chest and the monster inside perk up and take notice.

Dear god, not now! There was no way I could focus on controlling the dark force inside me while still getting away unscathed.

The beast leaned closer, his face only a hairsbreadth away from mine.

A strange, intriguing scent teased my senses. This close my eyes automatically zoomed in on the jagged, white line starting at the left of his nose, running past his lips, and ending just under his strong jawline.

A warrior's scar.

A startled, embarrassingly feminine noise burst out of me when his nose touched my skin, stroking from my temple up to my hair and making goosebumps erupt all over my skin.

Before I could stammer out a question, he reared back, silver eyes widening, and the dark, masculine slashes of his brows raised almost to his hairline. He looked almost . . . bewildered.

"W-what are you d-doing?" I leaned back, small pebbles digging into my palms. All my instincts screamed at me to flee, but I couldn't get my legs to work.

The beast didn't reply. With a narrowed, predatory stare he moved back into my personal space, determination clear in the set line of his jaw and compressed lips. Again, the word *beast* floated through my mind, accompanied by *feral* and *untamed* as I imagined him stalking his prey, making it wild with panic before chasing it into some unknown trap and delivering the killing blow.

The mental image, so reminiscent of my own monster, was enough to pull me out of my fear-spiral and remind me that I had my own beast to control. It was right there, lurking beneath the surface, ready to tear free and commit unspeakable crimes.

Not good, Hope! Even my inner voice sounded shaky. Although the beast in front of me terrified me with his hulking frame and scarred face, I was more scared of the thing living inside me.

It had already ruined my life once, taken away the one—

I took a deep breath and shoved my monster back down to the deepest recesses of my mind, ignoring the sense of hopelessness that engulfed me when it disappeared and left me vulnerable once again.

I snuck a peek at the beast standing so close the scent of him washed over me—he smelled like pine cones and raw masculinity, if such a thing had a scent—and met his glare with a wince.

My muscles tensed, readying for flight at the way his narrowed gaze focused on me. His head dipped down and he . . .

Sniffed?

Did the beast just smell me?

I turned my head sideways and drew a small, discreet breath in through my nose.

Ewww!

I smelled like dirt, blood, and sweat. Embarrassed, and confused as to *why* I was embarrassed, I cringed. But why should I care what the big, scary man thought of me? I'd been tortured, nearly killed. If anyone was entitled to stink, it was me!

The small, defiant pep talk sounded good in my head, but to say it out loud?

The thought alone had me trembling.

When I gathered enough courage to meet his gaze again, he was running his hands through shoulder-length, midnight-black hair and shaking his head in grim confusion. Turning and giving me a clear view of his profile, he glared—I didn't think he'd stopped glaring and scowling this entire time—and mouthed something to the first guy still standing by the car, staring at me intently.

While the beast was distracted, I took a moment to study him. I looked up and up and . . . up. He was huge. Even bigger than the first guy. Standing up, I'd probably reach no higher than his chest. The plain black tee he wore stretched taut across a wide chest; the short sleeves looked like they were about to burst from the thick biceps pushing against the tight material.

To say he filled out his shirt would be an understatement.

My eyes raced across broad, muscular shoulders, up to a thick neck, and stopped at the jawline where the jagged scar from his face ended. Covered in black scruff, his jaw was square and powerful. The light silver of the eyes I had so admired were deep-seated under prominent, black brows, lending him a dangerous air. The fierce scowl he sported made him seem even less approachable.

He was the epitome of dark, dangerous, and terrifying.

Consider me terrified.

"Get up," he said gruffly.

I shivered at his voice, so low and rough it was almost a growl.

When I didn't follow his command, just sat there blinking at the savage male looming above me with his arms crossed impatiently over a wide chest, one black brow raised while waiting for my supplication, he made a low, chuffing sound, bent his considerable frame, and simply lifted me straight up.

The hands spanning the entirety of my ribcage were warm, shooting small sparks up my spine and stirring something I didn't recognize. My whole world narrowed down to the heat emanating from those rough, calloused hands. For a second, I forgot the nauseating terror that had haunted me for the last decade.

But just for a second.

"Let me go!" The hoarse, pleading whisper sounded nothing like the demanding shout I wanted it to be. I gripped his hands and tried to pry them off me, dread once more clawing at my insides when all my waning strength was not enough to budge even one of his fingers.

The beast's scowl grew even more ferocious—an amazing feat considering how terrifying he already appeared—but he carefully lowered me until my shaky feet hit the ground.

Of course, my traitorous leg was still injured, immediately giving out. Only his quick reflexes saved me from yet another tumble.

"Foolish female," he rumbled as he reached out and grabbed me. Glowering, lips pressed tightly together, he looked like he'd gladly strangle me where I stood.

I quickly lowered my eyes, hunched my shoulders, and averted my face in preparation for the pain to come. His hands were so big, one hit had the potential to knock me unconscious.

My lip disappeared between my teeth, and I bit down hard to stop the whimper stuck in the vicinity of my throat before closing my eyes.

In captivity, I'd learned that the expectation of pain was almost as bad as the pain itself, especially when I knew exactly what was to come.

The tight grip on my arm loosened and when nothing else happened, I darted a glimpse up at the beast's face, quickly wishing I hadn't. His firm lips were twisted in disgust, silver glare so molten it should have melted the skin off my bones. A lock of black hair fell across one eye, which he almost immediately batted away with one of his huge hands. Hands that were covered in thin, white lines.

Scars. So many scars.

A sliver of sympathy made a home inside my hollow chest.

"Ash," he roared, making me wince.

My poor ears.

The beast noticed my discomfort—was thoroughly annoyed by it, if the dark glower he aimed at me was any indication—and huffed. "Take her."

Take her? Take *her? What does that mean?*

Could they be Hunters after all?

No. No.

Terror swamped, an icy torrent threatening to drown me. The throbbing in my leg intensifying with my fear, and I must have made a sound—probably something like a choked gurgle—because both the beast and the first man, the one I assumed was Ash, whipped their heads around and frowned down at me.

Ash's intense blue gaze penetrated the hazy terror, dispersing it piece by piece until my heaving breaths slowed to a trickle.

"You are scaring the girl, Ruarc," Ash admonished lightly, eyes still on mine.

Ruarc grunted, unconcerned.

"What is your name?" Ash took a slow step toward us.

"H-Hope," I whispered, silently cursing my vocal cords for sounding so timid when I was trying my hardest to appear strong.

"Hello, Hope," Ash said. Although his face was devoid of any emotions, there was something comforting in the way he looked at me. "I'm Ash," he continued and patted himself once on the chest, something I found vaguely strange but appealing at the same time. "The male standing with you is Ruarc. He will not hurt you." Ash took another step, his piercing, intelligent eyes exuding a slow-burning patience that had me leaning closer, hungry for the calm in those blue depths.

Ruarc made a weird, huffing sound that snapped me out of my fascination. When I looked back at Ash, it was with suspicion instead of wonder. *How did he do that?*

"W-what did he m-mean when he . . . When he said to take me?" I addressed Ash. Despite his weird voodoo eye magic, he still felt safer than the beast.

Ruarc.

Ruarc scowled. "Hospital." The grip on my arm tightened.

"No!" I pulled against the restraining hold, only aware of the blood rushing through my veins and the stark terror it carried.

Both men stilled at my outburst. Something hot and dangerous lurked behind Ruarc's silver eyes, but it was Ash who spoke in a voice so quiet I barely heard it. "Why do you not want to go to the hospital?"

Something about his tone held me captive. "I . . . I just . . ." I racked my brain for a plausible reason for why a woman in her twenties, obviously hurt, wouldn't want to go to the hospital. "I'm afraid of needles," I blurted.

"You are afraid of needles," Ash repeated slowly. He shot a quick look at Ruarc who continued to glare.

Cold tendrils of fear coiled deep in my belly. *They don't believe you,* my subconscious screamed. I was frozen, terrified they would somehow be connected to the Hunters, or simply ignore my wishes and take me to the hospital regardless of what I said. I hadn't had many choices in the last eighteen years, and the thought of this one being taken away from me turned my stomach with a sharpness that threatened to make me hurl.

I tried to speak, mouth opening before snapping shut again. *I'm not good at this.* I had no practice making up stories, and I couldn't just tell them the real reason: that I was fleeing for my life and the Hunters had contacts *everywhere*. The hospitals would be one of the first places they'd look.

"I-I can't *stand* doctors." I put as much of my desperation as I could into my voice, hoping my fear of the Hunters would lend truth to my words.

Ruarc sucked in a harsh breath and scanned my face. After a second, fierce determination filled his hard features and he nodded once at Ash.

I didn't know what it meant, but I followed his gaze, almost stumbling when I glimpsed his raw, painful grimace. It was gone and replaced by a neutral, thoughtful expression so quickly I thought I may have imagined it.

"Ash," Ruarc growled. His body was taut, on the verge of movement, but he held his powerful frame still, waiting.

"Yes." Ash nodded once and my world turned upside down.

4

HOPE

Despite my outrage at being carried like a sack of potatoes, I didn't dare complain. Partly because despite the broadness of Ruarc's shoulders, I was terrified he would accidentally drop me if I so much as wriggled my little toe, and partly because my mind was wailing in panic, making it hard to concentrate on anything besides the danger I found myself in with my imminent kidnapping.

Not only did I know nothing about these guys—they could be serial killers for all I knew—but they were built like warriors. Even though Ash exuded a quiet confidence, I could sense the restrained power in him. It showed in the predatory gait he couldn't quite hide, his easy steps, and broad shoulders.

So yeah, Ash was scary in his own deceptively calm way, but Ruarc was downright terrifying. There was nothing deceptive about him, just pure masculine power wrapped in a beastly exterior obviously meant for destruction. If someone were to ask me what I thought he did for a living, I would've guessed he was an ancient Viking warrior who relished in his choice of profession of raiding and maiming.

By the time the world righted itself and I was once again

on solid ground—closer to the car, but still a few feet away—I was shaking uncontrollably, convinced I was about to be chopped up and put in the back of their trunk.

This is it, I thought. *It was all for nothing.*

As I battled dread and the ever-present fear that'd been my constant companion these last eighteen years, a strange tingle began in the tips of my fingers. It grew, slid up my arms, tickled my neck seductively, and filled my mind with a fiery red glow.

Rage had a distinct taste, alluring yet bitter. It tempted, beckoned, and though I knew it would leave me hollow and alone if I listened to its beguiling voice, I didn't fight it.

Giving in, I closed my eyes and called to the darkness inside me, begged it for help. I steeled myself for the loss of control, for the brutality of my monster and—

Nothing happened.

My eyes flew open, heart hammering at an alarming speed. The shaking got worse as the rage fled like it had never been, leaving me alone—completely alone this time—with the terror of awaiting a fate sure to be gruesome.

"Be calm." Ash's deep, centered voice floated through my mind. His hand was gentle but firm as he squeezed my shoulder. "No one here is going to hurt you, Hope."

Tilting my head back, I met his bright blue gaze and the tightness in my chest loosened. I could finally breathe.

"W-where are you taking me?" I whispered.

"Home." He nodded at something behind me. I was tempted to turn around to see what it was, but I was loath to take my eyes off him until I knew exactly what would happen to me—and why.

"Th-that's not necessary," I said. "I'm f-fine. I'm fine," I repeated when Ruarc made a rude sound of disagreement. "If you could just give me a ride into the city, I would really appreciate it. I don't need . . ." I trailed off at the firm shake of Ash's head, the lone feather in his hair bobbing precariously.

How is that thing staying put?

"Idiotic females," Ruarc grumbled. He rolled his eyes in a way that clearly stated we—females as a whole—were all moronic. I wanted to say something to defend my gender, almost did too, but his scowl scared me off.

"Ruarc," Ash said softly, "wait in the car." When the other man failed to heed his order, I could have sworn I heard a warning growl coming from Ash. A sound that belonged in the jungle, not among humans.

Keeping my eye on the bigger threat—the angry beast that was Ruarc—seemed like a good idea, but I still snuck a peek at Ash, and when I did . . . Gone was the calm, pensive man from a moment ago. In his stead stood an inflexible wall of power with a will so strong I could feel it battering at my defenses. I had to stop myself from stepping toward the car and getting in myself.

After a few seconds of unbearable tension, Ruarc made an animal sound of his own and strode to the car.

I jumped at the loud, angry bang of the door slamming shut, and stood there alone with a man I had thought of as, if not safe, then at least safer than Ruarc.

While I stared at Ash, mouth gaping like a moron, his shoulders slowly lost their rigid tension. The unyielding light was gone from his eyes, replaced by tranquility.

I blinked, amazed at the quick transformation from raging thunderstorm to clear, still waters.

"Hope," he began, voice low and soothing, "you are clearly in dire need of help. You reek of fear and desperation. Wait —" He held up his hand, stopping my insulted sputtering before I could inform him of the fact that fear and desperation didn't have a smell and that it was rude to comment on it anyway.

Okay, I wouldn't have said that, but I sure did think it loudly.

"Let me finish, please." He was so polite, I couldn't stop

myself from nodding. "It does not matter to us what you are running from—yes, it is clear you are running," Ash said when I drew in a quick, startled breath. "We almost ran you over with our car. The least we can do is offer you a safe place to spend the night. And a warm meal. I promise you, you are free to leave whenever you want. We just want to make sure you are healthy enough to do so."

The sincerity in his voice, coupled with the observant, yet gentle way he was eyeing me, made me want to trust him. If he could see me, truly see me, and still look at me with kindness . . . Well, that was something I'd wanted for a long, long time.

Don't fool yourself, Hope. He doesn't know what you have done. What you are. *And if he did, he would look at you with contempt, not acceptance or kindness.*

But he had offered me a choice. My very first, freely-given choice. A sense of calm descended over me while a flutter of emotion I didn't recognize flapped its flimsy wings. It wasn't like I had anywhere else to go. With them, I'd have a roof over my head and I'd be away from the Hunters. At least for a night. I could always begin my search for my uncle tomorrow.

He's giving me a choice.

My heart stuttered, skipped a beat, then raced with renewed vigor. Or maybe I'd go once my leg was healed.

He's giving me a choice.

I lifted my chin, met his steady blue gaze and saw only compassion. "O-okay," I whispered, wondering if I'd just made the second biggest mistake of my life. "Okay."

With my attention shackled to Ash and my back to the car, I hadn't noticed the two figures appearing behind me. I didn't spot them until Ash moved, motioning for me to follow, and as soon as I saw them, I stopped. And I stared.

The two men waiting impatiently by the car were like the sun and the moon, but where the sun typically outshone the moon, here it was the opposite. The man I later found out to be Lucien was the most beautiful man I'd ever seen. He looked like a Greek god, carved from marble and forever untouchable by lowly humans.

His skin was pale, luminous like the moon, with no hint of a blemish to mar the perfection of his face. High, sharp cheekbones and a narrow, straight nose set the stage for a harsh kind of beauty that was almost painful to look at. Lips that would look soft and inviting on any other man were pressed into a thin line of displeasure. Instead of detracting from his looks, it gave him an air of unattainability, mocking anyone stupid enough to admire the masculine piece of art that would never belong to anyone but himself—or whichever goddess he found worthy.

His cold eyes were meadow green, framed by thick, sooty-black lashes and perfect eyebrows. A slightly narrow but sculpted jaw ended in a rectangular chin, the result of superb genetics or extreme luck. Tall, although not as tall as Ruarc, and lean rather than bulky, he was still muscular. Sculpted chest and shoulders gave way to narrow hips and long legs hugged by the expensive-looking suit he wore.

A low laugh snapped me out of my obvious gawking. "Enjoying the view, love?" the other, warmer man asked.

My cheeks flushed scarlet, and I looked away from Lucien, the ruthlessly handsome marble statue who was actually a flesh and blood man.

God, they must all think I am a complete moron, I thought, taking small comfort in the fact that at least Ruarc hadn't seen my idiocy—he'd folded his powerful frame into the car and was angrily fiddling with the radio last I checked.

Resisting the urge to fan my overly hot face, I squared my shoulders and looked back up, meeting Lucien's arctic, contemptuous stare. "Let her enjoy this experience, Jason," he said icily, his crisp, British accent cracking like a whip. "I sincerely doubt she's had the occasion to see males of my caliber." This was said matter-of-factly, not like he was bragging, but like he knew how gorgeous he was and was simply stating a fact he didn't much care about. "If the men of her acquaintance are anything like her, the view must be abysmal."

The cutting insult reverberated in my skull. I felt naked. Exposed. Like I was back on the slab in the basement of the Hunter compound, waiting for another nightmare to begin.

I wrapped my arms around my middle, hunched my shoulders, then cursed myself for caring what he thought, what anybody thought. I wasn't a great beauty, but I wasn't butt-ugly either. Granted, I stank a little, and yes, blood and dirt stuck to my hair—and various pieces of my clothing—but that didn't warrant such a cruel assessment, did it?

"Lucien." Ash's smooth voice was rough around the edges. With long strides, he moved away from the car and motioned Lucien over. "A word."

Without a backward glance, Lucien glided over to where Ash stood with his hands crossed over his chest. I couldn't make out what was said, but from the bored look on Lucien's face I didn't think he cared.

"Don't be sad, love," Jason said. Like Lucien, he had a slight, British accent, much more toned down and relaxed than the man who had just insulted me so thoroughly. "Lucien has had a stick up his ass since the day he was born. It's not likely to disappear any time soon. Not until some poor chap has had enough and pulls it out to beat the man with it."

A tremulous smile fought its way onto my face. My stinging eyes were glued to the ground, but it didn't seem to bother Jason. I wanted to look at him, wanted to see if his smile was as warm as the humor in his voice, but I wasn't ready yet. My feelings confused me. Dealing with these . . . these *men* confused me. I hadn't exactly been socializing during the last decade; all my knowledge of the real world came from the few movies and books I'd been allowed during my first few years at the compound.

I willed my eyes to stay clear, blinking a few times to make sure there was no excess water to give away my hurt feelings. It was stupid, really. I had no reason to care what these men thought. And I had never cared about my looks, or lack thereof, before. So why did Lucien get to me?

Maybe it wasn't what he'd said, but *how* he'd said it. And that the others had heard him. I felt devalued and small. And worried. What if they left me here to fend for myself? A few minutes ago I hadn't even been planning on going with them, and now I was worried about being left behind. If I caused conflict between them, they would surely decide I wasn't worth the effort.

When Ash's smooth voice rose to a heated whisper, my insides shriveled up and I felt sick. *This is my fault. They are arguing because of me.*

"It's fine," I said in a small voice. When no one replied, I cleared my throat nervously and repeated myself, a little louder this time. "It's fine. Really." When three sets of male eyes stared at me with various degrees of skepticism, my words died in my throat. I wanted to tell them it was okay, they could leave and I'd be fine. But I just couldn't bring myself to say it.

I needed help. Just for tonight. When my wounds were cleaned and my belly was full, I would head out on my own. After a little nap, maybe. If they let me.

God, I'm pathetic.

No one said anything. My skin itched uncomfortably, a sure sign they were all staring at me. I didn't know what to do or what to say, so I remained quiet. A gentle hand on my elbow startled me and made me look up. Warm, chocolate-colored eyes smiled down at me, sparkling with mischief and charm.

With a start, I realized I hadn't really gotten a good look at Jason. Next to Lucien, he'd kind of disappeared. It wasn't easy to measure up to the cold, untouchable beauty that was Lucien, but the more I saw of Jason, the more vibrant he became.

I shook my head and tried to look at him objectively. He was the shortest of the guys. The top of my head reached as far as his chin. He was exceptionally well built, more compact than lean, with well-defined pectorals and a ridged abdomen that could easily be seen due to his tight-fitting, canary yellow shirt.

That's . . . bright, I thought and felt my mouth twitch.

His arms were corded, veins almost angry looking, especially the ones in his neck. In a word he looked strong.

I let my eyes wander back up to his face, absentmindedly noting how his playful smile widened and showed off straight, white teeth. His dark eyebrows wiggled suggestively at me before he shook his head, his brown hair moving in tandem. It was cut a little shorter on the sides, the medium length on top looking both stylish and playful.

My face heated.

"Do you want to know a secret, love?" He leaned in close and all I could smell was his delicious aftershave—something dark, yet sweet with a hint of rain after a thunderstorm. *Electric*. Voice lowered to a conspiratorial whisper, he continued, "To not be afraid, all you have to do is pretend. After a while, you'll forget you're pretending, and just like that"—he snapped his fingers, a strange smile spreading across his face—"you are a new person." The look in his warm, brown eyes was suddenly serious. "But even if you forget, always remember the cause of your fear so that one day, when you are stronger and your fear is gone, you can come back and destroy what caused it to begin with."

My breath left me in an audible whoosh. Could I do that? Could I get over my fear of the Hunters and maybe, just maybe, one day destroy them?

I peeked up at Jason. What was *he* afraid of? Had he managed to wipe his fear, and the cause of it, out of existence?

"Don't worry, love." With a wink and a playful grin that so quickly erased the brief glimpse into his serious side, he held the passenger door open for me. "You're in good hands now."

5

RUARC

THE DRIVE HOME HAD BEEN TENSE AS FUCK. THE LITTLE female had shrunk with each mile, shoulders curling and spine bending until it had looked like she was about to disappear.

And with each wince, each tiny whimper, the anger in my belly had grown hotter.

I'd never been happier to get out of the car than when Ash finally parked.

"Here you go, lovely lady," Jason said with a flourish, bending at the waist in a strange looking bow and waving the little female, Hope, inside our house.

I fumed, annoyed at the ease with which he interacted with her and that damned, charming smile of his. Maybe I should punch him?

Would she still grace him with her shy smile if his nose was crooked and he was missing a few teeth?

"Move," I grumbled and shoved him out of the way. I wanted to check the house before the little female walked into a potentially dangerous situation. There'd been no Strays in our territory in weeks, not after what I'd done the last time, but couldn't hurt to be careful.

I drew in a breath through my nose, sorting through all the smells. The woodsy scent of polished oak hung in the air —Lucien had been making shit again—and the familiar smell of my brothers. No intruders.

I grunted, satisfied it was safe, and jerked my chin in the direction of the kitchen where we kept the first aid supplies.

Someone had to make sure Hope was looked after, and ever since she'd squared her shoulders and met my gaze head on, her wounded eyes pleading for someone to show her some kindness, I'd wanted that someone to be me.

I put the first aid box on the kitchen table and waited.

"This way," Jason said. His voice was light and cheerful— it always sounded like he was in on a joke no one else understood. Didn't think I'd ever seen the bastard without a perpetual smirk on his smug face.

Except for the times my fist was buried in his eye socket, I thought to myself and bared my teeth in satisfaction.

A slow, hesitant shuffling made my ears twitch. She sounded like prey. *Not good.* Someone had to teach the little female to hide her fear, otherwise she'd end up as someone's dinner.

Growling at the offensive thought, I almost didn't notice her faltering in the doorway. With effort, I tried to force my mouth to stretch into a smile. To put her at ease.

She flinched and took a step back, looking nervous as hell.

I dropped the smile.

Fucking Jason, I thought grimly. *He gets the sweet, shy smiles while I get the flinching and the terror.*

It was not the first time a female had been horrified after looking at me, but it bothered me that my burly frame and scarred face seemed to scare this one.

Made me want to growl at her.

Squashing the urge, I gestured to one of the empty chairs around the big kitchen table. It was situated next to a window and overlooked a part of our big backyard. From this angle, nothing was visible beyond the tall hedge that separated the yard from the rest of our land. "Sit."

"I . . . I-I'm okay," she stuttered, color creeping up her neck.

"Sit," I repeated, tilting my head and studying her. With a stiff, stilted walk, she crept toward the chair, all the while looking at me like I was going to pounce.

Prey, my instincts stated. I doubted it was her natural state. Someone had terrified her, probably abused her. Based on her actions, the frightened way she had interacted with us, the evasiveness and general unease she displayed in our vicinity, the bruises, wounds and various cuts, the most obvious explanation was that she was running from someone. Someone who'd hurt her.

A low, furious growl slipped from my throat. Hope's hand shot up to her neck, hiding her most vulnerable spot.

"Ruarc, stop terrifying the girl," Jason scolded, eyes alight with pleasure.

I didn't know what he found more amusing, my lack of social graces or how uncomfortable I was around this small, slip of a girl.

"Sit down, love. Ash will take a look at your injuries in a few minutes," Jason told her.

The little female stared at the chairs around the table. Brown eyes wide, her hands picked at her ruined clothing as her gaze skipped from chair to chair.

"W-where should I sit?" she asked in a small voice.

Jason's eyebrow climbed up, and he shot me a look filled with concern. The wily bastard may be a pain in my ass, but he had a good heart. No worthy, honorable male could look at an abused female and not feel helpless rage and a good dose of concern.

"There," I said, pointing to a chair at random. Instinct told me directing her was better than making her agonize over an insignificant choice.

My chest warmed when she graced me with a small, trembling smile.

Fuck me . . .

That smile, even unsure and hesitant, was one of the most beautiful things I'd ever seen. Dazed, I fell down into the closest chair, ignoring the warning creak from the wood.

Another of Lucien's damned creations. The annoying bastard could at least make furniture that didn't threaten to break when I sat down. He knew I was heavy, dammit! Though my size had served me well in my turbulent youth, sometimes it could be a real pain. Females took one look at my big frame and scarred face, and immediately judged me to be a brutal bastard. It didn't help that I wasn't all charm and easy smiles like Jason.

"So . . ." Jason said when it became apparent the female wouldn't talk. Her eyes were glued to her clenched hands on the table, which annoyed the shit out of me.

Want those eyes on me.

Bloody hell . . . Didn't just want those eyes on me, wanted to learn all her secrets, the reason for that stark pain in her eyes. Wanted to help her through the nightmare that haunted her, to destroy her enemies.

Bloody hell was right.

"Want to tell us what happened to you, love?"

Even if I hadn't been watching her so closely, there would have been no way to miss the terror clouding her expressive eyes or the way her breathing picked up at Jason's question.

"I . . . I fell."

My hands clenched and disappointment soured my mouth. Why would she protect the bastard who did this to her? She couldn't be so stupid as to love him or anything ridiculous like that?

Blood curdling at the thought, I scowled at her.

Foolish female.

Her face fell, making me feel like a brute, so I growled under my breath and felt my scowl grow more pronounced.

"Ignore the grumpy bastard, little Hope. He continuously gets out of bed on the wrong side."

I kicked Jason under the table, ignoring his choked laugh, and turned to the little female. "No lies." I detested lies. Either tell the truth or keep quiet. There was no honor in lies.

No honor in making females cry, either . . .

Disgusted with myself, I watched with growing horror as Hope's beautiful, soft eyes filled with moisture. She blinked furiously a few times, and I thanked my lucky stars that no tears fell.

"I just . . . I can't go back!"

Anguished, brown eyes stared up at me and my heart constricted painfully.

"Never," I swore, meaning it with every fiber of my being. Whoever was after her would have to go through me, and what a pleasant thought that was. Grim satisfaction swelled in my chest as I imagined ripping her abuser apart.

When Jason failed to chime in and offer his reassurances like a good male should in this type of situation, I leaned back in my chair, crossed my arms over my chest, and glared. He tilted his head, questioning. I jutted my chin out at Hope, hoping the asshat would get the message.

"Oh, right," he finally said, looking like a light bulb should be flashing over his head. "Ruarc is right, love. You don't ever have to go back. There are ways to deal with abusive situations. Shelters, for one. You could also go to the police. With your physical evidence it should be a slam dunk case, and we would be happy to help you until the bastard who did this to you is behind bars."

I grunted in agreement, but Hope didn't react like she was supposed to. Instead of being properly calmed by our promise of protection, panic flashed in her expressive, soulful eyes. Her small, pale hands were clenched around the table, almost like she was afraid she would drift away if she didn't have anything solid to hold on to. Her chest rose and fell in sharp, rapid movements, the sound of her panicked heart deafening to my sensitive ears.

"No, please," she gasped. "I can't—it's not safe! I-I just have to disappear!"

I was on my feet before I knew what happened. An angry snarl broke free from the deepest recesses of my chest, and this time I ignored Hope's fear at my aggression. It wasn't aimed at her so she had no reason to be afraid.

"What's his name?" I hissed.

What little color Hope had left vanished. Her whole body trembled as her mouth worked without a sound.

"Ruarc . . ." Jason started, but I growled at him, a low, angry sound that he knew to respect.

"A name."

"I-I . . . oh, god!" Hope cried, burying her head in her hands while her shoulders heaved with silent tears. Her fear in the face of her nameless tormentor drove me to the brink of mindless rage.

"Look at her!" I demanded, unsure if I was talking to Jason or Ash, who'd just entered the room and was staring at Hope with an unreadable expression. "The male who did this needs killing!"

"I'm s-sorry!"

Hope's muffled cry infuriated me further. The bastard had taught her to apologize even when she had done nothing wrong. Something broke with a loud crack and my foot stung. Hope jumped at the sound, but didn't look up. If anything, she hunched her shoulders even more.

Fuck! The damned chair can't even handle a good kick.
I fumed.

And why the fuck was Hope jumping at every loud noise?

Didn't she understand we were honorable males? Did she actually think we would hurt her, a defenseless, wounded female?

I snarled louder, furiously indignant.

Ash shot me a dark look and moved over to where the little female was sitting, head still in her hands, her tiny body shaking. He put a hand on her back and rubbed in small circles.

"Shhh," he crooned. "Take a deep breath for me." When Hope didn't respond, he leaned down and spoke softly right into her ear. "You are safe. No one here wants to hurt you. You are safe." He repeated himself over and over until her small frame stopped shaking and only the occasional shiver ran through her.

"Look at me," he said, using the same voice he used when he needed to bring one of us down from a killing rage.

Tormented, watery eyes peeked up through lashes wet with tears.

"Good girl," Ash whispered, still stroking her back. "You do not have to tell us anything you are not ready for. Understand?"

A shaky nod, Hope's gaze darting to Jason, then me. She groaned and her hands jerked in her lap, like she wanted to hide behind them again.

Ash followed her gaze, a small crease appearing between his brows. "They will not push you either." The steel in his voice warned us against arguing.

"We won't," Jason agreed, unusually subdued as he stared at Hope's tearstained cheeks.

The sight of her pain was almost too much. A growl slipped out as my anger grew. Anger at Hope for refusing to give me a name. Anger at Ash for not letting me push her harder. But most of all, I was fighting the bloodlust building at each averted look, each tear on the little female's pale cheeks. I wanted to maim and kill the fucker who'd hurt her, to really make him suffer.

Those that prey on the innocent need to die. Painfully.

"Ruarc . . ." Ash waited, a hard, impatient glint in his normally unruffled features.

"Fine!" I snapped.

"I'm sorry," Hope said again, voice barely above a whisper. "I don't mean to cause all this—this trouble." She waved her hand around in a gesture I took to include all three of us.

"You have nothing to be sorry about, Hope. When you are ready to tell us, we will be here to listen. In the meantime, I am going to take a look at your wounds."

I stalked from the room, unable to look at her injuries without killing someone.

Where the fuck is Lucien? I thought darkly. He was always up for some sparring, and I had to get this fucked up day out of my system before I went on a rampage and destroyed every single room in the house.

6

HOPE

"Lucien!" the big, angry beast bellowed from the other room. "Outside!" A door slammed shut and we were left in uneasy silence. I looked down, avoiding eye contact. If only the floor could open up and swallow me whole.

"Well, that was dramatic," Jason said, winking when he saw me peek up at him.

My cheeks heated and I ducked my head. Jason seemed so . . . so *happy*. Genuinely happy. During the whole half-hour drive, he'd cracked jokes, smiled, and laughed. He didn't seem to care when Ruarc grumbled at him or when Lucien's silence grew cutting.

Jason was free to be himself.

To not be afraid, all you have to do is pretend.

Something in my chest squeezed painfully. Which Jason was the real one? The one who'd spoken so starkly about fear and vengeance, or the playful charmer grinning down at me?

"Do not mind him," Ash said and reached for the first aid box. "I will need to cut some of your clothes away to get a good look at your injuries." His expression gentled when I blanched at the mention of losing my clothes—filthy as they were. "There is no need to worry. I will wait for your permission before removing anything."

"O-okay." My voice shook as I eyed the scissors he withdrew. The glossy metal glinted in the kitchen light and a wave of dizziness made me sway in my chair. Memories of various pieces of sharp, metallic objects and the damage they could inflict sliced through my brain.

Jason drew in a deep breath, eyes narrowing dangerously. "What's wrong, love?"

"Nothing," I whispered, pushing the memories away. "You can . . . I mean . . . my leg. You can start with my leg."

Where did my courage go? Or did I never have any to begin with?

Tilting his head, Ash studied me. Lurking behind his stormy blue eyes was a flash of cool intellect, of something ancient stretching it's mighty legs and whispering across the space between us. But then it disappeared and I wondered if my exhaustion and blood loss were making me imagine things that weren't there.

"Hmm," Ash murmured and glanced at the scissors. Something flickered across his face, something I couldn't read.

"I'll be in my room. Holler if you need me." Jason rose and left the room with a stiff gait, leaving me alone with Ash.

I jumped when he reached out. Rather than take offense, he waited in silence until my breathing calmed and the hot flush on my face receded before trying again. The touch of his hand was a featherlight caress as it glided over my knee.

"I see a lot of blood on your left leg, Hope. Where does the injury stem from?"

"Right above my ankle." I pointed to the painful, throbbing spot where the metal teeth had hurt me.

With exquisite care, Ash lifted my foot into his lap. After I gave another nod of permission, he cut a line from the bottom of my pants to just below my knee. I couldn't help the soft gasp that escaped me—my wound hurt, but it was the terrible feeling of metal against my bare skin I objected to—and I pretended not to notice the tightness around Ash's eyes or the way his slightly-too-wide lips pressed together.

When he moved the dirty fabric aside I was disappointed to see my injury hadn't even begun to heal.

They must have used the special metal.

My monster gave me a few unique abilities—the Hunters had been fascinated with my extrapolated healing—but the only skill I'd ever cared about was its ability to focus so intently on one thing that everything else took a backseat. It had helped me through some bad stuff. Like when Matthew had died . . .

Afraid I would break down and sob like a baby, I tried to think about something else. Anything else. Like Ruarc. I hated that I'd made him angry. I didn't know why I cared, but the way he'd looked at me when I'd lied about my injuries had made my stomach drop.

Ash sucked in a breath and looked up from my mangled calf with a glare.

Great, I've pissed off another one, I thought morosely.

"Why did you not tell me it was this bad?"

"I'm sorry," I whispered. I couldn't seem to do anything right.

Ash stared at me, then looked down at my leg before drawing in a deep breath. "Let me get you some painkillers." His voice was smooth. Too smooth.

"That's okay. Really, you don't have to go through the troub—" Before I could finish my sentence he rose abruptly, still careful with my foot when he placed it down on the chair he had vacated.

"It is not okay, Hope." His brows were furrowed, framing eyes that had gone hard. "None of this is okay."

I looked down, biting down on my trembling lip. "I'm sor—"

"Do not dare apologize." The command was quiet. Deadly. "You have nothing, *nothing*, to be sorry for."

Tears filled my eyes again, and this time I didn't bother trying to stop them. I felt like I had been living in a deep, dark abyss of pain, dread, and loneliness, but now . . . now someone was there, throwing me a rope, offering me a life-line—if I was brave enough to grab it.

"Just . . . wait here. I will get you some pills."

While I waited, I thought about how stupid I'd been. For months, ever since I'd hatched my foolhardy plan of escape, I'd clung to *one* thought, to *one* plan. My uncle. As though he'd magically heal me, somehow destroy the Hunters single-handedly, and find a way to deliver me from the monster within.

A despairing girl's dream.

If I found my uncle, there was a chance he'd take me in. But what more could he do? What could *I* do, wounded as I was, hunted by the very people I'd only just escaped?

You could stay here, the weaker part of me whispered seductively. *At least for a little while. Who could it hurt?*

My stomach rolled. If the Hunters found me, they would kill everyone I'd been in contact with. They wouldn't want their secrets spilled, their atrocities revealed to the world. That would bring attention and scrutiny, and though they seemed the ultimate evil, they, too, feared . . . someone. Or something. Whispers carried when one had nothing to do but sit in a cell all day, and the prisoners not yet broken occasionally communicated with each other.

The Hunters' fear would be deadly to me and anyone who knew their secrets. That much I knew.

The thought of Ruarc's fierce, silver eyes going dull and lifeless as they stared up at nothing made me want to gag. Or of death stopping Jason's easy smiles and cheeky winks. And what if Ash's quiet comfort was lost forever?

And though it was clear Lucien couldn't stand me, he'd

allowed me into his home. If he died, the world would mourn one of its most beautiful creations, a man who'd probably been shaped like his experiences, just like I had. Like we all were.

Inconceivable.

Even having known them for less than a day, I couldn't imagine a world where they were gone.

Gone because of me . . .

"Take these." Ash was back. He held out three small pills. "They will dull the pain and make you a little drowsy, which you will probably need to be able to sleep tonight."

I reached out, hesitating before accepting them. What if they knocked me out and one of the guys hurt me? What if they were trying to make me defenseless so they could imprison me, or . . . do things to me? What if they were biding their time to take me back to the Hunters?

I shuddered.

"They are just painkillers, Hope," Ash said quietly, placing a glass of water on the table next to me. "If we wanted to hurt you, do you think you could have stopped us in your state?"

Chills crawled beneath my skin and my gaze shot up, searching his steady, blue eyes, looking for any hint of malice or deception. His honesty, although scary, was just what I needed.

I knew they could have hurt me. I was injured, scared to death, and so exhausted I could probably sleep outside on the sidewalk—rain, snow, or a hurricane be damned. But I did have a weapon. A deadly one I was reluctant to unleash. They remained unaware of my monster, and that meant I could afford to trust.

Or pretend to trust.

I took the pills, a guilty, pinching sensation in my gut when his eyes warmed. Ignoring my conscience—this was about surviving, after all—I threw my head back and swallowed.

Ash sat back down, gently maneuvering my foot until it rested on his right knee and the small towel he'd placed there.

A few minutes passed in silence while Ash waited for the medicine to kick in. I pretended to study my injured leg while sneaking peeks at him as often as I dared.

My eyes kept catching on the beautiful feather peeking up from his dark mane. What did it signify? And why was his hair so long? It hung down his back like a silk curtain, almost as long as mine.

Compared to Ruarc, Ash seemed so in control. So present, if that made sense? Leaning back in his chair, eyes closed and expression peaceful, he looked completely at ease. I wondered what he was thinking about. Was he meditating?

"No," Ash said, a small, crooked smile pulling at his lips and revealing nice, even teeth and a small dimple in his cheek. It softened his otherwise sharp features, gentling the severity of the too-high, too-sharp cheekbones and harsh, slashing eyebrows.

"No, what?" I couldn't tear my eyes away from that smile.

"No, I am not meditating," he said, smile broadening.

"Oh." I ducked my head, embarrassed at having said my thoughts out loud.

I can't believe I keep getting caught staring at these men, I thought, mortified. *And that I keep saying my thoughts out loud like a crazy person*. Although that flaw wasn't really my fault. I'd taken to talking to myself while in captivity. Sometimes I went days without any form of human contact. It had gotten lonely.

Ash shook his head, lip twitching, but didn't say anything more about my slip up. "Let's take a look at your leg."

When he didn't move, I turned questioning eyes to him and found him studying me, one brow arched. Blushing, I realized he was waiting for my permission to continue.

51

I nodded, regretting it as soon as he tipped the bottle he was holding and poured a liquid that burned like acid.

I yelped. Short and sharp, mostly because the unexpectedness of the pain had stolen my breath. Ash jerked back and I froze, shame rising at the weakness my outburst revealed.

"The painkillers are not working." Darkness flashed over his face, tightening his expression.

We both ignored the thundering footsteps racing down the stairs and Jason's stilted curse when Ruarc slammed into him in the doorway. They stood there for a few seconds before Ruarc let loose a frustrated roar that made me shrink in my seat, and they both left the way they'd come.

I blinked at the empty doorway.

"I am sorry, but I cannot give you more pills, Hope," Ash said.

"It's fine." This time it wasn't a lie. Now that I knew it was coming I could handle the pain.

"It will hurt."

"I know."

"You will have to sit still so I do not accidentally injure you further. Would you like me to ask one of the others to hold your leg steady?"

Pure, unadulterated panic swarmed.

No!

My damaged, inner self was in a state of complete and utter terror. The thought of hands on me, holding me down, hurting me while I was helpless to resist . . .

I was going to be sick.

"Hope . . . Hope." Ash's sharp voice cut through the haze in my mind and my eyes snapped to his. His pupils were pinpricks, the icy blue of his irises swallowing them until they seemed to glow. His breathing was labored and his mouth looked . . . wrong. Like it was too small for his teeth.

Am I hallucinating?

"Take a deep breath for me, *banajaanh*. That's it. One more, deep and cleansing. Relax. You are safe."

I concentrated on Ash, on his reassuring voice and the slight strain buried deep below layers of leashed control.

"Wh-what does it mean?" I asked, focusing on the strangely beautiful word I hadn't understood, rather than the slowly receding panic I knew could come back and devour me whole if I gave it any sort of power.

Ash studied me, nostrils flaring. "It means baby bird. Or nestling."

I blinked. "I am not a bird."

"I know."

Sensing I wouldn't get a better explanation than that, I changed the subject. "What language is that?"

"Ojibwe," he said shortly.

I should probably have let it go, but I was curious about him and why he'd called me a baby bird in a language I'd never even heard of. "What is Ojibwe?"

Ash was silent for a long time, so long I worried I'd gravely offended him. When he replied, his face was devoid of any expression. "Ojibwe is a Native American tribe."

A vague memory of watching a cartoon with Native Americans when I was little flashed through my mind. I only remembered their bow and arrows and the feathers in their hair.

My gaze zeroed in on the playful feather bobbing above Ash's head. White and brown, tipped with red. *Pretty.* I looked around the roomy kitchen, wondering if he had a bow and arrows hidden somewhere too. I'd always wanted to try shoot one. Would I sound stupid if I admitted to knowing next to nothing about his people?

"Are you a Native American then?" I asked, intensely curious about this gentle, powerful man who had gone out of his way to help me.

The way he looked at me was disconcerting. Head cocked to the side, lips pursed, brows lowered in contemplation.

"Do you know where you are, Hope?"

"Do I know where I am?" Why was he asking me that?

When he simply nodded, I looked around, taking in the marble countertops, the roomy cooking area with fancy-looking cooking equipment I had never seen before, the windows showing the faint outline of the moon against the dark sky.

It was obvious, wasn't it?

"Uhm, yes. We are in your kitchen?" It came out more like a question than a definitive statement, but I was starting to get a little spooked. Was he crazy? Was that tight control of his hiding someone with mental instability?

Releasing a deep sigh, he shook his head. "I mean do you know *where* you are, what city, what state?"

Not understanding what this had to do with him possibly being Native American, I tapped my fingers together as nerves shot through me. How had this conversation taken such a strange, uncomfortable turn. Would he send me away if I didn't know? Was it a test? If I didn't answer correctly, would he assume *I* was the crazy one and send me to whatever place crazy people lived?

"I—I wasn't really told . . . I mean—it's not where I grew up, but . . . after we moved, I just didn't . . ." Why was I such an idiot? Couldn't I come up with *one* decent lie to cover for the fact that I hadn't been outside the Hunter facility since I was taken there as a child?

Ash blanched. When he began rubbing his temples with both hands, I wondered what he was thinking, what conclusions he'd drawn from my inadvertent revelation.

"He will never hurt you again," he said hoarsely. "I can't believe . . . he didn't even let you outside . . ."

Feeling sick, I covered my stomach with my hands and hung my head in shame. I felt terrible, absolutely *terrible* for letting these people think that I was running from an abusive dad. Or spouse. Or whatever.

I wasn't clear on what they thought, and I wouldn't be asking either. Anything was better than me telling them the truth. A truth that would eventually lead them to ask questions like *how* and *why*. And that could never happen. Telling them about the Hunters would put their lives at risk, and if they found out why I was there, what I had done . . .

I closed my eyes against the tears that threatened. If they knew, they'd hand me back to the Hunters and I would rather *die* than go back there. So I kept my mouth closed and let Ash draw whatever conclusions he wanted, comforting myself with the thought that no matter what he imagined, it could never be as bad as the truth.

ASH

The horror of what the poor girl had endured was silver in my veins. I had to fight to keep my face clear of the contempt I felt for her captor. In the state she was in, it was possible she would mistake the emotion, believing it aimed at her.

"Your wound needs stitching." I spoke to her bowed head. The sour scent of shame drifted through the air, mixing with her natural scent and corrupting what should have been pure. Even without my excellent senses I would have known her emotions. Shame kept her shoulders curled and guilt made itself known in the form of nervous fingers picking at threadbare clothes.

A victim. The cold thought stroked across my awareness.

She did not look up, keeping her chin tucked against her chest. "O-okay."

That one, quivering word told a story that had violence rising through my blood. She asked no questions, posed no refusal.

I gritted my teeth and waited for her to meet my gaze. She needed reassurance now, needed to understand that she was innocent and that victims bore no blame for the actions of their abuser.

An image of my mother appeared in my mind. Not from the last time I saw her, but from before, when her eyes shone with kindness, not pain, and her skin was smooth and undamaged. She had been pretty, my mother. Gentle. Kind.

The rush of fury that always followed these thoughts was neither unexpected nor allowed to fester. I shoved it away with the same ruthlessness my kind was known for and focused on my breathing.

Stay calm. First comes the breath, then the spirit, and then the rest can follow.

Three breaths later and I had leashed the rage prodding at my beast.

The girl's head remained bowed.

While I waited for her to gather her courage, I mentally scrolled through the events and conversations of the past few hours. When I got to the conversations about her abuse, I paused.

Something does not add up.

Her guilt was a heavy constant, shame always nipping at its heels. The desperation and panic I sensed within her were easily explained as left over feelings from the abuse it was clear she had suffered, but her fidgeting and her agitation seemed out of place. As though she was hiding something.

I toyed with the idea that her situation was not quite what it seemed, but no matter the circumstances I constructed in my mind based on her behavior, nothing truly fit.

What do I know?

Someone had hurt her. She was too pale; the illusion of paper-thin skin could only be achieved by not seeing sunlight for prolonged periods of time. Streaks of dirt marred her translucent skin, while long, brown hair hung in a tangled mess down her back. Her face was drawn and her soft, brown eyes reflected anguish and desperation.

The way she flinched at loud noises and sudden movements was disturbing—a behavior one generally developed when being beaten at regular intervals.

The whole thing left a sour taste in my mouth. The girl was clearly a victim, but every time someone referred to her abuser, she seemed . . . uncomfortable. And not because she was terrified—although she was—but because she was hiding something. When Ruarc had wanted to know the bastard's name she had all but fainted.

Could it be because they are powerful? I mused. *Or that there are more than one? A cult or a society, perhaps?* Whatever her demons, they kept her prisoner.

"Could you—I mean, I am ready for you to continue."

The small, anxious voice snapped me out of my reflections. When I looked down, I saw a set jaw, wide eyes, and a pulse that beat to the drums of terror. She was scared, but determined to survive.

A sharp pain burrowed between my ribs.

Poor girl. So much pain for one so young.

Just a fledgling.

Careful not to jostle her leg any more than necessary, I gently lifted her foot back into my lap and picked up the only needle in the first-aid kit. It was still inside its packaging. I unwrapped it, watching her eyes for any sign of anxiety.

No more than a twinge.

"Brace yourself, *banajaanh*," I warned gently, hating the thought of causing her more pain. "This will hurt."

HOPE

Ash was right. It did hurt. It hurt so much I had to bite my lip to keep from screaming. I was determined that no sign of weakness would escape me. No whimper, cry, or scream would betray my pain. If I'd learned anything in my years as a captive, it was how to deal with pain. And how important it was to hide your vulnerabilities from men.

"Only a few more to go, *banajaanh*," Ash said quietly. If I hadn't glanced up, I would have thought he was as calm as a lake on a windless day. His voice was more than pleasant. Both soothing and hypnotic, deep and low. But his eyes told a different story. The story of a raging storm. Brutal and violent, like the tear of flesh under steel.

Unable to look away, I watched as the corner of his eyes tightened with each pull of the needle, how shadows clouded his expression with every indrawn breath I couldn't quite stifle.

Almost as though hurting me hurt him.

With a sigh, my shoulders relaxed and the pain dulled. It didn't go away, not at all, but the sharp knife that was pain lost its edge and each cut felt a bit hollower.

A man who feels pain when those around him feel pain won't intentionally hurt anyone else. Not unless they have to.

That, more than anything, brought forth the first tendrils of trust. Trust that maybe not everyone was out to hurt me. And trust that men like these wouldn't align themselves with a group as evil and sadistic as the Hunters.

Ash must have noticed the change in me for when he next met my gaze, the storm had quieted. "Are you all right, Hope?"

I nodded, quickly looking away. Although I wanted to believe he had no intention of hurting me, I still found it difficult to maintain eye contact. The Hunters had trained me well.

Too well.

Plus, Ash was just too intense. When he looked at me, I couldn't help but feel as though he could see straight through me. Like I was a wisp of a cloud, easily parted by the tornado that was his presence. But unlike the tornado, Ash's surface reflected a calm sort of tranquility while his eyes occasionally showed the glimpse of the wild power he kept restrained. The burn of his scrutiny felt like a brand against my skin. Although I couldn't see him, I *knew* he was watching me. Studying. Learning.

A thrill of fear shot through me. My secrets were dark and ugly. Nothing I would ever want someone like him to know. Someone who was probably a much better person than I'd ever been.

A tug followed by a sharp pinch let me know it was safe to look back up. Ash's dark head was bent over my calf as he worked with a gentle but precise hand.

"Last one," he warned before quickly finishing the last suture and tying off the thread. He then cleaned the wound one more time before wrapping everything securely with a soft bandage. "You did well."

A warm glow filled me at the praise. "Thank you. For fixing me up, I mean."

He inclined his head, but there was a tightness around his mouth I didn't understand, and when he remained silent as he put the bottle of antiseptic back into the first aid kit, I felt this strange compulsion to talk to him, to bare my soul and tell him all about my problems.

But since I couldn't do that, I blurted out the first thing that came to mind. "I've never had stitches before."

"Is that so?"

It could have been my imagination, but I could've sworn I saw a flicker of relief lighten his serious expression.

"Yes, first-timer!"

The sharp focus he suddenly directed my way made me squirm. "You have not had cuts that needed tending, then?"

"Well, yeah, but they healed on their own—" My words turned to dust in my mouth at the look of rage that swept over his sharp features. Instinctively, I scooted back, forgetting I was on a chair and effectively trapped with a man that suddenly seemed much more dangerous than the Hunters ever had.

But as fast as he'd transformed into something resembling a whirlwind of blades—sharp and deadly, and with the potential to kill us all—his features evened out until he looked as tranquil as the calm lake once more.

"I see. And did you often have to wait for wounds to heal on their own?"

"No," I quickly replied. Too quickly. Ash's brows rose, but all he did was nod. And somehow that nod made me feel as tall as a worm, and about as ugly as one too, because all he'd ever done was help me and all I could do was lie and tell half-truths.

And he seemed to know it. Understand it, even. Was that possible, or was my imagination running wild?

"H-have you had stitches before?"

If he knew I was trying to change the subject, he didn't let it show. Leaning forward and resting his elbows on his knees, he pierced me with that shrewd gaze of his. "Not for a long time."

"When you were young?"

He looked thoughtful, then said, "Old enough."

It was strange, but the way he said so little, revealed so little, didn't put me off or make me feel shut out. Instead, it relieved the pressure of the conversation, making me feel at ease and spiking my curiosity.

"Old enough for what?" I asked, suddenly wanting to talk to him as long as he'd let me.

His eyes flickered over me and his expression lightened. Without noticing, I'd leaned forward, eager for not a single word to be lost as he spoke. It was unlike me and it instantly made me wary.

"To not need them any longer."

"How old was that?"

A dark emotion flickered behind his eyes. "Sixteen."

Sixteen . . .

My throat closed. "Oh."

I didn't pretend to understand the dark pain I sensed in him or the strangeness of his statement—what did age have to do with stitches?—instead, I pretended to study my surroundings while digesting all these new emotions, these new experiences.

"Who are you, Hope?" Ash's smooth voice cut through my thoughts like the Hunters' metal through flesh. Piercing eyes bored deep, flayed layer after layer in search of something I suddenly feared he would find.

This man . . . he saw too much. Understood things about me I still didn't.

He was dangerous.

A stranger.

What was I thinking? When had I forgotten about my perilous situation and how fast those closest could betray and wound? And when had I started speaking so freely, letting my curiosity get the better of me? I had to remember I didn't know these men. Not really. They didn't know my secrets, and should they ever learn the truth of my past . . .

Fear was lead in my veins, chills upon my skin, but Ash was still looking at me with those intense eyes, waiting for me to answer.

"I . . . I'm just m-me." I tried my best to stop the shakes I knew would lash my voice, but to no avail.

Ash drew back, mouth tensing. "I apologize. I did not mean to cause you distress."

"It is the cause of her distress that worries me," a cool voice announced from behind.

I jumped in my seat and turned my head until I could see the man in the doorway.

Lucien.

My palms grew damp.

Ash leaned back in his chair. "Now is not a good time, Lucien."

Lucien ignored him. "Who are you, Hope?" he asked, coming to a stop behind me so I had to keep my neck twisted if I wanted to keep my eyes on him.

Which I did.

"Or is the better question, *what* are you?"

For once, terror was not my enemy. It made me freeze, stopped my reaction from showing and revealing the truth of the matter—that *what* was more important than *who*. I didn't even know what the monster inside me was. I only knew what it was capable of.

Heat branded me when Ash grabbed my frozen hand. Concern marred his lowered brows, concern and something else. Suspicion? Worry? "We will not hurt you, *banajaanh*. Regardless of your answer." He gave my hand a reassuring squeeze.

I was not reassured. They were too close. Two strange men, boxing me in and making me feel trapped. My breath came in short, uneven bursts and my lips went numb.

Have to pretend. Have to throw them off.

"I-I don't kn-know what you m-mean."

Thankfully, Lucien moved to stand next to where Ash was sitting, no longer trapping me between them. With narrowed eyes and head tilted to the side, he looked like an avenging angel. An angry, suspicious angel whose nostrils flared with every indrawn breath. Each rise and fall of his chest seemed to anger him more, until he shook his head in disgust and left the room as abruptly as he had entered it.

Still holding my hand, Ash studied me with a thoughtful expression before letting go.

I couldn't decide whether I was more relieved or disappointed. It had been a long time since I'd been touched without the intention of bringing harm, and the comfort I'd derived from his warmth was more than I knew how to deal with.

Fear of discovery slipped. It had been stupid of me to worry about that at all. What kind of people would ever suspect another of harboring a monster? To most, humans were humans, and although they'd asked *what* I was, they had probably meant it as most did, what kind of person and what kind of job. What I was, what I *had been*, was a captive.

But now? I just didn't know.

7

HOPE

THE PAIN OF THE STITCHES, LUCIEN'S SUSPICION, THE WAY ASH seemed to see past my defenses to the withered, ugly thing inside, these things were nothing compared to the trauma my body had already gone through with the Hunters' torture and my escape. But added all together it left me wrung out, tired beyond measure, and feeling like each second dragged on for an eternity. When Ash suggested a break—mentioning something about tea—before moving on to my other injuries, I gave a grateful nod and rested my head in the cradle of my arms on the kitchen table.

The next thing I knew was the fuzzy quality of a dream. It began with pain. Not deep enough to jolt me awake, but enough to tense my body even in sleep. Cold metal pressed against my skin. My heart stuttered. But then it was gone and I relaxed. After a while, I dreamed of floating. Of deep voices murmuring. Of being enveloped in strong, capable arms while comforting heat warmed my stiff limbs and something soft and heavy draped over my body.

And then . . . Then there was nothing.

When I woke up, the first thing I noticed was the wonderful smells surrounding me. Clean sheets, fresh daisies, and the mouthwatering scent of a full breakfast.

Is that pancakes? I wondered, filled with disbelief. My stomach rumbled, hunger a sudden sharp bite, and I sat up to take in the room I found myself in. It was large and airy, the bed situated in one of the outer corners, right below a window I guessed to be just big enough for me to fit through. There was only one door and no furniture except for the large, king-sized bed, a double dresser, and the nightstand on the right of me that contained the cause of one of the delicious, fresh aromas I had woken up to: a large vase filled with daisies.

I sat up, mindful of my sore body. I was still fully clothed, barring the scraps of fabric that had been cut away by my leg and midriff, and I smelled—

Scrambling out from the covers, heart beating erratically, pulse pounding, I ran my hands down my body, feeling for clean skin, for patches without grime.

There were none.

A huge sigh of relief left my distressed lungs and I collapsed back down.

They didn't bathe me.

My heart slowed.

When I'd remembered the blood and dirt coating my skin and seen the contrast to these clean, fresh sheets, I'd known a moment of stark panic. *Too dirty for this untarnished white*, I'd thought. And I desperately didn't want any of the guys to see me naked. My undernourished, damaged body aside, being naked in front of *anyone*, especially while unconscious, left me feeling like hundreds of insects were trying to crawl up my throat and out of my mouth.

I swung my legs down the side of the bed, fighting the darkness closing in at the corners of my vision. *Not healed yet, then.* Pristine, white bandages climbed up my foot, circling my ankle before ending midway up my calf. Thinking about all the stitches necessary to close that wound made my throat close and saliva fill my mouth.

I swallowed and winced at the pain in my sides.

After my body had given out on me, Ash must have finished his doctoring. There was an uncomfortably tight bandage wrapped around my upper body from my waist to just below the thin piece of clothing still covering my breasts. I wasn't sure what the bandages were for, but when I moved, a terrible, piercing pain burrowed into my lungs, spreading through my ribs and chest.

What the . . .

I gingerly skimmed my fingers over the surface of the bandage. Either the monster had blocked this pain during my escape, or I'd been too preoccupied by the throbbing in my leg to take notice of other injuries.

I struggled to remember what Gregory had done to my ribs—I'd drifted in and out of consciousness near the end of my last torture session, and the memories were hazy at best. Did I want to know?

No.

The pain made it hard to breathe, but I knew from experience it wouldn't take more than a few days to heal completely.

Bracing my hands on the bed, I got up and crept to the door. It opened with a small creak, giving me my first look at the second floor of the guys' big house.

Do they all live here together? It had seemed that way, but that was strange, wasn't it? As far as I remembered only families tended to live together. I doubted they were closely related—they looked nothing alike—but maybe they were distant cousins or something.

Or just friends?

I slowly made my way down the hall, curious about where each of the seven doors on this floor led. *What a strange layout*, I thought, fascinated by the wide, furniture-free hall. The child in me imagined that each door led into a strange and riveting new place. The door with the snowflake sticker on the front would definitely lead to a winter wonder paradise.

Pausing outside the snowflake door, I studied the cute sticker. It looked like something I could've had as a child, all sparkly and adorable. Tracing each line of the design, totally absorbed, I didn't notice the door opening until I tumbled forward.

"Morning, love," Jason greeted cheerfully as he caught me against his body. "Beautiful way to start the day." He held me to his chest and grinned down at me, sunny brown eyes slowly turning into molten fire as they stared into my own.

I was clearing my throat nervously when I noticed that the chiseled chest my face was pressed into was, in fact, naked.

Stuttering meaningless nonsense, I pushed away from him and lowered my gaze so I wouldn't stare.

Do his abs have abs?

Naked except for a pair of boxers, his broad body was a wall of muscle. A wall I was busy ogling.

"I'm so sorry!" I squeaked and covered my eyes, face surely a bright, flaming red. The large bulge in his boxers had startled me, and when I stepped back, eyes tightly closed, I tripped over my own feet.

Strong arms caught me before I hit the floor and I was right back where I started, pressed against a mostly naked man.

"Y-you can let me go now," I stammered.

"Do I smell?"

I looked up at his suddenly serious face, wrinkling my nose in confusion. "Err, no, I don't think so?"

"Are you sure, love?"

"Uhm, yes?" It wasn't like I had sniffed him or anything,

but I couldn't exactly stop breathing and with my face so close to his skin, I could easily pick up on his darkly sweet scent. He smelled of virile, healthy male.

Virile? Healthy? When did I go crazy and start thinking these things had their own scents?

"Why does it matter?" I asked. *Unless . . .* Did *I* smell? God, was that why he asked? Mortification swept through me as I remembered I hadn't washed yet.

I should ask for a shower.

"Well . . ." Jason started, looking down at me with his face scrunched up in an overly dramatic way, like he was pondering one of the most important questions of his life. "Since you are so eager to get away from me, I can only assume you were either being suffocated by my stench, or you are so hungry you would risk falling down the stairs in your hurry to get some food." He grinned cheekily. "Since we have established that I smell divine"—*wait, when had we established that?*—"we should get some food in you."

Gaze riveted on Jason's mischievous smile, I didn't protest when he led me down the stairs. The steady hand at my elbow kept me upright when my leg threatened to buckle under my weight, and with each step I was acutely aware of his nearness. Of the heat radiating off his almost naked body. Of the powerful muscles bunching under his sun-bronzed skin.

"Shouldn't you put on some clothes?" I blurted when we reached the spacious living room and Jason's naked stomach brushed against my arm.

"Tired of the view already, love?"

"I—I wasn't . . . I mean, I wasn't looking," I stuttered.

Jason grinned and waggled his eyebrows at me. "Then I must be doing something wrong."

Face burning, I chose to remain silent.

What is happening?

Was he mocking me or inviting me to look? Or maybe he

was doing something else entirely? Life with the Hunters had not prepared me for normal human interaction.

If only my freedom came with a manual. Something suspiciously close to loss settled like a boulder in my stomach.

"Hey," Jason said, concern marring his handsome face. "I didn't mean to make you uncomfortable." Running a hand through his mussed-up brown hair, he swapped his weight from foot to foot and cleared his throat. "Look, I'm—"

A roaring wall of muscle slammed into him, throwing his body clear across the room, and rather than throw myself to the side, I stood and watched. Rooted to the spot. A strange haze took hold of my mind, my thoughts slow, disjointed.

No sharp corners. That's good.

This room, as the others I'd seen, was sparsely furnished. A huge sofa occupied the back wall, facing the biggest TV I had ever seen, a low table between them. An almost empty bookcase stood by the door leading to the hallway between the living room and the kitchen. The rest of the room was just empty space with four massive chairs placed in a seemingly random fashion—two by the table, one by the bookcase, and one by the window facing the front of the house.

Strange.

A vague sort of wonder at the tidiness of the place drifted through my mind. Despite four men sharing this place, there was not a thing out of place. No clutter or dirty dishes or clothes lying around.

Is that normal?

A loud crack echoed across the room and my haze broke. I flinched at the sound, watched Jason's muscular frame land in a heap next to the couch, and tried to stop the full body shaking I hadn't noticed until now.

The unexpected violence made my throat go dry—a desert storm raged inside me, stealing all the moisture from every pore, making my body feel like it was shriveling up and dying.

My feet remained glued to the ground.

The violent scene played again and again behind my eyes. The thunderous roar. The thud of impact. Jason's body flying across the room. The sound he made as he crashed against the wall.

When my muscles finally thawed, I started toward Jason, intent on making sure he was all right. But before I reached him, a massive wall of muscle flew past me.

I dropped to the ground, struggling to breathe past the tightening of my throat.

A deafening silence urged me to look, to peek through my fingers. Then I wished I hadn't. Ruarc lunged at Jason, not making a sound. A predator on the hunt.

Making my body as small as possible, not thinking clearly enough to vacate the premises, I focused on stopping as many of my frightened whimpers as possible. Sounds of prey attracted predators, especially those of the human variety— I'd learned that the hard way. It was better to be silent. Hide my fear.

If I could.

I clamped both hands over my mouth as the battle raged on. The air was suddenly filled with brutal roars and savage snarls. Glass shattered. Fabric tore.

Would the savage animals turn on me next?

I dragged myself off to a corner, curling up into a small ball, and closed my eyes.

"Enough." Ash's voice. The quiet command held so much power it nearly made my heart halt its racing beats.

All sounds abated.

I couldn't bring myself to open my eyes—I already knew what I would see. Mangled bodies, a room in ruin, blood . . . I didn't need any more of those memories, so I stayed in my world of darkness and focused on my breathing.

A gentle hand touched my shoulder and the terror that

had kept me frozen in place gave way to a rush of adrenaline so powerful it felt like I had been hit by lightning.

I bolted.

My legs scrambled under me and slid on the wooden floors. I ignored the frantic voices calling behind me, the meaty sound of a fist hitting flesh, and focused on getting up the stairs as fast as possible. Having forgotten all about my ruined leg, it came as a shock when it gave out and I fell-face first into the stairs.

The throbbing pain radiating from my lip told me two things. One, my lip was definitely split. And two, I was still very much alive. If I wanted to stay that way, I had to get away from the mindless violence downstairs.

The bed I'd woken up in seemed to my panicked mind the safest place to be. Adrenaline was a mindless instructor and my body wanted to obey; anything to get away from the danger in the living room.

"Hope . . ." The pained plea was enough to make me stumble up the rest of the stairs and into my room. There, I used trembling fingers to lock the door, all the while thanking whatever deity ruled over monsters like me that there was a key in the lock.

I slumped onto the bed. My heart sounded like a thousand horses galloping through a cobbled street. I couldn't get enough oxygen into my lungs, and each time my breath wheezed past my split lip, it throbbed.

I have to calm down.

I focused on my breathing and finally managed to fill my oxygen-deprived brain with enough of the glorious element that made life possible to start using my other senses.

My hearing recovered first and I flinched at the harsh whispers from the other side of the door. Scuffling ensued, then, "Hope?"

Silence.

"Hope?" Again, followed by a soft knock on the door.

Now that my pulse had stopped fluttering like a leaf stuck in a tornado, reason slowly returned. But try as I might, I could not understand what had happened. One second I'd been talking to Jason and the next Ruarc had attacked like a manic beast! What kind of people were they? And what could Jason possibly have done to deserve that rage? Had he hurt someone Ruarc loved? Was he dangerous? Or was Ruarc the dangerous one? He certainly had seemed deranged.

"*Banajaanh*," Ash said softly, the strangely melodic word soothing my frazzled nerves. "Please open the door so I can make sure you are not injured."

"Me?" I blurted in disbelief.

There was no reply, just a tentative turn of the door handle followed by a muffled curse and more shuffling.

"P-please just go away." I pulled on the covers, making a little cave, and scrambled inside. Alone in the dark I finally felt my shaking limbs still, and I pretended I didn't care that the solitude that had nearly broken me during my captivity now brought me solace.

8

HOPE

Shortly after I heard Ash leave, a much more sinister sound reached my straining ears.

"Hope . . ."

Ruarc.

I cowered under the blankets, as though they could protect me against the violence Ruarc had proved himself capable of.

Why was he still here?

"Hope . . ." A mournful call not suited to such a rough voice.

What did he want?

I grabbed the pillow and squeezed it against my chest. Fear once more flooded my senses, my breath coming in short, choppy bursts that seemed to deprive me of oxygen rather than fill my lungs. When I closed my eyes, all I could see was Jason flying through the air and the vicious attack that followed.

The strength in Ruarc's powerful body . . .

He could easily break down the door.

A small whimper pushed past my dry throat.

"Hope?" The voice grew louder. "You okay?"

If I kept ignoring him, would it enrage him? Would he come bursting through that door and punish me for my disobedience?

A sigh, then the sound of rustling fabric followed by a soft thud. "Wait till you're ready," the gruff voice said, sounding an awful lot like he'd settled down on the floor with his back to the door.

Was he planning on staying there until I came out?

"Please . . ." I wanted him to leave, but if I asked again would he get mad? He was so big. So powerful. One hit from those meaty, scarred fists might separate my head from my shoulders.

"Don't—" He cut himself off. Waited. Then words that sounded pushed through clenched teeth, "I'll wait."

Wait for what? I didn't dare ask.

Several tense minutes passed in utter silence. Enough time for the adrenaline to leave my body and exhaustion to take its place. My eyelids grew heavy, occasionally sliding shut only for me to force them back open. I couldn't go to sleep. Not with Ruarc so close.

And yet . . .

The more time that passed without incident, the harder it was to cling to my fear. Even replaying the violent attack in my head was no longer enough, and the next time my eyelids slid shut, they stayed that way until sleep was brutally ripped away and I jerked upright.

It was dark. Blinking did nothing to dispel the heavy shadows. I couldn't see. Couldn't move. Something heavy weighed down my chest. I threw my arms out, but they were trapped. Locked against my sides by . . .

A blanket?

I gripped the soft material and yanked the blanket off. The sunlight streaming through the window burned my eyes.

"Hope?" A hoarse inquiry.

"I . . . I'm sleeping."

"You were whimpering."

Was I?

I rubbed at my chest, felt my racing heart begin to calm. How much time had passed? And why was Ruarc still here, waiting? If he wanted in so badly, why hadn't he used force? What was stopping him? This was his house, his property. He could do what he wanted and there was no one to stop him.

Least of all me.

I shivered.

In the hallway, Ruarc shifted. A strange sound drifted through the door, something halfway between a groan and a growl. It drowned out the complaint of hunger rumbling from my empty stomach, and fear finally gave way to annoyance. I needed sleep. Awake, the incessant hunger pangs would eventually drive me to seek food, and with Ruarc right outside, neither option seemed possible.

"Go away," I muttered, exhaustion making me careless.

But when Ruarc replied, it was not with mindless rage, but more of that deep, hoarse voice that pushed a flutter of sympathy past my defenses. "No."

Sighing, I lay back down, intent on ignoring him until he went away. But my eyes felt gritty, my limbs too heavy, my head too big and filled with fuzz, and it didn't take long before I succumbed to my body's demand and fell asleep.

A couple of hours later, I jerked awake once more. At first, I didn't understand what had woken me, but then I heard it. The whisper of stealthy feet across the floor. Four steps. Pause. Four steps. Pause. Four steps. Pause.

Ruarc was . . . pacing?

He'd stayed. All this time, he'd stayed. Why? And why did that fact inspire a warm, unwelcome glow in my chest?

"Hope?" A mournful query.

Sighing, I climbed out of the bed and winced at the agony radiating from my calf all the way up to my knee. At least my lip felt much better. It still hurt, but the throb had given away to a dull ache.

"Yes?" My voice sounded as tired as I felt. Exhaustion, mental and physical, prodded at me despite the long nap.

He cleared his throat, a low, masculine sound that made my eye twitch. "Can we talk?" After a second he hesitantly added, "Please."

I twisted my shirt around and around one finger while I weighed the pros and cons of staying in this room for all eternity and never eating again. Intimately familiar with hunger, I knew the hollow feeling would die once a few days had passed, the need to eat replaced by the need to sleep.

But the low sigh from the hall carried so much regret I had no choice.

I reluctantly limped over to the door. The moment the lock clicked, I jumped back, half expecting Ruarc to burst in with that terrifying roar he'd used on Jason.

Instead, he slowly pushed the door open and lowered his gaze to the floor.

It looked wrong. Unnatural. I'd never seen him look anything less than wholly in control. Assertive and dominant. This display of self-doubt didn't suit his character at all.

You've only known him for a day.

When he didn't speak, I took the time to study him. Wide shoulders curled in a defeated posture, a wretched expression on his drawn face, scarred hands clenched into fists . . .

He looked terrible.

"Sorry." His voice was low and raspy, like he was out of practice. "Didn't mean to scare you this morning."

I stared. Was that it? No explanation, no reason for his outburst, just . . . an apology?

I was about to close the door in his face when he gave a heavy sigh and dragged a hand through his black hair. Every now and again he glanced up at me, studying my expression before looking back down at the floor.

What had brought this big, strong man so low? It couldn't simply be scaring me, could it?

His gaze darted to my bruised lip, lingered for a moment as something dark flashed over his expression. Then he jerked his chin down and swallowed hard.

He was upset I'd been hurt? But . . . I'd done it to myself.

A numbing tingle spread from my chest and up my throat. I'd been utterly terrified, and all this time Ruarc had been waiting to apologize. Because he'd scared me. Because I'd gotten hurt.

"I . . . I forgive you."

Ruarc blinked. Once. Twice. Then he stepped back. He seemed dazed, looking up and down the hall like he didn't quite know what to do. After a long, taut moment, he dipped his chin and turned to leave.

"Wait!"

He looked back over his shoulder, silver eyes expectant.

"Is . . . is Jason okay?"

A flinch, then every muscle in his body seemed to tightened. One of his hands moved to rub along the white line on his face. My eyes followed the movement and I found myself wondering how he'd survived the injury that had left him with such a terrible scar. Whoever had hurt him, they must have wanted him dead. Had he fought back? Killed? I couldn't imagine him running from a fight, but—

Ruarc's hand jerked down to his side.

My face heated, but Ruarc didn't mention my rude staring. Instead, he looked away, baring his teeth at the floor.

"Yes." Forced through a clenched jaw, the word sounded like rocks grinding together. The harsh lines of his face were drawn into a deep scowl, and before I could say anything else, he spun on his heels, stalked down the hall, and disappeared into a room at the far end.

The door slammed shut behind him.

9

HOPE

Where is everyone? I thought warily as I walked through the empty house a few minutes later. After the commotion from this morning, I was uneasy about seeing the men again. I couldn't seem to stop myself from acting like a moron around them. If I wasn't ogling one of them, I was either sobbing my heart out or screaming like a banshee fleeing for her life.

They must think I am crazy. And maybe I was.

Peeking around the corner to make sure the kitchen was empty, I let out a sigh of relief and limped inside. The light streaming through the closed windows bounced off marble countertops, making them gleam with a lustrous shine. Black should not shine, but this black did. It shone and shimmered, the dark color a startling contrast to the otherwise bright room. Glossy, white cupboards rose above the wide sink and hid beneath the long line of the counter. Polished, white tiles covered the floor, while the walls and ceiling were painted with more white. Had there been some beige thrown in, maybe a splash of color somewhere, the kitchen would have been softer, a tad more feminine, but the stark white next to inky black made for a harshly masculine flavor that wasn't at all unpleasant.

The long table I'd been seated at the day before stood far enough to the right that it was beyond the cooking area of the kitchen, and behind it the windows made way to a door that was unlike any door I'd ever seen. Except for the bottom, the whole of it was made of glass, and through the translucent material I saw a beautiful porch stretch across the grassy landscape.

In the light of day, with sunlight caressing each tile it passed, what had last night felt too big, too foreign to be anything but scary, now offered a moment of calm respite.

My stomach rumbled.

I opened my eyes, unaware they'd closed, and looked around. Besides a cutting board, a block of wood that held knives and the like, and some equipment I couldn't remember seeing before, the countertops were empty. Equally disappointing to my grumbling belly, the large table held no food, only an empty, wooden bowl.

I had miscalculated. Happy no one was there, I hadn't thought about what that meant for my stomach. I couldn't just take food out of the fridge, that would be stealing.

My hand rubbed distracted circles over my middle. Hunger gnawed.

A throat cleared behind me and a high-pitched squeak flew from my mouth. I spun around, hand clutching at my chest.

"Sorry, love." Jason flashed a grin that made me think he found my startled rabbit act funny, and crossed to where I stood in a loose-limbed gait that somehow looked both predatory and playful at the same time. "I didn't mean to startle you."

"It's okay." It was a breathless acceptance. The flutter of my racing pulse left me flustered, wary. But when I glanced down at Jason's feet, it wasn't because I was hiding—not entirely—but because I wondered how he moved without making a sound.

Are these guys ninjas?

"Up here, love." There was a smile in that smooth voice.

My eyes snapped up to meet his, but as soon as they did, a swarm of delicate wings fluttered in my stomach and I allowed my gaze to wander. Such soft-looking lips. Smooth and inviting. A jaw that was too strong to be narrow, but not wide enough to be square. Golden skin without a hint of stubble or—

"Jason!" My hand lifted, wanting to touch, to feel, make sure. "You're . . . you're okay!"

He didn't have a mark on him. No bruises, no torn skin, no open wounds. Nothing. His powerful, toned body looked no worse for wear.

Impossible!

I could have sworn I'd seen Ruarc slug him in the face at least twice—and the sheer power behind the blows should have knocked him unconscious for at least a day.

Jason's smile dimmed, a hint of regret creeping into his golden eyes. With slow movements, probably as to not startle me again, he came closer and scanned my face. When I didn't move or say anything, he closed the space between us until our bodies were almost touching. Standing next to him, I felt astonishingly tiny. It wasn't his height—out of all of them Jason was the shortest and though my head only reached his chin, the difference wasn't as big as with the others. It wasn't his height and it wasn't his wide shoulders, the powerful chest, or the strong arms, but his presence. He was so . . . *alive*. So very *alive* and crackling with energy.

Leaning down, he gently touched my bruised lip and grimaced, some of that energy pulling inward.

"I'm truly sorry about this." His tone was low and apologetic, nothing like the cheerfulness from this morning.

Thrown by the tenderness in his touch and not knowing

how I felt about someone touching me at all, I took a small step back. "I-it's not your fault," I stammered, lowering my gaze.

Jason dropped his hand and I watched as it opened and closed reflexively at his side before I peeked up at him. His eyebrows were drawn together, eyes slightly narrowed.

He didn't say anything at first, just studied me. Being the sole focus of his magnetic gaze made me squirm. I wasn't used to being the center of attention unless something bad was going to happen.

When he finally spoke, his voice was back to its normal lighthearted state. "Ash, good of you to join us, old chap," Jason said, eyes never leaving my face.

Not having heard anything, I turned in time to see Ash step into the room.

Okay, now it's just spooky.

Ash moved like the offspring of a ghost and a tiger—feet not making a sound, muscles rolling beneath taut skin, pace sure and unhurried.

"Hi," I said warily, worried he was angry with the way I'd behaved this morning.

At my tone, he halted. The bright light streaming through the windows bathed him in a faint glow, and eyes that had made me think of stormy oceans last night now seemed to glow with a bright, white light. The pale blue roamed over my body, lingering on my bruised lip, exposed stomach and bandaged leg. And once he'd finished his inspection, his gaze moved to capture mine and time stood still. A connection flared to life between us, bright and beautiful. I could hardly breathe. I wanted to reach out and touch the invisible thread that linked us, but before I could move it shattered, leaving me with a feeling of such stark isolation that, for a moment, I felt completely and utterly alone.

What was *that?*

I searched Ash's face, desperate to see if he'd felt it too, but when our eyes locked the connection was still gone and Ash looked . . . *normal*. Had it all been in my head?

"How are you feeling?"

"I'm . . . fine, I think. My leg is pretty sore, though," I quickly added, when he crossed his arms over his chest and raised his brows at me.

"You had three bruised ribs, love,' Jason said. "And it looked like a t-rex had chewed on your foot."

Ash tilted his head. "How is your breathing?"

"Are you in any pain?"

"You should sit."

I was barely aware of my lips parting, of the wistful sigh that slipped between them. Their concern was a balm soothing my fractured soul. I couldn't remember the last time someone had cared if I was injured. As long as it hadn't been life-threatening, the Hunters had just thrown me into my cell and waited for me to heal.

Forcing back the sudden moisture in my eyes, I took a deep breath and carefully used my finger to feel along the edge of each rib. "Good," I said with what felt like a wobbly smile, happy to be able to tell them the truth for once.

Neither of them returned my smile. Ash actually frowned, while Jason just looked bewildered.

Shouldn't this be good news?

"No lingering soreness?" Ash asked, nodding at Jason while I thought about my reply.

"Erhm, a little?" I was baffled. Did they want me to be hurt? No, of course they didn't. As concerned as they'd been over every little—

Oh god, I was so stupid! Of course they were confused. I had forgotten that normal people didn't heal as fast as me. Maybe they thought I had been faking my injuries last night? Or maybe they—

A startled gasp broke free when strong, warm hands cupped my hips and lifted me clear off the floor. Jason's lightly stubbled chin rubbed along my neck as he drew in a deep breath.

"W-what are you—aah!" A short, sharp giggle tore out of me as he repeated the same motion on the other side, tickling my sensitive throat. Both men froze.

My legs dangled uselessly in the air. The longer they remained unmoving, staring, the more my discomfort grew. I squirmed in Jason's grip. "Can you put me down now?"

Without a word, he lowered me back down to solid ground. I tilted my head up and caught his slow head shake— I didn't know if Ash's sigh was in reply to said head shake or something else, but when Jason saw me looking, the confused grimace was wiped off his face and replaced by a charming grin.

"I think you need a shower, love." He grinned at my appalled expression, eyes twinkling cheekily, but something else was lurking there too. A curious concern that clouded his handsome features, making his brazen smile look slightly forced.

"Did you . . . did you just sniff me?" My voice shook. I hated being embarrassed, and the low simmer of irritation growing in my chest was startling. Feelings like anger had been useless to me for so long I'd forgotten how it felt. When showing any form of heated emotion resulted in more pain, one quickly learned to suppress the dangerous emotions. Over time I'd stopped feeling them all together.

"Behave, Jason." Ash caught my gaze and gestured to one of the chairs in front of him. "Take a seat."

"I-I'd rather take a quick shower, if it's not too much trouble?"

A low, comforting rumble sounded from Ash. "A shower can wait, Hope. We need to get some food in you, and I would like to take another look at your injuries."

The steel behind his soft-spoken words had me lowering myself into a chair before I realized what I was doing.

Ash sat down facing me. He undid my bandage, ignoring Jason's sharply indrawn breath when my calf was revealed. "It has stopped bleeding and there are no signs of infection," he murmured. "As long as we keep an eye on it I see no reason why it should not heal completely."

Tension I hadn't been aware of flowed out of me. Having a permanently damaged leg would be a big hindrance if I was going to be living a life on the run or try to make my way to Canada.

"How long do you think it will take to heal?" Since the Hunters had used the strange metal in their teeth-contraption I would heal just a little faster than a normal human. Unfortunately I had no clue what *normal* was.

Ash searched my face. "I do not know," he said, and shot Jason a look I couldn't decipher before looking back at me. When he next spoke, there was something hypnotic in both his voice and the pale blue depths of his eyes. "What happened to your foot?"

A will not my own, indomitable like a mountain cutting through the skyline, flooded my mind. It pushed, urged me to reveal the truth behind my injuries, prodded at the secrets buried in my soul. The strange, intrusive sensation made something inside me stir. My monster flexed its presence, and suddenly the pressure was gone.

"I stepped on something," I mumbled and looked away, breaking the strange eye contact.

The scrape of a chair against the floor, then Jason's presence behind me. He leaned close, so close his breath whispered across the back of my neck.

"What did you step on, love?" Jason murmured, his words worming their way into my chest, curling around my heart where I could pretend his concern meant he cared for me. At least a little.

"I-I'm not sure." I was frazzled. Their heat enveloped me; Jason at my back, chin almost resting on my shoulder, and

Ash in front of me, using that penetrating gaze of his to peel back my layers one by one. Suddenly I got scared. A small whimper left my throat and Jason immediately rose. He stepped away and to my right, where I could see him but not feel him. "I . . . I didn't see it at first. It was dark and I was—" Would it reveal too much if I told them I was running? "I . . . I stepped right on it. It had these huge, metal teeth that snapped over my leg. I thought it went through the bone at first, but it obviously didn't."

When I finished speaking, neither of the men spoke. They stared at me with wide, unblinking eyes slowly filling with the first embers of fury. It made me wonder if I had said something wrong, revealed something I shouldn't have.

"Do you . . . do you mean a bear trap?" Jason asked, disbelief etched into every line of his face.

"I don't know." I hung my head, ashamed that there was so much I didn't know, that I hadn't been given the opportunity to learn.

"It could've snapped her leg right off, Ash!" Jason exclaimed, and this time there was definitely anger in his voice.

"Unless they were modified for people." Even though Ash's tone was calm, the corded muscles in his neck and the vein throbbing by his left eye told a different story. "Hope, were these traps meant to keep others away or prevent someone from leaving?"

I recoiled. Jason's eyes widened.

"Son of a bitch!" he shouted, teeth bared in a scary grimace. Watching him lose his cool heightened my own panic. It was chilling, seeing the lips that were normally curved in a charming smile now pulled back over teeth that looked a little too sharp.

Would he attack me now, like Ruarc had attacked him earlier, without provocation or reason?

I shrank back in my chair, trying to make myself invisible.

Ash rose slowly, eyes locked on Jason. "Out."

Visibly struggling for a second or two, Jason ended up jerking his chin then striding from the room.

Oh my god.

I was petrified. The last thing I wanted was a repeat of the fight this morning, especially if it involved me. Visions of the violence I had both witnessed and been exposed to in my years with the Hunters sprang to mind, making me want to vomit.

Ash took both my hands in his and started humming. At first I thought he had gone crazy, but after a few minutes my body reluctantly relaxed and I understood what he was doing. And why.

Another tendril of trust grew from the barren ground in my heart. A man who soothed instead of intimidated, healed instead of destroyed could never be in league with the Hunters. I'd go so far as to say he had to be a good man. A rare man.

After my breathing had slowed and I was no longer on the verge of terrified tears, Ash picked up the fresh bandages he'd left on the table earlier and wrapped my leg back up.

"This has to stay dry, Hope," he said quietly. "A shower would be difficult, but if you want to take a bath you can leave your leg up at the edge while you relax."

The thought of stewing in my own filth did not appeal. He must have seen it on my face, because his lips twitched and his eyes warmed.

"There is a showerhead in the bath. Use it before you fill the tub, but remember to leave your bandage alone."

"I will. And, Ash," I said, before I lost my courage. "I . . . I just want to say . . . thank you."

He looked at me and though his lips never curved, there was something in his expression that made a warm glow begin in my chest. "You are welcome."

Ash somehow managed to look both impassive and disapproving when I tried to leave without accepting the apple he pressed into my hand.

"Eat," he said, and while it was not an order, not truly, the way he looked at me—one brow raised in the mildest of rebukes—made me close my hands around his offering and bring it to my mouth.

The apple disappeared embarrassingly fast.

"Another?"

I shook my head. My skin itched. Blood and dirt and sweat acted as a physical reminder of what I'd been through. It had to go.

"Upstairs, then, I think." He took my elbow and escorted me up the stairs—mindful of my limp. "Here," he said, opening the door next to my room. "You will find towels under the sink and soap in the left cabinet. I will bring you some clothes."

I didn't say anything when he left. I couldn't. Ash had opened the door to the nicest bathroom I'd ever seen, and I was busy ogling. At the Hunter compound, I'd been one of the lucky ones. My cell had been one of the few with a small door attached. A door leading to a tiny, square room with a toilet and a sink. The room had been so small that I couldn't put my arms straight out to my sides without scraping them against the cold, cement walls.

The unlucky captives had been given a bucket and nothing else.

One man in particular stood out in my memory. He'd been afforded no privacy, was guarded around the clock, and occupied one of the smallest cells—just large enough for him to lay down on the floor and sleep. I'd seen him only twice in passing, and both times I'd been terrified by the snarling, ravaging beast that had once been a man. He'd been broken. The Hunters had broken him.

"Here." A hand on my shoulder dissolved the uneasy memories. Ash passed me a small pile of folded clothes. "They will be too large, but they are warm and clean."

"Thank you."

He dipped his chin. "We will have dinner once you are done."

After Ash left—and I rushed to lock the door behind him —I allowed myself a moment to bask in my opulent surroundings. Pure white tiles covered the floors and walls— I was starting to see a theme—the sheer brilliance of their brightness hard to look at directly. A massive tub took up the whole back wall, and I wondered briefly if they used it as a pool. It was certainly big enough for three or four people to lounge in, but as large as the guys were, they wouldn't be able to do much more than to lie back and relax.

An image popped into my head, that of Ruarc's considerable frame filling the bath, of his wide shoulders leaning against the porcelain surface, of long, powerful legs sprawling across the bottom of the tub, of his wet, naked skin glistening with droplets and—

Heat flamed at my face. I shook my head, banishing the strange thought.

What's wrong with you, Hope?

To the right of the tub loomed a shower nearly as large as the bath. A bench of sorts occupied the corner of one wall— why would anyone need a bench in their shower?—and a fancy-looking control panel attached below the first of four showerheads.

The bathroom boasted two sinks, a mirror above each, with several cabinets below. I found the bottled soap Ash had mentioned and put down the pile of clothes before pulling out the biggest, fluffiest towel I'd ever seen.

Everything in this house is oversized.

Not that I minded. I was looking forward to soaking in the tub.

I undressed and removed the bandages around my healed ribs. The cool surface of the tub had the skin along my back pebbling. My foot went over the edge, leaving me in a very undignified position, but I didn't care.

I was about to have a bath. My first in over eighteen years.

After fumbling with the knobs for the showerhead attached to the bath—cursing when I got scolded by hot water—I finally got everything to work. Scrubbing my body clean while keeping my bandage dry proved difficult, but not impossible, and soon nearly half the bottle was empty. By the time I allowed myself to lean back and let the tub fill, my limbs felt heavy.

I dozed for a while, and when I next opened my eyes, my head felt foggy and my skin was pruned. Memories of bath time when I'd been a child intruded and a smile pushed past the sudden lump in my throat. How I'd giggled when my dad pretended to be horrified after I played too long in the bath, oohing and aahing and acting as though I was gravely injured when I held up my wrinkly fingers. And when I got a little older, how I'd done the same with—

Agony stabbed at my heart, quick and brutal.

The heat from the bath no longer held any appeal.

I dried, then dressed in the clothes Ash had lent me. The sleeves of the baggy, black shirt had to be rolled up several times before my hands could poke out, and I could barely walk in the sweatpants, even after I'd done the same with the legs. But, like he'd said, they were warm and clean, and the material was soft. Softer than any I'd worn during my captivity.

Feeling strangely vulnerable in my borrowed clothes and clean skin, I headed downstairs.

The heady smell of food lured me into the kitchen where, to my horror, all four men were gathered. The big kitchen table was filled with different dishes and five place settings had been readied. They obviously meant for me to eat with them and based on the cold look Lucien sent my way, they'd been waiting for me.

I blushed, embarrassed at taking so long.

They must think I am a total weirdo.

"Hope." With warm eyes and an open expression, Ash pulled out a chair between himself and Jason. "You must be starving. Please have a seat."

Smiling hesitantly and feeling very underdressed—especially compared to Lucien who was wearing a stiff but beautiful blue suit with a white dress shirt underneath—I nonetheless felt grateful Ash somehow knew who I was most comfortable with. Opposite Ash sat Lucien, and next to him —across from me—Ruarc.

I murmured a polite, "Thank you," before folding my hands in my lap. With a glance at the guys out of the corner of my eyes, I waited to see how they would start. I'd never been to a dinner party before, and I didn't know the rules.

"Eat until you're bursting, love," Jason said with a wink and began filling his plate. "At this table it's eat or be eaten. You should see these two"—he pointed between Ash and Ruarc—"when they've missed a meal. You do more than blink and every morsel is gone." He grabbed a little of everything, expertly spooning tender looking meat, some sort of potatoes and steamed vegetables onto his plate.

Ruarc growled, glaring daggers at Jason's grinning face before turning to me. "Here," he grumbled and leaned over so he could pick up my plate. "What do you want?"

Every single muscle in my body froze as I stared out at the feast laid before me. At least six different vegetable dishes

—all looking equally delicious—and three different sets of meat, several sides I had never seen and, of course, potatoes. Never in my life had I had a choice like this. When I was young I'd eaten what my dad put in front of me, and when I was held by the Hunters I had been more concerned about eating at all than *what* I was eating.

I nervously tapped my fingers together below the table.

What if I picked the wrong thing? What if one of them got offended by my choice? I didn't know most of these dishes and I couldn't guarantee I would like them. I'd still eat it, but they'd be able to tell by my expression that I didn't enjoy it. I wasn't a good enough liar to school my features into showing what I wanted it to show instead of the truth.

It didn't help that Lucien was watching Ruarc's outstretched hand with disapproval.

My face got hot—strange considering my stomach felt like I had swallowed several tons of ice—and my breathing grew choppy. By now all the men were staring at me, waiting for me to decide, or at least say something. Anything.

I swallowed hard, unable to look at any of them. My tongue felt heavy and awkward, incapable of speech.

Just don't cry, please don't cry. For some reason heated moisture gathered behind my eyelids.

Why is this so hard? It's just a damned meal!

How had I become this pathetic person who quivered in terror at the aspect of making such a small decision?

Just as I was about to have a full on panic attack, Ash's big, calloused hand squeezed mine gently. "Give her some of the beef, the glazed carrots, a portion of fries and the mixed vegetables." He turned to me and lowered his voice. "Only eat what you like. It does not matter if you leave some, or if you want to try something else. There is plenty to go around."

The horrible feeling that had been building in my chest immediately alleviated. I tried to smile, but the trembling, embarrassed thing twisting my lips was about as believable as a Hunter claiming 'this wouldn't hurt.' I allowed the ugly thing to slip away, and settled on a nod instead, heavy with unexpressed gratitude.

Ruarc filled my plate. A low, angry rumble spilled from his mouth, the sound so animalistic it made me question my own sanity. Did normal people generally go around making these kinds of noises and I had simply forgotten that very strange fact, or was I going crazy?

Ruarc's straight, white teeth were bared, his jaw clenched. He refused to make eye contact when he handed me my plate, and instead glared down at the table. Occasionally he shifted his angry attention to include Ash and Jason as well, but never me.

Does that mean he isn't mad at me, or that he is trying to communicate that I am a huge pain in the ass?

Probably the latter.

A deep ache started in my chest at that thought. I pushed it away and took a small bite of the meat.

"Oh my god . . ." I couldn't stop my low groan of pleasure. It was . . . heavenly. The flavor exploded on my tongue, unlike anything I'd ever tasted, and the succulent meat melted in my mouth.

When I opened my eyes, everyone was silent. Ruarc's silver eyes were slightly glazed, his mouth partially opened, and I found myself staring at his lower lip. When it wasn't twisted in a scary scowl it looked soft and biteable—a little fuller than the upper one.

I tore my eyes away and blushed furiously.

Biteable lip? What the hell am I thinking?

I turned away from Ruarc and happened to lock eyes with Lucien. His were frosted over, disdainful, condemning me for a crime I had not been aware I was committing. I shuddered in visceral response to that icy look, to the contempt bleeding through his cold mask.

How could someone look so filled with hate, yet seem as

unemotional as a marble statue? The only thing that gave away his emotions were his eyes. His expression remained dispassionate, the hand not holding his fork lay relaxed on the table. Not even his mouth curled or tensed, or did any such thing a mouth did when the person attached to it harbored strong emotions.

Did he even feel them, or were they buried so deep as to only touch his surface thoughts when he allowed it?

I tore my eyes away, vaguely aware of my fork clattering against my plate.

Jason bumped me with his shoulder. "Try the chips, love. They are absolutely"—he popped one into his mouth, chewed slowly, and winked—"divine."

"Bastard," Ruarc spat, making me jump. He pointed a threatening finger at Jason and glared, the white scar on his face standing out in stark contrast as a vein started to pulsate in his temple. If I were Jason I would've been out of my chair, sprinting across the room, and heading for the safety of the outside as fast as I possibly could.

But Jason only grinned, completely oblivious to the terrible danger he found himself in.

Lucien coughed, fixing his cold stare on me while addressing the men. "Surely you could attempt to behave like civilized beings for the remainder of our meal? No need to behave like ruffians simply because we are in the presence of a street urchin."

I didn't know what a street urchin was, but the way he said it made me think it wasn't flattering. Based on the dangerous glower on Ruarc's harsh face, he had a problem with the insult as well. Or maybe he just didn't like being told he wasn't acting civilized.

Before Ruarc could lunge at Lucien, Ash abruptly stood. "That is not how we treat guests." His voice was dark, but still low and controlled.

Lucien rose stiffly, back ramrod straight. "She is *not* a

guest." His voice dripped with disdain. "We do not know anything about her or her reason for being here. I, for one, am not buying her 'poor, abused female act.' Throw her out and good riddance, I say."

A cold shiver raced up my spine. Why did he hate me so much? My chin trembled and I cursed my own weakness, even as my gaze refused to leave the hands clenched in my lap.

He's right. Lucien is right.

I'd bring nothing but trouble to their doorstep. Hunters aside, they were already fighting because of me and although I hadn't exactly known them long, it was easy to see a deep camaraderie and love existing between them—even if their violent confrontations left me stumped.

I couldn't pretend to understand the urge to beat up someone you loved, but maybe it was just a guy thing?

"Do you think the girl mangled her own leg then, Lucien?" Jason asked, a mocking half smile on his lips.

What if they throw me out?

My breath caught. I'd only been here a day, and yet the thought of leaving left a bitter taste on my tongue. What had happened to my plan to find my uncle? To live far away from the Hunters, so far they'd never find me, the safety of family surrounding me.

He might not even know I exist.

That particular worry was batted away before it could take root. I knew I had to leave eventually—seeking shelter with my uncle was the only thing that made sense—but not yet. Not so soon. Not until I'd healed. Not until this new world made sense to me. Not until I'd gotten a small taste of the friendship these guys shared between them, enough to keep me company on the lonely years ahead. Not until—

"Damned if I know, but I find it dastardly suspicious the way she just happened to be in our way. We never did make that meeting, did we?" Lucien turned to spear me with a *look*.

"But perhaps we should ask the wench herself, although I have my doubts a suitable explanation is forthcoming. From what I can tell, she is obnoxiously tight-lipped."

Heat rose in my cheeks as I accepted the truth of his blow. Lucien was right in a way. I had been dishonest. I hadn't told them the whole truth, but how could I? Even if they were the best of men they would throw me out on my head if they knew the truth about me, about what I'd done. I squeezed my eyes shut and waited for them to order me gone.

A sudden movement made me throw my hands up to protect my head—something I'd learned was imperative when around angry men. When a deafening roar sounded, followed by a heavy crash, I peeked through my fingers.

Ruarc's breathing was harsh. His broad, muscular chest rose and fell rapidly beneath his tight, black t-shirt. I followed his enraged glare to where Lucien was crouching. A broken porcelain bowl lay scattered behind him. The wall behind his head was smeared with sauce, dripping in slow rivulets like pooling blood, and vegetables spread out on the ground looking like broken toys.

Lucien stared at the shattered bowl, eyes comically wide before narrowing. He stood up, casually dusted off his clothes, and faced Ruarc. "This type of behavior is beneath you, Ruarc."

A menacing rumble erupted from Ruarc's chest. If my muscles hadn't already been locked in adrenaline induced fright, that sound would have done the trick.

"After the betrayal you suffered I'd have thought you smarter than this." Lucien's gaze cut to me. "But if you are determined to be made a fool once more I cannot stop you."

Ruarc froze. Even his chest was still, as if he no longer needed air. A menacing hush fell over the room. A tick started below one glowing, silver eye. A fisted hand clenched and jerked upward—toward his face—before being yanked back to his side. My eyes were unwittingly drawn to his scar, and in the silence that followed I wondered if it pained him still.

I should have known the utter stillness was a prelude to something terrible. Ruarc exploded into motion. With a vicious snarl, he threw a punch. Lucien ducked and Ruarc followed up, his teeth snapping at the air where Lucien's neck had been only a second before. The two men took full advantage of the empty floor space between the table and the door, lunging and throwing punches that, when connected, made a sickeningly thud.

At first, I thought Ruarc would wipe the floor with Lucien, but although he was much bigger—both in height and in pure muscle—Lucien was a hurricane of rapid movements, faster than anyone I'd ever seen. He fought smoothly, effectively, and with a cool, distanced quality that made Ruarc's heated attack ineffective.

The fight—or rather, the savage battle—ended after just a few seconds when both Ash and Jason threw themselves into the fray, subduing Ruarc after a few moments of intensely quiet wrestling. When they all stood there, breathing heavily, Ash grabbed Ruarc's shoulder and gave it a squeeze. He said something, too quiet for me to hear it, but the effect on Ruarc was immediate.

I watched in amazement as his shoulders slumped, eyes closing and brows drawing together like he was in pain. Then he nodded slowly, and Ash took a step back.

My chest constricted in a moment of sympathetic pain when I saw a flash of torment in Ruarc's silver eyes. I wondered what Lucien had meant; who had betrayed Ruarc and what had happened? It must have been pretty bad to bring forth such blind fury and pain.

Lucien, who'd watched the exchange with a clenched jaw, raised a single eyebrow. "You are simply proving my point, Ruarc. Already she has us fighting amongst ourselves when we all know who the real enemy is."

Was he . . . was he talking about me? How could I be the enemy? I hadn't done anything to them.

"Enough," Ash said. He dragged a hand across his face before glancing at my shaking hands and frowning. "I understand your reservations, Lucien, but whatever you may think I can assure you; Hope is innocent of the crimes you imagine."

The guilt I carried at my deception grew arms and tried to strangle me. Here Ash was trying to defend me when all I had done was lie and hide the truth from him.

You are a coward, my subconscious screamed at me.

"That remains to be seen," Lucien replied with cold look in my direction.

Darting a glance over at Ruarc, my heart twisted when I thought I saw a flicker of uncertainty cross his harshly masculine face. When he noticed my attention, his beautiful eyes shuttered and he frowned.

Just as well, I thought, stubbornly ignoring the ache in my chest. *He is clearly extremely volatile.* Twice now I'd seen him brutally attack someone I felt sure he considered a friend, or at the very least a roommate. If I, a relative stranger, pissed him off I could only imagine what he'd do.

"Well," Jason drawled. "I think I've had enough of brawling for today. What do you say, love, would you like to bring your dinner outside with me? The weather is sublime and we have a lovely view."

Ruarc shot Jason a grumpy scowl while I struggled to come up with a reply. I wasn't so sure being alone with Jason was a good idea. It seemed he took pleasure in riling up the others, especially Ruarc, and I had the impression he was an unapologetic flirt.

Not that I knew much about flirting.

I looked down, searching my lap for the answers, and was surprised when Jason said, "Excellent," and took my filled plate and marched to the doorway. In a gallant bow, he waved me forward. "After you, fair maiden."

Cheeks flushing at being the center of attention once again, I cringed at the harsh squeal of my chair scraping against the floor, and walked over to Jason. Ignoring the hot stares I felt burning a hole in my back, I grabbed the elbow he offered me for support as we walked through the living room and out to the terrace.

10

JASON

Hope ate quickly. Studiously. Enjoying each morsel, but not taking the time to savor the flavors on her tongue. Almost like she feared it would be taken away and not given back, leaving her to starve.

My mood darkened, but when she blushed and put the empty plate down beside her, I found myself . . . distracted.

Her head tipped back, her lashes fluttered, and her gaze lifted to the darkened sky, taking in the vast expanse of space, the glittering stars, the thin clouds that seemed like a veil between our world and the next.

Something on her face loosened, and something in my stomach twisted.

"This is nice," she said quietly, swinging her feet.

She sat on the porch-swing Ruarc had insisted Lucien make when we first moved here. It was sturdy—Lucien was good at what he did—but whenever Ruarc used it, the damned thing groaned liked it was dying. I'd never understood why he'd wanted it, but now . . . Watching Hope use her small feet to gently sway the airborne bench back and forth, a sweet expression on her too-serious face, I had to admit I was glad.

"Look over there," I said and pointed to the tree line about a hundred yards from us. "A trail starts by the old, covered well. If you follow it for about half an hour, you'll end up by a beautiful lake surrounded by sloping hills and a small waterfall." I watched her deep brown eyes go round with wonder. "If you want, I'll take you there one day, love." The endearment rolled right off my tongue. Natural. Easy.

"I . . . maybe. One day." Her hollowed cheeks reddened, and the slow burn of anger churned in my gut. Whoever hurt her had also neglected to feed her properly. How much had this slip of a girl had to endure?

"Here," I said, handing her the small box I'd brought outside. "Sweet dessert for a sweet lady."

"Wh-what is it?"

The way her voice shook made me frown. Did I make her nervous? Or was she just unused to receiving gifts?

"Open it and see." Giving her my most charming smile, I walked over and sat next to her on the swing. She looked at me, eyes clouded with wariness, and I resisted the urge to throw my arm over the back of the swing, not wanting to make her too uncomfortable.

Although, being a little uncomfortable is healthy, I thought. The sooner she got used to being around us the better. It would make the time she spent here much less stressful.

My grin widened as I watched her carefully lift the lid off the box. She was so cute. I refused to dwell on the reason for her hesitancy, wanting instead to focus on the future and what I could do to help her while she was here.

"Is it . . . chocolate?" Hope asked, wonder in her soft voice.

My chest warmed. It felt good, making her happy. If only in a superficial way. "That it is, love. Have a bite."

"I've never had chocolate before." She took a small nibble, unaware she'd just blown my mind.

How is that possible?

"You've never had chocolate?"

"When I was little, I wasn't allowed." Her sad smile didn't seem to lament that particular rule. It was more . . . wistful. "And while I was with—" She stopped abruptly, eyes going impossibly wide.

"When you were . . ." I prompted, keeping my voice calm and steady. I knew this was important. She'd almost let something slip. A name, maybe?

"I—I . . ." She stopped, looked up at me with her heart in her eyes. There was so much pain there.

"It's all right, love," I assured her. "Just tell me about the chocolate." I couldn't bear to pressure her. Ruarc would probably curse me later for not pushing—I knew for a fact the stealthy beast was listening to every word we were saying —but I couldn't bring myself to be the cause of any more of her pain.

What was the point of dwelling on the past? Like me, she should forget everything that brought her sorrow and focus on the life she'd not yet lived. The future could be a happy place; you just had to will it into existence.

"I just—I haven't had any before," she finished lamely, taking another nibble of the succulent, dark treat. A part of me wanted to force-feed her every single one in the box. She desperately needed to put on weight, preferably until she had a healthy glow and was nicely rounded. I didn't understand why, but the thought of her going hungry bothered me.

Probably because I know how it feels.

"Then this will taste even better." I smiled at her again, a big, playful smile meant to reassure. It seemed to work—she returned it with a tiny, shy one of her own.

Before that moment, I would have described her as plain. The fact that she was underweight obviously had something to do with it, but she didn't have any striking features. Her face was heart-shaped, charming but way too thin. With hollowed cheeks and limp, brown hair, she looked haggard.

Obviously mistreated.

Her nose was tiny with a stubborn tilt at the end.

Cute.

She had rosebud lips, full and inviting.

Beautiful.

But the rest of her was pretty much just skin and bones. We all towered above her, and Ruarc looked like a giant when they stood side by side. It didn't help that she had a waist so small I could span it with my hands.

But looking at her now, with her tiny, shy smile and down-turned eyes, I found her almost . . . pretty. Her eyes were by far her best feature. They were endless wells you could lose your soul in, the color matching the chocolate she was enjoying, only filled with so many emotions it almost made me dizzy.

Too expressive.

That would hurt her when not among friends. If one paid enough attention, I'd bet her eyes would reveal every emotion, every thought before it crossed her mind.

Suddenly transfixed, I stared as she popped the rest of the chocolate into her luscious mouth, closed her eyes, and moaned.

"This is . . . incredible."

Yes. Yes, it is.

11

HOPE

JASON'S TAWNY EYES WERE LOCKED ON MINE. THE COLOR I'D previously found a pleasing, warm brown had transformed until his eyes resembled liquid gold.

Like the sun, I thought, mesmerized by the change.

Gone was the playful, flirtatious boy-next-door. The raw, masculine power staring back at me was definitely all man. A scary yet thrilling tension danced in the air, making the fine hairs on my neck rise.

Searching my face, Jason slowly reached out and tucked a stray lock behind my ear. The motion, the closeness in the act, frightened me, made me think of the violence of men.

Ruarc's snarling face flashed through my mind.

I had to remember that I didn't know these men. Even though they hadn't hurt me yet, it didn't mean they wouldn't.

Before his hand could make contact, I jerked back. It was pure reflex, something I'd learned while under the care of the Hunters.

"S-sorry," I whispered, unsure how he would react.

A dark laugh rasped up his throat. "Never be sorry for following your instincts, love." His intense gaze left me to roam over the garden before fixating on something far away.

There was a weird quality to his voice when he spoke next. "Always do what makes you happy."

Happiness was the furthest from my mind. Safety and survival was all that mattered. To find a way to be out of the Hunters reach for good without forfeiting my life.

Maybe if I stayed here long enough the Hunters would stop looking for me. I could make my way to Canada, find my uncle before they could kill me.

Relieved he wasn't angry with me, I decided to let the subject drop. "Could I ask you a question?"

Attention back on me, he lifted an eyebrow and waved his hand, as if to say, 'by all means.'

I wasn't sure how to ask without being intrusive, so I hesitated.

"Don't worry, love, I won't take offense. Ask whatever your little heart desires to know."

"Are you guys related?" Before he could answer, I plowed ahead, worried I would lose my nerve if I didn't get it all out now. "I mean, you all live here together, right? And normally only family lives together. Unless I remember wrong . . ." I trailed off. Could I be wrong about that? Did friends live together? Or maybe . . . maybe they were more than friends. Unsure why the thought depressed me, I peeked up at Jason. His eyes were sparkling with repressed laughter.

"We are . . . business partners," he said, grinning down at me. "And friends, you could say. But, yes, we are family. Family by choice, rather than blood. We have known each other for many, many years, and although they annoy the piss out of me sometimes"—his eyes warmed and his voice deepened with feeling—"I would die for them."

Sorrow flooded me. I could *feel* how much he meant those words. Had anyone ever felt that way about me?

"How long have you known Ruarc?" I asked, thinking about the vicious fight they'd been in earlier and wondering if maybe I hadn't overreacted. The careless way Jason responded when confronted with Ruarc's rage indicated he didn't think Ruarc would seriously harm him.

"Ruarc, eh?" The way he looked at me was unnerving. Before I could freak out under his scrutiny, he averted his gaze and replied, "Around twenty years or so."

"Twenty?" That was a surprise. "You must have been young when you met."

"Hmm?" He stared at me, then blinked slowly. The way his eyes widened just a crack made me think something I'd said was troubling him. "Oh, yes. Erm . . . quite young."

"So you are childhood friends, then?"

Jason laughed, a loud guffaw that made me jump in my seat when it blasted out of him. "That's rich, love."

I raised my brows in confusion. If they weren't childhood friends, then that would put Jason between thirty and forty years old depending on when he considered childhood to end. "How-how old are you?" Heat crept up my neck. Concentrating on forcing it back, I wondered if I'd overstepped. My mother once told me you should never ask people their age, but I hadn't been able to stop myself. Jason looked younger than the others. I would have guessed twenty-five, maybe, with the others being around thirty. But then again, I hadn't had much practice over the years. None of the Hunters ever revealed their age to me, and I hadn't asked.

It hadn't mattered.

"Ah-ah-ah." He waggled a playful finger in my face. "If I tell you my age, you have to tell me yours."

I could have sworn there was an instant of some calculating emotion behind his vigilant gaze, but it was gone so fast I could have imagined it. Revealing my age was of little concern to me. Knowing more about them, however, had somehow become paramount.

"I'm—" With a start I realized I didn't remember my own

age. A wave of sadness cascaded over me, drowning me in its heartache. How had my life gone so wrong?

You know how . . .

Something ugly inside me reared its head, accusing me with flashes of images of things best forgotten.

So as not to awaken suspicion—or maybe I just didn't want him to look at me with pity when he realized how truly damaged I was—I blurted out the first number that seemed reasonably close, "Twenty-three!"

Jason leaned back, raising both eyebrows and looking me up and down. I didn't know if he was reacting to my near-shout or if he thought the age seemed wrong, but it made me squirm with discomfort.

When he ended his examination, I let out a relieved breath.

"You're so tiny, it's hard to imagine . . ." His voice was low and distant.

Imagine what? I wanted to know, but I didn't want him to ask any more questions about my age.

I was sent to the Hunters when I was six. It's been eighteen years . . .

After doing the math I realized I was actually twenty-four. A quarter of my life gone with nothing to show for it. At least my first few years in that place hadn't been so bad. Besides the devastating loneliness and wondering if my mother would ever-

I shook my head, determined not to think of it.

"S-so?" It was his turn.

Jason peered down at me, a cryptic expression on his handsome face. Then he blinked once, and it was as if all his previous thoughts disappeared. "I am twenty-eight."

"That's all?" I wrinkled my brow. That would mean he was eight when he met Ruarc. Wasn't eight considered being a child, still?

"You wound me, love." He clutched at his chest. "Do I look

106

so ancient to you, then? I would have you know, both Ash and Lucien are older than me, and Ruarc would be a valued item at a museum. If they didn't mind his surly nature, that is," he added as an afterthought.

That threw me. I would have guessed Ash was the oldest of them. And I very much doubted Ruarc was over thirty-five, if that.

"Then . . . then you have known Ruarc since you were a child? Doesn't that make you childhood friends?" I didn't want to fixate on this one thing, I just found it odd. Even more so when Jason looked momentarily startled.

"Oh, right. Well, I suppose it took us a while to become friends." His wry smile broadened as he lifted his gaze to the night sky. "You could say Ruarc found me a little annoying at first. But I grew on him."

"Like unwanted mold," a gruff voice said from behind.

I spun around in my seat.

Ruarc hesitated in the doorway, the scar on his face illuminated by the porch light.

"Meaning you sometimes want mold to grow on you?" Jason ribbed, grinning like a lunatic.

With a dark glare, Ruarc turned to Jason, his massive arms crossed over his broad chest. "Watch it, boy," he growled, eyes narrowing.

"See?" Jason gently poked my side with his elbow and nodded toward Ruarc. "Ancient *and* surly."

Casting a disgusted look at Jason, Ruarc strode across the patio and leaned against the railing, facing me.

Forced to turn back around or end up sitting with my back to them, I eyed Ruarc while my stomach danced with nerves. Of all the men in this house, Ruarc made me feel the most unsettled.

There was just something about him, something I couldn't put my finger on. My feelings for him ranged from wildly terrified to deeply sympathetic, with several different stops along the way. His capacity for violence and his volatile nature scared the crap out of me. But the other sides of him, the rage he displayed when a hint of my tormented past came up, the gruff way he'd apologized when he'd scared me, the mysterious betrayal in his past, his vicious scar . . . it made something inside me ache with a shared sort of pain.

Eyes locked on me, Ruarc grunted and jerked his chin.

Perplexed, I stayed silent, looking to Jason for guidance.

"Don't look at me, love. We have yet to decipher Ruarc's preferred method of communication. It consists of grunts, growls, and chin dips."

With eyes that were rapidly narrowing, Ruarc bared his teeth in a chilling grimace. "Leave, pup."

Jason held his hands up in a placating gesture of surrender and chuckled. "What if I promise to behave?" The wicked glint in his golden eyes betrayed his intent.

When Ruarc didn't reply, Jason sobered. "Consider the circumstances," he said to Ruarc, casting a meaningful glance my way.

Ruarc took his time scrutinizing me. My skin prickled in a not-entirely-unpleasant fashion where his silver gaze lingered. With a small frown, he inclined his head at Jason.

Glancing back and forth between them, I bit my lip and tried to figure them out. There was no true bite to Ruarc's words, no unease in Jason's eyes when the other man growled at him. They clearly cared about each other, in a strange, bickering type of way.

"So, my sweet," Jason started, brows drawn together and one finger tapping his toned thigh. "What are your plans now?"

"My plans?"

"Yes, what are you going to do when you are off on your merry way?" Jason ignored Ruarc's low grumble and focused solely on me.

Oh.

Sweat gathered at the back of my neck. Did they want me to leave? I wasn't ready, didn't have a clue how I'd find my uncle, much less make my way to Canada. The thought of being on my own again made my hands shake.

"I . . . I don't know." Despair was crawling up my throat, threatening to choke the very life from me. I'd never been on my own before—even at the compound when loneliness threatened to break me in a way the Hunters' torture hadn't managed, I at least had the crazed ravings of the other prisoners to keep me company. But here, out in the real world? I had no idea how to survive. How would I get money? I had no education, no experience. In fact, my lack of knowledge on all things in this world made me woefully unprepared for just about everything in life.

And did I want to spend the rest of my life on the run?

Not really, a small voice inside me answered. But how could I live a life free of the Hunters? How could I be free of my past and the monster living inside me, clawing every day to get out and ruin my life once again?

"Look what you did!" Ruarc barked, bodily removing Jason from his spot next to me and taking his place.

I was so shaken, so lost in my own thoughts about the future, that I wasn't the slightest bit alarmed at the display of power. That was probably also why I didn't react when one of Ruarc's huge, calloused hands patted my back with startling tenderness.

How can someone so big be so gentle? The question popped into my head, a sidetrack to my rising panic at my upcoming eviction.

"Love, please take a big breath for me." Jason dropped to his knees in front of me and clasped my trembling hands in his. "I didn't mean to make you worry. You're welcome to stay here as long as you want."

"'Course she is welcome," Ruarc snarled, glaring at Jason

with an expression that clearly stated this was all the other man's fault.

Taking a deep breath to calm my nerves and slow my racing heart, I peeked up at them. "B-but why? You don't owe me anything. Why are you being so nice?"

Ruarc frowned down at me, the big hand at my back that had been rubbing slow, soothing circles stopped moving. "There is no honor in hurting females," he said gruffly and looked away.

Jason rolled his eyes. "What Ruarc is trying to say," he started, ignoring Ruarc's annoyed grumble, "is that whoever hurt you was a coward. A slimy, unworthy piece of scum who should never have been allowed to walk the earth. Leaving you to fend for yourself would make us just as unworthy. Besides," he added with a grin, "having you around will be fun. Please try bother Lucien as much as possible while you're here."

I choked on a watery chuckle, for once not burning up with embarrassment when I did something strange. Their generosity, their kindness touched me deeply and stole my voice.

Both guys cleared their throats awkwardly while I sniffed and avoided eye contact, trying to get my emotions under control. Even though they seemed a little uncomfortable at my emotional display, they comforted me in their own ways; Jason squeezed my hands, thumbs gently stroking my pale skin, and Ruarc stared straight ahead and continued his soft exploration of my back with his huge-as-a-lion-paw hand. Sometimes his mouth twitched, like he wanted to say something, but he remained silent.

When I had my emotions under control I looked up at them with a warm glow heating my chest. "Thank you."

Later that night, while wind tickled the glass panes of the windows and the guys' voices had long since quieted, I found myself at the bottom of the stairs. The warm glow that had carried me through the hours between dinner and the moment I had lain down to sleep had disappeared, leaving me cold and small and so very alone.

I wasn't sure what I was doing or why I'd left the comfort of my borrowed bed. All I knew was the itch right beneath my skin, the violent thrashing of my stomach, and the prickle biting at my neck when I squeezed my eyes together and pretended I was safe.

What am I doing?

The sound of my bare feet sliding across the hardware floor whispered at the edges of my hearing. While the rest of the house slept, I crept across the living room and out into the hallway. There, I stopped. Stared at the door that led to the outside. If I wanted to leave, could I?

Metal shone, the door handle an unfinished smile that lured me closer. Not so I could escape my temporary shelter, but so I could make sure I hadn't traded one cage for another.

I'd been locked away for so long . . .

They wouldn't keep me against my will, I was almost sure. But something in me twisted with the first stirrings of panic.

Would the door be locked?

My eyes searched for a key, but it was just the door and me and that same half-finished metal smile.

"Just try it," I whispered to my shaking hand. It twitched but didn't turn the handle.

My pulse raced and my mouth went dry, and still I stared at the unmoving door while my grip grew damp and threatened to slide right off.

Tremors worked their way up to my wrist, past my elbow,

until my shoulder got infected and my whole body began shaking.

What am I doing?

I'd been given a reprieve, a place to rest, to heal, to gather my strength. I should be grateful, not filled with this restless fear.

What am I doing?

The sky. I had to see the sky. Had to know I could run if I needed, that I could be free. Outside. Where there was air.

Air.

My throat closed. One minute I was breathing, the next I clawed at my neck with my free hand, feeling for the rope that had to be cutting off my air—why else would I be choking?—but I felt only skin.

I stumbled against the barricade blocking my escape, still clutching that damned handle.

Bright, red spots dotted my vision.

My shoulder pushed against an unyielding surface, then my back. My knees buckled. I slid down to the floor, still not breathing.

Tendons in my shoulder screamed in pain.

I looked up, saw my arm outstretched, my hand fisted around . . . something.

What am I doing?

I blinked. And then, because they felt so heavy, I let my eyelids droop.

My lips tingled.

My fingers went numb.

I sagged, and then I was falling.

Pain bloomed in the back of my head, and suddenly I could breathe.

I gulped down several mouthfuls of air, opened my eyes and found that I was lying flat on the ground. My lower half remained in the hallway while my upper back, shoulders, and head lay on the front porch.

Outside.

Wooden planks painted white—so much white—made a sort of porch roof supported by the house itself and pretty pillars I hadn't noticed when I'd been brought inside last night. Intricate designs spiraled up each side, no two alike.

For a few minutes all I did was stare at those pretty pillars. That, and breathe.

Then I sat up, struggled to my feet, and went back inside. The itch under my skin settled, the thrashing in my stomach slowed to an uneasy roll.

I closed the door. Slipped back upstairs. Lay down in my borrowed bed.

My breath was slow, almost even. My body was tired. My brain exhausted. But I couldn't sleep.

What am I doing?

12

HOPE

THE NEXT MORNING I WAS TREMBLING WITH NERVES. AFTER my little adventure the night before, I'd spent a restless night tossing and turning and worrying about the future, until finally I'd decided I needed to ask for help. What else could I do?

Finding my uncle had seemed such a clear goal when I'd been trapped at the Hunter compound, but now that I was in the real world . . . Even if I somehow managed to find my way to Canada, it was still the matter of locating him in a country the size of—well, I didn't really know how big it was, but it was a country. A whole country!

You've never even met the man . . .

That was another thing. No matter what my father had said, my uncle might not want to help me. He might want nothing to do with me at all.

I was stuck. And no matter what I decided, I had no means to pursue my goals. I didn't know how the world worked outside the few movies and books I'd been exposed to. Asking the guys too many questions would raise suspicions and divulge much more of my past than I was comfortable with—which meant I had to learn on my own.

Since leaving the house right then was out of the question, I could focus on the second most important thing to my safety and future plans: money.

The world revolved around money, that much I'd learned from listening to the Hunters complain about their bosses, salaries, and the co-workers they felt were over-valued. Earning money required a job, so that would be my first step. Convincing Ash to help me find a job.

It would be difficult; I'd have to ask for help and reveal some of my weaknesses without actually revealing most of my past. I also didn't want to be a burden, and I already owed these guys so much. Without them I would most likely have been back in Hunter custody by now.

Besides that, how would I get a job when I was terrified of leaving the house and had no qualifications? Even if I could magically summon up a valid ID—which I didn't have —there was still the small matter of having the whole Hunter army after me.

Maybe it would be better if I ran, tried to find my way to Canada right away.

But how? I had no money, no experience with the real world. The Hunters would find me in no time, or I would die from starvation or exposure.

With a heavy sigh, I slipped from my room to search for Ash. There was no point in putting it off. The longer I obsessed about all the flaws in my plan, the more nervous I became. If I didn't stop, I would end up melted into a pool of screaming terror.

It would not be a pretty sight.

A flash of movement made me look up. "Lucien," I automatically called out, regretting my hasty cry as soon as it left my mouth and Lucien halted his long strides.

Rigid stance in place and back ramrod straight, he turned and arched a perfect, black eyebrow that somehow seemed to mock me. The frosty indifference in his cold, green eyes made my stomach feel like it was filled with acid.

"Uhm, never mind," I whispered, hoping he would take that as his chance to leave.

He didn't.

"I rather doubt you would have stopped me if you did not have something of perceived importance on your mind," he replied in a voice dripping with derision. "Instead of further squandering my time I suggest you spit it out so I can get on with my day."

I should have been used to his haughty, disdainful attitude and strange manner of speaking by now, but it stunned me into silence.

"Well?" he said, scanning me from head to toe—and if his expression was any indication he found me lacking in every way.

"C-could you . . . could you tell me where Ash is?" Silently cursing my high-pitched, panicked tone, I kept my gaze glued to the ground. Seeing the scorn on his face when he looked at me did not appeal. In fact, it made me feel bad. Unworthy, somehow, and even more ashamed of my past than I already was.

"Why?" The simple question was loaded with suspicion.

"I-I just want to talk to him about something."

"Is that so?" With three, long strides he closed the distance between us. Towering over me, his upper lip curled in distaste. "And what, pray tell, do you wish to speak to him about?"

"It's p-private."

"If you are considering deceiving Ash, little girl, I suggest you reconsider." He lowered his voice to a harsh whisper. "I *will* learn your secrets. You best pray they are not too dark."

With that ominous warning he left me shaking and alone in the hall. My secrets *were* dark.

If they found out . . .

The possibility alone made me shudder. I would have to watch out around Lucien—he was the only one who seemed suspicious of me. Maybe he was the only one who saw me for what I truly was.

A monster.

Courage lost, I turned back around and sought solace in my room. I would talk to Ash in a few minutes. I just had to stop shaking first.

ASH

"Ash?" The hesitant voice on the other side of the door broke my concentration as effectively as one of Ruarc's vicious snarls. The plans laid out in front of me blurred together until all I could see in my mind's eye was Hope's pale, sunken face.

"Come in," I called out. As I sat back and waited for her to enter, I gathered up the documents. It would be better if she remained unaware of who we were and what we did.

Peeking around the door, Hope paused in the doorway.

I stood, motioning her forward. "Please have a seat." Indicating the only other chair in the room, I waited for her to sit before I took my place on the other side of the desk.

In an attempt to look non-threatening, I leaned my elbows on the flat surface between us, wound my fingers together and rested my chin on top. Looking innocuous was a skill I had acquired early in life.

"What can I do for you?" I asked when she failed to speak. I made sure to keep my tone gentle, gaze locked on hers— which proved impossible when she dipped her head and stared at the floor. It saddened me that she seemed incapable of maintaining eye contact. Without realizing it she was relinquishing her status, making herself less than I was sure she could be.

"I . . . I need help," she blurted. A faint smell of fear stirred the predator in me.

She is not prey, I silently informed it.

There was no reply, of course, but I felt its interest as it perked its metaphorical ears and gave the female in front of me its undivided attention.

"Did something happen?" Dismay wound through me at the possibility of her being harmed while under our protection.

"Nothing new, no." Her voice wavered, hands shaking while they picked at a loose thread in her pants. "I've just been thinking about the future. Honestly, it's the first time in a long time I've allowed myself to think further ahead than a few days."

That startling revelation told me much more about her situation than I was sure she intended. For one, it told me she had not been certain of her own survival. When a being, animal and human alike, was trapped in an impossible situation, the only focus was on surviving the day. Thoughts of tomorrow would be left alone until baser needs—such as safety, nourishment, and shelter—were met.

Instead of questioning her about these new revelations, I nodded my head for her to continue. If I pushed her she would close down. Of that, I was certain.

"I have nowhere to go," she whispered. Her eyes resembled deep, reflective wells, showing me a brief glimpse into her damaged psyche, and my insides clenched. "When I leave here I will be all alone. I don't have any skills. I have no work experience . . . I—" Her voice broke.

I leaned across the desk, clasping her hands between my own. Hers were so small, completely dwarfed by my dark, work-hardened palms. Her despair—the defeated curl of her shoulders, her shallow breathing—made my chest feel hollow.

"Do not worry, *banajaanh*. We will protect you." The

promise was out of my mouth before I had time to think. I should not have given it without speaking to my brothers, not in these uncertain times. With the new developments up North and Rederick baying for human blood, having one underfoot could only complicate our lives.

And yet . . .

"I-thank you, really, but that's not something I can ask you to do. It's not why I—"

"It's not up for debate." Prepared to soothe her should my firm tone startle her, I was pleased at the unexpected spark of fire that briefly lit her eyes.

"I—no." She shook her head. "That's not . . . I mean, I wanted to ask you if you could h-help me f-find a . . . a *job*."

Her stuttering, the way she clenched her eyes shut when she had forced the sentence out was telling. It was obvious she was terrified at the prospect.

But why?

Deciding to reward her bravery, I pretended to consider the matter. "What kind of job are you looking for?"

Wide-eyed, she gaped at me. "You'll help me?"

"Of course," I said smoothly. "Do you have a job preference, an education perhaps?" If she did it would be much easier to find out more about her.

"No." She looked down at her lap. The thread from her pants was curled around a trembling finger. "I never went to school."

Only the centuries of studied control kept my face from revealing my astonishment. All of my theories about her shattered. Whatever had happened to her, it had to have happened at a young age. Why else had she never attended school?

With my throat suddenly dry I had to swallow a few times before I could speak. The more I learned about her, of her past, the darker her situation appeared. "I see." A feral presence rolled beneath my skin. It took all my concentra-

119

tion, all my control to keep it from introducing itself to the scared, human girl and her trembling request for help. "We could enroll you in school, get you started on your education."

"No!" The sudden cry echoed in the room, several emotions flashing across her face; surprise—probably at the unexpected volume of her own voice—fear, distrust.

The last one pierced me.

Trust takes time. My mother's words drifted across my mind. I had to remember that the girl had been through hell.

"I . . . I just need to find a job."

Disturbed, I wondered why she was so opposed to the possibility of school. "If you are running from someone," I began, noting how she flinched at my words, "we can enroll you under a different name. No one would know."

For a moment, her eyes filled with naked longing. Then, with a shake of her head, she deflated and looked back down. The thread she had been picking on had doubled in length.

I decided to put her out of her misery. "If you are sure . . ." I waited for her subdued nod before continuing. "We have been looking for someone to help around the house; cleaning, cooking, that sort of thing."

Hope leaned forward. "Like a maid?"

"Of sorts. Room and board is, of course, included. You will stay here and—" I halted my explanation, narrowing my eyes when Hope closed her eyes, took a deep breath and released a sigh filled with pure relief.

She did not seem to notice that I had stopped speaking.

Strange.

Looking back, I saw our conversation through new eyes. Her distress at the mention of school. The way she had battled against herself, forced herself to try to find a job. The relief when I had offered her one.

No, that was not right. Her relief had come when I told her she could stay here.

Clenching my hands, I silently berated myself for my own blindness.

"Seeing as you do not have any clothes, would you like me to take you to one of the stores in town and get you some supplies?"

The immediate acceleration of her heartbeat confirmed my suspicion.

"N-no, that's o-okay." She gripped the desk and looked up at me. "I-I don't have any money—"

"Consider it an advance," I interrupted.

She lowered her lashes, unable to hold my gaze. A sign she was about to lie or, at the very best, tell a half truth. "I-I don't want to take advantage of your kindness. Being allowed to stay here . . . It's more than I could have hoped for," she said, sincerity ringing in her clear, soft tones. "I don't need any clothes right now. The sweats you provided are more than enough."

There it was. The lie. Nothing big or important, but it clearly bothered her nonetheless.

No point pushing for more today.

I cleared my throat. "As I said, we need someone to help with the cleaning and cooking—"

"I can't cook," she blurted. Taking a deep breath, she met my gaze and said, "T-to be honest, I don't know much about cleaning either. But . . . I can learn," she quickly added, eyes wide and searching. Her poor bottom lip once again got dragged between her blunt front teeth and chewed.

"We will teach you everything you need to know."

She sagged back into her chair. "Thank you," she whispered.

Had she met so little kindness in her short life?

"You're welcome." I almost choked on the words. It felt wrong, somehow, to accept her gratitude when I was offering so little. "Let us discuss your salary."

She nodded, but didn't reply.

"Would you say fifteen hundred is fair?"

"Not paying me at all would be fair considering I'm pretty much useless and you are already giving me both food and a place to stay."

Feeling my eyes narrow and lips pressing together, I forced my hands to unclench. "You are not useless." My voice was quiet, but I made sure to put enough pressure behind it for her to take notice.

She surprised me when her gaze darted up at me before looking back down, not acknowledging my soft-spoken warning at all.

"Fifteen hundred a month is more than fair," she said. "It should probably be less . . ."

A month?

Since she clearly had no notion of her own value—and would probably argue the point with me—I decided not to correct her. In two weeks she would get paid three thousand and if she had a problem with that, then tough.

Having made my decision, I rose.

"We will take turns teaching you to cook, but until your leg is healed you will not do any cleaning." Holding my hand up to stop the protest already forming on her lip, I continued. "Since you have not had breakfast yet, head over to the kitchen and get some food."

After thanking me one more time in her quiet, serious voice, she left. Her small steps were still hesitant, her back slightly bowed, as if expecting a blow at any moment, but at least she had stopped chewing on her lip.

13

HOPE

After leaving Ash's office there was a new lightness to my steps.

I have a job!

Squelching the urge to squeal, I hurried to the kitchen.

"Morning." Ruarc's deep, gruff voice drowned out the sizzling sound from the stove.

"Good morning," I replied, hesitating in the doorway.

Ruarc turned away from the stove, narrowing his eyes at me. "Something wrong?"

"Um . . . no." I took a few steps forward. "D-do you need help?" Ruarc seemed to know his way around the kitchen. Maybe he could start teaching me right away?

Instead of answering, he raised his brows with a frown. "Sit."

I'll take that as a no . . .

Hobbling over to the chair, I sat down with a sigh. In all the excitement I had almost forgotten about my leg. The deep, painful throb was back with a vengeance.

A rumbling sound of thinly veiled disgust made me look around for the source. "Idiotic female," Ruarc growled.

"E-excuse me?"

"Your leg." He jerked his chin at it, like I was too stupid to know what he was talking about. "Should stay off it."

"I know," I snapped. There was a beat of silence, a moment where horror replaced annoyance, where blood rushed from my face and my stomach flipped with gut-wrenching fear.

I'd . . . I'd just snapped at a male five times my size.

I cringed, not wanting to look at him, not wanting to see the rage on his face at my display of temper or feel the meaty impact of his fists meeting my tender flesh.

But a few seconds passed without repercussions. And then a few more. Eventually, I gathered my courage and flicked my eyes over his face. Silvery orbs stole my breath as he met my gaze head on.

As though he'd been waiting for me to be brave.

A tug on the corner of his lips. An attempt at a smile? Out of place on his harsh, scarred face, and looking rather painful, it was still beautiful. Filled with a savage sort of satisfaction that froze me in place.

"Good," he grunted and turned around.

Good? That was his only response to my angry display? No yelling, no hitting, nothing at all?

As the shocking fear left my body, I found myself relaxing into the chair and studying the bulky male as he removed an omelet from the pan. If one could get over the sheer size of him, the wild, shoulder length hair, the scruff on his jaw and around his mouth, and the scary frown normally tugging his lips downward, he was actually quite appealing.

In a masculine, untamed kind of way.

"Is that for me?" I asked when he put a plate in front of me, nearly overflowing with food.

A sharp nod, then a groan from the chair next to mine as he sat.

Taking a tentative bite, I hummed in appreciation at the flavor. "It's good!"

"Hmm."

"How did you learn how to cook?"

"My sire."

Sire? What a strange way of putting it.

I took another bite, chewing thoughtfully. "Were you close?"

"No." His voice was flat, lip curling. "He was a real bastard."

"Oh, I'm sorry . . ." Sympathy tugged at my heart. I missed my own father terribly, and couldn't imagine ever describing him as anything less than a loving, doting dad. "At least he taught you how to cook."

Ruarc snorted. "Had a choice. Eat with the hounds, or learn to cook."

Appalled, I reached out and put my hand over his.

He stilled and his eyes shot to my face.

"That's terrible," I whispered, wanting to offer him comfort.

His eyes shuttered and he pulled his hand away. "Eat."

It didn't bother me. I knew how it felt to have a wound inside your soul, pestering and weeping, growing bigger and bigger every day until it threatened to consume you. If he didn't want to talk about it now, that was fine.

I could be patient.

Someday, though, someday I would find a way to help him. I owed him that much. I owed them all.

"Who hurt you?" The sudden question made me choke on a mouthful of delicious eggs.

"W-what?"

Eyes narrowing, he jerked his chin at me.

Blood froze in my veins. I looked down, half expecting to see some new, undiscovered injury in the vicinity of his nod. Instead, my fear trumpet my confusion when I understood what he meant.

I can't tell them!

I closed my eyes.

They could never know! Even if I didn't tell them the reason behind my captivity—only letting them in on the horrors inflicted on me, and by whom—it would end in death.

Either mine or theirs.

The Hunters would kill anyone who tried to help me, regardless if said help came in the form of vengeance or through the justice system. I knew for a fact the Hunters had infiltrated various important branches of the government—local police forces being one of the first.

"I . . ." I shook my head, staring down at the uneaten food on my plate. A week ago I wouldn't even have dreamed about a meal like this.

"What happened?" A harshly impatient demand.

"I c-can't tell you."

"Bullshit!" he growled and jumped to his feet. His silver glare bored into me. "A name."

"I can't!" How could I tell him a name, when there were many? How could I sign Ruarc's death warrant for the *possibility* that I would be able to sleep at night? There was no way he could take on the Hunters, and that's exactly what I was afraid he would try to do.

With a savage roar, Ruarc swung around and knocked the empty pan off the counter. The loud, unexpected clatter rang in my ears.

I sat frozen in my seat. It wasn't until my lungs started burning that I noticed I'd been holding my breath. What was I supposed to do? How could I calm the feral beast in front of me.

The feral *injured* beast.

For even amongst my fear, I felt his pain as if it was my own. An open, throbbing wound that had the power to fester on the soul faster than it could on flesh.

Spinning back around, mouth open in a savage snarl, Ruarc glared at me. Instead of yelling—like I expected—he paused, took a deep breath and closed his eyes briefly. "Eat," he snapped, and waited for me to get my shaky hands to obey. The previous delicious eggs tasted like dirt in my dry mouth.

After watching me force down a few bites, he pointed an accusing finger at my leg. "Better not see you trying to walk on your own. Need help, you let me know."

I nodded my acquiescence, not bothering to inform him I wouldn't be needing any help. I would get to wherever I needed to go by myself, even if I had to crawl.

The sound of a throat being cleared made me look to the doorway.

Oh no.

Lucien strolled into the room, arching a perfectly sculpted brow at Ruarc before pulling out the chair next to mine.

"May I?" he asked, waiting for my wary nod before sitting.

His politeness made alarms ring in my brain. Granted, I hadn't spent a lot of time in his presence, but the few hours we had shared had all been doused in miserable embarrassment—for me.

"Ash requested that I take a look at your leg." His voice was flat, cold eyes somehow managing to convey his distaste at this task.

"About time," Ruarc grumbled.

I glanced at him, silently pleading for a way out of what I was sure would be a very uncomfortable experience. His crossed arms and raised eyebrows suggested he would not take my side.

"That . . . that's okay, really. I'm fine."

"It is not up for debate," Lucien said.

"B-but . . . it's *my* leg."

He ignored me. With a cold mask of indifference, he rolled up the material covering my injury.

A dark rumble made Lucien pause. "Is there a problem, Ruarc?"

If looks could kill Lucien would be nothing more than a bad memory.

"No," Ruarc gritted out through clenched teeth. His jaw was so tight it looked on the verge of snapping.

Eyes flashing dangerously, Lucien turned his attention back on my torn flesh. He used both a careful touch and meticulous examination to rule out infection and any worsening—which he icily told me he'd expected someone as weak as me to succumb to—before applying a new bandage.

Letting out a relieved breath as soon as his touch disappeared, I tried to force my tense body to relax. I'd half expected him to be rough. For his fingers to dig into my tender flesh and tear open new wounds. His painstaking, careful exam had been unexpected. Despite the revulsion I had seen in his eyes at the task he had been given, he'd only used soft touches.

Maybe he isn't so bad after all?

"A contraption made of steel did this?" he questioned. Kneeling on the floor in front of me, a tilt to his head, he would have looked almost earnest if the cold dispassion in his eyes had been absent.

"Y-yes." *And the other, strange metal that slows my healing*, I added in my head.

His cynical smile spread across his face. "And your other injuries, the bruises and sprained ribs . . . they occurred during this same *fall*. The result of stepping on said contraption?"

At my wary nod his smile grew so many sharp edges I worried it would cut me. "How old are you, Hope?"

It was the first time Lucien had used my actual name.

"Twenty-four."

"Hmm." His calculating eyes narrowed dangerously, sending shivers of dread up my spine. When the slow 'tap-tap' of his well-manicured fingernails striking the hard table reached my ears, my shoulders curled protectively over my chest. A ball of trepidation sunk into my stomach, settling down as if it was going to stay for a while.

"If I am not mistaken, and I rarely am, you informed Jason that you were twenty-three." He let the evidence of my dishonesty hang in the air, somehow lending more weight to the silent accusation.

How could such a small thing inspire this much fear in me? "I-I must have misspoke."

"One could wonder," Lucien continued silkily, "how much of what comes out of your deceitful, little mouth is the truth. Lying about small, inconspicuous details, like your age . . . What atrocities are you hiding?"

Rooted in place as the ugly ring of truth in his words wormed its way beneath my flesh, I concentrated on trying to stop my hands from shaking. I couldn't do anything about the warmth in my cheeks, or the shameful nausea I felt over my secrets, but I could do my best to hide it from them.

"N-no, I just . . . I—"

"Enough!" Ruarc thundered, shooting Lucien a ferocious glare. He stalked forward and knelt in front of me. "You okay?" He searched my gaze, frown deepening at whatever he saw.

I nodded, not trusting my voice.

"She is fine. Scrambling for a story to cover her duplicity, no doubt." Lucien's cold eyes bored into me. A chill spread through my flesh, and I trembled.

"I said, enough!"

Even knowing Ruarc's fury wasn't aimed my way, I couldn't help the flinch that drew his heated, silvery glare away from Lucien. Even though he frightened me, something warm uncurled within at the way he'd tried to protect me.

Next to me, Lucien remained unaffected by Ruarc's rage. Icy composure in place, he pressed his lips together and rose stiffly. Without another word, he left.

Breathing heavily, neck pulled taut, Ruarc gripped the chair on each side of me and squeezed so hard the wood groaned. "Fuck!"

I reached out, hesitated, then put my hand over his. "T-thank you," I whispered.

His bowed head shot up. As the tension slowly left his body, he bared his teeth in what I could only assume was meant to be some type of grin. "Thought I scared you," he grumbled.

"Only a little."

More teeth showed. "Good." Ignoring my flushed face, he yanked me into his arms and carried me out the door like I weighed nothing.

"What are you doing?" I screeched, clutching at his shirt.

Please don't drop me.

I had a thing for heights and as tall as Ruarc was, I was sure a drop would be painful.

"Taking you outside."

"But . . . why?" His long strides made the distance pass in a blur.

"Because." He kicked open the door, obviously not caring about damaging their property.

"That's not an answer!"

"Tough."

"Ruarc!" Despite my fear of heights, my body was relaxed. It seemed secretly thrilled at being handled with such expert care, such strength.

Traitor.

"Female," Ruarc replied, baring his teeth in another attempt at a grin when I scowled up at him.

"That's not my name!"

"Hm."

"Ruarc . . ." I tried to make my tone stern.

"Hush," he chided.

Why, the nerve!

Deciding to give him what he wanted, I pressed my lips together and turned my head away. Silently fuming, I vowed not to say another word and see how he liked it, the reticent beast.

Keeping my vow turned out to be easy. There was just so much to look at!

Following a trodden path, Ruarc carried me around the corner of the house. Once we reached the patio I'd eaten at just the day before, he turned his back to the house and strode across the lush, green lawn until we reached a row of tall bushes prefaced by a narrow fence snaking the edges of their garden.

Not able to see through the thick vegetation, I'd assumed the fence marked the line between the guys' property and a neighbor, but I'd yet to see another house or any indication of other people than the four I was now staying with.

Without saying a word, Ruarc opened a crooked gate that had been all but hidden from view—it was oddly charming with elusive designs etched into each pillar and a dash of silvery strands flowing across the top beam.

My earlier annoyance had all but fled in the wake of this beautiful exploration—even if it was from a height I wasn't comfortable with, and enclosed by thick, muscular arms—but I was determined to not reward his high-handedness by breaking the silence. When he came to a stop, I crushed my curiosity and acted unaffected as I stared down at my hands.

With a low, rough chuckle I felt all the way down to my toes, Ruarc let go of my legs, letting me slide to the ground. The incredible heat from his body, the toned flesh dragging against mine created a reaction I didn't understand, a reaction that made me blush and step away.

Springy grass met my bare feet. I wiggled my toes and enjoyed the crisp sensation.

Grass. Fresh, natural, wonderful grass.

How had I gone eighteen years without the prickle of nature between my toes?

A gentle touch to my shoulder had me turn around. Ruarc looked down on me with an expression akin to indulgence. His eyes flashed with humor—unexpected and delightful—as he urged my eyes to rise.

I gasped in delight at the sight that greeted me and forgot all about my vow of silence. "Is that . . . ?"

"Yep."

Oh my.

A whole different world lay behind the ridiculously tall hedges. A beautiful garden made way to several small fields, a pond where a family of ducks were floating in the sunlight, a small stable, and a pasture with four horses and . . .

Is that a donkey?

Blinking at the bizarre animal, a slow smile spilled across my face.

"What . . . what is this?" I asked. My voice was breathless, but I didn't care. I'd found paradise. Or at least something that looked like it.

Ignoring my question, Ruarc jerked his chin to the bench at my right. "Sit."

Guess we were back to that.

I stifled the urge to bark like a dog, too grateful to him for showing me this. Whatever this was.

As I sat down I noticed swift movement out of the corner of my eye. Swiveling, I saw a flash of striking gray and brown fur streaking past a gap in the treeline far behind the pasture.

"Did you see that?" I exclaimed, squinting to get a better look.

"No."

At his clipped tone, I dragged my gaze away from the trees and looked up at him. His jaw was clenched, silver eyes hard.

"It was something big. Maybe a bear?" I wondered out loud.

"Your past . . ." The rough quality to his voice became more pronounced. Deeper. "What is safe?"

I swallowed. How did we get back to this again?

"What do you mean 'safe'?" I asked tiredly.

His brows drew together like I was the one who didn't make sense. "To ask."

"Huh?"

He glared through eyes narrowing in irritation. "Safe to ask," he growled.

Oh . . .

Warmth glowed in my chest. He was asking me what I was comfortable discussing? Despite his gruff manners, Ruarc was kind of . . . nice.

"My childhood, I guess." Wasn't much there, but at least it would give him something else to focus on.

"That all?" Disbelief was clear in his voice.

"M-maybe other things too. Normal things?"

"Fine." Gritted out through a clenched jaw. "Any siblings?"

I sucked in a breath, feeling like someone had hit me with a sledgehammer. Such a mundane question, yet I hadn't expected it. My eyes filled with tears and there was nothing I could do about it. "N-no," I pushed out through trembling lips.

"Fuck!" Ruarc shot out of his seat, pacing in front of me and muttering under his breath.

I didn't dare move. If I left this bench I was sure I would

collapse right there on the grass. Staring down at my feet, I concentrated on pushing unwanted memories back.

Maybe I could get out of this situation without bawling. That would be nice.

I didn't notice Ruarc moving until I felt his breath on my forehead. When I looked up, his face was inches from mine, angry glare withering my insides. "Just tell me," he snapped.

"T-tell you what?" I hated the way my voice shook. A tear fell, creating a hot trail down my cheek. I was weak. Weak and scared, just like I'd been my whole life.

When Ruarc spoke again, his voice wasn't quite as sharp. "Who hurt you."

"I—" The rest of my sentence died off when Ruarc spun around and placed himself square in front of me, aggression leaking through his every pore.

"Fancy meeting you here," a cheery voice called out and Jason emerged from the bushes. Hair disheveled, the top two buttons on his shirt were left open and showing me a glimpse of taut, golden skin. Dirt streaked across one cheekbone, giving him a boyish look, and a few spots marred his blue jeans.

I slumped in my seat. Despite his messy appearance he wore a charming grin, and I instinctively knew he would not pressure me about things I'd rather not discuss.

Ruarc, on the other hand, was dangerous to my mental walls. He was too pushy, too interested in my past. Seeing a woman who'd been mistreated seemed to infuriate him, and I was worried he would dig too deep, maybe even get hurt because of me.

Or find out my secret . . .

The thought of him looking at me with disgust was too much to bear.

Stiff with tension, Ruarc turned back to me. "Hope?"

I knew he wanted me to finish my sentence, but I didn't

know what I'd been about to say. Whatever it was, it would probably have been bad. Revealing.

Instead of answering, I shook my head, a frightened yelp leaving me when Ruarc jerked back. With a dark look at me and a warning growl at Jason, he left.

"Do you like horses, love?" Jason asked lightly, taking Ruarc's empty seat.

It didn't seem like the other man's furious departure bothered him in the slightest. Meanwhile I was still reeling from Ruarc's sudden mood change. Never had I seen someone who could go from zero to enraged in such a short time.

Shaking my head, I pushed thoughts of Ruarc aside and focused on Jason. "Yes, I do actually. When I was a little girl I was obsessed with ponies. I wanted a pink one. With a silver mane." I smiled at the memory. I had been so young then. Still believing pink ponies existed. Still believing the world was a safe place.

Jason chuckled, the warm, masculine sound sending spikes of heat over my skin. "I'm afraid we don't have any pink ponies for you, love. But we do have a sweet, normal-colored one in the stables."

"Really?"

He grinned at my hopeful tone. "Mhm . . . do you want to meet him?"

Filled with longing, I met his sparkling, amber eyes. "I do. I really, really do!"

RUARC

CARELESS PUP.

What the hell was he thinking, running around the woods this close to the house?

Furious, I swept inside. The door slammed behind me, making me grit my teeth and think back to Hope's terrified expression. No wonder I scared her. Was too big, too strong. Hell, I'd nearly destroyed the door just coming inside.

"Ash!" I bellowed. "Lucien!"

Jason, with his easy smiles and that canny way of always knowing what to say . . . My jaw went tight, the big ugly scar marring my face pulling uncomfortably at the healthy skin. Hands fisted at my side, I resisted the urge to touch it.

"In here," Ash called back.

I stalked into the kitchen, found Ash staring out the window while a finger tapped restlessly at the table.

Not like him.

Always controlled, Ash rarely showed any signs of agitation. While I lost my temper at the first bristling of fur, he kept himself tightly leashed.

A low growl slipped up my throat, my gaze going to the

chair I'd knocked down earlier when Lucien had pissed me off. He had to stop being mean to the little female.

"Did something happen?" Voice carefully neutral, Ash studied me with the same intense scrutiny he'd perfected over the years before getting to his feet and tilting his head. "You need to spar."

It wasn't a question so I didn't bother answering.

"Where is Hope?"

"By the stables," I bit out. "With *Jason*."

"Out back, then."

"Don't get it," I grumbled, stalking over to the back door —waiting impatiently. "She won't talk to me."

"She needs time, Ruarc. I have a feeling trust is a commodity that girl has not been able to afford in a long time."

"Time!" I spat, and hit the door so hard it flew open and crashed into the wall. *Fucking hell!* Needed to learn how to control my temper. Kept losing it around her, around the little female who was so scared but was trying so hard to be brave. "We kill whoever hurt her *now,* she'll stop being scared!"

A tic appeared at the side of Ash's jaw. "I do not believe it is that easy."

"Sure as hell should be!"

The other male chose to remain quiet. We went out the door, across the yard, entering the woods on the opposite side of the stables—Ash walking without a sound, me stomping and growling and cursing under my breath. Every branch that hit my face received a snarl in return. A few got snapped off by a furious jab, a few more got torn to shreds.

Ever since I saw the little female, all big wounded eyes, stark terror written across that pale, heart-shaped face, I'd wanted to protect her. Seeing a female mistreated, especially one so small and defenseless . . .

A dark growl vibrated in my chest.

"Calm, *niijikiwenh*," Ash murmured.

"Am fucking calm, brother," I shot back. Finally, *finally* we'd reached our destination. The clearing was big enough that we'd have plenty of space to move, the ground free of roots and relatively even. It wasn't our usual sparring place. The big rocks by the narrow stream were ones we used to relax after a run. They soaked up the rays from above even on cool days, heating tired bodies and helping with digestion after a hunt.

I tore off my shirt and tossed it at the nearest rock, impatiently waiting while Ash unbuttoned his and folded it neatly on top. Instead of being back at the house and taking care of the female, I was about to do what I did best; fight. Despite the restless energy coursing through me, my mind was with her, with *Hope*.

Needs to eat more, I thought darkly, considering all the possible reasons why she'd been starved. Wanted to see her body fill out and lose that gaunt look. Wanted to slay her demons so she could feel safe. Wanted her to not be so damned scared all the time!

Was what I should have said, instead of snapping at her.

Needed to learn to curb my temper before I scared her off for good.

"Ready?"

My gaze shot to Ash, took in the slow burn of anger in his eyes, the uneven rise and fall of his chest.

He needs this too, I realized. Was a reason Ash was always so controlled, a reason he never lost his temper. And it was a damned good one.

"Ready."

JASON

Once inside the stables, Hope's whole demeanor changed.

138

For the first time I got a glimpse into the woman she could have been—could still become. Wary excitement shone in her big eyes, a nervous smile curved her full lips. And while a hint of fear still peeked through—almost as though she worried this fleeting happiness would be taken away too—she didn't seem afraid.

Then she limped, and I was reminded of all she'd been through and how frail she still was.

I frowned.

"I-is everything okay?" she asked, voice soft and unsure. She tucked a stray lock of hair behind her ear, fiddling with the limp length.

Her stammering bothered me. It meant she was nervous, and I didn't want her to feel that way around me. "Of course, love," I said, forcing my face to produce a smile. "This way."

I offered her my elbow and slowly guided her to the correct stall. Carrying her hadn't been an option. My clothes were filthy from my romp through the woods, not to mention Hope was clearly uncomfortable with intimacy. Despite what Ruarc thought, carrying someone was an intimate act and not something you did with skittish little lambs like Hope.

The brute got away with it, though.

"Oh!" Hope's hand shot to her mouth. With wide eyes, she took a hesitant step forward, waiting right outside the pony's box. "He's adorable." She smiled at me, her eyes coming alive with joy. "What's his name?"

I couldn't respond. My heart hurt too much. How could something so small bring her so much pleasure? Had she led a life so dark that even the smallest consideration to her happiness lit up her face like a kid on fucking Christmas morning?

"Jason?" The vulnerability in her voice tore me out of my brooding.

139

I had to clear my throat twice before I could answer. "Snowflake."

"But . . . but he is completely black?" The confusion on her face was endearing. The way she scrunched up her pert little nose, the rounding of her perfectly shaped lips . . .

Adorable.

"Ruarc named him," I forced out. "No one has been able to figure out why."

Hope nodded, eyes already back on Snowflake. "Can I . . . can I pet him?"

Fascinated by the way she nibbled on her bottom lip, I almost didn't hear her. "Oh, yes. Of course you can, love." I had to get it together. I was supposed to cheer the girl up, make her forget about her torment for a little while. Gawking at her and wondering how I could make that sweet smile a permanent fixture was not on the agenda, for Christ's sake.

A sad, wistful smile parted her lips. "His muzzle is so soft . . ."

The melancholy note in her voice rubbed me the wrong way. She needed to have some fun, find something to forget her old wounds, and that was exactly why I'd brought her to the stables. "Now that we are here, love, do you want to take a tumble in the hay?" I waggled my eyebrows, hoping to startle a laugh out of her.

"W-what?" A blush crept up her neck.

"The hay, love," I continued innocently. "Throwing yourself in it can be quite cathartic."

Her blush receded and she looked at me with wide, guileless eyes. "Like in the movies?"

The movies?

I pushed the question aside and nodded. "If you can tear yourself away from old Snowflake over there."

The pony chuffed, and Hope laughed. The sound was soft

and titillating, but hesitant, and ending almost as soon as it began—like the sheer act of laughing startled her.

I forced my fists to unclench, to not reach for her.

Whispering something to a happy Snowflake, Hope gave his muzzle one last stroke.

"Where is this hay?" she asked, eyes already a little brighter than when I'd found her with Ruarc. The pushy bastard was pressuring her to reveal her past when what she really needed was to follow my example and focus on the present.

Smile, Hope. Just smile and you'll eventually feel better.

"This way." I placed her hand in the crook of my arm, taking slow, measured steps to make sure she didn't strain her damaged foot.

Her head swiveled from side to side as we walked. Pointing to the different equipment we passed, she asked questions about everything. If I didn't know the answer she'd look up at me, questions brimming in her soulful eyes.

"Ask me anything, love." This indulgent, protective side of me was new. It wasn't entirely comfortable, but I liked her too much like this—inquisitive and open—to fight it. Even though I could feel her hesitation like a dull throb in my bones, I knew it wasn't from fear. Not really. The girl wasn't scared of me, but someone had taught her to be wary. Even of people she wouldn't normally fear.

My face pulled into a frown.

"I don't want to be rude," she started, licking her lips, "but why do you have all this stuff if you don't know what it's for?"

"I'm not much of a horseman. This is all Ash's doing. He rehabilitates horses. And ponies," I added as an afterthought. "Although Snowflake belongs to Ruarc. Again, don't ask me why."

Her mouth gaped open before pulling up into an incredulous smile. "Really? Ruarc picked Snowflake?" A small giggle escaped her. The sweet, thrilling sound took me by surprise, and I jerked back as my dick got hard.

What the hell?

The way my body heated, quickly and with a force I'd never experienced, was inconvenient. Very inconvenient.

Attempting to ignore my body's response, I opened the door to the hayroom and guided her through. "Really."

"That is . . . kind of sweet," she whispered.

My eyes snapped to her face. Her perfect lips were parted just enough to catch a glimpse of small, even teeth, and her eyes had a strange sheen to them.

I could no more stop the rumble that forced its way up my throat than I could stop my next breath. "I don't think I have ever heard a female describe Ruarc as sweet," I muttered.

Startled eyes shot up to mine before she ducked her head, a tinge of pink staining her cheeks again. "O-oh . . . I . . . I just meant . . ."

Her discomfort unnerved me, made me remember that the goal was for her to have some fun. Pushing away the strange feeling that had damned near gutted me, I winked and gave her my most charming grin. "Don't worry, love," I lowered my voice, leaning down and breathing directly into her ear when I whispered, "I'm sure you are much, *much*, sweeter . . ."

When I drew back, her whole face was beet-red. "O-oh."

Throwing back my head, I laughed until a sharp nudge to my ribs made me look down with genuine amusement. Hope was staring at her own elbow like she had never seen it before.

"I . . . I'm sorry," she stammered. "I don't know why I did that."

Delighted at my victory, I leaned back against the wall and grinned. I probably looked like the Cheshire cat. "I teased you. You retaliated. That's a good thing, love."

She fiddled with the large shirt hanging off her emaciated frame, and I made a mental note to buy her more chocolate.

Much more chocolate.

"What . . . what kind of horses does Ash work with?"

Busy studying her body to decide just how many calories I needed to get in her every day for her to fill out some, I replied absentmindedly, "He deals with the lost causes. The badly abused or mistreated horses that no one else takes a chance on."

Deafening silence followed.

I glanced up, and the look on her face made me take a step back. Her gaunt features had gone even paler than normal, her expressive, brown eyes were drowning in a well of sorrow so deep I marveled she was still standing.

"Oh, sweetheart," I whispered, reaching out to cup her chin. When she jerked back I dropped my hand and sighed. "It's not about you. You are not like the horses."

"T-that's a lie." Her voice shook. "I'm *just* like the horses. A hopeless case." She turned around, limped toward the open doorway.

You're a bloody fool, Jason. My words had been careless, mindless. I'd been too busy planning for her future, her recovery, to guard my tongue the way I should when speaking to someone with trauma.

"Hope! Wait a minute." Catching up, I placed a tentative hand on her shoulder, but she brushed it off. I moved ahead of her, forcing her to hear me. "You are not a hopeless case. Surely you know that?" Desperate to salvage what had begun as a promising morning, I searched her down-turned eyes. The bright sheen of unshed tears nearly brought me to my knees. If a careless comment about horses was enough to inspire this much pain, I had more work ahead of me than I'd thought.

"C-can we go now, please?" Her voice was small. Wavering.

"Of course. As long as you lean on me. Ruarc will have my head if I let you walk on your own." My attempt at inserting some humor into the conversation went unappreciated. With a bent head, Hope was silent as she hobbled next to me all the way back to the house—dutifully holding on to my arm, but otherwise avoiding all contact.

She was withdrawing.

I recognized the signs. Hell, I'd seen them in the mirror every day for years. The best thing to do would be to give her some time to collect herself. A few hours, at the most. Then I would return and force her back into the world. Moving forward was always the best option, and I intended to help Hope do just that.

"Thanks," Hope whispered as we stopped outside her room.

"Any time, love." I gave her hand a gentle squeeze and watched as she went inside.

When the door closed, I let my smile die and slumped against her door. What had hurt her so deeply that she thought herself a lost cause? What had she been through? What kind of abuse had she suffered? Who was responsible? And during her darkest hour, why had no one ever thought to step in and help the sweet girl?

"Mooning imbecile," Lucien muttered as he walked past me.

Annoyed at being caught off guard, I leapt away from Hope's door, following Lucien down the hall.

"I'd be happy to moon you anytime, Lucien, just say the word!" Forcing my grin back in place, I chided myself for letting it slip.

To not be miserable, you have to be happy. If you can't be happy, pretend. The words I'd lived by for too many years to keep count floated through my head. I embraced them. I would be happy, dammit, or I would bloody well pretend until it happened.

15

HOPE

After my meltdown with Jason I needed some time to decompress. I *had* to figure out a way to deal with my new circumstances without breaking down in tears every time something reminded me of what I was and what I'd been through.

Figure it out, I told myself as I paced around the borrowed room. Unfortunately, my limp had not improved. In fact, the throbbing got worse the more I paced, but I couldn't make myself be still. Restless energy pulsed underneath my skin, making it crawl like a thousand insects scurrying just below the surface.

Everything felt tight; my clothes, my body. Every surface, every nook and cranny. Even my gums were itching.

Rubbing my index finger over the tingling in my mouth, I slumped down on the bed. It was no use. I couldn't get the sensations to stop, and I couldn't stop thinking about Ruarc. And Jason. They were so different, yet they were both trying to help me in their own way.

Maybe I should talk to them, tell them a little?

Just considering it made my stomach clench painfully as saliva gathered in my mouth. If I told them some of my story they'd demand to know the rest, and I couldn't, I *wouldn't*, expose my secrets.

I pictured their faces when they found out what I'd done . . .

"No," I whispered, clutching at my chest.

But what other options did I have? Thanks to the guys I had a job and a place to stay. A place I was *safe*. At least for the time being. And later, after I had saved up some money and had healed, maybe I could find my way up to Canada and my uncle?

You will never be free of the Hunters, a scared voice in the back of my mind reminded me. *No matter how far and how fast you run, they'll find you.*

But . . . would the Hunters find me if I stayed here? There was nothing connecting me to the guys, so as long as I was vigilant and didn't venture off the property I should be safe.

Right?

I put my head in my hands and released a shaky snort. I was fooling myself. The only way I would ever be free of the Hunters was if they were all dead . . .

My breath froze and I shot up from the bed, ignoring the discomfort in my calf.

If the Hunters were dead I would be free. Free to live. Free to explore. Free to love, too, maybe? And the others, the few left at the compound, they could be free too.

Was I . . . was I actually considering *killing*? For what, justice? Freedom? Love?

Who'd ever love you?

I swallowed hard and pushed the dark thought away. Could I even kill the Hunters by myself?

No.

There was no question in my mind, no blind hope that I'd one day be strong enough. I was only one person. One very scared, very weak person, and they were many and powerful.

Seeing even one of them again would bring me to my knees with terror.

So then how could I get to them? How could I destroy them?

A memory, foggy and drifting out of my grasp as soon as I tried to catch it. But . . . it was a start. The Hunters *had* been scared of someone. I couldn't remember who, or what they were called, but I remembered the hushed voices, the smell of fear. The Hunters feared someone—or something—I just had to find out what.

And if I couldn't, I'd have to find another way.

Biting my lip, I considered my options. Even if I found some way to destroy them, with the help of others or on my own, would I be able to go through with it? Could I live with the death of every Hunter at the compound on my conscience?

Yes.

The clarity of my conviction, my lack of hesitation was chilling. Yes, the Hunters were evil, and yes, they had put me through unimaginable suffering, but was that justification enough to sign their death warrant?

An image of the young boy they had brought in two years prior tumbled into my head.

Three days he'd been there. Either he'd died or—

My hands clenched and I had to close my eyes against the angry prickling behind my eyelids.

They will never stop. Not unless someone makes them.

If it was only about me I'd probably decide to run. But it wasn't just about me. It was about all the nameless people they'd hurt—and would continue to hurt—children, teenagers, and adults. Just because they only had adults now, didn't mean they wouldn't take another child in the future, and no person, regardless of age or what they'd done, deserved the treatment the Hunters doled out.

Decision forming in my mind, I felt a strange mix of relief

and blinding terror. The terror was easily explained, but the relief . . . That came from making a choice. I would fight. I would find whatever or whoever the Hunters feared, or I would find a way to destroy them on my own.

But I'd have to be smart.

In the back of my mind, my father's words replayed on a loop. He'd told me to seek out uncle Gavril if I ever needed help. He'd sounded so sure of my welcome. But even if I somehow found him, even if he agreed to help me, how could I bring the Hunters to another's doorstep? Someone who had no idea what I was, what I'd done, who was after me.

I pushed all thoughts of my uncle out of my head. What was the point worrying about that now? No, I should focus on healing and learning about the world. The decision about my uncle could be put off until I'd saved some money and discovered everything I could about whatever the Hunters feared. Only when I was fully prepared could I come up with a plan. A plan that included ridding the world of the stain that was the Hunters.

The thought caused tendrils of dread to squeeze my lungs until I could barely breathe.

You have to do it, Hope. You have to find a way to stop them.

And maybe after the Hunters were all gone I'd find a way to rid myself of the darkness in my soul. If I could, if the monster within could be torn away, maybe then I could find a place to call home. Even if the only home I could currently imagine was occupied by four potent men who all inspired different kinds of fear in me.

A fear I wasn't so certain I didn't like.

LUCIEN

The moment I stepped foot inside my home, I felt the urge to pace.

Damned human!

She was to blame for my immediate discomfort. She was to blame for the agitation plaguing me, the lack of peace.

Our home had been invaded by a girl drowning in secrets, and I despised secrets. Not only due to my role in our pack—a role I'd perfected to the point I could take one look at any individual and immediately find their pressure points—but due to the confines of my upbringing.

Secrets and lies. Fuel for the *ton.* Their duplicity, their willingness to overlook the horrors inflicted behind closed doors was as disgusting as the women's salacious looks and unwanted attention.

They're all the same.

I closed the door behind me, and drew in a deep breath. The female's scent lingered in the living room. Could she not stay in her own quarters? Her presence . . . disturbed me. The open vulnerability in those dark eyes of hers made a mockery of all my beliefs—from the trade I excelled at to the tight rein I held over my own emotions. How could she think to display her own weakness in such careless fashion? Did she have no understanding for all the ways it could be used against her?

I scoffed.

I could no more believe her innocence than I could believe the lies that fell from her lips. Lips that should be as emaciated and unappealing as the rest of her.

No, looking into the wounded depths of her seemingly guileless eyes, I wished to strike, to wound, to destroy whatever dreams lay behind that deceptively unguarded expression and ensure she left us—me—alone. Yet, I also wished to soothe.

The ridiculous notion, the urge to draw her near and erase her fears, left me cold. Seething.

My lips peeled back from my teeth before I was aware of my own lack of control. Tension coiled around my neck.

Intolerable.

Closing my senses to the damned girl, I walked through the living room. "Hello?" One of my brothers always stayed home when I was out doing what I did. They waited in case I came back injured or missed the agreed upon time.

"Kitchen."

I followed the sound of the curt voice. Ruarc may very well be impetuous and prone to reckless behavior, but god help any who'd think to hurt his family. I believed it to be one of the reasons he chose to stay at the house while I was gone—so he'd be the first to know should I have need of him.

"I have news." I halted in the doorway, taking in the scene I'd walked in on. "What in god's name happened?"

Ruarc, a fierce scowl tugging at the scar he'd done nothing to deserve, spun on his heels. "The pup," he growled with a glare at a subdued Jason, "upset Hope."

The mention of the human girl soured my stomach as resentment festered. "It takes little to upset her. You can hardly blame Jason for her many faults."

Two pairs of eyes glared at me.

"Ruarc's right," Jason said. He righted the chair that lay on its back in the middle of the floor and slumped down in its seat. "I didn't think before I spoke."

"It was an honest mistake." Leaning against the counter next to the sink, Ash wore an impassive expression. "Give her time."

The way Ruarc scowled told me it was not the first time he'd received that particular advice.

"I was careless."

Jason's dejected tone rubbed me the wrong way. Again, this was all *her* fault. Damn the girl for going around arousing trouble where none had previously existed. I would not allow her to mess with my brothers' heads.

My jaw clenched, irritation rubbing me raw for allowing any emotion to control any part of me.

But look at Ruarc! He'd been in a state of volatile temper ever since the girl had intruded on our lives. We'd existed in a comfortable familiarity before she forced her way into our midsts, and by god, as soon as I rid myself of the troublesome chit, we'd go back to that. To a Ruarc who was grumpy but not quite so prone to violent outbursts. To a mischievous, mayhem inducing Jason—his pranks were often annoying, to be sure, but in a way I'd grown used to. Rather that, than have him brooding and second guessing himself for speaking out of turn.

How dare the human make my brother feel bad for a mere slip of the tongue?

"What did you say to her?" The question was out before I could stop it, and I swallowed the silent curse that wished to follow.

Ruarc growled, began to pace.

"I accidentally drew a parallel between her and the abused horses Ash works with." He grimaced. "Well, I didn't mention her, but what I said about the horses . . . Like I said, it was careless."

"Where is she now?"

"In her room."

Good. Perhaps she'd stay there and save me the trouble of chasing her off.

"You have news?" Ash asked, kicking off the counter and taking the chair next to Jason.

"There's been . . . chatter." Ignoring Ruarc's furious pacing and Jason's glum spirits, I joined them at the table. Thoughts of the girl got pushed aside as I concentrated on what I'd learned. Out of all my sources, Hank was among the most reliable. He would simply not dare lie.

"What kind of chatter?"

"Our kind seen with theirs."

A storm gathered behind Ash's hard gaze. "Why has this not been reported to the Council?"

"It is only chatter at this point." Useless in many ways, but occasionally with some truth to it. "No original source can be found." Not even by Hank. "They keep dying." Which was the only reason Hank's secret remained safely locked away in the vault of my mind. Dealing in secrets was, by nature, a profession that didn't lend itself to many friends. And though I'd never call Hank a friend, I would prefer he stayed alive.

"And their captives?"

"As far as I know they remain the same. Brainwashed." The girl's wide, terrified eyes flashed through my mind. As much as I'd have enjoyed accusing her of being on their side, even I knew the Hunters simply did not bother with humans. "After what happened when Samuel's nymph returned . . ."

Quiet descended. When Arabella came back, claiming she'd escaped the Hunters' secret compound, Samuel had been over the moon.

Until she'd betrayed him.

He should never have trusted her.

"That was not the only instance," Ash mused. "To this day, the only ones returned have been twisted in some way. How do they convince them to turn against their own? How do they make youngsters barely through their third Ascension attack their own dams?"

Jason leaned against the wall, blew a breath out the corner of his mouth. "Blood magic?"

"The *Others* hold no sway over us," I told the youngest of us, unsurprised at his lack of knowledge. Information about the other supernaturals was hard to come by and even harder to keep. The Council had long since seized all the lore books and horded them with a greed that rivaled a sorceress' lust for gold. "We're naturally immune to most of their magic. Though, like the witches, they are able to track us should they wish to pay the price."

Jason shuddered.

Ruarc, who'd finally ceased his endless pacing, set his jaw and looked to Ash. "What now?"

"I am not convinced this is for us to worry about." He leaned back, tilted his head. "I am more concerned about the whispers from the North. Do they still intend on supporting Rederick when the time comes?"

"Yes." That had not been difficult to ascertain. Ruthless, merciless leaders inspired little loyalty, and loose lips grew looser when faced with the choices I offered.

"Hm." Ash closed his eyes.

We waited.

I did not envy him the burden of responsibility. The games the others of our kind played meant little to me, but I knew many of these issues were close to my brothers' hearts.

Ruarc, ever impatient, renewed his pacing, while Jason stared off into space with an expression I did not care for. Longing. Regret. When he acknowledged my gaze, I arched a brow, receiving an impudent eye-roll in response.

Pups.

"I think," Ash began, "it is time to begin speaking with the others. Whatever Rederick is plotting, it can only be bad, and I would hate for us to be unprepared should we need to attend the next Assembly."

"And the Hunters?" Ruarc asked, a bite to his voice.

"We will report it to the Council and leave it be for now, but Lucien"—Ash turned to me—"it would not hurt to keep an eye on a potentially dangerous situation."

I inclined my head.

A potentially dangerous situation . . .

The Hunters were not the only ones with secrets I wished to uncover.

HOPE

After spending the rest of the day alone, wavering between strengthening my resolve and panicking at the dumb choice I was planning to make, I decided to go to bed.

Jason had been up several times, trying to get me to join them for various meals and activities, but I hadn't felt ready to face them, and as soon as my head hit the pillow I fell into a restless sleep.

The only dreams I could remember having in the last eighteen years all centered around my father; I would see his face, partly obscured by shadows, I would smell his cologne, diluted and faint, but there, and I would hear his laugh, though it was like hearing it through a deep, all-consuming fog.

He was there, yet not.

For some reason I'd never suffered from nightmares—or if I had, I never remembered them. It was strange, considering the horrors I'd faced during my captivity. Maybe my brain had been too exhausted dealing with the current trauma to put me through more terrors when I was at my most vulnerable.

Or maybe I just hadn't slept deeply enough.

My first two nights with the guys I hadn't dreamed at all. The adrenaline pumping through my system and my body's need to heal probably had something to do with that. And it was probably why this nightmare caught me so completely off guard. One minute I was lying down in bed, the next I was back in my old cell.

I blinked in confusion, taking in the bare, gray walls, the dark, flickering fluorescent light, and the bars closing me off from the world.

No, no, no!

The familiar, haunting horror from my days with the Hunters slid between my ribs, scraped dirty nails up my spine, taunted me, froze me, left me with a feeling of dread so all-encompassing that, for a moment, my heart simply stopped beating.

My teeth chattered. I was cold. So very cold. The kind of cold that never truly leaves you. The kind that got etched into the cells of your being so you never forgot, never felt completely warm again.

"No!" My despairing wail bounced off the encroaching walls, echoing back at me. The sound was shrill, filled with the agony of *knowing*.

The deep breath I drew in to ward off my hysteria did more harm than good. The scent of this place was one I feared would forever haunt me. The stench of blood, sweat, and dirty bodies mixed with the overlaying, cloying smell of bleach and peroxide.

When I was young I'd never dreamed fear could have a scent. That the stench of pain could follow you through your dreams and haunt your every waking moment.

But it did.

And this place was the root of it all.

On the verge of hyperventilating, I ran to the bars lining the front of my cell, grabbed hold, and pulled with all the strength I possessed. But it was no use. Even with my monster's strength, I could not as much as dent the reinforced metal material. Gasping, legs shaking and terror zapping my strength, I resorted to hammering the bars with my fists. Blow after blow glanced off material that refused to yield.

Have to get out!

I kept swinging, kept hitting, until my knuckles split and blood dripped down my wrists.

The bars refused to bend.

With an air of desperation, I tried to push my head through the bars, but they were too narrow. "Hello?" I called out, wishing another prisoner would answer, someone sane, someone who dared defy the Hunters and allow me a moment of companionship in my terror.

No one answered. I couldn't see anyone, hear anyone. *Feel* anyone.

Alone. I was all alone.

The cell opposite me was empty. It had been empty for months. Ever since Matthew—

I was going to be sick.

I'd stared at that cell for weeks. Hating myself for wishing they'd bring someone else, another person I could talk to, even if that meant that person would suffer too.

The bouts of isolation were one of the Hunters' crueler tools.

"Open 391," a dark voice called.

Instantly every hair on my body stood at attention. Dread crawled like spiders down my throat, making me gag as fear swarmed.

In juxtaposition to my earlier need to escape, all I wanted now was to stay in this cell forever.

The cell-door creaked and moaned as it disappeared into a narrow slot in the wall. The sound had me recoiling in the corner I'd fled to—furthest away from the yawning opening —as tormented memories pummeled at my psyche.

And that voice. I knew that voice.

Dave.

"No, no, no—"

"Hello, princess." A chilling smile spread across a face with deep-set features and eyes that gleamed with twisted pleasure.

"S-stop c-calling me t-that." *Princess . . .* Whispered as I lay dying. Murmured in my ear as metal parted flesh and blood cooled around my body. A nickname I'd earned as a child simply for asking for another blanket during a cold winter.

Dave's twisted smile disappeared in a flash. "You know

better than that," he said. "Now, do I have to come in and get you or will you do as you're told?"

If experience had taught me anything, it was that resisting would make everything ten times worse. During my more rebellious days, I hadn't cared, but now . . . now I was too close to breaking.

Unfolding my frozen body from my hiding spot was like jumping off a cliff knowing only pain waited at the bottom. My limbs were stiff and unwilling, wracked by convulsive shivering.

A body has a way of remembering, and mine was loath to experience what was to come.

I tried, I really did, but each time I mentally yanked at an arm or ordered my feet to move, terror would paralyze me, leaving me as defenseless as a newborn baby.

But then Dave took a step forward and my body remembered that, too. I scurried out, neck bent and eyes locked on the floor.

Never make eye contact. Always obey. Don't contradict them.

All the prisoners lived by these rules. Or they died by them.

"Come on." With a rough yank on my arm, I was half-dragged down an eerily familiar corridor. Cells lined each side of narrow hall. Dead eyes followed us as we passed, their owners no longer looking human as they huddled in the corners and muttered to themselves. A few faces showed relief at not being chosen, but those were the new ones.

No relief could be found after you'd experienced all the Hunters had to offer.

I didn't know what was done to all the others, the souls without a monster to protect them, but whatever it was left them as hollow-eyed and broken as I felt. Though, in many of my darkest hours, I'd envied them.

The ones who'd died.

The metal floors reverberated with each step of Dave's

heavy boots, each clank like a backhand to the face. I hunched further and further down, curling at the waist to protect my more fragile parts only to be yanked upright by the hair while Dave's ugly laugh rang in my ears.

The closer we got to the stairs, the harder my heart beat until the irregular thump-thump was all I could hear. That, and the blood rushing through my veins.

When we got to the stairs, my legs felt like lead. It took all my power to drag them onto the dirty cement floor separating the holding cells from the darker, more nefarious parts of their operation. Once at the bottom, saliva filled my mouth and I forced my nausea back.

If I threw up on Dave he'd make me regret it.

"You know where to go," he said while dark amusement twisted his face into the mask of the monster he truly was. Dave liked inflicting pain. The bulge in his jeans told me it was going to be a bad day.

At least they aren't allowed to rape me.

I took comfort where I could.

"What are you waiting for?" Dave used a hand on my back to push me into the place I feared more than any other room on this earth. "Get going!"

I stumbled forward, landing hard on my knees. My breathing was labored, my eyes tightly shut. I didn't want to open them. Didn't want to see what waited for me today.

While I lay crumpled on the floor like a heap of old garbage, Dave locked the doors and started the preparations. The near-silent rustle of fabric as he changed his clothing felt like a jagged rock scraping at my chest. The snap of his plastic gloves made me whimper. The metallic clang of various equipment threatened my hold on my bladder.

A small, helpless whimper escaped before I could contain it. Cold terror gnawed at my gut, made my breath come in chopping, irregular gusts of air.

When Dave hoisted me up my sanity fled. Unyielding,

cold metal met my back and my body went taught as a bow about to snap. My mind threatened to shatter, every nerve ending in my body vibrated in preparation for what was to come. Each strap fastened over my unwilling body peeled away a layer of my sense of self-worth, replacing it with fear, anguish, despair, and glass shattering in my skull.

And then it began.

Dave loved his work. He relished my pain and soaked up my screams. Knives were his specialty, but he had an affinity for anything metal. Barbed wire. Cutters. Scissors.

It didn't take long for my vocal cords to tear. For the sounds I made to echo in my head, and in my head only as I swallowed mouthfuls of blood.

It was only when I was on the edge of the beautiful cliff of oblivion that he paused.

"Do it," he whispered. The excitement in his voice was almost worse than the metal piercing my flesh. "Come on, princess. You know what we want. Do it, and this will all be over."

Lies. It would never be over. Not if I gave them what they wanted. Not if I allowed them the use of the monster that had destroyed my life and sent me down this wretched path.

"I . . ." *I'd rather die*, I tried to say, but I couldn't speak. The only sounds I could make was broken whimpers and the wet rasp of my blood-filled lungs. But somehow, Dave saw it on my face, read it in my eyes.

He smiled, lifted his hand, and began again.

16

LUCIEN

My eyes snapped open. I couldn't quite understand what had pulled me from my restless slumber, but then a blood-curdling scream ripped open the quiet night, made it bleed with all the agony contained in that one sound, and I knew this was not the first time her voice rent the air.

Barely a second passed before I was out of the bed, teeth bared and ready to defend our territory. A familiar, old fear turned my insides rancid until I remembered I was no longer a small, defenseless child.

No, never defenseless, simply uneducated, I reminded myself as I threw on a shirt.

Another shriek tore past my defenses, flaying me open with ancient memories that were quickly and brutally squashed. However, my hand still shook when I reached for the door-handle.

Unacceptable.

Cold rage unfurled in my stomach, straightening my spine and quickening my steps. Icy tendrils engulfed my heart and traveled through my blood until the cold was all I could feel.

"Hope!" An unholy roar erupted from Ruarc as he skidded

around the corner, barreling down the hallway toward Hope's door.

What in damnation is going on?

A third scream split the air. Claws shot from my finger as the chilling sound ended on a wet gurgle and a whispered plea for mercy, "Dave, please . . ." Hope's broken rasp sliced through my bones, deep and aching. For a moment I was transported through time, to a place long gone where the whimpers of despair were uttered by me.

Ignoring the pain those screams invoked, I let familiar, arctic hatred fill me. Pain, sorrow, despair . . . *feelings* were a weakness, and weaknesses had to be purged.

Rebuilding my defenses piece by piece, I followed the destruction Ruarc left in his wake. The gorged marks in the floor displeased me, proof as they were of Ruarc's shameful lack of control. Nothing had been the same since we took in the stray human. There was no peace to be found, only chaos.

What kind of trouble is the wench stirring up now?

I followed Ruarc at a more sedate pace, watched with disgust as he tore Hope's door off its hinges in his rush to get to her.

The screaming had ceased; the time for haste was past. Either the human would be fine or she would not.

With clenched fists, I stepped into her room, dismissing my thundering heart and twisted gut as unimportant. Concern for a girl who promised nothing but trouble would be illogical. Absurd.

Beneath me.

Even so, my gaze hunted for the human in the dim room, not ceasing until she was found. And when she was, my gaze swept across every inch of skin in search of an injury while blood rushed to my head. My heart quickened, and I found myself with a burning ball of acid eating at my gut.

My reaction enraged me. Almost as much as her appearance did. Pale, hollowed cheeks were twisted in a pained grimace, her teeth were bared in an expression of abject misery. Her eyes were open, glossed over with the kind of agony one can never truly purge from one's memory, nor one's soul.

At the sight of her obvious suffering, the feeling that filled me was so foreign, so repellent that the ice in my veins momentarily melted, replaced by an unnatural heat.

Because of her.

Bitter hatred, the kind usually reserved for my dam and sire, coated my tongue. My loathing of her was malicious— yet another feeling I held her responsible for. The wench was dangerous, and I would not rest until she was gone. Her and her bloody secrets had no place in our lives. She was an unknown, a danger to my brothers, our home. And she was most definitely hiding something.

If I hadn't known it before, one look at her terror-stricken face proved her troubled past. A past a part of me wanted to root out and kill.

Damnation!

She had to go.

HOPE

Nightmare and reality briefly overlapped as the sound of wood splintering jerked me upright. The bindings were gone. The agonizing pain faded into the night.

I blinked, disorientated, glanced at the door.

That explains the noise . . .

The door was gone. In its place stood a massive, hulking shadow. Back-lit from the soft glow of the hallway, the outline of the beast's powerful frame revealed nothing except for a wild mane, dark stubble and luminous, silver eyes.

The eyes gave him away, and not a moment too soon. I'd

162

just been about to release the shriek of terror bottled in my surprisingly sore throat when I recognized the shadow as Ruarc.

His eyes were frenzied, hair wild and tousled as it fell past his jaw. A black shirt stretched taut over a powerful chest that heaved with each breath, breaths he sucked in between lips that looked . . . *wrong*. Thinner than normal and barely containing his teeth, the tip of two canines peeked out on each side.

Lucien stood right behind him, looking as untidy as I'd ever seen him. Ruffled hair, sweats not unlike those Ruarc wore hung low on his lean frame, and a white dress-shirt halfway buttoned covered his upper body. His face was ashen, eyes no longer cold but raging like a volcanic storm. When they landed on me I read something familiar in them. A feeling I knew better than most.

Fear.

It only lasted a second. Clenched fists straightened, flexed and released. And if his hands shook once, it was too dark to tell. When his glare swept across my frame next, the familiar, humorless expression was back, his gaze cold and distant once more.

Before I could rub my hands over my eyes to make sure I wasn't dreaming, Ruarc was there. I was yanked out of the bed and placed between him and the wall so quickly my head spun.

Thank god I chose to sleep in my sweats.

The thought of being dragged out of bed naked filled me with mortification and a good dose of fear.

I made a small noise in my throat, about to ask what was happening when one of Ruarc's hands reached out behind him and settled on my shoulder.

"Where are they?" he snarled, reeking of violence.

"W-who?" If someone was here, in the *one* room I'd claimed as mine in this massive house, it would be the

163

Hunters. Shivers wracked my limbs and my breath caught somewhere in the vicinity of my throat.

"The ones that made you scream!"

"What?"

The thick muscles in Ruarc's shoulders flexed as he scoured the room. "Someone hurt you. Heard you scream."

Once I realized what he was talking about, what had happened, my shivering stopped. In its place a deep humiliation took root. It seeped to the surface of my skin and heated my face, made my skin crawl.

"There's no . . . no one here," I mumbled. Rationally I knew I had nothing to be ashamed of. The Hunters did. *They* were the ones who should feel disgraced, *they* were the ones who'd done wrong. But somehow . . . somehow I felt dirty. Like each instrument of pain used to hurt me had stripped away layers of my humanity, leaving a filthy casing of shame in its wake.

"What?" Ruarc's voice was still stained with bloodshed. He didn't look at me, just continued scanning the room like some hidden danger was moments away from attacking us. The massive expanse of his back was like a brick wall in front of me, protecting me from perceived harm.

"Another bid for attention, perhaps." Lucien's voice was different. The cold, mocking tones were replaced by a hoarse, almost hateful note.

"W-what? N-no," I protested as Ruarc's hand tightened on my shoulder. "I just . . . I had a n-nightmare."

"A nightmare?" Lucien scoffed.

I wanted to sink into the floor. Disappear from sight. A nightmare should *not* have reduced me to this sort of mess!

Ruarc must have decided the room was safe, for he turned to me, silver eyes glowing with danger, and searched my face. I couldn't handle the scrutiny. Not now. Not when the feeling of Dave's hands was so fresh in my mind, when remembered pain still flared beneath my skin.

I broke the connection, staring at the floor and willing my eyes to stay dry.

"I'm s-sorry I woke you. It's just . . ." I couldn't continue. It had felt so real.

So raw.

Ruarc cupped the back of my head, drawing me into his body and engulfing me in a full body hug. His heat flowed into me, thawing the cold terror that had my heart in a vice grip and belying my belief that I'd never get warm again.

With a shuddering exhale, I wrapped my arms around him and leaned into his warm embrace. For the first time in years I felt almost safe. The steady thump of his heartbeat, the soothing circles he rubbed on my back, the faint scent of pine cones and wilderness I only associated with Ruarc, it all came together in a seamless blend that left me with a feeling of being protected.

Cherished.

And then he started humming in that deep, rumbling voice of his. My breath caught. Black spots danced in my vision and my body went tight.

The humming proved my undoing.

Ruarc tipped my head up, glancing down at me with concern etched into the hard lines of his harsh face, and . . .

I broke.

A single sob burst from me, the first drop in a storm of sorrow. My hands flew to my mouth, trying to force the sound back in and stem the inevitable flood of anguish.

The savage rage that had been burning in Ruarc's gaze receded to make room for something else, a milder emotion maybe.

The dam shoring my defenses crumbled. Hysterical sobs wracked my body with such force I briefly wondered if they would tear me apart. The thought didn't sadden me as it should, for at least then I would be at peace.

I was so lost to my grief, I barely noticed when Ruarc

lifted me like I weighed nothing, and sat down on the bed with me sideways on his lap. His palm came back up to cup my head, pulling it against his chest, and I was grateful. His palm was so big. It was like a wall between me and the real world, dimming the harsh glare from the overhead lamp and muffling the keening cries pouring out from the ragged wound in my soul.

A strange noise began in Ruarc's chest. A soft vibration that gave way to a low, haunting melody. His voice wasn't made for singing, it was too deep, too gruff and gravelly, but to me it was the most beautiful sound I'd ever heard.

The words were foreign, the vowels lengthened and the R's hard and drawn out.

After a while his voice quieted and I had to strain to hear the music he created. Holding my breath—and effectively my sobs—I stilled, ear pressed to his chest as I focused on listening. The way the vibrations carried the sound up from his lungs fascinated me.

"Calm, *m'eudail*," Ruarc murmured into my hair, his lips a whisper-soft touch.

"This is ludicrous," Lucien muttered.

The body beneath mine stiffened. I felt his lungs contracting, preparing a furious reply, no doubt, but before he could speak there were two more loud bangs echoing in the otherwise silent house. Stunned, I watched through blurry eyes as Lucien spun around to face the new threat.

Terror once more engulfed me, locking my limbs with a cold that should have frozen the tears coating my face. The heat I'd stolen from Ruarc's strong body seeped out of me and left me a shivering mess.

The Hunters had found me.

Oh god, please, no!

The guys, the wonderful men who'd taken me in and helped me would die because of me.

I tensed as I prepared to leap away, to meet the Hunters halfway in an attempt to spare the guys' lives.

I wouldn't let them die because of me.

"Ruarc!" Jason shouted from somewhere downstairs and my whole body went limp. I never thought his voice—panicked as it was—could sound so sweet.

Without making a sound Ash and Jason suddenly appeared in the doorway—both looking disheveled with streaks of dirt marring the bare skin on their arms and faces.

I gaped at them. There'd been no footsteps on the stairs, no creaks from the floorboards in the hall, and as fast as they had gotten here, they must have run.

Maybe they really are ninjas.

Jason pushed past Lucien, eyes going straight to me where I sat curled up on Ruarc's lap. His generous lips flattened, twin lines appearing between his eyes. "What happened?" he rasped.

I was too exhausted, too scared to leave Ruarc's warm protection and face the reality pushing at my mind to try to explain.

It was Lucien who answered for me. "The chit woke us by screaming the house down."

Arms tightened around me. I was too wrecked to complain.

Ash glanced at Lucien with an alertness that bordered on alarm. Whatever he saw made him turn back to Ruarc, brows drawing together in concern. "Ruarc?" He didn't do more than a quick scan of me, like I wasn't in the room.

Can he somehow sense that I am tainted? The thought sent a sharp jab of pain between my ribs.

"T'was nothing." The gruffness in Ruarc's voice had deepened and he sounded different, somehow. Like a part of him —something he'd left behind a long time ago—was peeking out. "Hope . . ." He trailed off, the big palm petting my back stilled while the rest of him thrummed with feral energy. "She had a nightmare," he bit out.

"A nightmare?" Jason repeated, dragging the word out like he didn't quite know what to do with it.

"Aye," Ruarc growled.

Jason's mouth dropped open and he gaped at Ruarc.

"Well, seeing as no one is hurt we should get some rest." Ash nodded once at Ruarc, then moved his piercing, blue gaze to me. He didn't say anything. He didn't have to. There was a quiet awareness in his gaze that unsettled me; like he knew what had happened and felt sorry for me.

I wanted to bawl.

"Lucien, Jason, if I could have a word?"

Jason looked strange without his confident grin. The playful glimmer in his eyes was gone and there was a stiffness around his mouth I didn't like.

He looked haunted.

Dragging the back of his hand across his mouth, he gave a jerky nod. "Night, love."

And then he left.

Lucien was slower to follow. He swept his gaze over both of us, jaw clenching. It looked like he wanted to speak, but in the end he followed Jason without a word.

When they were gone, Ash walked over to the door that had come to lean against the wall, lifted it, and carried it the short distance to the doorway. He did something—I heard a hard click and a soft groan—and then it looked as good as new.

Except for a small crack in the middle of the frame.

As soon as Ash left and closed the door behind him, Ruarc took hold of my chin and tilted my head up. His eyes were hard, yet not devoid of sympathy. With a heavy sigh, he rubbed his thumb across my lower lip.

I gasped, lip tingling where his thumb had caressed.

"It's time," he said gruffly.

Pretending I didn't know what he meant, I deflected. "Y-you sound different."

The hand resting on my hip flexed. "No." It was a statement. One not inviting questions despite the fact that I was right; he *had* sounded different. "Hope . . ." He hesitated. "Tell me. Please."

The *'please'* made my eyes sting. A part of me wanted to talk about it. Wanted to get it all out in the open in the hopes that the poison of my experience would leave with the purging of words. But what if it made it worse? What if the same disgust I already felt deep in my soul was reflected in his eyes?

"I . . . I don't know if I can."

Ruarc settled back against the headboard, dragging me further up his body. The warm, steely muscles under his shirt would have felt delicious at any other time, but I was too torn to really appreciate it.

He bent his head until his cheek rested on top of my head. "It'll help," he murmured, his hot breath sending shivers up my spine. "Give me some of it."

In his deep, gruff voice I heard the unspoken promise; sharing my burden would lighten it, make it easier to bear and his shoulders were broad enough for us both.

"I . . ." I trailed off. What could I safely share? Did I want to share anything at all?

Yes. Yes I do. The memories were like venom in my blood. What if I let out just a bit of it?

"I was . . . held captive."

Ruarc's arms tightened around me, but he didn't speak. His silence helped, made me feel like I could go on. Questions would make it harder.

"For many years . . . by e-evil m-men." God, this was hard. My voice shook and my hands trembled where I clutched them together in my lap. "They did . . . they didn't treat me well."

169

A deep, dark rumble greeted my confession. Even though I could feel the violence in the way his corded muscles shook with repressed anger, see it in the fisted hands at his sides, and hear it in his harsh breaths, I wasn't scared.

Not of him.

"T-they are never going to s-stop. They want me back—"

Ruarc tensed below me. "Never," he snarled. "You will never go back."

The grim vow made me catch my breath. He looked so ferocious; wild and untamed like a proud mountain no man, beast, nor monster could ever hope to conquer. His strong jaw clenched, the white, slashing scar proof of his perseverance. He seemed like a battle-hardened warrior, baptized in blood and death.

The brutal violence contained so close to the surface should have terrified me, repulsed me, even, but something inside of me rejoiced. *A worthy male*, it seemed to whisper. *A powerful male.*

I couldn't tear my eyes off him, this harsh warrior glaring down at me. Glaring, not because he was angry with me, but because he was angry *for* me.

He's angry on my *behalf.*

I softened, clutched at his shirt. Here was a man who wanted to protect me, who—

"No," I whispered as the truth hit me and my blood ran cold. "They kill people," I whispered. "Me being here . . . it's not safe for you. Any of you." There, I'd said it. Even as dread flooded my body, I also felt relief. Now he knew, well not the whole truth, but some of it. They would make me leave, as they should. If I brought death here . . .

My stomach revolted.

As I began making plans of leaving, a dark chuckle drifted down from the big male.

"If they come here . . ." Ruarc bared his teeth in a chilling smile that promised death to anyone fool enough to challenge him. "They will die."

They will die?

I blinked up at him, took in the confident arrogance of his expression, and reared back. Sitting on my heels next to him rather than on him, I already missed his heat, his protection, but I had to look him in the eye when I tried to explain why his words were dangerous.

I needed to know he truly understood how serious my situation was. That the threat to me was real, nothing to scoff at or wave away just because he was a physically superior male specimen.

"Ruarc," I began, yelping when he dragged me right back onto his lap.

"Right here," he grumbled. "You feel that?" He put my hand over his chest. "*I* am safe."

My heart skipped a beat, warmth and terror fighting for supremacy.

I have to make him understand so he doesn't get hurt.

"Ruarc, y-you can't . . . You can't go to the authorities—" His snort interrupted me. "I'm serious! They have people everywhere. It's not safe."

"Wasn't planning on it," he replied in the same arrogant voice.

The starch went out of my spine and I melted into him.

Thank god.

"Killing them will be better."

I jerked back up.

"Ruarc!" My heartbeat accelerated. I could almost feel the blood pumping through my veins. "You can't! T-they'll *kill* you." I could barely get the words out. It was too foul a notion.

"No." Said with complete confidence. His voice, so low and deadly, was almost enough to convince me.

Almost.

But I'd seen first hand what the Hunters were capable of, and I had the nightmares to prove it.

"You don't k-know them. They are terrible, evil creatures." I couldn't even refer to them as human, although I knew they must be. Only humanity could hate with such passion and perform such utter atrocities on those they deemed lesser.

"So am I," he replied and bared his teeth in what I could only hope was meant to be an assuring smile.

"You're not!" I protested, appalled he would ever refer to himself as evil. Dangerous, yes. Volatile and violent, probably. But not evil.

Never evil.

If he were, he wouldn't have comforted me after I relived one of the many horrors I had experienced. He wouldn't have vowed to protect me.

With his mouth set in a grim line, he narrowed his eyes at me. Before he could start arguing, I spoke, "Please promise me you won't try to find them."

He tensed. "Fool female!" he pushed out through clenched teeth, and though it shouldn't have, the insult hurt. "I'd *never* make a promise like that!"

His lack of faith in me hurt too, as did his belief I didn't know what I was talking about. Why couldn't he be reasonable? He'd get himself killed!

Suddenly I was furious. Jerking away, I crossed my arms over my chest and huffed. "Well, you'll never find them without me, and I'll *never* tell you anything more!"

Every single muscle in his body tightened. A low growl built in his chest, rumbling like thunder.

This time, he was the one who pulled away. With stilted movements he put me against the headrest, careful of my injured foot. Once I was settled, he surged off the bed and stood with his back to me. The corded muscles in his powerful neck looked like they were about to snap.

One moment he was standing still, brooding and dangerous, the next he exploded into motion. Halfway to the door he spun back around, glaring at me. "You," he growled, pointing a long index finger at me. "Stubborn, foolhearted female!" Breathing heavily, he stalked forward until he stood at the end of the bed, towering over me.

I bit my bottom lip to keep it from trembling. He didn't have to keep insulting me! I was just trying to protect him. "Well, you are . . . you are the most . . . the most—" The most confusing man alive? The most appealing, maybe?

No, don't even think that, I scolded myself.

"What?" he snarled.

"The most hardheaded!" I yelled.

"Need a hard head to deal with you!" His thunderous roar echoed in my ears. The way he was glaring at me, all furious anger and heated frustration, abruptly made me nervous.

What am I doing? I shouldn't be provoking someone as explosive as Ruarc.

Especially not a *man.*

The fight seeped out of me. I slumped, fighting back the ever-present tears. When had I become this person who always seemed to be on the verge of crying?

Weak. Helpless.

During my captivity at the hands of the Hunters I'd barely ever cried.

"I . . ." I didn't know what to say. My voice was low, trembling.

Ruarc shifted, heated gaze examining my face.

I bent my neck, unable to look at him.

"Jesus . . ." He took a step toward me and I couldn't help but cringe. It was an automatic reaction, born from years of experiencing the not-so-tender care of men.

He came to an abrupt halt. Out of the corner of my eye I saw him run a hand over the ragged scar on his face. Then a harsh exhale, almost angry.

I risked a quick glance up.

Clenched jaw, jerky movements as he dragged his palm over his stubble, eyes unreadable. What bothered me the most, though, was the slight slump to his shoulders, like he was tasting defeat.

I did that.

Tears stung my eyes, but I blinked them back. Something I'd done had caused Ruarc emotional pain. It didn't matter that it barely showed. Even if it was something minuscule I never wanted to be the reason he hurt.

Not after everything he'd done for me.

"Ruarc . . ." He wouldn't look at me. "Ruarc, I—"

"It's fine." He made a slashing motion in the air, as if he was cutting the last few minutes from his memory. His eye twitched.

A sick feeling of dread slithered through my body like a hungry, venomous snake. Ruarc's clipped tones, how he was not looking at me, the hard jaw and clenching fists made the air feel heavy.

Suffocating.

He opened his mouth, paused, then pressed his lips tightly together. Without looking at me, he left the room.

The soft sound of the door closing behind him sounded like a gunshot to me, piercing deeper than a bullet ever could.

I didn't understand why, but I felt like I'd lost something vital.

With stiff limbs and a burdened soul, I crawled under the covers, curled up into a ball, and pressed a pillow to my face to muffle my sobs. The weak, wretched creature I'd become disgusted me.

No wonder Ruarc had left.

What kind of woman flinched and recoiled just because a man was angry?

A part of me, a very small, very stubborn part, told me to

give myself a break. After what I'd been through my reaction was probably not *that* unusual, and feeling sorry for myself wasn't going to change anything.

But . . . what was?

Sniffling, I wondered about that until I fell asleep.

And that time, thank god, I didn't dream.

17

ASH

"More than one!" Ruarc roared. If we had been anywhere else, it was likely he would have punched through the wall. That he curbed his temper was testimony to the close bonds of our pack. He would never want to damage Lucien's work-room, not when the other male considered it his sanctuary.

Situated far enough from the main house that the noise did not disturb—despite our enhanced hearing—the single room was larger than that of a normal shed. We had built it ourselves, from sturdy material Lucien had picked out, and while he might never show it, we all knew how much he enjoyed the quiet and solitude that came with his work away from pack politics and the intelligence gathering he was so very good at.

The workshop sported only a single window—not tall, but wide enough to create the airflow Lucien required, each wall serving a purpose.

Shelves lined the back wall, every inch of space filled with various materials. Oils and polish—from home-made beeswax and raw linseed oil, to Danish oil for a durable satin finish—were stacked neatly, sorted by use and the wood for which they were best suited. The scent they created was one I had come to enjoy for the simple fact it smelled like home. Small wood-samples filled boxes of exactly the same dimensions, labeled by Lucien's exact handwriting. One shelf was dedicated to smaller tools, such as several different measuring devices, rolls of sandpaper, various clamps, a random orbital sander, and several more items I had seen Lucien use on more than one occasion. While another shelf held paints their owner seldom used, and the last carried the heavier equipment.

To the right rose a massive bench. Power-tools sat in spots made specifically for each item and its purpose. A fine layer of sawdust he could never quite be rid of had drenched the pores of the work-bench. Their scents—pine, birch, oak, all the woods Lucien used—blended with those of the oils and the paint. No matter how much Lucien aired out, the smell always lingered, and I imagined it would eventually soak into the male himself.

But it was the left wall that never failed to hold my attention. While all the furniture Lucien made was either sold or used in our home, he occasionally created what could only be described as art. Wooden figurines, their details so fine I doubted even Michelangelo would find them flawed, delicate frames made for pictures that had never seen the light of day, and wooden canvasses filled with landscapes carved by the most precise of instruments.

Lucien may not have been a painter, but what he created was art, and his landscapes were as beautiful as those created by master painters.

"They had their filthy hands on her!"

Anger rose, swiftly and unbidden at Ruarc's furious words. It took all my control to keep from jerking back, from showing how his words affected me. A female in pain was bad enough, but one being abused, repeatedly and purposely hurt?

That was something no decent male could stand for.

"Are you sure?" Jason rasped.

"Aye!" The Scottish accent Ruarc had all but buried rose to the surface.

Twice in one day. The volatile male was close to reaching his limits.

"What exactly did the wench say?" Lucien leaned back against his work-bench, cool tones at odds with the way his fingers clenched around the edge.

The way he spoke of Hope made me want to bare my teeth. Hostility had eroded his normally cold logic, and while he had always had a suspicious nature, it seemed the little human brought out the worst in him.

"Why are you such a bastard to her, Lucien?" Jason asked, a hard edge to his voice and a tightness around his eyes I had not seen for years.

"How many reasons do you need? Do you not care that she is dishonest? That her story is filled with holes? The very day we were to confer with Quentin and his damned pack she appears out of nowhere, refusing to answer our questions and handing out untruths as though she believes them. Do not tell me you haven't smelled the lies she spews."

"She is scared!" Jason countered. "The way you attack her at every turn doesn't help."

The newfound animosity between my brothers unsettled me. Friction was common in a pack such as ours, fights breaking out whenever tensions ran high, but I had never seen Jason this shaken, nor Lucien so on edge.

"Perhaps she is scared due to her own treachery. She is hiding something, possibly aiding some Strays in an attempt to take over our territory. Thus, she is scared of being caught!"

"Do you know how ridiculous you sound? Helping Strays . . ." Jason pushed away from the wall and glared at

Lucien. "Like those mangy beasts could ever organize enough to even attempt any sort of infiltration."

"They have in the past." Green eyes cooled. "Ever since Ruarc prevented their last attempt they've been chomping at the bit to try again. The human girl would be a perfect accomplice—"

"Bullshit!" Ruarc roared. His eyes had grown more reflective as his control slipped. When fangs grew and pushed against his bottom lip, I heaved a tired sigh and stepped in. A hollow pit gaped in the bottom of my stomach as I moved to the center of the room and waited for their attention.

Once given, the familiarity of solitude uncurled its mighty wings and settled in my bones. "Calm yourself, *niijikiwenh,*" I addressed Ruarc, the old tongue flowing easily as I reminded him of our ties, of the family we had all chosen, rather than been born into.

Brothers in truth.

I made sure to keep my expression tranquil and my voice steady. They had need of my strength.

They already have too many burdens to carry. All of them.

I drew my gaze over the three males that were my family, before settling on Ruarc. "When you are ready, *niijikiwenh,* please tell us what you learned from Hope." It could not have been much or we would already have been out there, searching for her abusers. "We must try to understand her situation before we can decide what is to be done. And no, Ruarc," I added before his temper had time to ignite, "that does *not* mean we will kick her out."

"Perhaps we should," Lucien said.

Eyes narrowed to thin slits, Ruarc bared his teeth. His nostrils flared as he scented Lucien's aggravation, though it quickly faded. It took a great deal of restraint to block our fighting impulse when risen, but Lucien controlled his beast, not the other way around. Rarely stirred beyond a cold anger, he seldom brawled outside the Assembly grounds.

With a gruff sound of acknowledgment for Lucien, Ruarc shared Hope's story. Or as much of it as he had gleaned. Hostility poured off him in waves as he spoke, while vengeance shone a quiet promise in eyes that had lost all pretense of humanity.

Only animal remained.

When he was done, I understood the fury driving him. It took root in me as well.

But it is not only fury . . .

Breathing in through my nose, I picked up the faint scent of an emotion I could not place. It was hollow. Akin to grief, but not quite the same.

Instead of picking at the threads to unravel Ruarc's mystery, I gave him his privacy and turned my thoughts to Hope. The more of her past that was revealed, the darker a picture was painted. The concept of her, helpless and alone, at the mercy of a group of people I could only assume was some kind of mercenary organization, left me feeling closer to the edge than I had in a long time.

Memories of blood and death tugged at my soul. The terrified cries of my people, the people I had condemned without regret, rang in my ears. The nightmarish scene from my youth was one I kept close. A reminder of what would happen should I lose control once more.

Taking a deep breath in an attempt to center myself, I clawed my way back in charge and focused on the one thing I could control; what came next.

"Did they . . ." Jason swallowed hard. "Do you think they . . ." He trailed off, uncharacteristically at a loss for words.

The unspoken question hung heavy in the air, affecting us all with its ugly ramifications. While Ruarc looked on the verge of tearing out of his skin, Jason looked as nauseous as I felt, and even Lucien seemed agitated.

"There is no way to know." I curled my fingers into a fist,

hiding the loss of control my claws signaled. The girl was getting to me. "Do not assume anything, but be aware of the possibility. Let her initiate touching, and do not crowd her."

Ruarc dropped his head into his hands and swore under his breath.

For a moment we were all silent, each of us trapped by whatever horror we suspected Hope had been subjected to.

The poor female.

It was Jason who collected himself first. "What now?"

They all looked to me, expectation heavy in their grave expressions. Their trust was an honor, their faith a gift, but some days the responsibility of our pack weighed so heavily on my shoulders I feared I would buckle under the pressure.

No . . . I would not let them down.

"Based on what Ruarc learned it seems Hope was kept by a group of men." I waited for Ruarc's angry growl to fade before continuing. "The only reason humans capture each other is for money or power. Hope could have been taken from a powerful or wealthy family to be used as leverage of some kind." The possibility disgusted me, and I rolled my head around on my shoulders in an attempt at alleviating a modicum of the tension thrumming through me. "Her fear of recapture could be a consequence of her trauma. Still, I would not want to rule out the possibility that she was right about the imminent danger this group poses to her. They may very well be powerful in the human world."

"Meaningless to us," Ruarc muttered as he paced a tight circle around the rest of us.

"Ruarc is right," Jason agreed. "Whoever they are, they can't get to her here. We should help her focus on the future. Give her the tools she needs to cope, of course, but also show her that she can still have fun."

Lucien's cold voice cut in, "Is there a particular reason you consider the silly chit our responsibility?"

Ruarc lunged forward. His claws shot out and swiped

Lucien across the chest. Before he could follow up on the attack, Lucien sidestepped while Jason got between them.

The small altercation was nothing new; with Ruarc's hot temper and Lucien's tendency to be blunt to the point of being unfeeling, their personalities often clashed. I had given up on civilizing them years ago.

"Lovely," Lucien said, looking down at the blood seeping through his shirt. His lip curled.

The wound would heal in a few hours, but the shirt was ruined.

I sighed. "That is not how we conduct our meetings, Ruarc." I may as well have been speaking to the wall for all the attention Ruarc paid me. Pushing him or using force to get my point across was pointless. Not to mention unpalatable. Being the leader of our small pack could be wearying. Isolating.

"I could ask you the same, Lucien," Jason said. "Is there a *particular reason* you detest Hope?"

With Lucien there was always a reason. Coldly logical to the point of being unfeeling, he saw things we did not and had saved our lives more times than I could count.

But his animosity toward Hope . . .

Ignoring Jason's question, he ran a hand over his bench and turned to me. "I would prefer to not take part in this little experiment. The duplicitous human is fooling you all, but if you insist on keeping her here I will have no part in it." He paused, cool gaze landing on Ruarc before he moved toward the door. "I will take no pleasure in proving you wrong. I only hope when I find her secret it won't be too late for you again, brother."

A flutter of anger crawled up my throat. It set my teeth on edge, tested my control.

The betrayal Lucien referred to was still fresh in the other male's mind despite the centuries that had passed.

Bitter fury lit Ruarc's eyes. "Leave then, you coward," he snarled at Lucien's retreating back.

Lucien stilled, his neck taut. The veins along his neck flushed against the pale skin, but he did not turn. With limbs that looked too stiff to move, he walked to the door and left us alone inside his sanctuary.

I felt a flicker of unease, of regret as the door closed behind him. True conflict weakened a pack. It pulled them apart, made them vulnerable. Had it been any other situation I would have gotten rid of the object of the conflict, but I could not stomach the thought of turning Hope away.

What kind of male would that make me? Make us?

Pinching the bridge of my nose between my fingers, I took a deep breath and prayed to *Gitchie Manitou* for patience and wisdom. "Until Hope confides in us there is little we can do. For now we must stay alert and let our instincts guide us. Look for anything out of the ordinary; a scent that does not belong, a sound coming at the wrong time, a shadow where none should be. If there are people after Hope and they dare intrude on our territory to find her"—a violent ripple of rage traveled through us all—"we will catch them."

"Think they'll come here?" Ruarc asked around a mouthful of sharp teeth.

"I doubt it." I walked over to the window, gazing up at our home—barely visible above the hedges, and nearly indistinguishable from the black night. "From what I know, human groups tend to cut their losses and run in these types of situations. That is, as long as the person who escaped does not have the means to destroy them."

Jason looked doubtful. "After telling Ruarc that it's too dangerous to go to the police, I would guess she doesn't have any concrete evidence."

"Or she believes any amount of evidence is insignificant in the face of the group's power and reach."

Ruarc growled. "Doesn't matter."

Tilting my head, I waited, and soon enough he bared his teeth, a thunderous rumble building in his chest.

Aggression pulsed up my spine in response, body thrumming to life with the power I always kept tightly leashed. Meeting his challenging glare head on, I pinned him with my gaze.

Silver eyes narrowed. If he'd been in his other form his ears would be flat against his head. He bared his teeth.

A roar in my ears. Claws speared through the tips of my fingers. I battled my own bloodlust, my need to make him submit. The *mahír fáinn* beat a drum of violence in my heart, a drum I fought with everything I was as I kept our eyes locked together.

"Calm, *niijikiwenh*," I said, putting all my considerable willpower behind the words.

Ruarc faltered.

Weaving peace with my mind, I willed him to remember, to gain control of his volatile nature.

He took a step back, his eyes cleared. With a deep breath, he shook his head. "Brother," he returned in kind, and I knew he was back.

We both looked away, forcing our instincts down. The significance behind Ruarc's aggression was worrisome, the human girl in our midst disrupting the careful balance we'd so painstakingly built while keeping our inner selves protected.

Cannot dwell on that. Not yet.

"You need to relax, Ruarc," Jason said with a grin and slapped Ruarc on the back. The deadly glare he got in return was thoroughly ignored.

Though I was glad to see some of the spirit return to Jason, it worried me how he seemed to push everything down, unwilling—or unable—to deal with the darker aspects of life. The tenebrous determination hiding behind his smile was another concern I would have to deal with.

Eventually.

"When you need to shed your skin, ensure you are out of sight from the house. No paws inside either, or the poor female may never recover."

Ruarc grunted his assent.

Jason looked thoughtful, but gave a nod of agreement. "One of us should be with her if she leaves the house. Just in case."

"I agree." *But it is not enough.* "We need to find out what it is we are dealing with. Jason, you have a human contact in the information business, do you not?"

"I do. Should I give him a call?"

"Yes, see if he knows anything about a group who has recently lost an asset. But do not reveal anything about Hope."

I headed for the door, sensing the others following close behind. Both Ruarc and Jason wanted to help Hope, and Spirit aid me, I did too. Despite Lucien's multiple warnings, I had made a decision that made me responsible for yet another life.

If this turns out to be a mistake I just put all their lives in danger, I thought as I silently made my way into the house.

Lucien, Jason, Ruarc. My responsibility. My brothers.

Not by blood, but by choice.

Could I risk that for a stranger? A small, helpless female with nightmares in her eyes?

I closed my eyes and saw her; thin, pale face, despair in each delicate line. In my mind, her eyes glowed like spun gold, beautiful and coveted, but with deep grooves gouged by instruments of horror. In the golden depths, I saw a well of pain so deep it beckoned me closer. Closer. But as I was about to lean in, drawn by the anguish I'd spotted there, my eyes flew open, my breath coming in harsh gasps.

She needs us.

I flexed my fingers.

185

The last time a woman needed you, your absence led to her death.

Pain struck hard and fast. The familiar taste of ash flooded my mouth. I remembered kneeling in the burnt out pyre while harsh whispers rang in my ears, my name a curse upon the lips of my tribe.

Askook.

Snake.

Crawling out of the dirt that day I had done the unforgivable. But then so had they. Bloodsoaked and with the scent of ash still burning in my gullet, I had left everything I had ever known behind, including my old name. Instead, I had taken the name Ash, so I would always remember.

The ferocity of man. The unfairness of the world. And the ease with which I killed.

The memories made me look to the sky and search for the same star that had guided me back when I rose from ashes and death, and survived my third Ascension. There was regret in me, and pain, but most of all there was fear.

I cannot lose my family again.

Sorrow fled as determination steeled my resolve. This was not the same. The past was dead. Gone. This time it would be different.

I would be different.

I would protect Hope, and I would protect my pack.

Or see the world burn as I died with them.

1 8

HOPE

Bleary eyed and fighting a losing battle against a yawn, I dragged my tired body out of bed. Surprisingly enough, the reason for my sleepless night wasn't so much my terrifying nightmare as it was the way Ruarc had left last night.

Dejected.

Like he'd given up on me.

Chest aching, I'd made it all the way to the bathroom before the absence of pain in my leg reached my tired brain. Why wasn't it hurting?

I closed the door and hurried over to the edge of the bathtub, taking a seat and peeling off the socks Ash had given me. The bandage underneath was no longer white; silverly swirls interlaced with a dark, almost black red covered the soft surface.

Curious, I pinched a flake of the dry liquid between two fingers and brought it to my nose.

Ugh!

My nose wrinkled at the scent of rot and blood.

Disgusting.

I undid the bandage, feeling my eyebrows climbing almost to my hairline as pale, unblemished skin was revealed.

No, not unblemished but . . . I squinted and there it was; a very faint, very healed scar. It wrapped around my ankle, spiraled up my calf, and traveled back down around on the other side. It looked like a monster had swallowed half my leg before taking a bite, only to spit it out again.

My injury was . . . healed.

The relief that filled me was euphoric. I could move. Run. My leg would no longer be dragging behind like so much dead weight, and—

Healed. It had healed.

A wave of dizziness drove me forward. I tried to remain seated, but my feet slid and I followed, slumping forward until my forehead rested on the cool tiles.

I'd healed.

I squeezed my eyes shut, but it made no difference. Open or closed, the black spots that danced across my vision made it impossible to see.

This was it. *Proof* that I wasn't human. *Proof* that something else, something sinister occupied the place inside where only *I* should be.

Shouldn't have happened.

The metal that had stopped me from healing at my normal speed should have left my leg mangled for however long it took a human to heal. Never before had this happened. Never before had I healed this quickly after being injured by that special Hunter metal.

Struggling to breathe, I flopped onto my side and peered down at my calf. At the faded, definitely-not-new scar.

An insidious, cold fear spread from my heart; brought numbness and tingling to my extremities.

Left me shaking.

If this was discovered, if one of the guys saw this . . . I could not explain this away. Lucien would convince the others I was hiding something, something big, and they'd throw me out.

I curled up in a ball, hugged my knees to my chest, and tried to stop shivering.

Where would I go? I was no closer to finding my uncle. I had no money. The job I'd been given was in this house, with these men. And outside the walls of their home lurked the dangers I'd done my best to escape.

The Hunters.

This . . . this was the only place I'd felt safe since I was a child.

The cold from the bathroom tiles had soaked through my body, my panic and fear increasing their effect until even my lips felt numb. I had to get up. Had to pull myself together.

The guys couldn't find out. They couldn't, and so I would not let them. It was that simple.

And that difficult.

Stiff and cold, I peeled myself off the floor. My knees still shook, my hands trembled as I grabbed hold of the edge of the bathtub, but I got to my feet.

How would I hide this from them?

Get rid of the evidence.

That was easier said than done. After running the bandage under water and scrubbing it for all I was worth without success, I bent and rummaged through the different soaps under the sink. Not knowing which to use, I tried a little of each, rubbing the cloth together until my hands were raw and the bandage regained most of its old white color. Then I wrung it out as best I could and placed it over the sink so it could dry while I showered.

I'd undressed and was about to step into the shower when the sound of a door opening whipped through the silent bathroom.

The lock!

I spun around and tried to yell "Occupied," but my vocal cords had frozen, my lungs had stopped working, and all I could do was gape as Jason's broad shoulders pushed through the door.

He was looking over his shoulder, grinning. "You tell him I want a rematch," he called out, and as he was turning I regained control of my body.

A high-pitched yelp tripped past my lips, and I lunged for the nearest towel.

Jason's head snapped forward, eyes widening as they took in my half-naked state, the towel clutched at my chest. His jaw went slack and he stumbled back, banging his head against the door frame in his haste to leave.

"Sorry, sorry!" He slammed the door shut behind him. There was another *thunk*, something hard hitting wood. "I . . . I didn't know you were in there."

My heart hammered in my chest. My pulse raced. The towel I clung to flapped like it was caught in the breeze, but it was only my hands shaking.

"I—"

The sound of his voice plunged my mind into icy water, and I lunged to the door. The sound of the lock clicking in place allowed me to exhale, and I realized I'd been holding my breath.

"Love, I . . ." Jason hesitated. "I didn't see anything—"

"Oh god!" I stepped back, held the towel away from my body, looked down. "Oh god . . ." I'd purposely avoided mirrors since I got here. Every time I caught a glimpse of my sunken cheeks, the dark circles under my eyes, the limp length of my hair, and the grotesque push of ribs against skin, I was reminded of my time at the compound. Dread, terror, shame . . . all emotions that would inevitably follow, but it wasn't the only reason I avoided mirrors.

I didn't want to see how ugly I'd become.

And I damned well didn't want any of *them* to see.

A soft rap at the door. "You have nothing to worry about, love. You had a towel. I—"

The rest of his words were drowned out by the pounding of my heart filling my ears. How vain could I possibly be? Why did I care if Jason had seen me almost . . . almost naked.

I touched the hollows of my cheeks.

What did it matter if the man with the charming smile, sun-kissed skin, and gorgeous amber eyes saw . . . all of this.

"I . . ." Whatever I had planned to say got stuck in my throat.

"You about to hop in the shower?"

"Y-yes," I stuttered, grateful he'd broken the horrible silence.

"Breakfast will be ready in fifteen." A short break, then, in a voice that was lower, a little hoarser than I was used to from him, "You okay?"

No. No, I was not okay. "Yes."

"Good." Another pause, this one taut. Strained. "I'll . . . I'll see you at breakfast."

"O-okay." Once he was gone, I brought my ugly, tainted body to the shower and tried to clear my mind. What had happened with Jason was not important. What was important was keeping my secrets and making sure I had an excuse ready the next time Ash wanted to change my bandage.

But how did one stop a male who'd proven to be both kind and honorable, when stopping him meant convincing him not to care?

JASON

Shit. Shit!

I stumbled down the stairs and took a seat on the first chair I saw.

Fuck me . . .

Her face when she'd realized I'd seen her . . . Pure devastation.

I closed my eyes, tried to banish the image I feared would be burnt into my mind for all eternity. Had a female ever looked so sad, so wounded, so agonizingly *raw*?

No. Never.

She had nothing to be ashamed of. *Nothing.* Yes, she was skinny—her towel had covered her private parts but before I'd turned, I'd caught a glimpse of a poking hip bone, a flash of a smooth, curving buttocks, and ribs that were too visible for my own peace of mind—but that lack of nourishment, her lack of flesh did not make her look weak or unappealing. Rather, it made me all the more aware of what she'd survived.

Who knew how long she'd been starved?

Years. It has to be years.

My teeth ground together as a wave of hot rage swept away pieces of my sanity. For years she'd been a captive, denied even her basic needs, and yet she had not broken. She had not succumbed to madness or cruelty or any of the thousands of other things that could have stolen her gentle spirit. No, Hope had survived. And while dying was easy, living was not.

She's strong.

But the way she'd looked at me, the hopeless, agonized look when she'd understood I was *seeing* her . . .

I tugged at the short strands of my hair, buried my face in my hands. How could I fix this? How could I wipe away the shame, the humiliation that had colored her face a startling red?

Groaning, I got to my feet and began pacing. Normally, I left anything unpleasant in the past. If I pretended nothing had happened, maybe she'd do the same? If I found a way to distract her, to take her mind off what had happened, would she try to forget? Should I allow her to forget?

Or would it be better to talk about it? To assure her that despite her obvious lack of food, she didn't look bad?

Don't go there, I told myself sternly, but it did no good. Again my mind brought back exactly what I'd walked in on, what I'd seen. And it wasn't unappealing. Far from it. There was something about her eyes that drew me in. Something about the sharp jut of a stubborn chin while her lips trembled with the attempt not to cry. The slender arch of her neck. The goodness of her soul. The body that housed it, that housed *her* would heal. It would fill out, flesh would cover bones, curves would appear and beg to be held, roundness would replace hollowness. And when it did . . .

My dick gave a jerk.

What the—

The fucker was hard.

Guilt robbed me of my breath. What the hell was I doing? Quickly, I brought to mind the anguish flashing over that pale face and breathed a sigh of relief when the asshole in my pants drained of blood.

"What did the chit do this time?" Lucien watched me from the doorway, the closest thing he got to a frown tugging on his lips.

"Nothing," I muttered.

He arched a brow.

"Really."

"If you say so." He crossed the room to the kitchen, hesitated in the doorway. "Do not let her muddle your mind."

Coming from Lucien, the show of concern might as well have been a declaration of brotherly love. He cared. We all knew he did, but sometimes I wished his caring would not result in the decimation of anyone he thought was a threat to his family. "She's not." I changed the subject, "What's for breakfast?"

"Food."

His dry humor pulled a reluctant grin from me. "Don't try that on Ruarc." He'd been in a terrible mood since he'd stormed out of Hope's room last night. "He's likely to rip you apart with his bare hands."

"Then he would struggle with his breakfast."

We walked into the kitchen, the male in question grumbling under his breath as he spotted us.

Lucien arched another brow and leaned casually against the fridge while I waited for him to explain his comment.

When it became clear he wouldn't say anything more unless I asked, I rolled my eyes and gave him what he so obviously wanted. "Why would he struggle with his breakfast?"

"Bear hands are not suited to hold a knife and fork."

Despite my bad mood, I couldn't help but laugh.

Lucien didn't smile, but his eyes warmed. He might not be the most affectionate brother in the world, but he didn't like to see any of us unhappy.

"Good one." I took the seat next to him, my thoughts returning to the human upstairs. If Lucien could distract me, why couldn't I simply distract Hope? Before another image of her anguished expression could renew the hollow ache in my chest, I started plotting. Ignoring bad things might not make them go away, but it sure as hell could make them stop hurting. At least for a little while.

RUARC

The little female was late.

I growled down at my bacon. The pig was lucky it was dead or I would've torn it to pieces with my bare hands.

The anger bubbling in my veins mixed with an emotion I hadn't felt in centuries. A cold, bitter, festering wound that made me question things better left alone. Things like why I was the way I was. Why I couldn't go a day without growling, snapping and snarling at others. Why I couldn't change the way females perceived me; like a dangerous, ugly brute who'd explode at the slightest provocation.

Why, why, why, I silently chanted as hot rage wound around me like hot mist. My sire's voice ripped through my mind, cold and filled with contempt; *Stop yer sniveling you worthless mongrel. If ye willnae do as ye're told, ye can bloody well starve oot here.* As a scrawny boy, barely seven summers, spending the dark, icy night on the moors all by myself had seemed a cruel and unusual punishment. Now I would have traded it for these *feelings* in a heartbeat.

"Has the food done something to offend you, Ruarc?" Lucien asked, a rare glimmer of humor in his otherwise cool eyes.

"Shut yer mouth." The words, sounding so like my father's, burned like hot coals on my tongue. The bloody accent had made an appearance more often than I was comfortable with lately, and I knew just who to blame.

The female in question padded into the kitchen, hesitating by the counter before taking a seat as far away from Jason as possible, and her part in my misery melted away.

I looked between them, taking in Jason's chagrined expression and Hope's blushing cheeks.

Just like that my fury returned tenfold. "What the bloody hell is going on?"

Hope's startled brown eyes peeked up at me. Quickly, before those soulful eyes could drain any of my righteous anger, I shifted my glare to Jason instead. Whatever the fool pup had been up to, it couldn't be good.

If he'd hurt her . . .

My chest vibrated with a vicious growl.

Instead of the apology I expected, Jason met my furious glare with a frown. "Nothing. Nothing is going on."

Nothing better have been going on or I'd bloody well ruin that pretty face of his.

"Hope?" I growled, never taking my eyes off Jason.

"I—what do you mean?" Her voice shook, and from the corner of my eye I could see her face was still crimson.

A red haze descended over my eyes and my heart sped up, getting ready to fight. It took everything in me to stay where I was, to not throw myself over the table and pummel Jason into the ground.

The aggression heating my blood was nothing new. But the force of the emotion, the speed it took me over . . . That was. A little light maiming was never off the table if my brothers pissed me off enough, but to really hurt them?

Never.

My mouth prickled as the Change stole over me.

If the little female looked up she would see that something wasn't right. That *I* wasn't right.

"Ruarc," Ash hissed, gesturing to my mouth.

Shit!

Without a word, I turned and stormed outside.

Letting my long, angry stride carry me while rage pounded at my skull, I continued until all I could see was trees. Furious at everyone; Jason for whatever he did to Hope, at Hope for what she made me feel, at Lucien for being a condescending bastard, at Ash for his enviable self-control, I cursed until I ran out of words while I tore off my clothes, pretending my destroyed shirt was Jason's face.

As I dropped to all fours and let the Change take me, one question echoed in my mind, provoking a livid storm of emotions best left buried; *why?*

19

HOPE

For the second time in less than twenty-four hours I'd driven Ruarc away. The uncomfortable heat warming my face was nothing compared to the hole in my chest. I hated that I bothered Ruarc so much that he felt the need to leave his own kitchen.

House, I amended as the heavy front door slammed shut.

"Do not let it bother you, Hope," Ash said. "Ruarc has always been quick to anger."

"I seem to bring it out in him."

Jason snorted. "We all do." The glance he threw me, accompanied by the lines between his drawn brows and the tightness around his mouth, made me think he wasn't any happier than I was about what had happened upstairs.

Probably feels bad about how horrible I look, I thought morosely.

He cleared his throat. "Do you know how to play poker?"

Ash groaned.

I stared at my food—anything to avoid looking into the face of the man who'd seen me half-naked and had run off so quickly he'd hit his head on the way. Poker . . . It sounded vaguely familiar. "The card game?"

"Yes, love, the card game."

The endearment had me glancing up, surprised. Even more so when I saw his grin. Not the full, confident grin he normally wore, but close enough that the mortification flooding me when I looked at him receded a drop. If he could pretend it had never happened, so could I.

"No, I . . . I don't."

"Want to learn?"

"Uhm . . . okay," I replied, not sure if spending more time with Jason was the right decision. "When?"

"How about after breakfast?"

"Sure." I glanced at Ash, wondering at the pained expression on his face and the way he kept staring down at his food. Were they upset Jason hadn't invited them along? Just as I was about to issue an invitation on Jason's behalf—grudgingly admitting to myself it would be rude to exclude Lucien—a thought struck me. "But . . . Don't you have work?" That was what *normal* people did, right, work?

"Not today, love," he said with a smile that made me strangely wary.

Despite my suspicion about this new activity, I had to admit I preferred him like this; all smiles and humor. It made it easier to forget my own embarrassment.

"What—I mean . . . How can you take so much time off?" I blushed, worried they would find my question rude or intrusive, especially considering how few of *their* questions I actually answered.

"I believe the chit is wondering what we do for a living," Lucien said, a sardonic twist to his firm lips. "Perhaps she is after our money."

"What? No!" How could he think that? The guys were the reason I was alive, the reason my escape had lasted longer than just a few hours. I would never steal from them or do anything to hurt them.

Except keep dangerous secrets.

Ash shot Lucien a look I couldn't decipher. His eyes were stern, mouth firm. "No one here believes that, Hope," he said, ignoring Lucien's polite sound of disagreement. "If there is anything you want to know about us, all you have to do is ask. We will not be offended."

I doubted Lucien saw it the same way.

Jason, who had been scowling at Lucien, chimed in, voice softening as he studied my face. "You don't have to be afraid here, love," he said. "Worst that can happen is you don't get an answer."

Looking up through my lashes, I searched his deep brown—not amber?—eyes. He seemed to mean what he was saying. Ash, too. And while a quick peek out of the corner of my eyes showed a cold and indifferent Lucien—the only hint of emotion the minute tightening around his eyes—their openness tightened my throat. No one had answered my questions in a very long time.

The burning curiosity I felt when around them urged me to pepper them with questions, but instead, I settled on a simple one. "Jason mentioned before that you are business partners. What kind of business do you run?"

Ash glanced at Jason before replying, "We own and oversee a . . . territory." His voice was careful. Neutral.

"Like you own land?" I asked in surprise before adding, "I thought you rehabilitated horses?"

Lucien's cold gaze raked over me, but it was Jason who answered. "He does that as well, love. Ash oversees our territory, but a few years ago we hired people to take care of the various businesses we own, leaving us with more free time." He paused, tilting his head while a playful grin tugged at the corners of his lips. "We have plenty of *leisure* time when we are not away on, erhm, business."

Ash gave Jason a hard look, getting a sheepish smile in return.

Curious.

Lucien broke the strange tension before I could puzzle it out. "Jason spends most of his *leisure* time with his many women," he said coldly while pinning me with his forest green gaze.

The words knocked the wind out of me, loosening a gasp lodged in my throat.

Lucien's eyes narrowed at the sound, but he didn't seem surprised. It rather seemed he was assessing my reactions. Cataloging the emotions he could read off my face. Somehow he'd known—or at least suspected—his words would hurt me, even though it had come as a complete shock to me when they did.

Jason jumped up, nearly knocking his chair over in the progress. The look he sent Lucien was filled with venom.

"My, I have shocked the girl."

"What is wrong with you?" Jason spat.

"I believe my dear mother could have given you a long list on the matter. Unfortunately for you, she is dead."

Another gasp. A lump that made swallowing difficult. What had happened in his life to make him so dispassionate about something so personal?

"Jason," Ash said calmly when it looked like Jason was about to jump over the table and attack Lucien. "Why don't you and Hope get started on your poker lesson a little earlier?"

The last thing I wanted right then was to be alone with Jason. Dark resentment radiated off him in waves, but the true reason I wanted to escape the constricting tension lay in the truth of my alarming emotions. Lucien's comment had gotten to me, and I didn't want Jason to know. Not when I didn't understand it myself. Why should I care that Jason was a womanizer? Just because I was woefully inexperienced didn't mean I should judge Jason for the . . . *stuff* he did with all his women.

Hope, you're a grown ass woman, you can at least think the word 'sex.' The inner scolding didn't work. Thinking about Jason in relation to . . . to *sex* was not a good idea.

"Fine," Jason muttered, scowling at Lucien while helping me out of my seat—if you can call jerking the seat back with me still in it, then hauling me up by the arm and practically dragging me out the room *'helping.'*

At my low sound of pain, Jason dropped my arm so fast I stumbled. "I'm so sorry, love." He stopped, steadying me before he looked away. Spitting out a low curse, he dragged a jerky hand through his hair. "I shouldn't have grabbed you like that. Lucien just . . ." He paused, glancing at the face I was trying desperately to keep devoid of feelings. Whatever he saw had steel appearing behind his eyes. He moved forward, raised his hand as if to touch me, though he dropped it before it made contact. "I'm sorry, love."

"I-it's okay." Despite the slight shaking, my voice didn't reveal any of my inner turmoil. The soreness in my arm was already gone, slight as it had been. The only reason I'd made any sound at all was because of the surprise of Jason's rushed exit.

"It's not okay. No man should treat you like that." The pained look he gave me melted my resolve to stay aloof.

"Really, Jason, I'm fine," I assured him and grabbed his hand, giving it a small squeeze.

He stared at our entwined fingers. "What Lucien said . . . I'm not like that. Not anymore."

A cold, slithering feeling curled in my stomach. I stepped away, breaking our touch while trying to contain the ugly sensation. Why did this bother me so much? "You don't have to explain," I said, and I meant it. Whatever he'd done in the past, it really wasn't any of my business. It wasn't as though the thought of him with another woman made something pierce my chest.

No. Not at all.

The heat of Jason's gaze roaming my face was disconcerting. I didn't want to look at him, didn't need to read the truth in his eyes. "Hope," he began, sounding disheartened. The stillness of his body belied the tension I heard when he spoke. "When I was younger . . ." He looked up, searching for words. His mouth opened and closed a few times. Whatever he wanted to say, it was difficult for him.

More than difficult, I thought as I watched his throat work without a sound.

Making an effort to make my voice sound as cheery as possible, I interrupted his silent struggle. "Teach me poker?" Before he could reply, I walked ahead of him to the living room. Unsure where he wanted me to sit, I waited for him as he slowly followed.

"Okay," he said and cleared his throat. When he spoke again, a false cheerfulness infused each word. "So this is what you do . . ."

Learning poker turned out to be harder than I'd thought, but at least it was a good distraction. Jason proved a patient teacher, going over each rule as many times as I needed without once getting annoyed when I struggled to understand the strange game. With the cards between us on the couch we shared, we'd played the first few rounds with them facing up.

While I'd tucked my legs against my body, feeling like a graceless sack of potatoes, Jason managed to both look casual and appealing despite his big frame. One leg bent, foot resting against the opposite knee, he'd twisted his torso to face me, and whenever he wasn't dealing he'd throw one arm across the back of the couch and lean forward, gaze locked on my face.

I had a feeling my cheeks had been a rosy red every since we sat down.

After my fourth loss in a row, Jason tossed his head and gave a dramatic sigh. "It's hopeless," he groaned. The back of his free hand found his forehead with dramatic flourish. "I'm afraid you will never be a decent poker player, love."

I smiled at his antics, enjoying the self-satisfied smirk he flashed at me in response. It was almost as if he took pleasure in my amusement. I wondered if that's why he was always so quick with a smile and a joke; to make others happy.

"It doesn't seem like a necessary skill."

Jason gaped at me in mock surprise. "Never say that! I happened to put bread on the table by playing poker as a young lad."

"Really?"

"Truly." His wide grin showed off two rows of even white teeth. Laughter sparkled in his amber eyes, giving him the look of a carefree, young boy. Although no one could mistake the wide-shouldered, muscular creature before me as anything less than a man.

"How do you make a living from a card game," I asked, suspicion narrowing my eyes.

"Gambling." He shuffled the cards, quick hands moving with an ease I found strangely compelling. "You do know what gambling is?"

I racked my brain, mentally flipping through each movie I'd been allowed to watch back in the early days with the Hunters.

Nothing.

I stared down at my hands, pretending the cards he'd just dealt held all my attention. How much of my past did I reveal when I was unable to comprehend what everyone else took for granted.

"Hope . . ."

I looked up in time to see Jason's smile dim. A soft glow shimmered behind his eyes, tantalizing and impossible in the way the colored deepened, changed, and then blazed like amber lit from within.

Drawn to that flickering, fragile light, I leaned closer, almost not hearing his next words.

"I made my money by betting on the right outcome in various games and events. Beating others in poker can also be lucrative. I did some hustling too, but don't tell Ash." A playful wink. "He likes to pretend I have always done things on the up and up. He kind of had to when he let me run the pack casino."

I blinked. In one mouthful he'd given me so much information I didn't know how to break it down. Without prodding about my lack of knowledge, he'd told me what gambling was—betting money and winning—that hustling was frowned upon, and that the guys owned a casino.

A rush of tender feelings coursed through me at his thoughtfulness, the way he volunteered information even though I was the polar opposite. Somehow, he didn't hold it against me, choosing instead to include me in their lives.

His openness enticed me to ask questions. Questions I'd never have asked if I remained at the Compound where speaking out of turn was met with swift reprisal. "What is a pack casino?"

Jason stilled, and that old fear came rushing back, freezing my breath and turning my insides to water. But then he blinked and made a made a dismissive hand gesture. "Oh, nothing, love, it's just a British turn of phrase. Americans just say 'casino.'"

I slumped back against the soft couch and breathed a sigh of relief.

We played a few more rounds—two of which I won, to my eternal surprise—and then Jason rose, his powerful legs encased in tight, dark jeans that hung low on his hips. "Up with you, love," he said, pulling me so close the heat from his body enveloped me. An electric current danced across my skin, drawing me closer, making my breath speed up in an unfamiliar reaction. Scary, yet . . . enticing.

A soft gasp escaped my parted lips as he cupped the back of my head, bending his neck and lowering his face until mere inches separated our mouths.

My gaze flew across his face, trying to understand what was happening, what he was thinking. A lazy grin played at his lips, his eyes held an emotion I couldn't quite decipher; something deeper than the moment called for, something heated and terrifying and—

He leaned closer and my breath caught.

"It's my turn to do the shopping." The murmured words made no sense to my foggy mind. All I could think about was his heat, the way his minty breath mingled with a delicious aftershave and the scent of stormy rain—a heady concoction that was pure Jason. The scent, *his* scent, filled my senses. My breath sped up, my chest heaved. The closer he got the more my head spun, and when dizziness hit, it was the good kind, the kind you wished could go on forever.

Jason stroked a finger across my cheek. "Come with me."

The spell broke as bands of cold dread tightened around my chest.

Leave the house? Leave the safety of this temporary shelter? I squeezed my eyes shut. Everything itched. Itched in a deep, throbbing, unrelenting manner that left me feeling as though my skin would melt off my bones. Leave? Go outside? Where the Hunters—

I stumbled back, almost falling headfirst into the couch behind us. "N-no!"

Jason followed, putting a hand on my shoulder to stabilize me. I shrugged it off, confused at my body's reaction, at the alien sensations coursing through it. But when I looked up, it was straight into glowing, amber eyes.

I shook my head, haunted by eyes unlike any I'd ever seen.

No, that's not right. Ruarc's eyes also seemed to glow. A time or two, having glimpsed them out of the corner of my eye, I'd thought they could have been pale gray, but whenever our eyes met they shone like liquid silver.

Questions raced through my mind, chased by confusion and my deep fear of leaving the bubble of safety that their home had become. Before I could stammer my way through an excuse as to why I couldn't go with him, Jason's hand gently squeezed my shoulder.

"Don't worry about it, sweetheart." He studied me, brows drawn together over serious eyes. "I thought it would be nice for you to pick out some things for yourself, but if you write a list I will make sure I get you whatever you need."

Relief made my voice wobble, "Oh." I swallowed a couple of times, but no words came. What could I say to someone who'd just proved he was thinking about me when he and his brothers were the only ones who had done so in a very, *very* long time?

The itchy feeling vanished. Dread became mist and drifted away. Warmth expanded in my chest. Having someone looking after me felt . . .

Wonderful.

He stroked a finger across my brow, the touch so gentle I barely felt it. I swallowed again, peeked up at him. Our eyes met, his warm and concerned, but devoid of the luminous shimmer that had so entranced me before.

Had I imagined the way he'd looked at me earlier? The way he'd made me feel with his touch, his closeness . . .

Did it mean anything?

Or am I reading too much into it? Having no experience with men—except for the Hunters who I was loath to refer to as men—it was impossible for me to know.

Shifting from foot to foot, uncomfortable and filled with the strangest feeling of heat, it suddenly dawned on me that Jason was waiting for a reply.

His lazy half grin made me frown. Was he laughing at me? I glowered back, surprised when his eyes glinted and he winked.

He winked . . .

Is he waiting for a list or something else?

Either way, I was lost. My brain was out of order; I couldn't think of a single thing I needed from the store. What would normal people ask for?

Pushing my mind back in time, I tried to think what I'd liked as a child. There had been these round, strawberry-cream flavored drops, but I had no clue what they were called. As for food, so far I had liked everything the guys put on the table and I doubted that would change.

"Don't be shy, love." Jason's smile widened. "Anything you want. Anything . . ." There was something in his voice. Something a little dark, a little wicked.

Heat rushed through me and gathered low in my belly.

Jason took another step forward, his right hand gliding over my side until his fingers spread across my lower back. With a small push I was pressed tightly against his muscled frame. I squirmed, my small breasts flattened against the steely abs of his upper abdomen, my cheek resting against his broad, sculpted chest. Something big and hard pushed uncomfortably against my belly, disappearing when he tilted his hips away. Something inside me clenched painfully at the loss.

What is happening to me?

My thoughts raced, the unbearable heat in my stomach unfurled and spread to my chest, my thighs. Even my fingertips tingled. A seed of fear took root deep in my heart, warning me I was in dangerous territory.

Jason's hot breath tickled my neck and blew all thoughts away, like a light breeze lulling a flame to sleep. "What do you want, love?" he murmured against my ear.

I wonder how many women he's said that to?

My throat constricted. What was I doing? Lucien had just revealed Jason's love of women—multiple women—something Jason himself had all but confirmed. In the past or not, I'd never measure up. And now . . . after having seen me half naked . . . now he knew. He had to know. I was . . . damaged. Beyond damaged, I was broken. And Jason was . . . Jason was . . .

Light. There was no other way to describe it, Jason was sunny and exciting and warm and kind. He was the breeze that tickled your neck in the spring, the bursting rays of morning-light in the summer. He was much more than I could ever deserve.

They all were. They'd saved my life, brought me into their home, fed me, clothed me, kept me safe. And what had I done in return?

"N-nothing. I don't need a-anything from the store." It took all my strength to push away from him, my body immediately mourning the absence of his warmth, the masculine strength of his body.

I could feel the reluctance in his hand as it left my back and dropped to his side. At his harsh exhale I glanced up, taking in his inviting lips before meeting his gaze. Once I did, I stumbled back. The burning heat in his amber eyes made them light up with a brilliant radiance.

It was beautiful and terrifying.

And completely inhuman.

"Jason," I choked out, unable to tear my eyes away from the exquisite brightness. At the sound of his name, Jason squeezed his eyes shut and violently shook his head. A low hiss rushed past taut lips that moments ago had seemed soft and supple.

Alarmed, I reached out to touch the wrist above his fisted hand. "A-are you okay?"

Before my fingers could make contact, he jerked back. "I'm fine," he snapped, then took a deep breath and continued in a calmer voice. "I'm good, love." The tension on his face, the tightness next to his eyes, told a different story. He grinned, but instead of warm humor, his eyes were cold and very unlike the Jason I had come to know. "Guess I know what you don't want."

Not giving me time to reply, he picked up the leather jacket slung across the back of the couch, and marched out the door, leaving me staring blankly after him.

Stomach in knots, chest tight and uncomfortable, I swallowed several times. The expression on his face as he'd left had been dark, a wry twist to his mouth that was almost self-deprecating.

And what he'd said . . .

Guess I know what you don't want.

Indecision paralyzed me; I didn't know what to do or what to think. Had we shared a moment? Had it all been in my head?

That would probably be for the best.

I could only bring danger into their lives. Danger and misery and secrets I could never, *ever* reveal. And what about Ruarc? And Ash? And the strange feelings they'd both invoked in me on separate occasions?

It was wrong. *I* was wrong.

Licking my dry lips, I took a wobbling step toward the stairs. It didn't look like Jason was going to be back anytime soon, and if he was I should probably make myself scarce. The thought of seeing him right then . . .

My insides took a nosedive.

There was no point standing around here. With the fragile way I was feeling, seeking solitude in my room for a few hours might be best. Maybe once I calmed down I could think straight and this whole thing would all make sense.

I trudged up the stairs, down the dark corridor, and walked into my barren room. It was spacious, but lacking any personal touches or decorations to give a warm, homey feeling. Even the bed looked uninviting to me at that moment, with its too-white sheets and its perfectly aligned pillows.

Even so, I flopped down onto the soft mattress and heaved another heavy sigh. In that moment, my insides matched the room; both of us barren and utterly hollow.

20

HOPE

I'VE MISSED SO MUCH, I THOUGHT SADLY AS I STARED OUT AT the beautiful scene playing out right outside my bedroom window. The waxing moon brought life to the dark landscape, its soft light a caress that tempered the night and illuminated what would otherwise be left in shadow.

Although it was not yet fully night, the moon greeted the world like a long lost lover, a little too eager and much too happy to see the day's reluctant farewell.

Though I'd managed to avoid Jason the rest of the day it had come at a price. Faking a headache had allowed me to stay alone in my room, a tray of food brought up by a much too conscientious Ash while guilt throbbed at my temples and summoned a faint echo of the headache I'd never had.

After years spent in solitude, being alone was the last thing I wanted, but at the same time I felt the draw of my empty room like I had the cell that represented safety when the Hunters were in the mood to play.

Shivering, I banished the ugly thoughts and pressed my nose closer to the cool glass. A deer stood in the middle of the garden. Bathed in the faint light cast off the silvery moon, it looked elegant and ethereal.

Beautiful.

Crickets sang and leaves rustled, and the deer munched on a plant right below my window. I smiled, felt the peace of the moment settle around me like a well-loved blanket. Back at the Hunter compound the nights had seemed impossibly long, the silence deafening and only interrupted when a particularly evil Hunter decided to play outside the rules.

Then the screams would break up the monotonous infinity while the captives cowered and wished for silence once more.

Movement to the right drew my gaze, and my smile widened at the sight. Another deer flicked its ears, one foot lifted as it pondered its next move. Would it dare dart across the yard, lit as it was by the soft glow coming from the house, or would it disappear from view as its elegant legs carried it back into the thick bushes surrounding the guys' garden?

A sharp knock on the door made me draw in a quick breath, and both deer leapt away.

I sighed and turned away from my gawking. Nature would still be there tomorrow, and hopefully so would I.

"Who is it?" I called out, glad my voice didn't shake and give away my fear. Even after three days of being safely tucked away in the guys' home, I still couldn't bring myself to open the door without knowing who was on the other side.

A beat of silence followed my inquiry, then a cool, distinct voice, "Lucien."

Lucien? Why on earth was he here?

I hurried to the door, cursing the overlarge clothes I'd borrowed from my saviors as I nearly stumbled over the hem of my sweatpants. Letting the door open a tiny crack, I peered outside. "Yes?"

An arrogantly arched brow met my inquiry. "Were you sleeping?" His gaze raked over me, took in the roomy sweats and baggy shirt, and his nostrils flared. For a second I thought I saw something igniting in those arctic eyes, but when I did a double take his expression was closed, face set in an icy mask of disdain.

"No."

He, of course, was dressed to perfection. The stark white dress-shirt he wore so well clung to his broad chest and lean torso. Black slacks hung off his trim hips.

He was beautiful and intimidating, and altogether too mean for my liking.

"May I come in?" His tone was polite enough, but the way he looked at me—like I was beneath him in some way—made me wish I could say no.

"S-sure." I stepped back, not stopping until I was standing beneath the large window on the opposite wall and wishing I was out in the garden with the deer.

Lucien entered and, to my relief, left the door open behind him. Again, his perfectly sculpted eyebrow rose—this time with a hint of amusement when he saw how far away I was standing. "You do know a few feet between us would not stop me if I intended you harm?" With the room shrouded in darkness, the moon bouncing off the wall and lending shadows a place to play, his amusement took on a sinister twist.

I tensed and my mouth went dry. If he was trying to intimidate me, he had succeeded.

"Are you afraid?"

"N-no."

"Liar."

There was something about Lucien that instinctively made me think he was dangerous. The pure silk of his voice —cold but smooth, almost lethal—and the glacier stare he wielded with such deadly precision was more than daunting. And yet . . .

"I'm n-not."

The way he stared out at the world, forest green orbs

resembling the sharpest icicles, made me think he'd seen or experienced more pain than he let on.

Despite my fear of him, another feeling stirred . . .

Compassion.

Don't be stupid, Hope. For all you know there is no great tragedy in his past and he was just born mean.

Although I doubted the other guys would consider someone who was 'just mean' their family. There had to be more to him than that.

Lucien sighed, looking as bored as a marble statue could possibly look without changing his dispassionate expression. "This is getting tedious," he said dryly. "You must know I'm not a rabid animal waiting to pounce on you as soon as we're alone?" His mouth twisted with distaste. "Despite what you may think, I am not ruled by emotions and my"—his nostrils flared—"*distaste* for you is benign. At least until I either gather proof of your deceit or you should attempt to hurt my brothers."

A rock formed in my stomach at his thinly veiled warning. I wanted to ask him why he disliked me so much, no, why he hated me so much—distaste was definitely too mild of a word for the derision dripping from every word he uttered in my presence—but I was too intimidated.

"I would never do anything to hurt your . . . your brothers." I took a deep breath and attempted a smile. No doubt it appeared as wobbly and stilted as I was feeling. "Jason said you all chose each other, that you *chose* to be a family." A sentiment I found vastly beautiful. "It must have been nice to meet people you just click with. People you can trust unequivocally."

Lucien bristled at my wistfulness. "That is none of your business."

I deflated.

Making friends with Lucien seemed impossible. Every advance was rebuffed, his cold facade as impenetrable as the

Hunters compound. "I'm sorry." I inched backward and grasped at the window sill behind me. "I . . . I didn't mean to intrude."

Green eyes narrowed to thin slits. "Then why did you?"

That was a good question. Lucien threw me off balance. His icy stare and cold contempt upset the small fragments of frail equilibrium I clung to for dear life. He unsettled me. Shook me in a way that left my soul quivering in a dark corner, confused by the mix of emotions he stirred.

And being around someone who hated me without trying to fix it went against my nature. I *wanted* Lucien to like me. Or if not like me, to at least stop hating me.

Unable to answer his question without inviting more, I looked away. The brief silence that followed scraped against my mind like steel-tipped claws. It was almost a relief when he spoke.

Almost.

"Yet another mystery you refuse to shed light on."

"T-there is no *mystery*," I denied, hoping I sounded more convincing to his ears than I did mine.

"Oh, is there not? Then, pray tell, who are you? Where did you come from? How did you *happen* to run into *our* car?" He took a step closer, a threat in the predatory way he moved. "Who stole your freedom and abused you?" A brow arched. "Or was it all a lie to earn our sympathies and a place to stay while you work your petty magic?"

No. No!

My mouth went bone dry. Guilt prodded its sharp talons against my sides, and I shook my head in denial. Lucien was wrong. *Wrong.* I wasn't out to hurt them. I didn't want to lie.

But you will, and you are.

And Lucien *knew*. He somehow saw my deception, sensed the ugly, terrible secrets I kept buried under miles of self-loathing and pain. He *knew* and it was only a matter of time before he threw me out.

Fresh terror flooded my already crumbling defenses. It twisted, grew, sharpened with each panicked breath. Alone I'd get caught. They'd force me back.

Oh, god!

Visions of evil leers and flashing metal crowded my mind, of cutting and tearing and pain and blood. So much blood. Dave's face swam before me, that same, ugly smirk twisting his lips, the one he always wore when he inflicted pain.

When I couldn't take it anymore, when I thought I might be sick, the horror receded, only to be replaced by far more damaging memories. Memories of claws, and teeth, and my brother's crumpled body.

I struggled to rein it in, to banish visions that never failed to bring me to my knees.

If Lucien ever found out about them, about the Hunters, they'd all be at risk. But if he knew of what came before, of the reason I had landed in that land of death and despair, if he knew what I was capable of . . .

He may just kill me.

And maybe that would be the right thing to do. Maybe he should kill me so he and his brothers could be safe.

But . . . I don't want to die.

A small, burgeoning hope—hope that I'd survive, that I wouldn't let my past repeat itself—slowed my racing heart. I shook my head and steeled my spine. "Just because I don't want to talk a-about . . . about what h-happened to m-me . . ." My voice broke, and out of the corner of my eye I thought I saw Lucien stiffen. I licked my suddenly dry lips before continuing, voice weak and shaking. "It d-doesn't mean I'm plotting against you. Ash and Jason and Ruarc . . . they've all been amazing, and if you all hadn't let me stay here I don't know what would have happened to me."

If Lucien was bothered that he'd been left off my list, he didn't show it. Expression inscrutable, he shifted to stare out the window.

While his attention was elsewhere and his profile was on display, I took full advantage. Studying him distracted me from the remnants of my fear, another emotion taking its place. Hair as black as the darkest night framed a hard face without any give. The cruel tilt to his hard mouth could have looked sensual if a smile ever graced those lips. Though they weren't plump, they were full enough that they'd have looked enticing if they weren't constantly either pressed tightly together or curled with distaste.

And his cheekbones . . . The sharpness complemented his face, but coupled with the hard glint in his cold, shuttered eyes, his unsmiling lips, and cutting jaw, it gave him a look of savage beauty; harsh, and deadly if crossed.

Occupied with thoughts of the beautiful man standing before me—why was he so cold and distant, why did he hate me so, and what would it be like to know the man underneath the frozen exterior?—I didn't notice when he turned around and pierced me with that cold gaze of his. It wasn't until his voice rose, fury tinging each, clipped word, that I realized I'd been staring blankly at him while he'd been speaking.

" . . . get on with it."

And I hadn't heard a word. I blurted the first thing that came to mind, "What?"

No one had ever accused me of being eloquent.

"Your bandage," he ground out through clenched teeth. The icy rage swirling in his startling, green eyes shocked me into stillness. For a moment, I couldn't breathe, confounded by how a beautiful nature-color like wintry-green could appear so cold and deadly. I kept staring up into his flashing eyes, confused as to why I was so captivated by the display of emotion.

And then it hit me. *Display of emotion . . .* When had the cold, contained man ever shown any emotion in my presence? Besides contempt or boredom, that was.

"W-what about it?" I whispered.

The icy glare Lucien aimed my way froze the breath in my lungs. "Are you deaf, wench?" he snapped. "I have come to change your bandage at Ash's behest." The task was obviously one he did not want. Though his eyes were still cold, something else lurked behind that icy wall, something hot and filled with the kind of anger that could not help but scorch anything it touched.

What would happen should that heated emotion ever break free of the ice encasing it?

With nostrils flaring and teeth clenching, Lucien was far removed from the cold, detached man that'd walked in here just a few minutes earlier. It was strange, in an abstract sort of way, when I realize I'd never seen him lose his temper, never seen him lose that icy calm that engulfed his whole exterior and made him seem oh-so-unapproachable. Even the other day when Ruarc had attacked him, Lucien had kept a clear head, not seeming the least bit bothered. If being attacked by an enraged giant didn't phase him, what could I have possibly done in the last few minutes to illicit the heated rage I could sense in him now?

"I, uhm . . ." What did he ask, again?

The bandages . . . But—my leg! I blinked several times in rapid succession, clinging to the windowsill until my fingers grew numb. My brain refused to work; I couldn't recall any of the excuses I'd practiced during my afternoon of solitude. "I . . . it's just that . . ." My panic woke the monster inside me. It stretched, languidly testing the bonds of its captivity.

The fine hair on my arms rose, the back of my neck prickled.

The monster pushed upward.

My pulse raced, and when my terrified, wide-eyed stare landed on Lucien, the spark of his heated fury was gone. He was drawing deep breaths in through his nose, eyes narrowed to thin slits as they searched the room. The clenched hands at his sides curled. Then suddenly he jerked his head to the window. Brushing past me, nearly knocking me over with the force of his determination, he opened it and stuck his head outside.

Confused at his bizarre behavior, I was nonetheless grateful for the reprieve. I closed my eyes, concentrating once again on shackling my inner monster while taking deep, even breaths.

With as much focus as I could muster, I looked deep inside and confronted the wild creature fighting to get free. With each slash of its wicked claws, I felt my composure crack. The uneven beat of my heart filled my ears while all I could smell, all I could feel was the savage darkness that shared my body, its incredible thirst for freedom.

Terrified of the bloody scene I risked waking up to should I lose control—worried for Lucien's safety despite how often he intimidated me—I pictured dozens of metal shackles binding the shapeless monster, both wishing and dreading I could see its face, just once, so I could understand what I was dealing with.

The struggle to force it down, bound and helpless in its cage, felt like it went on for hours, but in reality it could only have taken a minute or two. Once I was confident the monster was no longer a threat, I allowed myself three deep, cleansing breaths—breaths my poor lungs screamed for—and slumped against the bed.

While Lucien was occupied, I racked my brain for a believable excuse as to why the injury he meant to make sure was healing properly had, in fact, healed on its own.

There was none. He couldn't be allowed to see it.

"Uhm."

My hesitant voice snapped the taut man around. His eyes were wild, his nostrils flared and his mouth was slightly open. After sightlessly staring for a second or two, he closed the window and faced me with an inscrutable expression.

When I didn't immediately speak, icy disdain filled his eyes as he raked his gaze over me from head to toe, leaving me shivering with a feeling of not being good enough.

A feeling I was deeply familiar with.

"Is someone out there?" I gave a shaky nod to the window.

When he took too long to reply, I wondered if one of my tormentors lurked outside, using the shadows to hide his presence and biding his time until everyone was asleep so he could snatch me from my newfound safety.

But then Lucien shook his head. "It was nothing. For a moment I thought that perhaps . . ." His eyes chilled. "But of course, that would have been impossible."

He didn't make any sense, but I was not dumb enough to press him further.

"Shall we get on with it?" The frigid politeness matched the chill in his eyes.

Uh-oh. There was only one thing I could say. "N-no?"

Both his eyebrows shot up as he pinned me under his haughty stare.

"I . . . I asked Ash earlier," I improvised, hoping my voice didn't sound as unsure as I felt. I *hated* lying. "And he changed it for me. I told him . . ." I paused, swallowed hard, "I told him I wasn't comfortable with you doing it since you d-dislike me s-so much and—" The tightness squeezing my throat prevented me from continuing. Lucien was clearly disgusted with me, with my weakness and cowardice and probably a thousand other things.

"I see," he said, and I was surprised. Surprised he hadn't raised his voice, hadn't called me names. If he felt even an ounce of the loathing emanating from him, his self control was enviable. "I will take my leave, then." He turned stiffly, striding to the door. Once there, he paused. "If you want to be more than a stammering coward," he began, turning halfway so his face was in stark profile, "I would suggest you find a backbone and learn to deal with your fears."

He left.

LUCIEN

Infuriating, thankless female!

I slammed the door shut behind me and paced down the dimly lit corridor

Who does she think she is?

Instead of my usual, cold indifference, I was fuming. The hapless, defenseless *human* had rejected me. It didn't matter that her wariness in my presence was of my own doing. It didn't matter that she was the last female on earth I would want as my own with her fearful demeanor and shabby appearance. None of it mattered. Her rejection had stung when it ought to have bounced off my armor, crushed like a fly against a windshield.

The female twisted me up with laughable ease. It had to stop.

I yanked open the door to my quarters and continued my pacing. The room felt smaller, as though the walls had shrunk in my absence.

How dare she, a mere human, act as though I was beneath her? And after she'd been caught staring at my person with empty eyes, no doubt lusting for a night between my sheets.

A stab of desire at the picture she'd make naked in my bed caught me off guard. Fury beat a steady drum. I was not some baser beast ruled by my body, nor was I a mindless female willing to heedlessly share my body with every pretty face that happened by.

She's not pretty.

True. The wench was no great beauty with her pale skin

and too plump lips. Lips that would look delectable wrapped around—

I flexed my jaw, irritation banishing the image sheer will could not. The female was trouble. Already she'd caused tension between my brothers. Already her presence caused cracks to appear in the wall of ice I surrounded myself with.

Cursing soundly under my breath, I ceased my senseless pacing. There would be no peace inside these four walls, not this night. I left, taking care not to slam the door shut behind me. Such wasted display of emotion showed only weakness.

What was the female's endgame? Why did lies spill from her mouth, lies not of sweetest honey to lure and befuddle, but lies of barbed wire wrapped in fear. Bitter lies. Lies filled with regret and shame.

I shook my head and headed downstairs. The cold night-air beckoned, the scent I'd caught earlier luring me closer. Another female in *our* territory would be improbable. And as the human upstairs had proven, their gender brought nothing but trouble.

Still, I could not quite quench the curiosity that stirred.

Curiosity. Another flaw in the wall of ice.

All emotions were dangerous. The way I'd lost my grip on my fury when the female had stared at me like so many others over the years proved that. Although . . .

I called her a coward, but how many have still been standing after being exposed to the cold fury seething in my soul?

It was true she had stammered her way through a rejection of my reluctant offer to help, yet she had not backed down. Bold chin lifted, she'd squared her shoulders and told me no. Albeit in a quivering voice.

Had any female ever told me no before? Surely not since I was a child and at the mercy of my dam and sire.

Yet this female did. The same female who looked upon Ruarc's scarred visage, not with horror or disdain, but with sympathy and the same curiosity that drove me this very night.

Jealousy wound through my stomach, ugly and with a force I detested. On its heels nipped another emotion, one I was even more loath to feel; gratitude. I was . . . grateful that she had abstained from spurning Ruarc the same way most females did, and that fact had shards of icy fury bury under my skin, grating and cutting until the only emotion that remained was the cold anger I'd become so familiar with this last century.

Was this her plan? An insidious plot to burrow beneath our skin until she controlled us with the snap of her fragile, little fingers?

I had to admit, despite her lack of good looks, there was something about her that evoked thoughts better left forgotten. The dip of her pointy chin when she was uneasy, the elegant column of her slender neck, the hollow at the base of her throat a perfect spot for my lips to—

A wave of arctic fury chilled my blood.

Her plan was devious, but I would not be its victim.

Once outside I made my way to the ground below the human's window. The mysterious scent, if it had ever been, was long gone. I thought back to that moment, the one preceding the female's heavy stare as she cataloged each of my features as though looking at a horse she considered purchasing.

For the life of me I could not remember, could no longer recall the exact moment the strange, *female* scent made itself known.

Instead the memory was tainted by that of her stare.

My flesh rippled below the surface as I relived the creeping sensation of eyes upon my skin. I *detested* the hungry way females watched me. Their calculating inspection, their heated gaze, their slimy appreciation.

As though I was a piece of meat to be bartered for.

As though I could be bought, purchased with the right coin, the right information, the right touch . . .

Repellent.

It had been decades since my title last mattered, an eternity since women wanted the sought-after position of Duchess. Yet they still looked at me the same way they had when I walked among the *ton.*

Curse the male who spawned me!

The spitting image of my beastly sire, we shared more than our looks; his horrific temper, his propensity for violence, his cruelty, they were all a part of me. And as they did him, females only saw me as a thing to be coveted, failing to see the monster behind the mask.

The struggle I faced each day, the struggle to bury the violent, monstrous part I'd inherited from that loathsome male was one I faced with pleasure.

Each time I curbed my temper, a part of me gloated, gleefully aware I'd succeeded where my sire always failed.

Each time I replaced the hot, burning feeling of rage with one of cold determination, I did what my sire never could.

The bastard may have tried his best to mold me into a perfect carbon-copy of himself, but he'd failed. His fists had failed, his teeth and claws had failed, and his poisonous words had failed.

And now, a scared, mousy female was threatening to destroy everything I'd worked for. Threatening to snatch away the victory I so triumphantly lorded over my dead father.

No.

I stared up at the empty window, remembered the face of the female I'd left inside. *Curse her,* I thought in the blackest of moods. *Curse her and all the females like her.*

They had taught me to wield my beauty the same way I wielded my sword; with deadly precision and a lethal ruthlessness inherent in all of my species. It had made me one of the greatest spies among our kind, allowed me to taste the hollow victory that came from winning meaningless wars and gaining power I discovered held no interest.

The cost was too high. The price I paid each and every time hungry stares scraped against my skin was too great. The loathing clutching me in its sharp claws when I shared my body with those selfish, greedy females who wanted nothing more than the mindless pleasure any warm, attractive body could provide was too acute.

So then why had I allowed myself to be lured in by wide, wounded eyes and a quiet courage presented in the dip of a pointed chin, the squaring of thin, almost skeletal shoulders?

The fists curling at my sides spoke of loss of control, loss of the cold wall of ice that shielded me from dangerous emotions. Once more I cast a look up at the window sheltering the new female in our midst, and I made a vow right then and there, that no matter the cost, I *would* find her secrets before she could destroy us all.

21

HOPE

OVER THE NEXT FEW DAYS MY NERVES WERE SHOT. I KEPT waiting for Ash to barge into my room, eyes flashing with fury and demanding to know why I'd lied to Lucien about changing my bandage and taking care of my wound. I imagined his disbelieving face when I'd be forced to show them my thin scar—the only reminder of my injury—and all four men's tight, angry features as they showed me the door.

But nothing happened.

And while I tiptoed around, terrified my deception would be found out, I discovered they had a routine of sorts. And a bond that went as deep as any flesh and blood family I'd ever known.

Not that I'd known many.

Every day, all four men gathered for both breakfast and dinner. I had a feeling conversation would have flowed had I not been there, but as it were, Ruarc scowled a lot, Lucien was icily polite, and Ash watched everything with an inscrutable expression. Only Jason seemed to be himself, poking and prodding at his brothers, a huge grin cracking his face whenever he provoked a reaction. He even included me, seemingly determined to make me have fun.

And I probably would have, if not for the scars of my past and the fear that they would be uncovered.

Breakfast ended the same way each day, with Ruarc and Ash leaving the house only to return several hours later smelling like horses and sweat—a masculine combination I found appealing rather than unpleasant.

Lucien left around the same time, but he must have remained close. He appeared throughout the day, sometimes in response to one of the others calling him, other times to get a bite to eat or grab this or that. The scent of sharp citrus clung to his clothes—when he didn't smell inexplicably like pine and wood. But underneath it all he was just Lucien. And unlike the man, the smell beneath the others was warm, enticing, and dangerous. Like spring and summer and man rolled into one.

I found myself drawn to that smell, occasionally inhaling deeply when he was near. Once he'd caught me, and my cheeks had grown so hot I had rushed from the room to find the closest mirror, convinced my face was on fire.

Unlike the others, Jason didn't seem to have anything that needed to be done until later in the day. He stayed in the house with me, and only left after lunch when Ash returned to do whatever work he did in his office.

The first day after the incident that I—in my head— guiltily referred to as 'the great deception,' I was surprised to find Jason waiting for me with a pair of sunglasses in one hand, a box of strawberries in the other.

"We're going outside," he said with his usual, charming smile. His short hair was delightfully tousled and still wet from his shower, his blue shirt clung to his frame, and his jeans rode low on his narrow hips.

He looked good.

And I felt like a gray mouse standing next to a beautiful wolf.

"You'll need these, love." Ignoring my hesitation, he tilted my face back and slid the sunglasses over my eyes. "It's bright outside today." His hand lingered on my face, cupped my cheek while he stared down at me with an expression that was almost . . . tender?

My breath caught, my stomach tensed, and an explosion of butterflies burst to life inside me.

I didn't know what I was waiting for, why I wanted to run and shout and collapse to the floor all at the same time. Before I could figure it out, Jason drew back, held out his elbow with a lopsided smile, and winked. "You coming?"

The incident from the day before had apparently been erased from his memory. Or maybe it hadn't been a big deal to him? I'd expected stilted conversation and awkward silences. Maybe even accusing eyes to go with what he'd said after the weird moment we'd shared. But this . . .

This was better.

Much better.

I took his proffered elbow and allowed him to lead the way.

We spent an hour on the porch swing, eating strawberries and enjoying the sun. After so many years in a cell, just being outside was a luxury. Jason didn't miss the way I stretched my neck and closed my eyes, enjoying the beam of light caressing my face. And neither did he miss the way my skin flushed.

Two or three minutes after we went outside, he rushed inside for a cap—a bright yellow one that I suspected matched his shirt from that first day—and plopped it down on my head despite my protests that I'd never once burned.

"And how many days have you spent in the sun lately?"

I halted my protest and let him steer the rest of our conversation. It didn't take me long to notice that while he rarely stopped talking—a relief since my talking skills were rusty after mainly chattering out loud to myself for the last eighteen years—he didn't reveal much about himself or his past. He spoke mostly of this place and told a few stories about his brothers that revealed nothing about any of them except that they clearly loved each other like family.

Longing swept over me with brutal force.

Family. A place to belong. Love.

Things I'd had once upon a time, before I'd destroyed everything. Things I no longer deserved, would never deserve again. But knowing this did nothing to stop the yearning that built with every day I remained with this strange but tight-knit family.

A yearning I could ill afford to harbor.

I was still struggling with my feelings by the time Jason brought me back inside and left for work. Maybe that was why Ash's offer to show me their library a few minutes later left me reeling with excitement.

He led me past the kitchen, ignoring the door to his office on the left, and carried on to the end of the hall.

"You're welcome here any time," Ash said. He tried to usher me past him, but I was frozen in the doorway.

Their library was . . . heaven.

Big, even bigger than their living room, and so light and airy it was better suited to a ballroom than a library. Three of the four walls were lined with shelves carrying more books than I'd ever seen. A desk sat along the back wall, three big windows behind it spilling in light. The ceiling was high, higher than the other rooms, and I wondered if this was two floors with no rooms above. Several comfy looking chairs were scattered all around the room, and the floor-space in the middle had been claimed by two rows of standing shelves —also holding books.

Everywhere I looked: books. For a girl who'd clung to sanity with the few—very few—books she'd been allowed access to . . .

I swallowed. Hard.

"Choose any book." Ash nodded at the desk. "And when

you are finished, if you cannot remember where it goes, place it on the desk and one of us will put it back."

I turned to face him, a big, hard rock lodged in my throat. "Thank you."

His gaze swept over my face, moved to look at the room behind me, and then went back to me. "I will be in my office. Come find me if you need anything."

I stared after him until he disappeared behind the door to his office. Then I stared some more. Did he know the gift he'd given me?

So many books.

I stepped inside and slowly turned in a full circle, awed. Where should I start?

Even if I spent the next ten years reading, I wouldn't be able to get through all of these books. And I knew so little. This was the perfect opportunity to learn, a chance to gain an understanding of a world I'd barely had time to live in before I was ripped away by the Hunters.

The Hunters . . .

A cold shiver traveled up my spine and bit at my neck with teeth made of ice. If I was serious about moving on, if I was going to rid the world of their evil once and for all, I had to start somewhere. Learning about the thing they feared— the thing I was no closer to discovering now than I'd been five days ago—would be my first step.

Could that type of information be found here, in the library of four men who had about as much in common with the Hunters as this house had with my old cell?

No. I doubted the existence of such books in the first place. But then what should I be looking for? This was too good an opportunity to waste.

I turned in a circle, gaze sweeping over the endless choices. Countless titles. Novels across tons of different genres. A couple with the word 'biography' stamped across the spine. Non-fiction designed to teach and enlighten.

I need to learn . . .

I walked over to the shelf with titles on woodworking and the keeping of animals, dragging my hand over the worn spines. These books had been *read*. More than once. They weren't for show, they hadn't been bought and left forgotten. No, someone had studied them, closely observed—

I stopped, gaze caught on a big tome on the right.

An atlas.

I ran over and pulled it out, careful not to jostle its neighbors. To end the Hunters' evil reign I'd need help. Resources. And though I hadn't decided if I could bring that kind of trouble to my uncle—I'd never met him and he'd never cared enough to come check on us after my father died so why would he help me now?—it couldn't hurt to be prepared. If I was going to find him I'd need to know where I was going. The name of a place was not the same as studying its location, seeing a map and learning its surroundings.

I moved to a comfortable looking chair, sat down with the atlas open on my lap, and located Canada.

I spent the rest of the day in the library, devouring everything I could find about my uncle's country and searching for any mention of his family, the Sânriglas. They weren't mentioned, and while that wasn't unexpected, it left me with a strange mix of despair and relief.

The relief came as a surprise, a surprise I didn't understand. But before I could dwell on it, movement outside distracted me.

It was the third time I'd spotted Ruarc from my seat in the library. The first time, he'd watched me through the window, an unreadable expression on his hard face, before disappearing into the woods. The second time, I'd felt a prickle of awareness along my neck, but when I'd turned Ruarc had been walking toward the forest only to disappear among the trees with startling ease. And now he was striding along the edge of the forest, covered in bits of leaves and patches of dirt. He glanced my way, a scowl taking over his features when our eyes met.

He moved like a predator. Even from this distance, I could see the flex of muscle beneath his tight, black clothes, the determined jut of his jaw. Power rolled off him in waves, and it wouldn't have surprised me to see birds taking to the sky and critters jumping out of his way.

It wasn't that he looked angry, I realized with a jolt, but determined. Stubborn. Obsessive, even. Like whatever task he'd taken on held his full attention, and nothing could stop him from finishing what he'd started.

A shudder of something that wasn't quite fear captured my body. My eyes remained glued to the powerful male as he stalked out of sight. And when he was gone, it took me several long minutes before I could concentrate on the book I'd been reading.

The next day, straight after breakfast, I went back and scoured the library. I made a careful note of each title containing knowledge that I felt could be of use; navigation, hiking, crime novels that might help me learn how to avoid being caught, and even a book about business—maybe it would help me understand the Hunters better? Money, I'd come to understand, motivated people in ways I'd yet to wrap my mind around.

Unfortunately, I'd found no books that looked like they would mention the Hunters. None that would be of use to my other *problem* either. While I'd told myself the likelihood of finding anything about the evil inside me was less than zero, I couldn't help but feel somewhat disappointed to be proven right. A small part of me had hoped to find a book titled *'The monster inside and how to destroy it,'* or something equally damning to the thing that shared my body. But no such luck.

Restless, frustrated with my lack of progress, I walked along the shelves. My right hand glided over the spines of each book I passed, my lips mouthing the titles. There were so many. Most of them interesting, a few I desperately wanted to read, even fewer I thought I *should* read. I plucked a book off the shelf, turned it to read the blurb when my gaze caught on the book my free hand rest on.

'The Descendants of the Fae.'

I did a double take, but the title never changed. *The Fae? As in—*

A sudden tension between my shoulder blades, a weight to the air that hadn't been there before. I spun around.

Ash was leaning against the door frame, eyes flicking over the volume I'd touched but not pulled out. "Do you need help finding anything?"

"No, I . . . I'm okay." I quickly placed the first book back where it had been and stepped away from the shelf.

"Books might be one of the greatest treasures created by sentient life," he said with a curious tilt of his head. "Each one carries its own secrets, answers to questions you might not realize you have been seeking. Each word, painstakingly chosen. Each chapter meticulously penned. Or typed, as it may be." He straightened, and the effect was immediate. Every molecule of air around him sizzled with energy, with something I could sense but not understand. "Did you find what you are looking for?"

H-how did he know? I could have been reading for pleasure—I wanted to, I wanted to more than I wanted to take on the impossible task I'd set before me—and nothing else. "I . . ." No words would follow.

Gaze locked on my face, Ash merely nodded. "Would you like to watch a movie?"

I startled, as much from the sudden change of subject as what he'd said. "With . . . with you?"

One corner of his mouth tipped up and my cheeks burned. "That is the idea."

"I-yes."

"Good." He kicked off from the frame and held the door open for me.

I hurried out, remembering last second to not move too smoothly, in case he wondered where my limp had gone. "Are the others coming too?"

Though I'd spent five days here already, I still didn't know what Ruarc did with his time once he and Ash were finished in the stables—though finished was probably the wrong word seeing as they went back out before bed every night, probably to feed the animals. He *seemed* to do what could only be described as patrolling. I occasionally saw him roaming the gardens, disappearing into the woods only to reappear a few hours later, often bringing back half the forest in his hair and on his clothes. He'd never told me exactly what he did, and I'd never asked.

Questions invited questions, another reason why I'd refrained from asking all the ones burning on my tongue.

"Only you and I." Ash led me into the living room and bade me take a seat. "I will be right back."

While I waited for him to return, it hit me that I was never alone in the house. One of them always stayed behind if the others left. I wondered if it was because of me. Were they keeping an eye on me or were they protecting me?

Does it matter?

No. Not when, for the first time in so long I wanted to cry, I felt safe.

I don't want to leave.

The thought left me cold. What . . . what about the Hunters? They would never stop hunting me. They would hurt any soul who gave me shelter. And they would keep ruining lives, shattering their victims' sense of self until all that remained were broken husks and crushed dreams.

Somehow, someway, I had to stop them. Even if I could quell my conscience and disregard their victims, I had no hope of a real life as long as the Hunters existed. But . . .

What could a single person do faced with such evil?

Nothing.

I harbored a monster, a darkness that might be able to do *some* damage, but regardless of the cost, I would never allow it to be unleashed. Not the way it had been when—

A ragged hole opened in my chest, its edges made of acid that ate through my insides until the breath I didn't realize I'd been holding was forced from my lungs in a powerful gush that sounded suspiciously like a sob.

My eyes shot to the door, but either Ash hadn't heard me over the strange popping sound from the kitchen—it sounded like tiny, muted explosions, the scent winding through the house was a mix of butter and salt—or he'd decided to give me some privacy.

I shook my head and pushed thoughts of the past back into the tiny box in the back of my mind. The box I never allowed myself to open.

My focus belonged to the here and now, the future, not the past. I kept telling myself I'd leave when I grew stronger, when I had the means to reach my uncle without dying on the way there. But even the possibility of finding the last member of my family had lost some of its shine.

I'm happy here.

The thought snuck past my defenses, filling me with such dread I thought I might pass out.

Happy? I can't be happy.

Well, maybe contented was a better word?

Doesn't matter. This is temporary.

Nothing had changed. The Hunters were still out there, still hunting me. And I was . . . lost.

"Here," Ash said—I hadn't been aware of his return, too lost in my own miserable dilemma—and placed a huge bowl of popcorn in my lap. He sat down, close enough that I was very aware of his presence, of his enticing scent, the steel below the smoothness of his skin.

Next to him, I felt small. Vulnerable. Protected. And a part of me had already begun to mourn those feelings, to miss them. Because in a small corner of my soul lived a piece of me, a piece uncorrupted by fear and indecision, a piece not yet twisted by the Hunters' torment, a piece that knew what the rest of me was not yet ready to admit.

No matter what, I could not stay.

22

ASH

"Where are the others?" Lucien crossed the room, stopped by the edge of my desk, and glanced down at the form I was filling out. One brow arched as he pointed to a number at the bottom. "That seems excessive, does it not?"

The amount of feed I was ordering might have been considered excessive, but I had another three horses arriving in a few months for rehabilitation, and I liked Ray, the owner of the little feed shop in town. "Ruarc is making sure no Strays cross into our territory, and Jason took Hope outside." I ignored the annoyed sound he made and signed my name. "Their shop is struggling. If I order more feed than we can use, we can always donate it to the Jensen farm."

Lucien shook his head. "Always the bleeding heart."

I made a non-committal sound and changed the subject. "Have you heard anything more about Rederick?"

"Unfortunately, yes." He turned one of the chairs and took a seat. "It seems possible he has gathered support from a Council member. I do not know who, and it may be speculation, but if he has . . ."

"The battle will be harder than we thought."

"Are you certain it is one worth fighting?"

I swallowed the flare of heat urging a vehement response. The pen I had been holding clattered against the desk. "You think we should leave them to their fate and do nothing? If Rederick gets his way in this, it is only a matter of time before the old laws are brought back. Will you sit by and watch as humans become prey?"

"Humans . . ." He scoffed. "What have they ever done for us?"

"There are innocents among them."

"More so than there are sinners?"

I met the cool, green gaze of my brother. For as long as I had known him, Lucien had chosen to encase his inner self in a cage made of ice. But despite the harsh lessons that scarred him, he was far from heartless. "And the females," I asked. "The children?"

He stiffened. "Their males will protect them."

"Will they?"

A sound that was almost a growl, the closest to anger he permitted these days. "They should."

"You and I both know who suffers when males no longer value honor."

Had I not known him so well, I would have missed the way his mouth tensed at my words, the single moment he allowed himself to feel before the bars came crashing back down.

These flashes of emotions had been happening more often recently, and it gave me hope that one day Lucien would choose to step out of the prison he had made for himself.

He gave a curt nod. Not an easy agreement, but agreement nonetheless.

We sat in silence for a few short moments. I could not stop thinking about the human among us, and from the sudden curl to his lip, I suspected Lucien was doing the same.

It was . . . nice having a female around. Courteous and kind, albeit a bit timid—though that was to be expected—she had a soothing presence.

It had surprised me how much I had enjoyed watching movies with her. Her soft-spoken questions, the small gasps of surprise she could not quite stifle—too involved in what was happening on the screen—and the way her lower lip disappeared between her teeth when the stakes were high.

But most of all, I enjoyed the heat from her small body as she edged closer, forgetting her innate nervousness, the fear her abusers had taught her, and seeking comfort from my nearness. Trusting me, if only a little.

How long had it been since I had allowed myself the company of a female? Decades, at the very least. My attempts at casual relationships had all ended the same—with hurt and anger and accusations. The thought of endless sexual partners and one-night stands had never appealed—I required, at the very least, to like the person I was with, to be more than strangers—but I could not allow myself anything more than casual affection.

The risks were too great.

Besides, solitude suited me and I was never truly alone. I had my brothers.

"Gideon's pack will take our side," Lucien said suddenly. "His enforcer told me they're looking at—"

A noise that did not belong.

Tires.

We rose simultaneously.

Not Jason. Not Ruarc. Not one of ours.

My fingers curled. Claws pressed against flesh, eager to tear out. Eager to draw blood.

Lucien tilted his head, closed his eyes. "I don't know it."

The side of my beast that was only cold, only violent, roared in my head.

Intruders. Strangers. In my territory!

The urge to tear through the closest wall and get outside pounded at my skull. A low growl slipped past my still-human teeth.

Lucien met my gaze, and in his eyes I saw the same fury, the same inexplicable dread that shifted the floor beneath my feet. This felt different than any other time. This was different.

Hope.

The sound that had demanded our attention was still faint, but close enough that I itched to shed my skin.

"Where, exactly, did Jason take the human?" Lucien asked, proving that, despite his hostility toward her, the thought of an intruder coming across Hope was not one he was willing to entertain.

I stilled. "Out back."

"You're sure?"

"No."

The sound grew louder, a smooth hum of a motor joining the turn of four wheels, and suddenly I was moving. Running. Lucien at my heels.

The front door slammed behind us, and I barely noticed the clear sky and brilliant sun. I threw up a hand to shield my eyes, gaze sweeping across our property. The dense forest at the end of our driveaway blocked the small, winding road from view.

So I waited.

A few minutes later, a black Sedan rolled into view.

The fury swelling in my chest gave my beast the opportunity to encroach, and soon its coldly calculating presence swept through me at an alarming speed.

Lucien stepped closer. We stood shoulder to shoulder, a thrumming energy of violence alive in us both.

Intruders. Our land. Destroy, a sibilant voice whispered through my mind.

The car stopped. A man emerged. With the wind at our

backs, it took me precious seconds to catch his scent; rich, smoky, dark. A scent that reminded my beast of flesh tearing and our mouths filling with blood. And when I recognized what it meant, an unyielding need to defend rolled beneath my skin along with the beast I kept so tightly leashed it vibrated against its restraints.

You are the master of your body. I drew a deep breath in through my mouth, blocking the infuriating scent.

"And who might you be?" Lucien asked. Only a fool would fail to recognize the deadly threat hiding in that seemingly civil greeting.

The man stopped. Tall, slender, dark-haired. I did not know who he was, and it did not matter. All my energy was spent trying not to launch myself at the stranger who dared step foot onto my land without permission.

"I'm Kieran," he said. His voice, like most of his kind, was deep and smooth. Hypnotic, I had been told, to humans. He did not move from his spot, choosing instead to stand still and keep his hands loose at his sides. "I would have gone through formal channels, but I don't have the time. Not now." He smiled, but it was a bitter thing. Tainted, somehow.

"You know whose territory you have invaded?" Lucien asked.

Kieran's gaze flicked to me. "I do."

I infused my voice with a calm I did not feel, "Then your need must be great."

His shoulders lowered half an inch. "It is."

"Why have you come?"

"I've come for a word with your spymaster." Kieran turned to Lucien. "I need your help."

If Kieran thought it strange that we invited him into our home, he did not show it. He took a seat in the chair Lucien indicated—with Hope out of the house, my office was the only place I would allow a stranger to step foot in—and waited.

"What can we do for you?" Rather than keep the desk between us, I had chosen to sit opposite our visitor in one of the office's extra chairs. Lucien stood a little behind me to the right. He'd donned his cold, unreadable mask, and was watching our guest with eyes that missed nothing.

"My brother . . ." A pained grimace swept over Kieran's face. "His Blood—his mate—has been taken."

I stiffened. "When?"

"Three days ago."

Three days? Sympathy welled as I imagined myself in his brother's shoes. Had it been me . . .

"Why bring this to us?" Lucien asked.

"She's one of yours. Half," he corrected, a slight quiver to that one word that could have been either anger or grief. "And another has claimed her."

"Did she go willingly?"

"No." There was no mistaking the fury claiming his voice. Smoke as dark as the blackest night swirled in his eyes, and his features grew sharper as his true face emerged. "She was stolen."

"Who?" A quiet whisper. Lucien strode forward, his hand clenching around the top of my chair. "Who took her?"

"Wellington. We searched every inch of his pack's territory, but there are no signs of either of them. His alpha claims no knowledge, but he is hiding something."

"What makes you so sure?"

Kieran took a moment to reply, and when he did, fangs flashed with each word. "He claimed she was a valued member of the pack, and as such would let us know if she came back. They said . . ." Here he stopped, hissed out a breath. "They said they wouldn't dream of stealing her choice of whom to take as a mate."

"A lie?" I asked, already knowing what was coming. Being a half-breed came with its own set of challenges. Ones that were not deserved, and certainly not fair.

He inclined his head. "Help us find them and my nest will . . . owe you." His reluctance was to be expected; their kind never reneged on a promise. "You have my word."

Lucien looked at me, and that look said it all. He knew. He always knew. "Wellington travels between two packs," he began, and by the time he was done speaking he had proven his reputation as spymaster was well deserved, even if it was a title he did not particularly care for.

Many chose to refine a talent despite disdain for the art.

"Thank you." A heavy exhale, then a slow breath. "My brother and I are in your de—" Kieran stilled. He drew in another deep breath, opened his mouth, and . . . snapped it shut again. Slowly, too slowly, he looked at the door. "You have someone else living with you?"

All my muscles tensed. I concentrated on keeping my face neutral, but before I could reply I heard Lucien's hissed response, "No."

Kieran fixed his gaze on Lucien, eyes a swirling mass of smoke. "There's another scent here. Female."

"One of Jason's conquests," Lucien said, ice dripping from each syllable.

"She is staying with you?"

"You have gotten what you came for." I found my feet and inclined my head at the door.

Kieran rose too, his movements that of a wary predator aware he was moments away from becoming prey. "I would like to meet her."

"No."

Kieran stilled. "Are you protecting her or yourselves, I wonder."

"Neither." Lucien strode across the room and opened the

door. He stared at the other male with eyes that were thin slits of glowing green. "It's time you left."

Kieran did not budge.

Did he think we would allow him near the human we harbored? A stranger, a male who could rip out her throat faster than she could cry warning?

Cold anger scraped along my mind. Keeping my voice low and my tone even required all the control I had so painstakingly worked to gain after my last Ascension. "Leave."

To Kieran's credit, he did not flinch at the thunder in my voice, nor the beast using my eyes to watch him. A wary look crossed his face, but he held his ground. "Are you holding her against her will?"

My vision narrowed until all I could see was Kieran. "We are not." He made the mistake of looking directly at me, and I captured his gaze. "Leave."

He visibly struggled against the command, chin jerking as he tried to break the contact.

I would not allow it.

"See him out, Lucien. And follow him until he is off our land."

HOPE

I groaned and shook my head at Jason's offering. *Another* piece of chocolate. If I hadn't known better I would have thought he was trying to spoil me. "I'm stuffed."

I'd stayed with the guys for six days and seven nights— had it only been a week since I'd been tied down to a cold table, my skin split, my insides on display while Gregory rooted around inside me? Had it only been a week since terror had kept my limbs frozen, since despair ate at my soul until I wished my eyes would no longer open each morning?—it seemed both an eternity and a blink of an eye.

I shuddered, but before the memory of that awful place left me spiraling, I reminded myself of last night's decision; to give myself some time. Time where I tried not to agonize over my future. Time where the Hunters didn't rule my every thought. Time where I wasn't choking on the choices before me; to stay or to go, to fight or to flee, to sacrifice everything or live with crushing guilt.

Postponing the decision would not make it easier, but after I'd finished the movie with Ash last night, when I lay in bed unable to sleep for the suffocating pressure in my chest, I'd realized I was in no condition to fight the Hunters. At least not yet. And I still knew too little. I needed time—I'd only been free a week, surely I could take a little more time? —not to mention I'd yet to begin my work with the guys and earn the money I'd need to . . . well, to do anything.

Jason wiggled his eyebrows, pulling my attention back to the present, and popped the offending piece between his lips. "More for me."

He seemed right at home out here, sitting on a blanket on the grass, the remnants of our meal between us while he slowly chewed and watched me. The sun caressed his face, turned his hair to a wonderful golden brown. Amber eyes glowed with humor and warmth, and he always kept a devastating grin ready to be unleashed.

The comparison I'd struck when I first saw him came rushing back, and now more than ever I knew I'd been right.

Jason was like the sun—warm and bright and cheery.

"What are you thinking about love?"

Heat raced up my neck. I'd been caught staring. Again. "N-nothing."

"Doesn't look like nothing." A quick flash of a smile that made heat spread to my cheeks. "Tell me."

"Shouldn't we head back?"

"Oh, no you don't!" He grabbed my chin, gaze sweeping over my face before locking on mine. The grin that had been playing about his lips slowly slipped away. His regard grew heavy, almost a pressure over my skin.

My breath caught.

"Hope . . ." A rueful smile curved his lips. "You're not what I expected."

"W-what did you expect?" I asked, almost fearing the answer.

But rather than reply, a tender look entered his eyes, his thumb brushing across my cheekbone before he let his hand drop to his side. "We should head back."

Baffled, and warm in a way that could not be attributed to the sun, I could only nod and watch as he packed up our little picnic.

The wicker basket looked all wrong when held in Jason's big hands. The dusting of fine, golden hair down his arms looked utterly masculine, the veins in his forearms strangely attractive. Muscles moved and flexed beneath tanned skin, and the small, girly basket was transferred to Jason's left hand. With his right, he cupped my elbow and led me around the big rock we'd leaned against, and set a languid pace back toward the house.

"Have you . . . have you been on many picnics?" I asked when the silence became too much. My heart was still galloping from the unexpected touch earlier, and I needed a distraction.

"No," he said with some surprise, "this was my first."

Something warm bloomed in my chest.

"What about you, love? Have you been on a picnic before?"

"Once. Before I . . ." My voice trailed off and whatever peace I'd found during our meal vanished like it had never been. A shiver raced up my spine.

Jason stopped, and suddenly his arm was around my

shoulder, pulling me close. "You don't have to tell me," he said, tipping my face up to meet his gaze. "Everyone has secrets, and everyone has things they'd rather not talk about. Personally, I much prefer to remember the good things in life."

"And the bad?" I whispered.

"The bad can go to hell."

I averted my gaze before I could give into the pressure behind my eyes or blurt out the questions I was dying to ask. What secrets hid in Jason's past? And were they the reason for the far-away look he sometimes wore? The look I'd only caught glimpses of during my time here.

The desire to know him, to know them all, had steadily been growing. But I couldn't give in. Not before I was ready to share my own story, and I knew that was one thing I could never do.

The silence dragged on, each second stretched unbearably thin. But when I glanced back up at Jason he wasn't frowning down at me or expecting a reply. No, he was simply waiting, face turned toward the sun, eyes closed, enjoying the nice day.

In that moment, it was all I could do not to hug him.

"Home?" he asked in a lazy voice, still bathing his face in the sun's warm rays. Still not looking at me. Not pressuring.

Before I could reply, a prickle at the back of my neck made me turn. I frowned at the forest some fifty feet away. Had something moved? I scanned the treeline, confused at the unease slithering up my back when all I saw was . . . nothing. Nothing prowled beneath the cover of the canopy. Nothing moved beyond the leaves swaying in the gentle breeze. The smell of spring teased my senses, of grass and flowers and . . . smoke?

I shook my head.

Dust had been kicked up somewhere, carried by the wind, probably, but I couldn't see any smoke. Just the dust. Dust that hovered above the ground as it flew through the air. Dust that looked a little like smoke, maybe?

"Jason . . . Jason, look." I pointed the dark mass speeding toward us. Now that it was closer, I saw it wasn't dust and it didn't leave a trail that grew fainter with every foot it traveled. Rather, it looked like a cloud of smoke, moving as though it had a mind of its own.

Jason followed the line of my finger. His eyes widened, and threw himself in front of me while spitting a curse. The force of his hand against my chest had me stumble back several steps. By the time I regained my balance and looked back, a strange man had come out of nowhere and was leaping at Jason.

"*Run!*" Jason yelled an instant before the man hit him in the chest, and down they both went.

"Jason!" Heart pounding, I launched myself at the man who'd hit him. They were both on the ground, rolling in near silence, fists flying through the air with a speed I could barely comprehend. Fear tightened my throat, squeezed my ribs, but I grabbed hold of the man's arm and yanked as hard as I could.

It was enough for them to get to their feet, apart. The stranger half turned, looked at me like *I* was crazy, and shook me off.

Then he attacked in a flurry of arms and something that flashed white. A weapon of some kind? And somehow Jason blocked and countered each hit like he'd been born to fight.

The fear fled, a distant, strangled cry in the back of my mind. Not important. Not when Jason was in danger. Not when I'd brought danger into his life. Though I didn't recognize the stranger, there was no doubt in my mind he was a Hunter sent to bring me back, and having recognized Jason as the greater threat would try to eliminate him before grabbing me.

I looked around for a weapon. Anything I could use to hurt the man trying to hurt Jason.

Grass. More grass. A stick. *Too small.* But then . . . *a rock?* It was big enough to fill my palm. I tested its weight. With a good hit in it could probably do some damage.

While they traded punches, big bodies reeling from the force of each impact, I snuck up behind them. I lifted my rock. Swung. And hit—

Air?

They'd somehow moved several feet in the second it had taken me to raise my rock.

"Leave him alone," I cried, heart nearly stopping when Jason ducked under the strangers arm and threw his hand out too fast for me to see.

When the Hunter stumbled back, his cheek was split open in four long gashes. I blinked, but still saw no weapon.

A terrifying rumble rose through the air, then the two men crashed again. Jason must have spotted me, for he roared and threw the Hunter over his back, spun around and snarled at me. "Fucking *run!*"

While his attention was at me, the other man managed to somehow leap to his feet from a prone position on the ground, and was running at Jason.

"Look out!" I screamed, and started running too. The hand holding my rock waved wildly as I prepared to attack.

Jason's jaw dropped open, and when he tried to turn I realized my mistake. I'd distracted him.

The Hunter's fist connected with the back of Jason's head.

A sickening thud sounded, and Jason crumbled to the ground.

"No!" I rushed to his side, threw myself over his body and used my own as a shield. "Don't hurt him, don't hurt him!" Sobs tore from my throat. "I won't run again, just don't hurt him." I'd go back. I'd go back right now if only he wouldn't hurt Jason or the others.

Oh my god, the others! If they came out now, the Hunter would probably kill them.

My grip on the rock tightened. I'd bash the Hunter's head in before I'd let him hurt the guys who'd saved me!

I waited for him to draw one of their horrible weapons, for metal to pierce my body and shred my flesh. Maybe it wouldn't go through me. Maybe Jason would be okay.

"Please," I cried, "please."

A hand on my upper arm, the touch gentle. I swung my rock at his head, but he ducked and plucked it out of my fist with startling ease.

I blinked up at the Hunter, wondering how someone so evil could look at me with such concern, with such warm, compassionate eyes.

Then I was in the air, my stomach meeting the hard edge of a shoulder, and the scenery flew by with such speed I thought I was going to be sick.

I must have passed out. When I next opened my eyes we were deep in the woods, and the man had come to a stop. He lifted me and placed me gently on my feet. He even supported me when I swayed.

"Lily," he breathed. The name set my brain to throbbing. One hand rose to brush my hair away from my face.

I batted it away. "S-stay back."

"It's me." His voice was low. Smooth. Much too captivating. "Kieran."

"I . . . I don't know you."

Kieran stepped closer, and I instinctively flinched. The silence that followed had me fold my arms around my stomach and shiver. It was threatening. Cold. Filled with as much rage as a silence could be. "What," he bit out, "have they done to you?"

My head snapped back and I looked at him, really looked at him. He looked . . . furious, and his eyes. Something was wrong with his eyes. "W-who?"

His nostrils flared, his eyes closed. He leaned closer, breathing in. Then all color drained from his already pale face. When he looked back down at me, it was like seeing a man whose hope had been suddenly and irrevocably killed. "Lily?"

That name . . . it itched at my mind like a slippery needle. I should have been able to catch it before it burrowed, but each time I reached for it, I pricked myself at the sharp point and had to retreat before the discomfort in my mind bloomed into pain. "I'm . . . I'm Hope."

The man recoiled.

Not a Hunter, then?

My knees gave out and I dropped to the ground.

Please, please, please.

Cold, slightly damp leaves met the seat of my pants. "Are you . . . are you here to take me to the compound?"

I couldn't afford to believe otherwise. Not until I knew for sure. To believe I had escaped yet again only to be forced back there . . . I stared down at my hands while I waited for the answer that would seal my fate.

"The compound?"

The confusion in his voice was too real to be faked.

A horrible sound born in the pit of my stomach forced its way up my throat. I wanted to weep with relief, to rail against this stranger for making me taste the despair that had once haunted my every waking moment. But instead, my mind whirled and thoughts of Jason moved to the forefront. "Why did you attack Jason? Will he be okay? Oh, god, tell me he'll be okay!"

"I . . . I thought you were her."

"W-who?" I glanced up, took in the dark eyes, the inky-black hair, and a face that I might have found attractive if not for what he'd done. And suddenly an explosion of rage swelled from the depths of my soul. "You hurt him because of a *mistake*!"

"I thought you were she," he muttered. "I—Of course I noticed you were much too young but I thought perhaps you had been turned. That *she* had been turned." It was his turn to look away. "You are so . . . so much like her."

A mistake. It was all a mistake.

I staggered to my feet, keeping a wary eye on the stranger. There was something wrong with him. What he was saying made no sense. "Okay. I'll . . . I'll just go then."

He waved a hand. "Please. And my sincerest apologies to both you and your males."

I edged backward, keeping the unbalanced man in my sights for as long as possible. When he remained still—face averted, a slump to his shoulders that spoke of emotions I'd rather not attribute to my kidnapper and Jason's attacker—I turned and ran.

The guys were *not* happy.

I counted my lucky stars they'd found me on the forest floor after a root snared my foot, and not sprinting and weaving through the trees like I'd never been injured. Not that any of them had reacted well at seeing me sprawled on the ground.

"You sure you're okay, love?" Jason asked me for the fifth time since we'd returned to the house, earning a sour look from Ruarc. The bigger male seemed to blame Jason for my short stint as a kidnap victim.

"I really am fine. Though my pants need a wash."

A vein throbbed near Ruarc's temple. He grabbed my elbow and led me past the others, depositing me on the oversized couch in the living room.

Earlier, after they'd assured themselves I wasn't hurt, they'd brought me to the kitchen, made me drink a swallow of some disgusting, brown-ish liquid that had burned on the way down and filled my stomach with an almost pleasing heat, and asked me question after question about what had happened. The temperature had seemed to drop several degrees when Jason, in a much too quiet voice, had explained how I hadn't run, but had instead thrown myself at Kieran in an attempt to help. And now that they were done interrogating me, it seemed Ruarc had something to say about that choice.

I crossed my arms over my chest and looked down at my hands. I couldn't bring myself to meet Ruarc's furious gaze. Standing with his feet a good distance apart, arms crossed over a wide chest—a chest that heaved with the force of his breaths—he reminded me of a warrior preparing to battle.

Or a bull about to charge.

If he grew horns and tossed his head, he wouldn't need to change anything else. He already had the wide shoulders, the powerful build, the rage I imagined flowed through the big animals when they attacked to defend their herd. Yes, he was definitely bull-like, except he was too tall to be stocky, and his neck wasn't *that* thick. Muscled, but tall. Wide and strong, but also somehow lean. Or, not lean but . . .

Proportionate.

A chilling growl shattered the thoughts I was hiding behind and brought my attention back to the man towering above me. "Should've run."

I opened my mouth to protest, but he cut me off with a *look*. The kind that seemed so very *male* and so very confident he was right, that I ended up gaping up at him like an idiot.

"Happens again, you run. Got it?"

"But Jason was—"

"Don't care," he growled. "You should've run."

A dip in the couch and then the scent of horses and hay. Ash grabbed my hand and gave it a light squeeze. "We can take care of ourselves, *banajaanh*."

It wasn't the same as saying *I* couldn't take care of *my*self, but it sure felt that way. I peeked at him, once again unable to reconcile this Ash—calm, steady, in control—with the Ash I'd caught a glimpse of earlier. When they'd first found me there'd been something off about him. Something in the stiffness around his mouth. The dangerous tilt of his head. The unnatural stillness he'd exhibited as Jason and Ruarc rushed to my side while Lucien took off in the direction I'd fled from.

He'd brought to mind a lethal predator at the verge of losing control.

"I couldn't leave him there." I directed my explanation at Ash rather than the raging energy that was Ruarc. "Not while that lunatic was trying to hurt him!"

"We appreciate your bravery," Ash said, ignoring both the angry sound coming from Ruarc and the exasperated sigh from Jason. "But you are more of a hindrance than a help in a situation like that. Not because you are weak," he added gently when I hung my head. "But because you are not trained to fight. We are."

He made no mention of my size or the fact that I was severely lacking in muscle. If not for my adrenaline, I'd probably have collapsed after my first minute of sprinting through the dense woods.

I need to get stronger.

"And because I told you to run, dammit," Jason added.

"Should've made her run," Ruarc grumbled.

"How was I supposed to have done that? Ask the v—ask Kieran to stop the fight and wait while I escort Hope back to the house?"

Ruarc growled.

"Do you guys . . . do you know him?" I realized then that while they'd listened to my story—seeming as confused as I was with Kieran's actions—they hadn't shown surprise when I told them who had taken me.

"No," Ruarc snarled, but the look he shot Ash was filled with recrimination.

"I do not know him, Ruarc," Ash said. "We met him for the first time today."

"Was he . . . was he here for me?"

Lucien's mouth tightened in the way it always did when I'd said something that displeased him. "Not everything is about you."

"He called me Lily." Saying it out loud had a weird sensation snake through my head.

"Lily?" Lucien stalked across the room. Grabbed my chin. Tilted my head up. "Anything else you've failed to tell us?"

Ruarc snarled and broke Lucien's hold on me before stepping between us. "Not the point!"

"Then what is?"

He spun around, Lucien forgotten, and scowled down at me. "Should've run!"

"I don't know any Lily," Jason muttered. He took a seat on the other side of me and paid no mind to the furious male looming above all three of us. He looked at Ash. "You?"

"None Kieran would risk so much to help."

Help? It hadn't felt like he'd been trying to help.

"Did he say anything else when he called you Lily?" Ash asked.

I thought back. "Nothing except what I already told you. Although he did seem a bit . . . crazy."

"Crazy how?"

"Well . . ." My eyes shifted to the side. "Something about me being too young to be the one he was looking for. But then why would he take me?"

"Fuck's sake."

Startled, I looked back at Ruarc.

"Pointless," he snapped, then pointed an accusing finger at my chest. "You run when someone attacks you. Hear me? You run!"

"But he didn't attack me. He attacked Jason."

A strangled sound from Jason. Dark thunderclouds rolled across Ruarc's expression. He looked ready to blow.

"You. Run."

"I . . . sorry?"

Ruarc glared down at me.

"I won't do it again?"

Ruarc glared harder. Was it the question in my voice that had the vein in his temple pulsate? I didn't want to lie to Ruarc, but of course I would do it again. I'd do it again in a heartbeat if it meant saving one of the guys.

They'd saved me first.

"Really, I—Won't you say something?" The silent glaring was making my chest feel tight, like I was letting him down, and that outraged disappointment had become a vice squeezing me tighter and tighter until I either popped or he gave in.

Ruarc kept glaring.

"Please?"

The glare narrowed. His jaw bunched as he opened his mouth, closed it again. Anger churned in the flat press of his lips.

"Ruarc?" My voice quivered.

A beastly sound erupted and silver eyes flashed. Then I got my wish. "Don't you fucking ever do that again!"

A spark of fear lit at all that anger, and I flinched back. But before the spark could grow from a small flame to the blazing terror I knew myself capable of, Ash squeezed my hand.

My whole world narrowed down to rough calluses over warm flesh. To the heat of his thigh pressing against mine. To the gaze burning my cheek, wanting to capture mine, waiting for me to turn my head and take refuge in the peace, the comfort, the protection he offered.

And suddenly it didn't matter that Ruarc snapped and

snarled. It didn't matter that I had been kidnapped by a lunatic, however briefly. Nothing mattered except this. Except them. I was safe. *They* were safe.

I listened with half an ear to Jason half-heartedly scolding me for not running, to Ruarc's scathing lecture, to Ash's low reassurances. I listened to Lucien drawing Ash away and quietly discussing whatever was on their minds, to the low huff Ruarc made as he took Ash's spot next to me and the pat-pat of his reluctant forgiveness as he tapped my knee. And then I listened to Jason teasing Ruarc, to the low rumble of Ruarc's response, to the laughter that response inspired in Jason, and I thought to myself that this, *this* was what it was like to have a family. *This* was what it was like to have a home.

And then I couldn't breathe.

23

HOPE

THE NEXT MORNING I WAS BENT OVER, RUMMAGING THROUGH the cupboard under the sink, when my skin started prickling. The fine hairs at the back of my neck rose with a chilled shiver, the kind that lets you know someone is watching.

"Ow!" In my haste to turn around, my head banged against the sink. I rubbed at the offending spot, blinking back unbidden tears as I tried to make out the blurry figure standing in the doorway. Correction, the blurry figure marching across the white tiles and coming to a crouch in front of me.

"You all right?" The low, deep rumble couldn't belong to anyone other than Ruarc. The wild, clean scent of forest and man swept over me, and when my vision cleared I came face to face with broad shoulders and a wide chest.

"I'm fine," I muttered, embarrassed at how easily I startled.

If the Hunters don't get me, maybe someone will frighten me into stepping off a cliff, I thought dryly.

One of Ruarc's big palms cupped the back of my head, protecting it from further harm as he helped me to my feet. "Good."

Even while standing, the sheer size of him threatened to overwhelm. It wasn't fair that a man could grow so big, look so powerful, and yet still be so gentle. It went against all the laws of men I'd been taught at the hands of the Hunters.

The wide expanse of Ruarc's chest was covered by a tight-fitting, black shirt, showing off his strong shoulders, and the muscular torso tapering down to his waist. The same color sweatpants hugged his powerful legs, allowing me to catch a glimpse of corded muscles beneath the fabric.

"What're you looking for?"

My eyes shot to his, heat creeping up my neck and staining my cheeks a color I could only guess was a deep, startling red.

Oh god, he caught me eyeballing his body like a piece of meat.

I hadn't meant to, really, but I couldn't stop my eyes from roaming when he was standing so close, when his raw, masculine scent overwhelmed my senses, and his very essence—that of a potent, fierce male—seeped through my skin.

"E-excuse me?"

His molten, silver eyes left a scorching trail of heat where they raked across my body, causing a strange warmth to spike in my blood. After a leisurely study of my face, he jerked his chin at the cupboard I'd been riffling through. "Need something?"

"I . . . ah, I was actually looking for some soap."

"Soap?" The casual way he was leaning against the counter was deceiving. Eyes narrowed, lips compressed, he was as far from relaxed as I was.

"For the floors," I admitted, not daring to lie. Ruarc had a strange way of sniffing out untruths, and I knew he hated dishonesty. I had a feeling honesty—and honor in general—was very important to him.

"For the floors . . ." he repeated through clenched teeth.

The way he was glaring at me was unnerving. My hands

twitched and I had no idea why. It wasn't like I had a weapon handy, and even if I had, there was no way I would be using it on him. Disregarding the fact that I didn't want to hurt him, I was fairly certain—no, make that one hundred percent certain—he could break my neck faster than I could so much as make a fist.

He wouldn't hurt you, a small voice in my head insisted, although it sounded rather unsure.

"I . . ." The uncomfortable prickling in my chest warned me I better explain before my breathing became labored, something it always did when fear trespassed. "I-I wanted to learn what soaps should be used where so I can do a good job."

A vein began pulsating in Ruarc's temple. "Sit down." His eyes flashed with warning when I hesitated, his jaw tightening.

I sat.

When his massive body followed, folded in a graceful crouch, my breath caught. How a man of this size could move like that was beyond my understanding.

"Shouldn't be working," he muttered under his breath and reached for my foot.

I yanked it back. "What are you doing?" I squeaked.

"Checking your injury," he growled back, dragging my foot into his lap. The furious glare he shot me when I once again tugged against his grip was more terrifying for the stillness coming over him. "Don't. Move."

My hands grew clammy, and I suddenly felt trapped. If he uncovered the smooth, nearly unblemished skin beneath the bandage I only wore to lend credence to my deception, he'd also uncover a truth I'd protect with my dying breath.

I held on to the chair for dear life, not that it would do me much good if Ruarc decided to use his considerable strength against me. "Please . . . please don't."

He lifted his head,. examined my face. "Why?"

"I . . ." *Yes, Hope, why?* I said the first thing that came to mind, "It hurts."

Shame threatened to drown me when he jerked back, letting go of my foot as though it was hot coals he was holding instead of flesh and blood.

"Shit! Sorry." His gruff voice was hoarse, almost as if he was the one hurting.

"I-it's okay," I stammered. "It's not your fault."

He rose, movements stiff and stilted, the complete opposite of his graceful descent earlier. "How bad?"

"Not *that* bad, but—"

"Lucien!" Ruarc bellowed.

Lucien? Why would he—

"No!" I protested, heart beating so hard each thud felt like a hammer against my chest. "It's not that b—"

"Lucien!" Ruarc stalked over to the door, kicked it open and repeated his bellow.

I jumped to my feet, legs rubber that tried their best to be stiff when all they wanted was to crumble to the floor. "Ruarc, don't." I rushed over to his side, grabbed his elbow with hands that shook so it would be impossible to miss.

The angry male turned. Lips firmed. Eyes narrowed. "What"—disbelief dripped from that one, clipped syllable —"are you doing?"

Can't let him talk to Lucien. "Please . . . please don't make a big deal out of this." I searched his face, that proud, stubborn, harsh face, and saw not anger at my disobedience, but anger made hard by worry. "I'm fine. My leg is fine. It only hurts when its poked and prodded at, and if you call Lucien he'll do just that. And only because you worried."

The lie tasted bitter, but desperation made even the bitterest pill easy to swallow.

Ruarc stared down at my foot, the one now carrying my

full weight. "Fine," he bit out, and I sagged against him in relief.

Probably not my best move.

The hand that had found my arm sometime in the last minute tightened, and then I was lifted up and marched across the room until my butt once more met the hard wood of one of their kitchen chairs. Ruarc stood above me, arms crossed over his chest, glaring daggers.

"No cleaning," he proclaimed, jaw jutting out with masculine conviction. "Stay off that leg."

That . . . that wasn't quite what I had expected.

Too ashamed to meet his gaze—each lie I told them another heavy rock on the grave of my conscience—I just nodded. I'd find the soaps when no one was around, and then I'd make their home sparkle. It was the least I could do.

A heavy silence followed. I chewed on my bottom lip, gripped the edge of my chair when nerves made me want to pick apart the seams on my clothes. My right eye felt funny, like it wanted to twitch but couldn't quite get there.

After a few seconds that felt like hours, I finally darted a quick glance up, regretting it as soon as his fierce gaze locked on mine. Was he angry with me? Could he tell I'd lied about my foot?

No, he would have said something. Ruarc would never mince words. If he suspected me of lying he would surely yell at me and demand the truth.

"Teach me to cook?" I blurted.

He cocked his head. "Why?" The soft sound his fingers made as they tapped against his thighs distracted me.

"Why? Because . . ." I stared at him. How did I explain my need to feel useful, to not be the useless creature I had been my whole life, trapped and alone. Ruarc had a family. Even if the others weren't his biological brothers, they were still his brothers. And he had a job, a purpose in life.

Not to mention the near miss yesterday had left me with an urgent feeling beating away at my skull. I needed to work so I could save up money and eventually make my own way in the world, leaving the guys safe from the Hunters' wrath.

"I want to be useful. You guys . . . you're letting me stay here, have given me a job and you feed me and . . . I haven't held up my end of the bargain. You won't let me clean"—I pretended I didn't hear his rude snort—"so the least I could do is cook."

Ruarc's broad chest heaved with the depth of his sigh. "You don't owe us."

"I—maybe not, but I'd like to help."

Five seconds ticked by. I knew, I counted them all. Then Ruarc grunted. As communication went, it was lacking, but the slight incline of his head accompanying the grunt had to mean yes.

"Thank you!" I jumped up, disregarding the glare Ruarc aimed at my leg as excitement made me careless. Finally, finally I'd contribute and have something to spend my time on other than obsessing over my bleak future! "When do we start?" Without thinking, I put my hand on his arm. Hard, bunching muscles greeted my palm, his skin smooth over the steel below. Heat fluttered in my belly, but I ignored it, giving the big male a smile to thank him for helping me out.

Ruarc stilled. Unreadable, silver eyes locked on my face, tracing the path of my lips until my smile faltered, drowned by a new wave of heat I felt straight down to my soul.

"Tomorrow." The dark, husky tone drifted over my skin like tendrils of smoke, leaving me shivering with a feeling I didn't understand. He cleared his throat, breaking eye contact, and I let my hand fall. It hung uselessly at my side, the weight suddenly uncomfortable and foreign.

"We'll start with breakfast." His abrupt command startled me out of the strange trance I seemed to fall into around him. "Maybe we can—" He cleared his throat again, looked down at the floor, ground his jaw. When he looked back up it was with a black scowl. "Don't be late!" he snarled. Without another glance my way, he stormed out.

"You didn't give me a time—"

He was already gone.

"Why is Ruarc so . . ." I trailed off, searching for the right word. The movie Jason had invited me to watch kept playing in the background while I thought. The heat from his body might as well have been a bonfire, lapping at my skin like tongues of pleasant fire. Despite the huge couch, he'd chosen to sit close enough that our thighs touched every time one of us moved.

Head tilted, he watched me struggle to get my thoughts in order.

Angry? Volatile?

Wounded? The word drifted up through my mind, breaking free of layers upon layers of swirling thoughts before pushing at me with an insistence I found startling. The vicious scar slashing across his face was visible for the world to gaze upon, but what about the internal injuries, the emotional damage caused by things that leave scars? What had Lucien said the other day, something about—

"Vicious? Savage? Completely and utterly nuts?" Jason's devilish grin sent my heart into overdrive and momentarily distracted me from thoughts of his brothers. As I fought the blush I just knew was trying to crawl up my neck, Jason stared straight ahead, seemingly taken with the movie playing on the big TV. But the way his smile grew, the way his eyes seemed to laugh at me as my face grew hotter and hotter, made me think he was very aware of what was going on around him.

"Jason!" I exclaimed, swiveling my head to make sure no one had heard. "That's not what I meant! It's just . . . he doesn't seem very happy."

Jason threw his head back and laughed. A deep, belly-aching sound that drew forth my own mirth. I tried in vain to stop my amusement from showing, but my mouth kept twitching with the urge to smile.

I probably looked like a lunatic having a stroke.

"That's an understatement if I ever heard one," Jason choked out between big gulps of air. "Ruarc not seeming happy . . ." Jason shook his head, a big grin plastered to his handsome face. "Just thank your lucky stars you haven't seen him truly enraged."

Really? I thought back to his brawl with Lucien. *He seemed pretty enraged then.*

"I can see your doubt, love, but I can assure you, Ruarc has been extremely well behaved around you."

"If you say so . . ." My gaze slid back to the movie playing out on the big screen. "What is this, exactly?" A horribly deformed man-wolf was half running, half limping across the screen, big, ugly teeth bared in a fearsome snarl.

"It's called, *A werewolf in the city.*" His amber eyes widened in glee as a particular nasty attack took place. "You can't make this shit up."

"Apparently someone can," I sniffed, feeling strangely disturbed by his choice in movies. There was something about it that tugged on a dark corner of my mind, urging me to look closer.

I didn't like it. Not one bit.

Jason just flashed me another one of his mischievous grins. "Don't be scared, love. I'll protect you." Turning, he got to his knees in the couch and hovered above me, making claws of his long fingers. "Before the big, bad wolf eats your heart!"

I jumped back, heart thumping in my chest as a playful

growl vibrated in his throat. "Jason!" I was torn between embarrassment—I didn't want to be so easily scared—and a reluctant admiration of his knack for imitating sounds. "Don't scare me like that!"

"Sorry, love," he replied, not looking the least bit sorry. In fact, when he sat back down he looked rather pleased with himself.

"How do you make that sound?" I tried to keep the curiosity out of my voice, going for more of a huffy annoyance instead. I feared I failed miserably when his upper lip twitched, and he put thumb and index finger to his chin, striking a thoughtful pose.

"Well, love, it starts right here." He put his hand over the middle of my chest, his thumb grazing the top of my breast and sending rivulets of shivers down my back. "Take a deep breath"—he followed his own instructions—"and let your chest contract lightly. Push the air up into your throat, and aid it by vibrating your vocal cords slightly." A wolfish smile bared his teeth while a low growl rose from his chest. The shivers down my back multiplied.

From fear or something else?

"You try it."

"No, that's okay . . ." I didn't want to make a fool of myself by snorting like a rabid dog.

"Come on, love, just try it. What's the worst that could happen?"

That I fail miserably. Then you'll have another reason to see why I'm not good enough for you.

Wait, where had that come from? God, I was pathetic.

"Fine," I said, just to crush the idiotic thoughts I was having and to prove to myself I didn't *like* Jason.

The object of my idiotic thoughts wiggled his eyebrows.

I took a deep breath, thought about the terrifying noise he'd made, and tried to imitate it.

The sound that erupted from my throat was so foreign that I didn't think it had come from me. Only Jason's wide eyes and the slight, surprised 'O' he was making with his mouth convinced me that it had.

Compared to Jason's growl, it was nothing of course. It was like comparing an angry lion's roar to a tiny kitten's playful squeak. Even so I was proud at my attempt. The sound had been softer, less aggressive—and definitely less wolflike—but it had potential.

Jason leaned in until his warm nose pressed against my neck. My whole body locked down as something in my lower belly gave a tight squeeze. Goosebumps erupted along my neck and chest as Jason dragged his nose from the bottom of my neck all the way behind my ear.

"Oh!" Was it my imagination, or had he nipped at the sensitive skin there? "W-what are you doing?"

"Just checking," he murmured, slowly pulling his head away.

When I gathered myself enough to meet his eyes, they were glowing a deep, beckoning amber. I licked my lips, lost in his heat, his scent. "Checking what?"

"If you smell like wolf."

"W-what?"

"Mmm . . ." he shook his head and flashed me a devastating grin.

The moment was gone, shattered into a million, shiny pieces that would never be.

"Well?" I demanded, ignoring the heat coursing through my molten veins.

If he can pretend nothing happened, then by god, so can I!

"Well what?"

"Do I?"

That innocent smile was surely feigned? "Do you what, love?"

"Do I smell like . . . like wolf?" I gritted out.

Still grinning, Jason shook his head, eyes sparkling as they roamed my face. He lingered on my lips, but only for a moment. Something flickered in his eyes, but was gone before I could put a name to it. "What a silly question," he said. "Why would you smell like wolf?"

"Jason . . ." The name was a warning. I would not let him see me smile. When had I become comfortable enough to do more than meekly agree with whatever he said? Disagreeing with him, pretending to be stern, even when I was laughing inside, it was heaven. Freeing.

"Hope," he mocked. Even pretending to be serious, he couldn't quite hide the grin tugging at his lips.

"You are hopeless!" I threw my hands up in the air, huffing loudly, then crossed them over my chest in a manner I hoped looked intimidating.

"That's just because I don't have you, love."

Startled, my gaze shot to his. Amusement and something else warmed his gaze while I gaped up at him like a moron.

"You are Hope." He pointed at me. "All the way over there . . ." Only an inch or so separated us. "Leaving me without you. Thereby, I am . . . hopeless."

Heat flushed through my veins, found my heart, and met with solid ice.

I looked away, trying not to show the gaping loneliness that suddenly expanded inside me, swallowing yet another part of my wounded soul. I wanted . . . I wanted so badly to . . .

To what?

"Well, it's not as funny when you have to explain it," he muttered, smile gone.

When I glanced back at him, his brows were lowered, the corner of his lips edging down. He cleared his throat. "Should we finish the movie?"

"Yeah."

We finished the movie in silence. I couldn't begin to guess what thoughts made Jason's normally cheery face clouded with darkness, but me? I kept wondering what it would feel like to be part of a family, to have someone like Jason at my side to shed light on the shadows that clung to my heart.

Probably pretty damned great . . .

JASON

The change that came over Hope was as sad as it was telling. Loneliness clung to her small frame like a heavy shroud, growing heavier and darker as she distanced herself by curling her shoulders and lowering her head.

I moved a little closer, needing to dispel whatever darkness tried to pull her under.

The couch dipped beneath my weight.

Hope peeked up at me, dark eyes peering out from the curtain of hair shielding her face from my view.

A man could drown in those eyes.

What the hell?

These were dangerous thoughts. I'd wanted to help the woman, to teach her how to let go of the past and start living in the present. My plans did not include me seducing the poor girl.

I swore softly under my breath, pasting a weak grin on my face when Hope's eyes turned questioning. Beautiful. Soft. Pools of emotions too easy to read.

What the hell, Jason?

When had I started waxing poetically about a girl I barely knew? It was madness. Pure, unequivocal madness.

"Are you okay?" Her soft, dulcet voice still carried too much hesitation. If I'd ever doubted a spine of steel existed beneath the damaged she'd suffered, those doubts would have been wiped away with the way she threw herself at

269

Kieran to protect me. She could have run, but she'd chosen to fight.

What she'd been through . . . you either broke or came out stronger, and Hope sure as hell wasn't broken.

"Never better, love," I replied.

Another unsure glance in my direction. I held her gaze and gave her my best smile.

A beautiful, soft blush colored her cheeks as she shyly looked away. I kept an eye on her, pleased that the color was staying despite her going back to watch the bloody gore fest on the screen.

Before I could tease her about her blush, I became aware of another presence. We had company. Not wanting to disturb Hope—who was still staring blankly at the screen—I threw a quick glance over my shoulder.

Lucien. Standing in the doorway staring at Hope with an unreadable mask in place, he looked like a silent sentinel.

He must have felt my gaze for his eyes snapped to mine, annoyance brimming, and I couldn't help but tease him. Tilting my head in a silent question, I raised my brows and gave him an arrogant smile.

With the kind of deadly silence I was convinced he'd been born into, Lucien bared his teeth. Along with the narrow-eyed glare he aimed my way, it should have been threatening enough to silence me—and had I been anyone else, anyone not considered a brother, I probably wouldn't have survived that look—but the devil in me loved riling the haughty male. So instead of backing down, I threw an arm around Hope, sent Lucien an innocent grin, and enjoyed the sight of his teeth grinding together.

But since this was Lucien—cold, controlled, stick-in-the-mud Lucien—it didn't take him longer than a few seconds before all traces of emotions were wiped away. He sent Hope an inscrutable look before leaving.

A self-satisfied smirk spread across my face before I

remembered the arm I'd thrown around Hope. Suppressing the flash of joy piercing my heart at the feel of her warm, trusting body pressed up against my side, I looked down at the little female and grinned when she winced at the bloodshed on the screen.

"I'll let you pick the next one."

24

HOPE

THE NEXT MORNING, I HURRIED DOWN THE STAIRS BEFORE THE first rays of the sun could warm the pillow I'd begrudgingly vacated. Since Ruarc hadn't told me what time we would start preparing for breakfast, I'd gotten up at five-thirty in the morning, determined to convince him I would be an apt student; always on time, always prepared.

Or, as prepared as I can be, I thought glumly, looking down at the pencil and sheet of paper I'd found in the desk in the library the night before.

Looking around the spacious kitchen, I let out a sigh of relief. Ruarc wasn't here yet, which meant I had some time to battle the eager butterflies trying to escape my stomach by crawling up my throat.

Ugh . . . Shaking off the disturbing visual accompanying that thought, I took a seat by the table. Ruarc would probably be here any minute. I couldn't wait to see what he'd teach me first.

Occupying myself by picturing the different possibilities, I barely noticed the passage of time. It wasn't until a gruff voice spoke right by my ear that I realized I'd fallen asleep.

"W-what?" I stammered, jerking upright.

"What're you doing?" Ruarc glowered down at me.

"I . . . I was waiting for you."

He frowned. "Why?"

My heart sank. Had he already forgotten about our cooking lessons? "So you could teach me. T-to cook. Like you said yesterday."

"How long?" Ruarc cocked his head, his broad shoulders and compressed lips making him look more like an angry warrior than a patient teacher.

"How long, um, what?" I stared up at him, shoulders sagging when I saw the vein by his temple. It was pulsating. That couldn't be good . . .

But how am I supposed to know what he means when he refuses to finish a sentence! I gritted my teeth, resolving to hide the shiver of fear I always felt when he looked so angry and forbidding.

"How long have you been here?" The words were harsh and clipped, pushed out as they were through a tightly clenched jaw.

Was I supposed to have gone to find him when I got up, or was there another way I had failed? "Uhm . . ." I looked out the window, noting the clear, blue skies and beaming sunshine. "I'm not sure."

Ruarc closed his eyes, pinching the bridge of his nose between two fingers. "Fine. It's fine."

I blinked up at him, trying to figure out what was happening. "Should I have looked for you?"

"No!" he snarled, before repeating in a slightly more modulated voice, "No."

Did he not want me here? It was a possibility that hadn't occurred to me before, but now that it had . . .

Ouch.

I squeezed the dull gray material of my shirt—another one of Ash's—between one hand. It hurt knowing I was, yet again, unwanted. A bother. Someone to be hidden away and forgotten.

Wanting nothing more than to slink back upstairs to lick my wounds, I cleared my throat awkwardly. "Well, then . . ." I attempted a brave face, upset at the wobble I felt when I tried to smile, "I'll just go back upstairs."

When I tried to stand a heavy weight pressed down on my shoulders. Twisting my neck to see what had stopped me, I swallowed hard.

Ruarc's big, heavy palm covered every inch of skin from the bottom of my neck to the top of my arm. A long finger rested over my collarbone, the calluses on his hands sending sparks of lightning up and down my spine.

In the past, a heavy hand anywhere on my body would have sent me into panicked shivers while cold sweat broke out on every surface of my body. But now . . .

This touch didn't feel foreign or wrong. It felt . . . nice. Nice in a way I'd forgotten touch could be. I looked down, marveling at the harsh contrast between his lightly tanned, calloused hand and my too-pale, unblemished skin. A frown tugged at my lips when my eyes were drawn to the myriad of crisscrossing, thin lines covering his hands, and the lighter, more spread out white scars on his fingers.

"Why?" he grumbled, turning around and putting a pan on the stove. "Giving up?"

"No!" The response was automatic. A quick, instinctual denial of a perceived weakness. "You seemed angry, I . . . I thought maybe—"

Ruarc spun around, pinning me with a glare. "You want to learn or not?"

"I do!" I stood as well, inching closer to his spot by the stove. "I'm sorry," I said, not quite knowing what I was apologizing for.

Ruarc grunted.

Well, at least he didn't ignore me. That was a start, right?

The next half hour flew by. Ruarc didn't say much, but then he didn't have to. He conveyed most his thoughts by glowering, glaring, or grunting. *The three g's,* as I silently dubbed them. Once in a blue moon—or less, since I wasn't quite sure how often they occurred—he would give me a rare half-nod, the highest of compliments in Ruarc's limited vocabulary.

"No," he snapped as my hand hovered over the pan brimming with the beginnings of an omelet. "Salt at the end." He didn't explain why he had salted the mix before it went in the pan, or why it was okay to salt the fried tomatoes in the pan but not the eggs. And I didn't ask. Instead, I shook my head and obeyed the master—a truly apt description if you based the term on the incredible flavor of the dishes he not-so-graciously let me help him prepare, rather than his teaching skill.

While we were waiting for the omelet to finish, Ruarc turned to me, a strange expression hovering over his harsh features. Breaking eye contact—something I'd noticed Ruarc rarely, if ever, did—he glowered at his hands.

Curious, I followed his gaze. They looked normal to me. Although his right hand did keep jerking; like he was stopping himself from repeating some nervous habit.

When he noticed me watching he stiffened. Accusing silver eyes met mine and I was floored by the pain hidden in their depths. Immediately, my heart ached for him. Ached for whatever had happened to him, or whoever he'd lost. Before I could say anything, offer a measure of comfort or a kind word, the pain was gone from his eyes, leaving only a glowing fury behind.

Without thinking, I reached out. Before my fingers could curl around his, he reared back, piercing me with the ferocity of his reaction.

"Do you . . . Do you *pity* me?" The quiet rage in his voice sent chills down my neck. My heart thumped. Once. Twice.

Then it swelled, swallowing my fear and leaving behind a feeling of kinship.

"I would never." A solemn promise. This was important to him—I felt it in my bones. And I understood. Here we were, two grown people who both feared—or in Ruarc's case, detested—pity and all the terrible feelings that particular response dredged up.

The glower didn't leave his face, but after searching my eyes, the stiffness left his body and he drew a deep breath. "Good."

That's it?

Gathering my courage, I asked, "Why would you think I pitied you?"

Instead of answering, he cursed under his breath and jerked the pan off the stove.

"Ruarc?"

He glared. "Taste this." A fork was shoved under my nose with so much force it would have gone straight through me if Ruarc had less control of his limbs.

Taking a small bite of the newly cooked omelet, I moaned at the flavor. "It's good!"

Ruarc's only reply was a grunt. At least it sounded a little less angry than his previous ones, which I considered progress.

"Ruarc . . ." Taking another deep breath, I was about to repeat my question when I noticed his tense shoulders. I paused, taking a moment to look a little closer. There was a strain around his eyes, his lips were pressed together and his neck was pulled taut. Every line of his body screamed of his discomfort. Did I want to add to that, possibly bring up bad memories by asking questions that would only satisfy my own curiosity?

The answer was a resounding *'no.'*

"What are we making for dinner later?" I was rewarded

for my choice when some of the tension buried in his muscles dissolved.

He looked at me, took his time studying my face, like he was committing it to memory, before his lips curled back in a toothy half-grimace-half-smile that pulled at his scar and made him look even more menacing than before. And yet . . .

I'd never been less scared of him.

"Lamb," he grumbled.

I returned his smile with a hesitant one of my own. "Sounds good."

That terrifying-but-appealing smile of his was gone, but I could have sworn the corners of his mouth curled up when I brushed my hair away to peek up at him.

Would I see it again?

A bubbling sensation sparkled in my throat. It took my confused mind a moment to understand what it was, and the realization was shocking. It was a giggle. It was trapped in my throat, and as soon as I recognized it, it disappeared.

And it was all because of him. Because of Ruarc. He'd made me want to laugh with that smile that wasn't a smile.

Had he always showed his amusement that way, or was it something he'd picked up to make potential enemies wary? It would work, too. A man that looked terrifying even when grinning from ear to ear was a man to be feared. The way his eyes warmed kind of ruined the 'terror-effect' but maybe he—

It isn't an act.

The muscles in my legs quivered. I wanted to sink to the floor.

Eyes can't pretend, they can't lie. So the smile wasn't something he'd practiced. Ruarc . . . Ruarc didn't know how to smile.

Sadness gathered like a heavy cloud in my chest. He'd bared his teeth in an imitation of a smile, like the muscles were unused to moving that way. Had he lived a life so devoid of happiness that he'd never learned that simple, human expression? Even I, despite my stay with the Hunters, had my early childhood to look back on when everything else lent itself to despair. Why didn't Ruarc have that?

Any humor I may have felt was wiped away, leaving behind a horrible sensation in the pit of my stomach. It felt heavy. Nauseating. Carried the cloying sensation of guilt and pain.

"What?" Ruarc snapped, voice cracking like the barbed end of a whip.

Whatever emotion had shown on my face, Ruarc had not approved.

I won't add to his pain, I won't, I told myself, trying to think of a plausible excuse. It was hard, especially when I had no idea what I had looked like. "I was just thinking . . ."

Ruarc glared, eyes hard and unforgiving.

"About the lamb."

His eye twitched.

"Poor lamb," I sighed, knowing it sounded like I meant it because . . . well, I kind of did.

He looked startled, eyes roamed over my face. Looking for clues, maybe? Then, his face cracked and I saw all the teeth I could ever wish to see as he showed me a full-on display of pearly-white chompers.

Err, I mean, as he showed me a startling grin.

I blinked up at him, amazed at the gift he'd given me and feeling sad at how quickly it disappeared.

"Don't," he commanded, voice a smidgen less surly than normal, "or you won't be able to do it."

"Do what?"

"Slaughter her."

"What!" I shrieked, spinning around while my eyes ran over every inch of the room; as though the poor lamb was hiding somewhere in the kitchen.

"It's part of your cooking training." His lip twitched. Probably in anticipation of eating the hapless animal.

"I can't!" Dear god, how could he ask me to kill an innocent creature?

Oh, hypocrisy. I was willing to eat the little darling, but not if it was not already dead?

Ruarc leaned back against the counter. "Then you fail."

"Fail?"

"Your training." He was staring at me with a strange intensity.

"I-I . . ." I couldn't kill anything. I just couldn't. With pleading eyes, I silently begged him for mercy. I could eat vegetables. Really, for the rest of my life, I would eat nothing that required killing. If I stuck to a vegetarian diet he couldn't possibly force me to—

Wait . . . Why was his eye twitching? And his mouth . . . it was jerking. And was that a tooth peeking out?

"Are you . . . are you *laughing* at me?"

A few more teeth showed as a short burst of sound broke from his wide chest. It sounded rusty, unused. Just a short bark of a laugh, and then it was gone.

"You were joking?" A small, hopeful smile spread across my face.

"Yes."

"That's . . . that's great," I said. "I really couldn't kill anything." A small shudder of revulsion rippled over my skin, and Ruarc stiffened.

"The salt," he suddenly growled, turning to stare daggers at the salt shaker I'd left next to me on the counter.

I looked down at the item in question and tried to understand what brought on this abrupt change of emotion. It seemed every time things went better with Ruarc, I did or said something to upset him. And every time, without exception, I had no idea what it was that I did wrong.

And it doesn't help that the man can go from amused to a killing rage faster than I can blink.

Not meeting his glare, I silently handed him the salt, watching from the corner of my eye as he shook it over the finished omelet with a vigor that, to even my untrained eye, promised way too much salt.

"Did-did I do something wrong?"

"No." Plates clattered against the counter as Ruarc yanked them out of the cupboards. The ugly screech of metal and porcelain colliding filled the air when utensils were carelessly thrown on top.

The sound made me shudder with remembrance, and Ruarc stopped to look at me. His silver eyes were hard, but after taking a deep breath, he stilled. A strange expression descended over his face, and then, with mechanical movements, he began setting the table. This time he was more careful, and the ugly noise ceased along with my trembling.

"H-here, let me help," I offered with a small step toward him.

His harsh features were tight, eyes flaring when he growled, "No."

Feeling myself deflating, I turned and closed my eyes. I just needed a moment to recover my equilibrium, to let go of the confusion and sadness that swamped me at how this had turned out.

At least I heard him laugh.

It hadn't been a nice sound by any means; harsh and low and growly, the rusty sound had grated at my ears, but it had still made heat spread through my limbs, made my heart grow lighter and freer.

I want to hear it again.

Once the table was set, Ruarc pointed to a chair with a raised eyebrow and a look in his eyes that clearly stated I better obey or else. After I adhered to his caveman demands he proceeded to ignore me.

Jason, Ash, and Lucien all came strolling in a few minutes later. A cheery greeting from Jason, followed by a warm-but-reserved, "Good morning," from Ash, were both better than the regal nod Lucien deigned to offer me, eyes just as cold and disdainful as ever.

When we were all seated, the other guys pretended to ignore Ruarc's bad mood. In fact, no one spoke to him until they tried the omelet.

"Jesus," Jason sputtered, choking and spitting the food out into a folded napkin. "What on earth happened to the eggs?"

A furious glare and a snarled, "Nothing," from Ruarc followed.

"No, really, they taste like you sprinkled them with fertilizer."

A plate went flying as Ruarc smashed his fist down onto the table. "Quiet!"

"Jason," Ash began, voice so calm you wouldn't think he had almost been hit in the face with a plate full of cheese, "this was Hope's first attempt. We should—"

"Wasn't Hope," Ruarc interrupted with an angry grumble.

Lucien arched a brow. "That *is* surprising," he said, raising his glass to his perfect lips and taking a sip of water. I didn't know what came over me, maybe I was just fed up with his hostile behavior, but suddenly I found a piece of my spine. Attempting to imitate Ruarc, I scrunched up my face, narrowed my eyes and sent him my best glare.

Lucien choked and water went flying across the table. For a second not a sound could be heard. Having lost my courage as the tense silence stretched, I shrank back in my chair, waiting for the blowback sure to follow. Instead, Jason let loose a deep, belly laugh, the same one he'd shared with me the day before. It warmed me all the way down to my toes, and I dared a tiny, grateful smile in return.

Even Ash seemed amused. His eyes were warm when they rested on me, and, even though his expression was mostly unreadable, one corner of his mouth tilted up ever so slightly. "Did Ruarc teach you that fearsome grimace, *banajaanh?*"

I was about to admit that, yes, he had inspired it, but one quick glance at the man in question convinced me otherwise. Ruarc's mouth was set in a grim line, expression dark and foreboding. Both eyebrows were lowered over stormy eyes, glaring at everyone who dared look his way.

Oh, no. What had I been thinking? Ruarc probably thought I was mocking him, or making fun of his grumpiness.

Trying to show him I was sorry, that I would never intentionally set out to make him feel bad, I sent him a small, apologetic smile, and shook my head at Ash. "No, I just . . . no," I finished, for once not caring that I sounded like a ninny.

Ruarc's burning eyes bored into me from across the table, pinning me in my seat with their intensity. His gaze lingered on my lips before he jerked his head away, glowering at his food and muttering under his breath.

The whole thing was a disaster. The cooking had been fun, but Ruarc clearly disliked being around me. Not that I blamed him. Always saying the wrong thing, always doing the wrong thing . . . it felt terrible, like a weight around my heart.

I slumped in my seat, chewing at my bottom lip. I only had two choices; either I could try to avoid Ruarc from now on, or I would need to find some courage and ask him what I'd done to rub him the wrong way.

Maybe it was something I could fix?

25

RUARC

Bloody hell. Bloody hell!

The little female was impossible! Either she cowered and shrunk away, making me feel like a mean, hulking beast, or she graced me with a hesitant smile—one of the ones that looked a little like she was surprising herself with the action but couldn't quite help herself. A smile like that reminded me of all the reasons why this was a bloody bad idea, not to mention the knife piercing my gut every time she said or did something that made me think of her past. Knowing she'd gone through so much shit in life that the idea of smiling was surprising to her made my blood boil.

The other reason why her smiles were so deadly was the reaction they elicited in me. A feeling of possibility, of a light at the end of my dark, dark days. Those tiny smiles, those beautiful, lethal smiles . . . they made me wish for things I knew could never be.

"Bloody hell," I muttered, skewering Jason with a lethal glare when he raised a questioning brow at me.

It wasn't meant for you, you idiot.

That was another thing. My surliness. Hard as I tried, I couldn't curb it. Didn't stand a chance. During our lessons I'd

283

tried not to snarl. Tried not to glare at the little female, but it'd proved impossible.

When she bit her lip, concentrating hard on whatever task was before her, I got hard. So hard I wanted to punch through the wall.

When she ducked her head to hide a shy smile, I was hit by the certainty that *I* would *never* make her smile like that.

When she stared up at my ugly mug or studied my scarred hands, I felt like the biggest brute in the world, and all I wanted to do was lash out at her for a judgment she hadn't delivered.

And probably never would.

The worst, the absolute worst, was when she flinched. It'd happened when I'd made a sudden move, reaching for the spices above her head, throwing a fork into the sink next to her. Innocent, everyday occurrences done a little too fast, a little too sudden, and she'd flinch. Either that, or jerk back. Sometimes she'd even throw a hand in front of her face, as if to shield herself from harm.

The fury that took hold of me when that happened was so dark, so hideous, I wondered how it didn't burst from me and sear the floor with its acidity. Wanted to rip off the heads of the motherfucker *lithbhárs* who'd hurt her, but I didn't know who they were!

She won't tell me!

That, again, had poisonous rage flowing through my blood, twisting my insides until breathing became difficult.

When that shit happened—when my rage got away from me—I knew she felt my tension. She probably didn't understand how or why, but I had a feeling the little female was more in tune with others than she thought. It was there in her eyes, the concern that made them round and big, the light that would not be extinguished no matter what was done to her.

It floored me. It amazed me. It made me turn into a bloody fool.

"Bloody hell . . ." No one commented this time, but Hope stared down at her food with huge, wounded eyes.

You see? You will never do anything but cause her pain.

I snarled at my own thoughts. A female like her was too fragile for a savage animal like me. I'd end up hurting her, either physically—accidentally, due to my size and what I was—or emotionally when I didn't respond how I should, or I was too abrupt with her. Hell, looking at her now, hanging her head and looking fucking miserable, I would say I'd already accomplished that.

"Goddammit!" I banged my fists on the table, losing control of my temper once again. Three heads shot up while one, the most important one, shrunk further back in her seat, looking for all the world like she wanted nothing more than to disappear. "Going out," I snarled, fighting the Change as I stormed outside. With my teeth elongating and tearing a strip of flesh off the inside of my lip, I chided myself.

The little female had gone through something terrible; the abuse she'd suffered was clear in the way she carried herself, the hesitant tone she used when talking, the nightmares that made her scream as if someone was tearing strips off of *her* flesh.

Claws shot out from my fingers as the familiar, hot fury filled me. I threw my head back and roared. I roared for the female, for the horror she'd been through, and for my past—the hideous betrayal that had left me too scarred to be any good to anyone.

But most of all, I roared for the loss. The loss of something I hadn't even had a chance to experience.

Dunnae fool yerself, boy, my sire's voice taunted in my mind, *ye never stood a chance.*

Hundreds of years after his death, the evil man could still

get in my head. It made me weak, as foolish as the taunts ringing in my ears claimed.

Growling, I dropped to all fours. *No more,* I thought. *Never again.* Banishing the bastard to the furthest corner in my mind, I took off running. A run would clear my head. Maybe when I came back, I would have some answers.

Not bloody likely.

26

ASH

A LIGHT BREEZE RUSTLED LEAVES AND LIFTED STRANDS OF Hope's hair, allowing them to caress her face in a dance she must have found annoying. She batted them away with a wave of a not-quite-steady hand. "W-what are we doing out here?" she asked in a trembling voice, eyeing the trees to our left as though waiting for something—or someone—to pounce.

The scene with Ruarc at the kitchen table had stolen her newly found fire, and once more she was stammering and unsure, smelling of fear.

At least the scent is more subtle now. Lessened.

"I thought you may like to spend some time with the horses. If your leg feels up to it, of course," I added. Lucien had not mentioned any complications which could only mean it was healing nicely.

"Oh . . ." She peeked up at me. "That-that would be nice." A cautious smile formed on her lips, giving her pallid shade a hint of a blush.

A few days of decent food and rest had been transformative. Her face was no longer as gaunt as it had been, her

287

cheeks not as hollow. If she lifted her shirt her ribs would not be protruding like vulnerable sticks ready to be broken.

Improved but not healed.

Making sure to keep my eyes off her lest she felt threatened or uncomfortable, I kept my pace slow and even. The last thing I wanted was for her to stumble or hurt herself further. So far there had been no signs of discomfort, no tension around her eyes, no smell of rot or blood on the air. But the way her leg had looked that first day . . .

My hands curled into fists.

"You must tell me if you are overtaxing your leg. I do not want your injury to worsen." Even though I kept my eyes off her, her sharp, indrawn breath and sudden halt alerted me to her distress. Her face, when I turned, was ashen and her lips trembled.

Alarmed, I reached out a hand to steady her quivering form. "Are you all right? Do you need to sit down?"

She ducked her head, refusing to meet my gaze. "No." A shrug, the gesture dismissive but for the way her chin kept dropping. Nervous hands fiddled with the string holding her sweatpants up, her bottom lip disappearing between her front teeth.

Something was not right.

"Hmm." I took my time assessing her movements. She must have felt my gaze caressing her smooth skin, but not once did she look up. Her eyes glued to the ground, her thin shoulders hunched, she looked like a terrified child convicted of crimes that shamed her deeply.

Guilt colored the otherwise pleasant scent of her skin.

Strange . . .

Guilt and shame should not cloud a victim's eyes. Were the emotions misplaced, rooted from the same dark corner of the subconsciousness of those harmed by others and left to believe they were to blame? Or did she feel shame for relying on strangers to help her, for the fuss we made over her injuries? Guilt for her wrongful belief of putting us out?

Whatever the reason, pushing her would do more harm than good. She would only open up when she was comfortable, and so I would be patient.

"Would you like to continue?" If she said no, I would escort her back and try this another day.

She met my eyes for a moment before averting them. "Yes, please." A breath of relief.

If she knew what I had planned once we reached the stables her relief would be short-lived. I had no misconceptions about what this would mean. If everything went according to my plan, Hope would reveal some things about her past today that would most likely haunt me. And to get her to trust me enough to share, even just one experience, I would have to share first.

My jaw ground together.

"Do you enjoy it?" Hope asked as we resumed our walk. Grass, wet from the night's rain, reached up to share its moisture with the bottom of her sweatpants. Rolled up as they were, she would not feel the dampness unless she walked outside for hours. "Rehabilitating horses, I mean," she added with a faint blush.

"I do."

She looked up at me, a line appearing between her delicate brows. "What . . . what about it do you like the most?"

She wants to know more. Talk to her.

A tall order for someone like me. I was not used to explaining myself. Not used to sharing, either. Everyone considered Ruarc to be the reticent one, but while he was a man of few words, he *could* share if need be. For me, keeping emotions and events to myself had been a matter of survival since I was a child. Breaking that habit would be tough.

"There is not an aspect of it I do not like. Except for seeing the trauma inflicted on some of the poor animals," I added. "But the rest I love. In particular the moment trust re-enters the equation. The day the horse sees that, finally, there is a person who will not harm him. Once I have earned their trust the rest of the journey is one of understanding."

Hope blinked up at me, a sheen of moisture making her eyes shine beautifully. "That's . . ." She cleared her throat. "That's really nice."

"Hmm." My reply must not have been sufficient—she was still looking up at me with her wide, soulful eyes, like she was waiting for me to expand.

Or maybe she wanted me to reciprocate, show an interest in her life?

No, that would just bring back bad memories for her and make her shut down before I was ready.

As we came up to the stables, the window of opportunity was closing; Hope's eyes were back to staring at the ground, her shoulders hunched.

Keeping my tone even and non-threatening, I held the door open for her. "I thought I would introduce you to a mare who is almost ready to go home."

She nodded and hurried past me, careful not to brush up against me as she went.

"She is right over here," I said, leading the way.

The mare in question was beautiful; a coat as black as the deepest ocean on a moonless night, with an elegant head and wide, curious eyes. The scars marking her face and body were faint, nothing like the open gashes she had sported when she arrived.

"Hope, this is Dancing Queen. Queenie to her friends."

"Hi, Queenie," Hope murmured, a slight smile warming her face and making her look a little less lost. She reached out, looking pleased when Queenie nuzzled her palm.

"Queenie used to be a racehorse," I murmured, keeping one eye on Hope as I told her the horse's story. "When her owners realized she was never going to place, they sold her to the highest bidder. Unfortunately, the man who bought her was cruel and had no knowledge on the right way to train a horse. He used violence to push the poor girl past her limits. Almost killed her."

"That's terrible," Hope whispered. "How did you save her?"

"The man was spotted beating the horse by someone who cares about animals. They called me, and here we are."

Sad eyes glued on the horse, she asked, "How did you get him to give her up?"

With great pleasure, I thought, remembering how the man had looked after Ruarc and I were done with him. "We convinced him it was in his best interest to find a different hobby."

Her shoulders tensed, but she kept petting the horse. "Good," she said fiercely, making me think she understood some of what had transpired.

"Would you like to brush her?"

The way her eyes lit up brought a shocking sadness to my heart. Every time we showed her kindness or consideration she was so clearly surprised and delighted. It was as though no one had ever shown her anything but pain.

"I would love to! If she likes it, that is," Hope added.

I nodded, reaching for the small tack box I had left outside the stall a few hours earlier. "Try this one," I said and passed her Queenie's favorite.

Hope accepted the round, plastic brush, her small, delicate hands turning it over as she examined the rounded, square rubber-teeth sticking out at regular intervals. "What kind of brush is this?"

"It is called a Curry Comb. Rub it in a circular motion, like this." I made a smooth circle in the air with my right hand. "Queenie loves it. The massage feels good and it is healthy for her blood flow."

Hope nodded, a determined tilt to her chin. "Got it."

"Take this side." I guided her over to Queenie's right. "I will start on the left." I ducked under the mare's neck to stand on the opposite side. The top of Hope's head barely reached the mare's back, making it hard for her to see me.

Just as well, I thought. *It will make it easier for her to talk when the time comes.*

Working my greater height to my advantage, I peered down across Queenie's back and watched the top of her head as she gingerly touched the brush to the soft fur in front of her.

"Do not be afraid of pushing too hard." I lifted my matching brush, using firm strokes that made Queenie grunt with pleasure. "Experiment with the pressure. Watch her eyes and ears for signs of discomfort. If she dislikes what you are doing, her eyes will widen, she may step away from you and her ears may flatten against the back of her head. If she closes her eyes, sighs and lowers her head like that, it means she is enjoying it."

"Okay," Hope whispered. "Thank you."

Her next few strokes were firmer. She kept a careful watch on Queenie, and a slow smile spread across her face as the mare closed her eyes, head lowering in relaxation.

"Very good." I wanted her to feel useful. To feel as though she excelled at something, even if it was just brushing a horse. The way Hope carried herself, the lack of confidence shining through her clear, brown eyes made me suspect she felt inadequate, insecure, and it made me doubt she had rarely, if ever, had the opportunity to learn something she enjoyed.

I should teach her to ride.

"You're different here," Hope murmured. She kept her head down, making it impossible for me to see her expression. "You sound so at peace. Not that you normally don't," she added, picking up speed. "I just mean . . . oh, I don't know. It's just different."

"Hmm." I took a moment to think about her words. "I have always felt at home with animals, especially horses. They are an unusually perceptive species. If you are calm and treat them well they will repay you a thousand times. They will give you peace in times of distress, and comfort in times of sorrow. Most animals are gifted at sensing your emotions, horses in particular."

The sharp sound of Hope's next indrawn breath was like a knife to my heart.

I glanced over at her, my chest constricting at the sheen of tears in her eyes as she lifted her face to stare at the scar Queenie had just below her eye. With a trembling hand, she gently traced the white line with her thumb.

"Will she ever be okay?"

Her tremulous voice stoked the anger I kept under lock and key, tempting my beast into a hunt that could only end with death.

A hunt I knew Ruarc, in particular, hungered for.

I took a deep, calming breath, letting the familiar scent of horse and hay relax my tense shoulders. Another inhale and a different scent prodded something in my brain. It wasn't Hope's sweet scent, but a complex pattern buried below the surface. Underneath her honeyed fragrance lay something sharper, something that stirred a longing in me I did not understand, nor wished to examine.

I cleared my throat, focusing on Hope's question. "Queenie will always have scars. Some you can see, like the one below her eye, and some you cannot. It is the hidden scars, the ones deep inside, that are the most difficult to overcome." I paused, waiting for a reaction. Except for her quickened breathing and the scent of sorrow in the air, she gave no outward appearance of having heard me. "Luckily for me," I continued, stroking the mare's smooth neck, "Queenie is a fighter. I saw it on her first day here; the fire in her eyes, her determination. She was not aware of it then, but that's what saved her. Not me or anything I could have done, but her own will."

A soft sniff came from Hope's bent head. Her shoulders were curled inward, protecting herself.

I went back to brushing Queenie. If I wanted her to talk, to open up and show me some of her scars, I would have to be patient.

After a few minutes of silence, I was rewarded by a faint whisper. "I . . . I want to be strong too."

"You are strong, *banajaanh*," I replied, keeping my voice soft and soothing. "It takes strength to survive, to open your eyes each day and *remember*."

A small whimper tore from her throat, raw and desolate.

Ah, little bird with broken wings. You long for flight.

I fought against the desire to rush to her side, gather her in my arms, comfort her and keep her safe. But I knew if I did that, I would be doing her a disservice. She needed to talk, to purge some of these things from her soul and to *know* that there was no judgment here. Only acceptance.

"I-I d-don't want to r-remember."

"I know."

I let the quiet settle around us. A quiet only broken by Queenie's faint sighs and rumbles when we hit a particularly good spot with the brushes, and Hope's occasional, heartbreaking sniffles.

Her pain was a spear through my heart.

"It-it wasn't always b-bad," she stammered, making every muscle in my body tense with the need to go to her. "In the beginning . . . at first they treated me okay."

"Hmm." It was difficult to keep my anger at bay, to not clench my fists and grit my teeth while I raged against the unfairness of the world. But I exercised the tight control I always surrounded myself with and kept my voice calm and noncommittal while inside a detached fury grew.

A peculiar cold spread through my veins as a calculating

presence made itself known. Violence was a melody sung in blood, vengeance a terrible, silent roar through the sky. We watched the little female. Weighed her mettle against what was known. Assessed the torn but not quite broken spirit.

And we felt . . . something.

The ice spread, reached out, took control of my hands and—

I drew in three deep breaths, urging my flesh to follow my spirit, to allow me back in control.

The scent of fresh dirt, of blooming flowers, of green trees filled my senses, and the cold receded.

Just in time, I thought as Hope's fragile voice drifted up past Queenie.

"I-I mean . . . it was boring. In the beginning I had very little to do, and I was grateful when they took an interest in me. It meant a break from the monotonous waiting and sitting around." She stopped, took a deep breath. "T-then one day . . . one day it c-changed and I would have given a-anything, *anything*, to go back to the boredom."

Fury rose once more. Swift. Unbidden.

Thank the Great Spirit for Hope's human ways, I thought. Had she been like me, the scent of my anger would have coated her tongue, the quickened thud of my heart as I struggled to curb my lethal response would have echoed in her ears. I, of all people, knew how important it was to always be in control, to never let instinct rule the mind or control the body.

Listen to your instincts, yes. Feel them and the emotion they brought forth, yes. Process and learn, but never let them rule.

Despite that knowledge, I had to fight for control, fight against the feral nature of my beast as it clawed to get out, to destroy. And all in response to my own, wild emotions.

When Hope hesitated, the only sound I could squeeze through my tight chest was a soft chuff. It was a low, soothing sound, meant to comfort our young, and it seemed to work on females too.

Thank the spirits.

"I f-feel s-so d-d-dirty," she choked out, a heart-wrenching sob following her devastating confession.

That's it.

I could no more ignore her sorrow than I could stop breathing.

As Hope fought against her emotions, one hand clutched to her lips to stem the flood of anguish spilling from her in heaving cries, I ducked around Queenie and came to the grieving female's side. Taking a chance, I touched her arm, then her shoulder. When she did not object—only stood there, staring at the ground with near-silent tears running down her pale cheeks—my heart stopped, my breath caught, and when the blood once again rushed through my veins, I was no longer the same.

I gathered the fragile body against my own, wondering if she knew how much strength resided within her delicate bones, the resilience of a mind refusing to break. Did she know the great power it took to not only survive, but to live with demons so great you felt their weights like iron around your neck? Should she fail to understand it now, there was no doubt in my mind that Hope would survive. That she would endure and, eventually, thrive. She simply needed a little help.

"You are *not* dirty," I pushed out, swallowing twice around the painful lump in my throat. "You are strong and resilient, and no matter what they did to you"—my hands shook as I grabbed her shoulders and pulled her against my chest—"you are *not* dirty. You are *not* to blame for the actions of others, nor your own," I added, keeping her cheek trapped against me when she tried to pull back, probably to argue my point. "*Listen,*" I emphasized, knowing how important it was that my next point stuck, "you cannot be held responsible for anything you did in the name of survival. And you cannot, *you cannot*, hold yourself responsible for what was done *to you*."

By the time I finished speaking, Hope's small frame shook with the force of her sobs. Instead of pulling away, she clung to my shoulders while her tears soaked through my shirt.

"It was not your fault," I said adamantly. "And you *will* be all right. One day you will wake up and realize it has been a full day since you last thought of your trauma. And then it will be a week. Then a month. A year."

She made a choked sound of disagreement.

"It is the truth, *banajaanh*. You survived. Now all that's left is to heal. If Queenie here can do it"—I turned us so we faced the drowsy mare—"you can do it. And we will be here for you. Every step of the way."

The sobs were slowing down, but her wispy body still trembled in my arms. How someone could hurt an innocent —especially someone as good as Hope—made a familiar, deadly wrath twist through my belly.

I closed my eyes, concentrating on my surroundings, on the waif-like girl in my arms, her chilled, velvet skin, her sweet scent, and the soft, hiccuping breaths fanning across my chest hot enough to leave me feeling branded through my shirt.

An unwelcome feeling slipped through my veins, tearing my thoughts away from Hope.

Concentrate on your surroundings, on what is safe.

I refocused my mind, picking up on the faint sounds of the horses moving around in their stalls, the swish of their tails, their sighs and grunts.

Hope's small palm as it glides across my chest.

I took a step back, almost dropping Hope in the hay. "Sorry." My heart gave a painful squeeze as I steadied her.

"T-that's okay." Her face was ravaged by grief. Wet, pale

cheeks, a red nose, bloodshot eyes. She was a mess. And I had never seen anyone more beautiful.

What is happening to me?

It had been centuries since I was stirred in this way—not since that fateful day I lost my name, rising from the ashes a broken man.

The silence between us lengthened. If I didn't fix this she would never open up again.

"Forgive me, *banajaanh*," I began, unsure how to explain my sudden urge for distance. "I did not mean to take advantage of your grief."

Using the back of her hand to wipe tears from her cheek, she lifted her soulful, brown eyes to mine. "Y-you didn't. I feel . . ." Her long, dark lashes fluttered as she sighed. "I feel like . . . like some of the poison was drained." She looked back up at me, a world of sorrow reflected in the deep pools of her eyes. "It probably won't last, but it's a start."

Without thinking, I clasped her hand in my own, marveling at how small she felt, how fragile her thin bones seemed swallowed up in my grip. "It will get better with time. Talking about it helps."

She blinked up at me, a hesitant, tremulous smile hovering over her mouth. "I don't think I can say any more. At least not now . . . but thank you. Thank you for listening."

"Whenever you feel the need, my door is always open for you."

She let go of my hand, a silent plea for space to process, or maybe to think.

"Should we finish with Queenie before she falls asleep?" I slipped around the sleepy mare to pick up my discarded brush.

"Yes. Please." It was barely above a whisper, but then I did not require an answer, not when her eyes revealed so much of her emotions.

If she wanted to pretend everything was okay I would support her.

So we went back to pretending. She pretended to feel better, that nothing was amiss and she hadn't just revealed a little more about her mysterious, dark past, while I pretended being near her did not arouse feelings in me I long since thought dead.

Feelings I would have preferred stayed dead.

What would happen if pretending was no longer an option?

I never wanted to find out.

27

HOPE

I couldn't stop shivering.

Ever since Ash brought me back to the house an hour ago, an insidious cold had penetrated deep into my soul, making me want to burrow under blankets and hibernate for a year or two.

The more time passed, the colder I felt, until my teeth chattered and my hands trembled with the ice in my veins.

What was I thinking? I shouldn't have told Ash anything. If he ever found out the truth—

Another shiver wracked my body. After how he'd made me feel today the thought of seeing the warmth in eyes turn to disgust and hatred was more than I could bear.

I closed my eyes and tried to think about something else. Anything, as long as it didn't involve the guys and the contempt they would shower me with if they knew my secrets.

Hot chocolate!

The image of a steaming cup of sweet goodness popped into my head. It'd always seemed to make me feel better when I was young. Unfortunately, I had no clue how to make it. As a child, it had just appeared in front of me when it was the most needed, courtesy of my amazing father.

How hard could it be?

The harsh glare of the midday sun shone through the large windows in the guys' kitchen. Its bright blaze tickled my skin, a promise of warmth that I couldn't feel.

As I bounced on the balls of my feet in front of a kitchen cabinet—attempting to thaw my frozen limbs while searching for the magical drink of hot chocolate—a shadow loomed above me.

I twisted around, hand shooting to my chest as if to stop my galloping heart from escaping during its mad frenzy.

"Hope," Ruarc muttered darkly as he brushed past me.

"R-Ruarc." My teeth smashed together, mangling his name with the force of my shivers.

His abrupt halt startled me almost as much as the stillness in his body when he turned to face me. Compressed lips, brows lowered in an angry scowl, but when his luminous eyes studied my face, his expression altered.

"What's wrong?" He tilted his head. "You've been . . . *crying*?" An ominous growl erupted from his chest, raising all the fine hairs along my neck.

"I-oh," I exclaimed as, in a blur of motion, he appeared in front of me. He tilted my head back with his long index finger, examining my face.

"You *have*!" he snarled, twisting his head to look behind us, as though the reason for my tears were lurking in the corner. "I will kill him!"

"You—what?" Alarmed, I took a step back, pretending my rapid breathing was *not* a sign of fear when Ruarc followed so close there was less than an inch of space between us.

"Ash! He did this!"

"What?"

The continuous growl rumbling in his chest rose in volume. "He made you cry!"

I gasped. "No! Just . . . we just talked. I-I wasn't sad because of him!"

Ruarc didn't look convinced. The mulish way his chin jutted out, the dark, slashing brows lowered as far as they could go, it all spoke of a furious man not ready to let go of his misconceptions.

"Then what?" His hard eyes searched my own.

"I . . . I don't really want to talk about it."

Please don't make me say it all again. Please . . .

"Why not?"

"Because its painful!" I blurted and the cold shivers that had temporarily stopped came back with a vengeance.

"But you can talk to Ash?"

I didn't know what to say, so I averted my gaze and stared at the tiled floor.

Why did *I* speak to Ash? I asked myself, aware of Ruarc's harsh breathing above me. *I didn't reveal much, at least I don't think I did.*

Ruarc's face suddenly hovered inches from my own. "Hope," he hissed, and if I wasn't so cold, if I hadn't just had an emotional upheaval leaving me drained and heartbroken, I would have found it funny that this massive, proud man was bending at the waist—almost doubling over—just to glare at me.

"Why can you talk to Ash and not—" He stopped as a particularly harsh tremor shook my frame. "You cold?"

"N-no," I lied, pressing my teeth together to stop them from making that terrible noise.

Ruarc narrowed his eyes, the silver orbs growing hard until they looked like flat, unyielding metal. "Do *not* lie to me!"

I shrank back, unsure whether the lump in my stomach was caused by fear or shame. "Sorry," I muttered, unable to look at him.

Ruarc grunted.

After several tense seconds of squirming, waiting for him to question me further, I couldn't take it anymore. Sneaking a quick peek, I held my breath as my eyes darted to his face.

His jaw was a taut line, brows slightly raised as he studied me.

"What?" I squeaked when I grew too uncomfortable with his perusal.

"You're afraid."

Of him? I . . . wasn't. A realization that came as a shock. True, he sometimes scared me, and true, I found him intimidating. The feelings he evoked in me *did* make me afraid, but I wasn't scared of *him*, not really. "N-no . . ."

Ruarc rolled his eyes, a gesture I would have found faintly endearing on such a big, scary-looking man if it hadn't been so insulting. "You want tea?"

The abrupt subject change threw me. "Um . . ." What I wanted was hot chocolate. If I told him no, would he be upset?

"Yes or no, Hope."

"Uh, sure."

For the longest time he simply stared at me. His gaze roamed across my face, lingering on my eyes for so long I was afraid he was trying to see straight through to my weary, damaged soul.

"Lie." His jaw clenched.

Asking for what I wanted shouldn't be this hard, should it?

"I'm sorry." When my lower lip wobbled, I drew it between my teeth in an attempt to hide the emotional response from Ruarc. I hated being this weak.

"Tell me," he demanded, closing the distance between us while tilting my chin up until I was looking into his magnetic eyes. "What do you want to drink?"

I blinked slowly up at him, caught in a seductive web of emotions I didn't quite understand and the harsh beauty that was Ruarc. Despite his scarred face, the brutal angle of his cheekbones and his severe, slashing brows, he was a perfect example of the kind of fierce, savage warriors that mother-nature was capable of producing. And there was beauty in that. An unmerciful, violent kind of beauty generally reserved for predators in the wild, but beauty nonetheless.

The way he looked at me, with such intensity, such naked *need* . . . Need to understand? To help?

"I . . . I want . . ." My voice was breathless, uneven. My body was thrumming with a kind of sensation I had never felt before. It was new. Exhilarating.

And it terrified me.

Ruarc's fiery gaze trailed down to my lips, his pupils dilating until only a faint circle of glowing silver remained.

A soft gasp parted my lips, and he jerked back; his eyes wild and nostrils flaring. The sudden distance, the alarming way he was staring at me both combined to chase back the warmth that had enveloped my body at his nearness.

"I—"

A rumbling that sounded unnervingly like thunder filled the space around us. Eyes glued to me, Ruarc's chest expanded as another rumble cracked through the air. Deeper than a growl, a heavy bass sound I could feel down to my marrow, the rumble caressed my skin, my senses, and nudged at my slumbering monster.

"W-what are you doing?"

The sound grew and my breath caught, a gasp flying from my lips.

Ruarc's glowing, silver gaze shot to my mouth. He shook his head. Once, twice. Then, taking a step back, he leaned against the counter behind him, rubbing a big palm over his jaw.

The rumbling stopped.

The scary, potent sound had evoked a response deep inside me. A primal instinct I hadn't been aware of existed. It was as though a whole new sense had unfurled, had reached up through me and basked in the thunder Ruarc had created. And now that it was gone I felt its absence keenly.

A muttered apology rasped from Ruarc's throat. There were lines of tension between his shuttered eyes, and his mouth was set in a grim line.

"I-it's okay." Every fiber of my being wanted to ask what had happened, what that terrifying, amazing thrum of sound had been, and what it meant. But before I could think of a way to phrase my question Lucien strode into the kitchen. His eyes skimmed over me before he turned his head dismissively, but once he looked at Ruarc he came to an abrupt stop.

"What happened?" he asked in a chilled voice. When Ruarc failed to respond, he turned to me, eyes narrowed with suspicion. "What did you do?"

Ruarc, with his teeth bared, stepped forward, blocking Lucien's view of me with his substantial bulk. "Lucien, so help me . . ." he growled.

Lucien drew back, a hint of surprise coloring his skin before his expression closed. His beautiful, green eyes were just as frosty as ever, and his dark eyebrows were raised just enough to give him a haughty, superior look.

A beat of silence followed Ruarc's outburst, then Lucien visibly stiffened. His spine straightening until it looked so taut I was surprised it didn't snap straight off. "Very well," he said, moving past us to pull a container out of the fridge. His eyebrows rose as Ruarc moved with him, keeping himself between me and Lucien at all times. "Don't be so dramatic," he said in a dry voice. "I'm not going to attack the chit."

Ruarc's only response was more of the same, deep rumble from before. This time, having experienced it once before, I let the sound carry through my body, filling the empty parts of my soul, and rejoicing in its radiance.

Nothing else existed but that sound, that feeling. Everything changed as my vision adjusted to make room for something I didn't understand.

The quiet luster of the sun suddenly seemed to shine with a brilliance that surpassed anything else I'd ever seen. Bright light spilled in through the uncovered windows, casting a warm glow over the kitchen that banished all shadows and left the room as luminous as the brightest of pearls. The white kitchen tiles no longer looked white, instead they shimmered an almost golden color and made the space seem less utilitarian and more of a home.

No sound could be heard over the deep, growling thunder echoing through Ruarc's broad chest. A song of power, of hunger, of need, it silenced all else, as though every creature felt the need to quiet down and listen to the powerful display of the male in front of me.

Even Lucien held his tongue as he stared at Ruarc with an expression I'd never seen on his face before. All his movements had ceased, it didn't even look like he drew breath. His mouth parted, a tiny space between his lips that revealed even, white teeth.

"Have you gone mad?" he breathed, a look of horror stamped across his perfect features.

Another rumble, then Ruarc's deep voice as he denied the accusation. "No."

"You cannot be serious!"

"I am," Ruarc snarled, rolling his tense shoulders.

The display before me shot shivers of need down my back. A clawed hand clutched at my heart and made its beat uneven. Painful.

What was happening? The crackling tension between the two men had the back of my nape prickling with sensation. I was lost. And uncomfortable. Something was happening here, something important that, for the life of me, I couldn't understand. All I knew was that my skin crawled, my heart felt too big for my chest, my gums itched, and my body felt too small.

Too fragile.

Something inside me wanted to tear out and greet the radiant world I'd somehow stumbled into.

Oh, no! I clutched at my chest as sudden, violent terror surged through me, momentarily stealing my breath and my thoughts with it.

It's happening, oh no, oh no, oh no!

I silently chanted a refusal in my head, gaze darting around the room to look for a way out. The brightness was receding, shadows once again appearing in every corner, every hidden nook and cranny until the dark was all I could see. The monster had only escaped once. And the one time I'd been too weak to contain it I'd lost everything . . .

And taken an innocent life with me.

"You cannot mean to . . . with *her*! Have you—" Lucien's surprisingly heated voice was quickly lost to the insidious fear slithering through my mind. The sound of voices arguing faded out, and their cadence changed.

" . . .clearly terrified."

"None of your—"

"It is if she—"

Too busy struggling with my panic, nothing registered until Lucien stood shoulder to shoulder with Ruarc, both men staring down at me with such strange expressions a part of me took notice and pulled me back from the panic that had taken root.

Lucien, who was always hard to read, looked *strange*. His normally composed face was drawn, tension seeping into lines around his mouth. There was a strange flickering in his eyes, like two emotions warred within him, neither relenting in their unwavering struggle to be victorious.

Ruarc, on the other hand, was much easier to read. Even in my scramble to push back the advancing terror rapidly taking over my body, I could see his pain as clearly as I felt my own. His face was twisted into a savage grimace; hurt and anger fought for supremacy in his glowing, silver eyes.

"Would never hurt you," he said. The words sounded torn from his throat, painful and raw, drawing me out of my panicking mind.

"W-what?"

Ruarc huffed, releasing a stream of hot air that left my skin tingling where it touched. The strange crawling in my skin receded. The monster calming.

Thank you, god!

"Not gonna hurt you," he muttered.

"I . . . I know," I said, confused by his statement, and further confused when Ruarc's brows lifted in surprise.

"You know?" Lucien asked slowly, staring at me like he'd never seen me before.

"Y-yes."

"Then why are you reeking of terror?"

Ruarc glared at him but didn't interrupt. He watched me with a strange intensity, waiting for me to explain myself.

Shivering, I wrapped my hands around my stomach. I couldn't tell them about the dark *thing* living inside me. "I-I wasn't."

Ruarc's gaze hardened, and my stomach clenched with shame. The thought of disappointing him made me want to crawl in bed and stay there for at least a week.

"I mean . . . I—" I swallowed hard. If I couldn't lie and I couldn't tell the truth, what option was left? "I . . . I don't . . . I would prefer not to say," I finished lamely, peeking up at Ruarc.

His was the approval I craved.

It was easy to ignore Lucien's disbelieving look, the suspicion gathering in his cold eyes. He'd made it clear several times that he despised me, that he thought I was a fraud, a liar, a . . .

Stop it, Hope, I scolded myself. *You don't care what Lucien thinks, remember?*

Ruarc, on the other hand . . . His opinion meant a great deal to me, and I desperately wanted him to understand that I was trying. My solution wasn't perfect, but at least it was the truth.

Ruarc's hard eyes studied me, almost urging me to speak.

Keeping my mouth shut and the excuses at bay was difficult, but I didn't want to lie to him again, to see angry disapproval form on his face.

After a few seconds he gave me a begrudging nod, sending pangs of relief through my strained muscles.

"This is insanity," Lucien muttered, a tired note overtaking the chill in his voice. "With your"—he gestured toward Ruarc, who bared his teeth in reply—"and not pursuing answers. Do you not want to know *why* she is scared? At least find out before—"

Ruarc's jaw clenched, and he jerked his head once, an angry, non-verbal *'no'* stopping any further protests. "But," he growled, pinning me in place with the force of his glare, "we *will* talk about this soon."

Swallowing hard, I gave him a tiny nod all the while telling myself it would be okay. The next time he brought it up, I would tell him I wasn't ready and after enough time passed he would forget all about it.

Right?

Lucien turned his frown to me. Something lurked in his eyes, something I hadn't seen on him before and couldn't quite understand. The way he looked at me, head slightly tilted with an expression of deep concentration, made me think maybe he didn't understand me either.

When he noticed me staring back his eyes shuttered, face once again an unreadable, cold mask.

"Come." Ruarc's sudden command startled me. Almost as

much as the heat from his hand on my lower back as he urged me toward the door. "Let's eat."

The sudden change of topic left me reeling. "B-but the food is here," I said dumbly and strained my neck to look at the empty mugs we left behind. I still hadn't gotten my hot chocolate.

"She's right, Ruarc," Lucien interjected. It annoyed me that his voice could sound so smooth while practically freezing in his mouth. "The food is, indeed, *here*."

Ruarc didn't stop or look back. "Take-out."

I knew what take-out was, but only because it had been the source of an argument between my jailers one day. One of the Hunters had left the premises during guard duty to get take-out, explaining how he had been hungry and only one store around offered food to go. He hadn't thought it was a big deal, since there was another guard stationed with him.

I had never seen that particular guard again.

"No, please, let's just eat here," I pleaded, stopping in the doorway. I wasn't ready to go out in the real world. What if a Hunter saw me?

"Why?" Ruarc studied me, one brow arched in challenge, and I suddenly understood what he was doing. He wanted me to communicate, to reveal things about myself. Like why I didn't want to leave the house.

"It's . . . easier?"

Ruarc's scowl grew more pronounced. "No," he snapped. "It's easier with take-out." He grabbed my hand, entwining our fingers in an intimate hold that sent flutters to my belly. "Come."

"Excellent," Lucien interjected, the set of his hard mouth suggesting he found *nothing* excellent right then. "I could use some food myself."

Ruarc let go of my hand and slowly turned. "What?"

Lucien ignored him, quickly ducking around the bigger male when it looked like a fist to the jaw might be imminent.

He walked ahead of us, probably not even noticing Ruarc's angry growls or the way he tugged me along behind him.

"Ruarc . . ." I dug my heels in and refused to move. The grip around my wrist didn't so much as tighten, its owner too in-tune with my movements. As soon as I stopped moving, he did as well. "I really don't want to go." Just thinking about leaving the safety of the house made fingers of dread crawl up my spine.

"Why?" Ruarc asked in a dark voice, making it abundantly clear that I would be going unless I had a valid reason not to.

My brain chose that moment to cease all functionality. "Uh . . ."

"What I thought." Ruarc's angry strides were far longer than my own and after a few steps he ended up dragging me behind him. As we rounded the corner I bumped my hip into the living room table.

"Ow!" My free hand immediately went to rub the offending area, and I almost crashed into Ruarc's back when he came to an abrupt stop.

Silver eyes raked over me, pausing at my smarting hip. Was that a hint of remorse softening his gaze. "Let me see."

"Oh, it's . . . it's nothing." I didn't want to bare any skin in front of him, especially not when Lucien was waiting by the door, an inscrutable expression on his cold, marble face.

A roll of silver eyes, a muttering about 'foolish females,' then I was yanked up into strong arms and pressed against a wide, powerful chest.

"W-what are you doing?" I squeaked, flailing until Ruarc's arms tightened around me in a firm but gentle warning to be still.

"Better this way," he muttered, not really answering my question at all. A gentle touch to my neck was followed by his big paw-like hand as it stroked absentmindedly down my back while he walked.

As soon as he carried me out the door, shadows leapt in

my soul and my fear intensified. The brisk breeze slapping at my face chilled me more than it should have, while the warm rays of the sun barely registered.

"Keys?"

Ruarc's voice renewed my urgency, and I racked my brain trying to think of a reason he would accept as to why I had to stay. I instinctively knew if I told him about the danger I was in he would lock me in the house and never even suggest us leaving again, but I couldn't tell him. And he wouldn't accept a lie.

The warm scent of spring washed over me as Lucien passed us. His skin seemed almost luminous where the sun-kissed its flawless surface. "I have the keys."

I shuddered when Ruarc's arms tightened around me. "I'll drive," he said and waited for Lucien to open the door to the passenger side, then carefully arranged me in the seat. Before I could offer a single protest, he'd locked the seatbelt in place around me and gotten in on the driver's side.

And so, unable to think of a reasonable excuse as to why all of this was completely unacceptable—struggling to think at all when I'd been held in Ruarc's strong, firm arms—we left the safety of the house and ventured out into a world infested by danger, Hunters, and whatever other monsters went bump in the night.

28

LUCIEN

I had to be out of my mind. It was the only reasonable explanation as to why I'd joined this ridiculous venture. Spending time with the human girl was high on my list of torturous activities, but after Ruarc's demented display what choice did I have?

What had possessed the male to offer Challenge for the ridiculous, dishonest, deceitful female? And why did that fact prod at my temper and cause everything inside me to tighten?

A humorless half-smile tugged at my lips.

This. This was why I abhorred emotions. They made you weak, preyed at logic and rational thought. And should they take root and touch your soul, you risked a festering wound that could ultimately destroy.

"W-where are we going?" Hope asked in that quiet, unassuming voice of hers. The voice that screamed *prey* and *innocent* and *helpless*, all things meant to lower a male's guard for the surprise attack that was sure to follow.

Manipulating. Deceiving. The whispered mistrust coiled like a snake ready to strike, originating in the rational part of my brain, the part impervious to the human's beguiling, brown eyes and soft manner.

I flexed my jaw and stared out of the window. Now, more than ever, it was imperative that I discovered the girl's secrets. I could not let her trap Ruarc, nor could I allow my stubborn brother to make a mistake he was sure to regret for the rest of his life.

A life that would be severely shortened if he does what I fear he will.

I clenched my fists, purging my mind of all preconceptions in an effort to better understand the strange female with the utterly ridiculous name.

Hope. Who in their right mind would name their child thusly?

"Depends." Ruarc glanced at me in the rearview mirror. I had opted to sit in the back to easier observe the girl and her interactions with the male she'd set her sights on. "Lucien's not picky." He turned back to the little wench while keeping one eye on the road. "What do you want?"

"W-whatever is closest." Hope wrung her small hands in her lap. The twisting limbs held my gaze as the same unfamiliar feeling I'd choked on when Ruarc's intentions had become clear rose once more. It took great effort to keep the troublesome emotions at bay and my expression closed.

Squash it, I silently commanded. *Feelings are for the weak.*

I was here to observe, to learn, and to make sure Ruarc did not fall for the human's many lies. Why could she not answer a simple question with a simple truth? Why did she shy from innocent questions, evade all inquires as to her past? What dark secrets hid behind those eyes that revealed every lie?

Though, not every word from her luscious lips was a falsehood. I was loath to admit it, but some aspects of her tale made sense. Take her apparent inability to make any kind of decision on her own, for example. Many times I'd watched panic cloud her expression when faced with even the simplest decision, like what to eat for breakfast. A plausible explanation for this debilitating weakness could be a more prolonged captivity than we had first believed, which fit with the few crumbs of story she'd fed Ruarc. Indecision was a failing often acquired after a lengthy period of being denied choices.

Or after invariably being punished for making the wrong ones.

Rage rose with a quickness that nearly stole the breath from my lungs. The amount of punishment it would have had to take for this result to solidify . . .

A growl stirred in my chest.

The light crinkle of abused leather as Ruarc squeezed the life out of his seat reached my sensitive ears and broke through my fury. If I hadn't been trained from an early age to hide my emotions, my face would no doubt have been twisted with the same anger reflected on Ruarc's scarred visage.

I suppressed a snort of disdain. Ruarc never could control his emotions; they ran hot and close to the surface.

Keeping my expression blank, I examined him. The tension around his mouth spoke of words unsaid, the bleakness in his eyes of a quiet anger. He was troubled. Deeply so.

The idiot cares about the girl. A fact that had become painfully plain during his display back at the house. His claim had come as a horrifying surprise, not simply because she was human, but because of the reaction it had inspired in me.

"Burgers or pizza?" Ruarc asked her. There was a warning in his voice the girl would be smart to heed.

When she failed to reply, I found myself leaning forward, interested in what she would say. Too interested.

But I needed to understand the chit. If I didn't, how would I be able to stop her from destroying our pack?

Swallowing hard, she threw me a quick glance before

lowering her lashes and addressing Ruarc, "W-what do you want?"

Ruarc's jaw clenched.

Wrong answer. I sat back, waiting for satisfaction to fill me at the prospect of watching Ruarc chew her head off, but instead, the always-present ice in my gut grew sharp edges, poking and prodding until I had to look down, disturbed when no gaping wound greeted my narrowed eyes.

Claws tearing through tender flesh would have been preferable to any emotional reaction. I was not weak. I would not be weak. Not like my parents, whose inability to shut off their emotions had led them down the path of destruction.

"Not what I asked," Ruarc growled, glaring at the road. "What do *you* want?"

"Oh, um . . ." The girl fiddled with the string keeping the ridiculously large sweatpants in place. "L-Lucien? What . . . um . . . what would you prefer?"

I was stunned. The wench avoided me whenever possible, why on earth would she drag me into this? Unless she was trying to create tension between Ruarc and I to further her own agenda? "Either way," I replied coolly.

"I didn't ask Lucien," Ruarc snapped, hands whitening from clenching the wheel too tightly, "I asked you."

The chit looked stricken. At the sight of her pale face filling with embarrassment, my own hands tightened into fists as impotent rage swam to the surface of my emotions.

What the devil?

Ruthlessly, I crushed the unfamiliar fury until cold indifference was the only thing remaining. It was safe. Familiar. And the numbness it dragged over my ugly soul felt like heaven.

"I'm sorry," Hope whispered. "I-I just don't . . ." She trailed off, blinking furiously down at her lap.

Ruarc sighed, the heavy sound carrying a mix of anger and despondence. "Have you ever had either?"

"Only . . . only pizza."

"You liked it?"

"Y-yes."

"Good." Ruarc turned off the little dirt road separating our home from the acres and acres of untamed land surrounding our house. That land was part of our territory. Our home.

The nearest pizza place was in the small town fifteen minutes down the road. The town consisted of one grocery store, a couple of food places, a tack shop, a feed store, and one clothing store that served all the humans in the nearby area. There were a few other places in the town square as well, but nothing noteworthy.

It never ceased to amaze me how little was needed for humans to gather like a flock of sheep.

While we drove, I found myself studying the girl more intently than I had planned. I told myself it was simply so I could catch her in a lie—eventually all dishonesty was found out—but it was more than that. The delectable spot behind her ear, so warm and sensitive, called to me. And how would those plump lips feel against my skin? Would her core taste as tantalizing as her scent promised?

She was a complex puzzle, all innocence and warmth spiced with deceit and secrets.

My gaze was drawn to her neck. Long, elegant, and much too pretty for a female who spun webs of lies like they were drops of rain to be sipped, one at a time. She fiddled with the string on her pants once more, and I found myself picturing them intertwined with mine, so much smaller, so trusting, clenching with pleasure as I sent her over her peak.

Arousal tore through my ice-walls like a flaming sword. I had to grit my teeth to swallow a groan, and the muscles along my back strained with the effort it took to keep still.

Fool!

"Not far," Ruarc muttered to himself. Every now and again he would direct a narrowed-eyed look at the blasted chit, making her shrink a little further back in her seat while Ruarc gritted his teeth together and pretended her fear didn't make his control slip and his fury build.

After a few minutes of this, Ruarc's eyes were thin slits of glowing silver.

I leaned forward, chafing at the way the girl flinched away from my proximity, and looked at Ruarc's eyes.

His glowing, silver eyes.

"Ruarc." It was a warning, a reminder of where we were, who was with us.

His teeth snapped together inches from my face, a quick warning to back off. The fool had lost his mind.

I turned to the vexing female. She was watching Ruarc with cautious curiosity, not at all what I wanted to see. I would much rather she cowered in the corner than having her pay attention to our exchange and potentially learning our secrets.

"What are you looking at?" My tone was a knife, cutting and flashing steel. Her startled eyes darted to me before lowering, and suddenly I felt completely on edge.

"Lucien . . ." Ruarc's growl was deeper than it should have been. It was an unmistakable threat from one male to another.

I leaned back. "Fine." The car was not the place to hash this out, alas I would wait. Perhaps Ash would be the better person to turn to, he had always been better at communicating with Ruarc than I.

The cold shards in my gut came back. If something was not done . . . Ruarc might decide to pursue Hope.

Not possible. It is not done.

But if he did?

Who was this dratted female who'd invaded our territory

and made a home in its heart? Who had she once been? And who had put the deep shadows in her eyes? A sudden, irrational urge to find the blackguard responsible raged through me. Was she an innocent victim or a darned good actress with a penchant for cruelty? For it was cruel, to make my brothers worry if no dark past haunted her steps. The possibility that she was a spy meant to tear us apart had occurred to me, but what kind of spy told lies that her eyes gave away as soon as they passed her lips?

It does not matter.

I would find out eventually, and either way I would protect my brothers against making a mistake that would end them.

Jerking my head around, I stared out at the passing landscape. This too would end. In a hundred years from now, I doubted I would even remember the name *'Hope.'*

HOPE

The charged silence in the small car had my scalp prickling as I tried not to fidget.

Lucien was unusually quiet. His blank stare drifted over the passing scenery, and every once in a while two lines appeared between his brows, a storm brewing in his cold eyes. I found myself shrinking in my seat, wondering what emotions lurked beneath Lucien's marble mask, and if they would spill over and cut me down with them.

Drawing closer to the door, I peeked up at Ruarc. If Lucien was a storm waiting to happen, Ruarc was a volcano *wanting* to erupt. His jaw was clenched so tightly I was surprised his teeth hadn't shattered, and his eyes were furious slits promising death to any who might disturb him.

Wisely, I kept quiet.

After a few minutes, the car turned and slowed down.

The scenery changed from unending forest to an open, paved square indicating the start of town. A handful of stores stood side to side, filling every inch of space in the allotted area. Their cheery signs advertised everything from food to clothes and even an antique store.

This was it? This was the 'big city' I'd been terrified to enter? It wasn't a city at all, barely even a town. If a Hunter was lurking here . . . Even the thought was ludicrous.

Don't get too comfortable, Hope, the smarter part of my brain warned. Even if it was unlikely, I still had to be careful.

Ruarc parked the car in the middle of the square, claiming one of five parking slots. "Out." His voice was short and clipped.

I'd never met a man with such a commanding presence, such strength. It had to infuriate him how pathetic I was; unable to make even the simplest choice.

Before I could move, my door opened and Ruarc's angry face leaned over me. With a click, he unbuckled my seatbelt, moving back and holding the door open for me.

"Thank you," I mumbled, surprised he was being so nice when he was clearly still upset. Not that I blamed him.

Silently demanding I follow, Ruarc jerked his head in the direction Lucien had disappeared to—a quaint shop with a bright yellow door and a cheerful sign that read: '*Grandma Guccelli's pizzeria.*'

I ducked my head, pulling my dark hair as far forward as I could to obscure my face. Though unlikely a Hunter would be lurking around any of the stores, I'd prefer not to take any chances. Not while the familiar, old fear skated across my skin and played havoc on my insides.

Ruarc's long legs carried him several feet ahead of me, leaving me to scurry after him. It suited me just fine. If someone was waiting for us inside, Ruarc's powerful frame would block me from view.

Just before entering the pizzeria, Ruarc turned. "What're

you doing?" A brow arched, narrowed eyes resting at my slumped shoulders.

With a nervous glance behind, I shifted from foot to foot. Being out in the open was making me jittery. With no buildings in the middle of the square, just those five parking spots, this made an ideal hunting ground if one were scouting for prey.

That's what I am. Prey.

The feeling didn't sit right, and I swallowed hard. "Can . . . can we go in?" I asked in a small voice, hoping he wouldn't notice how badly my hands were shaking.

Of course, his unnerving gaze immediately honed in on my trembling limbs. His jaw went taught, lips compressing. Was he angry with me again? I hated that he always saw my weaknesses.

Instead of commenting, he grabbed my hand, linking our fingers together in the same, intimate hold he'd used earlier. Warmth migrated from his grip, shooting up my arm and settling like a protective layer around my chest.

"Come." His dark mutter was as much a command as always, but this time there was a hint of softness to his voice.

When I hesitated, still looking over my shoulder—just in case someone was watching us—he tugged on our entwined hands, pulling me ahead of him and shielding my vulnerable back with his own body. When he started walking he lay his arm across my shoulder and chest, forearm resting against my collar bone, pressing my back against his front with every step we took.

The restrictive hold should have scared me, made alarm bells go off in my head, but instead, all my muscles relaxed. A sigh slipped between my parted lips, my heart slowed down, and my head felt heavy enough that tipping it back and leaning it against the broad chest at my back felt natural.

I was completely boxed in by broad shoulders, strong arms, and a warm, hard stomach. All I could feel was Ruarc.

All I could smell was his wild, forest smell, both spicy and seductive at the same time.

"You ordered?" he asked Lucien, voice gruff.

My eyes flew open.

When did I close them?

We were inside the little pizza place. Lucien was leaning against the counter, eyes glittering dangerously as his gaze raked over Ruarc's protective hold. "No," he said flatly.

"Anything you don't like?" Ruarc asked me, mouth almost touching my ear. The scruff along his jaw tickled my bare skin, and I shivered.

"N-no," I whispered, breathless with the fluttering feeling he stirred to life. "Oh!" There was something I didn't like. Could I say so? Would it make him angry? What if he wanted it on his pizza and I ruined it for him?

"What?" His hot breath drifted across my cheek.

"I, um . . . I don't really like asparagus." I wrinkled my nose, remembering the foul tasting things from when I was a little girl.

Lucien snorted. "Who in their right mind puts asparagus on their pizza?"

My cheeks flamed, and suddenly the arm around me felt confining. Too tight. I wanted to escape, become invisible, disappear through the floor.

I shouldn't have said anything, I thought, leaning away from Ruarc. Him seeing me like this, like some dumb ninny who knew nothing about the world . . .

My stomach clenched.

To my surprise, Ruarc's hold firmed. He dragged me back against his body, giving me a quick squeeze, before leaning down to whisper in my ear, "Proud of you."

Everything inside me stilled.

Proud of you.

Three little words, uttered in that deep, gruff voice, and suddenly I felt lighter.

Proud of you.

Warmth radiated through my body, and a strange kaleidoscope of emotions crashed into my chest, threatening to make me laugh and cry at the same time. It was silly, getting so wound up over such casual praise, but it was the first time anyone had told me they were proud of me since I was a child. Since the *before*. Before my monster made its presence known. Before I had taken a life. Before I had become a prisoner in every way a person could.

My sight grew blurry, my knees weakened. I shook my head, trying to clear my vision, and gripped Ruarc's forearm with both hands. Words were beyond me, but I managed a squeeze, hoping he would understand how grateful I was for those three words.

For once, sharing my opinion had been worth it.

Lips brushed my temple, a quick, soft nuzzle that short-circuited all my senses and sent my mind reeling.

I lifted a shaking hand, touching the blazing skin Ruarc had caressed with such gentle affection—

No. It's not possible.

I wouldn't, couldn't, let myself believe that. That Ruarc held any feelings for me, least of all affection. If anything, he was trying to reward me for finally doing what he wanted. For sharing my opinion.

But why does that matter so much to him if he doesn't care for you? A traitorous voice whispered, raising hopes destined to be crushed under a wave of reality soon enough.

"Here you go," a kind voice said, ripping me out of my thoughts.

When I looked up, Lucien's glacier stare was fixed on my face. The intent way he studied me didn't stop, even as he accepted five large pizza boxes from an elderly man—maybe in his sixties—who was all wrinkled smiles and bushy brows. His large, kind eyes were the type you automatically trusted, and they crinkled at the corners when he smiled at Lucien.

"Enjoy your dinner boys," he said with another grin, unfazed by the icy glare Lucien shot him in return, and winked at Ruarc. He turned to me, lowering his voice to a whisper, "And you, miss, don't let them boys starve ya! Appetites like wild beasts, ya hear me. Get in there and claim a whole pizza for yourself before there's only scraps left."

With another wink, he scrambled into the back, leaving me flabbergasted while Lucien—carrying the pizzas—marched out.

"Nice guy," Ruarc commented.

Outside, the sun shone, warm tendrils of light caressing exposed skin while a slight breeze ruffled hair and clothing alike.

I didn't feel it.

The only heat my skin absorbed was Ruarc's. The only air teasing at my nape was Ruarc's hot breath as he leaned down to whisper a reassurance in my ear. His scent surrounded me, his protective presence both shielded and chased away fear. From the moment he'd pulled me against his chest until the time he gently deposited me in my seat—buckling me in like I was something precious to be protected—no fear nipped at my heels, and my mind was blissfully at ease.

Lost in my own bubble, I startled when I spotted a young man running toward us.

"Ruarc!" he called out when he was still a good twenty feet away.

Ruarc turned. "Yeah?"

The boy—he looked to be around eighteen, with startling blue eyes, a mop of curly brown hair, and a pointed blade of a nose—jogged over, breathing hard but grinning. "Da got those treats you ordered for Snowflake. The apple cookies and the carrot sticks!"

If I hadn't known better I could have sworn embarrassment hid behind Ruarc's suddenly tight jaw. "You bring them?"

The boy didn't care about Ruarc's grumpy manners. He was still grinning when he produced four decent-sized packets from pockets that looked much to shallow to carry them. "Samples. To see if they're to Snowflake's liking. If they are, Da promised to order a whole bunch, just for you!"

The kid's enthusiasm almost spilled over, and I found myself smiling as I listened to the exchange.

"Thanks." Ruarc grabbed the horse treats and held out a couple of bills.

"No way," the boy said, both hands held up like he was warding off evil. "You guys keep our little feed and tack store in business almost all by yourselves. Da would have my hide if I took money from you for a sample."

Ruarc grunted, but put his money away. "Coming down tomorrow for Ash's order. It in yet?"

"Packed and ready to go!"

"Good." Ruarc turned, looking like he was about to close my door and head around to the driver's seat when the boy spoke up again.

"Wait!" His face suddenly flushed, gaze moving from Ruarc to me and back again. "You got a . . . a lady with you?"

I shrank back, bubble bursting and leaving nothing but unease behind.

The glare Ruarc shot the kid was accompanied by a dangerous growl.

"Whoa!" Blue eyes widened. "I just wanted to warn you."

"Yes?" Lucien's voice was pure silk.

"Some guy . . ." The boy cleared his throat. "Some guy has been going around making people uncomfortable. A stranger. He's been acting real shady, even old guy Gus thinks so. He told Da to keep Jenny home 'till the stranger's gone."

Ruarc crossed his arms and stared.

"Uhm . . . Word 'round town is he's staring at all the ladies." Here the boy threw a quick glance my way. Ruarc's stare became a glare. "Looks too intently. Bad intentions, that one."

"What does he look like?"

The youthful face scrunched up. "Pretty normal looking guy. 'Bout my height, dark hair, clean-shaven. He's got a tattoo at the back of one hand, one of them skulls, but pretty-like." He shook his head. "Ma says no matter how he tries to dress it up it still looks like a gang tattoo."

Whatever else they said was drowned out by the roar in my ears. *Jan. The kid is describing Jan.*

If I'd been alone I would have screamed. Since I wasn't I held my breath and hoped if I did it long enough I'd either pass out or be so distracted by my burning lungs that the terror spiking my sudden burst of adrenaline would magically disappear.

Jan. Jan was here. He was here, looking at women. Hunting.

Hunting me.

Bile rushed up my throat and I was forced to swallow, forced to breathe, forced to experience emotions that had once threatened to break me.

Ruarc closed my door and I was left in silence. Horrible, deafening silence. I was vaguely aware of him and Lucien speaking outside—I couldn't hear them but I saw their mouths moving out of the corner of my eye—but their presence failed to bring me any sort of comfort.

The Hunters were looking for me.

I knew they would be, I *knew*. So why couldn't I breathe? Why couldn't I think? Why were red spots dancing across the back of my closed eyelids?

A ragged gasp flew from the bottom of my lungs.

The Hunters were here. They'd . . . they'd found me.

29

HOPE

By the time Ruarc and Lucien got back in the car, my terror had given way to a welcome numbness. There was no doubt in my mind Ruarc would have sensed my fear—somehow they always seemed to know how I was feeling—and would have poked and prodded at the still open wound until I broke.

"What did Ash order?" I asked absentmindedly, not listening to the reply. Something about horses. Food?

My head was spinning. Each thought passing through my mind a fleeting, elusive mist I couldn't quite grasp. I barely felt the churning in my stomach, the tightness in my chest. Being numb was . . . good.

Until it wasn't.

Ruarc had been talking. I realized this the same way I'd once realized it had been five long years since I last saw the sun; with a detached sort of panic, knowing it mattered but unable to push through the fog clogging up all the space in my skull.

I drew in a deep breath.

I couldn't afford to panic, couldn't afford to go numb and

close my eyes to my surroundings. If the Hunters were here . . .

It doesn't mean they've found me.

True. The place would be crawling with Hunters if they knew I was near. So what did it mean? Why was Jan there?

My throat burned with the need to empty my guts. The thought of him, of Jan . . .

A shudder wracked my body.

"You cold?"

I looked at Ruarc, trying to read his expression, but I struggled to focus on his face. "No."

And I wasn't. Cold was doable. Cold was a sensation you could recover from, something you could combat with a warm bath or some hot chocolate. I wasn't cold. I was something much worse.

"You're trembling." A snarl in his voice.

I couldn't bring myself to care.

Were the Hunters searching all the towns around the compound, starting with those closest and working their way out? That seemed the most logical answer given what I knew. It would mean they'd move past this area in not too long, wouldn't it?

If I hadn't already been sitting I'd have sagged to the ground.

Lucien's cool voice drifted through my mind, but the words made no sense.

A warm hand grabbed mine. Ruarc. "What's wrong?"

"N-nothing." I had to leave. As soon as the Hunters had finished searching the areas close to the guys and it was safe for me to move on, I had to leave.

A deep, throbbing hurt squeezed my middle so hard I momentarily lost my breath.

When . . . when I left—

My heartbeat suddenly pounded at my temples. I squeezed my eyes shut and pulled my hand free.

In a few weeks I would leave to find my uncle—my breath turned to frost in my lungs, my fingers curled in my lap—I'd do what my father had told me. I would find my uncle and . . .

And what?

Put his life at risk? Somehow convince him to help me take down the Hunters? Make him help me in my search for whatever it was the Hunters feared? And how would I do that, how would I find what they were afraid of when I didn't even know if it was a person or a thing or an organization or what!

My eyes stung.

"What is wrong with the female?" Lucien angled his body between the two front seats, his cold gaze making my skin prickle where it touched.

"Don't know." The words sounded mangled. Hard and straddling a knife's edge of temper. "Hope? Hope!" Ruarc snapped, and the harshness of his tone startled me enough to snap me out of the fog I'd been lost in.

"Sorry. I . . ."

Lucien muttered something under his breath, and Ruarc growled.

"What. Is. Wrong." Not a questions as much as a demand. I had a feeling he'd be glaring at me if he wasn't driving and paying attention to the road.

The town was far enough away now that the tree line began thickening, the road growing narrow as the forest grew dense. We were almost home.

Home.

"I . . ." Tears pressed at the back of my eyes, but I refused to let them fall. "I remembered something. But I don't want to talk about it," I added, giving as much truth as I could without revealing too much.

Another growl from Ruarc, an annoyed sound from

Lucien, and though neither of them pressed—to my surprise —the rest of the drive passed in taut silence.

I kept my hands in my lap and stared out the window until we reached the big ranch house that had come to represent a feeling I struggled to put into words. A feeling I'd have to give up to keep the guys out of reach of the Hunters. And a feeling I'd probably never have again, not with the impossible task I'd set before myself.

Find the Hunters' weakness, use it against them, make sure they can never hurt anyone ever again.

But I was only one person. One weak, cowardly person. What difference could I really make?

The car stopped. Lucien grabbed the pizzas and Ruarc came around the car and helped me out before I could move on my own. When his hand found my lower back, my soul thawed and I had to fight the impulse to lean into his body and allow his strength to carry my own weak heart. Thoughts of Hunters, of my uncle, of the few captives left at the compound, they all drifted to the back of my mind, disappearing behind a door with a padlock and flashing warning signs screaming 'stay away.'

For today, at least, I would pretend none of the rest mattered. That I was home. That the guys were my family and that I was not a monster. For today I would pretend the noose around my neck wasn't tightening with every second I stayed. That leaving was a choice, rather than an inevitability. Only for today.

"You are back," Ash stated when we walked into the living room. He rose with the fluid grace all the guys seemed to possess, looking first at me, then to Ruarc, standing so close the heat from his big frame swept against my skin like unrelenting waves of a tropical sea. "Did everything go smoothly?"

Ruarc grunted. "Brought pizzas."

"Hmm." Ash glanced at Lucien as he marched into the kitchen leaving the five pizzas on the massive, living room table. "Would you like to eat here, Hope?" he asked, peeling away a layer of my soul with those piercing eyes of his. "There is a new movie I think you may enjoy, and I thought we could all watch it while we eat."

Ever since I'd let it slip that I loved movies—quickly muttering something about being hungry and fleeing before I could reveal the sad reason why—Ash had surprised me with a new movie every day, tracking my likes and dislikes with an attentiveness I found startling.

I swallowed hard and looked up at Ruarc. "W-what do you think?" He wanted me to make my own decisions, but if I said yes and Lucien didn't want me there I'd only create conflict between them when he returned.

Ruarc took his time, keeping me hostage with his stare as he searched my face. Finally, after what seemed to me to be years, he inclined his head tersely. "We will watch," he told Ash, keeping his eyes locked on mine.

I lowered my gaze. My body felt strange. Heavy and uncomfortable.

With a harsh exhale, Ruarc led me to the middle seat on the massive couch. "Sit," he grumbled, then turned to Ash who sat down on my right. "Jason?"

"On his way in. He had a problem with a Stray."

The atmosphere grew chilly. Ruarc took the seat to my left and casually threw one arm across the headrest behind me. With one foot resting on the opposite knee, he should have looked relaxed, at ease, but something about him made me think of a dangerous predator biding his time.

"Does . . . does Jason work with animals as well?" I asked, hesitating at the weird look passing between them.

"No." Ruarc's response was clipped, making it clear the subject was closed.

"Oh . . . Okay."

A sharp sigh had me crane my head looking straight up into Ruarc's luminous eyes. They narrowed. His mouth opened, like he was about to speak, but without a single word it snapped shut with an audible click of teeth, and he remained quiet.

The next few minutes passed in uneasy silence. Busy avoiding eye-contact, I used my hair as a shield and peeked at the guys through the dark curtain. Ash watched Ruarc with a quiet intensity while Ruarc grumbled angrily under his breath.

When Lucien came back—plates stacked in his one hand, glasses in the other—his cold eyes unerringly shot to the one part of me touching Ruarc; the thigh pressed against his.

"You seem to have taken my seat," he said coolly.

Ruarc bared his teeth in a chilling grimace. "Mine now."

The hardness in Lucien's expression made me draw back, but he said nothing, only placed the plates and glasses on the table and sat down in a comfortable looking chair a little to the right of the rest of us.

"Honey, I'm home!" a cheery voice sang from the entrance. The tanned man owning said voice kicked off his shoes, flashed me a grin, and stopped. Nose twitching, Jason took one look at the pizza boxes and threw himself over the stack like a lion taking down a gazelle. Picking through them, he drew out the third from the top. "This is mine," he said, grinning at me when I gaped at him.

"Why that one?" I asked.

He smirked, tapped his nose with his index finger. "Superior nose, love. I could smell the pepperoni."

For some reason, his words made Ruarc growl, a low, threatening sound that didn't seem to phase Jason in the least.

"I will get us something to drink." Ash's calm voice was like a balm to the tension in my shoulders but as soon as he left the room, Jason claimed his seat, scooting closer until I was almost sitting in his lap and dragging another low growl from Ruarc.

Trying to diffuse the puzzling tension, I turned to Jason. "How did you smell the pepperoni when all the pizzas were on top of each other, and all had the lid on?"

His eyes sparkled. "Ah! Genetic superiority, love. But don't fret," he added with such dramatic flourish I couldn't quite stop my mouth from pulling up into a reluctant smile. "Very few are blessed with my excellent genes so you needn't feel bad. Just look at Lucien, over there. Terrible genetics."

I gasped, whipped around to look at the man whose beauty intimidated me every day. "Jason," I scolded in a soft whisper, "you know that is far from the truth!"

Lucien's perfectly sculpted brow rose, his mouth curling with disdain. "Excuse me?" he said in a voice so cold I shivered.

"I . . . I just meant . . ."

The longer I stared at him—I couldn't look away, my instinct screaming that danger lay ahead—the frostier his eyes grew. "Enchanted by beauty, are you?" There was no expression on his face, no emotion. "It is to be expected, I suppose, from someone who has none of their own."

My mouth fell open on a silent protest. What did he—

Had he just said—

Oh my god . . .

I cringed. I knew I was no great beauty, but to say it to my face . . . and in front of others, guys I admired and—

An eruption of terrible snarls and growls followed Jason and Ruarc as they leapt from the couch.

Those sounds . . .

Inhuman.

"You cold-hearted bastard!" Ruarc roared, teeth flashing

dangerously. He stalked forward, seemingly incensed at Lucien's lack of response.

Jason snarled words were no less hard, "You should be ashamed of yourself, Lucien! Telling lies and hurting a female for no other reason than—"

"Fools." With a voice that was as quiet as it was lethal, Lucien rose. "You are both fools. Trailing behind the wench like pups not yet out of their dens. What possible reason . . ." The words died off, and I felt his gaze like a burning touch.

Lifting my head, I saw him staring fixedly at my cheek.

Miserable, I swiped at whatever had drawn his attention. Something wet touched my finger.

Am I . . . am I crying? Aghast, I drew back and felt the rest of my face.

Dry.

Instead of relief, my insides shriveled. One tear. One tiny little tear and I'd proven yet again how weak I was. How stupid.

Why had I not laughed at Lucien's insult? Being called ugly was far from the worst thing that had been thrown my way. So why did it hurt? Why did my face burn and my throat feel tight and scratchy?

"I . . ." Lucien shook his head, dismay etched across his marble face as he stared at me.

Ruarc swiveled around, followed Lucien's gaze. A fierce frown twisted his expression, a low, threatening sound spilling from his throat. He marched back to where I sat and gathered me in his arms. If he felt how stiff I was, he didn't show it. He simply pulled me onto his lap.

Heat engulfed me as his big body curled around me. Protecting me. Shielding me from Lucien and his harsh truths.

"He's a fucking moron."

I stiffened, hating that I'd caused strife between them, but Ruarc only held me tighter, growling into my hair.

W-what are these sounds?

Then Jason was there, no trace of his previous humor left on his suddenly hard face. While Ruarc held me, murmuring foreign words into my hair, Jason leaned down and cupped my cheek. "He is wrong," he whispered, tilting my face to meet his determined, amber eyes. "You are beautiful."

Wrenching my head away, I tried to swallow my disagreement. The harsh sound that escaped my lips was foreign and ugly—not quite a sob but close enough to make me wish I was alone.

Jason's lie, well meaning as it was, felt like a kick to the chest—and I knew what that felt like, having experienced several. It was almost worse than Lucien's hateful words, for at least Lucien was honest in his dislike.

"Go." Ruarc's command was a harsh exhalation, the words carrying an inflexible decree my legs wanted to follow even though I knew it wasn't aimed at me.

For once, Lucien didn't say anything. He left in silence, despite Ash's low, "Lucien," from the doorway, and not a sound was heard until a door upstairs closed on a soft whisper.

Surrounded by warm, male bodies, I should have felt trapped. Afraid. But instead, I buried my head in Ruarc's strong chest and tried to ignore the hot shame that insisted I retreat and lick my wounds in private. His hold on me tightened, almost as if he knew my thoughts, and I sniffled. There was something to be said for being held like this.

Jason was leaning in as well, stroking my back in slow, soothing circles. And while I was here, surrounded by his closest friends, his family, Lucien was upstairs. Alone. After having been chased out of his own living room by a woman he detested.

Guilt sat like lead in my belly.

A deep sigh, a slight dip in the couch, and Ash's familiar scent washed over me. He smelled faintly of the horses he worked with every day, but underneath there was the smell of male; a musky, appealing scent that somehow carried with it the feeling of endless plains and a beckoning sun.

"Hope . . . *banajaanh*," he began, sounding as if he was in pain. "That had nothing to do with you. Do you understand?"

I shook my head. Of course it was because of me.

A heavy sigh, a warm touch. "What he said is not the truth. Not the world's truth, and not his truth."

Another lie. I gripped Ruarc's shirt tighter—comforted by the low rumble echoing in his chest—determined to shut out words bringing only more humiliation. Did they think I couldn't handle the truth? Did I appear so weak that I couldn't even stand to be called *ugly*? Appearances didn't matter. Life mattered. Freedom mattered. Having people who loved you . . .

"You must understand . . . Lucien has had a tough life. Sometimes he reacts to words and situations we find innocent, because they are a trigger for him. What he said had nothing to do with you and everything to do with the past." Earnest words spoken in a calm, quiet voice. They buried under my skin, soothing the hurt I had no business feeling in the first place.

"Ash is right, love," Jason injected. "Ignore Lucien. His words don't matter. Not when no one here agrees."

"It's okay," I said softly. "You don't have to lie to me. I know I'm not pretty, and that's okay. Really," I added as three pairs of eyes stared at me in disbelief. "I'd actually prefer it if you were all just honest and admitted you agree with Lu—"

"Not a chance!" Ruarc snarled, squeezing me so tight I let out a pained whimper.

His arms immediately loosened.

"Love . . ." Jason ducked his head to catch my gaze. "We don't agree with what Lucien said. I doubt he even agrees with himself, the wanker." A crooked smile tugged at the corner of his lips. "Why would we?"

336

Their vehement disagreement left me bewildered. I threw a quick glance at Ash, seeing nothing but an inscrutable expression, before looking back to study Jason. A slight flaring of his eyes, a heated emotion peeking out before bleeding into nothingness.

What did Ruarc think? With his chin resting on the top of my head, his broad frame cradling my much smaller form, I couldn't see his face. But I could feel the tension in his hard body, the tightening of his powerful muscles.

"Thanks, guys," I whispered. I couldn't bring myself to actually believe that they found me even close to beautiful—and I couldn't allow myself to care—but despite my lack of faith in their words, the fact that they cared enough to comfort me, to offer lies that surely tasted sour on their tongues was heartwarming in its own way.

Ash patted my hand. "Let us eat." The pizza boxes were still spread out before us on the table. A delicious scent drifted up, teasing my nostrils when he opened each lid. "We all prefer different toppings. Have one from each, if you want. Then you can see which you like."

"She'll obviously prefer the pepperoni," Jason said. The playful sparkle in his amber eyes was back, and I was grateful for the distraction.

"The Hawaiian is pretty decent." Ash nodded to the one closest to him.

"Are you kidding me? It's got pinapple. *Pineapple*." Jason shuddered. "That's like ordering pizza with slices of apple or banana or raspberries. Have you ever heard of raspberry pizza?"

"No," Ash said, face impassive. "But it sounds delicious."

Jason sputtered, a sound between a laugh and a moan fighting free, and though Ash didn't laugh, one corner of his mouth tipped up. I couldn't help the small smile I flashed in response.

There was so much food on the table, I'd have thought it

could have fed us all for at least a week if I hadn't already seen how much these guys could eat.

"Which one is Lucien's?"

Ruarc's hand squeezed my hip. "The vegetarian one."

"He . . . he doesn't eat meat?"

"He does," Ash replied. "But he prefers his pizza without."

"Weirdo," Jason said, but there was no heat behind the insult.

"Shouldn't we wait for him?" When no one spoke, I tried again. "He should be here with you guys, what happened wasn't . . . it wasn't a big deal."

"Was a big deal," Ruarc snapped. "Made you feel bad, made you c—"

"He will be down when he feels like it, Hope," Ash said and shot Ruarc a look I couldn't decipher. He gestured to the food. "Will you not eat?"

I looked over each pizza in turn, trying not to think about Lucien sitting alone upstairs while I was spending time with his family. Everything looked great, even the pizza covered in so many colorful toppings it could have been a piece of art. Biting my lip, I considered my choices while I waited for the others to start.

And waited.

And waited.

"A-aren't you gonna eat?"

"Ladies first." Jason flashed me a grin before waggling his brows at the pepperoni. "Be good little pepperoni and maybe the pretty lady will choose you."

The false compliment made me cringe, but it wasn't enough to distract me from the choice in front of me.

"I'll have . . . um . . ."

"That one," Ruarc said on a soft growl, pointing to the box on the far right. "Pass me two, Ash."

I could have kissed the grumpy man right then and there!

A curious tilt to his mouth, Ash did as Ruarc requested,

and soon I had a scrumptious-looking slice of my own.

In two bites half of Ruarc's pizza was gone. He jerked his chin at the TV. "Movie."

The rich sound of laughter filled the air and warmed my chest. Head thrown back, eyes glittering with humor, Jason looked so warm, so alive that I fought the urge to throw my arms around him and hug him until the strange feeling in my chest disappeared. "I see you're comfortable," he teased Ruarc, pointedly staring at the big palm that had somehow found its way to my thigh.

In typical Ruarc fashion, a grunt was his only reply.

The flutters in my chest eased at the first bite of delicious pizza. "This is so good!" I hummed to myself as my tastebuds exploded.

"You can never go wrong with ham, love," Jason agreed. "Although, if I were you, I'd choose the pepperoni. It's the best seller for a reason."

I peeked at his plate; two uneaten crusts and a half-eaten slice. "I can see that." I dared a teasing smile. "I guess now I can see how you sustain your bulk."

"Are you calling me fat?" Jason narrowed his eyes and gestured to various hard muscle on his body. "Do you see this? It's all muscle, baby."

Ruarc snorted, which led to a healthy debate where Jason listed all the reasons why he was the best looking of the guys, while Ruarc rolled his eyes at regular intervals, and Ash just shook his head, occasionally interjecting a quiet rebuttal of Jason's points.

As I leaned back, the warmth of Ruarc's protective hold seeping into every part of my body, I was amazed at the glow I felt inside. If my heart could have danced, this would surely be how it would feel; this luminescence in my chest, expanding and pushing, until I felt as light as a flower petal in the wind.

It felt like home.

30

JASON

You are beautiful.

The words, *my* words, continued to spin circles in my mind all through the night and into the next morning. It was her eyes, I decided. Those startlingly wide eyes. They were too kind, too pure for whatever brutalities she'd suffered.

My insides turned liquid as I remembered my first sight of the brutal gashes tearing at her legs. Blood had still been trailing down from the deep cuts around her calf when Ash tended it, her leg swollen, the skin shredded.

I made a mental note to ask Lucien how her injuries were healing—though I'd scented no blood or pain—and followed Ruarc down the slope leading to Lucien's workshop. The door was opened, the angry sound of a saw being dragged across wood sliced through the air.

The phone call that led us to have this impromptu meeting had not left us with much patience to spare.

"No." Lucien's clipped voice came between a brief break in the violent sawing. "Still no trace."

Ruarc cursed, knowing as well as I did what that meant.

Every night since the day Kieran had taken Hope, Lucien had been hunting, and every dawn he'd returned empty handed. His relentless pursuit had surprised me given the circumstances, but it didn't matter. Not when he hunted prey nearly impossible to track.

Once inside, the scent of freshly cut wood rose to greet us, and when I kicked the door shut, sawdust caught in the draft and danced in the air.

The bright light from the morning sun shone through the big windows, illuminating a drawn-looking Lucien hunched over his worktable.

"Were you out all night again?" I asked.

"Yes."

"Still looking for Kieran?"

The hand holding the wood steady clenched. "What else would I be doing?"

"I don't know." A grin tugged at my lips. "Practicing the art of seduction?"

Lucien turned. "What?"

"Hey, I don't know what you do with your free time, and I don't judge."

Ice filled his eyes. "Do you not?"

Was he referring to last night? That quick, my humor drained. "Only when people act like dicks."

Hope carried her scars for all the world to see—the way she agonized over the smallest choice, the way she cringed at loud noises, the way she often made herself look small, as if she could disappear, become invisible if only she could curl her shoulders just so—and yet no sharp edges stood ready to cut the hands that reached for her, no bitter words left her tongue when provoked, no malice lay in wait beneath her kindness.

How did some people come through horrors coated with kindness and compassion, while others became tainted by it?

I gritted my teeth against the familiar sensation slithering past my ribs to attack my heart, and forced my lips to form a carefree smile.

"This what you want to waste time on?" Ruarc crossed his arms, one finger tapping at the opposite forearm. Though he spoke to us, his gaze drifted to the window.

Thinking about Hope?

I sure was.

Making the sweet human smile had become something of a game to me. A game where the prize was witnessing the fruit of my labor and knowing *I* was the reason her lips parted and her small, white teeth flashed.

"No," I admitted, and though his eyes still glittered dangerously, Lucien turned back to his project.

"Kieran is proving as elusive as the rest of his kind. Even I cannot find him," he said.

"I am not sure finding him should be a priority." Ash moved to stand next to Lucien, watching as the other male worked. "He did let her go, which he would not have done unless it was as he said; a case of mistaken identity."

"I don't really care why he took her, only that the bastard did." It still burned that he'd knocked me unconscious, that I'd failed to protect her when it had mattered the most.

This was just one of the many reasons why it was dangerous to keep a human around. These new laws being tossed around made matters worse, not to mention the unpredictability of the Council. Even if a male *wanted* to pursue someone like Hope, it would be impossible.

Can't pursue her without telling her what we are, can't tell her unless she's bound to us.

A shot of adrenaline spiked my heartbeat. Why was I thinking about pursuing our guest? And why the fuck did that make my dick hard?

Disgusted with myself and knowing the horror and fear Hope would feel if she knew what I was thinking, I tore through the ugly part of my mind until I was satisfied there'd be no more surprise hard-ons.

At least not during this meeting.

"Want him dead for laying hands on her," Ruarc snarled under his breath. His gaze remained fixed on the sights beyond the window, the muscles along his shoulders lay in corded ropes below his shirt. "But he didn't hurt her. And now his nest owes us."

I hated it when the grumpy asshole used logic instead of his volatile emotions. I hated it even more when he was right. *Dammit.* "Looks like you get to stay home tonight, Lucien," I said.

He was done with the saw and put the wood away in favor of plucking a half-formed wooden figurine off the nearest shelf. A short knife found its way into his other hand, and he began carving. "We will see."

Ruarc snorted and the nail on the finger that never stopped tapping grew sharp. A drop of blood welled where it pierced his skin. "Get to it."

"You all heard the call," Ash said. "Our only option is to prepare as best we can."

"No," Ruarc growled, still staring through the window. "They can bloody well turn back around."

"I would turn them away if I could, Ruarc, but they are thirty minutes out and if we do not wish a war we need to deal with the issue now, before the Assembly vote."

"Fuck the Assembly," Ruarc spat.

I nodded in agreement. If the other packs were dumb enough to vote for this new law, if the Council were too pigheaded to put a stop to it, they could all drown in their own blood for all I cared. Rederick, the alpha of the South-East Colorado pack, was a fanatic, and anyone that followed a fanatic was an idiot.

"Fool notion," Lucien said. He continued to carve his figurine, the knife making long, swirling marks I recognized as feathers. "If there is a war do you imagine we will be safe, that *Hope* will be safe?" He cut Ruarc a cold glare. "You forget we are also in Colorado. Our territory is not so far removed that the battle won't spill over. And even if it missed us . . ." He carved a deep groove, the beginning of a beak. "If Rederick's law passes no humans will be safe, and I, for one, shall not stand by and see them all slaughtered."

Ash placed his hand on Lucien's shoulder, and though he didn't smile, his eyes warmed.

"There won't be a war." Ruarc finally tore his gaze away from the window and turned to face us. "I'll take care of Rederick."

"You would have to go through his entire pack first," I said.

A dangerous light entered the stubborn male's eyes. "So be it."

"Absurd." Lucien smacked his palm against the wooden bench, put down his work, and turned to face Ruarc. "Do you imagine we would allow you to go by yourself, Ruarc? They are fifty strong!" He drew in a deep breath. "Even if we all went, even if we requested aid from Blake's pack, our chances of winning are slim at best."

Ruarc replied with a wordless snarl.

Ash shook his head. Lines of strain had appeared at the side of his mouth, and when he spoke he barely moved his lips. "Even without Rederick, the proposal would be brought to the Assembly. There are too many who hunger for the old ways, and the Hunters provide the fuel needed to ignite outrage. We need to meet with Blake and gather our allies. Without a strong opposition the Council may decide to invoke the old laws."

"Can they do that?" I asked.

"Yes," Ash replied. "They have done so in the past and may do it again if given cause. They were never meant to have the power they do, and if its threatened . . ."

"War," Ruarc growled.

"War," Ash agreed.

Something built in my chest, a furious, bitter sound I

forced myself to swallow. If Ash was right—which he tended to be—we had no choice. "How long will they stay?"

"One night."

Too long.

I looked to Ruarc. The big male shook his head, sending his mane of hair flying. "A night too long."

Dragging a hand through my own, much shorter hair, I frowned. Did Hope prefer longer hair?

"There is nothing to be done about it now," Lucien stated in his usual, cool voice. "Blake is not a radical, and I do not believe he will attempt to harm the human."

"He better not!"

A deadly silence descended on the heels of Ruarc's snarled decree. It grew, expanded through the workshop, too taut, too tense, like a balloon pushed to the edge of its capabilities. It hovered there, ready to explode into shards of silver, ready to cut, to burst, to destroy.

"He will *not* harm Hope." A quiet, quiet promise, fangs and claws carved to become words. The silence imploded, and all that power, all that taut tension drew back into the male responsible.

There was a reason Ash was our leader, a reason he was equally feared and respected among our kind. Though he'd never once spoken of it, we all felt the power he struggled to keep contained. The same power that drove lesser males to insatiable, unspeakable violence.

Mahír fáinn.

"Well then," I said, shaking off the last of my unease. "What's the plan Mr. Bossman?"

Lucien rolled his eyes.

Was it my fault that I was the only one who found that funny?

"Ruarc and Lucien, you should be there when they arrive. Jason, you keep Hope away from the house. Do not let her out of your sight."

"Aye, aye, Captain." I shot Ash a mock salute, grinning at Ruarc's snarl and the glare he shot my way as he stalked out, probably heading back to the house to squeeze in some time with our little human before our *guests* arrived.

The enforcer was needed while I was free to play my games and try to lighten the shadows darkening Hope's bright light. If only I could show her the way, teach her to stuff her past into a small, metal box and shove it so far back in her mind that she'd never have to look at it again.

"Do you know who Blake is bringing?"

Lucien took a moment to consider Ash's question. "Zakhar, most likely. Perhaps Dakota if they are planning another stop."

Ash stilled. "Dakota has an uncle up north. If Blake thinks those family ties will help them reason with Mason . . ."

The pack ruled by Mason Bellard up north was rotten to the core. A few years back Ash had been passing through on one of his yearly treks, and the stories he'd come back with were so atrocious even Lucien hadn't been able to hide his disgust.

"They'll be here soon," I interjected, wanting to end this conversation so I could join Ruarc in seeking out some Hope time. "Anything else we should expect?"

"The stables," Lucien said with a jaw that looked stiff and unyielding. "They cannot sleep in the house."

Ash nodded, then, "And keep Hope out of their sight."

"Do not let her wander on her own. Who knows what trouble the wench will stir up."

"Lucien . . ."

"She's a menace!" he snapped.

I rolled my eyes. "Okay so . . . We keep them away from Hope, make sure we're on the same page with this whole Rederick thing, warn them about Mason, and convince them that sleeping in the stable is for their benefit." I grinned. "What could go wrong?"

31

HOPE

QUEENIE NUZZLED MY PALM. THE SOFT SWIPE OF HER EAGER muzzle as she searched for hidden treats was almost enough to distract me from all the questions buzzing through my mind.

The phone call Ash had received shortly after breakfast had caused quite the uproar. His short, clipped replies had held all the guys' attention; Ruarc had looked on the verge of bursting from his chair while eyeing the phone with a destructive glint in his stormy, silver eyes, and Jason had lost the charming grin he'd aimed my way just seconds before.

After Ash hung up, he'd muttered a quick goodbye while Jason had said something about seeing me in a few minutes.

As I'd looked out the window, staring after their fast retreating backs, I'd wondered what all the fuss was about. They clearly hadn't wanted me hearing whatever they were going to discuss—having entered a building far out of my hearing. Maybe it was some kind of business meeting?

"You're much easier to understand, aren't you Queenie?" I murmured, scratching under her chin. I was glad I'd chosen to come out to the stables while the guys were busy. It was so peaceful in here, the only sounds soft and natural; horses chewing and softly blowing air out their noses, quiet nickers and the occasional scraping of hooves. I could understand why Ash spent so much time out here.

Queenie's ears flickered just as my own ears picked up the sound of raised voices. My mouth went dry.

Calm down, Hope, don't let your imagination run wild, I told myself sternly. Just because someone was upset didn't mean trouble would follow.

With light steps I made my way to the open door, popping my head out an inch or so—just enough so I could peek around the frame.

A furious Ruarc stormed across the field separating the stables from the tall, majestic hedge hiding the house. When his glowing eyes found me he came to an abrupt stop, mouth moving in what I could only assume was a low curse. Running a hand through his hair, he closed the distance between us a little too quickly for my comfort.

"Where have you been?" he demanded, taking hold of my shoulders and giving me a slight shake. His voice was rougher than usual, a hard edge biting into his words.

"H-here?"

Despite his obvious anger, he treated me with care. His hold, though tight, was not harsh. It struck me as odd how such big, rough hands could be so gentle.

Ruarc growled, a sound that seemed a mix of ire and relief. "Couldn't find you," he muttered. For a brief moment, he leaned down, letting his forehead rest intimately against mine. I breathed in his enticing scent, forgetting all my worries as I let him hold me.

"Sorry," I offered when my brain caught up with his words. "You were all busy so I thought I would visit Queenie."

Ruarc jerked his head back, eyes narrowing dangerously. "You came by yourself?"

"Uhm, yes?" Who else would I have gone with?

"You shouldn't go alone," he gritted out through a clenched jaw, tugging me under one arm and glaring across the landscape beyond the stables. A vein pulsated near his temple.

"I know the way back," I muttered when he kept his angry gaze glued to something in the distance. "And I wasn't snooping."

Narrowed eyes shot to mine, the unnatural glow beautiful despite his anger. "I know," he snapped. "Just don't—"

A shadow came barreling around the corner of the barn, nearly crashing into us. "Ruarc," Jason hissed. Puffs of hot air drifted over my cheek as he panted, standing so close I could count each individual fleck of gold in his eyes. Eyes that were rapidly changing between warm brown and glowing amber. "Why the hell did you slam the door in my face? Didn't you see me?"

I inched away from Ruarc, my attention glued to Jason's inhuman eyes. That . . . that couldn't be normal. Eyes weren't supposed to change color like that, and they definitely shouldn't glow.

Ruarc bared his teeth. "I did."

"I searched the whole house before I realized—Oh, forget it." Jason threw his hands up and shook his head. Then he turned to me, a slow smile spreading over his face as his now brown gaze stopped its perusal and stared at the top of my head. His grin widened as he plucked something out of my hair. "Hay."

"Hi," I replied, confused when his smile grew.

"No, love. Hay." He twirled the offending piece of hay between nimble fingers.

"Oh. Right." For reasons I didn't understand, my eyes locked on those hands, a blush staining my cheeks.

Ruarc growled again, a more menacing sound this time. "C'mere." He gripped my hand and tugged.

I stumbled back into his body, his right arm ending around my waist, our sides plastered together.

"Oh," I breathed.

So warm. He was so very warm. Heat emanated off his big frame like he was a giant, live coal. My cheek pressed against the coarse material of his shirt, the chest below rock hard and solid. Everywhere we touched, I burned like I was being branded.

The scent of him swept over me. Rich. Masculine. Wild.

I looked up, past his broad shoulders, past his scar, past the dark scruff covering his jaw.

My breath hitched.

The look in his molten, silver eyes made something low in my belly clench. He dipped his chin, stared down at me in a way that was purely Ruarc; pushing, demanding, sheltering. And offering all of himself for me to judge.

A flutter in my chest, my heart skipping a beat before racing, racing, racing . . . If it beat any faster I'd pass out.

Ruarc's gaze moved to my parted lips. Parted to allow the rush of air struggling to escape my tight lungs.

Everything inside me clenched.

What is happening to me?

Right before my chest could explode, Jason snorted. Whatever strange spell had seized me in its exhilarating hold collapsed. I looked away, blushed when I spotted Jason rolling his eyes at Ruarc and muttering something under his breath.

Ruarc didn't seem bothered in the least. There was a grim sort of satisfaction in the way his lips tugged up at the corners, displaying two sharp canines.

Those look a little too *sharp, don't they?* I thought, staring at gleaming, white teeth that rivaled any wild predator's. As I watched, his lips firmed, hiding the canines from view. The hand holding mine clenched once before relaxing, and he began walking us toward the house.

Jason cleared his throat, coming up on my other side. "Would you like to watch a movie with us, love?"

"A movie? I—Yes, I'd like that." I was still shaky. How could these men, these relative strangers, inspire such intense, foreign sensations? What did they mean? Why did my body feel warm and shivery at the same time, while flutters contracted my belly in a way that was far from unpleasant?

"Don't concentrate so hard, love," Jason teased. "You don't have to pick the movie. Ruarc will." He clapped Ruarc on the shoulder, expression so impish he suddenly looked five years younger.

Ruarc glared back. "Pup . . ."

Jason snatched his hand back, and I wondered if there had been some hidden warning in that one word.

"Relax, you big grump." A quick laugh and a dodge as Jason moved far enough away that Ruarc's lazy swipe missed him. "Your taste isn't *that* bad. You selected a good movie back in ninety-three . . ."

Opting to ignore the teasing, Ruarc opened the gate between the hedges that separated their backyard from the rest of their property, and led me through. His attentiveness brought a smile to my face and a lightness to my steps. The way his big palm engulfed mine, the way his other hand held my elbow, guiding me over a root here and a big rock there, the way he kept scanning the landscape as if making sure no threat loomed in the distance made me feel protected. Cared for. Intellectually, I knew these gestures of protectiveness wouldn't save me from an attack if the Hunters found me, but somehow, being near him, having him take care of me in his very Ruarc-y way . . .

It made me feel safe.

Of course, it couldn't last, and when that feeling of safety shattered, it shattered with such ferocity that I wondered how the two men next to me hadn't heard it break.

I became the marble statue I'd compared Lucien to, unable to move, unable to breathe, unable to do anything but stand frozen and stare.

"God dammit!" Ruarc snarled, glaring at the strangers in our backyard. Jason leapt ahead of me, both of them using their bodies to shield me from view.

To shield me . . .

I was still a statue. My lungs screamed for air and my tongue felt thick and dry. But now that they'd tried to hide me, I knew the threat was real and terror punched down my throat. It was like trying to swallow the ocean; for every bit of water pouring into my stomach, a gallon more waited its turn. It would never end. I'd be left a bloated corpse, drowned by the kind of primordial fear that left you shivering in a corner, unable to open your eyes for fear of what you'd see.

Someone said something, but all I heard was a buzz.

My mind swam with images, drowned me in possibilities, each one worse than the next. Then my treacherous brain conjured an image that shriveled my lungs until what little air they'd been able to draw through my tight throat died. An image of the Hunter I despised the most.

All I could see was him, his dark thin frame as he leaned over me, glasses almost falling off his crooked nose while he scribbled notes in his journal. All I could smell was blood. My blood. Metallic and sharp, rapidly cooling on skin that felt frozen. Knives. So many knives. Silver gleaming in the low, yellow light from the overhead lamp. And all I could hear was the scrape of his pen. The sound of something being crossed out. The sound that meant it would start all over again.

My lungs burned, and far, far away, I heard voices.

"They're early." Jason. But not the normal Jason. A hard-edged, chilling Jason.

"Fuck!" A snarl. Violent and furious. Ruarc.

I blinked, and though the silver knives disappeared, I saw only blackness. Blackness tinged with red spots.

"Jason!" A hiss. Then hands on my shoulders.

"Hope? Hope!"

Gathered against a wide chest, Ruarc's wild scent replaced the smell of my blood. My knees buckled, but I was already close to the ground.

He's kneeling?

"Deep breaths, Hope," Ruarc said. A huge hand came to lay flat against my chest, pressing ever so slightly.

My lungs contracted, and my mouth opened in an airless gasp.

"Breathe." The heat from Ruarc's palm seeped into my skin. Somehow, it melted the constraints squeezing my lungs, and the first, thin slice of air was gulped down. "There you go, *m'eudail*. Again."

I gulped down another mouthful, my burning lungs screaming.

"Is she having a panic attack?"

I sensed rather than saw Jason squatting next to us. He grabbed one of my hands, brought it to his mouth.

Ruarc ignored him. "You're safe," he murmured in a gruff voice, stroking my face with his free hand. "Take a slow breath in, hold it for a second, then out."

I did as he said, his steady focus stabilizing me. Once. Twice. Finally my lungs stopped their painful protest, and my breathing grew smoother.

I opened my eyes.

"Thank you." My voice was hoarse and wispy, the sound of helplessness made into being.

Too weak. You're too weak, Hope.

Why couldn't I let go of my fear? Of what had been done to me?

I *knew* it wasn't realistic to expect to be one-hundred-

353

percent trauma-free after only a bit over a week, but did I have to be *this* pathetic?

"Hope . . ." A finger nudged my chin up, forcing me to meet Ruarc's gaze. It burned. "Don't be sad." A command, but a soft one.

I blinked back sudden, unbidden tears, and then my face was buried in his chest while Jason stroked my head.

"You don't have to be scared, love," Jason whispered near my ear. "The males that are here . . . We know them. They aren't here for you. In fact," he added, pausing midstroke, "they were scheduled to arrive. Remember Ash's phone call this morning?"

I nodded jerkily, Ruarc's shirt rasping against my wet cheek. The fact that they were expected slowed my racing heart. If they'd called in advance, they couldn't be too dangerous. They wouldn't have been allowed entrance if they were.

At some point, I must have begun to trust the guys, because I believed they wouldn't knowingly put me in danger.

"You see, love," Jason said with forced cheer. "There is nothing for you to worry about."

Pulling away from Ruarc, I brushed the hair blocking my view aside. "Then why—" I took a deep breath, gathering my courage. Why was it so hard to question them? To believe that I deserved answers? "Wh-why did you react like—Why did you jump in front of me?"

The way Ruarc tensed made me think Jason was under-playing it when he said, "It just took us by surprise, love. That's all. They weren't supposed to be here for another hour or so."

"Really?" I looked at Ruarc, trying to read the emotions playing across his rugged features. Mouth set in a grim line, expression taut, slashing eyebrows pulled low over glowering eyes . . . He looked ready to commit murder. More so when the vein at his temple began pulsing, and I could hear the grind of his teeth.

But then he looked down at me and I was too slow to hide the way my hands shook. There was a sound, like thunder in the distance, before his expression softened and he put his hand at the back of my neck. "You're safe." The statement held utter confidence and was devoid of any trace of doubt. It was said the same way you would explain to a child seeing the dark for the first time that no matter how it seemed, the sun would always rise again tomorrow.

I slumped, allowed myself to relax, to give into the hand at my neck pulling me closer. "Okay," I whispered into the crook of his throat. "Okay." More fear drained away as Ruarc dragged his nose over my temple.

A strangled sound, half growl and half something else. I pulled back, peeking up at Jason's frowning face, and something akin to shame boiled up and left a ragged tear in my chest.

What am I doing?

Before I could dwell on any foreign feelings, Jason tensed and let loose a furious growl. Ruarc jumped to his feet, spun around, and snarled with such savage aggression that all the hairs on my body rose.

"What a warm welcome," an unfamiliar voice drawled.

I scrambled to my feet but couldn't see the owner of the voice—Jason and Ruarc stood with their backs to me, blocking the stranger from view.

"Move." Ruarc's voice was warbled, like he was trying to speak with his mouth filled with glass.

Someone else laughed, a tinny sound I instantly disliked. "What are you hiding there, man?"

Ruarc stepped forward, his whole body vibrating with fury. Before he could throw himself at the newcomers and tear them to pieces—and there was no doubt in my mind that was exactly what would happen if a confrontation ensued—Jason put a hand on his shoulder. Their eyes met. Ruarc's glowing with violence while Jason's showed steely restrain. Silent communication seemed to pass between them until Ruarc jerked his chin in a gesture only Jason understood.

"Mind your manners, Tim," the first voice said, much harsher now than the laid back humor of before.

"Blake," Jason inclined his head, the movement stiff. "Why are you not at the house with Ash?"

"Heard something here, thought maybe it was Ash coming back from the stables."

I tried to peek around the guys, but Jason's firm grip on my arm stopped me in my tracks. "He's not."

"I can see that." There was humor in Blake's voice, warmth too. It was clear he knew my guys.

The *guys, not* my *guys*, I silently corrected.

Sudden snarls erupted, and I stumbled back. My foot got caught on something, and down I went.

"Hope!" Jason's frantic call would have worried me if I wasn't concentrating so hard on calming my erratic heart. Three strange faces hovered above Ruarc's shoulder as he knelt in front of me, feverishly running his hands all over my body.

"You hurt?" he growled.

I shook my head, unable to make my dry throat cooperate enough to form words.

"Sorry if we scared you, darling," the voice I knew as Blake drawled. He was tall, almost as tall as Ruarc, with striking features you rarely saw outside magazines. The way he carried himself made him seem older than he surely was, maybe around thirty-five? His short, black hair was tousled with a carelessness that bordered on indifference—and who could have blamed him? A man that good-looking didn't need to primp.

To his right, a veritable giant stood guard. His expressionless face, bald head, and dark eyes made him seem downright scary.

"It's . . . it's human!" the man with the thin voice gasped. The one they'd called Tim.

My gaze flew to his mouth, not believing he'd said what I thought he had.

Did he call me an 'it'? And said I was human, like that was abnormal?

I froze while my gaze was still locked on his lips. Was it some kind of cruel prank? Did he somehow sense the monster inside me, calling me human to throw me off?

A sneer twisted his face, and a low, threatening sound rose from a frame I would have thought much too thin to create such a sinister sound. He took a step toward me, menace radiating from every inch, lips peeling back to reveal teeth that—

A terrible roar tore through the air, hanging there like a dreadful storm about to descend and wreak havoc on the world. Ruarc was a blur. He crashed into Tim, and the other man went down, limbs flailing and eyes wide.

Ruarc put a hand around Tim's throat and snarled.

For a single moment, they were still. Then Tim bared his teeth and looked around Ruarc. He found me, beady eyes dragging up my front with a slow insolence that made my skin crawl. "The human bitch shou—"

All hell broke loose. The noises they made would forever stay with me. The meaty thuds of fists striking flesh. The quiet, almost soundless grunts they made when a punch landed. The thunder crashing in Ruarc's chest.

Though Tim had gotten up when Ruarc had followed his gaze to look at me, it didn't take Ruarc long to knock him back down. Once more, Ruarc had Tim by the throat, but instead of giving up, the other male clawed at Ruarc's arm, leaving deep, bloodied gouges.

"J-Jason?" I tugged on the nearest sleeve, unable to look

away from the brutal battle. Though Tim was still fighting, trying to reach Ruarc's face with one hand and throwing dirt at his eyes with the other, he stood no chance. Lying there, he had no choice but to accept the merciless beating being delivered in grim silence.

Nausea bubbled, my stomach cramped. I looked to Jason, hoping he would put a stop to the fight, but to my disbelief, he looked completely on board. Mouth an unforgiving line of grisly satisfaction, the steel I occasionally glimpsed in his eyes returned in full force.

He had no intention of stopping this fight.

This was not a side of him I'd been allowed to see. This steely-eyed stranger had hidden beneath Jason's quick wit and playful smiles. What other aspects of himself did he hide away from the world?

A guttural cry tore from Tim.

"S-stop," I croaked, terrified Ruarc would kill the man. Not because I harbored any love for Tim, but because I didn't want Ruarc to go to jail!

Or commit murder, my mind added as an afterthought. No one deserved to carry around that sort of guilt.

The scary man, the one I didn't know the name of, jerked around to stare at me. There was something in his eyes, something dead and flat that terrified me to my core. Whatever it was, he didn't let it bleed into the rest of his expression, almost like he'd contained it to his eyes, to that one part of him, and wouldn't let it touch anything else.

I shivered.

"That's probably enough, don't you think?" Rather than be upset at the beating of one of his friends, Blake sounded bored.

Growling, Ruarc delivered one last punch, got to his feet, and slowly stepped to my side.

He wouldn't meet my gaze.

A gasp flew out before I could stop it. "Your hand!" Blood

coated the skin, the crisscrossing of white scars invisible below the dark red fluid. Reaching out, I carefully ran my finger over his knuckles in search of broken bones and open wounds.

"Not hurt," he grunted in that gruff way of his.

I gaped at him, realizing all the blood belonged to Tim.

The gashes on his arms . . . I could no longer see them. Had my eyes played tricks on me? Was it not wounds but blood from Tim sprayed in a weird pattern?

"Not bad," Jason said. He shot me a grin, dissolving the tension among the guys left standing.

Ruarc bared his teeth. I wasn't sure if it was meant to be a threat or another attempt at smiling, but I guessed the latter. "Pup needed to learn," he growled, casting a disgusted glance at the motionless man on the ground.

"Is he . . . is he dead?" While the aspect disturbed me, I was fully prepared to help Ruarc find a shovel and hide the body.

Blake threw his head back and roared with laughter. "Dead? Hah!" He kicked at Tim's foot. "Get up, boy. Show the lady how very alive you are."

Fascination warred with disbelief as I watched Tim peel himself off the ground. Once he was standing, swaying like he hadn't quite caught his balance, he sent me a look filled with so much hate I automatically took a step back.

That time, Jason was the one who threw the punch, sending Tim flying a few feet before he landed with a dull thud.

I cringed at the sound, but when bile rose in my throat it was not in response to Tim, but something else. A feeling of wrongness. Of something I should have already felt but hadn't.

My gut kept churning, and I spun in a circle, looking for what was missing. What was wrong.

Could it be—

An ugly feeling slithered up my spine, and then I knew. The thing wrong with this picture was . . . me.

I'd just seen a man beaten within an inch of his life, and I'd barely reacted. In fact, it hadn't really bothered me too much. If Tim had only submitted, Ruarc wouldn't have—

Wouldn't have what? Why was I not more bothered when violence of any kind usually sent me fleeing? Was it Tim? I'd taken an instant dislike to the man, to his lanky build and hateful eyes, but that wasn't reason enough. Did it have something to do with the evil inside me?

Dear god, is the monster affecting me more than I know?

"Well, Zakh, it looks like Ruarc and Jason share your opinion about Tim." Blake grinned at the scary, bald giant. *Zakh*, I presumed.

The big man scoffed and pivoted in the direction of the house, the graceful movement so fast it was almost a blur. The only other person I'd seen who could rival his speed was Lucien, but with Zakh's bulky build, I'd assumed he would be slow.

"Wh-where's he going?" My whispered question was aimed at Ruarc, but it was Blake who answered.

"To find Ash." Blake glanced at Ruarc's tight jaw before his speculative gaze landed on me. He perused me with a distant interest, an interest that seemed to grow when Ruarc dragged me into his side, put an arm around my shoulder, and glared. "As you may have guessed, I am Blake," he said. "I'm an old friend of Ash's." His lips spread in a movie-star smile. "Who might you be?"

"Oh. Uhm . . . I—" Before I could finish my sentence, a dark growl spilled from Ruarc.

"Her name's Hope," he said as the delicious vibrations of his aggressive warning danced across my skin. "All you need to know."

Blake's smile widened, showing a hint of sharp fangs—did all the men have fangs these days? "How fascinating."

A low chuckle broke the rising tension. "Don't mind Ruarc. He is just a smidgen"— Jason held up two fingers less than an inch apart—"protective."

Blake laughed, a deep rolling sound of humor that untangled a piece of the anxiety in my belly.

A very small piece.

"Sounds like Ruarc," Blake said with another warm smile. He had a dimple on the right side of his mouth. It was cute, but my observation was more of a 'huh' than any real admiration.

Another growl, then Ruarc grabbed my elbow and hoisted me in the air. I landed snug against his chest, one arm around my back and one under my knees.

I considered protesting, but I felt safer with Ruarc's arms around me.

"Might as well go back to the house," Jason said before Ruarc could take off. "Better she's around all of us now that they've seen her."

32

RUARC

The rise and fall of Hope's melodic voice filtered through my brain—assuring me she was all right—while I glared at the office door. Was their fault, damned interlopers, that I was stuck here forced on the alert while Jason took advantage of my preoccupation.

Every time he made Hope's voice lighten with contained laughter, my emotions were at war. On the one hand, the sound of her happiness was a balm to my battered senses, but on the other hand . . .

Another male was making my Hope smile.

Unacceptable.

Jason chuckled, a rich sound of seductive amusement he'd no doubt practiced to perfection. My fists curled under the kitchen table, wanting nothing more than to give that jaw a good, solid punch.

"Quiet," I snarled at him, unease piercing my chest when Hope startled. I turned to her, trying to make my voice milder. "Not you."

She nodded, the corner of her lips lifting to a half-smile. It took all my willpower to tear my eyes away from the softness I saw in her eyes and back to the door I was guarding.

It was imperative no one exited without my knowledge. Especially with *Tim* there.

I growled.

Jason grinned. "What do you think upset him now? The sound of birds singing? The wind blowing? Me breathing? Oh, definitely me breathing," he said, without giving me the satisfaction of wincing under the fierce scowl I leveled at him. Instead, the smug bastard shot me a challenging grin that had me considering leaping across the table and biting his nose right off.

It would grow back . . . in a week or so. The thought made me bare my teeth in good humor. The little female wouldn't like looking at him while he healed.

"He's scary when he looks like that, isn't he, love?" Jason's conspiratory whisper reheated the anger simmering in my gut. Anger that grew at Hope's lowered gaze, the hint of a smile curving lush lips.

Damned pup!

Fury melted on my tongue and grew teeth of its own, but before I could give Jason's shin a good kick, the door opened.

I snapped to attention, tuning out even the warmth that was Hope. The first person out the door was Blake, of course. The Riverland's alpha barely glanced my way before locking eyes on Hope.

My fangs lengthened in my mouth, a fact I took full advantage of when I gave him a good look at the weapons I would use to tear his throat out should he come near my little female.

The madman smiled at me. A full, warm spectacle of a smile that made me instantly suspicious.

Where the fuck has all the fear gone?

Males used to piss their pants when I turned my considerable temper in their direction. Not shoot me grins or smile like they were pleased.

363

I grumbled under my breath, watching as Blake whispered something to his second, Zakhar.

There was a male I didn't mind; a vicious bastard who shared my reluctance to yammer when a frown was just as effective. From Russia originally, Zakh had immigrated long before the cold war, finding his particular talents better appreciated in a war-torn America. Some said he'd fought for the South, but I knew better. If that asshole had been fighting for the South, the world would have been a much different place.

Zakh nodded and followed him outside my line of vision. I bristled, torn between going after them to make sure they weren't plotting anything nefarious, and staying here with Hope.

I stayed.

Lucien walked out next. The cold fury swirling in his green eyes when they locked on Tim pleased me. Lucien allowed the smallest space between his body and the door, forcing Tim to squeeze against the wall in order to pass. As the weaselly male slipped past, Lucien grabbed his arm and spoke in words too soft for me to pick up.

A grim smile pulled at my lips. Whatever had been said caused the weasel to lose what little color he had left, his Adam's apple bobbing like a duck in a pond with each nervous swallow.

Run, weasel, run.

He scurried away with my glare burning into his back. One of his fisted hands twitched. Could he feel my desire to give chase? He'd threatened Hope. *Threatened* a female under *my* protection.

Claws burst from the tips of my fingers and dug into the wooden table. I grabbed a bowl of fruit, using it to cover the marks I'd left, then curled my hands into fists to hide the proof of my violent upheaval.

Guilt rose when I remembered the care Lucien had taken

with crafting the furniture I'd just gouged, but I shook it off, pushed my chair back and jerked my chin at Jason. "Stay here."

He'd guard the little female while I was gone.

I left the kitchen before Hope's questioning gaze could halt my step. Inside the office, I unclenched my hands so my bloody claws would stop tearing at my flesh.

"All good?" I asked Ash when he closed the door behind him.

"I am not sure," he said. He walked past Lucien and took a seat on the wide couch Jason had insisted on moving in here, claiming the wooden seats were not comfortable for the long hours we sometimes spent in here. "There is a restlessness in Blake I have not sensed in the past. He is eager to put a stop to Rederick's plotting, but he does not wish to wait for the Council to gather."

I grunted. I knew how Blake felt. I, too, wanted to hunt the Black Mountain Pack, wanted to feel their blood dripping between my fangs before they could bring their ridiculous agenda before the Assembly. Too bad a little bloodshed wouldn't fix anything.

"Blake will wait," Lucien said, a chilling expression on his face as his gaze locked on the front door. "I don't believe he's our biggest issue."

Ash frowned, a sight so rare I did a double take. "I agree. The youngster Blake brought, Tim—"

A vicious snarl ripped from my chest before I could stop it. "Pup's all *wrong*."

"I agree," Ash said. "And I think Blake sensed it, too, long before today. A youngster that aggressive toward a female, regardless of species . . ." The air grew chilly. "No, this was a test for him, perhaps to see how he would act around another pack. And the way Zakh glared at him during the meeting indicates failure."

Lucien's upper lip curled. "Good riddance."

"Even if Blake waits, which I believe he will, there are those that agree with Rederick," Ash said. "Blake does not have enough allies to guarantee the vote goes in our favor."

I bristled. "How stupid can they be?"

"We haven't exactly made friends," Lucien said with a glance in my direction. I'd been the enforcer for as long as we'd been a pack, and I was not known for my diplomatic skills. More than a few half-dead strays had limped away from our territory—even more hadn't been able to leave at all—and while strays didn't hold grudges, Alphas did.

Damned if I hadn't pissed off nearly all of them at some point.

"No, we have not." Ash sighed and ran a hand through his hair. It was rare for him to show this much emotion. I experienced a flicker of regret for all the times I'd lost my temper with potential allies in the past. "Ruarc, you and I will need to schedule a trip over to Jorgen's territory. Although they are few, they have ties with many of the larger packs. We need as many of them on our side as we can get, or this may be the start of another war."

"Can't leave," I muttered. "Take Lucien."

"Why me?"

"Don't care about Hope."

Lucien crossed his arms and sent me a piercing look. "And I suppose you do?"

"Yes."

"So much so that you can't stand to be parted from her for a day?"

I squared my shoulders and glared back. "Yes." Our short time together had taught me many things about the little female. A pure heart beat in her chest. A bright soul shone in eyes that revealed deep emotions and too many nightmares. She cared for others, maybe too much, and not enough for herself. Next to her I was a brute, a savage, a giant, scarred male that spoke too little and snarled too much. And yet she'd held my hand, uncaring of their rough calluses and ugly scars. She'd let me hold her without stinking of fear, and instead of pity or disgust, understanding flashed across her expressive, heart-shaped face when she stared at the disfiguring scar twisting up my jaw and pulling at my lip.

"You are being utterly ridiculous." Lucien turned pale, green eyes to Ash. "She's human. *Human*! She's been here for less than two weeks and he's already this attached. What happens if she returns his sentiments? What happens if the Council finds ou—"

"Back. Off."

Ash stepped between us. "Ruarc is no youngling, Lucien. We cannot control his actions."

"You mean to do nothing while he destroys himself?"

All my muscles tensed, got ready to leap past our Alpha and tackle Lucien to the ground.

He dares imply she wouldn't be worth it?

Female like her was too good for me. I'd settle for being a . . . a *friend*. Protector. Wanted to-*needed* to chase off those shadows clouding her bright eyes. Damned if I'd let Lucien's ridiculous fears stand in the way! As if she'd ever want me back.

A vicious snarl scraping up my throat.

"Calm yourself, *niijikiwenh*." Ash's gaze was steady, the bright blues of his eyes resembling a calm sky, draining some of my anger. "You know Lucien means well. And you, Lucien . . . There are better ways to illustrate your concern."

I grunted. It was difficult for us all to put aside our protective instincts. The bonds between brothers, especially the ones you chose for yourself, didn't allow for carelessness or indifference. I understood his need to protect me, but the idea that I needed protecting from Hope?

Ridiculous.

"By the time I am proven right it will be too late."

"Take your fucking opinion and shove it!" I snarled back.

367

Lucien's frosty glare filled with cold, detached anger. "Use your head for once, you stubborn fool! You know nothing about the wench, besides the drivel she sees fit to share and the lies spewing from her deceitful lips. You've detested liars your whole life, when the devil did that change?"

A white hot rage roared through me. Gums itched, canines grew. Pain burned through nerve-endings in my fingers, and when I looked down at my clenched fists, blood ran in shiny rivulets down my scarred skin. That I'd pierced my own flesh barely registered as the roaring in my ears grew. All my focus was drawn to the male threatening my place with Hope. The male I was now convinced wanted me out of the way so he could steal my place at her side.

Never!

"I know she's kind," I pushed out. Talking was a bitch when your teeth weren't made for a human mouth. "I know her compassion is greater than her sense of self preservation. She's brave and—"

"Brave? The girl is scared of everything. She stammers when she speaks and she jumps at all sudden movements." Lucien ground his teeth together. "Calling her brave is like claiming the rain is dry."

"She's brave," I snarled. "Maybe it's not the loud kind of courage of a male preparing to fight, but it's courage all the same. She threw herself at Kieran to save Jason, for fuck's sake!" The memory of that folly never failed to stir the coals of my fury. The thought of what could have happened . . . I bit my cheek, tasted blood, drew in three breaths.

Lucien crossed his arms and stared.

"To have gone through what she has . . ." I shook my head, marveling at her quiet strength and her will to continue fighting to survive when most would have given up. "She escaped," I reminded him.

"You do not know what she has been through," Lucien replied with no inflection to his tone. "She claims to have been abused. Claims to have escaped. For all we know she was never held captive to begin with."

Fury snapped my spine straight, and I saw red. My next words were said with a killing quiet that Lucien better fucking hope he heeded, or my teeth were going to find his throat. "Never, *never*, question her abuse to me again!" My voice rose. "You think she abused herself? You think she stepped on a bear-trap on *purpose*?"

"Where are her scars?" Lucien retorted, the careful control he always kept wrapped around himself slipping. "If she was abused and held captive, shouldn't she be riddled with scars? Humans do not heal like we do!"

For a second, he made me doubt—where *were* her scars? —but then I pictured Hope's pale face, her wounded eyes and the expression of utter torment that came over her whenever she noticed that she gave away her fear, and my doubt vanished in a cloud of certainty.

My little female has faced enough pain in her life. I won't add to it by questioning the few secrets she has trusted enough to share with us.

No. Fucking. Way.

"I'm done with this." I turned my back on them both. Ash should have fucking joined in and supported the female. No way he'd failed to see what I had.

I'd lived longer. Fought longer. But Ash saw things others didn't. Wise. Perceptive. Controlled. He *knew* things other didn't. Understood them.

So why the fuck didn't he chime in now?

Lucien watched me through narrowed eyes but said nothing. I stopped glaring at him in favor of glaring at Ash.

"Give us a moment, Lucien," Ash said.

Out of the corner of my eye I saw Lucien give a stilted nod, then he left. The door closed with a quiet click.

"I do not want to leave Hope either." Ash's admittance softened the feral edges of my temper. "The thought of leaving her with less protection does not sit well with me. Not now before we know all that has happened to her."

I offered a grunt of agreement.

"But Ruarc . . ." A wave of unease went through me at Ash's penetrating stare. "We need the votes. Think of Hope. And think of the other innocents that may suffer should Rederick win."

He was right. Goddammit, he was right. "Fine. But we're back in twelve hours." This I wouldn't budge on.

Ash nodded. "Twelve hours."

Fixing my gaze at the opposite wall so I wouldn't have to look at him, I muttered, "Sorry about the allies."

"No need to be. If you had not done what you did, I probably would have. And that would not have ended well."

Depends if you consider a bloodbath an acceptable outcome.

"Is Jason with Hope?" Ash asked after a brief pause. The thread of unease in his voice made my hackles rise.

"Yes," I growled.

"Good. Let us go out there and see how our guests act in a more casual setting."

ASH

While Jason kept Hope contained to the kitchen and away from prying eyes, Lucien had gathered our guest at the front of the house. When Ruarc and I joined them, Blake was leaning against the sturdy rail curving our rather narrow front porch, while Zakh glowered at Tim with his arms crossed and his back against the house.

He was not the only one.

Tim was staring sullenly at one of the white-painted columns supporting the porch-cover, his right hand clenching around the wood while the left curled at his side. It looked like he was doing everything in his power to avoid

Lucien's frozen gaze without outright staring down at his feet and conceding power.

"What do you know of Rederick's supporters, Lucien?" Blake asked after the silence stretched too thin.

Lucien shifted his gaze to Blake, and Tim shuddered with the reprieve.

I listened with half an ear as the others spoke, choosing instead to contemplate our options. The next Assembly was several weeks away. Weeks in which the Black Mountain Pack could wreak their havoc *if* they were brazen enough to act without the Council's approval.

Doing so would mean war. Countless lives lost. Packs destroyed and families ruined.

Will another war be the key to stop the rapid spread of the rot that infests so many of our brethren?

Both sides would suffer heavy losses, but the side that struck first would lose more as the merciless hand of the Council punished those without regard for our laws.

Could we afford to strike first? Could we afford not to?

I did not know. Clarity remained hidden in shadows of gray, and I found myself . . .

Preoccupied.

As it often did these days, my mind circled back to the human we harbored; the female with the broken wings who carried secrets and guilt so heavy they threatened to crumble what remained of her defenses.

If forced into a war, each member of our pack would need to fight, and none would be left to protect her when her demons came knocking.

I cannot put her safety above my pack, yet I cannot conceive of leaving her to fend for herself.

A choice that should not have been difficult remained an impossible puzzle.

"—same mistake again." The sneering voice dragged me back to the present, my attention settling on Tim.

Had he already forgotten his fear?

Blake's hard eyes dug into the younger male's back while Zakh stood silent and still, guarding his alpha while keeping the new pup close at hand. With each word the youngster spoke, Blake's expression tightened.

"*What* did you just say?" Ruarc spoke with a lethal quiet that had both Blake and Zakh take a step back—removing themselves from the equation and letting us know they would not protect their pack-mate.

"You heard me!" Tim's eyes were wide, nervous, but he refused to back down. A youth's folly. "I've heard a lot about you. You are rather famous, you know."

"I wouldn't go there if I were you," Blake said.

When Tim ignored his alpha, Zakh shook his head in typical enforcer fashion and stared stonily ahead.

The lack of repercussion was not a go-ahead, as Tim seemed to believe, but rather the pack getting tired of him repeating his mistakes. He would learn or he would not, but either way, Blake and Zakh were done with their coddling.

"Ruarc the raider. Ruarc the king," Tim taunted, stepping head to head with the male who had already beaten him into submission once that day. His thirst to avenge his humiliation looked a lot like stupidity. "Ruarc, the famous leader who got his face disfigured because he was too—"

"Stop that!" A distinctly feminine cry of outrage cut through Tim's tirade. As one, we all turned. Chest heaving, an angry flush staining her cheeks, Hope glared at Tim while Jason looked over her shoulder with a sheepish smile and a shrug, as if to say; 'what did you want me to do?'

"Stay out of this, filthy human!"

Hope's gasp was lost in the fog that followed. A violent urge to punish Tim's insult rose, and with it came a feeling, a terrible, icy cold that washed over me, through me, and threatened to take my body as its own.

No, I told it, while its unyielding present battered at each cell, its rage a poison in my blood. *No.*

Rather than give in, I honed the violence turning to ice in my veins into a controlled force of will, and when my gaze pinned Tim in place, I allowed him a glimpse of what lived inside me, of what prowled beneath the surface of my skin.

Beady eyes widened and bloodless lips parted in a silent scream.

I blinked, and he stumbled back, drops of sweat gathering along his hairline.

"Y-you—"

No one paid Tim's stuttering any heed. Not when Hope hissed—the sound that of an angry kitten filled with all the confidence of a full grown tiger—and stepped forward.

"You take that back," she shouted. The female who'd spent most her time haunted by fear now stood with her feet apart, indignant fury snapping her brows together and making her eyes spit fire.

Tim sputtered, glanced at me.

I said nothing. Did nothing. I was captivated by the iridescent soul shining in her eyes. By the angry flush across her cheeks. By the conflicting emotions I often sensed at war within her.

Her hands shook, but she did not let her fear stop her.

Neither would I.

"Take it back!" Hope cried again.

Tim scoffed, having gained confidence from the lack of interference. "Why would I do that? It's only the truth, you are a filthy hu—"

"Not that!" Hope interrupted, taking a small step toward the fearless youngster who kept insulting her. "About Ruarc! He isn't disfigured at all! Scars show character! They are a badge of honor showing that the person carrying them has been through—"

Tim threw his head back and laughed.

Teeth clenching, I fought the urge to knock Tim down. This was Hope's battle, and her defense of Ruarc was beautiful to behold. Not only was she doing what a true packmate would do, but she was saying something we had all been trying to convince Ruarc of for years.

"You gotta be kidding me!" Tim chortled. "Look at him." He gestured toward Ruarc, not seeming to comprehend the danger he was courting. "I am sure he was ugly even before his face was mutilated, but with that scar? He's hideous."

Ruarc showed no outward reaction to the taunt. He kept his stony gaze locked on Hope, waiting for her reaction.

He thinks she will agree with Tim.

A terrible, high pitched shriek of rage ripped from Hope. If I had been in my other form I would have lowered my head and whined at the dreadful sound.

"Y-you monster!" She stood nose to nose with Tim, having moved when we were all busy shrinking away from her battlecry. Jason quickly hurried to stand beside her, keeping one eye on Tim at all times. "He is *not* deformed!"

Ruarc's strangled, "Hope . . ." bounced off her. The angry female did not look back, nor did she give any indication she had heard him.

Fearless. In defense of others, she proved fearless.

She jabbed a finger into Tim's chest, the larger male staring at the offending digit with equal parts disbelief and disgust. "*You're* the deformed one! Twisted up and ugly inside. Who attacks someone based on their looks for no reason at all?"

"No reason?" Tim gaped, the sneer he'd sported faltering. "The fucker almost killed me!"

"It seems the lesson he tried to teach you did not take." Lucien's cool voice cut like deadly claws ripping at prey's flesh, making not only Tim blanch, but Hope as well.

Casting Lucien a quick glance, she took a deep breath, her

small, tense shoulders lowering a half inch or so, and turned back to Tim.

I watched her trembling hands tighten into fists, and admiration swelled. She shook, and yet she did not back down. Fear would not conquer her now, not when she was rising to the defense of another. She felt it, yes, but it did not rule her.

Many of our kind made the mistake of thinking fear equaled weakness. But fear was imperative to life, to living. The day I woke up utterly without fear would be the day I had lost everything, for it would mean I either had nothing left to lose or that I stopped caring about the consequences of my actions.

"Ruarc only—only did that to protect me," Hope stammered. "If you're upset about what happened y-you should t-take it out on m-me, not him."

A thunderous silence followed her demand, broken only when Lucien made a choked sound of disbelief.

Tim glared with ugly intent. "Oh, believe me, I will!"

The color leeched out of Hope's skin, her lower lip trembled.

Four low growls threatened death, Tim's only warning should he try hurt our Hope.

Our Hope?

He glanced at Ruarc, hateful eyes gliding over the other male's face, lingering on Ruarc's tense jaw, glowing eyes, and the stony expression he kept firmly in place. When Tim looked back at Hope, a stubborn tilt angled his narrow jaw. "Did you know Ruarc was married?" he asked, looking pleased when the brave little female recoiled like she had been hit.

He was trying to hurt her . . .

Slowly, afraid I might lose control should I move too fast, I let my gaze move from Hope to Blake. The color left his face, and he shook his head once. He did not care what happened to the worthless male at this point.

Good.

To Tim, Ruarc may have looked uncaring but that could not have been further from the truth. His past was a vicious scar every bit as visible as the ones gouged into his skin.

"You're married?" Hope turned to Ruarc, the anguish in her expression a testament to the budding feelings I had suspected she harbored. Only for him, or—

Air hissed past my lips. My mind closed.

"I was." The words were barely audible through Ruarc's clenched jaw. "Not anymore."

Tim levelled a nasty smirk at Hope. "And here he goes again, being led around by his dick. The last bitch that tricked him got his face. I wonder what you will take from him?"

Hope went ashen. Her hands trembled, her shoulders hunched, and she averted her gaze.

Guilt. Guilt and pain.

A seed of doubt sprung.

What was she hiding? A future betrayal? A deadly secret? Or was the reason Tim's remark got such a strong reaction that *she* was married?

Something hot and uncomfortable speared me.

Has my objectivity been obliterated by the little human? Am I putting my pack in danger by letting her stay with us?

The burden of responsibility dragged against my neck like a heavy anchor caught at the bottom of the sea. It tugged and pulled, demanding I act before its chain ripped into my throat.

So I looked at her, searched the soul shining in down-turned eyes, and despite the guilt written across her expressive face, I could not believe she would seek to harm us. She was too good, too selfless.

She had risked her life to save Jason. And she had defended Ruarc when doing so no doubt terrified her.

She would not betray us.

Tim opened his mouth, malice twisting his lips.

"Hope will take nothing," I said, and stepped forward before he could speak. Hope quivered at my side, and a quick glance down showed me a bent neck, a curtain of long, dark hair now hiding her face from view. "She is not the kind of person who takes."

"So she is paying for the roof over her head? The food in her belly?"

"Careful," I said, knowing full well Tim was past heeding warnings, past sensing the treacherous waters he was treading. Sharks abounded here, and the pup did not sense it.

The pack he had grown up in had done him a great disservice.

Tim drew his eyes up Hope's body, lingering on breasts and lips. "That means *no*, so does she offer other . . . *services* in lieu of payment?"

The sound of furious growls were but a distant noise. My hand shot out and wrapped around the offensive male's throat. A choked cry squeezed past his parted lips before my grip tightened.

I loosened the shackles I kept wrapped around my beast. Cold violence clashed with the earthy, protective sense of *pack. Family.* I leaned in until my mouth was right by Tim's ear—I did not want Hope to overhear. "You need to be careful, youngling." The slow drag of a growl resonated in the rasp of my voice, and the urge to squeeze harder, to destroy this creature before he could harm our human pounded at my mind.

He threatened our human.

Claws slowly extended, pricked against soft, vulnerable flesh.

He has no respect for pack.

377

The corner of my lip lifted. Ending him would be so easy.

He thinks humans deserves no protection.

Blood welled at Tim's throat. Just one drop.

He kicked his feet.

Satisfaction was a slow, uncurling fire in my chest, and it was also a warning. A warning I should heed before regaining control became impossible.

"The female is under pack protection." My lips barely moved with the soft-spoken words. "Harm her and the next time we need a demonstration to scare off the monster I will give you to Ruarc."

The sudden stench of renewed terror permeated the air. It would not have surprised me had he leaked. Eyes wide and face going purple, Tim looked over my shoulder at Ruarc. Whatever he saw on the enforcer's face—or whatever rumors he recalled—had him flailing in my grip and clawing at my hand.

I gave him one last squeeze before letting go. He tumbled to the ground, clutched at his throat while gulping down big mouthfuls of air.

Satisfied he would not soon forget this lesson, I stepped back and concentrated on finding my center. Each time my control slipped it was a little harder to regain it. Age had a way of wearing on a soul, especially when time carried so many burdens and no one to share them with.

"I-I am w-working . . . I *will* be working to pay—"

My hand found Hope's trembling shoulder and put a stop to her shaky explanation.

"You don't need to defend yourself, love," Jason said in a hard voice. "It's Tim who should be explaining himself."

The male in question staggered to his feet and glared down at the ground. "How could you put one of her kind above one of your own? Our ancestors meant for *us* to rule, not *them*!"

Confusion pinched Hope's face, but though she clearly

did not understand what Tim meant, she stood her ground and blocked Ruarc from Tim's view. Or she would have, had she been anywhere near his height and width. It was as though she didn't want Tim to refocus on Ruarc, and would rather hear Tim continue to abuse her than to watch Ruarc suffer.

"Is this the kind of trash you allow into your den, Blake?" Lucien asked.

Blake stroked two fingers down his throat, lip curling. "He's the nephew of our only female, raised in a pack supporting Rederick. Her brother asked that we take him in and give him a chance." He swallowed, shook his head. "I see now it was a mistake."

"You can't be serious?" Tim gaped up at his potential pack mates. "Over a filthy hu—"

"Enough." Lucien's cold command cut through the air. With Hope trembling before Tim but refusing to back down, and with Jason's bulging arms straining with the effort of holding a snarling Ruarc back, Lucien strolled over to where Tim was standing. He cast a quick look back at me, and I nodded.

If he wanted to do this, all the better. Ruarc would go too far and I could not interfere in another alpha's pack.

"That's quite enough," he said again. Face devoid of all emotions, he stared at Tim until the other man dropped his gaze. "I challenge."

"Heard," Blake called out.

"Seconded," Zakh muttered.

Tim gasped, wide eyes roaming over both members of the pack he had been so sure would accept him. "You can't let him do this! It's barbaric!"

"It is fitting then, as you seem determined to live in the past," Lucien replied.

A near crazed expression overtook Tim as he glared at Hope. "This is all your fault!" Before he could do anything he would regret, Blake and Zakh closed in on him and pulled him a few steps away.

Hope finally took a step back. She looked like a lost lamb, gaze darting back and forth between the new arrivals as they began arguing among themselves in quiet whispers. Another step, onto my foot this time.

"Oh, s-sorry," she mumbled, peeking up at me with those big brown eyes. "W-what's happening?"

"Nothing yet." It was the truth. The Challenge would take place the next day at dawn.

Something on her face told me she was unhappy with my avoidance, but she simply said, "Okay," and backed away until she was inside.

Her light steps carried her around the corner, out of sight, and then there was just the sound of her hurrying up the stairs and slamming the door to her room.

"I'll go," Ruarc growled.

33

HOPE

"WHAT WERE YOU THINKING?" RUARC ROARED, HIS HANDS ON my shoulders tightening. "You could have been hurt!"

A few seconds after I'd left the ugly confrontation downstairs, he'd come charging after me like an angry bull, shaking me until my teeth clattered while snarling something about careless females.

I blinked. Watched his eyes narrow into thin slits. Rage and pain swirled in a sea of glowing silver, blending until the sharp emotions were indistinguishable from one another.

Had I done that?

"I just . . . I didn't think that—"

"Damn right you didn't think!" The force of his growled admonishment left me temporarily speechless. He was *furious*.

But why?

I lowered my gaze, unable to look at that wide, tense jaw or those angry, black eyebrows as they snapped together. "I . . ." I didn't know what to say, how to explain. When I'd overheard Tim's rant against Ruarc, something in me had snapped. A small, fragile part of me, a part I'd thought long dead, had expanded its wings in a burst of indignant fury.

How *dared* Tim speak like that about Ruarc?

The feel of a molten gaze burning my face, of Ruarc's rough palm sliding past my shoulder and down my arm, rubbing against my bare skin, raising gooseflesh where it touched.

I shivered, waited for him to speak, for further chastisement. But instead of yelling at me, he crushed me to his chest, burrowed his nose in my neck, and drew a deep breath.

"Hope, my Hope," he rasped, desperate hands running over my body in a way that didn't feel intrusive, but rather like he wanted to assure himself I was okay. It was the kind of touch my soul craved, like a light had been lit and shone upon the damaged, shriveled thing. I could feel it stretching inside me, unfurling like a withered flower touched by the sun for the very first time.

My eyes closed, my head fell back.

How did I survive eighteen years without this?

His hands slowed, then stilled. They were back on my shoulders, two heavy weights that felt no more restrictive than the blanket I wrapped around myself at night.

"I'm sorry," I murmured, wanting to soothe him the way he'd soothed me.

Ruarc leaned back and shook his head. "What you said . . ." His voice deepened, his eyes searched mine. "You mean it?"

With a shaking hand, I reached out and cupped his strong jaw. Short, black hairs scraped against my fingers and tickled my palm. Not stubble, not a beard, either.

Just Ruarc.

"Every word," I whispered.

Before my touch-drugged brain turned back on, before fear and insecurity burrowed deeper in my heart and forced me to run away, Ruarc moved.

The first taste of his lips was a savage, all consuming

experience. He wasn't gentle. He didn't hold back or hesitate. His mouth descended on mine with such hunger, such passion my mind emptied of all thoughts but him.

His taste.

His touch.

His scent.

I couldn't breathe. My heart pounded in my ears.

One of his big hands held my nape, the other pressed against my lower back. They didn't roam. They didn't touch beyond their burning borders. They stayed excruciatingly still.

My stomach dipped and rose, bottomed out and flew through the air.

His tongue swept across mine, tasting sweet yet dangerous. Wild yet tender.

Firm lips moved. His hands flexed.

His scent was everywhere. Masculine. Untamed. Predatory. He smelled of forest and horses and man.

He pressed closer. A sound I would never forget rumbled from his chest, a snarled, desperate, hungry sound that made heat erupt someplace low and throbbing.

Ruarc licked and tasted every inch of my mouth until his flavor was branded onto the very essence of my being.

And then he shook. Vibrated, almost. The arms I'd wrapped around his neck moved with the bunching muscles of his shoulders.

Wrenching away, breathing heavily, his eyes burned. "*A chuisle*," he murmured, his mouth hovering so close each breath was shared. The hand at my nape moved to my face and his touch gentled until each finger slipping over my cheek felt like silk covered wind. His bright, silver eyes glowed with heat, explored every aspect of my face like he was as desperate to imprint the memory as I was.

When he next bent his head, his kiss was a velvet caress.

With aching tenderness, he brushed his lips across mine, the touch elusive and fleeting.

Maddening.

I moaned and he did it again. This time his lips lingered at the corner of my mouth where he pressed a sweet, torturous kiss.

I couldn't breathe.

I couldn't breathe, I couldn't breathe, I couldn't breathe.

"You okay?" A hoarse whisper. His hands skimmed up the line of my arms where they remained curled around his neck. He loosened my hold, intertwined our fingers and brought one of my hands to his lips. Eyes locked on mine, he kissed the inside of my wrist.

My breath hitched.

I didn't care if I ever got it back.

Ruarc's gaze slid across my face, tracking every movement, every twitch and jerk like his life depended on it. Yet still he maintained the distance between us.

It was all I could do to not whimper at the loss. I wanted his lips back on mine. Wanted his taste in my mouth. Wanted that big, muscular body wrapped around mine, all that power, all that heat washing over me until we were indistinguishable from each other.

Instead, I nodded.

Once more his eyes searched my face. I didn't know what he was looking for, but despite the tension around his mouth, the rapid rise and fall of his broad chest, there was a strange, masculine satisfaction hiding in the press of his lips. "Good."

Tension curled like an electric whip in my stomach. A whip that cracked down my back and froze every cell in my body when Ruarc began guiding me toward the bed.

My heart simply stopped beating.

I'm not ready for this!

Visions of grotesque acts assaulted my mind, put together

by my imagination after all the taunts slung by the Hunters. I didn't know what went on between a man and a woman when they had sex, but I knew it was done in a bed. Based on the Hunters descriptions it was something I wanted to avoid at all cost.

My feet refused to move, my breathing became shallow.

Ruarc noticed my frozen limbs—how could he not?—and immediately stopped. The gentleness he showed then was something I'd come to depend on around him—a gentleness that stood in stark contrast to his scarred visage and towering frame. He pressed another kiss to my wrist and shored my trust with four simple words; "Let me hold you."

Ugly thoughts dissolved.

This was Ruarc. He would never hurt me.

"O-okay." I followed him to the bed. He always moved with such purpose, such determination. Almost as if he was angry about where he was going.

The bed groaned under his weight, and if I hadn't known better I would've thought the slight grimace that overtook his face was embarrassment.

"Bed's too small," he muttered, waving me closer.

It was true. The bed that had felt so luxurious to me was dwarfed by the massive man in its middle. Ruarc's strong back was propped against the headboard, his long, powerful legs reaching almost the full length even though he wasn't lying down. Broad shoulders took up nearly one third of its width.

"How tall are you?" I blurted, staring at his feet.

His big feet. His big, bare feet.

"Tall." He plucked me up and settled me between his thighs. Strong arms wrapped around my middle and pulled me against hard-packed muscles and flesh so hot I felt his heat through our clothes.

Ruarc buried his face in the crook of my neck and inhaled. "Mmm."

His mouth moved up the column of my throat, then . . .

A swift, wet caress, my body flooding with heat.

Did he just . . . Did he just lick me?

My heart beat once, hard and fluttery at the same time, and then it stopped. Not for long, maybe two or three seconds. And when it started again it raced.

"Comfortable?" he asked, a smile in his voice.

"I . . . I think so?" I wiggled my rump to test, felt the hard, pole-like *thing* pressing against my lower back, and blushed so hard I nearly passed out. "Y-yes."

Ruarc groaned, a thoroughly male sound, then placed his big palm across my belly and held me still. "Good. Now talk."

"Talk? W-what do you mean?"

A deep growl worked its way out of his chest. "Need to know. So I can protect you."

The world stopped spinning.

He wants to know about the Hunters.

An icy web of dread tightened around my lungs. "I-I don't want . . . I can't . . ." Anything I revealed would either put him in danger or destroy another piece of my battered soul.

The Hunters.

My monster.

The day I—

My throat closed. Just closed. Small sips of air fought down into lungs that suddenly ached.

I was so damned *weak*!

Before I could spiral into a full blown panic attack, Ruarc tightened his hold and brought one hand up to my heart. There it lay, pressing, calming, melting the suffocating web of ice and frost and despair.

Small, comforting sounds brushed past my ears until my breathing evened out. Only then did he relax, pressing a quick kiss behind my ear.

"Tell me . . ." He swallowed hard. "What you are comfortable with."

The reluctance in those hard-pressed words said it all. He wanted to know everything, wanted to push until my soul lay bare before him and all my secrets spilled out into the open.

But he didn't.

He let *me* decide.

And because he did, I was struck by the urge to *give*. To *share*. To *compromise* any way I could. Because that was exactly what he'd done.

"I don't know where to start," I whispered.

His hand curled against my chest, the myriad of thin white scars moving with the motion. "Tell me why you are scared."

I instinctively knew he didn't mean now. He was asking why I was scared when we were out in public, why I didn't want to leave their property, why sometimes even leaving the house shot shards of terror up my spine. "B-because . . ." I gathered all my courage, determined to push this one truth out before he asked for a truth I couldn't give. "They're . . . still looking for me."

Stillness behind me. His chest stopped moving. The warm puffs of air that had been tickling the sensitive skin on my neck ceased.

"Ruarc?"

A finger twitched. "How do you know?" A silky whisper, violence hidden in velvet-wrapped words.

"I . . . I just do."

Don't ask why, please don't.

The silent plea was answered. Ruarc tightened his hold on me and growled, a drawn out thunderous sound that rumbled from his chest. "Doesn't matter." His arms around me shook with strain. "They come, they die."

I knew his words were meant to reassure—a part of me even believed him—but I knew the Hunters. Knew what they were capable of. If they did come for me . . .

We'd all die.

387

Ruarc placed a finger under my chin. Tilted my face sideways. Pinned me in place with a fierce gaze. "No one will hurt you as long as I live."

My breath caught.

Silver eyes burned. "Hear me?" His chin lowered in a stubborn, male way. "*No one.*"

What if you don't live?

The thought was so horrible I had to swallow a sob.

"What else?"

Still reeling from his vow—he couldn't mean it, I was basically a stranger and definitely not worthy of Ruarc's life —I peeked up at him and scrunched my nose in confusion.

He tapped the tip, lips twitching. "What else scares you, *a chuisle?*"

Rather than answer, I jumped on the distraction he'd provided. "What does that mean? You've called me that before."

His eyes bored into mine. "You first."

"I . . ." I had to tell him. It wasn't like I could hide my intimate fears from him forever. "Uhm . . . what this means, I guess." I gestured between us. "And, uhm, *sex.*" Pretty sure my face was crimson.

I turned away so he wouldn't see the full extent of my humiliation. There was no way I wanted him to think I was some scared, ignorant, little girl, but if I didn't tell him the truth he might push for more than I was ready to give.

A fierce snarl ripped through the air, startling me into looking back at him. "Did they . . ." The savage fury twisting his expression was nothing compared to his eyes. The luminous silver seemed to swirl, drawing me in, while a murderous glint misted over his pupils until his expression looked strangely blank. "They rape you?"

A violent shudder rippled through me, and for a moment, Ruarc's face was a canvas of agony. But as quickly as the volatile emotions emerged, they also retreated, and his face became a blank mask.

Squashed against his chest, strong arms became steel bars. Not a prison but a protective cage. A place of safety. A refuge.

"Don't have to answer," he whispered against my hair, a shudder wracking his large, muscular torso. "Doesn't change anything." The steely bands around my middle tightened until he blew out a harsh breath. "Either way, they'll pay."

His unequivocal support was a balm to my sullied soul. I had *not* been raped, but I had been violated in other ways, and his rasped confession gave me room to dream, to wish, to hope.

I knew he'd turn away in disgust if he ever learned it all, but in this moment, turning his words over and over in my mind, *'doesn't change anything,'* I could pretend he'd see past the horrible things I'd done, the monster that I was, and still have murder in his eyes when thinking I'd been hurt.

"No," I finally said. I had to clear my throat twice before I could say anything else, but I couldn't let him believe this. Not when the belief made his hand curl against my stomach, the knuckles white and angry. "Nothing like that. It was just . . . words."

I didn't add how damaging the words were, or how, when they'd first started torturing me, I'd waited for that inevitable degradation every day. Each threat, each taunt had made the anticipation slowly chip away at my sense of self until I almost wanted it to happen. Just to have it over with.

Of course, after I'd overheard a Hunter curse the fact that rape wasn't allowed I'd wept with relief. It was the only time during my captivity I'd felt grateful.

Ruarc seemed to deflate behind me. A ragged sigh slipped past his firm lips, and he moved to rest his chin against the top of my head. "They still die," he said, but some of the feral rage in his voice had given way to hard relief. Oh, the violence was still there, dripping off each clipped syllable like acid eroding rock, but less. As though maybe instead of torturing my tormentors for ten years, he'd limit himself to a few months.

I almost snorted at the strangeness of my imagination.

"*A chuisle* is an endearment. Directly translated, it means 'my pulse.'"

It took me a moment to register the abrupt change. "My pulse?" I repeated, tracing the white line of one of the many faded scars slicing across the back of his hands.

"Yes," he grumbled. If Ruarc was the kind of person who squirmed, I had a feeling he would be doing so now.

My pulse. It was kind of lovely. And it made me consider things. Like the way his lips had felt against mine, the care he always showed me, and the gentle, protective side so at odds with the rest of his personality.

Butterflies danced in my stomach as I eyed the harsh lines of his face.

At some point I'd stopped seeing the rough, savage features as scary, and begun to simply accept them as a part of Ruarc. A part of the first man who'd ever made me feel safe.

Among other things.

The ragged scar tearing through his flesh had become a mark of strength. The broad nose—broken at some point and never healed right—suited his powerful presence. His square jaw was very attractive and I found it suited his unapologetic, forceful personality. The same with the shadow of scruff he never seemed to be without. And his eyes . . .

I've always loved his eyes, I thought as I stared into pools of glowing silver that only reflected acceptance and an emotion I couldn't quite decipher.

"Are you my boyfriend?" I blurted, immediately clapping

both hands to my mouth in horror while my question hung between us like a bloated fly.

What had I just said? Where was my brain-to-mouth filter? Had eighteen years of torturous captivity completely eroded my grasp of normal society?

What's wrong with you, Hope?

"Yes." It was a grunt.

My eyes snapped to his, watched the hard press of his lips, the way he tossed his head like he was upset.

"Boyfriend . . ." he grumbled. Another emotion flitted across his face. Disappointment? Regret?

I swallowed hard, trying to squash my growing horror. Did he feel like he had to say yes? Did he feel sorry for me? *Pity?*

Tentacles wrapped around the undigested food in my stomach and heaved. I . . . I was going to be sick. "It—It's okay," I forced out. "You don't have to—"

The world spun on its axis, and suddenly I was facing Ruarc. He'd put me on my knees between his legs, one hand wrapped around my upper arm, the other holding my chin and forcing me to meet his gaze.

His glittering, furious gaze.

"Too late," he snapped. "You're mine now."

The possessive grip on my chin didn't loosen until I jerked my head in a small nod. Then, all he did was glare down at me, as if gauging my sincerity, eyes narrowed and assessing.

Hesitantly, I reached up and placed my hand over his.

He startled. Stared.

Next to his, my skin seemed pale. Luminous, almost. And his hand was more than twice mine in size. So rough. So masculine. So strong and capable and *gentle*.

Ruarc made a sound, a gruff, growly grunt that tickled at my belly, and then his hold transferred from my chin to the back of my neck. There was a hardness to his features, a sharpness that called to mind a hungry wolf when he pulled me close and rubbed his face against the side of my throat.

"Mine," he growled, and I felt teeth scrape against my flesh.

Heat erupted in my belly. My skin pebbled. But when he pulled back and stared down at me I smiled despite the strange shivers working through my body.

Ruarc . . . Ruarc wanted me.

It wasn't about pity or feeling pressured or any number of other weird things that had flown through my mind and spread its creeping doubt. No, he wanted me.

Me!

While I struggled to accept the amazing, astounding fact that this incredible man wanted me as his girlfriend—a damaged, fragile creature who jumped at loud sounds and was terrified of leaving the house—Ruarc's jaw jutted out as though he was preparing for a fight.

"I want names," he growled.

"Names?" It took me a second to realize what he was asking, and when I did, it was like having eaten a bowl of candy only to be told the candy had been made from worms. "B-but . . . you said I only had to tell you what I was c-comfortable with."

Ruarc's expression closed, brows smoothing out from the tense 'V' they had been molded into and some of the intensity in his gaze blanketing. With a jerk of his chin he let me know I was right.

So why did I feel like I'd just been punched in the gut?

"At least . . . at least not yet," I whispered, knowing full well I could never tell him—although part of me wanted to.

The muscles along his shoulders flexed, as though he was struggling to hold himself. "Soon."

"I . . . I have questions too . . ." I trailed off, hesitant to ask him anything he wasn't prepared to answer.

But Ruarc didn't seem upset at my timid half-request. Instead, he seemed to relax.

"Course." He gently guided me down on my side and slid down the bed. When he turned his expectant gaze on me, he was lying on his back, one hand propped behind his head and the other wrapped around my shoulder. My cheek rested on his wide chest and my front was plastered to his side. If I so much as wriggled, a possessive palm would push against my lower back, making sure our bodies stayed glued together.

I felt . . . safe.

Ruarc was hard all over. Like steel made flesh. And he was warm. So warm I thought he could have melted even the coldest of nightmares. And when he tilted my face up, looked down at me in that way that almost seemed angry but was really just intensely Ruarc, I knew what I wanted to ask.

"What happened?" Using a featherlight touch, I touched his scar.

As soon as I felt the raised edge of his old injury, he jerked back and grabbed my hand. His eyes shuttered, expression closing until all that remained was a blank look hiding depths of impenetrable pain.

"Nothing." The tone was so forbidding I didn't dare push.

Hurt, I pulled my hand out of his hold and looked away. I understood keeping secrets; there were plenty of things I was unable to tell him. But I'd shared more than I was comfortable with because he'd asked. The fact that he was unwilling to do the same made my insides twist with a cold, hopeless feeling.

"Okay."

The chest I'd rested so comfortably against a few minutes ago suddenly felt foreign. When Ruarc sighed, my stiff neck moved with the rise and fall of his breath, but only because his grip on me prevented me from moving away.

"Sorry." The gruff exhalation was barely a word, more of a dark sound of regret.

"It's fine," I muttered.

"No." He used a finger under my chin to force my gaze back up. "I'm no good at this."

A whip cracked past my ribs. Was he already tired of me? "At what?"

"This." He gestured between us, adding another stripe to my flayed heart. "Talking."

Oh!

I gave him a small, relieved smile. "I'm not either."

Ruarc rolled his eyes. "Females are always good at talking."

"Known many?" Although I made an effort to keep my voice light, a trace of uncertainty colored the question.

He gave me *a look*. A 'don't-be-daft' kind of look, and traced my lips with one calloused finger. "Not for centuries."

Anxiety slipped away, replaced by a warm glow. Centuries must mean it had been so long he could barely remember.

A very good answer.

Drawing invisible patterns on the black shirt covering his chest, I dared one last question. "Will you . . . will you tell me one day?"

He stilled. Then a gruff, "Yes. Soon." The hand resting on my shoulder flexed. "There are . . . *things* you must know for the story to make sense."

His foreboding words sent tendrils of unease down my spine, but I crushed them the same way I crushed the crippling insecurity I felt when I thought too long about how a man like Ruarc could want a woman like me. And how I was going to face the others when they heard about our . . . relationship. And how I must have lost my damned mind to enter a relationship when I knew it was only a matter of weeks before I had to leave.

Leave . . . I still have to leave.

My stomach dropped to my feet. Nothing had changed. I still couldn't stay, only now when I left I'd have a knife twisting my belly and another piercing my heart.

"Cold?" Ruarc rubbed at the pebbled flesh on my arms, a scowl twisting his lips. Before I could reply, he pulled the blanket over us both and nuzzled the top of my head. "Hungry?"

I shook my head, mouth too dry to speak.

"Should eat. It's past dinner."

"What . . . what about the others?" Sitting across the table from Tim was the last thing I wanted.

"They'll eat without us."

"But you always eat together."

"Not today," Ruarc growled. He stroked a hand down my side, resting it in the dip of my hip. "I'll be right back."

He left, and when he returned it was with leftovers from the day before—a delicious pie with the most tender crust—a laptop, and several DVDs.

"Borrowed it from Jason," he said in a gruff voice. "Thought we could watch something."

Like a . . . a date? Suddenly my stomach was alive with somersaulting butterflies.

I have a boyfriend. I actually have a boyfriend.

I forgot all my worries, all the ugly thoughts and reasons we shouldn't be together, and allowed Ruarc to sweep me up in this beautiful—temporary—fantasy.

"That'd be great." I beamed up at him and scooted back.

We ended up watching two comedies—though Ruarc never let go enough to laugh, a lazy sort of heat filled his gaze every time I did, and he watched me more than he watched the movie—and one thriller.

The fear I expected never came. Not when a woman was chased through the streets by men with guns, and not when her enemies closed in and it looked like all was lost. Instead, I dozed off, safe with Ruarc wrapped around my back, his bicep under my head, his bristled cheek rubbing across my hair whenever he brushed his lips across my temple. And halfway through the movie I was sound asleep.

I didn't wake up when Ruarc extracted himself from our tangled position. I didn't wake up when he walked out on silent feet. I didn't wake up when the door closed and I was left alone.

I didn't wake up, but I was vaguely aware. And when he left, the nightmare he'd kept at bay with his presence hunted me down and swallowed me whole.

34

HOPE

Lily!

Someone was screaming.

The scent of blood. Of salt. The sound of harsh, broken sobs. A man.

And above me, an endless white.

Lily!

The world melted at the corners and dragged me down.

Down. Down. Down.

All around me rose cold, cement walls. Grey. Forbidding. Streaked with old splashes of a red so dark it appeared black.

And across the narrow corridor that separated us, a startling splash of blood-red hair. The color—and the wild, springy curls— concealed the wound splitting open his skull.

"Matthew . . ." My voice was so weak the whisper was caught by the greedy nothingness of this place.

"You did this." A short, plump figure slapped his hand against my cell-door. "He had to die because of you."

No!

I doubled over, the blooming pain in my stomach more than regret. More than despair. A hole the size of my fist had opened up beneath my palm, the wound gushing blood so fast the floor soon flooded.

I was drowning. Drowning in blood.

"Are you ready?" Jan looked over the other Hunter's shoulder. A tattoo flashed. Bones and flowers.

"No. No!"

The door opened. Jan stepped inside. His lips smiled but nothing else on his face moved. "We have an appointment."

The floor disappeared and I fell.

Shredding pain. Agony. Nerve-endings burned.

Then the hole in my stomach disappeared. A line was cut from my throat to my pelvis. My ribs were cracked. Spread open. Air touched my heart.

"Matthew?" His name slipped past torn lips. Under my back, a cold, hard table. Straps across my thighs, feet, shoulders, neck, arms, wrists.

"Dead," Jan said. He reached inside, palmed my heart.

Squeezed.

"They're all dead."

I scrambled out of bed, tripping over my own feet and lunging back up. My chest heaved. My breath was short and choppy. I couldn't see, couldn't sweep the room for hidden monsters.

It was too dark.

I stumbled over to the window, yanked the flimsy curtain apart, pressed my back against the cool surface. The faint glow from the moon hidden behind gloomy clouds gave me just enough light to see that I was alone.

There were no Hunters to torture me, no Matthew dying in a pool of his own blood, and no bars to keep me locked in with the monsters.

I was alone.

The erratic beating of my heart slowed from a gallop to a trot. I forced my fingers to uncurl and took a deep breath.

I was still on edge.

Even after my breathing slowed, even after the nightmare fractured into wisps of transparent memory, I couldn't shake my unease. My skin felt sensitive, like every slight disturbance in the air were shards of cutting glass. Like the shirt I wore was made of tiny needles.

Shivers danced like falling ice over my body.

I was freezing.

I tiptoed across the cold floor to the hoodie hanging over the lone dresser in the corner. As soon as I dragged it over my head, the wild scent of forest and pine cones enveloped me.

Ruarc.

I buried my face in the neckline and took a deep breath, letting his scent wash over me. He'd replaced the hoodie I'd borrowed from Ash with one of his own. One steeped in the beautifully wild scent that was Ruarc.

A trembling smile stole over my lips only to be wiped away by another shudder.

Judging by the blackness outside, it was the middle of the night. I should have gone back to sleep but . . .

To my eyes, the bed rose from the floor like a craggy mountain. Hard. Terrifying. Threatening to throw me off and land me in the midst of another nightmare.

Don't want to sleep.

I turned and rushed to the door. Maybe some food would settle my nerves.

Eerie silence followed me all the way downstairs. The house was normally teeming with life, male voices rising and falling, the sound of a TV playing or food being cooked or doors opening and closing. This silence, this horrible, deafening silence was made sinister by the absence of all the noise I'd grown used to.

It's night, you coward. They're probably just sleeping.

I made my way to the kitchen. Once there, my bare feet slapped against the tiled floor like mini explosions. Cringing, I went up on the balls of my feet and tried to be quiet.

A groan. Long and drawn out.

I jumped, dropped the knife I'd just picked up and spun around.

But there was no one there.

Another groan, and my shoulders drooped.

It's just the house. The house's settling.

Movements rushed and choppy, I spread peanut butter on a piece of bread and attempted to ignore the way my skin crawled.

Stupid. You're being stupid, Hope, I scolded myself. *There's nothing to be scared of, the guys are right upstairs and you're safe. The Hunters don't know where you are or they'd have stormed the place by now.*

It was nearly impossible to turn my back to the door, to put everything away without throwing looks over my shoulder, jumping at every shadow, every whisper of wind outside. Fear had taken root and was not letting go.

Plate with food in hand, I hurried out of the kitchen and toward the stairs. The creak of a door opening upstairs had me freeze with one foot in the air.

Who was awake at this time?

I put my foot down on the floor, avoiding the first step and backing up.

It could be Lucien. Or one of the *guests*. I'd forgotten to ask where they were sleeping.

Fighting against the overwhelming urge to seek shelter in my room, I turned and rushed through the living room, into the kitchen, and out the back-door.

Fresh air slapped me in the face and brought me to a halt. The night sky was nearly black, with a few heavy, gray clouds hovering on the horizon and blocking most of the faint moonlight.

My skin prickled, but I felt better being outside. There was so much land sprawled out in front of me, so much open space. I could run here. Run and run and run and no one would be able to catch me.

Curling up on the swing, I started eating and let my mind wander. My foot pushed at the ground, and my seat swayed. Soundless at first, then with a sudden, horrible screech of metal.

I jumped, nearly falling off the swing.

An owl hooted in the distance.

The sudden lump in my throat made swallowing impossible. I rubbed a hand over my burning eyes, wishing for courage, for the ability to forget.

For no more nightmares.

My heart was heavy when I finally sat back down, my mouth dry. I made the swing move again, prepared for the ugly sound this time, and gritted my teeth when the urge to jump *still* manifested.

I rubbed a hand over my tight chest and picked up my plate.

The food tasted as gray as the stormy clouds overhead.

Giving up on eating, I tilted my head all the way back, watched the rapidly darkening clouds rolling across the sky, felt the sharp wind shooting past me. Nature was as beautiful as it was daunting. I would never get tired of it. Never forget what a privileged—

"Hello, *human*."

I didn't scream. I had no air in my lungs for that. Instead, my head snapped toward the voice while my feet tried to carry my body away from this new threat.

The result was me toppling over before quickly righting myself and scooting as far back on the swing as I could go.

"T-Tim," I choked out. My mouth felt so dry the name hurt coming out. "W-what—where are the others?"

My eyes swept past him, but there was no one there. He'd come out here alone.

"Out." He stepped away from the door leading into the kitchen and prowled closer. His eyes were wild and unfocused and the bruises that had decorated his face earlier were gone.

How . . . how's that possible?

"And you're out here all alone . . ." He dragged out the last word while putting his hand on the swing. I looked up—unable to breathe—as it glided over the top frame. The wood groaned under the force of his grip, and when he slapped his other hand to the frame, moving to stand over me, he tilted his head down and watched me from eyes that glittered. "Imagine that."

Every fiber of my being was screaming at me to *run* to *get away* to *flee the predator stalking me*. But my mind refused to believe I was in any real danger.

The guys wouldn't let anyone hurt me.

Ruarc wouldn't let anyone hurt me.

And what could Tim do? What would he *dare* do after the beating he'd already taken?

No, my terror was cowardice, emotional scars that would fade with time.

I was safe.

I was safe.

I was *safe*.

And still I shrank back as far as I could go, pressing my back against hard wood, breathing shallow and uneven. "W-what do y-you want?"

The sides of his lips pulled up into a grotesque smile that revealed rows of sharp teeth. Unnaturally sharp teeth. Deadly teeth.

Not human, my mind whispered.

"Isn't it obvious?" His eyes glowed a pale yellow. They fixated on my chest and stole the air from my lungs. "I want to see what all the fuss is about."

My heart raced. Not with forceful beats but with shallow, stumbling little claps that made my head woozy and the top of my chest feel too light.

My eyes darted to the right, then the left. I could feel them tumbling around in my skull, desperate and terrified, like a mouse being hunted by a lion.

Too far.

Only a few feet separated me from the door but it might as well have been ten miles. With Tim blocking the way I didn't stand a chance.

"Try." His voice held a note of excitement. "See how far you get."

"P-please."

The black of his pupils bled through his irises, swallowing the pale yellow until darkness was all that remained. "Please, what?

"L-let me g-go."

His tongue darted between sharp teeth and licked his lips. "Why?"

He . . . he wanted me to beg.

My mind blanked, my throat tightened, my vision narrowed. Tim was just like the Hunters. He would feed on my fear, take pleasure in my pain, win with every wound he inflicted.

I threw myself to the side and tried to dart under his arms.

As soon as I was on my feet, he grabbed my shoulders and threw me back down. My backside hit the swinging bench with enough force that I bit down hard on my tongue.

Blood. I tasted blood.

"Do you know what you did?" he hissed. "What you cost me?"

"I—"

"Quiet!" He looked away. His jaw worked soundlessly. "If it weren't for you . . ." A pause. A shake of his head. A low growl followed by a glare. "I guess it doesn't matter anymore. Now I just want to see why they were all so worked up over a *human*."

He ducked down to his haunches and reached out.

Cruel hands dug into the tender flesh above my breasts, and my heart flat-lined. I yanked against his hold, choked on a scream that refused to tear past my rapidly closing throat while mindless terror gouged its clawed fingers through my shoulder blades.

I was yanked up from the bench and pushed against the railing with terrifying ease.

"R-Ruarc w-will k-k-kill y-you!"

Tim snorted and tightened his punishing grip until I whimpered. Then he smiled, a cruel, ugly thing, and yanked.

My scream was silenced by the hand he clapped over my face. White-hot pain traveled up my arm, piercing my shoulder where it felt my arm might fall out of its socket. "He won't care," Tim whispered into my ear. He sounded so sure that doubt took root. "You're nothing to them. A plaything. Something new and shiny. They would've tired of you eventually, I'm just speeding up the process."

I was choking. The hand covering my mouth and nose didn't just steal my breath, it had my stomach turn with revulsion. It smelled wrong. All wrong.

I couldn't breathe.

My feet kicked at Tim, but he only stepped closer, pushing his body against mine, forcing a leg between my thighs and—

Tim removed his hand, wrapped it around my throat instead. "Scream all you want, human. There's no one here to hear you."

My insides turned to a frozen wasteland. Of all the things

he could've said, that was the most terrifying. If no one was here, I was completely at his mercy. And he was so much stronger than me.

He snickered, and that cold, merciless sound told me everything I needed to know.

Tim would hurt me in ways I'd never been hurt before unless I could escape.

I let go of the hand squeezing my throat, curled my fingers into claws, and dragged my nails down his face.

He cursed and loosened his hold.

It was enough.

I pulled with all my might. Ducked. Avoided the arm shooting out. Scrambled to reach the door. Angry hisses behind me, feet stomping on wooden planks.

My hand reached out, one finger brushed the door handle and—

A burning pain in my scalp. My head snapped back with such force my body followed.

"No!" I tried to yell, tried to scream, but my lungs were starved for air, terror making my breathing too shallow to produce enough force. My cry was a reed-thin, barely-there sound that was swept away on the wind.

Then I was on the ground, Tim's hand in my hair, Tim's breath in my face, Tim's fingers digging into my flesh.

Blackness crept in around the corners until only a pinprick of sight remained.

And then Tim's snarling face rushed toward me. "You'll pay for that!" He rolled on top of me, his weight all *wrong*, too *heavy*, *crushing* my lungs and my spirit and the wall protecting my mind.

Wild with panic, I kicked and bit and clawed to get away, to hurt him, to do *something* before he violated me in a way I knew I wouldn't survive.

I'd been through too much. I'd break.

Tim hissed when a flailing limb hit him in the face, but he didn't let me get away again.

He was too strong, easily overpowered me, and caught both my arms in a tight grip above my head. Slowly, his furious stare molded into something uglier, something darker, and he used his claws—*claws?*—to rip my shirt open.

Cool air blew across my vulnerable skin and I writhed. Muscles strained with effort, shook with exhaustion.

Too weak.

Lips peeled back in hideous victory, Tim leered down at my bare breasts.

Crippling shame descended, followed by a hopelessness so encompassing I briefly wished I could die.

This can't happen!

My taut body twisted and turned, bucked against Tim's iron grip.

Tim ground my cheek against the cold patio.

Silent sobs tore my throat to broken tatters.

Tim shredded my pants.

Hot tears ran rivulets down my cheeks.

Tim ran his free hand from my knee up my thigh, until he touched the soft fabric of my borrowed boxers.

My stomach revolted, twisted, dipped, shrunk and expanded with waves of nausea. I kicked both my legs up, trying to dislodge him.

Tim would not be budged.

I was swamped by feelings of disgust, despair, crippling shame. But by far the most dominating emotion was the feeling of helplessness. At not being able to *fight*. No matter what I did, I couldn't stop this nightmare. I was too weak, or Tim was too strong. My body an unwilling participant in what would be a gruesome act meant to degrade and destroy, while my mind was held hostage, forced to witness the very thing that would annihilate it.

A long, despairing wail left me as my body was crushed under his weight.

Tim plucked at my boxers.

My mind threatened to break.

"These have to go," the evil on top of me said while he licked his lips and gripped the front of the boxers.

He'd tear them, now, and leave me completely bare, completely helpless, completely destroyed.

Inside my mind I felt a vague echo of fury. Of something dark and deadly. Something wanting to escape.

A glimmer of hope.

My monster!

I wanted to cry with relief. Why hadn't I thought about that? I dug deep, tried to open the cage that always kept it contained. I pulled and yanked but the door wouldn't yield. It felt heavy, stuck. Like pulling an anchor through water and mud.

The cage was stuck. It didn't want to be opened. Yet I could feel the monster's urgency, the desire to kill bubbling from the other side of that tightly shut door.

Why couldn't I open it?

I gave one last mental heave only to be slapped down so hard my ears wouldn't stop ringing.

The force of the devastation that filled me then was unlike anything I'd ever felt before.

A complete lack of hope.

There was nothing I could do. I couldn't save myself, couldn't stop Tim. Even my monster had given up on me.

I would have to endure this nightmare. Endure and pray that it would not break me. That both body and mind would survive long enough that I could see justice be done and Tim be destroyed.

A cold, deadly rage bloomed in my chest and for the first time in my life all I could think, all I could smell, see, hear and imagine, was blood. Tim's blood.

Tim's blood in my mouth as I tore out his throat. Tim's blood on my face as his life poured out of his body. Tim's blood everywhere but inside him, leaving his eyes lifeless and unseeing for all eternity.

But then Tim lowered his face and grinned down at me, and all that remained was fear.

"Cry. Scream. *Fight!*" Slowly, so slowly I thought I would die, he stroked a hand down my belly and gripped my boxers between two clawed fingers. "It won't make a lick of difference . . ."

I gathered all my strength and shrieked my pain and my rage.

The muscles along his arm tightened. His lips drew back. He smiled.

35

LUCIEN

The human female was not in her room.

No heartbeat, no soft breaths, no sleepy sounds. Her room was empty.

What was the wench up to?

I paced up and down the hallway. Once. Twice. Three times.

Where was she?

Suspicion bubbled up from the depths of my core. It stung. Like acid flowing over my inner armor, causing boils and tears in material I had thought impenetrable.

I should never have lowered my guard.

My fingers twitched with the urge to curl, but I suppressed it and allowed my face to settle into its most natural expression. The cold indifference I showed the world had been mistaken for a mask by silly females in the past, but in reality it was what I was. *Who* I was.

Cold. Unfeeling. Impenetrable.

Are you still?

Ignoring the sneaking doubt the same as I did all emotions, I moved with purposeful silence.

No female upstairs. Living room empty. Kitchen . . . A few crumbs on the counter. Perhaps enjoying a midnight snack?

Alone?

A silent snarl curled my mouth.

A deep inhalation revealed only the female's lingering scent. Ash had dragged Ruarc and Jason out on a hunt with the visiting pack—to keep them away from the human—but it would not have surprised me to learn of Ruarc's premature return.

The fool is determined to be the cause of his own destruction.

No matter the cost, I would not allow Ruarc to die for a female.

When I neared the back door, my legs grew roots and refused to move. Fur I didn't possess wanted to bristle in warning. I stared.

Something didn't feel right.

My vision shrunk until the door loomed before me, dark and impossibly ominous. I couldn't tear my gaze away.

Silent. Everything went silent while I tried to understand why my instincts were roaring.

I lifted my face, used both nose and mouth to taste the air.

Something in me chafed at the smell lingering on my tongue. There was an odd scent in the air, one that did not belong. It smelled like stark terror interwoven with a predators fierce anger. And it smelled decidedly female.

There was another scent, too. *Other.* Not pack.

A quiet, quiet growl rose in my throat. Alert energy rushed through each cell, but despite the crackling chaos I remained calm. Detached.

The steady cold I was accustomed to enveloped my heart, my lungs, my very being. A dense barrier, thick with snow and ice and metal forged in blood, it guarded against weakness, it forbade emotion from wrestling control from the mind.

But then . . . a muffled wail.

It snuck beneath the door, smashed into my chest, and shattered my carefully constructed armor as though it had never been. The anguish in that simple sound made everything inside me come to a crashing halt.

My breath.

My blood.

My heart.

I stood there. Frozen like I hadn't been since I was a child seeking a safe haven from the terrors of the night. But this time the fear wasn't for myself. It was for the female who had uttered the torturous cry.

A cruel voice issued a taunt and my mind went blank. Something dark swept through me. Something dark and deadly and hideously destructive.

Rage.

It struck. Battered. Melted ice and turned the blood in my veins to knives.

My hands curled.

I crept through the door without making a sound. And what I saw, what awaited . . . My blood curdled.

My vision flashed from dark red to black. Claws sprouted from my fingers. Long, sharp fangs cut my lips as they sprang from my upper and lower jaw.

The frozen wasteland of my soul ignited with volcanic heat.

And I. Did. Not. Care.

A male—a male not of our pack—lay on top of the female under our protection. Vile threats flew from his lips. His claws were out. Touching. About to *rip*. And her shirt . . .

Her shirt was *torn*.

Nothing else registered. A roar thundered in my ears. Swiped at my mind. Silenced everything else. It grew louder and louder until I felt an answering explosion build in my chest.

And then I was moving so fast everything blurred.

I reached them. Did not make a sound. Dug my claws into the worthless cretin's back and threw him off my—*the female*.

Bloodied claws dug into my palms.

In the back of my mind a familiar, cold voice urged caution. Warned that if I did not stop to rebuild my icy fortress it may be lost for good.

I paid it no heed.

A thud. His body crashing into cold earth with a *thump*.

My head swiveled, noted where he'd landed.

I followed.

Then Tim lay at my feet, as powerless as Hope had just been and about to feel pain far surpassing what he would've inflicted upon her had I not arrived in time.

If I hadn't gone to find her . . .

The roar in my ears was joined by drums. Battledrums.

This male . . . this male would die.

Incredulous eyes blinked up at me, and I smiled.

How could I begin to describe the pleasure I took from his paling face, from the knowledge of his own death stamped across wan features?

I couldn't.

But I *could* ensure what happened here today would be beyond what even the worm at my feet could ever have imagined.

I bared my teeth in a cold smile, dark anticipatory pleasure stretching my lips as my true nature was given room to grow.

And then . . .

A lightning quick strike. A bloodcurdling scream. A smaller, wetter *thump*.

I watched with deadly satisfaction as blood sprayed from the writhing, vile *meat* on the ground. So much more flesh to take . . .

Another menacing smile stretched my lips taut as I wondered what I would remove next.

36

HOPE

T<small>HE TERRIBLE WEIGHT CRUSHING ME LIFTED AND</small> I <small>COULD</small> finally breathe.

I scrambled to get up, to get away, to *run*, but my legs couldn't hold me. Water had replaced muscles, jello had replaced bones. I was a mass of rolling, gasping, heaving *goo* —a two year old would move faster.

Tim. Where was Tim?

He'll come back!

Just as I managed to peel my head off the porch, a terrible, high-pitched scream cut through the cold night.

Goosebumps rose like mounds of angry ants under my skin. What . . . what was that?

Hands trembling, thighs shaking, feet twitching, it took me several tries before I managed to stand. I blinked. And then I blinked again.

The earlier clouds had broken, leaving a lone beam of moonlight shining through on the horrific scene playing out about ten feet from where I stood.

Tim writhing on the ground.

Tim making hideous, pain-filled little noises.

Tim slapping at the grass, rolling from side to side, mouth wide open, eyes squeezed shut only to blink open and roll around in his head.

Above Tim loomed an avenging angel with a smile so savage, so cruel, I could barely stand to look at it.

I rubbed my eyes, but no matter how long I did that or how many times I blinked, the scene didn't change. Lucien was towering above the blubbering mess on the ground, a brutal, inhuman smile twisting his harsh beauty into a terrifying, cutting mask.

His lips moved, but I couldn't make out what he was saying. The low, silken voice wouldn't let a single word carry, but by the way Tim reacted, he'd heard every word and would rather face the devil himself than Lucien.

I took a shaky step forward, then another, stumbling onto the damp grass, eyes glued to Lucien. I didn't know what I was doing or what I wanted, but I had to get to him. I had to . . . had to—

Another cloud parted. My stomach dropped.

"L-Lucien?" His name was less than a whisper, caught in a gasp and twisted in my dry mouth. His arm . . . his arm was covered in blood.

I tried to rush forward, but my gaze snagged on something on the ground, something pale and pallid, lying in the grass above Tim's head.

A piece of flesh.

My eyes shot to Tim's groin where blood was spurting through a ragged hole in his pants.

Oh my god.

Lucien had ripped off Tim's . . . Tim's *man-part*.

As if only then remembering my presence, Lucien turned. Slowly. Glittering eyes examined me from head to toe, catching on my ripped pants and the boxers revealed underneath.

That terrible smile that made him look like a murderous god come down to exterminate his humans vanished, replaced by something worse, something far deadlier.

Before he could get a good look at my exposed breasts, I used an arm to cover them, fighting another wave of searing shame. As I lowered my head and averted my gaze—unable to stop the betraying wobble of my lower lip—Lucien snapped out a, "Stay there," to Tim and advanced on me.

Careful not to touch me, he stopped and kept his gaze fixed on my face, never once dipping below my neck. "Are you hurt?" His voice was a razor wire wrapping around my throat, but instead of digging into my skin and cutting off my air, its touch became a caress. A promise.

A promise of violence and protection and outrage.

"Hope?"

Startled, I glanced down at my arms, only now feeling the burning ache Tim's claws had left behind.

Lucien followed my gaze. "I will kill him for you." Cold eyes burned into mine. "Turn away."

Those words . . . My brain refused to understand. I kept getting distracted by Tim's low moans, by the stench of blood and urine and fear. My eyes darted from Tim's writhing form to his bloody, torn off appendage to Lucien's glittering eyes.

Everything was so—so far away.

I will kill him for you.

An ugly part of me rejoiced in the violence of that offer, the violence already perpetrated. If Lucien hadn't ripped it off, the thing that was now the reason for Tim's pain would have torn through me and destroyed a piece of my soul that I could never have gotten back. But . . . another part of me was horrified. Mostly at myself for not being more horrified.

"No," I said, surprising both of us. "I . . . I don't want you to kill him."

"May I ask why not?" A silken question. No need to yell when violence lurked in eyes that burned.

I took a deep breath, glad I finally *could*. "Because—because I don't want to be the cause of anyone's death. And maybe if . . . if *he*"—I couldn't bring myself to say his name out loud—"is given a second chance he'll do something good with it."

Emotionless mask slowly sliding back into place, Lucien listened with a cocked head. "As you wish."

Just like that my legs gave out. Before I could hit the ground, Lucien was there. He hooked one arm beneath my knees, the other supporting my back, and lifted.

"I have you."

I'd never been this close to him before. With my cheek resting against his chiseled chest, his scent washed over me; tantalizing, heated, like when the spring air turns to summer and all you can smell is life. Vibrant and vital and vivid.

I'd thought being this close to him would freak me out—not that I'd made it a habit to fantasize about being in Lucien's arms—but despite our rocky relationship and the disdain he so often showed me, I couldn't help but relax.

Lucien made a sound deep in his throat, turned, and took two steps toward the house before going unnaturally still.

"W-what is it?" I asked when he turned and cocked his head. Listening? Shivers ran up and down my arms and legs, my fingers digging into Lucien's hard bicep.

"Don't be afraid," he said, turning us to face the woods. "They are returning."

They? They who?

I was shaking too violently to ask, but I had a pretty good idea who it would be.

None of the guys had come rushing out when Tim started shrieking in pain. Not even Ruarc. He would have come—unless he was too far away to have heard.

Holding onto Lucien for dear life, I lifted my head and

followed his gaze. At first, I couldn't see anything, just the dark edge of the forest surrounding their property, but after a minute or two the bushes—and even the trees—shook as they parted.

A shape took form in the shadow, a gigantic monster of a man with a wide chest, powerful, long legs, and arms strong enough to ward off most the evil in this world.

But not the Hunters, I reminded myself, watching Ruarc shooting from the woods at a breakneck speed. His chest had been left bare, black sweatpants covered his lower half. This far away I couldn't see his face, but I would have known him anywhere with his glowing silver eyes and wild, black mane.

An inhuman roar rattled the trees, and somewhere on the ground Tim whined.

Lucien's arms tightened around me. He was marble at my back, flesh and blood marble. And when Ruarc reached us, the marble turned to ice.

With excruciating care, Ruarc gently scooped me into his own embrace and turned his back on Lucien, shielding me with his body.

"*A chuisle*," he whispered against my neck as he breathed me in. His voice was surprisingly hoarse, the low tones thrumming with emotion.

He was strong enough—and big enough—to hold me pressed against him with one arm under my knees, his palm cradling my hip. The other shook as it ran over every inch of my body with a desperate, searching touch. When he encountered the forearm blocking my chest, he used a gentle but firm touch to lift it away and peer at what he probably thought was an injury.

"N-no . . ." More a gasp than a word, and too late at that. My breasts were once again bared to the cold night air, and my eyes stung with unshed tears at the thought that this, too, was tarnished.

The first time Ruarc saw me, any part of me, shouldn't be

during trauma, at a time when the cold clutch of shock still held me in a tight grip and my whispered denial couldn't tear past my numb lips fast enough to stop another humiliation from taking place.

But Ruarc was Ruarc and as soon as he saw my torn shirt and what lay beneath, he averted his gaze and released my hand so fast it smacked against my chest.

His whole body was rigid, vibrating with contained violence. He hissed a breath through clenched teeth. "Who?"

One word. So much rage.

I looked at him, and the look on his face yanked at my heart. The narrow slits of his eyes glowed with fury, his jaw was so tense it looked about to shatter, his lips were compressed into two, tight lines, broken by the descent of deadly fangs.

He looked magnificent. And not human.

Not human. Ruarc's not human.

My gaze remained locked on those sharp, inhuman fangs. If I drew breath, I wasn't aware of it.

He's not human.

"Who?"

Too quiet. His voice had gone too quiet.

I pushed the revelation to the back of my mind—*later, he'll tell me later*—and focused on his question. "I—"

A withering snarl shook his chest, eyes locked on Lucien who'd taken a step closer. "Don't you fucking come near her!"

"It wasn't him." I was surprised at how brittle my voice sounded. "Lucien saved me."

Both men stilled, and something flickered across Lucien's inscrutable expression, something that made my heart squirm and my face grow hot.

Ruarc growled. "Then who the fu—"

A moan from behind, Ruarc keeping his body between

me and the sound, twisting his neck with enough force that the bones creaked.

A beat of silence.

Another.

Time crawled by, one deafening second at a time. Then, with such deliberate slowness that the locked muscles of his big frame barely twitched beneath the skin, he slowly, so very slowly, turned and faced Tim.

"What," he said, with a voice that could have cut through the earth itself, "are you doing here?"

The injured man took one look at Ruarc's face and promptly scooted backward. The blood from his wound had slowed to a consistent trickle, but like a predator, Ruarc's gaze immediately zeroed in on the source of the slippery, wet substance Tim had left behind.

He stared. He stared at what Tim no longer had. He shook. And then Ruarc opened his mouth and roared.

Holy—

I shrunk back and clapped both my hands over my ears, watching the man on the ground doing the same while curling into a ball and weeping.

It went on and on. Louder and louder. Deep and hard and so very furious.

The harrowing sound reverberated through the air, through me, through the very ground itself. And when it was over I sagged against the male responsible for the ringing in my ears.

Ruarc glanced down at me, and whatever he saw on my face had the harsh lines of his face tighten further. He glared at Tim, wouldn't look at me. "Go with Lucien."

"No!" The denial rang hollow. I cleared my throat, swallowed another batch of tears, and touched Ruarc scarred cheek. "I need you, Ruarc," I mumbled, and when he looked down at me, I let him see the devastation I felt, the guilt and the shame, the horror and the pain. I lay it all bare, ignoring the feeling of weakness accompanying my shaking hands, my trembling lips, the tears that filled my eyes when I looked up at the face of the one man I knew on some deep level that I could trust.

Alone, he'll kill Tim.

I couldn't let him live with murder on his conscience. Not when I know what it did to one's soul.

"Stay with me."

The cheek under my palm twitched. Ruarc shook; the arm holding me shook and the thumb finding its way to stroke my face shook. His eyes reflected a fury so deep I couldn't help but shake with him, but in the end he crushed me to his chest, buried his face in my hair, and jerked his head in the smallest, most reluctant nod to ever have existed.

"You hurt?" His voice was hoarse. Thick, almost. And something told me if the answer was 'yes' it wouldn't matter what I said next.

He'd rip Tim to pieces.

I clamped my lips together to stop them from wobbling. The concern and anger he felt on my behalf . . . I wasn't sure why, but it made my throat tighten and my eyes prickle. "N-no."

"You've bled." Accusing eyes scanned every piece of my exposed skin.

"Merely a scrape," Lucien interjected, earning himself a glare. "She will heal."

I stopped listening as Ruarc growled a reply. Chills shot up and down my back. I was so cold. And the loud moans Tim kept making was turning my stomach. Despite what he'd done to me, I didn't feel the need to witness any more of his suffering. The violence he'd been subjected to had been severe. Traumatic. And even if it hadn't been, I had no desire to spend any more time sharing the same air as him.

I want to be far away, I thought, willing Ruarc to walk me inside.

But where would Tim go? He would need a hospital, wouldn't he?

"W-what now?" I asked in a shaky voice, interrupting their harsh whispers.

Lucien shot me a grim look. "Now we wait."

"Shouldn't he go to a . . . a hospital?"

"No," Lucien replied. "Ash will be here soon."

I twisted my neck to look up at Ruarc and asked in a small voice, "Can we go inside now?"

A rattling breath, then his lips brushing my temple. "Soon."

"What will Ash do?"

A hint of a smile lurked in Lucien's cold eyes. It was the same kind of cruel, terrifying smile that had found its way to his lips when he'd dismembered Tim. And while the rest of his face remained a blank mask, that chilling smile prowled beneath the surface, just waiting for an excuse to be unleashed. "The right thing."

The air froze in my lungs.

"He better," Ruarc snarled.

"W-what does that mean?"

Ruarc cupped my head and pressed the side of my face back into his chest. "Nothing."

"Ruarc . . ."

"Listen to your keeper," Lucien said, tone too soft for me to take offense at the words themselves. He turned his gaze to Ruarc. "How far out were you?"

"Half a mile. Other's had to take care of the—of things."

"Did he say who was pulling the strings?"

Ruarc made a sound of disgust. "No."

"Shame."

After a few minutes of waiting—which I spent curled up in Ruarc's strong arms, trying to forget the last few minutes

421

had ever happened and blocking out Tim's continuous moans—there was movement at the edge of the forest. A tree rustled. Leaves parted. And Ash emerged from the shadows, Blake following a few steps behind.

I squinted, trying to spot Jason and the other guy—what was his name again—Z-something—but they were nowhere to be seen.

Ash's expression was unreadable, devoid of any clue as to his emotions. He stopped before he reached us and looked down at the blood and the lone piece of flesh discarded in the grass. Blake joined him, stared at Tim with hard eyes. "What did you do, Tim?"

Tim moaned, his fingers raking across the ground and leaving deep claw marks.

Not human.

Blake's upper lip curled. He dismissed the other man with a shake of his head and looked at Lucien.

Ash did the same, but when he spoke his words were as flat as his eyes. "What happened?"

A cold hand seemed to tightened around my throat. I didn't want to talk about it. Didn't want to relieve it again so soon.

Or ever.

Shivers took me prisoner, and Ruarc reacted as though each was a personal affront to my safety. He stepped back, turned us sideways so most of his body blocked me from sight. Twisting his head to keep the others in his line of vision, he bared his teeth and rumbled. The shock of hearing that sound again, the deep, dangerous sound that always made something tighten deep in my belly, chased my shivers away.

"Ruarc?" Horror pulled Blake's mouth down into a frown. "What are you doing?"

The booming sound tumbling from Ruarc's chest lowered into a growl—no less menacing but not nearly as deafening.

"I believe what happened here is quite obvious," Lucien said, ignoring Blake's question in favor of Ash's. "But I know our laws and it needs to be said. If Hope will allow it, I will recount the incident."

"I—" Throat too tight to speak, I simply nodded. Better he tell it than I.

When Lucien began, I squeezed Ruarc's arm, jerking my head at the house.

"Not yet," he said gruffly.

I didn't understand. Why did I have to be here for this?

Not wanting to listen, I closed my ears to Lucien's detached re-telling. Occasionally his voice rose, a hint of something dangerous cutting through his words only to be swallowed by his cold composure. Blake's droll tones interjected here and there, but I didn't pay attention to what he said. Instead, I focused on Ruarc. On the harsh, angry breaths in my ear, the clenching of his hand on my hip, the way his teeth gnashed together.

At one point I thought he would attack Lucien. The steady rumble he'd first made that day in the kitchen returned tenfold, roaring like unfettered thunder in the sky until his chest vibrated with the force of the sound. But he never moved. He stood there like my personal harbor in a tremendous storm, keeping me safe and using his massive body to spare me the sight of Tim.

I wondered how much that cost him. The inaction.

"What did you say?" Fury tore Ruarc's words apart and left them bleeding in the air.

"She wants him to live," Lucien said. "Has some silly notion he may change and do some good one day."

Silence. A vibration in the chest at my back, then, "Are you insane?"

The furious roar startled a gasp from my lungs and I shrank back, blinking back tears. His anger felt . . .

Cutting.

"Ruarc!" Lucien snapped.

Ruarc tensed, looked down at me, then jerked his gaze away and clenched his jaw. "Probably in shock," he muttered. "Doesn't know what she wants."

"I do!" I was still shaky but at least I'd found my voice again. "I don't want to be the reason he dies. And who knows"—I shrugged, wiped at the wetness on my cheeks —"maybe he will save someone else in the future."

Ruarc glared but kept his voice low. "He has to die."

"No." I turned my head so he couldn't intimidate me with that fiery silver gaze.

"Hope . . ."

"Ruarc is right," Lucien said. "He should die."

I looked from Lucien to Ruarc. From cold detachment to stubborn determination. Why wasn't anyone putting a stop to this? Why didn't Ash say something? He hadn't spoken once. Not since Lucien started recapping the horrible incident.

Why won't he look at me? I thought, trying to catch his eye while craning my neck to see around Ruarc. *Look at me!*

And then he did.

Ruarc moved and Ash's still frame filled my line of vision. Long, *long* black hair gathered in a bun at the back of his neck. A lone feather bobbed above his head. The wide lips, the flat nose, the cheekbones that were almost too high. And those eyes . . .

Intense blue eyes flickered with a white-hot flame, and although his expression gave nothing away I could almost see the heat flaring beneath his skin.

Fire, I thought, unable to look away. *An undying, ravenous fire.*

If I'd glanced away I would have missed what came next, that's how fast he moved. One second he was standing next to Blake, inscrutable gaze studying the hand I couldn't seem to stop from shaking and the salty tracks of tears on my cheeks and the way my chest moved with each choppy breath, the next he was in front of me and Ruarc, an impenetrable wall blocking Tim from sight.

The way he'd moved, faster than my mind could comprehend . . .

Not human.

The only clue as to what happened was that quick flash of movement, a splash of something dark, and Ash himself.

A thump, the sound wet and somehow deeply sinister. I strained my neck, trying to see around them, to see Tim, but I failed.

Tim . . . Tim wasn't moaning any longer.

I looked up at Ash's empty expression, looked at the flecks of something glistening nearly black around the collar of his shirt, looked down at his hands—

Not human.

Deadly, black claws tipped his fingers, each digit dripping with a dark, sticky substance that had to be blood. The coppery smell strained around us like a cloud about to burst.

"It is done." Ever neutral, his tone this time carried an edge. A splash of darkness, of the kind of heavy responsibility belonging to he who was solely judge, jury, and executioner.

Dazed, I looked between them, between all of them; their grim faces and flat eyes and set mouths. "W-what is done?"

Ruarc pressed me closer to his chest and strode toward the house. "Nothing, *a chuisle.*"

I twisted in his grip, grabbed his shoulders and heaved myself up, wildly searching the space behind him for Ash. "What did you do?" Dread was an insidious whisper in my ear, chanting; *not human, not human, not human*, over and over and over again, until finally Ash's burning eyes locked on mine and everything went quiet. "What did you do?"

"I did what was necessary."

425

My hands became icicles slipping down Ruarc's shoulders and my body turned to stone.

Ruarc grunted, repositioned me when I would have fallen, and kept walking.

This . . . this was all my fault.

One more death. One more mark on your soul.

How many could I take? How many marks were needed to forever coat a soul in a layer of slimy black?

I tried to tell myself that Tim had it coming, that this was not another innocent life laid at my feet, but even remembering his evil smile as he prepared to violate me didn't lessen the guilt. It didn't stop the trembling of my body, the coldness seeping into my flesh.

Not human.

Tim had not been human. Ruarc was not human. Ash was not human. None of them were human.

And I couldn't find it in me to care.

A nose dragged over my temple. A deep, hoarse voice muttered something that was drowned out by the numbing drone in my ears.

Who was I kidding? If I reacted like this to the death of my would-be-rapist how could I trick myself into thinking I could be responsible for all of the Hunters' deaths?

It's different, my mind insisted. *The Hunters will never stop. They'll kill and torture and maim until there is no one left.*

But if that was my reason for destroying the Hunters . . . What would have stopped Tim from attempting to rape the next girl who got in my way? Had I been about to let another, future woman suffer his violence just because I was too weak to take a life?

"—something to drink." Ash. His words drifted through my mind.

"Kitchen." Short and snarly, it vibrated out of the chest I was cradled against.

"Take care of your mess," Lucien said in a deadly tone

from somewhere behind me. An affronted noise followed. It sounded like Blake.

"And her? She's seen too much, she knows too much. When the Council finds out . . ."

The words sounded vaguely ominous to my tired brain, more so when three chilling growls echoed through the living room. Ruarc stopped and, without turning around, pushed out, "And will you tell?"

"No." Clipped and short. Offended? "But what is your end-game here, Ruarc? You know what will happen if—"

"My life!" Ruarc growled.

"You are throwing it away." Lucien. Sounding pained.

"And her life?" Blake asked. "You don't have time before the Assembly to do what is needed! Not to mention it may not take."

Ruarc went utterly still. "You don't know what you're talking about."

"Don't I? Ruarc . . . you have no good options left. The Council—"

"Fuck the bloody Council and fuck their rules! She's *mine*!"

"You can't be serious?"

"Deadly serious."

"But what—"

"I'll protect her!"

An itch at the side of my face made me turn to find Lucien staring at me in a way that was almost hopeless. Then he closed his eyes, turned, and marched away.

"What is happening to your pack, Ash?" Blake asked, voice fading as Ruarc followed Lucien into the kitchen and used his foot to slam the door shut behind us.

Gait stiff, Lucien crossed the tiled floor and leaned his back against the opposite kitchen counter. "This may not be exactly what I warned you about," he began in a voice dripping ice, "but it is headed in the same direction regardless of what you may claim."

"Save it." With exquisite gentleness, Ruarc lowered me into the nearest chair.

Wincing, I kept my arms crossed over my bare breasts. My shirt, the shirt Tim had ripped down the middle, hung in tatters off my shoulders.

"I'll kill him all over again," Ruarc muttered with a murderous scowl, his glare searching the kitchen.

A vein in Lucien's temple pulsed.

I looked away. The cold shock was receding, leaving me closer to uncontrollable sobs and hot, devastating shame. I couldn't bear to look at Lucien, didn't want to see the censure in eyes that always looked at me with cruel disdain. I didn't want to see his triumph when his worst suspicions were confirmed about me. That I was dirty. Not worthy of the help they'd given me.

Tainted.

Why didn't my monster save me?

As Ruarc moved to furiously rifle through the cupboards and drawers, making enough noise that my ears hurt, Lucien pulled his white dress-shirt over his head.

"Here," he said, holding out the crisp-looking material.

My eyes were drawn to that smooth, marble-like skin against my will. His body looked both muscular and lean, with a powerful chest only a little less wide than Ash's, and strong, capable arms. His stomach was a thing of art, all carved ridges and toned muscles. His hips were narrow, a cut 'V' disappearing into his slacks, and like his face, his body was perfectly symmetrical, every inch accounted for, every piece of flesh molded to perfection.

My mouth went dry.

His body was every woman's dream; so flawless even Michelangelo would weep at its beauty.

How would the rest of his body look? Would his legs be as toned as the rest of him? And what about—

428

I slammed my eyes shut, guilt an endless barrage against my soul. How could I be checking out another man just a few hours after gaining a boyfriend?

And half an hour after being assaulted by a man trying to rape you?

Opening my eyes and keeping them locked on the floor, I reached out a trembling hand to take the offered shirt, but a savage snarl froze me in place. Ruarc's lethal glare wavered between my outstretched arm and Lucien's shirt.

I snatched my hand back, cheeks burning.

Ruarc leapt across the room and swiped the shirt away from Lucien. Bringing it to his face he inhaled.

Another snarl, disgust lacing his expression.

"I-it's okay," I whispered to my feet. "I'll . . . I'll get something from my room instead."

In my hurry to escape and get some clothes, I rose too fast. As a black wave of dizziness swamped me, Ruarc's hand shot out and grabbed my shoulder. With a muffled curse, he guided me back down, kneeling in front of me so he could look at my face.

"Sorry." His voice was all gruff apology. "You . . ." He rubbed a hand over his jaw, jerked it away and stared at it as though it had betrayed him somehow. "Fucking hell—Turn!" he snarled at Lucien so abruptly I jerked in my seat.

Lucien turned with a sound that was almost a growl, giving me another reason to startle. Had I ever heard the controlled, rigid man make a sound like that?

Glaring at Lucien's back, Ruarc put his body between us for good measure and lifted one of my hands away from my body. Careful not to hurt me, he threaded the sleeve over my arm and wrapped Lucien's shirt around my back.

"Switch," he said in a low voice, jerking his chin at the arm covering my breasts.

My face heated a million degrees, but I did as he said and watched with wonder as he tenderly covered me up without peeking—making sure I was covered the whole time—buttoning each, tiny button with hands that looked way too big for such a delicate task.

"Thank you," I whispered when he was done.

"Should have been here," he rasped, cupping the back of my head and moving so our foreheads were touching. "Bastard hurt you . . ."

My heart clenched at the anguish and guilt in his eyes. "It wasn't your fault."

Ruarc shuddered and went on as if he hadn't heart me. "Thinking about what he could've done . . ." He squeezed his eyes shut.

"It wasn't your fault," I repeated in a softer voice. "I shouldn't have . . . shouldn't have gone out by myself—"

He jerked back. "You did *what?*"

I gaped at him, mind drawing a blank from his abrupt change from tender and caring to furious and demanding. Had he not known? "I—"

Before I could defend myself, Ruarc's accusing glare snapped to Lucien. "You didn't stop her?"

"I did not hear her," Lucien said. "She was sneaking around the house. I wasn't aware she was missing until I walked past her empty room."

"I didn't sneak!" I twisted on the hard chair. "I was just hungry and thought—"

"Do that again and you're going over my knee," Ruarc snapped, the angry veins in his neck straining against his skin.

A startled breath whistled past my teeth. "W-what?"

"Do *not* threaten her!"

My head whipped around, wondering why Lucien defended me and why he suddenly looked like he'd been chewing rocks.

"She's *mine!*" Ruarc snarled.

"Then treat her like it!"

Silence reigned while I counted each beat of my racing heart. I'd gotten all the way to twenty—not daring to speak while the guys looked like they were plotting murder—then Lucien shook his head and looked away, expression going back to being cold and distant.

Ruarc rose to his full height, towering over me. "Don't you ever, *ever*, go anywhere alone again." It was one of the longest sentences I'd ever heard him make, and he said it with such fury, such conviction, I was convinced the consequences would be dire if I didn't follow his command.

What possessed me to say what I did next, I had no idea. "Y-you . . . you can't t-tell me what to d-do."

His eyes widened for a second, then narrowed. He doubled over and lowered his face until our noses touched. "Watch me."

Something in me snapped. I didn't know what, or why, but his harsh words buried their way into my heart and started tearing apart the tender flesh.

Deep down I knew he was just looking out for me, but I couldn't help but wonder if maybe he thought I was to blame for what had happened. Maybe he thought I had brought it on myself, somehow. And maybe his order to not go anywhere alone was because he didn't trust me anymore.

Throat constricting, eyes growing hot and achy, I swallowed back tears and lowered my gaze. I opened my mouth to say—I didn't know what—but all that came out was a stilted, ugly sob.

"Fuck!" Ruarc's voice carried a mixture of horror and anger, and then he was back on his knees, trying in vain to catch my gaze while stroking his hands down my arms, my back, my hair.

A strangled noise from Lucien did what Ruarc couldn't. I glanced his way, but he wasn't looking back at me. He was staring at the opposite wall, brows drawn low over eyes that gave nothing away.

Ruarc cupped my cheek. "*A chuisle*, I—"

The door burst open, splinters flying to reveal a heaving bare chest, enraged amber eyes, and a twisted mouth forced slightly open by elongating fangs.

As soon as Jason took in my discarded shirt on the floor —I would burn the ripped material as soon as I had a moment alone—Lucien's non-expression, and the hole in my pants with the boxers underneath, horror filled his face.

I burst into tears. Loud, wailing tears. Broken sobs strangled my voice, erupting with such force that they squeezed my chest and halted my breaths.

It felt like dying.

Broken, I bent at the waist, yanking my hands to my face to hide from the world. Calloused palms brushed over the back of my hands, and I shied away. The touch grew firmer, desperate even, but I couldn't remove my hands, couldn't let them see me like this, all shattered into a thousand ugly pieces that made no sense.

Why can't I stop crying?

Why can't I be normal?

Why am I so pathetically weak?

A furious snarl startled the tears right out of me, and I looked up in time to see Lucien pummel his fist into Ruarc's face. Before I could intervene, Jason threw himself into the mix, howling with pain as a fist collided with his eye.

For a frozen moment all I could do was watch, then an elbow split Ruarc's lip and something inside me twisted violently.

"Stop!" I shrieked. When no one listened I threw myself in the melee, catching a flash of silver eyes—wide with what looked like panic—and a dying snarl before I curled my body around Ruarc to shield his vulnerable face against more punishing blows.

A hammer smashed into my shoulder. Or maybe it was a fist. Whatever it was, it hurt. It really, really hurt, and I couldn't stop the pained whimper clawing up my throat any more than I could stop my body from being wrenched to the side by the force of impact.

Everything stopped. All movement, all sound, all breathing. Except mine. Mine still came in harsh little gasps as I clutched my arm to my chest, but everyone else was completely still.

For about three seconds.

Then Ruarc roared and threw the others off like they were weightless. His silver eyes sparked like lightning, and when he turned his glare my way I felt it like a snap of electricity dancing over my skin.

Gawking up at him from the floor where I'd landed, I was torn between awe at his strength and a healthy dose of respect for his temper. With his mouth set in a grim line, jaw hard and unforgiving, I expected his hands to be rough, but when he helped me to my feet it was with all the care one would show a newborn baby.

Jason and Lucien also got up, but instead of keeping wary eyes on Ruarc—the man who'd just thrown them around like ragdolls—they both stared at me with varying degrees of disbelief.

I looked away.

With gentle hands—a complete contrast to the hard glare he was pinning me with—Ruarc felt along my shoulder. I winced when he touched a tender spot, but nothing felt broken.

"Lucky," he said in a flat voice.

Jason laughed, but the sound felt off. "Lucky? She was damned near killed!"

Lucien didn't say anything. Just stood there. Staring.

Ruarc shook his head, eyes still flashing with anger as he looked at me. "Our fault."

Jason sputtered. "How is it our fault?"

"She doesn't know."

Sneaking a careful peek at Ruarc, my brain reluctantly tried to put the pieces together.

Not human. They're not human.

I shoved the thought away.

Can't deal with one more thing tonight, I just can't.

"That's not an excuse!" Jason snapped. "She should know not to throw herself between males fighting like that."

I scowled at Jason. His mouth snapped shut and he turned his hard glare on me.

Lucien made a weird sound, halfway between a laugh and a choked growl. "Unbelievable."

I felt myself shrinking under the force of their combined anger. They were all so mad.

All I'd done was try to protect Ruarc. It hadn't even been a conscious decision, I'd just reacted to seeing him hurt.

Stupid.

Unwilling to cause any more trouble than I already had, I stared at the floor and tried not to fidget. My stomach was twisted into a mass of knots. Turbulent emotions tumbled through me, one after another until I thought I'd be sick. If my mind lingered on Tim, what he had tried to do or what happened to him, the shaking began again so I tried to blank my mind and think of the sky.

The open, star-kissed sky that could never be contained or imprisoned. Would always be free.

After a few seconds of tense silence, Ruarc growled low in his throat. "Clusterfuck." Then he scooped me up in his arms and stormed out of the room.

Despite my unease at his anger, I knew—deep down— he'd never hurt me, so I kept quiet while he carried me up the stairs, threw open the door to my room with more force than necessary, and slammed it shut behind us with his elbow. I didn't speak when he gently placed me on the bed and yanked the cover over my lightly trembling form. I didn't say a word when he growled, first at the door, then at the window, and then, it seemed, at his feet. And I kept my mouth shut and watched him pace around the room in tight circles that should have made him dizzy.

It made me dizzy.

After a few minutes he joined me on the bed, lying flat on his back and staring up at the ceiling. The dangerous fury I'd sensed prowling beneath his skin seemed to have simmered down.

When he spoke, it was without looking at me, without any expression on his face whatsoever, and with a gruffness that made my heart clench. "Wanna talk about it?"

"N-no."

"Tomorrow then," he said and I recognized it for the resolute command it was. Ruarc wanted to hear the story from me, probably wanted to know what had happened *before* Lucien arrived at the scene.

I thought about it, and though I was loath to relive this evening, it might help. After all, when I'd revealed pieces of my past before, it had felt like a wound being drained—painful but ultimately healing.

Tomorrow.

I had questions I needed to ask too.

"Okay."

"Can I . . ." he cleared his throat, glaring at the ceiling and pressing his lips tightly together. "Can I stay?"

"Yes," I rushed out without an ounce of hesitation. I didn't want to be alone. "Only to sleep?" Said as a question, I hoped he would understand it wasn't really one at all.

He grunted an agreement.

Neither of us spoke for a moment. Then Ruarc rolled over and tucked me into his side. One arm went below my head, the other over my waist. He buried his face in my neck and breathed me in.

I melted into him, my body finally releasing some of its tension.

The arms around me tightened and all I could feel was him. His warmth, his protection, his embrace.

"I got you," he whispered. "I got you."

37

RUARC

Damn that fuckhead Blake, damn him to hell!

I wanted to snarl so badly I all but bit my lip in two trying to silence the roar building in my skull. Only thing keeping me quiet was not wanting to wake my female.

Blake, though . . . The bastard was right. Hope had seen too much. She'd seen claws and fangs and glowing eyes, seen all but our true selves, and though she hadn't said anything yet, I could read the questions in her expressive face when she looked at us.

She knew. Not everything, but enough to be considered a threat by the Council.

God-fucking-dammit!

Blake wouldn't tell them, but if Hope said one wrong thing to one wrong person . . .

And it wasn't like we could put her out and wish her luck —the thought alone was enough to make me want to tear someone to pieces—not while she was being hunted.

But by who?

Fuck, can't think about that. Not now.

Any lycan who came near our territory would be able to scent her. All it would take was one too-curious stray, one enemy spy, and all hell would break loose. They'd question why a human lived among us, they'd try to find out what she knew, and if they succeeded . . .

There was one way around our laws, one way a human would be allowed to live knowing the truth. It would take time, but if it worked? Fuck, if it worked, if she wanted it . . .

My heart thundered in my chest.

I'd never wanted anything as much as I wanted this. Her. She—

She was waking up. My female was waking up.

Propped up on my elbow, I drank in the sight of her with hungry eyes. She chased the darkness away, quieted the volatile emotions raging inside.

I ran my eyes over every inch of exposed skin, not really caring if she woke and saw me staring. So what if I was acting like a besotted fool?

I couldn't look away.

She arched her back in a stretch, one of those I'm-just-waking-up stretches. Long, black lashes fluttered against delicate skin. A soft sigh escaped inviting lips.

Achingly beautiful. And all mine.

Soon as her guileless eyes opened, her lips curved in a sweet smile of welcome and a surge of possessive lightning flared in my gut. Wanted to wrap her up and keep her away from everyone. Wanted to be the only one who ever saw that bed-rumpled hair, that gorgeous smile.

Then she blinked and her expression clouded.

Remembering last night.

I suppressed the violent growl building in my chest. Every time I thought about what had happened my heart twisted and the air in my lungs turned to spurs. It burned. Each breath burned. I wanted to resurrect the asshole who'd hurt my sweet, innocent female so I could tear him limb from limb.

One death just wasn't good enough.

438

Hope moved. Just an inch to the side, and one of her dainty hands came up to curl against her cheek.

Just like that my rage vanished.

"Morning." My voice was hoarse with need. The need to tie this exquisite creature to me for good. The need to savagely destroy anyone who threatened her physical or mental wellbeing. The need for *her*.

"Good morning." Her voice was soft. Vulnerable. Peeking up at me with huge eyes, her gaze drifted to my lips before she hurriedly looked away.

Everything I was demanded I kiss her. Devour her. Claim her until she would never even think about leaving my side for more than a few seconds at a time.

Possessive asshole that I was, I didn't want to share her time with anyone.

When she swallowed, the pulse in her neck beating faster, I could no longer hold back.

"Mine," I growled and grabbed her, mindful of her smaller, fragile bones. The squeak she let out as I dragged her across my chest egged me on. When she was lying on top of me, her tiny nose scrunching in confusion, I pulled her close and brushed my lips across hers.

Have to be careful, I reminded myself. *Don't want to scare her.*

At first, she didn't respond. Didn't as much as twitch. Then a moan broke free and she relaxed against me. I nibbled at her bottom lip, groaning long and loud when she opened for me. She tasted like the finest wine, the sweetest, most decadent treat.

When her tongue hesitantly came out to touch mine I hardened to the point of pain. Her inexperience was heady. Made the possession coursing through my veins sharpen with the knowledge she had never been intimate with another man.

At least not willingly.

My jaw tightened at the horrific possibility, the beast inside roaring.

Have to relax before I hurt her.

I buried my face in her neck and inhaled, letting her scent do what my mind couldn't. Then I sucked on the skin behind her ear, nibbled my way down her jaw, licked at her lips. Fusing our mouths together, I went deep. Tasting. Owning. Devouring.

A wicked, feminine moan.

My cock jerked, straining against my pants.

Thank fuck I didn't undress last night. Would scare the—

Her blunt little nails dug into my shoulders and all my thoughts fled.

Wanted her to mark me. Show the world I was hers.

That she was mine.

When her hips began moving on my stomach, I knew I'd made the right decision letting her be on top. If she'd been under me I wasn't sure I could've controlled myself. And this way she could set the pace. Feel safe.

Thundering footsteps from the stairs had my Hope tearing her mouth from mine with a sound of distress. Wide eyes flickered to the door, pupils dilated with arousal.

Jason.

Was going to murder that sneaky fucker! Knew for a fact he could walk the damned stairs without making a sound!

I squeezed Hope's hip and attempted a smile. She returned it with a tremulous one of her own.

"Hell of a way to start the day." I rolled us until we were side by side, our foreheads touching. Loved this feeling. Loved being with her. Her closeness and the fragile trust that had begun blooming in her eyes every time she looked at me.

Was addicted.

I'll never break that trust, I swore silently as another sweet smile broke out on her pale face. Still too skinny. Needed to feed her more, remove the translucent quality of her unblemished skin until she glowed with health.

"Mhm," Hope hummed. Her movements were hesitant, a little nervous when she reached up and put her palm against my cheek.

My heart wrenched violently. How long since I'd been touched like that?

Putting my hand on top of hers, I turned my face into her soft palm and kissed it. Her intoxicating scent washed over me. I drew it into my lungs, spun it around in my mind until it was forever entrenched in the deepest recesses of my being. "You. Are. Mine," I growled, knowing she couldn't possibly understand. Couldn't *know* what that truly meant.

Possessiveness surged through every inch of my being until she was all I could see. All I could smell. Taste. Feel.

Mine.

A playful sparkle lit her expressive eyes. "And you're mine."

My gaze shot to her smiling face, my breath froze.

A piece of my heart was claimed at those words, and it didn't surprise me to realize she already owned several.

Peace unlike anything I'd ever felt blanketed my soul. I knew she didn't understand what she was saying, how serious it was to me. But her declaration settled me in a way nothing else could've.

She was mine. No one could take her away. They so much as tried, I would tear them apart and scatter the bloody pieces across our territory until every living creature knew touching her was signing their own death warrant.

It was that certainty, that unequivocal feeling of possession and pride, that made my heart clench with dread at what was to come.

I had to tell her. Had to pray it wouldn't horrify her. She was so fragile, had been through so much . . .

I was terrified the truth would scare her away.

Never let her go!

That violent denial was accompanied by claws digging into the mattress. If she wanted to leave, could I let her?

A silent snarl reverberated through my skull with an unequivocal answer. *No. Fucking. Way.*

Somehow I had to convince her we weren't dangerous. At least not to her. Had to convince her to stay even if she wanted to run.

"So . . ." Hope's lip disappeared between her teeth, a nervous habit I'd begun to resent—no one was allowed to hurt her, not even Hope herself.

Not able to stop a soft growl, I gently pulled her lip free and rubbed my thumb over the abused flesh. "Tell me about last night."

A shaky nod.

I schooled my features to hide the burning rage flaying the skin off my bones whenever I thought about *Tim* and what that worthless piece of shit had done.

Hope didn't need my anger. She needed support. Comfort. All the tender shit no one had taught me. And I wanted to learn. For her.

Looking down at her trembling hands, Hope began speaking.

Her words cut me. Sliced through me like knives. One of them buried in my chest and stabbed and stabbed and stabbed.

Every shaky word, every choked sentence, and every silent tear that refused to fall plunged the knife deeper. I wanted to rage at the world. Wanted to rip Tim to pieces. Wanted to plant my fist into Lucien's perfect face for failing to realize she'd left the house.

But most of all I wanted to gather her into my arms and protect her against all the many dangers in this world.

"Then he . . . he t-tore my p-pants . . ." She made a choking sound and closed her eyes.

She might as well have ripped out my heart and staked it to the ground.

If Lucien hadn't arrived at that moment . . .

Fangs pierced my gums.

When the first tear fell I could no longer stop myself. With a ragged curse I shot forward. The trembling, traumatized female was nestled in my arms before she could object. "Enough," I growled and rearranged us on the bed until she was sitting between my thighs the way I liked it. Protected. Surrounded by me and the deadly weapons my particular brand of dangerous wielded. Weapons I would use to assure the destruction of all her enemies.

"Sorry," she whispered. Her chin drooping to her chest in a submissive gesture of defeat that made me grind my teeth.

"Not your fault," I growled, struggling to contain my fury. I tilted her head up so I could look down into her wounded eyes. "Never your fault."

Hope's rapid blinking caused more tears to fall. "A-are you mad at me?" she asked in a small voice.

Her words startled me into stillness. Why would I be mad at her? I examined her face, saw the guilt and shame written across her delicate features. And then it hit me.

The way I'd acted yesterday. Yelling at her when I found out she'd gone outside by herself.

Bloody moron.

"Course not," I said, voice hoarse, and pulled her closer. I couldn't stop myself from brushing a kiss over the spot right below her ear. Like a starved man I groaned as the wonderful scent of her filled my lungs. "Nothing you could've done," I added, for once not caring how gruff I sounded.

"I could have stayed inside."

"Wouldn't have mattered. He was set on hurting you and would've found a way." My grip on her tightened. "Doesn't

443

mean you are allowed out alone," I added with a growl. Didn't want her thinking it was her fault, but I'd be damned if I let her out of my sight ever again.

Hope's breath hitched and some of the tension left her. She relaxed against me, snuggling her face into my chest and squeezing the possessive hand that had somehow landed on her thigh.

"You really think so?"

"Know so."

"Thanks, Ruarc." She curled her small body against me, trusting that I wouldn't hurt her, that I wouldn't use my considerable strength, my size to bring her pain.

Can't lose this, I thought. *Can't lose her.*

The fact that I might once she learned the truth? It fucking gutted me.

3 8

HOPE

A STRANGE CALM HELD ME CAPTIVE AS RUARC TRACED CIRCLES over my hip.

His exciting, masculine scent tickled my nose, his heat warmed my body, and the affectionate way he nuzzled my neck soothed some long-forgotten wound deep in my heart. I didn't want the moment to end, but it was time. I'd put it off long enough.

When I looked up at him his shoulders tensed, almost like he knew what I was about to ask. "Will you tell me . . ." I took a deep breath and maintained eye contact—something I was normally not comfortable with—and watched wariness tighten his features. "Will you tell me what you are?"

The hand on my hip stilled. "Yes," he growled after a tense pause. "Need to get the others."

My mouth went dry.

For some reason I'd expected to be alone with Ruarc for this conversation. After what had happened yesterday, I wasn't sure I was ready to face the others. Tim's attack was still fresh in my mind; Lucien's vicious joy at tearing him apart, the terrible sound when Ash killed him, and the angry glares and accusatory looks last night in the kitchen. Even easygoing Jason had looked at me with fury in his glowing, amber eyes.

And today I'll find out why his eyes keep changing.

"Okay," I relented, accepting Ruarc's outstretched hand when he got up. "Do you think . . . do you think they're still upset with me?"

"Better not be," Ruarc grumbled, his hand squeezing mine as he guided me out to the hall.

No point dragging my feet.

Never letting go of my hand, Ruarc led me downstairs and stopped outside Ash's office. Muted voices drifted through partly opened door, one cool and cutting, the other angry and harsh. Then a third voice, much lower, and all the sound ceased.

Ruarc pulled me against his chest and rested his chin on top of my head. "Don't worry. I got you." His deep, rumbling voice soothed the ragged edges of my nerves.

Feeling shy, I hesitantly brought my arms around him as best I could and hugged him back. Firm lips pressed against my neck, a quick kiss that lanced heat straight to my belly, and before I could sink deeper into the embrace, he moved to open the door. Only his comforting hand at my lower back kept my knees from knocking together as we walked inside.

The spacious office seemed much smaller today, courtesy of the three huge males waiting for us inside. Sitting behind the big mahogany desk, Ash should have looked out of place with the bobbing feather twined in his hair and the calloused hands used to harder work than holding a pen. But he looked as at home here as he did in the stables, and I imagined he'd look just as at ease stalking through untamed plains as he hunted for his supper.

Meanwhile, Jason looked distinctly uncomfortable.

446

Seated in the middle of the large couch along the right wall, he refused to look at us when we entered and kept his gaze glued to the floor.

Lucien, perched on the armrest of the couch, looked as he always did. Cold and unapproachable.

Not waiting for an invitation, Ruarc ushered me forward.

I sat in the chair he pulled out for me, turning to look over my shoulder when I felt his comforting presence leave my side. Leaning against the bookshelf on the left, only a meter or so between us, he met my pleading gaze. His mouth tightened at the corners, but he jerked his chin at me, letting me know I should stay.

"Hope," Ash said, his striking blue eyes piercing me with their quiet intensity. "How are you feeling today?"

I swallowed hard. "G-good." *Please don't ask me about last night, please don't.*

He took his time studying me. Assessing. Then he tilted his head and spoke in soft, soothing tones. "We have some things we need to discuss, *banajaanh.*"

My mouth went dry. "Y-yes."

"Last night changed things."

Because of Tim? Because he'd been killed?

Guilt threatened to shred me in its deadly claws. Were they in trouble? Had the police found out? Or was it something else? Something to do with Ruarc and the reason he couldn't talk to me about all this by himself?

Not human. They're not human.

"What are you?" The hoarse question left my trembling lips for the second time that day, causing a shadow to pass over Ash's carefully collected expression, and when he spoke, his voice was a growl with its edges cut off.

"*Dè cháiní Bháan Mahír.*"

Those words . . .

My eyes drifted closed; my skin rippled over bones that felt those four words down to the marrow. I'd never heard anything like it, yet a part of me recognized the language, felt drawn to it.

I should have known this my whole life, I thought and leaned closer. "What . . . what does it mean?"

"It means 'Children of the White Wolf,'" Ash replied. The weight of his gaze was a physical thing, heavy and assessing and boring a hole straight through me. "We call ourselves lycans, but it is not our true name." He tilted his head in a way that was purely otherworldly. "We are the descendants of *Bháan Mahír* and *Céalen an amdúir*. We are *mahír*. We are *wolf*."

A balloon expanded through my chest, filling me with this light, strange air that made everything around me turn hazy.

Wolf . . . Wolf. Wolf. Wolf.

They weren't human and they weren't wolves. They were *Wolf*.

"I . . . But—" One word. One of them sounded familiar. "Lycan?" That one. It tickled at my subconscious, sounding of raised voices in a long forgotten memory and ugly taunts that slipped through my grasp before I could examine them too closely. Only when it was swept away by the black sea of memories better left forgotten, what he'd said sank in. "Wolf," I breathed. "As in . . . werewolves?"

Somewhere far away, Lucien scoffed. "Not werewolves. Lycans."

I blinked, found him still perched at the edge of the couch, a glow expanding through the breathtaking green of his irises.

"Werewolves are simple, slavering beasts created by the movie industry to entertain the masses." A sound of dismay. "Lycans have not fared much better, though the myths have gotten certain parts right. The term was coined centuries ago by the Greek and adopted by our kind when we got stuck in this world. 'Children of the White Wolf' is quite a mouthful when you're in a hurry. And the old language . . . Sadly there are only a handful species left who speak it."

This world? Our *species? Lycans?* I turned that last word over and over in my mind, trying to come to grips with what they were telling me.

It was difficult. Impossible. *True,* an insistence voice whispered through my mind.

"Are you okay, Hope?" Head tilted, those too-wide lips pressed together, Ash studied me with piercing intensity.

"I . . . I think so." Strange, but I felt almost relieved. Like I'd been walking around with blinders, hearing and feeling all these things I couldn't see, couldn't prove were there. Until now.

The guys had ripped the blinders away and awakened me to a brand-new world.

Lycans.

It made just about the right amount of sense. I'd been through too much to doubt the crazy truth when I heard it. At the Hunters' compound, I'd seen things, heard things that didn't make sense. And though all the monsters I'd ever seen had been human, a monster lived inside me as well. An unnatural, inhuman monster that caused my soul to fracture and left me half of what I was meant to be.

A cold prickle of awareness crept up the back of my neck. I turned and found Lucien eyeing me with an unnervingly blank expression. No contempt glinted in forest-green eyes, no mocking curl tugged at lips that ought to be soft and inviting, not hard and pressed together. But the longer I looked, the colder his eyes became, until even the arctic would freeze in the face of such chill.

"Just like that you accept the truth?" A soft, dangerous question. "Perhaps you already knew about us?"

449

"N-no?" Would he ever stop doubting me?

Not until he uncovers all your secrets.

I shuddered.

"Do you have any questions, Hope?" Ash asked, a welcome interruption from Lucien's suspicion.

I peeked at Jason while I gathered my thoughts. He blinked, but kept his head down. I'd grown used to his cheerful commentary, to his funny quips and warm, subtle support. His silence had me feeling . . . lost.

Was he still mad at me from last night? Or maybe . . .

I swallowed the sick feeling rushing up my throat.

Because of me, a life had been taken. The weight of such a burden was nearly impossible to bear.

Before the vice around my neck could tighten to the point of impeding my speech, I took a deep breath and answered Ash's question, "The language. What you said. The . . . the k-kainee bahan . . . something?" I stumbled over the pronunciation, stuttered as I tried to duplicate his words.

"*Dè cháiní Bháan Mahír.*" The cadence of Ash's voice changed when he spoke this language. He sounded vibrant. More alive. Just as he did when he spoke Ojibwe. "It's Fae."

I blinked. "Fae?"

An impatient grunt from behind, Ruarc's hand curling around my neck. "Doesn't matter. Get to it, Ash."

Fae? As in . . . faeries? Why would werewolves—oops, lycans —know Fae?

And more importantly . . . "Lycans. I . . . I guess that means you can turn into wolves?"

At Ash's cautious nod, a strangled noise escaped from the tight confines of my constricting throat. The sound dragged a hissed exhalation from Ruarc and an icy glare from Lucien.

I ignored both.

To be able to shed your skin and become something else. *Someone* else . . .

Fierce longing swept over me and suddenly I was

desperate to see their change, to attempt to understand what they were, what they *truly* were. I wanted to greet that hidden part of them—something I was unable to do with my own dual soul—to know them fully.

But asking to see the manifestation of their biggest secret would probably be rude, so I settled for a more open question. "What . . . what else can you do?"

"We are not so different from humans," Ash replied, frowning when Lucien made a sound of disagreement. "But our lives are prolonged and we are harder to kill."

I had so many questions. How long did they live? In what way were they harder to kill? Were there *other* things out there that were also real?

Things like . . . me?

My breathing grew rapid.

I couldn't ask. If I did, I'd have to tell them everything. Not only what I'd been through—and the thought of picking at the open wounds of my past did *not* appeal—but why. If they ever found out what I'd done to end up with the Hunters at the tender age of six . . .

No.

But . . . Tim had called me human. He'd seemed almost disgusted by it.

"How do you know if someone is human or . . . something else? Like a lycan," I hurried to add before the sudden pity in Ash's gaze unraveled me.

Why was he looking at me like that?

"There are several indications," Ash said in a strangely gentle voice. "But the easiest and most reliable way is scent." He tapped his nose. "Someone's scent cannot lie."

"You can *smell* what someone is?"

"Everything has a distinct scent. Grass. Water. Dirt. Cats and dogs and deer and bears. Everything, including lycans and humans. And below the scent that tells us *what* you are, lies the scent that tells us *who* you are."

"W-what do you mean?"

Ash spread his hands to his sides and leaned back in his chair. Watching me. "Your scent is human"—*boom* went my heart—"and it is also Hope. If you left a piece of clothing in a store, any lycan who knew you would be able to tell it belonged to you." He looked at Ruarc. "Ruarc's scent is lycan and—"

"Pine cones," I said numbly. The first layer of the complex scent that made Ruarc . . . Ruarc. I didn't have the energy to list any other.

Human. I'm . . . human.

A human abomination.

I guessed, in a way, it made sense. If there were such things as lycans in the world—*magic*—then it stood to reason any type of supernatural could exist. And maybe far up the branches of my family tree, a monster had lurked. A monster that had passed its genes to me.

But not to anyone else in my family, I thought.

They'd all been human. My mother, my father, my—

My vision went black, then red, then a startling white.

I gathered those treacherous thoughts and slammed them behind a heavy, metal door.

Shivers rushed up my back, scuttling like tiny insects and feeling just as unwelcome.

Other questions, I reminded myself before the silence grew any more strained. *You had other questions.*

One deep breath later, my brain had stopped screaming.

"I've noticed . . ." I hesitated, darting a glance at Jason, who was still silently avoiding us all. "Your eyes, especially Jason's, they sometimes change color. Or glow. Sometimes both."

Ash nodded. "Yes. When our emotions run high, the wolf bleeds out into our human form. The first sign is the eyes. Then come the claws and teeth. After that, fur sprouts and the ears can pop up."

Ears? Fur? While human?

It was hard to imagine the cold and unaffected Lucien with fur and wolf ears on top of his head. It was enough to twist my lips as I struggled not to smile. Then I remembered all the times it had seemed like there was something wrong with one of the guys' mouths. Was that the teeth growing?

"But . . . doesn't that cause problems? With humans seeing you? And why do Jason's eyes so often change from brown to amber, when none of you guys change eye color?"

"Jason is young," Ruarc grunted. "Less control."

To my right, Jason bristled. He shot a deadly glare Ruarc's way before he looked back down with his jaw clenched.

"Ruarc is right to a degree," Ash said. "Jason is the youngest of us and has the least practice controlling his wolf during times of heightened emotion. His wolf's eyes are amber, while his human eyes are brown. Most of the time our eyes are exactly the same in both forms, just a little brighter and maybe a little deeper in our wolf forms. The glow also comes from the wolf. Ruarc, on the other hand, has spent so much time as a wolf that his eyes remain silver regardless of his form, but the glow only occurs when he struggles with control."

I thought back to all the times I was struck dumb by Ruarc's luminous, silver gaze. Mostly I'd noticed the glow when he was angry. Furious even. Or when we'd been kissing.

My face heated and I stared into my lap, struggling with the meaning behind his behavior. Was it possible that I affected him as much as he affected me?

Don't be stupid, Hope.

Almost as if he'd read my mind, Ruarc shot me a wolfish grin—complete with the typical Ruarc twist; all teeth, very little smile—and gave me a wink.

A wink.

I almost fell off my chair.

"I believe there was a point to this other than Ruarc's flirting," a cold voice said.

"This must come as a shock to her, Lucien. She is allowed to ask whatever she needs." Ash tapped five fingers against the desk with the kind of contained impatience that spoke of power waiting to be unleashed. "You are free to ask questions whenever you want, Hope, but Lucien has a point, however poorly put. There is a reason we are telling you about us now."

Right away I knew I wasn't going to like where this was going.

39

HOPE

"Because of . . . because of Tim?" My voice shook.

"In part." Ash kept his face expressionless, but something hovered behind that blank mask, something sharp and cunning and so dangerous all the hairs on my arm rose and my monster jerked awake. "What he did to you yesterday, what you saw . . ." One by one his fingers stopped tapping to lay still against the desk's polished surface, and that stillness, that lack of movement seemed somehow . . . ominous. "Had it not happened . . . But it did. And with Ruarc's display, your relationship—"

My gaze shot to Ruarc. "You told them?"

An eerie silence descended. Thick and heavy, it swept through me like a tidal wave of hot, humid air as three pairs of eyes flashed and landed on me at the same time.

The lack of noise and movement, the utter stillness made my mind reel. I glanced at Ruarc, took in his glittering eyes and the hint of a smug, feral smile spilling across his face. My cheeks heated at the hungry way he looked at me. Like he wanted to devour me right there and then, in front of everyone.

"Told us *what?*" The pressure Jason put on that last word made it snap like the boom of a gun.

Again I looked to Ruarc, but he just stared back at me with the same heavy-lidded gaze. "I . . . I mean, we, uh . . . we only just decided to . . . to be together?"

Silver eyes narrowed. "We *are* together."

Jason flew out of his seat. "Are you kidding me?" When no one answered, he glared at Ruarc. "I know what you said to Blake, but I thought . . ." His breath was a harsh exhale, fingers lifting to press between brows that were drawn together. "You should have waited."

Tension snapped like a whip through the office.

"For what?" Ruarc snarled, his touch disappearing as he turned to face off against Jason. "For you?"

"Maybe!" As soon as the word flew from his mouth, Jason froze. His gaze darted to me, doing a quick scan of my face before his jaw set and he stared back at Ruarc.

"Choose your next words wisely, pup."

"Like you did?"

Ruarc snarled, and my chest felt tight. Hollow.

This is my fault.

My mouth opened but no words came out. I didn't know what to say, so I settled for looking at Jason, silently pleading for something . . . something I didn't understand. But when our eyes met, he jerked back, shook his head once, then dropped back down into the couch and looked away.

Dismissing us.

"Enough." Lucien rose with the fluid grace I now believed had something to do with his werewolf nature. His cold stare brushed past me only to settle on Ruarc—who bared his teeth in response but stopped snarling. "Though I admit I fail to see the need for such theatrics, if you insist on continuing you can do so in your own time. Away from the rest of us."

Arms already wrapped around my middle, I resisted the urge to draw up my knees and curl into a ball.

Ruarc uttered a low curse, then he . . . left.

A sick feeling spread from my chest, but before it could swallow me whole, Ruarc returned.

"Up," he barked, grabbing my arms and lifting me up when I didn't move fast enough. A huge black sweatshirt was wrapped around me. "Better?"

I glanced at Ash, looking for clues to this bizarre behavior, but he looked back at me with the same, blank expression he seemed to have perfected.

"You were shivering." Ruarc gave the arms I'd gone back to wrapping around my middle a pointed stare. "You tell me if you're cold."

Weird feelings popped up. Some banged at my skull, insisting I pay attention, while others stroked across my heart and made the poor organ work twice as hard.

It's just a sweater, Hope, don't be stupid.

But . . . he'd noticed. Ruarc noticed everything. And while it was unease that had made me cold, he'd seen and made an effort to fix it. To make me comfortable.

I whispered my thanks, got a one-armed hug in return—accompanied by a quick nuzzle to my neck—and was guided back down in my chair.

"We were not . . . aware of your relationship," Ash said while Ruarc fussed with the hood of my borrowed sweater, trying to make it lay flat. "I was referring to how Ruarc—" An unnatural pause while something flared in his eyes, there and gone in less than the time it took me to blink. "It does not matter any longer."

They hadn't known?

I darted a glance up at Ruarc.

He cocked his head. *What?*

I licked at my suddenly dry lips, trying to ask him for help with my eyes alone. They hadn't known, and I'd blurted it all out like a moron.

Fire flared and molten silver heated in time with a slow,

457

toothy smile that said one word, and one word alone. *Mine.*

My whole body flushed with a strange heat and something low in my body clenched.

Flustered, I cast my eyes away from the potent male in search of something safer, anything really. But what captured my attention was Ash. His gaze was still locked on my face, one of his fingers having renewed its slow tapping, the *tk-tk-tk* scraping along my nerves. His undivided attention was a lot to handle at any time—those blue, intelligent eyes seemed to see everything, noticed every insecurity, prodded at every secret—but under these circumstances it was nearly unbearable.

By the time he finally spoke, I was fidgeting and picking at the fabric of my pants. "If you want a relationship—a romantic relationship—with a lycan, there are certain aspects of our nature you need to be made aware of."

A small thread broke off between my nails. Staring down at it, I barely noticed when Ruarc went behind the desk and rooted around in one of the drawers. When he returned, he pulled at my hand, gently unwrapping the tight fists I hadn't been aware of making and placing something soft and semi-squishy in the palm of my hand.

I stared at the gray lump, uncomprehending.

"Squeeze it," he said gruffly, closing his hand around mine. "Can use it to keep your hands busy."

This time, a whole heap of strange feelings rattled between my ribs, kicking against the restraints of my human body and trying to reach the surface. Ruarc was . . . He was . . .

Not nearly as scary as he tried to be.

I smiled, and if it felt like my face was cracking it was nothing compared to the rest of me. "What is it?" Prodding at the weird mass left small indentions. I pulled on a small piece, fascinated when it tore off from the rest of the body only to reattach when I rubbed them together.

"Eraser."

"Really?" I remembered erasers. They were square and white and quite firm.

"It is a special kind," Ash said. "You can shape it into thin points, so it is easier to erase lines with a narrow margin."

"What's it used for?"

"Drawings," Ruarc said. He moved back to his place behind my chair and placed his left hand on my neck, squeezing gently. Then his thumb moved, putting slight pressure against tense spots.

A small sigh slipped past my lips. "You draw?"

"No."

"Then . . ." I trailed off, distracted by the tight circles he was making with his thumb. Besides relaxing me, the movement had springs coil in my lower belly.

"Lucien. For his designs." He pressed harder and my muscles turned to mush.

"What . . . what designs?"

Lucien said something. I couldn't hear what—too focused on what Ruarc was doing—but his tone conveyed as much cool displeasure as any words ever could.

"Feel good?" Ruarc growled near my ear.

"Mm . . ."

The rasp of a stubbled cheek against my own. "More?"

My head dropped back, lids so heavy I almost missed the way his lips tilted up at the corners.

His thumbs dipped down to my shoulders, pressed against a spot that made me groan—

"I've gotta get out of here."

I snapped upright in time to see Jason cross the room without moving his gaze off the floor. He didn't slam the door, but I almost wished he had. The quiet, almost careful way he closed it seemed infinitely worse somehow.

A heavy weight settled across my chest.

"Are you quite finished?" The snap in Lucien's voice could've made rock crack and bleed.

"S-sorry."

"Not your fault. I have that effect," Ruarc growled, a teasing sound to his deep voice. I hadn't known he could sound like that; light and almost carefree.

I gave him a smile, a tiny, timid one that broadened when he bared his teeth back at me.

I loved the scary but lovely affair that was Ruarc's version of a smile. It was almost enough to make me forget the look on Jason's face when he'd left, and the way I kept messing everything up.

Almost.

Then I looked at Ash and my smile slipped. He was frowning. Actually frowning. Not properly, not like I frowned and certainly not like Ruarc frowned—that man looked downright terrifying when angry—but a mild one, one that showed mostly around the eyes and only a little around the mouth.

"You should know, Hope," he began, watching Ruarc but speaking to me, "that you are free to leave here at any time."

A dark rumble erupted from the man—the lycan?—at my back, drowning out my sharp intake of breath.

"Of course, we want you to stay, but we will not force you." His eyes, still on Ruarc, hardened. "Not if you want to leave."

"I . . . O-okay."

"Our . . . courtship rituals . . . are a bit different from human ones. Our males are territorial, more aggressive than those of other species. Conflict between males can be . . . unpleasant. Especially if a female finds herself drawn to more than one male." Ash's finger kept tapping against the table while I tried to control the thundering drum that had suddenly replaced my heart. "Of course, if neither male is willing to back down and the female wants both, they may end up sharing her."

They may end up sharing her.

The drum battered at my ribs.

Share?

" . . .in control."

I held up a hand, head spinning. "Wh-what did you say?"

Ash did that thing where he tilted his head and studied me in a way that felt distinctly non-human. "All you need to do is say no."

"No, the other thing."

The hand Ruarc had placed on my neck tightened to the point of pain. I winced and he immediately let go, stroking his thumb across the sensitive skin in apology.

"The sharing?"

My nod was shaky at best, my mind a jumble of impossible thoughts.

"Are not the consequences of such a pairing more important than this?" Lucien cut in. "Should she not be made aware of what she'll take from y—"

"No," Ruarc snarled, but I barely heard him. All my focus was directed at Ash, waiting for what he would say next.

"Our females"—my stomach dipped at the use of *our* —"sometimes take more than one mate." He returned my attention with an intensity that threatened to flay me open and reveal all the ugly hidden inside.

"B-but . . ." I swallowed hard. The conversation was making me uncomfortable. Feelings I didn't understand bloomed in my chest only to be swallowed whole by crushing guilt. I couldn't even look at Ruarc. "Why would any man agree to share? Why not find someone he can keep to himself?"

A strange light glimmered in Ash's eyes. The corner of his

lips tilted ever so slightly down, and his voice lowered, got rougher. "At some point in your life, if you are lucky, you might meet someone who touches a part of you you had thought long dead. A part no other has been able to see, let alone reach. It could take you completely by surprise and be someone you would never expect, or it could be a person who buries under your skin in such a gradual way you do not notice until it is too late." His gaze grew sharper. Assessing. "If you meet someone like that, what does it matter if you have to share her? If the thought of losing this person is as appalling as the thought of losing a limb, you would do anything to keep her. Anything . . . as long as it meant you would be a part of her life."

My breath caught.

He's speaking from experience.

Some unnamed emotion set my heart to throbbing. Who was this faceless, nameless woman that Ash so obviously longed for?

And why do you care? I asked myself, too much of a coward to look for the answer.

"While Ash's view on the matter is *very* romantic," Lucien began, "there are other reasons for this practice. For one, the male lycans outnumber the females five to one. It may not always be a matter of choice, but a matter of necessity."

"Hardly," Ruarc snorted. "Could always mate with a human."

"And what of the consequences, Ruarc?" Lucien asked intently. "Think of what you will be giving up."

I fidgeted in my seat. What would Ruarc be giving up to be with me? A hope for a proper mate? A woman who was wolf, as he was, and thereby foregoing something they all possibly longed for? And kids . . .

"Told you to drop it," Ruarc snarled.

He probably wanted kids. Even if I'd wanted to bring children into the world—something I could never do while I continued to share my body with a monster—could he even have kids with a human, someone a whole different species?

Doesn't matter, I told myself firmly. You'll be gone long before this becomes an issue.

My eyes burned.

Lucien turned his glacier stare on Ruarc. "I was simply saying—"

"I think that's enough, Lucien." Ash gave a barely perceptible nod in my direction. "Some things must come in time."

I pushed all conflicting emotions down—no point dwelling on something that would never matter. "So . . . Human mates?"

"Humans are lesser," Lucien said coldly. "Most wolves consider them pests at best, meat at worst."

"Not lesser," Ruarc gritted out. "Different."

The only thing I heard was 'meat.' "You . . . you *eat* humans?"

"*We* do not," Lucien replied with a grimace. "But some do."

I struggled to swallow past a sudden wave of nausea.

"Do not worry, Hope," Ash said. "There are few who consider humans food. Humans are, in general, safe. But we can come back to your questions later. If you and Ruarc are pursuing a relationship, you need to know what to expect. The most important thing is that you always have a choice."

Adamantly putting aside the whole 'meat debacle' for the time being, I glanced at Ruarc. He looked tense, but there was no doubting the possessive glint in his eyes when he met my gaze. When the time came, *would* he let me go? Did I want him to?

Almost as though he'd heard my thoughts, his expression tightened until his jaw looked ready to snap.

"Ruarc?" There was steely expectancy in the way Ash called his name.

Blue and silver clashed. Several tense moments passed

before Ruarc snapped a clipped, "Yes." His biceps bunched below his black shirt when he rolled his shoulders. "Her choice."

Gaze lingering on Ruarc, it took a second before Ash looked back at me. "Other than that all you really need to know is that regardless of what happens between you and any of us"—my stomach flipped—"you'll always have a place here. A home."

A home . . .

I glanced over at Lucien. To my surprise, he didn't object. Instead, he gave a barely perceptible nod when he met my gaze, and for the first time, the coldness in his eyes didn't faze me.

"As long as you don't betray us, that is," he said, ruining the brief moment of peace with a chilling smile that was little less than a baring of teeth.

I flinched, and Ruarc turned to Lucien with a warning growl.

The sound that came out of Ash then shouldn't have made all the hairs on my body rise. It shouldn't have made my heart skip a beat and my mouth go dry.

But it did.

It wasn't a roar. It didn't resemble the rumble Ruarc sometimes made—the one that made my skin prickle and my blood heat. And it wasn't even a growl. It was quieter. Softer. And a primal part of me screamed that it was much more dangerous.

"Enough," he said, that one word so low I barely heard it. He closed his eyes and drew in several deep breaths, and when he flicked his gaze over my face, the blue had gone so pale it nearly resembled ice. Or a very hot fire. "It goes without saying you cannot tell anyone about what you have learned here." The blue deepened. "Our world's survival depends on secrecy, which is why our first and most important rule is to keep humans in the dark. All humans."

Uneasy skittered across my back. "I won't say anything." And I wouldn't even if I had someone to tell.

"Good," Lucien said. "The Council executes those that do not abide by their laws. They wouldn't simply kill you." A bitter twist of his lips. "They'd kill us as well."

My fingers bit into the sleeves of my borrowed sweater.

Thank god I hadn't eaten anything yet or it would all have come back up. One of my biggest reasons for leaving was to protect the guys from the Hunters, and they were telling me someone else might kill them? Because of me?

"Who . . . what is the Council?"

"Our leaders."

Leaders? The leaders of the lycans . . .

My eyes closed. A spark of something, something sharp and unfinished sliced through my mind. It cut until it found a quiet corner, dipped its root to test the soil . . . And then it grew. Swelled. Until I could taste the possibility on my tongue, the bitter flavor tinged with a wild, wild hope that seemed as inconceivable as escaping the Hunters had once been.

But then reality intruded and the world turned gray. None of it mattered. Not if the guys who'd rescued me might lose their lives.

"They'd . . . they'd k-kill you? Why?"

"We are accountable for you now, Hope. For you and your actions," Ash replied. "The moment we brought you, a human, in under our roof, you became our responsibility."

Trepidation was barbed wire wrapping around my middle, squeezing and tearing until I could barely breathe. "You never said what prompted this discussion, and I know it wasn't Ruarc," I added. "You were all here already. Waiting to talk. Why?"

"You deserved to know."

The words were delivered in his usual monotone, but his

jaw . . . A muscle jumped once at the side of his jaw, as if he was trying too hard not to grind his teeth.

"Is this about the Council and their rules? Will they find out—Oh, god, do they already know?"

"No."

I sagged in my chair.

"Tim's death was not your fault."

I jerked back, only Ruarc's hand coming to squeeze my shoulder kept me in my seat. "What?"

"Tim grew up in a pack that considered humans prey. That we"—his voice grew sharp edges—"protected you, treated you as pack . . . that's what sealed his fate. Once he decided to leave his old pack, his death became inevitable. If not here, then another place, another time. And most likely with many human victims left in his wake." A short pause. "Do you understand what I am saying, Hope? It was not your fault."

My left foot kicked out, catching the edge of the desk in my haste to get up, to run. "I don't—"

"Not your fault," Ruarc growled.

"No." It was not an agreement, but a desire to end this part of the conversation. It wasn't important. Not when I felt like I had a blade pressed against my neck, ready to cut. There was something they weren't telling me, something bad, something— "You still haven't told me why."

"Does it matter?" Ice and silk. Lucien's voice was ice and silk. "It's too late now."

"What's too late?"

"You have already seen too much," Ash said. "If you were to ask the wrong questions of the wrong people . . ." His eyes bored into mine. "Pieces of knowledge . . . suspicions . . . Those are often more dangerous than seeing the whole picture."

"Blake kindly reminded Ruarc of his precarious situation

before they left last night, and, of course, the muleheaded male made it worse," Lucien said.

"Don't remember you arguing," Ruarc growled back.

"Perhaps because you have the memory of a rock!"

"Rocks don't have memories."

"Exactly."

Squishy rubber gripped between my fingers, I twisted and twisted and twisted.

It sounded bad. The whole thing sounded really bad. Lucien's anger with Ruarc, how Ash said I'd seen too much, and the vague memory in the back of my head of Ruarc losing his temper with Blake.

They'd broken the rules and now the Council would try to kill them.

"What do we do?"

"About?"

"About you! You guys are in danger now that I know, aren't you?"

Lucien turned his head so slowly I had time to count the seconds. Six. It took him six seconds to look my way. "You are worried about *us*?"

"Of course I'm worried about you! Why wouldn't I be? You've just told me—" A lock of hair fell over my eye. I swiped it away, hoping they didn't notice how much I was shaking. "Look, there has to be some way out of this. Or around it. If the Council kills the people who fail to keep the lycan thing secret . . ." I trailed off at the unsettling quiet that had fallen over our little group. "What?"

Something flared in Ash's eyes and was gone before I could pinpoint the emotion behind it. "We are not currently in any danger."

They weren't? Then why—

"Oh. It's just me?" The notion didn't really disturb me. Better me than them. Especially when it would've been my fault

—if they hadn't saved me in the first place I would never have been in a position to see what I'd seen. And I had the whole Hunter section after me already. What was one more enemy?

"Oh?" Lucien impaled me with a stare made of iced-over swords. "*That* is your reaction to realizing your life could be forfeited? *Oh?*" His voice grew in volume, nostrils flaring with each, clipped enunciation. Why *this* was what got a reaction out of him, I would never understand. "And no, you are *not* in any danger. Not yet."

"Oh—I mean, uhm . . . Sorry?"

A strange half-growl came from Ruarc, while Ash tilted his head and once more drummed his fingers against the desk.

"Sorry?" Lucien gritted his teeth and speared me with another of those weaponized glares.

I looked down.

"Don't," was Ruarc's instant command. "You're not beneath him."

"What?" I was quickly losing control of this whole conversation. They'd flooded me with information—information I felt I'd handled quite well considering I'd just learned there were such things as werewolves—uh, *lycans*, prowling the darkness—but now my head was starting to spin.

"Lowering your gaze is a sign of submission," Ash explained. "When you instantly look down and keep your eyes away, you are telling the other wolf that you are *lesser*. That you accept his dominance over you, his place above you."

"I . . ." What on earth did you say to something like that? I'd learned to keep my eyes down as a captive. As a way of mollifying my tormentors and avoiding extra punishment for being 'cheeky' or 'thinking I was their equal.' It was a survival instinct—one I doubted I would be able to get rid of just like that.

"Can we get back to the part where the female *apologized* for thinking she was in danger?"

If Lucien's voice had been a whip, I'd have been flayed by now. I was about to apologize when Ruarc growled a warning.

Wait a minute. How do I know its a warning?

That struck me as odd, too. I'd often been able to tell what their various sounds meant. Was that an instinctual thing left over from the days when humans huddled in caves —aware of the dangers lurking right outside their unprotected shelters—or was it a thing lycans could control? Like a defense mechanism against humans, a way to communicate without words when the world was yet young and humans traveled in large packs and spoke a different language?

"Back off," Ruarc barked, and it was only then that I noticed how close Lucien was. He towered over me, staring at Ruarc with a strange light in his beautiful, cold eyes.

The screech of a chair sliding over hard floor made me cringe. With slow, controlled movements, Ash rose. "That's enough for one day."

"Wait," I cried, a thought having just occurred. "T-Tim he . . ." My voice broke, and three growls filled the room. It was freaky, but at the same time, I found it weirdly reassuring. "He scratched me. With his claws, I think." Acutely aware of Ruarc's protective heat behind me, and knowing the fury vibrating through him on my behalf could ignite at the smallest provocation, I aimed my next question at Ash. "Does that mean I'm . . . infected?" I didn't know a lot about werewolves, only what I'd seen in the few movies allowed me, but they all had that in common. Get bit or scratched and you turned furry on the next full moon. If werewolves were based on lycans it stood to reason they could share some similarities.

"No," Lucien snapped. "You can't catch wolf. It is *not* a disease."

469

My jaw fell open as Lucien stalked past us. "Lucien, that's not—"

The door slammed shut behind him.

I looked up at Ruarc, prepared to share a what-the-hell moment, but his jaw was as tight as Lucien's had been, and his eyes were shuttered with steel.

"I . . . I didn't mean it like that." I shot Ash a pleading look when Ruarc's expression remained the same. "I-I don't know anything about lycans. You said to ask questions . . ." My voice dropped off as my chest clenched painfully.

"Hope is right, Ruarc," Ash stated. "She needs to ask these things."

A jerky nod.

I swallowed back more pleas for understanding and stared glumly down at my hands.

"Hope." Ash looked at me in a way he never had before—intent, yes, but almost like what he was about to say was painful. "Lycans are born. Not made. You can never be changed."

I nodded—because he seemed to expect some kind of reply—but I didn't understand his somber tone. I didn't need to be wolf to care for Ruarc. Or to be with him, for whatever short time we had.

Biting my lip, I glanced up at my . . . my boyfriend.

Nothing.

Nothing in his eyes, nothing to give away his feelings, only the tense line of his jaw pulling on his scar and leaving his lips a grim line.

"I . . . I guess I should—"

"Let's go."

Before I could stutter a reply, Ruarc pulled me off the chair and out the door.

40

HOPE

My mind was reeling when Ruarc dragged me out of the office.

Werewolves . . . mating . . . several males? It was all too much. I hadn't even remembered to ask some of the questions burning a hole in my head. Like how old they were.

Centuries?

The thought was scary and felt utterly unreal, but Ruarc had used that word the other day. Maybe it wasn't a metaphor like I'd thought, but an actual, literal statement.

It wasn't until the smell of hot chocolate reached my nose that I realized we were in the kitchen. In a daze, I looked for Ruarc, finding him by the stove. The sleeves of his shirt were rolled up to expose thick forearms and angry looking veins as he furiously stirred a wooden spoon through hot liquid.

Some of the cocoa splashed out, landing on the back of Ruarc's palm. I gasped as the tan skin—interwoven with lines upon lines of thin, white scars—reddened.

He didn't seem to care. Instead, his pale, silver eyes were narrowed in my direction. "So?" Angry. Almost accusing.

"So?"

"I repulse you now?"

I stared at him, my body locked in place. What was he talking about?

His breath hissed out through clenched teeth. "Knew it. Don't blame you," he said, but his hands curled into tight fists.

With a hesitation stemming from years of being rejected, I moved until I stood right behind him and gingerly touched his back. He jerked away. "I . . . I don't know what is going on," I said, misery filling my voice and making it sound thick. Uneven. "You don't repulse—"

Ruarc spun around, lips pressed in a tight, uncompromising line. "Doesn't matter. Still want you." He shook his head, eyes filled with self-loathing. He ran a finger across his jaw by his scar, tracing the white line until it ended by his nose. "Hate this. Fucking scars and fucking lycans."

Catching my trembling bottom lip between my teeth, I tried to follow his jumbled thoughts. Did he . . . did he think I didn't want him anymore now that I knew what he was?

"No," I whispered, gathering my courage and putting my hand on his chest. This time he didn't jerk back. "The whole lycan thing . . . It doesn't change how I feel about you."

A violent shudder ripped through his body. He leaned down, putting his forehead against mine. "Can't let you go."

When I didn't pull away he lowered his head, moving slowly and watching me with an intent that bordered on obsessive. Still not breaking eye contact, he snaked an arm around my back, dragging me forward until I was flush against him.

He was so close now that I could count the specks of darker silver in his irises.

A sound, halfway between a moan and a whimper, stole past my lips, and finally his mouth came crashing down on mine.

That first touch of his mouth drained my lungs of air.

Calluses rubbed against my nape as his hand closed, the grip firm and possessive and so . . . so . . .

My eyes fluttered shut and a deep, unsettling throb began between my thighs.

He claimed me. There was no other word for it. His tongue invaded my mouth like a conqueror set on victory. He licked, nibbled, sucked, and bit until my mouth felt foreign; swollen and hot.

Lightning seemed to dance over my skin, leaving it pebbled and so sensitive each touch spilled fire across my flesh.

His free hand skimmed up my back, down to my waist, settling on my lower back and pressing me impossibly closer.

I moaned and clutched him closer.

"Mine," he growled and spun us around.

Then I was on the counter with my legs spread almost painfully wide to accommodate his large frame. He pulled me to the edge, my core pressing against the hardness in his jeans.

My whole body jerked as I felt him there; layers of clothes separated us, yet it was the most intimate moment I'd ever experienced. He moved, an involuntary jerk of his hips that immediately stilled and ended in a deep groan.

My stomach tightened, my breath halted, my eyes rolled back in my head.

I'd never felt anything like this.

Keeping a tight grip on my nape, Ruarc dragged his lips over my mouth and groaned again. The sound rumbled from his chest, powerful and male and so attractive I squirmed. And when he fused his mouth over mine once more, swallowing my soft whimpers, my nipples tightened with an invisible string connecting them to my lower belly and the pulsating point between my legs. Each thrust of Ruarc's tongue in my mouth sent signals to all three parts, and they fed off each other until I felt dizzy with the strange, almost painful pleasure coursing through my body.

It felt . . . It felt like . . . It was—

Like being tickled on the inside of the stomach. Not in a way that made me want to laugh, but in a way that made me want to squirm and collapse and moan and make it stop and make it go on forever and ever and ever—

"R-Ruarc . . ." His name was a plea on my lips. A plea for something I didn't understand.

My skin felt too tight. My body too tense. The tingling in my stomach was unbearable, and yet, exquisite in its torment.

It was light and it was dark and it was everything. And it was brand-new.

"Your taste," Ruarc growled against my lips, his tongue running along the seam in a hot caress that left them prickling. "Can't get enough."

If my life depended on a reply right then and there, death would have claimed me. There were no words in my mind, no thoughts, no worries. Only need. Need and a myriad of new, combustible sensations, igniting and exploding with every touch.

Ruarc's calloused hand gripping my nape.

Ruarc's mouth devouring mine.

Ruarc's tongue exploring, claiming, possessing.

A tug against my lower back. Our bodies as close as they could get. His scent invading me, his heat branding me, the deep bass of his voice making my toes curl with every word, every sound, every groan.

Exotic restlessness teased at my senses. It made me bury my fingers in Ruarc's silky hair. Made me arch into his body and rub my breasts wantonly against his chest.

Ruarc growled and pulled me impossibly tighter.

A fervent moan left my throat.

An inhuman snarl, then Ruarc was across the room. His breathing was ragged, eyes wild.

"Gotta stop," he rumbled, his voice a deep rasp.

I could barely hear him over the pounding in my ears. I stared, and whatever he saw on my face had him curse under his breath, close the distance between us, and bury his face in my neck.

"Smell so damned good," he groaned.

"You too," I whispered back, inhaling and letting his scent, that wild, masculine scent, stoke the flames smoldering in my belly.

A low, deep chuckle rumbled in his chest. "You hungry?"

"Not re—"

"Should eat." Having apparently decided, he pulled away with a reluctance that made my cheeks heat. "Will fix you something."

At some point he'd nudged the pot with cocoa off the stove. It stood steaming with chocolate goodness, the aroma nearly as delicious as Ruarc's own scent.

While I fidgeted—silently cursing whatever phenomenon that made every inch of my body super sensitive—Ruarc poured a cup and pressed it into my hand.

"For me?" I said, inwardly groaning at that ridiculous question.

"Sure as hell didn't make it for me."

My brows climbed up my forehead. "You don't like it?"

"Too sweet."

"Sweet is good!"

Ruarc grabbed a pan from one of the cupboards, placed it on the stove, and turned. Silver eyes dragged over every inch of my exposed skin so slowly and with such hunger that his gaze gliding over something so innocent as my arms somehow felt erotic. When he finally reached my face I was sure it had to be bright red.

"Yes," he growled. "Sweet is good."

Heat flared deep in my belly, and Ruarc turned back to the stove.

"Pass me those," he said, his voice a little too rough

I passed him the cloves of garlic he'd indicated with a typical Ruarc chin jerk and slid forward, preparing to jump down and help.

A heavy hand squeezed my leg. "Stay. Like having you near."

My stomach did a little tilt, spinning twice as fast when he stroked up my leg. Then he grabbed a plastic board and a knife and started to peel the garlic.

"You have questions."

The sudden change of subject extinguished the last of the flames, and I suddenly remembered that my world had just expanded.

"I . . . I do," I said at last, thinking about all the things I wanted to know, all the things I wouldn't know to ask. It wasn't just their age, but how their world worked and what other creatures inhabited it. It was how this whole thing would affect me and my relationship with him. And the Council . . .

The idea that had begun as a seed in Ash's office when my world had shifted to include lycans, was now a Thought that wouldn't stop growing. A Thought that, once it had found soil, refused to pull up its roots and leave. It grew impossibly large, until I feared it would all come pouring out and destroy everything.

But when I opened my mouth, it didn't come tumbling out, and neither did any of the important questions I needed to ask. Instead, what came spilling out was, "How did you get your scar?"

At first I didn't think he'd heard me. He didn't react at all, he didn't even flinch. But the garlic got sliced a little faster, and his knuckles were white around the knife. "Happened centuries ago," he said without once glancing up from his task.

"Centuries?"

His lip curled. "Yes. Wolves don't die of old age."

"Y-you're immortal?"

"No. Just very hard to kill." He poured some oil in the pan and went to the fridge. A red onion took the place of the cut garlic that was now gathered neatly at the edge of his cutting board. Metal flashed as he made quick work of the onion, slicing it into small pieces before throwing it into the pan. Then he looked at me, and there was so much unsaid in that shuttered look that I almost flinched. "Sure you want to know?"

"Yes," I said. "I'm sure."

Sure it was important that I knew. Sure we couldn't have a relationship while he carried whatever burden this was by himself.

Why does it matter if you're leaving soon?

Maybe . . . maybe I didn't have to. Eventually, yes—there was no happily ever after in my world—but maybe . . . not yet? Maybe not for a while.

"Grew up in Scotland," Ruarc began, eyes never leaving the knife clutching in his right hand. "Hard land. Hard people."

Onion sizzled in the pan, filling the kitchen with a sharp yet sweet scent.

I reached out and put my hand over his, stroking his scarred knuckles.

The knife clattered against the board.

"When I was a lad my sire, *Tighearnan*"—his nostrils flared—"sent me to foster with a clan who held an important territory. They were powerful and had many warriors, but they weren't wolves. My sire wanted their territory for himself and since a full on attack would have cost too much, he sent me instead. Told me to gain their trust, learn their

477

secrets, and lead the attack when the time was right. Still hadn't gone through my first shift, and at ten summers I was already behind. Tighearnan thought the mission would harden me, speed my development along."

"Oh, Ruarc," I whispered. "That wasn't right."

"Was what it was." He moved his hand so we were no longer touching, and grabbed a wooden spatula. "The chieftain had two daughters. The youngest, Fiona, was only three and was kept apart from the rest of us. The eldest, Ailsa, was my age. Fair of face and with a gentle soul, she was the first truly kind person I'd come across."

I struggled to keep my face blank in case Ruarc looked over, but he never did and I probably failed anyway.

I'd never been one to care about my looks—honestly, there had never been much reason to in the past. If I thought about it, I guessed it would have been nice if I didn't look quite so wan, if my ribs didn't stick out as much as they did, and maybe even if my hair was smooth and shiny instead of coarse and dull. It would have been nice to be beautiful, if only to please Ruarc. But looks had nothing to do with the knots in my belly or the ugly sparks of jealousy stabbing at my ribs.

No, this had everything to do with the last part of what he'd said. Not the fair-face-thing, but the gentle-soul-thing.

If Ruarc ever caught a glimpse of my soul, he'd see a steel strap made of teeth and poison and deeds so black even the Hunters found it abhorrent.

And he'd hate me.

Unaware of my dark thoughts, Ruarc continued his story, "She befriended me and three years passed. Convinced myself I'd been forgotten by my sire, and was . . . content. Life was still hard; back-breaking work, sword practice and the Fergus' firm rule dominated my days—"

"Sorry," I squeaked, hating to interrupt. "But who was 'the Fergus'?"

Ruarc lifted the wooden spoon and gave the onions a quick stir. "Fergus was the laird." He rolled the R so *Fergus* sounded like *Ferrrges*, and *laird* sounded like *lairrd*, with an extra hard D at the end. "Being away from my bastard of a sire was a blessing, but it was Ailsa who made me happy. She was my first friend, ye ken? Made me feel like kin—" Ruarc slammed the spoon into the pan and ran his now-empty hand through his hair. "Damned accent sneaks up on me," he growled. "Talking about this shit . . ."

Heart hurting for him, I inched closer. "We don't have to talk about it if it's too hard."

A frown took over his face. "It's fine." He finally looked at me, just a quick flick of his eyes, before he went back to glaring at the food he was preparing. "You deserve to know."

A heavy sensation weighing at my chest, I watched Ruarc get some vegetables out of the fridge with his jaw clenched tight and each movement stiff—like his joints had forgotten how to bend. He filled a pot with water, turned on the heat, and began cutting a bright red bell pepper into small squares.

"Let myself relax, told myself he'd forgotten all about me." His expression darkened, thunder brewing in bright, silver eyes. "Was a fool. Day I turned thirteen, day of my first shift, my sire found me. While I lay naked in the woods, unable to move from the pain of the first Change, he questioned me. Wanted to know all about the Fergus' fortress, his men; their numbers and weaknesses. I refused. He beat me until I passed out, but I never told him." Ruarc bared his teeth in a grim, violent smile. "Didn't tell him shit."

Tears pricked at the back of my eyes, but I didn't speak, didn't give in to the urge to reach out and comfort him. I had a feeling if I interrupted him now he wouldn't be able to finish the story. So instead, I waited and I hurt with him.

"He cursed me, told me I was no longer his son. Then he left." Ripples beneath his skin, like this body was a restraint and he was aching to tear free. "The relief was overwhelming. Was finally rid of the bastard who'd made my life a living hell."

My heart sped up; something bad was coming.

Ruarc tossed the bell pepper into the pan and reached for the next ingredient, something green I couldn't remember the name of but vaguely remembered not liking as a child. He stabbed the knife into the green mass, cutting hard and fast, decimating the thing until there was nothing left to cut.

Only broken pieces.

The knife tumbled carelessly onto the table. Ruarc closed his eyes, leaned forward with his hands clutching at the counter and his face paling until the white slash of his scar was barely visible.

"A few days later, Ailsa was dead." Said in such a flat voice it took my brain several seconds to digest his words. Long enough that Ruarc continued speaking and my shocked gasp went unheard. "Tighearnan found out about my friendship with Ailsa. Guessed she was the reason I didn't want to betray the Fergus clan. So he killed her."

"Ruarc, I . . . I'm so sorry."

His eyes flew open. "Don't," he snarled.

I put my hand on top of his, heart clenching when his fingers jerked away from my touch. "It wasn't your fault, Ruarc. You were a child."

"Was my fault. If I'd done as he said . . ." A growl that cut off before it started. "He wanted to punish me. Remind me that I was his property to do with as he pleased and that any resistance would be punished." His voice lowered to a deadly calm. "And that was the day I knew I'd one day kill my sire."

It hurt. *I* hurt. Ruarc had lost everything, and at such a young age.

We have that in common, I thought. *Though Ruarc was blameless in his loss while I . . . I wasn't.*

"Years later, when I was one and thirty, Fiona became engaged to a moron named Leod. Knew the man; a pretty fop with a penchant for cruelty. Had been married twice. Both wives dead." He scratched his cheek—right where his scar bisected his skin—the gesture almost unconscious. After a second, he jerked his hand away and glared down at the table. Or the knife? "Didn't want Fiona to be the third wife he killed, not sweet Ailsa's younger sister. Couldn't handle it."

I swallowed what little moisture was left in my mouth before I remembered the cup of hot chocolate. I took a small sip, grimacing when the sweetness hit my taste buds. It suddenly felt wrong. Cloying and ugly.

Watching Ruarc talk with obvious affection about another woman, even a dead one, had my stomach churning, but it was nothing compared to seeing his pain. To sit there, powerless, while he suffered.

How could I make this better?

"Watched him for a while. Was no doubt in my mind he would end up killing Fiona, and after a mere three days I had proof. Bastard attacked a twelve year old girl, would have raped her if I hadn't put an end to it. I killed him."

I killed him.

No emotion. Expression empty.

If I was going to be scared of him, now was the time.

But I wasn't.

So Ruarc had killed. It didn't really come as a surprise. I'd thought him a warrior when I'd first seen him, and I'd been right. He'd lived in a time of Scottish lairds, of feuding and territorial disputes. A time I couldn't even begin to imagine.

Besides . . . anyone who preyed on children didn't deserve to live.

"Good."

His eyes snapped to my face. Searching. Then he turned back to the stove, grabbed the mangled mess that had once been a vegetable, and threw it into the mix.

"*Good*, she says." He used the spatula to stir the hot oil

around the new addition, shook his head once, as if to shake my words free of his mind. "Went to see Fiona. Told her Leod was dead. She became hysterical." Something akin to regret flickered to life in his eyes. "Apparently she loved him, was taken in by his pretty face and charm. Let it slip she was pregnant. It would ruin her."

He spun around, speared me with a look that was almost a plea.

"Was my fault," he rasped. "My fault she lost her sister, my fault she lost her fiance, my fault she was ruined."

"No, Ruarc, that's not true!" I exclaimed. I inched closer, daring to cup his bristled jaw in my hands.

He jerked away with a feral snarl. "Don't!"

I dropped my hand, my heart sinking. I hated the pain he was feeling, the guilt and misery etched across his strong face.

I also hated how he pulled away from me. It left my heart a shriveled, useless thing.

"If it weren't for you she would have suffered for years under the hands of her fiance," I said, speaking to my knees now. "She would probably have died. And," I added, willing him to hear me, to know that I was right, "even if you hadn't been involved, your—Tighearnan—would have killed her and her entire family when he eventually invaded their territory. Ailsa would have died no matter what you did."

"I offered to marry her. Fiona," he said in a quiet voice. "She refused."

My eyes squeezed shut. I wasn't sure what shredded me more; that he'd asked someone to marry him, or that the idiotic woman had refused and crushed Ruarc's heart in the process.

His next words firmly pushed me away from hurt feelings and shoved my face into an ocean of black rage.

"She . . ." He faltered and looked at me. Jaw clenched, brows drawn together, his face changed until he was glaring.

"She didn't like me. Wasn't good enough for her, and she hated the way I looked. Too big. Too ugly. Not good with words."

"That bitch!"

Ruarc stared at my mouth.

"What?" There was a definite defensive note to my tone.

His lips twitched. "Nothing."

I crossed my arms over my chest. "Well, she was."

The twitching sped up until his mouth split in a wide grin; all his glorious, white teeth on display in a way that would terrify even the bravest man. "Not arguing, *a chuisle.*"

I melted a little at the wonderful endearment I had grown to love. "Okay then." I moved a little more, my side pressing against the forearm he was leaning on. I tensed as the memory of his earlier rejection hit, but nonetheless reached out and cupped his chin in my small palm. "I find you very handsome," I breathed and watched his pupils dilate.

It had taken me a while to admit it to myself, but it was true. I did find him handsome. Had since I first saw him. Well, at first I'd thought he was scary looking, definitely worthy of a couple of nightmares, but there was something infinitely attractive about his strength. The raw power held within such a large body.

Fiercely strong, yet exceedingly gentle.

Hesitatingly, as if he wasn't sure of his welcome, he reached out and brushed his hand over my cheek. "Would tell you to stop lying," he growled, "but I almost believe you mean that."

"I do."

Another one of those deep growls. Ruarc inched closer and pressed a kiss to the corner of my mouth. "Sweet. *Much* better than chocolate."

When he moved back to look at me, I almost fell off the counter as I instinctively chased his lips. Only his hand on my stomach stopped my forward momentum.

A small grin played on his lips, slowly disappearing the longer we looked at each other. "Want me to finish?"

"Only if you want to."

He grunted. After a minute where he put some rice in the now boiling water and gave the vegetables in the pan another quick stir, he continued, "After she refused me her father found out. He was furious. Commanded her to marry me. So she did."

Those three little words stole my breath. Something dark and unpleasant stirred to life in the place where my soul should have been, the place my monster occupied.

"I didn't love her, but I'd loved her sister so I tried to do right by her." He paused. Swallowed. "She wouldn't let me touch her. Could barely stand the sight of me. I . . . I accepted it. Understood how she felt." A bitter twist of his lips. "Did my best to protect and provide for the woman, but she was miserable." He angled his face away and rushed past the next sentence. "After a few years of watching her grow bitter and desolate, I decided to fake my death so she could move on."

The more I learned about Fiona the more I hated the woman. She'd made Ruarc feel like he wasn't good enough when all he'd done was try do right by her. She really was a—

"Wait, why would you have to fake your death?"

The look he gave me was inscrutable. "She was miserable with me. Better that way."

"Surely there were other options? You could have lived separate lives, lived apart." I put my hand on his arm. "Why did you do it, Ruarc? Why take such drastic measures?"

Silver eyes dulled, then sharpened to hard flint. "She would grow old. I wouldn't."

Reality came crashing down so hard I couldn't breathe.

Oh.

My insides tumbled to my feet.

Oh.

If I stayed with Ruarc—which I couldn't, so why was I

even thinking about this?—I'd eventually grow old while Ruarc stayed young and virile forever.

Suddenly the big windows that allowed the sun to stream into the room bothered me. The sun itself was my enemy. Each day it would rise and time would march on.

For me.

I knew how it would go, too. I could see it playing out in my mind as clearly as if it was already happening. Ruarc would stay faithful to the end. Even when I was old and wrinkled and he found me repellent, he'd stay with me. I'd watch him suffer, *grieve*, as I faded away bit by bit. Or worse, watch him eagerly await the day I died and released him from the prison his life would inevitably become.

But you're not staying, so it doesn't concern you, does it?

I blinked back tears and Ruarc's rugged face swam into focus. Arms braced on the counter on either side of my hips, he was leaning in until our noses almost touched.

"Don't." His voice was a dark rasp. "Where you go I'll follow."

What? What did that even mean?

Seizing my chin in a bruising grip, he glowered at me with such intensity I was momentarily stunned. "Whatever you're thinking, *stop*."

When he didn't relent, I whimpered. He'd never been rough with me before, not like this. A part of me was shocked. And maybe a little scared. But deep down, in a place I rarely ventured, I found that I treasured his strength. Treasured his urgency in making me understand.

"You're mine, Hope," he growled while his eyes grew darker, the swirling silver glowing from within. "No matter what. You. Are. Mine."

With a fierce snarl, he dove for my lips.

The first five seconds were nearly violent. He crushed my mouth beneath his, teeth clinking together, tongue invading, his grip just this side of painful. And I found myself responding with a rush of deep abandon.

I couldn't breathe, yet I didn't care. Air had ceased to be a necessity the moment Ruarc's powerful presence invaded my senses and took my mouth in a kiss so brutal, so fierce, so ferocious in its hunger, that only *he* mattered. Only his lips on mine. Only that tongue stroking, caressing, invading.

When he pulled back, I was panting. The tight grip on my chin had gone from painful to reassuring, and the palm that had, at some point, come to rest above my butt felt like a brand.

"Understand?" It was a sharp growl, heavy with meaning.

"Y-yes." My heart was a frenzied bird trying to escape a too small cage, and the lie only increased its hysteria.

Because I didn't understand. I couldn't.

I was trapped, caught between my heart and my mind. What was right and what was wrong.

And I didn't see a way out. Not without leaving too much of myself behind.

"Say it. Say you're mine."

I swallowed, the hunger in his eyes making me melt. "I'm yours."

A long groan tore from his throat and his grip on me tightened. "Always."

The warmth that had been pooling in my belly turned to ice, scattering until only a distant memory remained.

Always.

There were so many reasons why that was impossible. But . . .

I'm here now.

How vulnerable did I want to be? How close to the sun should I fly? Was it better to clutch at happiness with both hands, to bask in the glow of the closest thing to love I'd ever get, or to never know its touch at all and save myself the pain of having it wrenched away when the time came?

My mind felt murky, my head too heavy for my shoulders.

How long did I have?

The Thought was now a drum in my head, a fist around my heart. Not a plan, but an obsession.

An unfinished question.

Whatif-whatif-whatif.

"You okay?"

My eyes flew open, caught Ruarc's gaze sweeping over my face. He was still close enough that the scent of him wrapped around me like velvet ropes.

I forced my lips to move into a smile and pushed all my thoughts into the sturdiest mental box I could find. "Yeah."

"You went all pale."

"I just . . . felt a little lightheaded."

His eyes narrowed. Turned assessing. "You need breakfast."

"Maybe."

The silver were now only thin slits. "You sure there's nothing else?"

"Yep. So where did you go after you pretended to die?"

He tensed, extracted his limbs, and moved back to the stove. The vegetables got a good stir and was soon joined by cooked rice. He kept stirring, and with each scrape of the spatula his expression darkened.

"She was kidnapped before I could go through with it." His lips peeled back in a silent snarl, and for the first time I bore witness to the change that gave his voice that particular thickness; fangs. Long and sharp and deadly, rising from his lower jaw and dripping from his upper like stalactites waiting to tear flesh from bones if anyone was unlucky enough to be near when it snapped.

And then the rest of his teeth followed suit, no longer flat and dull—no longer human—but those of a wolf's.

For a couple of seconds I could only stare, until slowly, as if it required great effort, they returned to normal.

Or is it the wolf that's normal?

"My wife . . . Stolen," he snarled. "A female under *my* protection. Had to find her, save her."

The years had done nothing to dull his fury. The harsh lines of his face gave anger a natural threshold, making him look perfectly at home while volatile emotions raged.

"Know who took her?"

Mute, I shook my head.

"Tighearnan." He spat the name like it was something foul.

"No," I breathed.

"Exactly." Ruarc yanked the pan off the stove. "Had been hunting him for years, and there he was. With my wife." He slammed the pan down on the counter, not bothering with protection against the heat. It was marble, after all. "Said he would release her if I surrendered. Said he wanted his son back." A humorless smile twisted his firm lips. "What he wanted was a slave. A monster to control and send against his enemies. Knew it before I went, but what choice did I have?"

I pressed my lips tightly together, willing my stinging eyes to stop watering. Without saying a word, I jumped down from the counter and pushed my way under his arm until I could reach around his waist and give him a hug.

At first he remained stiff, unyielding. Then, when I pressed my face against the bottom of his chest—he was too tall for me to reach any higher—he exhaled. The sound was heavy. Harsh, almost. But when he pulled me tighter against him, using one arm to hug me to him, I knew I'd made the right decision.

"Went to him. Surrendered. It killed me to do that," he admitted. "To just give in. But I knew he would keep to the bargain. Was the only good thing about the bastard; he never broke his word."

I hummed softly and waited for him to continue.

"Brought me to the dungeons, to Fiona. Only . . . it was wrong. All wrong. She was smiling."

Chills erupted along my spine. *Please no. Please, god, no*, I chanted in my head. *Don't let it be what it seems. It's too cruel.*

"She was working with my sire."

My heart lurched.

"Was still in love with her old beau and resented me."

My throat went dry.

"Wanted to punish me for taking his place."

My vision blurred though no tears fell. Not yet.

I hurt for him, for the honorable, caring male who'd done everything to save the sister of a girl who'd been his best friend when he was thirteen. He'd given everything to keep Fiona safe and happy. Sacrificed everything.

And she'd betrayed him.

In a flat, cold voice, Ruarc said, "While I was chained to the wall, she spat on me."

I snapped my head back to stare up at him, almost tearing several ligaments in my neck. His expression was closed. Closed and distant.

"Told me . . . told me she hated me. That she could never love someone like me. Said she wanted a refined man with a genteel face, not some harsh-looking brute who's only talent lay in warring."

A burning sensation gathered in my chest. Loud and angry, it buzzed and buzzed until it was a roar I couldn't silence. My head was my enemy, conjuring up image after image of how Ruarc would have looked—before he was scarred, before he was hardened by this particular betrayal. How he would've strode into his father's domain, proud and unfearing, determined to save the wife who'd openly scorned him regardless of the cost to himself.

And he'd known the cost would be steep.

I saw his face when he realized something was wrong. Felt his heart stutter when the woman he'd come to save flashed a cruelly amused smile. Lived his horror, his shame, when he understood that the two people who should have loved him—his wife and his father—had conspired to destroy him.

And I heard him ask the one question I'd asked myself every night for years as I cried myself to sleep at the Hunters' compound; *what is so wrong with me that I can't be loved?*

"She was wrong. So wrong," I forced out. It was hard to speak.

A tightening in his jaw was the only indication he'd heard me. "Fiona took my sire's silver dagger and started carving. Said I was already so ugly no one would notice if I missed a few pieces."

A strangled sound worked its way up my dry throat only to die at my lips. How would I have felt if it had been my mother, not the Hunters, holding the knives used to hurt me?

"She tried to do more. Wanted to cut off my whole nose, but Tighearnan stopped her. He needed me somewhat whole if I were to be his vassal. She left shortly after."

Trying to swallow around the gritty lump in my throat, I tipped my head back so I could see his face.

There were lines of tension around his mouth and his eyes were hard and staring straight ahead.

He's so much braver than me.

He'd exposed internal scars and laid himself bare at my feet, and all because I'd asked. I doubted there was anything anyone could say to make me share the ugly things I'd experienced at the hands of the Hunters.

There'd been a time I thought that revealing what others did to me would be easy, but the viler the Hunters' actions and the crueler the words, the more I started believing I deserved it. That I'd somehow earned the torment they inflicted upon me and that their ugly whispers were truth spoken aloud.

Even when I didn't, their shame somehow became mine.

How could I speak about what had been done to me when it was so ugly, so evil, so disgusting that simply thinking about it made the bitter taste of bile appear on my tongue and shame turn to rot in my stomach?

Looking at Ruarc, I knew he believed Fiona's insults to be true. And yet he'd still shared it with me, letting me hear what he believed were the ugliest truths about himself.

How had he found the strength?

"How . . . how did you escape?" I asked, wanting to get the rest of the story over with so I could begin repairing some of the damage the telling had inflicted.

"Took three years before they grew careless. I broke free, killed him and left Scotland."

Good, I thought, fiercely glad he was dead. "And what about Fiona?"

"Couldn't harm her. She was Ailsa's little sister. I left and never looked back."

Something dark and vengeful rose up inside me. I wanted to hurt her. Even though I knew she was long dead, I wanted to hurt her for what she'd done to Ruarc.

He left her alone. He just . . . left.

That, more than anything else, proved once again that the streak of honor running through Ruarc's core, was so ingrained, so strong, that nothing could ever tear it apart.

"Thank you for telling me," I whispered when I could speak again.

Ruarc didn't reply, just stared straight ahead with flinty eyes.

Standing on the tip of my toes, I could almost reach his neck. I leaned in, pulled on his shirt until a fleck of bare skin was revealed, and brushed my lips over his collar bone.

He jolted at the touch, then flinched, before he finally looked down at me.

As our eyes met, I tried to infuse all my feelings into my gaze. The respect and admiration I felt for him, the desperate *want* I harbored for *him*—his body, his mind, his soul—the pain I felt at the terrible things he'd been through, and the very real awe at how he'd not only survived, but moved on and left the horrible woman without a backward glance.

It made me question my choices, my motives. Did I want to destroy the Hunters so I could keep what had happened to me from happening to anyone else, or did I want vengeance?

I didn't think revenge was what drove me, but maybe the darkest, vilest part of me, the part that sang my monster to sleep every night with promises of '*soon*,' maybe that part wanted something else?

As I stared up at Ruarc, trying to convince him with my eyes alone that he was *worthy*, that, to me, he was perfect in his imperfections, the bleakness in his eyes slowly retreated. They glowed, brighter than ever before. And then he slumped forward and buried his scarred face in my neck with a broken sound that split my heart in two.

Without thought, I embraced him. My lips searched for purchase against his silky hair. I wanted to offer comfort. Give back some of the safety he'd given me. The *home* I'd found in his arms. "Your past doesn't define you, Ruarc," I whispered as he crushed me to him. "Your scar isn't ugly, not at all. It's a badge of honor, proof that you have survived terrible things and come out the other side stronger."

A shudder went through him. He didn't speak, didn't make a sound, but neither did he move away.

"You are so handsome."

That got a reaction. A strangled sound of disagreement drifted up from where his face was pressed against my neck.

"You are," I insisted. "When I look at you I see someone strong. A protector and a warrior. An honorable man who would do anything to shield the people he cares about from harm."

Ruarc leaned back, tilting my face up. Wonder and something soft, something tender and foreign and bright stared down at me. "*A chuisle*," he breathed, cupping my face between his hands.

At that moment, he was my whole world.

We stopped speaking in favor of feeling, of touching. Sweet caresses and breathless kisses become our language, our only sounds that of Ruarc's possessive growls and my soft gasps whenever he found a particularly sensitive spot to graze with his teeth. Whatever it was he did with his mouth at the crook of my neck made my toes curl and my stomach feel like it was in free-fall.

When I pressed my body hard against him, sweeping my hand across steely muscle and digging my nails into the top of his shoulders, he yanked back with a snarl.

My heart hammered in my chest, but when I caught his wild gaze, it came to a crashing stutter, then a full stop.

A wild animal. He looks like a wild animal.

Though he looked human in all the ways that mattered, in that moment he seemed more wolf. Feral. Predatory. Ferociously hungry.

I shook my head, wanting to thump it against the wall.

How had I not seen it before?

Now that I knew, it seemed so obvious. Ruarc wasn't human. He wasn't even close. This form, this *human* form, could barely contain the animal that pushed against the flesh-prison that contained it, and for some reason, that fact comforted me.

After all, the monsters who'd hurt me had been nothing if not human.

"Food." One word, distorted by the sharp teeth crowding his mouth and the deep bass of his voice.

"M-me?" I squeaked, thinking, if only for a moment, that he'd lost it and I was on the menu.

His eyes flashed—heat and hunger—but he shook his head, turned, and grabbed a plate and a fork from the cupboard. "Made you breakfast," he growled, and dished up a plate of rice mixed with vegetables from the pan I'd all but forgotten.

As soon as the plate was heaped full, he thrust it into my hands, dragged both of his through his hair with another low snarl, and prowled across the floor while I stared.

"What?" he asked, when I didn't eat but just stood there. Unable to look away.

"Nothing."

He growled, but the sound was softer than it had been. "Eat."

"Will you . . . will you join me?"

He looked at me for so long I thought he was going to say no. But then he grabbed himself a plate and herded me to the table only to yank me down in his lap. "Feeding my female," he grumbled to himself, adjusting me until I was comfortable.

He proceeded to feed us both. I always got the first bite, and Ruarc seemed to only eat when I was busy chewing. It was nice. Intimate. And when we were done, it seemed very natural for me to throw my arms around his neck, bury my face against his chest, and close my eyes.

41

JASON

I᠎ᴛ ʜᴀᴅ ᴛᴀᴋᴇɴ ᴍᴇ ᴛᴇɴ ᴍɪɴᴜᴛᴇs ᴛᴏ ʀᴇᴀʟɪᴢᴇ ʜᴏᴡ ʙᴀᴅʟʏ I'ᴅ fucked up after the debacle in Ash's office. But by then, the damage had been done. I'd hurt her. By not looking at her, by staring at my feet while she tried in vain to catch my eye, and by losing my temper like a bloody child, I'd hurt her.

Of course, she didn't know I'd spent a sleepless night shaking with a mix of anger and blood-curdling terror. And that being near her brought it all back; how the air had smelled of fear and blood when Zakh and I had come back from our run. How I'd seen Tim's empty eyes staring at nothing from a skull that was no longer attached to his body. How my heart had been pounding as I sprinted up to the house, searching for a second body.

Hope's body.

And then bursting into the kitchen only to see her half-naked, shivering, a hole in her pants, the stench of fear permeating the air around her until the bitter taste coated the back of my tongue.

That moment had been like the end of a thousand feet fall, when you splatter against the pavement and your body is torn to pieces.

When she'd seen me, wrenching sobs had spilled from her like her heart was breaking.

And mine fucking had. It had cleaved straight into two deformed pieces and bled the kind of caustic blood that burned when it touched flesh.

I'd lost it. Utterly lost it. And when dawn had arrived and Ash informed me we had to tell her everything, I'd still been lost.

In the office, I hadn't been able to look at her for fear she'd see pain in my eyes and mistake it for pity. Or that she'd pick up on the anger jabbing at my temples—why the fuck had I not been there to protect her? Twice I'd failed her now. *Twice!*—and think it was directed at her.

It had taken all my energy to not look at her, to hide my emotions so I wouldn't pile on the hurt—or pressure her when her world was already being changed by what she was learning—and then . . . then she'd let it slip that she and Ruarc were a bloody couple.

Where had my damned smile been then? My jokes, my good humor, my fucking mantra of smiling until things no longer hurt? Why couldn't I have laughed it off instead of acting like a jealous dick?

I'd spent the rest of the day alternatively cursing Ruarc for being the first with a claim on Hope, and myself for my damned self-destructive streak.

But enough was enough.

I knew I had a lot to make up for if I were to bridge the gap that had opened between us like a giant, gaping chasm, but by god, I'd bloody well fix it.

What still got me was that Ruarc—grumpy, hard-headed Ruarc—had managed to win her over while I'd gallantly decided not to pursue her. To protect her. And then it hadn't even mattered, because Tim had attacked her and suddenly we had to tell her the truth.

And if that wasn't the piss-icing on the shit-cake I'd been

forced to shovel down, it sure as hell was the appetizer.

The main course—doubling as a kick to the nuts—was being hit in the face with the depth of my feelings for her when I'd done my best to keep them from getting involved at all.

How had that happened?

It was fucking terrifying to realize I'd gladly give up centuries of my life if it meant having a few decades—or even just a few days—with a person who gave me a reason to smile other than to numb the pain. I'd never thought I would truly want someone to *know me*. Not after I'd spent my whole existence trying to wipe out all memories of my past and who I really was.

And along came Hope, all bruised eyes and haunted expression, and I suddenly found myself thinking that maybe, just maybe, she'd accept the part of me that was too ugly for me to ever want to bring into the light.

So that evening, I marched myself down to help Ash make dinner. Ruarc was out hunting the Stray that had carelessly left his scent too close for comfort, and I was here, determined to at least soothe the ragged edges of the wound I'd inflicted and to once more make Hope comfortable around me.

After that . . . well, I had time, didn't I? And if Ruarc could get the sweet, little human to see past the grump-parade that was one of his main settings, then maybe I could convince her to look past my far more numerous flaws and finally claim a little piece of happiness for myself.

———

Once we were all seated around the table—minus Ruarc—Hope's subdued demeanor prickled at my conscience. Needing to fix what I'd broken, I forced a grin and nodded in the direction of the fridge. "I made pudding for dessert, love."

497

She didn't seem to know what to say to that, just kept her gaze locked on her food. "W-where's Ruarc?"

I gritted my teeth against the urge to yell at her, to force her gaze up and on me, to make sure she understood that she didn't need Ruarc when I was around. I, too, would take care of her. I, too, wanted her.

"He will be back in a few hours." Ash's face revealed as little as his words, but when Hope remained still, staring down at her place of mostly uneaten food, he tipped his head to the side and uncharacteristically added another morsel of information, "Pack business."

"Oh . . . okay."

"Not hungry, love?" I asked.

"Not really." She speared a carrot with her fork and brought it up to her mouth. I suppressed a groan as those full rose lips parted and imagined it was something else she was putting between them. "It's very good, though," she assured us as she finished chewing.

"You should eat up, regardless," Lucien inserted. "You would do well with some added weight."

Even though I agreed with Lucien, I couldn't stop myself from sending him a fierce frown when Hope paled and looked away. The shame in her expression didn't belong there. I wanted to wipe it off and watch her face fill with laughter and joy instead.

She needs to smile more.

"Only eat what you want, Hope. We often have leftovers," Ash said.

That was a lie. It was a rare occasion where food remained on the table after a meal. Being a lycan was hungry work.

"Want to play some cards, love? We can bring the pudding." I wiggled my brows, willing her to laugh.

She still looked uncomfortable, but her lips tipped up in a tiny, careful smile. "Okay."

Once she pushed her plate away, I went around the table and pulled out her chair, guiding her to the living room.

It was time to start rebuilding our friendship and get Hope to agree to spend some more time with me.

Alone.

A predatory grin pulled at my lips. With Ruarc busy with enforcer business for the next few hours, a plan began to take shape.

"You win again, love," I said affectionately as I placed my cards face down on the table. I had to work hard to hide my grin when her eyes narrowed with suspicion.

"Really?" She reached for my cards.

"Ah, ah," I admonished, putting them back in the deck. "You know the rules."

A cute, little frown appeared on her face—two tiny lines emerging between big, guileless eyes, mouth pursing in a way that made my mind leap to other, more interesting things.

"Then how do I know I won?"

I made my eyes go as wide as they could. "Are you insinuating that I'm *letting* you win?"

A reluctant smile tugged at the corners of her mouth. "Maybe."

"The whole point of poker is to win, love. I wouldn't pretend to lose just to see your gorgeous smile."

She blushed, a pretty pink stain over hollow cheeks.

She needs to eat more.

Scooping up the last bit of pudding, I put it in her bowl. "Eat up, love," I said with a grin. "Winning is hard work."

She eyed the pudding with a look that was part yearning, part apprehension. "I feel like it's talking to me," she admitted with a rueful smile.

Intrigued, I leaned forward. "What's it saying?"

"Well . . . it's a particularly arrogant pudding."

My interest grew. "Oh?"

She mimicked my posture, resting her elbows on her knees, and moved closer. "It thinks very highly of itself. Brags about its sweet taste, its chocolaty goodness."

"Then what's holding you back?"

Humor sparkled in her brown eyes. "It reminds me too much of you."

"Really?" I drawled. "You think I'm sweet?" Satisfaction curled in my stomach. Maybe she was recalling the last time we played poker; the intimate moment I'd all but ruined with my insecurities and insensitivities.

"I think *you* think you're sweet. Just like the arrogant pudding," she quipped, peeking up at me.

The little minx.

I threw my head back and laughed, happy when her uncertainty slipped away and her smile widened. My little jokester was not used to having fun. Definitely not used to telling jokes. But despite being a little awkward and uncertain of her reception, I found her incredibly charming.

And completely alluring.

"In that case," I murmured with a wicked smile, "I think you should enjoy it."

Her face flooded with color. "W-what?"

"The pudding, love," I said, pretending not to understand where her mind had gone. I pushed the bowl toward her and grinned. "Enjoy."

"Oh!" The way she stared at me—unfocused and a little bit lost—made my jeans uncomfortably tight.

With a jerk of my chin I indicated the bowl sitting under her unmoving fingers. "Before it runs away from you."

She shook herself out of her daze—a shame when she was so damned cute all flustered and sweet-looking. "Right."

While I dealt the next round, Hope finished off the

pudding. Fulfillment swam in my veins when her bowl was empty. It felt good providing for my little human and making sure she ate. I couldn't wait to see the gaunt look be replaced by some flesh. She would look great with rounded cheeks, I decided as I stared at her beautiful face. How had I ever thought her plain?

The mere notion was ridiculous.

When she smiled her whole face glowed with warmth. It transformed her from merely beautiful to absolutely stunning.

"Wish me luck, love," I said as I picked up my cards. Her delicate snort made me hide a grin behind my hand. When had this girl's happiness become so closely tied in with my own?

I froze.

Being dependent on someone else for my own joy was not something I'd ever wanted. It was downright scary.

We make our own happiness.

How many times had I told myself that as I stared at my reflection, forcing a smile until the act itself pressured my mind into feeling something resembling a shred of contentment?

What would I do if Hope didn't feel the same way? She was human, after all. She'd been through trauma. A trauma I knew next to nothing about. She wasn't wolf, wasn't brought up with the possibility of multiple mates. The concept might shock her. Repulse her.

And then where would I be?

My smile felt stiff, so I forced my face to relax and moved my mind away from thoughts better ignored.

"I bet two," Hope's melodious voice called out.

"Two what, love?"

She bit her lower lip. "Uh . . . two of these?" She held up two white chips.

"That's two dollars."

"You know that I don't have any money, right?"

Giving her a slow grin, I winked at her. "You do now." I laid out my cards, face up this time. "Nothing. Not even a pair."

Staring down at the cards, eyes wide with shock, she let out a trembling breath. "I . . . I really won?"

"You've been winning this whole time, love," I replied, choosing not to tell her this was the first hand I couldn't have beaten—unless I'd kept my three queens instead of discarding two of them.

When she lifted her head a wide, earnest smile spread across her face and lit up her eyes. "I've never won anything before," she confided.

My chest swelled, heart aching with both sweet delight at her clear pleasure and agonizing misery that her life had been so filled with pain that something as simple as winning a card game made her this happy.

"I have a feeling your streak is just starting."

"Can we go again?"

In that moment, with her eyes shining with excitement, I realized there was nothing she could ask me that I wouldn't do.

It was bloody terrifying.

"Of course, love. Why don't you deal?" My hands shook when I handed her the deck. With perfect clarity I suddenly saw my whole future laid out before me. One road began with Hope and was filled with unknown twists and turns. It was a shorter journey, sure, but one filled with excitement, joy and . . . maybe love?

The other journey continued my current existence. Part of a pack, a family I loved, but . . . without *her*. It stretched before me. Unending. Straightforward. Flat. And steeped in the same loneliness I'd existed in for years.

But hadn't I been happy? Or had I just been so good at pretending I'd even fooled myself?

42

HOPE

"Here you go, love," Jason said and pressed a twenty dollar bill into my hand.

I stared at it, half expecting it to jump up and bite me. "Jason . . . I can't take your money. I didn't have any to play with in the first place."

"You won it fair and square, love."

No part of me thought it was right to take the money, but something about the stubborn tilt to his jaw convinced me not to argue. Maybe I could slip it into his room another time?

"Well, thank you."

My grumbled, insincere reply pulled a laugh from Jason, and just like that I was mesmerized.

I loved it when he laughed, both the sound—rich and full of amusement—and the way he did it—full bodied and with all his heart. His head was thrown back, and my eyes were drawn to the strong column of his throat.

When his laughter died down, I was squirming in my seat, uncomfortable in a warm, tingly way I couldn't explain.

Jason watched me as I fidgeted. Tilting his head and

taking a deep breath, his gaze flickered over my face and lingered on my mouth.

Then he moved his eyes down my body and smiled, playful and with enough teeth showing to remind me of Ruarc. "You need to buy some clothes."

I followed his gaze. Ruarc had swapped out the old clothes I'd borrowed with some of his. All black, of course, and very comfortable, the sweats were so large I could have quadrupled in size and still had room to spare.

"I . . . I have to wait until I start working—"

"Bullshit."

I jerked back. His tone wasn't really harsh, but it was short. Not like Jason at all. "I don't have money yet and I—"

"Ash already told you he would take it out of your future salary." His voice gentled. "The truth, now, love."

"I . . ." Hanging my head, I racked my brain for a believable response other than; 'I'm too afraid to leave the house.' But was that still the truth? I'd left with Ruarc and Lucien, and nothing had happened. Well, not nothing. Discovering the Hunters were looking for me didn't count as nothing. But they hadn't found me, and by now they would've moved on. The town was small enough that I'd have been surprised if they looked for more than a day.

Jason slid closer and threw an arm around my shoulders. "Come on, sweetheart. Talk to me."

To say yes would probably be stupid. Careless, even. But I wanted to. And not because I was dying to get new clothes, but because I wanted to be brave. I wanted to stop making choices solely based on fear.

And if part of the reason I wanted to say yes was because I didn't want to disappoint Jason, was that so bad?

"You're right." I let my inner self loose for a victorious dance at Jason's startled look. "I'll go."

"Tomorrow, then," he said with a wide grin, having already swallowed his surprise. "I'll take you tomorrow."

The room shrunk around me, compressing my lungs. "T-tomorrow?"

"Yep." A flicker of uncertainty flashed through his amber eyes, and I knew then that I couldn't say no. Not any more. "Unless you have plans I'm not aware of?"

"I . . . no."

"Excellent!" Genuine excitement shone on his grinning face. He gave my shoulder a squeeze before pulling back, looking vibrant and alive and so handsome that my breath hitched. "Shall we say, right after breakfast?"

"O-okay."

Jumping to his feet, Jason looked down at me with a beaming smile. "You'll have a great time, love. Take a moment and write a list of all the things you want so you don't forget anything." Without waiting for me to reply, he sprang up from the couch, flashed me a grin, and left.

I guess I should make a list? Dread mixed with excitement. I'd never been shopping before, at least not that I could remember. While in the Hunters' care I hadn't really thought about clothes or material goods, although I often longed for books or movies—the few I'd had access to had been taken away years ago as punishment for my first escape attempt, and despite the physical pain they inflicted, losing those items had been the far greater blow.

I shook my head, dislodging painful memories, and pictured Jason's face just as I'd agreed to go. He'd given me one of his rarer smiles, the ones that went all the way to his eyes and made them shine with warmth.

Shopping will be fun, I decided as I got to my feet.

Maybe I could even get Ruarc to come with us, get his opinion. If not, I'd at least have Jason. The clothes he wore suited his personality, looking both stylish and comfortable. He'd know what I should buy.

Deciding I would let Jason or Ruarc pick out my clothes dissipated some of the dread coiling in my stomach. I wouldn't have to make a fool of myself by showing them I had no idea how to dress or pick out clothes.

Trudging up the stairs to wait for Ruarc to return, I tried to tell myself I wasn't scared. That this was just an innocent trip to a town I'd already been to. A town the Hunters had already searched.

There was no reason for them to still be there. No reason at all.

Everything would be all right. I'd get some new clothes, spend some time with Jason—and maybe Ruarc—and be back here before dark.

It would be okay. It would.

Chills masquerading as dead fingers trailed up my back.

The Hunters would never know.

"No," Ruarc stated with a look of grim determination. No trace remained of the passion he'd displayed a few minutes earlier when his lips had been devouring mine with a ferocious hunger that had my stomach fluttering like a million electric butterflies were trying to escape.

"No, you don't want to join?" I asked, making an effort to keep my face expressionless. I didn't want him to see that his brusque dismissal bothered me. So what if he didn't want to come shopping with us? I couldn't expect him to want to spend every second of his day with me just because I wanted to spend all of mine with him.

Silver eyes narrowed as they traced my face. "Can't," he said, crossing his arms over his broad chest. "Busy."

"Oh . . . what are you doing?"

"Work." His clipped, short answers sparked a flare of annoyance.

Mimicking his stance, I shot my chin out and met his

gaze head on. "Fine. I'll see you when I get back. If you're even here," I muttered.

A terrible stillness came over him. "*What*?" He stepped closer, looming above me with a fierce scowl.

Since his question hadn't really been a question, I kept my mouth shut.

Another step brought him near enough that his heat warmed the small space between our bodies. "You're not going."

The way he said it, the finality to his statement, no, his *order*, turned the flare of annoyance into blazing anger. Here I was, having escaped a lifetime of captivity only to be told what I could and could not do by my boyfriend of one day?

Without stopping to think, I shoved my finger into Ruarc's muscular chest, repressing a flare of fear as his upper lip curled to reveal a longer-than-normal fang. "You can't just decide what I do and when I do it. That's not how this works!"

"Oh, but it is," he said silkily, and grabbed my wrist. "You're staying."

"Am not!"

He tugged and I tumbled into his hard body. "You're. Not. Going." A vein throbbed in his temple. "Not without me. Not with *Jason*."

A shiver worked its way up my back at the menace he projected, and keeping my voice from shaking proved impossible. "Y-yes, I am."

"Goddammit!" he roared.

I jerked back, tripping over my own two feet only to be rescued by the very man I was trying to get some distance from. He made sure I was steady before letting me go, silver eyes boring a hole through my head.

I froze. Like a rabbit who'd just spotted a big, scary predator, all my muscles locked up.

"Can't keep you safe if I'm not there," he growled.

I hid my hands behind my back so he wouldn't see them tremble. "Jason will be there—"

In a blink he was in front of me, rumbling from that deep place in his chest that made my belly clench with feelings I wasn't yet ready to acknowledge. "No." His voice was pure steel as he glowered down at me. "You will *not* go."

I fixed my gaze at his throat so I wouldn't have to look into eyes that had become hard and uncompromising. "That's not fair, Ruarc," I whispered. "You can't just make my decisions for me while you go out and do whatever you want."

"Not doing what I *want*," he growled. "Have to. Pack business."

"Still . . . you can't . . . you can't forbid me to leave." As soon as that last word left my mouth, I knew I'd made a mistake. It was there in the way he jerked back, in his harsh inhale and the unforgiving line of his mouth.

Dark brows drew together into two deep slashes. When he spoke, the words were brutal and garbled, like his mouth was filled with razors—which wasn't far from the truth if the glimpses of sharp teeth I caught were anything to go by. "*Leave?*" A flash of wild fear, quickly eclipsed by the growing determination and rage filling his eyes. "Never!"

I flinched. He caught the minuscule movement and his eyes narrowed until they were thin slits of savage silver. My whole body trembled as every instinct I possessed screamed for me to flee. All thoughts of Ruarc fled my mind until I only saw a huge, furious stranger in his place. The rage he was radiating short-circuited my brain and brought back memories that had dread slither up my spine.

I stumbled back, squeezing my eyes shut when he followed.

Stalking me.

"You're not leaving," he snarled, invading my personal

space until my back hit the wall and his towering frame filled my entire field of vision.

I couldn't speak. The terror had left me numb and mute. Instead, I gave a jerky nod, not daring to open my eyes.

Time passed. A minute, five minutes, an hour. I couldn't tell. My ears strained. I picked up heavy breathing. Then a muttered curse, followed by a leaden exhale. A big palm cupped my shoulder, hesitated, then pulled me into a warm, male body. Lips brushed across my temple. Bristles dragged across my neck, forcing my skin to react with a shiver before I could control myself.

"Hope, I—"

"Ruarc?" Ash called from somewhere down the hall. "We have to leave or we will be late."

A muttered curse, then Ruarc's touch fell away. I kept my eyes closed while his stare dragged across my face. I felt it, like pinpricks of heat.

After an indeterminate amount of time, his knuckles stroked across my cheek. The caress felt strangely reluctant.

I kept my eyes closed and remained still.

Another heavy sigh, and then all the power drained out of the room, leaving me suddenly gasping for breath. My eyes shot open, taking in the empty room and the closed door. He'd left, and he'd taken all that energy, all that heat, all that wild fury with him.

His scent lingered after he left. Fitting, since I stayed frozen to the spot for several more minutes. I stood there until the frost in my veins melted and fear was shoved aside to make room for a bigger presence.

Anger.

It flowed through me, gathering in the pit of my stomach like a ball of heated lead. Anger mixed with heartache as I tried to sort through our argument.

I understood that I'd hurt him, even though I hadn't meant to. I could appreciate his protectiveness—in fact, it often made me feel safe and cared for—but this time it had felt too much like being under someone else's control; a feeling my body rejected with a violent bout of nausea.

And the way he'd roared at me, terrified me into submission . . .

It's not right.

Looking back, I realized he probably hadn't meant to scare me. And I shouldn't have let myself scare, I knew Ruarc wouldn't hurt me. But if I let him take away my choices I would never be able to become stronger, to respect myself and earn the respect of those around me.

Taking a deep, fortifying breath, I picked up a pen and a sheet of paper—borrowed from the library—and began making a shopping list. Maybe Ruarc wouldn't even be back by the time we left tomorrow. Maybe he'd be gone until we returned. Either way, I was going.

He might not be that mad . . .

43

HOPE

AFTER A RESTLESS NIGHT OF TOSSING AND TURNING, I WAS ready to get this shopping trip over and done with. My stomach rolled when I got up. My fingers shook when I got dressed. And my legs trembled when I walked downstairs.

No matter how many times I told myself I'd be safe, a small voice in the back of my head was screaming. Not a wordless scream either, but one filled with curses, rhetorical questions—mostly ones that left me questioning my own intelligence, or lack thereof—and incriminations.

Leaving the house was going to be absolutely nerve-wrecking.

At breakfast I kept quiet, acutely aware that both Ruarc and Ash had yet to return from whatever mysterious *errand* they'd gone on. Even Jason's relentless attempts at cheering me up failed. Not even when he made a stern face out of his eggs—a face that somehow wore the same cool expression as Lucien—did I manage a smile. And though Jason laughed uproariously when Lucien—without so much as a glance down at the plate—poured brown sauce all over his creation, the nerves in my stomach refused to settle.

Or they couldn't.

Back in my room, I fretted about what to wear for all of two minutes before realizing it didn't matter—it was either black sweats that were too large, or . . . black sweats that were too large.

I stared glumly at my reflection for a few long seconds before shaking my head.

"It's no use," I told the stranger looking back at me. "You're too scared."

Her lips were too full for her face—which was still too gaunt—and her eyes too large. Her shoulders were slightly hunched, as though expecting a blow at any moment, and her hands never stilled, continuously picking at her sleeves, her nails, her pants. A nervous gesture I immediately hated.

She wasn't me. Couldn't be me. But . . .

I recognized the fear pinching her expression, had felt it enough times for us to be intimately familiar.

"It's a short trip," I told her. "You've already been there. They . . . they're not looking there any longer."

The person looking back at me was not convinced.

I averted my gaze and said, "You'll be safe."

That time, the words weren't quite as hollow, so I kept my eyes on my feet, not looking at her while I spoke. "You'll be fine." My voice firmed. "Everything is fine, and staying here would be cowardly. You don't want to be scared for the rest of your life, do you?"

I threw a quick glance back at the mirror, relieved to see the bruised look had retreated and the stranger's chin jutted out at an angle I'd only ever seen on Ruarc.

Determined.

Stubborn.

I squared my shoulders, tried to envision Ruarc, and took a deep breath.

There. That's better.

I marched across the room and opened the door.

The squeak that flew from my lips when I saw Lucien on

the other side was loud enough that, for a moment, his cold mask cracked.

My heart lurched, gave a painful, slow beat, then crawled up my throat and stayed there.

Raw. It was the only word I could think of to describe what lay beneath his mask. Raw emotions. Raw pain. Raw wounds.

But the crack only existed for less than a second, the mask restored with the same cold perfection Lucien was made of. And I found myself questioning if what I'd seen had been real, or only a remnant of the ghost I'd seen in the mirror.

Projecting my wounds onto him.

"May I have a moment?" A cool inquiry.

I took too long to reply. Lucien arched two perfectly sculpted brows and looked pointedly over my shoulder.

"S-sure." I stepped back, sending him a furtive glance as he passed me and came to a stop in the middle of the room.

Trailing him was a waft of a darkly dangerous scent. It took all my willpower not to close my eyes and inhale, to taste the air in search of that elusive fragrance that was somehow spring and rain and thunder and forest, all mixed with his innate, masculine flavor.

My eyes snapped open.

Too late.

Lucien's rich, green eyes were heavy with consideration. Behind him, the bed loomed large and somehow insidious in the background, a stark, white contrast to the crisp, black suit he wore. It hugged his shoulders, highlighted the perfect 'V' of his body as it narrowed from his chest down to his hips.

I followed the lines of Lucien's lean body, marveling how he could look both sleek and muscular all at once.

Like a jaguar, I thought, *looking so inconspicuous with its grace, until its powerful hind legs bunch and it soars through the air and bites your head off.*

The mental image wasn't imaginary; I'd seen this happen in a nature documentary. One of the first the Hunters had given me during my first year.

From six until I was around fourteen, the compound hadn't been so bad—besides the staggering loneliness.

While I stared blindly at Lucien, I became aware of a continual, low sound. Its vibration reached through the air, wrapped around my skin, and delved down through flesh, bones, and marrow. There it settled, a deep, unsettling itch that held the promise of pleasure.

If only I would scratch it.

As soon as I raised my burning face—hoping to God he hadn't noticed my staring—the sound ceased.

The quiet that followed felt unnatural. Jarring.

And Lucien must have noticed. He was staring at me with a quiet intensity, upper lip curled in a familiar expression of derision.

I tried to gather my thoughts. Twice I opened my mouth only to close it without speaking. Eventually, what came tumbling out was the question I couldn't stop asking myself. "W-what do you want?"

Another arched brow. Then, slowly, as though it was pulled from the bottom of his weary—or, more likely, annoyed—soul, "Do you know how to defend yourself?"

I blinked. "Sorry?"

"When the coward attacked you"—a shadow passed behind his eyes—"did you have any notion of how to muster a defense?"

Ugly memories assaulted my senses. Remembered fear whipped my heart into a gallop, shame turned Lucien's scent bitter on my tongue, horror beat at my skull.

I'd been utterly powerless. Still was. "N-no."

"Would you like to learn?"

"Yes." The word shot from my mouth before I could stop it. Any hesitation I had about Lucien as my teacher drowned in the wake of that night. Of what had almost happened. And what hadn't.

My monster . . .

It hadn't been able to help. No matter how hard I'd yanked at the door of its cage, it had remained stuck.

I never wanted to feel that overwhelming, helpless despair ever again.

"Excellent."

"Why . . ." I licked my dry lips. "Why are you helping me?"

"Should I not?"

"I mean . . . you don't like me." It was a surprisingly painful thing to say out loud.

No response, just a steady, cool gaze that never moved beyond my face.

"Why would you help me, then?" I whispered.

"Does it matter?"

"It does to me."

A considerate narrowing of his eyes. "Enough to purchase the answer?"

I took half a step back before I knew what I was doing. "W-what do you mean?"

"Not that," he snapped. His eyes glittered dangerously. "An answer for an answer. A truth for a truth."

It was my turn to be quiet. With no way of knowing what he would ask—knowing a refusal once I heard the question would be an answer in itself—the offer was too risky.

Time slowed to a crawl while Lucien waited for a response that would never come. Eventually, his expression smoothed out to an unreadable wall of ice, and he rubbed his long index finger across his lower lip in an absent-minded way that held me mesmerized. "Very well, we will start tomorrow."

How could a man have such pretty lips? Lush and full—

when they weren't pressed together in a flat line of disdain like they were now. And how could a man's skin look so flawless, so smooth and marble-like at the same time? And those eyes, glittering with a chilling fury, those perfectly sculpted cheeks flushing with the faintest trace of color. Did he ever—

All my questions died a fiery death at the expression on his face. Cold, frozen with wrath. A wrath aimed at me.

The finger that had kept me entranced was jerked away from his lips, the look he shot me one of utter contempt.

"One would hope you are not as easily distracted as you appear." A quiet whisper that chilled me to my bones. "Allowing your eyes to wander where they should not go is a good way to get yourself hurt." Cool eyes swept over my face. "Let this be your first lesson; never get distracted when in close proximity to a dangerous male."

Frozen in place, I tried to lean as far away from him as I could.

He was right. Not only should I keep my guard up, especially around him, but I shouldn't be staring at him like that. Correction, I shouldn't be staring at him at all. If he'd been staring at my lips the way I'd stared at his—

I shook my head and tried to block his tempting scent from my senses. His words had been harsh, but the lesson would not be forgotten.

"I . . . It'll be the last time," I promised.

A minute stiffening of his shoulders, so small I wouldn't have seen it if I hadn't settled my eyes in the vicinity of his throat. "Good," he muttered. "Perfect."

I waited to see if he had anything else to add. And waited. And waited some more. A full minute passed, suffocatingly silent. I peeked up at him, heart stuttering at the expression on his face.

Again, that rawness from earlier, the wounds I'd thought

a reflection of my own. Silent, he stared out the window, transfixed by something I couldn't see.

His stillness bothered me. The pain I'd glimpsed bothered me even more. When Lucien was cold and distant I knew how to act. I could suppress the strange fluttering in my belly when he looked my way, and I could distance myself from his presence.

But when he was like this, almost . . . *vulnerable*, my heart ached for him in a way it had no business aching.

Lucien hated me.

He'd made no attempt to hide his disdain or mince the callous words he relentlessly threw my way. And I was with Ruarc. I was Ruarc's girlfriend.

I had no business feeling anything for Lucien at all.

"You ready, love?" The cheery voice cut through the tense silence a moment before Jason popped his head around the door. "Lucien?" His expression turned wary. "What are you doing here?"

Lucien had already turned away from the window and was facing the other man. "Jason."

Doing a quick sweep of the room, Jason's gaze zeroed in on my face. "You okay, love?"

I nodded at the same time Lucien interjected, "Why wouldn't she be?" There was a clear warning in his voice. A warning Jason didn't seem to care for.

Gait loose yet predatory, Jason moved to my side and used a gentle touch under my chin to tilt my head back.

A warm flutter came alive in my chest when his amber eyes roamed over my face. They lingered on my lips, a slow smile spreading across his face.

"Hi," he said simply, dragging an answering smile and a shy 'Hi' from me.

"Yes, hello." Lucien's sharp interruption cut through the warmth in my chest. Staring up at another man with an expression surely resembling moonstruck was *not* okay. In fact, it was abhorrent under the circumstances.

I took a step back, breaking the connection between us while a gnawing sensation ripped at my stomach.

"Now that we have all been properly introduced"—a hard note to that last word—"perhaps you can leave so I can finish what I started."

Jason bared his teeth. "And what, exactly, was that?"

"I don't believe that is any of your business."

"It is if you are upsetting Hope."

The temperature dropped several degrees as Lucien's flat mask morphed into an arctic glare. "I was not," he replied in a clipped tone. "And even if I was, should that not be *Ruarc's* concern?"

Jason clenched his jaw and glared right back. "You know that's not how it works."

"H-how what works?" I asked.

Lucien ignored me. "Ah, but does *she*?"

Two hard gazes swung in my direction.

"Uhm . . . maybe we should go?" I eyed the door with longing, wanting to escape the underlying tension I couldn't figure out.

One of these days I would have to sit down and find out everything I could about lycans and all their rules.

"Where are you going?" Lucien asked in a deceptively mild tone.

"Shopping."

"Where?"

"Where do you think?" Each word short and clipped, Jason sounded completely unlike the man I'd come to know and . . . care for?

Something inside me clenched and loosened.

When the hell had *that* happened? My whole life I'd had no one. Had cared for no one. Well, no one except—

Don't think about it.

With a desperation born from fear—fear of opening old wounds, fear of breaking down and crying in front of these men, fear of the shadowed *thing* that lived inside me—I switched gears and focused on the guys instead.

"I see." Lucien was leaning back against the windowsill, one ankle crossed over the other in a relaxed manner. His face was carefully blank, but the pulse in his neck beat against his skin in an angry pattern, and his index finger was tapping against his thigh. "I believe I shall join you."

"That won't be necessary," Jason said.

"Oh, but I insist."

Jason took a step forward, sparking something predatory within the colder male. Although Lucien's mouth remained pressed together in a firm line, something about him brought to mind the wild, petrifying smile that had stolen over his face after he'd torn Tim apart.

"Wait," I squeaked. "Maybe . . . maybe we should all just go?"

A beat of silence, then Jason turning a heated glare on Lucien. "I don't know what you think you're doing, but if you don't behave I will beat you until that perfect face of yours is nothing more than a bloody, distant memory."

Instead of replying, Lucien treated Jason to a leisurely, unimpressed once over.

A low growl slipped past Jason's lips.

"What should I bring?" My voice sounded too bright.

"Nothing, love," Jason said, still watching Lucien. "Just bring your beautiful self."

Lucien snorted.

Jason growled.

This would be fun.

44

HOPE

An hour later, our tense party entered the first store. Squashed between a supermarket and a bookstore, it was small and chaotic, a single room acting as the entire shop.

Heaps of colorful clothes were strewn on top of tables, hanging off racks, and folded casually on the shelves lining the walls. Everything existed without any particular order, jeans, dresses, sweaters, and shirts mingling everywhere.

I loved it.

The clothes were unique—made by a team of sisters who were among the small population who called this town their home, though their workshop, we were told, ran out of their garage.

A sweet lady in her late forties ran the shop itself. She was plump and beautiful with long, black hair hanging from a messy bun at the back of her head and a warm smile permanently etched into her face.

As soon as we walked into her store she descended upon us with a warm greeting, dragged me along to show me her favorite outfits—all a little too big for me, but as she so warmly put it, I would grow into them once I got some meat on my bones.

Rather than blush and mumble with shame, I actually felt my lips pull into a shy smile. It was impossible to take offense when she so clearly meant well.

She'd make a good mom.

The unexpected thought startled me into stillness.

"This one." Jason passed me a deep blue dress with a black belt around the waist and pointed at the dressing room.

While Lucien had been standing stiff and uncomfortable by the door—making me wonder yet again why on earth he'd wanted to come—Jason had taken an active role in the whole shopping escapade. Not only did he hand me clothes he thought would look good on me, he also helped me say yes or no to Margaret, the store owner, who never ran out of clothes to bring me.

I imagined a sheen of gratitude lighting up my eyes every time he made a decision for me—especially because he seemed to somehow sense when I liked something and when I didn't.

If he sometimes shot smug looks in Lucien's direction, I pretended not to notice.

"You sure?" I frowned at the pretty dress. It was beautiful but when would I be able to wear it? It didn't look like something you would wear around the house.

Jason grinned. "Oh, I'm sure, love. Go on, try it." He shooed me into the tiny dressing room at the back of the shop and closed the drapes.

Having already tried on four different pairs of jeans, several sweaters, and a bunch of shirts so soft I couldn't stop myself from rubbing the fabric over my cheek, I knew the drill.

Once I'd shimmied into the dress, I took a deep breath and stepped out.

Not a sound.

Jason's mouth dropped open, but he didn't speak, his eyes heated as they dragged up my body. Finally, he smiled; a slow, appreciative grin that made me fiddle with the hem of my dress and cast a glance over at Lucien.

I had to swallow my disappointment at his blank look. His cold gaze swept over me like I was just another display in the store, before it landed on the wall behind me.

Jason stood. "You look beautiful, darling."

Heat crept up my neck.

I was far from beautiful—and I knew it—but the way he looked at me, the glow in those amber eyes, the hungry curve of his lips . . . In that moment, he made me feel like maybe I was.

But only for a moment.

"Go change into the dark jeans and the top you liked so much, then we'll gather up the rest and go find you some underwear." With a lazy smile, Jason ushered me back and stood guard while I changed.

A few hours later my whole body ached and I'd happily chop off my feet if it meant never feeling this deep throb ever again.

Jason had ended up buying far more clothes than I was comfortable with. I'd been happy with one pair of jeans and two shirts, but even though I'd tried to tell him there was no way I could afford all of these clothes, he'd insisted we take everything I looked at twice. And when I'd mentioned money or that my work at their house hadn't exactly started yet, he'd scoffed and pretended he couldn't hear me.

To make matters worse, both men were carrying several shopping bags each, while I carried exactly zero. Every time I moved to grab one, one of them would snap it up before my brain registered they'd moved.

Lucien's default setting—cold and unmoving—had been replaced by one I liked even less; a glowering mountain of ice who tracked my every movement with narrowed, thoughtful eyes.

Those eyes . . . they made me uncomfortably aware of myself. Enough that I kept tripping over my own feet. Only Jason's quick reflexes saved me.

But despite this new development, not a single insult left Lucien's perfectly shaped lips.

No derogatory marks.

No low sounds of disdain.

Not even a mocking snort.

He carried my bags without a word of complaint despite the—anger?—that made those cold eyes so heavy with consideration.

Thank the gods for Jason. He'd been all irresistible charm and playful flirtation. He'd made this whole experience fun, despite the thousands of outfits I'd tried on and the myriad of little decisions he'd tricked me into making.

"How about some Italian, love?" he asked, tugging on the hand he'd claimed after we left the last shop.

"Sure." I gave him a shy smile before glancing back at Lucien's stone-cold features, wondering why he always walked a few steps behind us. "If that's okay with you?" I directed my question at Lucien.

Lucien stared at me, not saying a word. Then he gave a short nod and went back to scanning the crowd.

My shoulders slumped with defeat.

I didn't get it. Why was he here if he didn't want to interact with us at all?

A muttered curse pulled me from my glum thoughts. I glanced up, took in Jason's locked jaw and tight shoulders, and followed his gaze to see what had caught his attention.

Then I stumbled.

It was a woman. A staggeringly beautiful woman.

Jason's hand tightened around mine.

As if we'd practiced the movement a thousand times, we all came to a stop, waiting for her to spot us.

Jason's made a sound, halfway between a growl and a groan, casting me a quick glance before fixing his attention back where it belonged.

A weird sensation in my stomach, like a nauseating yank that left me hollow.

The moment the woman saw Jason, her whole demeanor changed. Her face went from relaxed and smiling, to intently focused. She spun around, somehow not tripping over her high heels, and came prowling toward us.

Shiny locks of blond hair cascaded down her back; complementing her fair complexion and blood red lips. She was dressed in a tight-fitting, gorgeous dress that accentuated her curves, and a predatory smile played on her lips.

Her innate confidence was a thing of beauty.

She stopped when her ample breasts were a hairsbreadth away from brushing up against Jason's arm. "Hi there, handsome." With a flick of her hair, she reached out to place a hand on his chest.

Red flecks sparked in my vision and I almost swayed. An ugly, slimy feeling slithered through me as I imagined all the parts of Jason she'd already touched.

The feeling didn't go away, even when Jason captured her wrist before she could make contact. It didn't disappear when his pupils shrank, or when he ground his teeth together and took a step back.

All I could think about was their bodies together. The admiration he must have felt for her, his expression when he moved above her.

I was going to be sick.

"Jenny." He inclined his head.

Ignoring me completely, *Jenny* moved with him, thrusting her shoulders back while giving him a practiced pout. "I've missed you. I haven't seen you in *ages*."

God, how I envied her easy confidence, the sexuality pouring off of her. I'd never be able to pull that off.

"I've been busy."

She cocked her hip and lowered her voice, "Too busy for me?"

The hand enveloped by Jason's big palm suddenly felt hot. Like holding a live coal.

What the hell was I doing? This other woman, this *Jenny*, clearly had some sort of claim on Jason, and here I was clinging to him like he was my boyfriend?

I yanked my hand free, pretending I didn't notice the way Jason glanced down at me, looking almost surprised before his lips compressed into a grim line.

When he looked back at Jenny, nothing was left of the normal Jason-charm. He set his jaw and didn't reply.

Pursing her lips, the beautiful, intimidating woman finally seemed to notice me. She flicked her gaze over my dull, brown hair, the new clothes clinging to a body that looked downright sickly, and the brand-new tennis shoes that went well with my new jeans. As she took in my shoes, her nose curled, and she looked away, dismissing me. "With *her*?"

A hot, uncomfortable feeling had me avert my eyes. I would have stepped away if not for Lucien's hands coming to rest on my shoulders and pulling me back against his torso. The hard muscles beneath his suit jumped at the contact, but otherwise he gave no indication he felt weird about us being so close when he'd always made sure to keep his distance.

Meanwhile, everywhere we touched, my skin burned.

Jason scowled. "That is none of your business."

"What happened to you?" Jenny demanded. Her eyes glided across every inch of his tall, powerful frame. "You used to be so . . . *friendly*."

I almost choked on my next breath.

Why do you care? You're with Ruarc, remember?

"Something amazing."

I looked down at the floor and tried to concentrate on anything but their conversation and the strange, heated presence at my back.

My conscience was right. It shouldn't matter to me what Jason had done—what he *did* with his time. It wasn't like we were more than friends. I was with Ruarc, and despite the fight we'd had, he made me happy.

"Amazing? Really?"

A strangled growl marked the end of Jason's patience. Out of the corner of my eye, I saw him cross his arms over his chest and scowl. "It was nice seeing you, Jenny."

"Wait," she cried as Jason made a move to walk around her. She reached for his arm, shot me a venomous stare that froze on her face when, for the first time, she noticed Lucien.

She stared. And stared some more. Pretty blue eyes glazed over, and a sound very much like a low moan tore from her throat.

"What is it, Jenny?" Impatience rolled off Jason in waves.

Eyes never leaving Lucien, she purred, "Introduce me to your friend?"

Uhm, what?

They were *not* interchangeable toys she could trade out when it suited her.

Instead of chewing her out, Jason grinned. "This, Jenny, is Lucien." He winked at Lucien and grabbed my wrist. "Come, love. Let's give these two delightful creatures a moment alone, shall we?"

He dragged me a few feet away and turned us so we could see the scene unfolding.

"Should we . . . should we leave them alone?" It felt weird spying on Lucien like this. And the ugly feeling in my stomach kept intensifying, not abating, even though we'd left Jenny behind.

What's wrong with you?

"Nah. Lucien won't be long," he said, still grinning. It wasn't until he looked down at me, gaze briefly resting on my hunched shoulders and the hands that wouldn't stop picking at my new shirt, that his smile fell. "Love," he began, gently interlacing our fingers so I had to stop my nervous habit and look up at him, "I've never been in a real relationship. I haven't really wanted to until now."

"Jenny?" I blurted, probably looking as confused and aghast as I felt. He'd practically pushed her at Lucien.

"No, love. Not Jenny."

I frowned. There was no one else around? The little street we'd stopped on was right between a lingerie shop—a place I'd walked around in with a permanent blush staining my cheeks while Jason picked out this and that—and a cute looking cafe.

"But . . ." He couldn't be talking about me. I was with Ruarc—which Jason *knew*. Besides, Jason was way, *way* too handsome for someone like me.

But so is Ruarc.

"Look at me, love," Jason murmured, his eyes soft. The way he was smiling—with a good amount of self-deprecation —caught at something inside me.

He does that a lot.

The ironic twist to his mouth, the darkness he almost succeeded in hiding behind charming smiles and playful banter. And the mocking glimmer in his eyes that was never directed at anyone but himself.

Or was it just my imagination?

I hoped it was. If not, Jason could be in the kind of pain that left your soul dragging behind you; too tired to lift its feet and too numb to care about the wounds it collected along the way.

"Jenny . . . She meant nothing to me. That doesn't sound very good," he added when he noticed my raised brows. "But it's the truth. I've spent the majority of my life focused on just having a good time, having fun, you know? But since I met you, things have changed." He looked down at our joined hands. "My priorities have changed."

I swallowed hard.

What . . . what did that mean?

An annoying flicker of wishful thinking ignited in my brain, chased away by doubt, self-loathing, and a huge heaping of guilt. What on earth was I doing? What was I *thinking*?

"—worth a million of you," Lucien hissed, drawing me out of my own head and back into reality.

Caught up in Jason, I'd forgotten about Jenny. Based on her affronted expression and the loud huff of air she spat out, whatever had happened between her and Lucien couldn't have been good.

Lucien's cold mask had slipped, but what lay beneath this time was only fury. Fire lashed through his green eyes, complementing the slight flush decorating his sharp cheekbones. Contempt spilled from him in waves, almost like heat. And through the fury snapping in the air around him, he still managed to be the most beautiful man I'd ever seen.

"You—you rude, frigid *bastard*," Jenny spat, spinning on her heels and stalking away.

Lucien tracked her retreating form until she was out of sight. "My parents were married, you half-witted harlot," he muttered, stiffening when Jason chuckled.

The hollow pit that had been my insides since we met Jenny filled with amusement.

Who was this man and why was this the first time I'd seen that dry humor?

He frowned. "Not a word out of you, pup," he warned, and strode past us.

Jason turned to me with a grin. "Didn't know he had it in him, did you, love?"

I shook my head.

No. No I hadn't.

The rest of the day passed in a blur. The restaurant Jason picked out served delicious food, pulling a moan from me at the first bite. He'd ordered for me—I'd been too busy mumbling incoherently down at my menu and avoiding the waiter's gaze—a pasta dish with a creamy, white sauce, and toasted garlic bread on the side.

Both men were strangely quiet during the meal. Jason occasionally fed me a piece from his own plate when there was something he wanted me to taste, but otherwise didn't speak.

Lucien didn't say a single word, and kept to his frosty silence during our visit to the last two shops. Occasionally, I would catch his gaze lingering on my face, a strange light in his brilliant, green eyes, but mostly he scanned each face we passed and kept up a chilly front.

I was too tired during the car ride home to care too much about the silence, but when Jason parked the car and Lucien stalked away without a word—though he did pick up a few bags—I couldn't stop myself from staring after him and feeling . . .

Guilty?

"Did I . . . Did I say something wrong?"

"No, love. You were a delight," Jason assured me before he vaulted from the car and rushed to my side.

He always moved with such a spring in his step, like he had a reserve of boundless energy pushing against his skin and urging him to hurry. Even when he sat still, he'd bounce a knee or move his hands—last time we watched a movie it was playing with my hair while I was hyper-aware of his closeness.

When he spoke, it was with his whole body; animated, a lot of gesturing, and looking so vibrantly *alive*.

It had been one of the first things I noticed about him, and the more time I spent with him, the more I came to believe that a spark of what made the world come alive—call it creation, or life, or whatever—existed inside Jason.

"What're you thinking so intently about?" he asked, having opened the door on my side without me noticing.

"Nothing, just . . ." I shook my head. "Nothing."

"It's a good look on you, love." He tapped a finger at my lip. "You have a lovely smile."

My hand shot up to feel the spot he'd touched, surprised at finding my lips curved.

When had that happened?

"Let's go put away your clothes." Jason reached for my waist and lifted me straight out of the car, chuckling at my startled cry.

He held me against his chest. He was warm. So warm. "We . . . we bought too much." My voice came out breathless.

Instead of putting me down, he placed me on the hood of the car and stepped between my legs.

Heat immediately flooded, dragging across nerve endings and making my skin prickle with awareness.

The heady scent that was Jason—dark, male, and with a hint of sweetness—enveloped me when he leaned closer. "We didn't buy nearly enough, love." His smooth voice drove liquid heat through my veins. "You deserve only the best."

A sharp pang pierced my heart.

I didn't deserve the best. Not even close. Not after what I'd done.

And look at you now, my conscience spat. *Lusting after Jason when you already have the perfect man wanting to be with you.*

God, what was I doing?

"Jason," I began, intent on pushing him away. But then . . .

Soft lips swept over mine in a soft caress that left me shaken.

Breathless.

Branded.

I shook. I trembled. I felt . . . heat bursting to life in my belly. Hands on my waist. His lips . . .

Once, twice, three times they gently brushed my own. And then they stayed.

He captured me in such a heartbreakingly tender kiss, I all but melted.

No tongue invaded my mouth. No nibbles teased at my lips. Instead, he stayed still. Feeling me. The velvet touch of his mouth a beautiful sensation, pushing with just the right amount of pressure, a soft, careful, heated touch that I somehow felt all the way down to my soul.

The perfection of the moment drew a soft sigh from my lungs, a sound Jason responded to with a savage growl.

Suddenly, a hand buried in my hair, the other finding the middle of my back and pulling me against a hard body.

Surrounding me, Jason's arms were bands of steel. They kept me close. Kept me safe.

My heart raced.

I moaned again, throwing my arms around his neck and arching into him.

His body vibrated with restraint, and his chest released a continuous rumble that I felt like a tug between my legs.

Despite the change, the taut tension of his big frame, the kiss remained the same; a soft press of lips as they molded to mine.

Intimate.

Warm.

Perfect.

Each shared hot breath was like a gust of heated glass exploding between us, but instead of cutting, the pieces melted and became more fire to heat our flames.

His whole body shook, letting me feel the power in those hands, in those broad shoulders and wide chest. I felt how contained he was, how much he was holding himself back.

His strength, his power . . .

He was hard all over.

Except his mouth.

That was soft. For several, long seconds.

It wasn't until he groaned and slanted his lips over mine to deepen the kiss that I remembered who I was. And who I'd given myself to.

I've told Ruarc I'm his . . .

I tore away with a mangled cry.

Jason immediately stepped back and dropped his arms to his sides.

What had I done? How could I have been so stupid?

"I . . . I didn't—" My voice shattered.

I would lose Ruarc. I would lose him.

My eyes burned.

He wouldn't put up with a betrayal like this. He shouldn't. He deserved better. More.

Not me. Not my baggage, not the evil hunting me, and not the darkness buried so deep inside me it had become a part of who I was.

I slid down the car, knees almost buckling when my feet hit the hard ground.

"Love . . ." Jason reached for me, but I ducked under his arm and sprinted up the driveway. "Wait!"

I had to get away. Had to get myself under control.

Ruarc couldn't see me like this.

I made a sound. A broken, hopeless whimper.

I owed him the truth, but not like this. Not while I bawled all over him, and his honor forced him to comfort me when I was the one who'd done wrong.

Knowing the good, kind heart that beat beneath that

massive chest, he might end up forgiving me just because I was a sad, pathetic creature.

The last thing I wanted was to manipulate him into forgiving me. Into being with me.

I slammed into the door, ignoring Jason's call for me to wait, and managed to get my trembling fingers to work the handle so I could get inside.

The door slammed open behind me.

Rushing through the living room, I found the stairs and sprinted up to my room.

Footsteps behind me. Too close.

I stumbled over the threshold. Turned. Slapped at the lock.

It clicked in place.

A low curse. Then, "Hope . . ." A soft knock. "Love, please open the door."

I buried my face in my hands to stem the sobs breaking through my tight throat.

"Don't cry." A ragged plea.

"P-please leave me a-alone."

A soft thud, like his head was resting against the door. When he next spoke, his voice was thick. No longer vibrant. "Please, sweetheart, give me a chance to—"

"G-go away!" I cried.

I couldn't hear what he had to say. I couldn't listen to his excuses. To all the reason why it had been a mistake, that he hadn't meant anything by it, that he could never care for someone like me. Whatever it was he wanted to say, my heart couldn't handle it.

Not when it was already splitting in two.

I will lose him. I will lose Ruarc.

I would lose them both.

When had this happened? When had I become this faithless, horrible creature?

For a long time, there was only the sound of my strangled breathing and the soft scrape of Jason moving in the hall.

Then he whispered, a torn, "I'm sorry," and was gone.

I staggered over to the bed, fell down, tried to halt the tears flowing down my cheeks.

When Ruarc got back I'd have to tell him what had happened. That I'd betrayed him.

With a sob, I buried my face in my pillow and let myself cry. By the time Ruarc was back, I was determined to be empty of tears so I could give him the explanation—and the out—he deserved.

He deserves so much better than me.

45

RUARC

THE VISE THAT HAD BEEN SQUEEZING MY HEART ALL DAY loosened slightly as I caught the scent of our territory.

Almost home.

The day had been a shit-storm of epic proportions. I'd been riding a sharp edge of fury from the moment I stormed out of the house and left my female in the hands of my pack brothers. Despite trusting them with my life, unease dogged my steps while I was away. Every time I closed my eyes, I saw Hope's big, wounded eyes staring up at me. Smelled the sharp scent of fear. Saw her blanching face and the tremors in her hands.

Hadn't felt right leaving her like that. But if I'd stayed we'd all have been in danger. I was the pack enforcer for a reason, and today I'd been needed, goddammit!

If a Stray hadn't left his fucking scent all over our property—getting as far as *the front-fucking-door*, I wouldn't have had to rush out last night. It had been years since one had dared get this close, and now that I had its scent I wouldn't stop hunting until it was caught.

What if it smelled Hope? Saw her?

A snarl erupted into the still night.

And of course, we'd had another pack to see. They'd had issues with Strays last year, so Ash had thought they might have known something.

Unfortunately, how I'd left shit with Hope had influenced me ever since.

The churning in my stomach had driven me nearly mad with rage. If the north-eastern pack hadn't feared us before, they damned well did today. Their alpha was a brainless twat, something he'd proven when he'd instigated a dominance play in the middle of our meeting. Although Ash thought I could've stopped it without tearing his throat out, my mood had been so foul, I'd reacted before my brain was fully caught up. Luckily for the alpha, a healer had been nearby.

Hope's pale face, eyes scrunched tightly shut, flashed behind my closed lids.

Fuck!

I snarled. The sound deeper, more menacing now that I was in my wolf-form.

Emotions battered at me from all sides. Mostly rage. Red hot rage that made my teeth ache with the desire to feel flesh tear.

But also feelings I wasn't used to, could barely recognize.

The guilt was easy. I was used to dealing with guilt. But the near panic thundering in my chest was foreign.

Have to get home.

Shouldn't have left in the first place. Should have stayed, apologized and made sure my female was all right before I even thought about stepping one foot out the door. But Ash had been waiting. And what did one say to a female after such a colossal fuck up? How could I explain the irrational fear driving my protective instincts when she mentioned leaving without me?

Or the possessive surge at the thought of her being alone with Jason?

I stopped by a shallow creek. The fresh water looked inviting, so I jumped in and made sure every inch of my fur scraped against the sand at the bottom. Once I was satisfied most of the blood was gone, I took off at a sprint.

The wind ruffled my fur and the cold dirt gave way beneath my paws.

Lucien's workshop came into view, and I skidded around the corner. Throwing my head back, I howled. Ash's answering howl was further away, but close enough that I didn't have to wait.

It took me less than a minute to get dressed; dark sweatpants and a black shirt. I gritted my teeth with impatience and jogged up to the house. Stepping inside, I slammed the door shut, and froze.

Something's wrong.

A metal rod had more give than my jaw. My teeth ground together, fangs growing and digging into my gums. The overwhelming scent of worked up male offended my nose and stirred the hot anger I'd been unable to shake all day.

A spike of my pulse, a burst of panic. What if my little female was hurt? What if Jason had hurt her?

A red haze floated over my vision as I recognized Jason as the owner of the riled, male scent. If he'd hurt my Hope . . .

I'll kill him.

As I stormed into the kitchen I tried to control my rage. Hope wouldn't like it if I hurt Jason for no reason. As much as it pained me, I knew she felt *something* for him, and even though he annoyed the shit out of me, I loved my brother.

"Jason," I barked at the gloomy figure slumped over a chair. A half-empty bottle of scotch dangled from his hand. He lifted his head, eyes dull, and opened his mouth.

Nothing.

I clenched my fists at my side.

Idiot.

No matter how much he drank he couldn't get drunk. Lycan metabolism. "Where's Hope?"

"Upstairs." His mouth formed a desolate grimace. "I messed up," he admitted and glanced down at the table. "She's upset."

"If you hurt her . . ." I didn't have to say anything more. He knew.

I spun on my heels and rushed up the stairs.

"Hope?" Her door was locked. I was about to kick it down when I heard the rustle of clothes on the other side of the door.

I fumed as I waited.

Fucking shit-show.

My vision narrowed further and further, until only a sliver of sight remained. The sound of my foot tapping against the floor pulled me out of thoughts of blood and gore —Jason's blood and gore—and dragged my focus to the other side of the door.

A click indicated the lock had been turned. I pushed my way inside, careful to not push the door into the fragile, precious package on the other side.

I scented her before I saw her. The sweet fragrance of her skin was tainted by a smell I never ever wanted to come off her. Fear. And hurt. The feeling kind, not the physical kind.

Fucking lucky for Jason.

Then I got my first glimpse of her. A growl rumbled in my throat.

Her eyes were red-rimmed, and a deep, anguished sadness shone in their depths. Her obvious pain brought out the savage fury always lurking beneath the surface of my being—especially where Hope was concerned—and nearly blinded me with it's intensity.

"Who do I kill," I growled, prepared to tear whoever hurt her limb from limb.

Her mouth opened, but no sound came out. Her eyes

were wide, startled. Her lip trembled, but she bit down on it, hard.

Too hard.

I frowned and reached out to rescue her ever-abused lip, but she jerked back, eyes brimming with tears.

My frown turned into a dark scowl. Someone had hurt her enough that she was wary of me.

It better fucking not be Jason!

My jaw hurt with the force I was using to press my teeth together so I wouldn't punch through the floor and bite Jason's face off.

"I . . ." She looked down at the floor. "I did s-something b-bad."

She did something bad? I stilled, scenting the air while I watched her fidget through narrowed eyes. *A bitter scent. Sour, almost. Wrapped in—*

Pain?

Understanding came, and with it, a black mood I fucking didn't need right then. I got it. The hunched shoulders. The self-loathing in her eyes. The way she didn't want to look at me.

She was ashamed.

Squaring my shoulders, I braced myself for her confession. Whatever it was, we would get through it. Even if I had to swallow this rage burning a hole in my stomach.

"I . . . Jason and I . . . we k-kissed." Her voice broke on the last word, body inching away until she stood sideways.

Like she was expecting a blow?

"Did he force you?" A deadly calm came over me as I waited for her reply. Images of a bloodied Jason tore through my mind. If he'd forced her . . .

"I kissed him back," she admitted on a whisper.

A ragged growl tore from my throat. Jealousy boiled.

There was no doubt in my mind I would have killed Jason if he was anyone else. Not my brother.

The thought of another man touching what was mine made fangs sprout from my gums and claws erupt from my fingertips.

As it were, Jason owed both of us an explanation. Had he forgotten Hope was human? He couldn't push her. Couldn't kiss her without a conversation first. Had to sit her down. Explain shit to her.

Fuck!

This day was getting worse and worse. The need to pummel Jason until his face was mush was one I seriously considered giving into. The pup had to learn, and who better to teach him than the older brother who loved him despite his flaws.

Life-threatening flaws.

I struggled with controlling the emotions wreaking havoc on my insides. Didn't know what to do. How to make this better for her. For my poor, little human who looked as fragile now as the day I met her.

Another savage growl made its way past my tight throat.

Muscles tight, body on full alert, I averted my gaze before the sight of her—shamefaced and devastated—made me do something I'd regret.

Jason should *never* have left her like this. Insecure and hurting.

"I'll be right back." The words were almost unintelligible, pushed out as they were between teeth that refused to unclench.

"Ruarc, I . . ." She drew in a deep breath and met my gaze head on. "I'm so sorry." The bright sheen in her eyes made me expel a harsh breath. Pain radiated off her, her pale face a mask of misery.

But she didn't cry.

Almost worse.

Seeing the shine in those eyes and knowing she was doing her damned best not to let a single tear fall . . .

I swore under my breath, torn between the need to comfort my little human and the need to teach Jason a lesson.

She won't feel better until she understands.

My instincts screamed at me to stay, to take care of my mate. But the logical part of me—the tiny spark that was shrinking in direct correlation to my growing need to kill—knew I had to deal with Jason first. Then we could *both* talk to Hope. It was the only way.

Still. Couldn't leave her like this.

"It's fine." I tried to modulate my voice. Make it soothing. But the gravelly sound that came out was hoarse and raspy. Ugly. Like I was. "I'll fix it."

Her eyes widened, then they filled with tears, causing her to look away. Misery was etched across her beautiful face, giving her a haunted look.

When she didn't reply—her convulsive swallowing made me think she couldn't—I could no longer hold myself back. With two long strides she was in grabbing distance. My arm shot out, pulling her tight against me.

Small. She was so small. Her head only reached my chest.

Gotta be careful.

Her body was too frail. One wrong move and I could seriously harm her.

The feeling of responsibility, of pride that she trusted me enough for this, and that she was mine—mine to cherish, mine to protect—was overwhelming.

Hugging her with one arm, I used the other to palm the back of her head and tilt her face. "Don't worry," I growled. With my throat as dry as bones, no other type of sound was possible. "It'll be okay."

Not knowing what else to say, I brushed a quick kiss over her forehead. Jason's lingering scent brought forth a surge of jealous rage, but I smothered it before it could tear another snarl out of me.

Doesn't matter. Jason is pack.

If I kept telling myself that, eventually the rage had to fade. Or at least soften around the edges.

In danger of being swept away by Hope—her scent, her vulnerability, her battered heart—I released her so I could find Jason.

Her choked cry ripped me apart.

Fuck!

That sound . . . Like a burning silver knife to the gut. Like acid raining on my insides. Like every bone in my body being pulled out and put back together—a little more crooked, a little more damaged than before.

Without looking back I rushed from the room, certain *one more* sound of pain, one request from her would make me stay. Even though I knew I shouldn't.

Had to find Jason. Needed him to help explain to Hope.

After I beat the shit out of him.

Baring my teeth in a grim smile, I headed to the kitchen.

46

HOPE

It took me several miserable minutes to stop staring at the empty space where Ruarc had been. The look in his eyes when I'd told him . . .

My stomach cramped with an empty, gut-wrenching feeling that made me want to vomit.

The surge of fury that had morphed his face into a savage grimace had been bad enough, but before that, right before the rage flooded in, I'd seen something worse. Something much worse.

A flash of pain.

I closed my eyes and dropped my head into my hands.

I'd hurt him. My beautiful, amazing, proud warrior. I'd hurt him. And hurting him made me feel like the lowest of the low. Like scum.

Hunter scum.

I brushed damp hair away from my face. My hands shook.

Knowing he'd never look at me the same way again, that the tender, protective look that was somehow both soft and savage with possessive fury all at the same time was lost forever . . .

Hollow. That was how I felt. Hollow and lost and so empty I feared a strong wind could carry me away.

He'd said he'd be right back . . .

I glanced at the closed door. Why would he bother? I wouldn't have come back for me. I'd betrayed him, I'd kissed another man. I'd—

The door flew open and banged against the wall. A dark shape sailed through the air, landing in a crumpled heap against the wall on the opposite side.

"J-Jason?"

The shape on the floor unfolded. A battered face turned to me, flashing a lopsided smile that showed teeth coated with red smudges. "Fancy seeing you here, love."

Oh my god! It took me several tries to blink back my tears. *This is all my fault.*

I shuffled forward, wanting nothing more than to run to Jason and make sure he was all right, but a peek over my shoulder stopped me in my tracks.

Ruarc closed the door behind him with a thunderous scowl. Bulging muscles played under the skin of his strong arms where they lay crossed over his chest. "Owes you an explanation," he growled, jerking his chin at Jason.

I turned back to Jason, feeling my stomach roll uneasily. If I went to him, would Ruarc see it as another betrayal? Would he hurt?

My gaze roamed over Jason's form. One eye swollen shut. A split lip. A bruised cheek. Dark marks covering his throat.

Had Ruarc *strangled* him?

I took a hesitant step toward the battered man on the floor and glanced at Ruarc. His forbidding, silver eyes tracked my every move like a true predator, but other than that, he gave no indication of his feelings.

I finally got close enough to kneel in front of Jason, my hands hovering above him, afraid to touch, to hurt. "Are you . . . are you okay?"

"Peachy keen," he said with a grin. His gaze moved over my shoulder to Ruarc, and when he looked back at me, his grin had disappeared. "I'm sorry, sweetheart. I should have made more of an effort to explain, and I shouldn't have kissed you." My heart sank. "I should have waited for Ruarc before taking that step."

"W-waited for Ruarc?"

Behind me, Ruarc huffed and muttered something that sounded suspiciously like, "Dumb pup."

"Waited for Ruarc," Jason confirmed. A hissing breath passed over his split bottom lip when he pushed himself into a sitting position. He got settled with his back against the wall, one leg raised and bent at the knee. "Lycan relationships aren't like human ones, love. They're a bit more complicated." He touched his lips. Frowned. "Multiple mates, remember?"

The breath I'd been about to exhale got stuck in my throat.

Multiple mates.

But . . . "I'm not lycan," I reminded them—as if they could forget. "Lucien said your males share because there aren't enough females. *Lycan* females. I'm . . . human."

Ruarc grumbled a curse under his breath. "Doesn't matter."

"But—"

"Perfect as you are," he said gruffly.

Tears pricked at my eyes where normally I would have smiled.

You betrayed him.

I could barely stand to lift my eyes and meet his gaze, but when I did, I saw no recrimination. No disgust and no hatred. Only something tender.

Then he turned to Jason and bared his teeth. "Continue."

Jason spread his hands in a 'what can you do' gesture. "We both like you, love. Obviously."

545

A strange numbness tingled in the tips of my fingers. I couldn't wrap my head around it. Couldn't bring myself to believe it was true. First Ruarc and now Jason?

What is so special about me?

Nothing. At least nothing good.

Unaware of the dark place my thoughts had gone, Jason continued, "And we want to be with you. Both of us."

"Why?"

Jason's expression darkened at the disgust he no doubt heard in my voice. "For so many reasons, but before we get into that, let me explain why what I did was wrong."

"It wasn't . . ." I bit my lip. "It wasn't just your fault."

Ruarc scoffed. "Was his fault." A dark glare in Jason's direction, one that seemed to say, 'are you gonna get to it or do I have to beat it out of you?'

"We've always known we might share a female," Jason said. "Not only because there's so few lycan females, but because if there's ever any trouble, we'd know the other members of our pack would die to protect our mate. A very important consideration when you live in a world as fraught with violence as we do."

Jason tilted his head and studied me. A slow smile tugged on his split lip, causing a droplet of blood to spill down his chin. Before I could think, I reached out and caught the glistening moisture on the pad of my index finger.

"I'm sorry you got hurt because of me," I whispered.

Since I'd arrived here, I'd caused so much friction.

"Not your fault," Ruarc growled. "Pup's an idiot."

The 'pup' flashed me a rueful smile. "He's right, love. Ruarc had sort of claimed you—"

With a savage snarl, Ruarc moved from his position by the door and crouched in front of Jason. The look on his face . . .

Primal fear kicked me in the chest, and for a moment, I

546

forgot that the male in front of us was one who'd never hurt me.

Ruarc's lips peeled away to show two rows of sharp, glistening teeth. "*Sort of?*" he hissed.

Jason met Ruarc's furious glare with a small grin. Either he was oblivious to the danger he was in, or he didn't care. "Well . . . maybe more than sort of," he admitted with a shrug and a wink my way. But then his expression sobered. "I should have talked to you first, mate."

Ruarc grunted in agreement and moved behind me. Strong arms came around my waist and—

I flew through the air and landed safely in his lap. Burying his nose in my neck, he inhaled. "Smell good."

"Ruarc, I'm . . . I'm so sorry."

He hugged me closer. "Nothing to be sorry about, *a chuisle*."

"But—"

"Nothing."

Engulfed by his warmth, I relaxed for the first time since kissing Jason. I felt safe. Protected. Cared for.

Ruarc nuzzled at my jawline, and I tilted my head back to stare up at the man I'd done nothing to deserve. "Thank you."

The way his eyes softened, it was possible he knew I wasn't really thanking him for accepting my apology, but for being him. For taking the time to understand, and for not leaving me when he'd had a good reason to.

The sound of Jason clearing his throat was followed by a hoarse chuckle when Ruarc's head whipped up and skewered Jason with a glare.

"Relax, old man," Jason joked. His fingers felt around the bruises on his neck, brows lowering in a wince when he touched a tender spot.

"Hurting, pup?"

"I've had worse."

Even though Jason was still smiling, I felt a twinge of discomfort. "Will you be okay, Jason?"

Ruarc snorted.

"No, love. I am doomed to carry Ruarc's necklace of bruises for the rest of my life."

My wide eyes bounced between them until I noticed the twitch at the end of Ruarc's lip.

"Very funny," I muttered.

"I thought so too." Jason turned his head, eyes landing on the bed. "Should we get more comfortable? The floor is not helping my bruises."

Ruarc stiffened. "No."

With a roll of his eyes and a slight wince, Jason relented. "Fine. You hog the bed and leave me to contend with the hard floor.."

A satisfied grunt from the man exploring my neck with distracting lips.

Jason rolled his eyes again before settling back against the wall and spearing me with a too-serious look. "We didn't have a set agreement to share or anything—god only knows wolves are too mercurial to decide something like that before they find their mate." He shot Ruarc a meaningful look and got a teeth-baring, scary smile in return. "But maybe . . . maybe sometime in the future? Yeah. The thought had occurred."

It had?

"Problem is, sometimes a member of a pack will meet someone on his own. Now, *normally,* males will court whoever they please as long as the female isn't officially mated, but it can cause a lot of friction within a pack—us being territorial assholes, and all that." He flashed a grin that was both charming and self-deprecating. "And this is when dealing with lycan, females, mind you."

Ruarc grumbled, but I barely heard it. My mind was busy digesting.

"Point is, you're human. I should've gotten Ruarc's permission first, and then I should've waited for him to explain everything to you before I made a move." His voice lowered. "I fucked up."

My heart clenched. "Jason . . . It wasn't your—"

"It was," he said harshly. "It was my fault. Not only did I fail to do what was right, I left you thinking you'd betrayed Ruarc." His expression darkened, leaving very little of the Jason I knew behind. "I left while you *cried*."

Ruarc stiffened. A slight tremor worked its way through his body, but he didn't make a sound. His head remained bent over my neck, but his mouth was still. No longer exploring.

Although I felt the seething anger rolling off him, the alarm I'd normally feel was missing. Not because his anger wasn't scary—it was—but because my brain had chosen that moment to unravel the threads Jason had dangled in front of me.

Share. Multiple mates. *Pack*.

They hadn't had a set agreement *yet*, but . . .

"You mean . . ." The rest got stuck in my throat. I swallowed and tried again. "You mean I should *mate* with everyone in your pack?"

Was mating . . . *sex*?

The shudder that went through me made Ruarc stiffen. "No," he growled at the same time Jason said, "Not exactly."

The male at my back was all hard muscles, tension making him rigid. With a deadly low tone, he repeated, "No."

Jason waved away Ruarc's objection. "It means that everything is up to you, love. If they are interested in you, they may court you. But you are not obligated to be with them. You can say no," he added in a gentle voice.

I took a deep breath to shore up my courage. "Is mating . . . does it mean . . . sex?" I whispered, and immediately felt my face go flaming hot.

You can't even say it without blushing.

I looked down.

"Of course not." Jason reached out to pat my hand. Before he could make contact, Ruarc jerked me back with a ripping snarl.

"Ignore him," Jason said, grinning. "Us males can be a bit . . . possessive. And no, mating does not mean sex. Although," he added with a wiggle of his brows, "sex is a fun part of it."

Heat flooded my belly while dread spiraled down my spine.

The two opposing sensations clashed, became entangled, warred while lightning struck and thunder boomed. Until finally they settled side by side in an uncomfortable stalemate. Waiting for the other to retreat.

And one did.

The head shrank, burned out when no new fuel urged it to burn hotter, and all that was left was the dread.

The idea of sex was . . . terrifying.

Images of the Hunters and their evil taunts swam up from a sea of ugly memories. Their cruel mocking. The horrifying threats. The painful grip on my inner thighs as they spread me open to '*look*' as they called it.

They'd never actually penetrated me, but they'd left a mark on my soul nonetheless.

"Jason!" Ruarc snapped.

Blinking, I glanced over at Jason, took in his ashen face and wide eyes, and wondered what the hell kind of scary glare Ruarc was aiming his way.

But Jason wasn't looking at Ruarc. He was staring at me.

"Sorry, love," he said, and his voice held a note I didn't recognize. A dangerous undertone broken by a scraping, hoarse edge. "A mate is kind of like a wife. Or husband. Only there is no such thing as divorce. Once you have chosen your mate—or mates—that's it."

Longing pierced my heart; left me torn open and bleeding.

If it wasn't for the fact that death stalked me and that the guys would hate me if they knew what I'd done, I might have gotten some silly fantasy in my head about Ruarc and me riding off into the sunset together.

Maybe even with Jason by our side.

"So there's some kind of ceremony?"

Ruarc grunted in the affirmative, earning a sharp look from Jason.

Did Ruarc . . . did he want *that* with *me*? Some of the things he'd said, the way acted around me . . . it almost sounded as if he looked at me as a potential mate.

But that's ridiculous, right?

"What . . . what does all this mean?" I asked, wringing my hands in my lap.

This time when Jason grinned at me, his injured eye opened.

He was already healing.

"It means, love, that both Ruarc and I want a relationship with you. It means that if we are as suited together as we believe, we could eventually become mated." His eyes glinted dangerously. "If you would have us, that is."

The sound of my heart beating was too loud. Could they hear it? "B-both of you?"

Jason gave me a slow nod, eyes glued to my face as he waited for my reaction.

I gave none.

I was completely frozen.

A burst of pure happiness shot through my soul and I felt light. So very light. But then apprehension set in, and with it, the world came crashing back down.

The Hunters.

Always the Hunters.

I would never be safe as long as they were alive, and neither would anyone associated with me.

And if not the Hunters, then me. The monster who'd destroyed my life so thoroughly that I still hadn't found all the pieces. And even if I did, I was too warped now, too broken and misshapen to ever fit them back together.

I couldn't stay. I couldn't stay. I couldn't stay.

But can you give them up?

Everything inside me locked up tight.

The thought of never seeing them again, of letting them move on and find a proper mate—a lycan mate—sent daggers slicing at my heart until only ribbons of torn muscle remained.

Knowing I had to say something, give them some sort of reaction despite my emotional turmoil, I squeaked out a tiny "Oh."

I wanted so badly to throw myself at them, to do everything in my power to make this work. To make them so happy that they'd eventually consider taking me as their mate.

But how could I do that when the Hunters were still alive and hunting me? How could I even attempt to make them love me when they didn't really know who I was? How could I consider staying when they'd hate me if they knew the truth?

I couldn't. But I couldn't give them up, either. Not unless every other choice was taken from me.

"I know it's a lot to digest, love. Take your time." After giving me an understanding smile, Jason leaned to the side, groaning, and slapped a hand against the floor. "Blasted uncomfortable," he muttered, shooting a glare at Ruarc.

The most self-satisfied grunt I'd ever heard came from the man keeping me locked against him, and I felt him smile against my neck.

All those teeth so close to my throat.

I smiled. I smiled because I wasn't afraid. Not in the least.

"You got any more questions, love?"

My smile fell.

This doesn't change anything, I told myself. *You can't have a happily ever after. At some point, your past* will *catch up with you.*

But as long as I was here . . .

"You said you can be possessive," I began carefully, remembering how Ruarc had snarled when Jason had tried to touch me, "wouldn't that cause a lot of jealousy and heartache?"

Ruarc moved his right arm up over my belly, heat flaring to life under his thrilling touch, until his hand found the spot right above my heart. A deep, satisfied rumble started in his chest. "No."

I shivered.

Jason rolled his eyes at Ruarc before shooting me a sheepish green. "It's nothing for you to worry about, love. There is bound to be some issues—not because we are wolves but because we are part human—but the males work that out among themselves." He raised both his brows. "Did you honestly think we would expect you to deal with this one's"—he nodded at Ruarc—"temperament alone?"

The rumble came to an abrupt end as Ruarc swiveled his head to Jason. I looked up just in time to catch the death-glare he aimed at the other man.

Jason opted to ignore him.

"So . . ." I glanced down at the arm Ruarc held around my waist. It was tan—covered in a light sprinkle of dark hair—with the veins in his forearm right below the surface. The man did not have an ounce of fat on him, just muscles upon muscles upon muscles. "Can any—any lycan . . . Uhm . . ."

"Spit it out, love."

A warm, uncomfortable flush climbed up my neck. "Does this mean that, as long as it's a lycan, it's okay for any person to, uhm, to kiss any of us?" I held my breath, heart racing.

A sharp bark left Ruarc. "What?" He'd gone rigid behind me.

Jason's gaze burned. With drawn brows and a clenched jaw, he stared at me like I had gone insane.

"No. Hope . . ." He took a deep breath. "If you kissed another man, someone *not* in our pack . . ."

"He would die," Ruarc's gravelly voice finished.

"D-die?"

"Die."

Die . . .

That was . . . that was crazy, wasn't it? And how crazy was I that their answer didn't send me fleeing, but left me relieved that they didn't want to share me?

At least not with anyone outside the pack.

I chewed on my bottom lip.

Was it bad they were willing to share me between themselves?

"A-and you?" I asked, pushing the rest aside for later.

You're good at that, Hope, the ugly mental voice that so resembled my mother's sneered. *How does it feel, living in denial?*

I chewed a little harder, startling when Ruarc suddenly— and gently—used two fingers to pop it out of my mouth.

"Don't," was all he said. Then he brushed his mouth over my cheek, growling a little under his breath.

Jason watched the exchange with eyes that had gone dark, pupils dilating and brown giving way to glowing amber. When he spoke, his voice was low, "What do you mean, love?"

"Can women—erm, *females*, kiss you?"

An angry growl tore from Ruarc as Jason slowly shook his head. "Of course not. A female attempting intimacy with a male who is already courting a mate will get hurt."

"Hurt?"

Something in Jason's expression told me everything I needed to know, even before the word left his mouth. "Yes."

"You would *hurt* her?"

"Yes," Ruarc answered and buried his head in my neck. He didn't look up again. Not even when Jason cleared his throat and muttered his name. Ruarc was, apparently, done with this conversation. He busied himself by alternatively smelling me, nibbling on my neck—which was so distracting it was hard just to keep my eyes open and not let my head fall back against his shoulder and moan—and dragging me tighter against him.

After staring at Ruarc for a minute and being utterly ignored, Jason sighed and shook his head. "A female wolf would expect it. If she came after one of us while we were courting you, it would be a threat to your life."

I gasped. Not because Ruarc had chosen that moment to press a kiss behind my ear. No, not at all. "W-what do you mean?"

"If a male has decided on mating a female, only her death would make him consider someone else." He paused for a minute, tipped his head to the side like he was thinking. "Although, both males and females can change their minds *before* the mating thing happens. During the courting phase. You know, if they're incompatible or whatever." He hit the empty air, like he was batting the thought away. "Either way, during the time before the bond snaps into place, females have been known to occasionally kill other females to get the mate they want. It rarely ends well, but it has been done."

"That's terrible!"

"Enough," Ruarc grumbled. "Time for Hope to sleep."

Wait, what?

"When was *that* decided?"

"Right now." The determined tilt to his chin told me everything I needed to know.

I wrinkled my nose and looked at Jason for help.

He was grinning.

"Alone?" he purred. The heat in his eyes made his grin look downright wicked.

"With me," Ruarc bit out and turned us sideways.

Dismissing Jason.

"But . . . but I still have questions!"

"Tomorrow." Ruarc lifted me off his lap and moved us to the head of the bed. There, he settled against the headboard, me sprawled on top of him.

Jason got up and made his way over to us. Shooting Ruarc a triumphant smile—which turned into a muffled grunt of pain as Ruarc elbowed him in the ribs—he leaned down and pressed a tender kiss to the corner of my mouth.

I was so startled I just sat there in Ruarc's arms, blinking up at both men. They wore identical expression of heat mixed with something tender.

"Your face . . ." I reached up and gingerly touched Jason's mouth. It was healed.

Jason grinned and grabbed my wrist. "We heal quickly," he said, and pressed an innocent kiss to the inside of my wrist.

Innocent . . .

Then why was I squirming?

Ruarc growled.

Still grinning, Jason released my hand. "Goodnight, love." He moved to the door, hesitated in the doorway.

"Close it," Ruarc growled.

Jason gave a mock salute, threw one lingering glance my way, then closed the door.

47

RUARC

THE LOOK ON MY FEMALE'S PRETTY FACE WHEN I STRIPPED OFF my shirt forced me to swallow a groan. Her wide eyes looked startled as they roamed over my bared torso, almost painfully wide.

If she kept staring at me like that the painful throb in my dick would escalate to full blown agony.

I suppressed the urge to flex my muscles and rolled into bed next to her.

"Hi," she squeaked, an adorable blush coating her cheeks.

I grunted in reply and, with a tug, had her sprawled halfway on top of me. Ignoring her sputtering, I arranged her so her face rested on my chest, her arms wound around my neck, and her shorter legs reached down to intertwine with mine.

They reached my knees.

Cute.

When I was satisfied, I put a finger under her chin to tilt her head up. "Okay?"

As her head moved down in a nod, I leaned in and captured her mouth in a possessive kiss. It was a good thing she moaned and pressed closer, because there was no way in hell I could've stopped.

My female tasted like ambrosia.

I ate at her lips, uncaring when our teeth occasionally clashed. All I wanted was to devour every inch of my sweet, delectable female. To drown in her scent. To make her as crazed as she made me.

I sucked her tongue into my mouth, groaning when she almost shot off the bed. She would have if I didn't have one hand on her lower back, the other entwined in her hair.

"Ruarc," she groaned, short little bursts of air escaping her swollen lips. She pulled back. "You . . . you're really not mad?" A world of insecurity shone in her soulful, wide eyes.

My insides boiled.

My female should never *feel like this.*

"No," I growled and her brows shot up before she looked down. Cowering. "Don't." I gripped her chin and forced her to meet my eyes. "Was Jason who made a mistake. Not you."

A sad shake of her head, gaze averted.

Another growl vibrated in my throat. "You're mine." I claimed her lips in a fierce kiss, chest swelling with satisfaction when she went pliant and her hot, little body melted into mine.

She squirmed, hips jerking and back arching, a sweet gasp whispering past kiss-swollen lips.

A low, guttural snarl tore from my throat.

Then she pressed her hips down, and *fuck me* . . .

While wiggling on top of me she'd aligned our bodies perfectly. Only a thin layer of clothes separating me from the sweet, feminine flesh between her legs.

Lust thundered in my veins, the urge to claim her beat at my skull. She was so fucking hot, my little female. So innocent and sweet and responsive.

So fucking mine . . .

Her gyrations drove me mad. Her breathless moans

forced me to swallow gallons of fierce possessiveness. The need to brand her with the mark of my teeth, with my scent, clawed at my mind.

She's not ready.

Knew it without a doubt. Knew it with the same surety I'd felt when I'd decided to claim her. But knowing didn't do shit for the furious roar of need beating against my ribs.

I wanted her. All of her. Her cries of passion as she came. The look of wonder on her face when she realized how much pleasure this big, scarred body could give her. The arch of her back as she spasmed around my cock.

Her love.

"Want to make you come." I licked at the corner of her mouth.

Tastes so good.

"W-what?" Glazed eyes stared down at me. Her hair was tousled, lying in soft waves around her expressive face.

"Make you come," I repeated on a growl. Words were becoming harder. Everything in me roared to touch her. Wanted to bind her to me until she could never, *ever* leave.

Not even if she wanted to.

Her lips twisted in confusion. "What . . . what do you mean?"

Forcing my brain to focus on the information revealed in her blank stare was difficult. When I understood, I stilled, and fierce joy mixed with the mindless need flowing through my veins.

She didn't know. No one had ever made her come before.

I'd be the first . . .

Joy was chased away by burning possession.

Mine!

The word was a snarl on my lips, a fire in my gut, a brand between my shoulders. I'd tattoo her fucking name on my back if I'd thought that'd convince the world to stay away from her.

Had I been in my other form, I would've roared a challenge to the sky. The thought of sharing her with *anyone*, even my brothers, made me want to tear someone to pieces.

Using my grip on her hair, I bent her head back until I could reach the sweet juncture between her neck and shoulder. Then I bit down. Not hard, just enough so she felt my teeth. So she'd know how it would feel when I finally marked her. "Want to give you pleasure."

"You mean . . . sex?" Her voice wavered.

"No." I placed my mouth over her pulse. "No sex." I licked the sensitive skin, then sucked it into my mouth.

A sweet gasp of surprise.

I bared my teeth in triumph. "Just touching. And licking."

For a moment she didn't reply. Might have held my breath. Then, her trembling voice uttered that magic word, "Y-yes."

I almost erupted from the bed. But that would've scared my female, and I needed her relaxed. And excited. And warm, and willing, and wet, and—

A snarl ripped from my chest.

Make my female feel good. So good.

I flipped us until she was below me and watched her cheeks flush with color.

"Ruarc . . ." Her hand came up, hesitated, and cupped my cheek.

I leaned into her touch, rubbing my bristled cheek against her soft palm. "My Hope."

A sweet smile curved her lips, and though her eyes were still wide, her pupils were dilated, her face flushed, her breathing uneven.

A possessive growl tore from my chest before I could think better of it. Had to taste her. Needed to. To lick and bite and touch until she gasped my name. Until all other names and all other words had fled from her brain, leaving mine the only one to ever pass her lush lips.

But I had to go slow. Even if it killed me.

My voice sounded rough when I told her to relax, disappearing into a hoarse rumble as I dragged my lips across her collarbone.

Small hands came up to wound through my hair.

The fragility of my female never ceased to surprise. To awe.

A fierce vow of protection repeated in my mind, the same one I'd already made her. She was so much smaller than me. So much more fragile. Made me even more determined to keep her feeling safe and protected.

With that thought in mind, I put my weight on my elbows and leaned down, placing our foreheads together and taking a moment to just *be*. To give her a chance to feel without expectations or pressure.

"Ruarc," she whispered, and when her hand came up to cup my cheek and her eyes closed while a soft sigh slipped past her lips, my heart all but exploded.

Trusts me.

She'd been betrayed in the past—I saw it every time I looked at her, the guarded shield clouding her eyes, the remembered pain haunting her—and still she trusted me.

My hands dug into the bed. Afraid to touch her. Afraid I'd lose control and hurt her.

Never! Another fierce vow.

Keeping my weight on one elbow, I brushed a lock of her away from her forehead. "You okay?"

She opened her eyes. "Yeah . . ." A soft sigh. "Yeah, I'm . . . good."

Big, brown eyes swimming with emotion, she tugged on my head, guiding me down into the first kiss she'd ever initiated between us.

"Ruarc . . ." A whisper against my lips.

Victory was a heady rush. Possession drummed in my ears.

She was *mine*.

I kissed her back. Clumsily, like I hadn't since I was a lad. Couldn't help it. With her, I lost all control.

Every sigh tearing from her throat made the beast roar in my head. Every soft moan drifting up past her perfect lips heated my blood to unbearable levels. Everywhere she touched, I was branded.

Have to taste her . . .

I kissed my way down her body, leaving small love-marks I'd later stare at with all the savage pride I'd never known I possessed.

When I got to the line of her jeans, I almost tore them apart with my bare hands.

Until I remembered that my female was human.

"Off?" My body shook while I watched her face, watched trepidation war with passion.

Passion won.

She gave a small nod.

Thank fuck!

I went slow. She was nervous, and that was okay. This was new for her.

New for me too, I realized with a clench of my heart, struggling to keep calm while need and a raging, obsessive possessiveness thundered through my veins.

This is . . . she's—

"Beautiful."

She immediately blushed a bright red and avoided my gaze.

I frowned. "You're beautiful, *a chuisle*."

"T-thank you."

She didn't believe me.

Teeth clenching, I growled, "You. are. Beautiful. And"—I licked at the spot right above her waistband—"you taste like fucking heaven."

"Ruarc!" She arched her back, little nails digging into my scalp.

Done with her ridiculous doubt—anyone who set eyes on her would want to make her theirs, dammit—I moved down her body.

She looked at me with wide, trusting eyes.

My heart ached.

Being as careful as my large, clumsy hands were capable of being, I undid the buttons of her jeans—jeans she'd bought with *Jason* and not me—and dragged them down her legs.

My gaze was drawn to the bandage covering her calf, and I scowled. How long did it take humans to heal?

"Still hurt?" I brushed my hand down her leg, stopping before I accidentally did something to aggravate her injury.

She blanched, but shook her head. "Y-you've seen me walk. It's basically healed, I . . . I just use the bandage so I won't have to look at the . . ." She hesitated. "Scab? The scab is ugly."

I pushed down the rage wanting to erupt at the reminder of her abuse. "But it's healed?"

"All good." She shook her leg and banged her foot down into the mattress with unnecessary force.

I growled and grabbed her knee. "Stop that."

She allowed me to put her leg back down, then grabbed at my arms. "Stop worrying." She bit her lip. "I . . ."

Vulnerable. She looked so vulnerable.

She's fine.

Lucien might not have said anything, but the cold bastard would keep his silence unless something needed to be told.

'She's fine' didn't count. Not to him.

Know she's fine.

If her injury had become infected or re-opened, I'd have scented it.

"Ruarc . . ."

Hating the stark vulnerability in her voice, I leaned down

and kissed her. Kissed her until she melted beneath me, until she arched her back and sweet moans spilled from her lips like drops of the sweetest honey.

Mine.

I drew back and looked down at my half-naked female.

Air was sucked from my lungs at the sight greeting me, leaving them straining.

I couldn't stop staring.

My mouth watered at the thin, lace panties barely covering her mound. Black. And so thin I could scent her arousal; the sweet fragrance of my female.

Proof that she wanted me.

A deep, savage snarl rose from the deepest recesses of my beastly soul, and if I'd doubted for a second Hope was made for me, that doubt would have vanished at her reaction.

She shivered.

Fucking *shivered*, and her lips parted on a moan.

This time, I was the one incapable of forming words. All I could think about was getting to that soft, hot flesh and making her scream my name.

Can't think. My female . . .

Her taste was so close. Her mound, waiting. Waiting for my tongue. But . . .

Couldn't move. Couldn't bring myself to remove that last piece of clothing shielding her.

Don't wanna scare her.

Somehow, Hope knew. With a nervous half-smile, she lifted her hips, telling me without words that it was okay.

Half a second later her panties lay shredded on the floor.

I parted her legs and just stared. Pink and flushed.

Perfect.

A fierce surge of possessiveness made my breath catch on a snarl.

No one else would ever see this. No one!

I ignored the part of me that knew I'd have to share. It

was possible I'd be beating up my pack brothers on a regular basis, but it would be worth it. Was no doubt in my mind they'd all agree it was worth it.

She's worth everything.

I breathed deep, took in her sweet scent, the slightly spicy undertone of her arousal. She smelled like desire. Like warm, hot female. Like coming home at the end of a battle. Like Hope. My Hope.

My balls ached to empty inside her. The steel my cock had become threatened to shred my pants. Wanted her. Wanted her so badly it hurt.

Want to see her convulse with pleasure, to know it was me who gave it to her.

I don't know how long I stared at her core, fighting the urge to bite her soft thighs, to mark her as mine and bind her to me for all eternity—with or without her permission.

She looked so soft. So inviting. So *mine*.

But when I drew a deep breath through my nose, eagerly taking in another lungful of her perfect, female scent, I caught the beginning rise of the only scent that had the power to stop me in my tracks. The only scent that could kill my desire at this point.

The scent of fear.

I pulled back. Looked up. Froze.

What the fuck?

Her face was ashen. Big eyes wide with emotions I knew all to well. Terror. Anguish. Fucking regret.

Already she regretted this. Regretted me.

Should have known.

I wasn't right for her. Was too big. Too ugly. Too scarred and savage and hard for someone like her. Someone so perfect.

"Sorry," I muttered and leaned further back.

My chest was splitting. Ripping straight down the middle

and exposing the useless muscle pumping acid into my blood.

But I'd gladly accept that pain if it meant my heart would fall out and stop. Fucking. Aching.

"R-Ruarc . . ." Hope's voice was barely audible. A whisper of a thin sound among the rustling of sheets as she covered herself up.

Hiding. From me.

"Don't." My tone was too harsh, but I couldn't help it. My female was scared of me.

I'd failed her.

My stomach heaved like I was going to be sick. Thick despair clawed at my throat, and I could no longer look at her. Couldn't bear to see disgust twisting her face or fear shining in eyes that had been so trusting, so *welcome* only minutes before.

"It's not y-you, Ruarc." Her voice broke. "It's . . . it's *them*."

My head snapped around, took in her too-pale face, the nightmares swimming in her eyes. "Who?"

She shuddered—at my too-soft voice or the expression on my face. Her throat worked as she attempted to swallow. To speak.

"Who?" I demanded. Was ready to fucking *murder*.

"The men who . . . who had me."

The men who had *her?*

My world went black. She said something else but I couldn't hear it over the roaring in my ears.

Rage licked up my chest. Wrapped around my heart. Burnt.

Took all my effort to keep my body still. To not explode out of my skin and rip the room to shreds in my fury. *They hurt her. They did something to her, something that made her fear—*

A loud, furious snarl.

Mine.

A roar.

Still mine.

Words refused to form on my tongue. My jaw clenched too tight for me to speak. Fangs had already descended, my beast howling for blood while rage blazed through us both.

Several seconds passed. I pushed. And pushed. And when the words came, they were warbled. Distorted. Ugly. "What. Happened."

I couldn't look at her. If she cried I would lose it. If I caught a glimpse of pain on her face, I would shed my human skin and go on a rampage unlike anything this world had seen since the Beast of *Gévaudan*.

"They would—" Her voice broke again, a soft sob escaping. The rage I felt in that moment flayed skin from muscle and stripped tendons and tissue from bones. It left nothing untouched, nothing alive. It burnt through me, maiming and destroying and annihilating, until all that was left was a smoking carcass and a few, brittle bones.

If I turned to her, if I showed her how close to the edge I was . . .

She'd run screaming from the room.

"Tell me." It was a command. Harsh and brutal and with edges that cut.

Couldn't help it. Was fucking *wrecked*.

Another sob.

Fangs pierced my bottom lip.

"They would . . . they would look at me. They'd look and scare me, but nothing else, okay?" Her voice rose at the end, shrill, like she was trying to convince us both it hadn't been that bad. That it wasn't enough to send me into a tailspin of murderous rage.

"They'd *what?*"

Another sob.

Another hole in my lip.

"They'd spread me and . . . look," she whispered.

And then it clicked. Her sudden fear. Her frozen body. It'd all happened when I stopped to memorize the beauty laid before me.

They'd forced her legs apart and splayed her open for their own amusement.

I pushed my rage down. Further and further, until it was buried in a red ball of destruction I would unleash when I was far, *far* away from my female.

When the *lithbhárs* who hurt her was within my grasp.

It took all my concentration and all my willpower to hide away the lethal fury riding me. When my claws retracted and my fangs shrank enough that I could run my tongue over them without cutting myself, I turned.

The sight greeting me pushed at my straining control until my whole body shook.

Hope's face was buried in her hands. Her shoulders were shaking. What little I could see of her face was pale, almost translucent. The fragility of her human state hit me straight in the chest, made me that much more aware of the grave responsibility I would gain if she became my mate.

When. *When* she became my mate.

I wanted this female. Wanted her with a fierceness bordering on the irrational. In the short time I'd known her, she'd come to mean everything. If she'd let me, I'd mate her right here, right now. And as soon as she was ready, she'd be mine. Consequences be damned!

"My Hope . . ." I tried for a croon. It came out sounding like rusted nails.

Her shoulders continued to shake. The soundless sorrow sent shards of silver spikes through my heart. The trauma she'd been through was peeking out in bits and pieces, shredding me more each time.

At some point she'd have to let it all out. Grief, anger, and sorrow. And I'd be there.

Every step of the way.

I'd stand guard while all her demons were expunged and her tormentors lay rotting in the ground. Preferably in pieces. Having died in agony. Dreadful agony. They would scream, and beg, and plead, and I'd tear them apart with my bare hands, slice them from hip to sternum, rip away arms and legs while they cried—

Claws shot from the tip of my fingers and sliced holes in the mattress.

I growled at my own carelessness and turned my thoughts away from her tormentors.

Several deep breaths later—after my claws had retracted and I was once again in control—I scooped Hope into my arms, settling with my back against the headboard and a heap of warm, shaking female in my lap.

I ignored her sobbing protests and lifted her chin. "Look at me," I demanded, annoyed when she kept her eyes squeezed shut. "Look. At. Me."

I felt like an asshole when her eyes flew open at my harsh tone, but needed her to see. To understand. "One day you'll tell me," I said, voice dark with promise, "and then I'll kill every last one."

My words did not stop her eyes from leaking, so I growled to show her just how serious I was. The tears slowed to a trickle, and my chest puffed up in satisfaction.

Until her big, wet eyes pierced me with accusation.

"D-don't g-growl a-at m-me," she cried, and I winced, rubbing a hand over my chest.

How the fuck did I fix this?

"Don't cry," I commanded, each tear another shred to my aching heart. She'd break me. If she continued this way, she'd fucking break me.

"I c-can't help i-it!"

With a muttered curse, I tilted her face up and kissed her. I made her sorrow mine. Kissed her face. Tasted each tear. Claimed the anguish making wet trails down her cheeks.

The salt on my tongue would serve as a reminder. A promise. And one day I'd look back at each of these tears. I'd remember the way she looked right now; the misery stark upon her pretty face. I'd remember, and I'd hunt down all those responsible.

I'd hunt them down and make them pay.

Tear by tear, they'd pay. Piece by piece. Scream by fucking scream. And when they were nothing but charred remains, their existence long forgotten, I'd spend the rest of my life erasing their memory from my female's tender heart.

Her tears finally slowed. I kissed away the last one, nuzzling her neck for good measure, and waited.

"You . . . you aren't repelled?"

Her voice was small. A little broken. A lot damaged. And her question was pure nonsense.

"*What?*" I felt like yelling at her, but didn't want her to cry again.

Wincing, I held my breath until I was sure she wouldn't start leaking again.

"Because of what they did . . ."

Had to bite back a curse. "Never. Why'd you think that?"

"You just . . . when I told you . . . you were so angry. You couldn't even look at me."

Shit!

I kept messing up. "Was angry. Scared of losing control. Of hurting you."

She stared up at me with wide eyes. Still not understanding.

"You're mine," I growled, willing her to understand. "Thought of you hurting makes me want to destroy the world."

Her eyes filled with tears again, but the tremulous smile trembling on her lips made up for it. "That's . . . that's one of the sweetest things anyone has ever said to me."

I grunted. "Dumbass people."

"Who?"

"Everyone you've been around."

Her smile grew. "But not you," she whispered.

"Not me," I agreed with an arrogant snort.

I would take care of her. Cherish her. Love her.

Kill everyone who'd ever hurt her.

Just had to figure out who they were . . .

48

HOPE

Warm, soothing light teased my closed eyelids and spilled across my face in a comforting kiss of heat. Throwing my arms over my head, I stretched, calves tightening and back arching off the mattress.

Why did stretching in the morning feel so incredible?

I blinked my eyes open, reveling in the morning sun streaming through the closed window, and rolled to my right.

The spot Ruarc had occupied during the night was empty, but not yet cool.

He must have just left.

A smile broke free.

He'd held me all night. The heat from his body had chased away the ice eating away at my soul. The strong arms engulfing me had kept even the most daring nightmares at bay. And his hot fury had calmed the bitter shame that had curdled in my stomach after I'd freaked out on him.

Thought of you hurting makes me want to destroy the world.

My smile grew so wide it hurt.

Those words . . .

And before that, before things had gone wrong, and

before he'd said the words I'd never forget, he'd been kissing me. Touching me.

My whole body had been flushed with sensations I'd never before experienced. Everything had felt hot. My skin had felt so sensitive that each brush of Ruarc's big, calloused palms had made my breath catch and my stomach contract with something too hot, too electric to be called something as simple as pleasure.

I sat up, wrapping the blanket around my shoulders to ward off the morning chill. The faint scent of pine cones and wild, earthy power hung in the air. My eyes drifted shut. Ruarc always smelled like forest mixed with something elusive, with words that couldn't possibly be a smell, and yet . . .

Wild. Power. Male.

Those were the words that popped into my head every time I caught the slightest hint of his scent.

I padded to the bathroom on bare feet and took a quick shower, surprised to catch a whiff of Ruarc's lingering scent when I descended the stairs. It was almost as though some of what made Ruarc, well, Ruarc, had attached to my skin, making a home within my body.

Not that I was complaining. I loved the way he smelled.

"You're looking particularly pleased with yourself this morning, love," Jason said. He stepped into view just as I hit the bottom of the stairs, his smooth, whiskey voice a caress up my spine. "Did my sweet, little human have some fun last night?"

"Jason!" I felt myself blush. "What—uhm, good morning?"

A charming grin curved his lips and lit up his eyes. "Where's my morning kiss?"

"M-morning k-kiss?"

He cocked his head. "We are dating now. Didn't you catch that during our chat last night?"

"Oh! Uhm . . ."

"Is my blushing flower a little shy?" Both his brows rose, leaving him looking like a faintly startled caricature of himself.

The ridiculous image stole a giggle straight out of my mouth.

"Ah, that's better." He stepped closer, forcing me to tilt my head if I wanted to keep watching him.

Which I did.

His cheeky grin made me wary, but at the same time butterflies danced in my stomach, flapping their wings in joyous excitement.

One hand snaked behind my back, fast—too fast for a human—and buried in my hair. A gentle pull later and his mouth hovered above mine. Our breaths mingled, his smelling faintly of mint spice.

"Good morning, sweetheart," Jason whispered, mouth brushing mine in a faint caress.

A small, startled gasp tore from my throat.

The space between us disappeared, and then he whisked my breath away with a kiss so tender I thought my heart might break.

It had never occurred to me that he'd be like this, all soft and gentle and heart-wrenchingly sweet.

He pressed featherlight kisses all over my mouth, lingering at one corner before giving my bottom lip a slow, tormenting lick.

Heat flared in my belly.

I pressed closer, spurred on by a deep, masculine groan. That sound, that deep, male sound gave me the courage to wrap my arms around his neck and cling to him, my body folding into his. Soft where he was hard. Yielding where he was unwavering.

Through all of that—the way I pressed myself against him, the frantic way I clung to him—the kiss stayed the same.

Just a tender press of lips, soft sighs, and the occasional provoking lick of his tongue.

The heat in my belly spread. Everything tingled. A deep arousal ignited in a sudden wave of burning passion. A passion I'd only just begun to recognize with Ruarc.

Just as I thought I would lose my mind, Jason pulled away. His eyes were heavy lidded, a flush creeping along his cheekbones. Lips that had just been teasing mine were slightly parted, allowing room for a few heavy exhales.

"And that's how you say good morning," he said, the rough quality of his voice telling me he'd been just as affected by our kiss as I had.

I couldn't reply. Couldn't do anything but stare up at him while I tried to push my brain into gear.

His low chuckle sent shivers up my spine. The sound was heavy with masculine satisfaction, filled with need and want and all things carnal. "We better go, love." He reached up and reluctantly pulled both my hands away from his neck.

My thoughts came slow, like they were covered in syrup and stuck together. "Where are we going?"

Another grin cascaded over his face. "Breakfast. Let's go." He pulled me against his chest and whispered in my ear, "Before I devour you where you stand."

I pressed my thighs together. "I . . . But . . . What?"

"You see, love, there's this one thing I can't stop thinking about, one question burned into my mind."

I shouldn't ask. I knew I shouldn't ask. "W-what question is that?"

Damn you, brain!

His grin changed to a carnal smile, wicked intentions gleaming in his amber eyes as he licked his lips like a wolf before a meal. "Why, how you would taste, of course."

Before I could stutter a reply, he walked away, leaving me standing with my jaw slack and my eyes wide and unseeing.

Two men? What were you thinking?
I was in so much trouble.

49

HOPE

Later that day, I was nestled into Ruarc's side—my legs thrown over his lap, his arm around my shoulders, my head on his chest—when Jason waltzed into the living room with a broad grin on his face and a square box carried under one arm.

"It's time," he pronounced with a serious expression. "Too many moons have passed since our last battle, and we have a new member to initiate."

"Initiate?"

"Yes, my sweet dove. You haven't lived until you've seen this one"—he arched a brow in Ruarc's direction—"battle it out on the board."

"Dove? Aren't doves just fancy pigeons?"

"It's a term of endearment, love. Don't ruin the moment."

I laughed, enjoying Jason's playfulness and the way he brandished his box when he spoke.

Eyes sparkling with mischief, Jason sauntered over to the couch where we sat. "You ready?"

"To battle? What, exactly, does that mean?"

Ruarc put his chin on top of my head and turned to Jason. "Looking for a whooping, pup?"

"As a matter of fact, I am." Jason flashed a grin. "Why don't you bend over and let me get started."

A quick extraction from our entangled limbs, and then Ruarc was on his feet, towering over Jason with his teeth bare in challenge. "Careful." The warning was accompanied by a low snarl, the threat in the terrifying sound so chilling I wrapped my arms around myself in an instinctive attempt to protect my vulnerable areas.

"Is this the place I'm meant to say, 'my, what big teeth you have'?"

I cringed, prepared to see fists flying, but instead, Ruarc's lips spread wider, turning an alarming baring of teeth into an alarm-baring-of-teeth-that-was-also-a-smile.

A smile I'd come to love.

Jason grinned back and thumped Ruarc on the back.

"The others?" Ruarc asked.

"Ash is bringing snacks, and Lucien is probably waiting till we're all ready. You know how he is," Jason added in a strangely neutral tone.

My stomach dropped.

It was my fault. If Lucien chose to miss this—whatever this was—it would be because of me.

And I couldn't even blame him.

His dislike of me, his suspicion . . . Everything he'd accused me of had been true—or if not everything, then most of it. I'd lied to them, misled them. Just being here put them in danger.

My hands tightened into fists. "I'll be upstairs."

"No, you won't." Before I could move, Ruarc sat down and lifted me onto his lap.

"But—"

"No buts!" Jason interjected. "Although, yours is particularly exquisite . . ."

I gasped, and Ruarc glared at Jason. "Behave," he said, but then his hand slid down my body and squeezed the butt in question. "Mmm." He growled into my ear, teeth baring in good humor at the goosebumps rising in tandem across my skin, like little toy soldiers ready to battle.

"Oh, I see how it is." Jason looked pointedly down at Ruarc's hand. "You playing favorites already, love?"

Even though I knew he was kidding, I couldn't help a quick stab of worry. Ruarc was my first real boyfriend, and he was quite protective.

I squirmed.

Did Jason expect me to change that, to make the rules myself? And, more importantly, should I?

I like how things are now, though. I like having Ruarc take charge. It makes things so much easier.

But easy wasn't a good reason for anyone to get hurt.

"I'll always be the favorite," Ruarc growled, squeezing my hip. A second later, his lips found their way to a spot behind my ear. There, he pressed a quick kiss to the sensitive skin, making me shiver. "Was smart enough to claim her first."

Jason threw back his head and roared with laughter, and just like that my worries disappeared. A smile tugged on my lips, and before long I was laughing with him.

"You hear that, love? I think your, err . . . *boyfriend's* ego is growing out of control."

"But, Jason," I began, determined not to worry about the way he'd stumbled over the boyfriend thing, "as long as I've known you—"

"Not long at all," Jason reminded me with a grin.

I smiled back. "That's true, but as long as I *have*"—I waited to see if he would interrupt again, but when he only raised a brow with silent expectation, I continued—"your ego has been like that. I don't know why you'd suddenly start worrying about it growing out of control."

A deep, rough chuckle rolled out of Ruarc like claps of muted thunder. "She got you there."

I was too surprised, too awe-struck by the beautiful sound to react. And I wasn't the only one.

For several seconds, Jason stared at Ruarc in silent wonder, until a slow, wide smile broke out across his face. This one was so warm, so heartfelt, that it made unbidden tears prick at my eyes.

"Brother," Jason said quietly. The two men shared a long look, neither speaking. Then, in tandem, they both turned to me. "Thank you."

I tilted my head. "For what?"

"For everything, *mo chridhe*," Ruarc said and buried his nose in my neck.

Warmth flooded my chest—even though I didn't quite understand—and my voice was low and hoarse when I replied, "I should be thanking you. Everything you've done for me—"

"Was nothing," Ruarc interrupted.

"It was everything, Ruarc," I whispered back.

"Are we interrupting?"

I twisted on Ruarc's lap and looked straight into a pair of piercing, blue eyes. The owner of said eyes held a bowl of popcorn in one hand, the other a pitcher of water.

The guys almost always drank water. Water or beer, with the occasional soda thrown in once in a blue moon.

Lucien walked past him, and my guard immediately rose to shield me from the crisp, cutting voice that would soon wonder out loud what, exactly, Ash thought they had interrupted.

But while I was shrinking into Ruarc's side, Lucien simply glanced at the box Jason had put on the table when the others walked in and made no comment.

"Nothing that can't be picked up again later." Jason took a seat on the couch next to me and Ruarc, kicked his feet up on the table, and shot me a sly wink.

Something hot and fervent pierced my heart. A hope, a wish for a future I could never have.

This . . . this was a taste of family, of belonging.

And I never wanted it to end.

"We waited," Ruarc said and jerked his chin at the table.

Ash followed his gaze. "Monopoly?" A smile broke over that too serious face, a smile that warmed his eyes and instantly transformed him from a controlled and guarded male, burdened by responsibility, to a carefree, younger version of himself. He took the last seat on the couch. "We have not played this since—"

"The berries," Lucien interrupted. A flicker of humor sparked in forest-green eyes as they swept over Jason. "I'm surprised," he drawled. "I seem to recall a young pup claiming monopoly was for the devil?"

A hint of color tinted Jason's cheeks. "I'd forgotten about that."

"Really?" Ash's brows rose. "I would think it hard to forget that distinctive color of red."

Lucien snorted, and if not for Ruarc's stubborn habit of keeping me wrapped up in his arms whenever he was near— a habit I'd come to adore—I'd have fallen out of my seat.

Lucien snorting?

Was the world ending?

"It wasn't simply red," he said, and this time his lips twitched, almost like he was on the verge of a smile. He joined us around the table—gracefully folding his lean frame into one of the two available chairs. "It was rose-red. Or so the lady claimed."

Jason cleared his throat. "I don't think Hope needs to hear the whole story—"

"She does," Ruarc interrupted in that low, gravelly voice that always seemed to drag across each of my nerve endings in a way that left me tingling.

"No, she doesn't. It has nothing to do with—"

"Monopoly?" Ash lifted the lid of the box and revealed a colorful cardboard surface, strange metal shapes, and various plastic pieces and cards. "Is it your *wish* that we pack it away?"

Ruarc grunted out a laugh, while Jason scowled.

"Let's just play," he grumbled.

"We will. And while we do I am sure Hope would appreciate another piece of insight into one of her mates."

As soon as the words left Ash's mouth, we all froze. Me, because I wasn't sure how to act around the others with our new dynamic, unsure if they even knew. The reason for Ruarc's and Jason's unease could be for the same reasons, but I doubted it.

Not knowing made me worry they regretted their commitment to me.

"Not mate. *Boyfriend*," Ruarc spat, and I tensed further.

We hadn't known each other long, but the way he disparaged our connection felt like a cheapening of what we had, regardless of my own uncertainty about our future.

Jason cleared his throat and gave a small shake of his head.

Ruarc stiffened, cursed, then tightened his grip on me. "Whatever you're thinking, don't," he growled in my ear.

"I . . . I wasn't—"

"Ruarc isn't a fan of the human courting terms, love," Jason said softly. "He is impatient, and since he can't call you mate he has to settle on terms he feels are . . . lesser."

He can't call you mate.

Because I was human?

"I understand." But I didn't. Not really.

"Be patient," Ash said, and I wasn't sure if he was talking to me or Ruarc. "These things take time."

Ruarc's only reply was a dark, unhappy sound.

A ball of lead had formed in my stomach, and while I tried to digest it, I sneaked a peek over at Lucien.

His gaze was fixed on a spot above my head, his hands curled around his chair's armrest.

His silence disturbed me.

"I'm the shoe!" Jason suddenly cried out.

"You're a shoe?" Confused, I glanced at this feet. "You're not even wearing shoes."

"Sadly my feet are too big for normal shoes, love."

Ruarc grunted. "That why you want the tiny shoe?"

"Ever heard of irony?"

"What's with the shoes?" I asked again, looking around and seeing all four men staring at the box with various expressions of humor. Even Lucien.

"You know what they say love." Jason wiggled his brows. "Big feet, big—"

"Shoes," Ash interrupted. "Big feet, big shoes."

Jason laughed, looked at my confused expression and laughed harder. "Exactly, oh wise one. Big shoes."

I shook my head. "I am so lost."

Leaning forward, Ruarc snatched something out of the box and held it in front of my face. "It's a game piece." He used his index finger to tilt my head back so I could meet his gaze. Molten silver traced the lines of my face, lingering on my mouth. "It's yours, *a chuisle*," he murmured and brushed a too-short kiss over my lips. Then he turned to Jason and glared. "For upsetting our female."

"She wasn't upset," Jason protested. He reached for the little metal piece, but Ruarc jerked it out of reach and placed it in my hand.

"Hope, love, my little turtledove." Jason turned comically large eyes at me. "I need my game piece. It brings me luck."

"I don't recall you ever winning, Jason, so I doubt it brings you luck," Lucien said dryly. He tapped a finger against his lip, tilted his head, and reluctantly looked my way. "You could offer it to him as payment for the story."

The devious idea took root, and I could feel my lips

stretch in a grin of my own as I looked at Jason. "Lucien has a point," I said. "I'll give you the shoe . . . if you tell the berry story."

Amber eyes widened. Jason blanched.

My stomach hollowed. "No, I—Don't worry." I reached over to give him the piece. "You don't have to tell me, it's okay." If anyone knew what it was to prefer certain truths to stay buried, it was me.

As my hand opened, Jason's eyes lit up.

I'd been played.

"Aha!" He snatched the piece away and gave me a triumphant smile. "I've bested you, fair maiden. Now that I have my shoe, I will be unbeatable and you will all tremble before your master!"

I blinked at him, took in his maniacal grin and the sparkling humor dancing across his face, and burst out laughing.

"I do not think you are suited to be a master, Jason," Ash said. He snatched the shoe out of the other man's hand and offered it to me. He didn't smile, but his eyes were warm. "A master's first job is to see to his partner's happiness."

"Have you met me?" Arms thrown to his sides indicate himself, Jason grinned. "All I do is spread joy."

Lucien rummaged through the box and withdrew a metal thimble. "That cannot be pleasant for her."

Amber eyes narrowed. "Pleasant for who?"

"Joy."

"And Joy is?"

Lucien looked up, face expressionless. "Why, the person you've been spreading."

For a second, Jason looked like he was going to pass out. Then his face twisted, relaxed, and finally gave into a smile so wide it nearly cracked his face in two. "You wily old fox!"

Lucien shrugged, placed the thimble on the board, and watched me with an expression that seemed to say, "Well?"

For some reason, my face went flaming hot, and I couldn't hold his stare. Was I supposed to have understood the joke? Commented? Laughed?

Knuckles brushed over the back of my hand, just a quick touch, there and gone again. "Should we team up and take down this egomaniac?" Ash asked, tipping his head in Jason's direction.

I immediately nodded.

"Ruarc, will you swap places so I can sit next to my teammate?"

A deep rumble vibrated in Ruarc's chest. "I'll join."

"Join?" I tilted my head and looked back at him.

He's so handsome.

Even wearing a scowl and pressing his lips tightly together, he was such a magnificent male. The scar slicing into his skin only made him seem more dangerous, more potent, and the scruff always covering his jaw made me want to rub up against—

"Your team."

"Oh, no, you don't." Lucien threw something. It arced through the air and would have hit Ruarc smack between his eyes if his hand hadn't shot up and caught it between two dexterous fingers. "You're with me."

"You can't all gang up against me like that!" Jason turned his puppy-dog eyes my way. "Tell them, love."

Holding back a laugh, I shook my head and smiled. "You and your ego brought this on yourselves."

Jason clutched at his chest and threw himself back against the couch. "You wound me!"

"I'll wound you," Ruarc muttered as he reluctantly put me down and moved to the chair next to Lucien. "Your fault."

"Somehow I believe you shall survive the separation," Lucien said.

Seeing them all together like this, teasing and having fun,

made my chest so tight I could barely breathe. They were a family. A *real* family.

Longing swept over me like a ten-foot wave, and I nearly drowned.

Was I strong enough to walk away when the time came? I could no longer picture my life without them. Without any of them. Even Lucien.

The most vivid memory I had of him didn't include any insults or harsh words, but the way he'd saved me. The terrifying smile he'd worn as he'd torn off the part of Tim that would have hurt me. The safety I'd found, if only briefly, in his arms that night. The way he'd averted his eyes when he'd seen the state of my clothes, the simmering fury in shaking hands, the careful way he touched me.

A slight shift in the couch and the scent of horses, man, and wild plains; Ash settling in next to me. "Do you know how to play?"

I'd played board games when I was young, but never monopoly. "No. Not really. Is that okay? Do you want me to switch teams? I could always—"

"It is all right, *banajaanh*," he said gently. "I will teach you."

In the end, my inexperience wasn't quite as much of a handicap as I'd thought. Ruarc kept trying to help me—to Lucien's consternation—and whenever I landed somewhere where I had to pay, he'd growl at whoever collected my taxes, even when it was his own teammate. Several times, I had to bite my lip to stifle a smile—certain Ruarc double his effort to make sure I won if he saw my amusement.

Ash, ever the gentleman, made sure we didn't take advantage of Ruarc's protective nature, focusing instead on helping me learn and on beating Jason, who took the whole thing with good humor. That was, when he wasn't pretending to be devastated by everyone trying to beat him, or cackling with manic glee whenever we landed on one of his properties.

"Will you stop making that god-awful noise?" Dice clenched in one hand, Lucien glared at Ruarc, who stopped growling at Jason long enough to bare his teeth at Lucien.

"He's touching her!"

"What of it?"

"She's mine!"

A strange glint entered Lucien's eyes. "I was under the impression you two were sharing."

Ruarc stared at Lucien as though he was an idiot. "But he's touching her!"

Lucien stared up at the ceiling and muttered under his breath.

Meanwhile, a grinning Jason moved his hand from my knee up to my thigh.

I fought the urge to squirm in place, very aware of Ash's nearness.

Suddenly a dark, thunderous sound boomed from Ruarc's chest, and Jason's hand disappeared. Ruarc dragged him by the neck away from the couch and threw him out into the hallway.

"Mine!" he snarled.

I jumped to my feet, gnawing at my lip and taking a hesitant step toward the hall.

This was what I'd been scared of. Two men and one woman; jealousy was bound to be a problem.

A noise, something clattering to the ground.

I rushed after my two guys, crashing into Ruarc in time to see Jason spring to his feet in a lithe move that would have made a gymnast proud.

"W-what are you doing?"

Patting imaginary dust off his pants, Jason grinned up at

me, completely ignoring the dangerous presence grumbling at my side. "Having some fun, love."

"It didn't seem like fun." I reluctantly stepped away as Jason moved past us and was surprised when Ruarc let him. In fact, Ruarc's anger seemed to have fled, and a pleased look passed over his rugged features. He grunted and turned, keeping hold of my elbow as he led us back to the couch.

I looked between them, felt my brows draw together in confusion. Why did they both seem to be in such a good mood?

"I don't understand this," I said as Ruarc deposited me next to Ash. He took the time to pin Jason down with a scowl before taking his original place next to Lucien.

"I cannot say I blame you," Ash said. "Ruarc and Jason have always had a strange relationship. Jason enjoys riling up Ruarc, and Ruarc enjoys putting Jason in his place. It has been a while," he added. "It is nice to see them having fun again."

"Fun?" Were my eyes bugging out of my head or did it just feel like it?

With a sly wink in my direction, Jason turned back to the board. "Come on sixes," he said and threw the die. Two threes peeked up at us, and Jason's victorious whoop was loud enough to make me wince. "You're all doomed now." Gleefully rubbing his hands together, he took a moment to include us all in a gloating sweep of his gaze, then reached over to pluck his new property out of Lucien's hands.

Apparently, Lucien always controlled the bank. Not only did he never cheat—cheating was apparently allowed as long as you didn't get caught—but his meticulous manner and sharp mind kept everyone else from cheating as well.

Mostly.

"Careful, youngling, or your confidence may prove to be your downfall." Lucien pointed at Jason's dwindling stack of cash. "A wrong step and you will be forced to sell." He leaned closer, lowering his voice until it was a cold whisper. "And then you may end up losing *everything*."

A shudder of unease rippled below my skin, but while I rubbed at my arms to get rid of the sudden chill, Jason only smiled.

"Can't lose something you never had, mate," he replied and picked up the die once more. "What do you think, love? Do I have another double in me?"

A calculated look flashed through Ruarc's eyes. "Wasn't that what got you in trouble before?"

Jason jerked, his throw going wild. Both dice tumbled off the table.

Ruarc bared his teeth in a wicked smile and gestured to the floor. "Every double you roll, you get a cherry."

There was a moment of silence, then Ruarc's deep, gravelly chuckle filled the air, and all the air in my lungs disappeared.

I loved that sound.

"Ruarc's first prank," Lucien said after the laughter died down. His upper lip twitched. "I'm confident Jason would have preferred Ruarc settled the manner in his usual way, instead of stealing a page out of his book."

"I'm used to the fists," Jason muttered. He picked up one dice, rolled it around in the palm of his hand, then picked up the other. "The prank was . . . new."

"When was this?" I made the mistake of looking at Lucien when I spoke, and as soon as I saw him stiffen, I winced and braced myself for a scathing reply.

None came. He only stared, a tick in his jaw, expression unreadable but not frozen.

Not yet.

Jason cleared his throat. "Five years ago, I think. I can't really remember what I'd done to piss off the beast, but instead of starting a fight, he just walked away." An accusing look at Ruarc. "That should have been my first clue."

589

Ruarc's jaw tensed and he glared at Jason. "Meaning?"

"Meaning that you *never* walk away from a fight, and you are *incapable* of controlling your temper."

Ruarc shot to his feet with a menacing growl. "Not true."

A lazy smile, Jason gesturing to Ruarc's aggressive stance. "Proving my point here. What do you think, love," he asked me. "Think I should have known?"

When Ruarc huffed and sat back down, scowling at Jason, a part of me wanted to rush over, climb into his lap and plant kisses all over his face. Only fear of what the others would think held me back.

"Know what?" I asked, distracted.

Hands on my waist. Quickly, before I could react, they pulled. Then I was pressed against Jason's side, his arm around my shoulders, his finger under my chin. He searched my gaze with eyes that turned from serious to playful in a flash, then leaned down and placed a smacking kiss on the tip of my nose.

When another growl rumbled from Ruarc, this one more grumpy than aggressive, Jason ignored it and kept his gaze locked on me. "Known that the old man had a plan. A monstrous, evil plan."

Amused, I turned to a still scowling Ruarc. "What did you do?"

"Nothing more than he deserved," he grumbled.

"That's a vicious lie, old man!"

"Watch it, pup."

"Typical." Jason rolled his eyes. "Old men are all the same, grumpy and envious of the young and virile."

Ruarc snarled a second before a thunk sounded. My eyes as wide as saucers, I turned just in time to see one of the metal pieces bounce of Jason's forehead. A tiny, red spot bloomed between his brows.

"Nice aim," Lucien said and snapped up the die.

"Excellent," Ash chimed in.

Jason narrowed his eyes at Ruarc. "You'll pay for that."

The slow smile Ruarc sent back was all teeth. "Try me."

Jason glared another second or two before turning away and absentmindedly rubbing at the spot the game piece had hit.

"You okay?" I whispered, leaning in to take a closer look.

Jason looked down at me, brows drawn together. Whatever devious thought flashed through his mind had a grin forming on his lips before he sent a quick, victorious glance in Ruarc's direction. "It hurts, love," he told me, tilting his head down. "Kiss it better?"

"Oh . . ." Tension gathered in my stomach. Everyone was staring.

So what?

Being uncomfortable wasn't a good reason to reject his request, innocent as it was. So I leaned in, prepared to kiss the rapidly fading mark, only to find Jason dipping his head at the last second and catching my lips between his teeth. He growled, a light, playful sound that spiraled tendrils of heat down my belly, and kissed me so deeply I felt it to my toes.

A deafening growl. A flash of movement. Then I found myself at the other side of Ash, blinking up into piercing, blue eyes.

"What . . ." I trailed off. I knew he must have lifted me, but it had happened so fast it almost seemed like magic.

"I thought it best to move you away from the trouble-maker before Ruarc lost his temper."

A quick glance over at Ruarc was all it took to convince me Ash was right.

"Spoilsport," Jason said in a voice dripping with self-satisfied smiles. He passed me die. "It's your turn, love."

I rolled, and the game continued.

"That's five hundred." Ruarc crossed thick arms over a massive chest and eyed Jason with grim satisfaction. "Reminds me of something."

Jason groaned. "Oh, come on! Haven't I suffered enough?"

"No."

A soft sound from Ash was all it took to draw my attention. "It began when Ruarc walked away from a fight. Jason's face when he thought he'd been let off the hook . . ." He'd tied his long mass of silky, black hair back in a knot, and when he shook his head, I thought for sure it would all come tumbling down around him. It didn't. The hair stayed magically put, and my gaze strayed to his temple, where a single braid dangled to his shoulder, bound at the bottom with a piece of red string. "I do not think I have ever seen Jason looking so stunned."

"And for good reason," Jason muttered.

Ash didn't smile, but amusement showed in the way his eyes crinkled at the corners. "When Ruarc joined us at the bar that night—"

"I thought he'd come to kill me." Jason sent me a look. "You know how unreasonable he can be."

"He can be a little . . . difficult at times," I agreed.

Ruarc huffed. "You shouldn't talk, female. See this?" He pointed at a spot on his head and glared. "You're making me gray. Lycans don't do gray."

"I'm not difficult! And there isn't any gray where you're pointing. All your hairs are black as night."

"Like his soul."

"Who went out against my orders?" Ruarc opted to ignore Jason's insult and pinned me with a silver glare. "Getting yourself into all kinds of trouble."

My jaw clenched, and something hot stirred in the depths of my soul. "You can't forbid me from doing things."

"I can."

"No, you can't!" The need to establish some ground rules

rose as something inside me strained for release. It pushed against my battered psyche. Ignited a fire I hadn't thought myself capable of. I was about to argue when I realized what was happening.

A vice tightened around my chest, squeezed all the air from my lungs. I froze. My breath froze. My muscles froze. The only movement inside was the stubborn beat of a heart that refused to pause, sluggishly working to pump blood through my veins.

Thump-thump-thuuump.

I pushed the monster back down, wrapped it back up in its chains, shoved it into a cage, and hung padlocks on the door.

When it was once again secured, I averted my gaze and slumped against Ash.

The heat from his body drove the cold away, and after a minute or so, my fingers and toes began prickling as they regained sensation.

Slowly, I became aware of a strained silence.

I looked up, caught by blue eyes that seemed to . . . change? A presence, something other than Ash, something ancient and cold and terrifying, stared back at me. Then it was gone, and Ash was the only one left.

He tilted his head. Assessing.

I jerked my gaze away, found Ruarc. The gloating I'd expected was nowhere to be seen.

Strange.

He'd won this argument. And even if he hadn't, he *could* kind of tell me what to do. In some ways. Sometimes.

Admit it, it makes you feel safe. And sometimes . . . sometimes it makes you tingle in places you have no business—

Cutting the thought off before it could fully form, I blushed and looked away again, refusing to meet anyone's gaze until the story continued.

"Hope?" Jason leaned forward so he could see my face.

"Love, you know I agree with you. Ruarc can be downright monstrous."

My head snapped up. "He isn't monstrous!" I gave Jason a good glare before turning to Ruarc with an apologetic look. "You aren't. I'm sorry if I made you feel like that."

Eyes wide, Ruarc looked from me to Jason before a slow smile tugged his lips away and showed a glimpse of white teeth. "Don't worry, *mo chridhe*. Jason likes exaggerating. Don't you, pup?"

Jason sighed. "Don't you start."

"So you were at a bar?"

"Brought cherry drops," Ruarc said. "In a big glass. Had to be at least fifty." A slow, toothy smile. "Jason's the kind of male who *has* to have what he's not allowed. So I refused to share."

"It was cruel, love. Downright cruel."

"Jason must have asked him at least as many times as there were candies in the glass." Lucien handed Ash two hundred monopoly-dollars for passing go. "Ruarc kept refusing."

"Made me think they were little drops of heaven," Jason said. "The way he hoarded them."

"Were they?" I asked.

"More like drops of hell."

Ash passed the die to Jason. "Ruarc eventually told him they could play for it. Jason agreed, but the way he groaned when Ruarc pulled up a monopoly box could be heard around the bar."

"Pup's horrible at the game," Ruarc agreed.

My gaze whipped around the room, following the person speaking with a fascination that bordered on the obsessive.

I was starved for information. Not the way I should have, not about general life and the things that would help me survive, but information about these four men. About their lives, their hopes and dreams, anything they deigned to give me.

If they'd known my thoughts, they'd probably have thought I was a creepy stalker.

"How did it work?"

Looking reasonably glum, Jason told me, "Every hundred I made off the big bully would buy me a drop. If he won the whole game, he'd get a dare."

"A dare?"

Ruarc grunted. "I'd tell him to do something and he'd have to do it."

"That's . . . risky."

"Pup was cocky."

"I did fine in the beginning," Jason argued. "And with each piece of candy I wrestled from this one's"—he jerked his thumb at Ruarc—"evil grasp, I grew more sure it was all worth it. They were delicious."

"So delicious you could not help but gloat," Ash said. Then he . . .

He *winked* at me.

My mouth snapped shut, catching the tip of my tongue between my front teeth.

Serious, unreadable Ash actually *winked*.

When Ruarc had winked at me I'd nearly fallen off my chair. When Ash winked, I'd almost bitten my tongue in two. If Lucien ever decided to jump on the wink-train, it would probably be to shock me into an early grave, for if he ever did wink . . .

I would burst into spontaneous flames.

"He was making a spectacle of himself," Lucien said, not looking at me but watching Jason move his game piece. "Pursing his lips, making sounds meant to annoy Ruarc. He had no idea the candy was coloring his lips a bright, cherry-red."

"Really?" I looked at Jason, tried to imagine what he'd look like with bright, red lips.

"Truly."

"In the end, it looked like he was wearing lipstick," Ash said. "And it did not take long for others to catch on. Jason was friends with most of them—having spent many nights in that particular bar, a bar for supernaturals—and most had been victim to one of his pranks in the past."

Ruarc snorted. "They started joining the fun. One told me my date looked pretty, another asked Jason 'How much for a blowjob?', and Jason"—he rubbed a hand over the scruff on his neck—"what did you say again?"

Jason frowned. "It was Gideon's enforcer."

"That's right," Ruarc growled. "You said 'I thought you only stuck your wick in sheep, you Scottish bastard.'" He leaned over the table and plucked a hundred dollar bill from Jason's stack. "Didn't think *this* Scot saw you land on my property, eh?"

Jason frowned harder.

"Sufficient to say, there were a lot more jokes before the game finished," Lucien said. "And when it did, Jason owed Ruarc a dare."

"There was this female at the bar. A genie—"

"A genie?" My head spun. A freaking *genie?* They were real?

"They're not that special, love," Jason said, casting a sour look at Ruarc. "Though they like to think they are."

"This particular genie was well known in the community," Ash said. "You see, a genie can only ever grant three wishes in their lifetime, and Lana—that was her name—boasted that she didn't need her powers to make a man's dream come true."

"Sex," Lucien said in a droll voice. "She was talking about sex."

An ugly feeling slithered through my stomach. It reached my heart, twisting. I looked at Jason.

"World class bitch," Ruarc growled.

"Really?"

He dipped his chin and grunted, Ruarc speak for yes.

"She did have a reputation that drew a lot of males," Ash said. "Lured by her looks and her promise of pleasure, they tended to overlook her less . . . favorable qualities."

Accusation in every line of his body, Jason pointed at Ruarc. "The bastard dared me to seduce her."

My stomach dropped. If he'd gone home with her . . .

How could I ever compare?

No matter what Jason had said, I wasn't pretty. Dull, brown eyes, even duller hair. A face that looked too gaunt, a body that needed time to heal before it would look healthy, let alone attractive.

Not to mention my utter lack of experience with both sex *and* relationships. Hell, I didn't even have experience with real *life*, having been locked up and tormented for most of it. And what did I do the first time Ruarc saw me . . . *bare?* I freaked out and spent the night crying into his shoulder.

God, I'm a mess.

A sharp pain in my bottom lip, and I realized I'd been chewing it. Again.

I looked up, past Ruarc's frown and into cool, green eyes. They narrowed, swept over my face, and returned to burrow into my soul; an icy presence that curled around me, dove deeper and deeper until it touched upon the leashed monster inside.

The monster stirred, interested, and before I could panic, Lucien spoke and the monster quieted. "She, of course, believed she was god's gift to men, but the only thing she had to offer was her body." His lips curled with distaste, and I realized it was the same look he'd given the woman we'd met when shopping, the same look he'd used to crush me under his heel like a bug, on more than one occasion.

What, exactly, brought it about?

Ruarc grunted again—agreeing with Lucien?—and held his palm up for Jason, who'd just landed on his property. Again. "Should have seen yourself," he said, accepting the money Jason begrudgingly handed over with a flash of teeth. "You were so cocky. Marched up to her, said whatever crap you say to pick up girls, a fucking arrogant grin in place. But that died quickly, didn't it?"

The glare Jason shot Ruarc was ruined by the touch of pink crawling up his neck.

"What did she say again?" A flash of fangs as Ruarc prodded at a temper I wasn't sure *could* explode.

Through gritted teeth, Jason pushed the rest of the story out, "She looked at me like I was dirt. Wrinkled her nose, and all, I kid you not." He wrinkled his own nose. "Then she said she doesn't date men who wear more makeup than she does. And that if she did, she certainly wouldn't date someone wearing *that* shade of lipstick. She said it clashed with my coloring." Dismay clung to his voice and pulled his mouth into another frown.

Ruarc threw his head back and roared with laughter. The deep, gravelly sound went straight to the place between my legs, tugging, teasing, and when it was joined by Ash's low chuckle and a short, faint sound of amusement from Lucien, the feeling in my lower belly was so intense, so strange and alarming that I slapped my hand over my belly as though I could bat the sensations away.

When the sounds of amusement died down, Jason was still a little pink around his neck, but he'd regained his good-natured humor. A self-deprecating grin gave him a devastatingly handsome appearance, and the way he was watching me, brows slightly raised, chin lowered, I suspected he *knew* the effect he was having on me.

"'Course, he didn't understand until he excused himself and went to the bathroom," Ruarc said with another gravelly laugh.

"Trying to salvage his pride, no doubt," Lucien said.

Ash stroked my arm. Just once. An innocent touch that did *not* make me aware of how close we were. How good he smelled. "When he left Lana, he looked so dejected. So sad."

"And then a minute later, we heard a roar of outrage," Lucien said. "And he came barreling out the door, marched up to the bar, and shook a finger in Ruarc's face, yelling that he'd gone too far."

"The anger did not last long," Ash said. His gaze drifted over my face. Lazy. Relaxed. The hand resting at the back of the couch, nearest me, came down and touched my hair, rubbed a few of the strands between two of his fingers. "A few days later he began laughing about it, though he has never forgotten the sting of Ruarc's one and only prank."

A light, airy feeling bubbled in my chest. I looked up at Ash, took in those wide lips, the harsh angles of a face that looked both sharp and impassive all at once. Took in the slow smile spreading across his face, the warmth in his eyes.

I tried not to laugh. I really did. But with grins still flashing among the guys, and Ruarc's and Jason's booming laughter ringing in my ears, the battle was lost.

The first peel of sound startled me. It startled me so much I clapped both hands over my mouth. I cast a pleading look Jason's way, not wanting him to feel bad, to feel like we were ganging up on him. But his grin only widened, and suddenly trills of giggles climbed up my throat and erupted, one after another, until my stomach hurt and I was heaving for breath.

When I finally got it under control and opened my eyes, it was to the sight of four pairs of eyes watching me with such quiet intensity all the humor drained, leaving only a warm buzz in its place.

A low growl. Ruarc standing and coming closer. Hands

under my arms, big arms engulfing me in heat. Safety. "You've got a beautiful laugh, *a chuisle*," Ruarc said. And if his voice was hoarse, none of the others commented.

I didn't understand the heavy . . . whatever it was, in the air. So I said nothing. In fact, I didn't speak again until he'd carried me upstairs, lay down next to me on the bed, and said, "Tell me something good."

And I did.

50

HOPE

DURING THE NEXT FEW DAYS, I WAS HIT BY SEVERAL BIG realizations, each one leaving me reeling.

The first one happened right after breakfast the morning after we'd played monopoly, when Ruarc pulled me out to the back porch and placed a cup of steaming hot cocoa in my hand. The scent rising from the cup hit me in the face like a sledgehammer. And like a sledgehammer, it destroyed the wall where memories of my dad had been hiding.

I saw his face, I felt his hand on my brow, I heard his voice telling me to go to my uncle if I was ever in trouble.

And I realized clinging to a memory from when I'd been five couldn't have been what he'd wanted. Yes, it had given me hope when I'd had nothing, something to hold close to when I'd felt all alone in this world. But my father wouldn't have wanted me to chase a pipe dream, to seek out a man I'd never met, who'd never once tried to find me.

Maybe if I was a kid and hadn't been through what I had, but not now.

I guessed a big reason why I'd wanted to find my uncle— why I'd felt like I *needed* to find my uncle—was so I wouldn't be alone in this impossible task I'd assigned myself. But if being alone was all that stood in my way, why didn't I ask the guys for help? Right now, why didn't I open my mouth and ask Ruarc to help me destroy the Hunters?

Because you don't want them to die.

Had I thought I'd feel differently about my uncle once I got to know him?

I've been an idiot.

I never would have been able to ask him for help, ask him to put his life in danger. And then I would have been stuck in Canada—in the exact same situation—just waiting for the right moment to leave so I wouldn't be responsible for yet another person dying.

This took me two full days to digest. Once I had, it was as though a small—minuscule—weight had been lifted off my shoulders. *One* choice made. *One* decision I wouldn't have to agonize over anymore.

Not that you've thought that much about your uncle since meeting the guys.

He'd been a comfort when I was trapped with the Hunters, imagining a life outside the compound, but . . . not any longer.

The second realization that hit me had been a long time in the making. It was simple. Ridiculous. Stupid.

And it didn't surprise me in the least.

I didn't want to leave.

I'd probably thought that exact thing several times over the last few weeks, but this was the only time I allowed it to really take root. The only time I'd truly listened.

I didn't want to leave.

It was impossible, a wish made by a child. But there it was nonetheless.

I didn't want to leave, I wanted to stay. For as long as they'd have me. Longer even. I wanted to stay for the rest of my life.

That night, I cried myself to sleep while Ruarc curled around me and tried his best to stem the flow of my tears.

"Don't cry," he said in such a rough, pained tone that it almost worked. Almost.

But I kept crying.

It was only when he started singing that I fell asleep. That deep, growly voice was utterly unsuited to singing, but it didn't matter.

I loved it.

I don't want to leave. I never want to leave.

My heart was breaking, crumbling, shattering. And it felt like it would never heal.

My third realization was a combination of things that culminated in the first headache I'd ever experienced.

Or maybe it was more of a mental ache?

Either way, it started with the Thought. Each day, it grew. Each day, it expanded beyond past borders and burrowed along pathways I'd never known existed.

I would eat, and there it was.

I would be cuddling up with Jason and watching a movie, and there it was.

I would be burning up with need while Ruarc pressed heated kisses to my neck, to my chest, dragging those big, strong hands down my body in a way that had my hips shoot off the bed, and there it was.

It never left.

It never slept.

It never gave me a moment's respite.

And one day, I reached the end of my frayed, burning rope.

I'll do it.

There. Decision made. I'd do it, and if I survived . . . if I survived, then I'd come back here and hope the guys still wanted me with them. That they'd forgive me.

Because living without them wasn't living at all.

Once decided, the *how* remained a huge, taunting question mark. The *when* . . .

I left that one alone.

I told myself it was because I had no choice—the Hunters needed time to believe I was long gone, that'd I'd run to another country and holed up somewhere—but I knew, even if all the answers presented themselves tomorrow, I knew I'd find a reason to wait. At least a little longer.

I needed a concrete plan, anyway. More than the Thought could provide. It would take a while to figure everything out —if it even could be done. A few months, at least.

Please let me have at least a few months.

And while I was here, I'd soak up as much happiness as I could.

How stupid I'd been, not knowing if I should let myself care, wondering if would be better to never know the warm glow of love so the loss wouldn't be as devastating.

This . . . what Ruarc and Jason made me feel, how they all made me feel . . . *this* was life.

How could I even considering walking to my death without ever truly *living*?

And so the days passed while I did my best to push the Thought and everything that came with it into a tiny corner of my mind.

Ruarc continued to teach me how to cook, his gruff manner extending to his teaching, but in a way I found adorable. Especially when he would absentmindedly press a kiss to my temple or the top of my head as he stormed around in his domain.

One day, Jason took me to see the waterfalls. It was magical, right up until the point he rushed me back home, muttering about a scent and bellowing for Ruarc when we were close enough—which was still quite far—for him to hear.

Being around Ruarc never ceased to amaze me. I loved the way he was constantly touching me; be it running his hands through my hair, holding me in his arms, or pressing his lips to mine. We spent a lot of time around the horses. It was strange to see such a huge man handle the big animals with such gentleness.

Strange but wonderful.

Dinners continued to be a time where everyone's presence was mandatory. It was an affair for the whole family—a family I longed to be a part of with every fiber of my being. Lucien had been absent twice in seven days, but when I asked where he was the subject was quickly changed. I suspected it had something to do with lycan business. Or pack business, as they called it.

Most nights, I sat squished between Ruarc and Jason. My head would eventually land on Ruarc's chest and my feet on Jason's lap. I didn't know how he did it, but Ruarc always made sure it happened that way.

And the nights . . .

Well, I had mixed feelings about the nights. Ruarc barred Jason from my room after nine. It was a rule Jason had accepted with good humor. Suspiciously good humor.

When I asked him about it, he only looked at me with wide eyes and a grin he couldn't quite suppress, and said, "I don't know what you're talking about, love."

I didn't push the matter because I loved the way Ruarc held me at night. It kept the nightmares mostly at bay, although I had woken up a few times with a scream stuck in my throat while Ruarc hovered above me, expression a mix of horror and such fiery rage it immediately soothed the frayed edges of my fear.

The only part of our nightly ritual I was confused about was when we said goodnight. Every single night, without fail, Jason would press a tender, lingering kiss to my lips while we stood outside my door. He never pushed further, never asked for anything more. It could have something to do with the terrifying, impatient presence waiting on the other side—the angry vein in Ruarc's forehead was always pulsating to its own, furious beat whenever Jason reluctantly released me and nudged me inside, which he always had to do because my brain ceased to function due to the warm feelings Jason's kisses inevitably invoked—but I somehow knew he was doing it for me.

Being patient.

And kind.

And playful.

All the qualities Jason's exhibited again and again

Ruarc on the other hand . . . Ruarc made my blood roar. He took his time. Kissing every part of my body—except the ones that ached. There were places I never knew could make me crazy, like the hollow of my elbow. Why did his open-mouthed kisses there make something pull deep inside my belly? But no matter how many breathless sighs escaped me, how much I writhed on the bed, he never smothered the fire. Instead, he stoked it. Made it into a living, being entity that wanted with an acute ache I didn't know how to sate.

Sometimes I wondered if he wanted me to ask for more. Wondered if he was waiting until I was ready to admit what I wanted. But that couldn't be right, could it? Ruarc was a pushy, dominating beast. If he wanted to go further, surely he'd push for more?

A small part of me thought that maybe he just didn't want me, but the other larger part—the part that had come to know and trust the man behind the grumpy mask—knew he was just that type of man. Honorable. Kind. Wanting to make me happy.

But while he was patient with me in that regard, I knew it was just a matter of time until he fell screaming off the cliff of patience and demanded to know the names of my tormentors. I could feel the moment sneaking up on me, closer every day. When the moment came . . .

I can't tell him.

Not until the Hunters were gone.

I had no doubt the guys would go tearing after them if they knew, and then . . . then they'd die.

Lycans or no lycans, the Hunters were too many. And they had weapons. So many weapons.

They're too strong. Too powerful.

Ugly sneers flashed through my mind. A face peering close, too close, while I lay strapped to a table. The sound of a pen scratching against paper; detailing my responses during the latest *session*.

I didn't know if it was possible to stop them. They loomed impossibly big in my mind, impossibly mighty. Indestructible. Invincible. Evil . . .

No, I couldn't tell them. I couldn't tell Ruarc. He'd get himself killed.

You could tell them everything except who. *Everything except* where. *If they don't know who they are or where to find them, they can't hunt them.*

I rejected that possibility with a violence that left me reeling.

No.

They'd push for more.

No.

It wouldn't work.

No.

Just no.

Because behind my desire to protect them, was something ugly. Something dark and slithering and cowardly.

Me.

I couldn't let them see *me, s*ee who I really was, what I'd done. Because then it would be all over. I'd lose them.

And losing them would destroy me. Seeing the warmth in their eyes turn to disgust would break me.

So I pushed it away to the same dark corner of my mind where the Thought lay in wait, and I lived.

For the first time in my life, I truly *lived.*

5 1

LUCIEN

A RAGING INFERNO WAS TEARING MY INSIDES TO PIECES.

It was crumbling.

The cold fortress I had built so painstakingly over the years—laying brick upon brick until the memory of my mother's hissed words; *I wish you had perished in my womb*, no longer phased me—was succumbing to the blazing fire that had started as a kindling only a few weeks ago.

Right around the time we'd taken in a guest.

I blamed *her*. The wench. The galling woman who wouldn't leave me be. Not until my world was left in ashes and my walls lay burning at my feet.

As though she'd heard my thoughts, the vexing creature in question turned around and fixed me with eyes that were deep, brown pools of innocence.

My god, the woman was determined to destroy me.

"Do you . . . do you want one, Lucien?"

Hope's hesitant voice made me arch a brow. Had I not been civil to her for the past week? Had I not gone out of my way to curb my acidic replies and inherent suspicion?

Then why the devil is she still so nervous around me?

Inwardly I seethed, while on the outside my face reflected

only the coldness that had been my entire existence until a few weeks ago.

Did I want the sugary treat she held in the palm of her hand like an offering?

"No, thank you."

My chest grew tight as I watched her face crumble. The nuisance of a woman was atrocious at hiding her emotions, and I refused to admit, even to myself, what a grand prize that would be. A woman unable to lie. A woman whose face would give away even the smallest falsehood. A woman whose only secrets would be those I allowed her to keep.

For someone who traded in lies and secrets, that was a beguiling temptation.

The female turned, giving me her back, and I had to bite back an ugly curse at the flash of pain I caught on her face. Then Ruarc's arm came to rest on her shoulders, offering her the comfort I couldn't.

Again I seethed.

As soon as she wasn't looking, Ruarc sent me a glare. Had he not had his arms full of warm female, a fist would probably be flying at my face. It wouldn't be the first time I took a punch to the face, but long gone were the days I couldn't fight back.

I had fallen prey to the female's strange curse, leaving me once again encased in a chilled armor of my own making.

"Why can't you be a bit nicer to her, mate?" Jason asked.

I shrugged, faking the indifference I used to feel. The indifference I *wanted* to feel. "I fail to see how politely declining hardened sugar is not being nice."

"You know better than that, Lucien."

The devil take him, I did. I knew better than to let pesky distractions such as *feelings* get in the way of my life.

"Should you not hurry along before your little *human* forgets all about you?" I stared pointedly at Ruarc who was taking advantage of Jason's distraction by stealing a kiss from the little pest.

She's ruining my life.

Jason stiffened. "It's fine," he bit out. After a moment, he shook his head and repeated it, this time with less severity and with a slight, cynical grin. "We know how to share. Most times," he added, the grin reaching his eyes.

I wanted to smack it away.

When I didn't reply, Jason shrugged and hurried to catch up with the other two, leaving me behind.

Devil take it, why had I decided to go on yet another shopping trip?

I followed a few paces behind, attempting to ignore the crushing loneliness that threatened to destroy my equilibrium. When Hope turned her face to Jason, a soft smile curling her lips, the hot fury I'd done my best to bury my whole life came rushing back to life. But this time it brought a well of pain to keep it company.

Casting a glance back at me, Hope's soulful eyes widened before showing gentle understanding. For a second I forgot who I was. Forgot who *she* was. All I wanted to do was pull her into my arms and never let go.

It infuriated me.

Drawing from the coldest part of me, I sent her a glacier glare. A tug on my lip told me it was curling. It was an image I had perfected. An image dripping with disdain as my cold, impenetrable wall fed off each emotion I ignored.

Perfect, I thought to myself as her face fell.

The sentiment rang hollow. Where I used to be coldly dispassionate, I now ran hot with emotion. It was all her fault, devil take her!

When we reached our destination—a bookstore Ruarc had insisted the female needed to see—my insides rolled at her blank expression. Below her carefully—if not successfully—constructed indifference, lay a world of hurt feelings. Feelings I, no doubt, was responsible for hurting.

Why couldn't I discontinue my abrasive behavior around her? We'd made a truce, of sorts, and I'd even offered to teach her how to defend herself.

Before I could recall exactly *why* that was necessary and fly into a blind rage, I let the cold wash over me, blanketing my feelings in a layer of imagined snow. From behind the frozen window of my soul, I watched a foreign, traitorous part of myself take control of my body and approach the chit.

"They have drawing supplies at the back," I told her, recalling watching her doodle on pieces of paper when no one was looking.

"Oh." She seemed afraid to meet my eyes; her gaze landing somewhere in the vicinity of my chest. "Thank you."

Two simple words. They shouldn't have had the impact they did, holding the breath in my lungs hostage until I felt as though I was drowning. "You're welcome," I choked out.

Still not raising her skittish gaze, Hope wandered into the store and looked around. Searching for one of the two males who held her affection, no doubt.

Could she ever look at me like that? With the certain knowledge that I would welcome her, would keep her safe?

Don't be foolish.

Half an hour later a brilliant smile was plastered to Hope's full lips. Every few seconds she would glance down into the tiny shopping bag Ruarc had allowed her to carry, and her eyes would sparkle. None of us had the heart to remove it from her tiny, clenched fists. Not when she looked at it with such naked longing.

I recognized her emotion. It was the same curious antici-pation riding me when I had new wood to work with. The feel of the material under my hands, the give and take as I shaped it until its form matched the image in my mind, was one of the few tasks left to me that gave me any type of pleasure.

Perhaps the girl and I had something else in common, after all.

I kept my distance while Ruarc placed the female on one of the many benches decorating the sidewalk in this small town. He stacked all the bags around her, cupped her face in his much-too-big hands, and kissed her. Jason did the same, and then they left, both of them jerking their chins in a gesture I knew meant they wanted me to watch her.

I inclined my head and waited for her inevitable attempt at conversation.

It did not take long.

The feel of her gaze lingering should have been abrasive —like my skin was being scraped by sandpaper—but, as usual, Hope was the exception to the rule. When I felt her eyes on my chest, instead of disgust, I felt . . . pleasantly warm? When she looked higher, hesitating by the annoying throb of my pulse, my first response was one of anticipation.

It lasted for about a second.

Then my teeth clenched in preparation.

When females looked at my face they all swooned. Or stared. Some bit their lips, their eyes heating with promises they believed I'd be pleased to receive. Others were more brazen, daring to put their hands on me, to touch when no permission—nor, to be frank, encouragement—had been given.

It never failed to sour my stomach.

This female, however, could never be predicted. I knew she found me attractive—my mother had often told me the beauty I inherited from my father was the devil's own work —but instead of lust twisting her expression, Hope met my gaze head on. A small, hesitant smile curved her lips, and the openness in her eyes invited conversation.

Not a heated embrace.

Not long, languid kisses.

Not her taste being burned into my mind or the touch of her silky skin branded into my palms.

No. She offered simple conversation. A reprieve from the frozen wastes of my existence, from loneliness and shadow and the numbness I'd come to crave.

Before I could make a fool of myself and throw away a century of perseverance, I turned my back, ignoring the poison ivy that dragged down my throat and scratched against my insides like little swipes of regret.

It was ridiculous. How could such a tiny, strange girl shatter my fortress with a mere look? How was it possible to want to pull her impossibly close and push her far, far away at the same time?

These last few weeks had been hell. Feelings I'd thought long dead to me had risen with a momentum I would have thought impossible a mere month ago.

They should have been dead.

Gone.

Instead, the haunting image of the female's pale, graceful face, the soft swell of her lips, and the tormented pain in her eyes continued to plague me. She was driving me to the brink of destruction, all the while wearing a hesitant smile, acceptance and welcome and *forgiveness* in every gesture, every word.

No matter how cruel my tongue.

I'd meant for my callousness to send her fleeing. Even in the beginning—when suspicion and contempt had ridden me like a stallion possessed—it had not taken her long to unravel the careful construction I'd painstakingly created to protect myself from the very thing now threatening to eat me alive.

And when I had to swallow a growl at the thought of her leaving, I knew I had failed. In every way.

In that moment, a part of me hated her. I hated her for what she had taken from me, and I hated her for the steep cost she would force my brothers to pay in order to keep her.

With a violent shove, I forced the emotions back before they made me weak. It was time to put the girl out of my mind once and for all. After I turned back to check on her. To make sure she was still there.

It wouldn't do to lose the nuisance of a woman before her males returned.

The acrid scent of terror was the first warning. I spun the rest of the way around, all senses on full alert.

My heart seized while I frantically searched for the little human.

There!

Sitting exactly where I'd left her.

It took me several precious seconds to recognize the second warning. Not because my mind was still reeling from the steep drop into panic, but because she was sitting with her face tilted, showing me only half her profile.

And the half I was seeing froze the blood in my veins.

She was devoid of color. Utterly white. Her lips were compressed and bloodless, her cheeks as pale as the first time I'd seen her. One hand fisted in her lap, clenched so tightly the skin was almost translucent with strain.

Every inch of her was shaking.

I leapt across the trashcan standing in my way and shoved a human male to the side in my haste to reach her.

"What is it?" Despite every effort to keep my voice emotionless, it came out a harsh bite.

She didn't respond. It was doubtful she'd even heard me. Her eyes remained unseeing. Glazed over and distant. It was as though she was in another world.

Or seeing something I do not?

And that was the third warning.

Narrowing my eyes, I followed her gaze. The girl was definitely staring at something.

Or someone.

A low warning rumble tumbled from my mouth before I could think. It was the sound of Claiming. Of Challenge. Of pure male idiocy.

After the last time I'd lost control, that day in Hope's bedroom, I'd promised myself I would never utter that ridiculous sound again. But right then I was glad of it. Anyone hearing that sound would cease being a threat and flee. Predator turned prey.

"Where," I asked again, my eyes scanning every inch of the street and every window in every shop. I wanted to throw my head back and howl the song of battle. Wanted to tear down the street and destroy whatever had put that strained, hollow look on her face. The look that made her eyes shut down until she looked less like herself and more like a victim.

For once, I didn't question what she made me feel. There was no time and my Hope was in danger. The only feeling clawing at my throat was the urge to kill. To destroy.

Protect.

Movement caught in the corner of my eye, and I whipped around.

Nothing.

Hope stared down at the ground, a glassy quality to her eyes. "I thought . . . I just . . . never mind." Her voice was soft. Too soft.

"That was not *nothing*," I hissed. "You saw something. Now explain yourself." I didn't care if I sounded like a bastard. If she'd seen what I believed she had seen . . .

Someone will die.

"Lucien," Ruarc snarled, coming around the corner at a sprint. "What the *fuck* did you do?"

I bit back the sharp retort burning a hole through my tongue. "I did nothing. The girl saw something, but she's refusing to answer my questions."

Ruarc's sharp gaze whipped to the annoyingly silent woman in question. "What. Happened?"

A burgeoning respect bloomed at her complete disregard of Ruarc's fury. I had seen grown men cower before that glare. The glare, coupled with his bared teeth and harsh voice . . . the fact that she wasn't intimidated impressed me against my will. A tiny slip of a girl like that should be huddling in a corner somewhere, not defiantly refusing to share with her potential mate.

But the fury burned across Ruarc's face couldn't quite hide his fear. His gaze roamed over every part of her in a near crazed frenzy—checking for injuries and making sure she had remained unharmed.

A male lycan protecting his female was even more dangerous than a starved vampire.

Against my will and better judgment, I followed him down the dark tunnel of protective rage.

"Jason!" I bellowed.

We waited in taut silence. Less than a minute later, Jason came sprinting down the street. His frantic gaze jumped straight to the quivering girl at our side.

The second he reached us, he gathered Hope into a hug. She was stiff, nearly unwilling, standing within the circle of his arms without hugging him back.

"What happened, love?" he asked, brushing a few strands of hair away from her face and tilting her chin up, forcing her to meet his gaze.

"N-nothing."

Ruarc went rigid.

Ruarc stiffened. "Stay here," he ordered Jason.

The look in his eyes was a perfect reflection of my own, churning chaos. He jerked his chin to the left, and I immediately knew what he wanted. Many a night we had hunted under the stars, but it had been a while since our prey was human.

"W-where are you going?"

Ruarc didn't answer.

"D-don't g-go." A hoarse, ragged plea that made fury sprout wings and tear out my back.

Ruarc ground his teeth, but remained silent.

While a feeling I refused to recognize gnawed at my marrow, I closed my eyes and prepared my body.

Three breaths later and the armor was back in place. It had changed; cracks had appeared in the black ice and some places had worn thin. But the armor was still intact.

Sharing one last speaking look with Ruarc, we took off in opposite directions.

Let the hunt begin.

52

HOPE

Did he see me?

My heart raced.

Did he see me?

Chills erupted.

Did he see me?

The question tumbled around in my brain, rattling my skull and pounding against the few remaining barriers in my mind until I was scared the monster inside would tear free.

What if he saw me?

Another chill dragged across my skin. All the fine hairs on my body rose like seaweed in a stormy ocean, and I shivered. Would I ever be able to relax again?

Through the endless cold ravaging my body, I was vaguely aware of the tense silence that filled the car. Ruarc hadn't said a word since he and Lucien came back from wherever they'd run off to. They'd trudged back after thirty minutes, looking defeated and furious all at once.

I should never have let them convince me to come here.

The despairing thought reminded me of my own guilt. If the Hunter had seen me, he would definitely have noticed one of the guys. I could end up being the reason they were targeted.

The reason they were killed.

I'd known going to the next town over was a bad idea, but since I'd refused to tell anyone the truth—to protect them, or at least that's what I told myself—I'd run out of excuses. If I'd known I would see Jan, I would've stayed in bed under the blankets while screaming myself hoarse.

Why was he still so close? He should have moved on by now, unless . . .

Unless he knew I was close.

I clutched at my chest, feeling like it was about to explode.

No. No, if the Hunters even suspected I was close to this area, the whole place would be crawling with Hunters. It had to be a coincidence.

That's all it is. A coincidence.

The car came to a stop, already home.

Home . . .

Could it still be my home after what had almost happened?

I barely noticed when the guys left the car. My door opened, throwing a gust of wind against my neck that raised chills in its wake. The night air was cool, the moon hanging low and heavy, casting creepy shadows in the dark.

"Out," Ruarc growled, his voice nothing more than a knife's edge. He stalked to my side and pulled me out of the car.

"Ruarc . . ." Jason trailed off when Ruarc brushed past him, me struggling to keep up. If not for his palm on my lower back, I'd have fallen.

I stumbled after him, brain on autopilot.

It wasn't until the door closed behind us and I took in the unfamiliar surroundings that my mind re-engaged. "W-where are we?"

The room was spacious, bigger than mine, with high ceilings, two large windows, and a huge bed taking up the back wall. The walls were a stark white, the floor the same. There were no pictures or knick knacks lying about, no excess furniture. A dresser leaned against the wall closest to the door—also white—while a small cabinet rested next to the bed.

The cabinet was black.

Ruarc stood with his back to me facing the windows. His shoulders were tense and high, the muscles of his neck corded. "My room."

My heart clenched. Ruarc had lived here for years, and yet there was nothing in the room that spoke of who he was, of who he'd been.

My gaze was drawn back to the black doors of the small cabinet. Did he keep anything in there? Pictures, mementos, books?

"Who'd you see, Hope?"

I flinched, dared a look.

Molten, silver eyes that burned.

There was no give there. Not anymore. His chin jutted out, his jaw was clenched, the dark slashes of his brows drawn low and angry.

I'd run out of time.

Shifting from foot to foot, I tried to think of an excuse, an answer that would satisfy a man who had reached the end of his patience. I wanted to give him what he wanted, I really did, but the thought of him knowing my deepest, darkest secrets, of him turning away from me when he learned what I truly was . . . It made my insides revolt until I struggled not to empty my stomach all over his pristine, white floors.

Worse, if he went searching for the Hunters, he'd be killed.

I couldn't bear it.

"It . . . it was nothing."

Thin slits of silver raked across my face. The feeling of being exposed was almost enough for me to cross my arms over my chest, to hide from his sight, but I stood still. Something was sneaking into his expression. Something cold and hard and terrifying.

Dread slapped at my face. The skin along my neck pebbled.

"No more lies." A harsh command spoken in a harsh tone.

Sweat coated my palms. "I can't—I don't know—"

"Enough!" The roar was deafening. "Who. Did. You. See?"

Should I tell him? *Could* I tell him? Would he think he was invulnerable just because he was a lycan? Would he try and take on the Hunters?

Would he expect everything, my soul laid bare?

He'll hate me.

Family was everything to him. Everything.

My eyes flickered over him, took in his furrowed brow, the hard, unyielding line of his jaw as he ground his teeth. When his muscles coiled in his shoulders, I knew I'd run out of time.

"Ruarc, I . . ." I took a step closer, my gut knotting when he didn't move. He didn't open his arms, didn't lean toward me like his instincts was urging him closer. All the things he always did . . .

Gone.

He drew in a deep breath, nostrils flaring. "Gotta tell me, Hope. Have to—" He shook his head. "*Need* to protect you. Can't if I don't know the enemy."

Pain bloomed in my chest and threatened to send me crashing to the floor.

He'd sealed his fate. With those words, Ruarc had sealed his fate. I no longer harbored any doubt he'd go after the Hunters. Not after what he'd just said.

"I . . . I can't. Please understand—"

Making a slashing motion through the air, Ruarc cut off

my sentence. There was a hard edge to his next words, "Don't. I can't . . . can't handle the lying. The mistrust." His eyes were cold, hard steel. "I'm done."

The world tilted on its axis and something in my stomach swelled. It swelled and swelled until there was no more space. It twisted. Shrieked. And then it raced up my throat and spewed from my mouth in a single, choked gasp.

"W-what?"

Done? He's . . . done?

It couldn't be real. I couldn't be losing the man I loved —*oh, god, I love him!*—because I was trying to protect him.

Ruarc snarled, a wordless, horrible sound. And when he spoke, it was with that snarl turning each of his words into razors. "You don't trust me."

The air in my lungs froze. Turned to ice. Shredding, tearing, rending ice.

I couldn't breathe.

Reaching out, I tried to touch him. He stepped away, and my heart jerked so hard I thought I might pass out.

I squeezed my eyes shut, willed the tears to retreat. All I wanted was to assure him that it wasn't true. I did trust him, I did. I just didn't want him to die.

Liar.

As if he'd heard me, Ruarc's eyes changed. Still hard— how could they be so hard?—but eaten through by the acid of disillusionment, of contempt.

The crack that went through my heart then was so wide, so deep, it seemed impossible that it could happen so quietly. Surely this kind of pain couldn't be contained to a single body? Contained without a sound?

How could the sound of a broken heart go unheard?

"Ruarc, p-please," I croaked, voice breaking.

He crossed his arms, eyes cold and dead. The way he looked at me made me want to shrivel up and die. I'd never thought he would give up on me. Never thought he would look at me with disgust.

Didn't you, though?

It had been my deepest fear, seeing the expression he wore right then. And *I'd* made it happen. I'd kept my mouth shut and made my worst fear into reality.

All because I was a coward.

When my first tear fell, I could almost see his temper deflating. He hesitated. Opened his mouth. But then his jaw hardened, teeth clenching. He took one step toward me, igniting a hope that stole the breath right out of my lungs, before he shook his head and stormed out.

Without looking back.

I collapsed to the floor, silent tears streaming down my face. I didn't have air to sob. I could barely breathe. My insides rolled, acres of barbed wire cutting through flesh and bone, shredding everything in its path.

It hurt. It hurt with a deep, throbbing ache that built and built and built until I thought my heart might explode.

I rolled onto my back, trying to breathe.

He left me.

Betrayal warred with bitter regret.

How could he leave me?

I should have told him the truth.

But he said he would always *be with me.*

I hadn't been honest.

He's gone. He's gone.

A sob tore from my throat, and I curled into a ball on the floor.

What have I done?

What have I done what have I done what have I done.

Ash

It was becoming harder and harder to stay away from Hope. Her scent was everywhere; lingering in the kitchen where she spent so much time with Ruarc, drifting down the hallway from the room she slept in, invading my mind even while I slept. Whenever I walked into the living room, the smell of her skin was so strong I could taste it in the back of my throat.

It was proving . . . challenging.

Especially when I went cold. When the beast pushed to the surface and craned my neck in search of more of that tantalizing scent.

I had not lost control since the day I was reborn, and I would not do so again. Not while I had a family to protect.

While I tried to keep my mind off the one person who could try my control, Ruarc came bounding down the stairs. Less than a minute later, Jason followed hot on his heels, looking like he wanted to kill.

I did not get involved. There was no need. Even though they fought more than anyone else in our little pack, Ruarc and Jason had always been close. Close in a way that siblings who annoyed the living daylights out of each other were close.

When both of them looked like that, I could only think of one reason for their strife.

Hope.

My wolf stretched inside my mind, its ears perking before lying flat in preparation for a hunt. For once we were in accord. We would seek out the sweet human and make sure she was unharmed.

I found her curled up on Ruarc's floor, cheeks wet with tears. They glistened like a thousand shiny stars upon her moonlit skin, beckoning me closer.

Cold curiosity—the beast pushing, straining, watching.

Hurt? A deep inhale. *No blood.* The first stirrings of anger. *Who?*

I pushed its disjointed thoughts away and felt my human heart ache for her sorrow.

"*Banajaanh*," I whispered, coming to kneel in front of her. "What is wrong?"

Her bony shoulders hunched further as her face sought refuge in her hands. She didn't reply.

The way her shoulders shook disturbed me. Such sadness should not be locked away in silence.

If I had carried any reservations, they fell away in that moment. "Come here, little bird." I placed one arm beneath her knees, the other around her shoulders. Silky skin met my calloused palms, and the flesh on her bare arms pebbled beneath my touch.

I forced back a growl.

When she failed to utter a word of protest, I lifted her into my lap. Disturbed by her slight weight, I hugged her close, acutely aware of her fragile bones and cold, clammy skin. I wanted her strong. Resilient. Even more so than she had needed to be to survive her past and all its horrors.

"You are all right, *banajaanh*," I murmured, stroking her hair. The dark, soft length no longer hung in knotted tangles around her face. It had softened, grown impossibly smooth, framing her pale face in a beautiful mass of silky tresses.

I continued to pet her while I pressed her against my chest, sharing my heat. Every few seconds, silly sounds of comfort and words of reassurance slipped from my mouth. Some were in the old language, and some came out fae.

She stilled for those, basking in the quiet comfort of our magical brethren's lyrical tongue.

For the first time in almost four hundred years, I had no control over what I was saying.

"Do not be sad," I crooned. "I am here."

"I-I ruined e-everything," she hiccuped, face still buried in her hands.

"What do you mean, *banajaanh?*"

626

"H-he h-hates m-me."

Surely she could not be talking about Ruarc? "No one hates you."

Big, tearfilled eyes were all I saw when she lowered her hands. "R-Ruarc does."

Even knowing it could not be true, I had to quell a burst of anger. Ruarc would never hurt her. Not on purpose. "I am sure that's not true." The fleck of bare skin behind her ear looked so inviting. So soft.

A deep need thrummed to life, and my arms tightened around the warm bundle of female in my arms. She lay still. Trusting. Accepting my comfort.

The unyielding predator I had come to accept as a part of myself, borrowed my eyes and studied the alluring creature in our arms. We cocked our head. Saw the trail of wetness on her soft skin. Smelled the pain of loss. Heard the thumping beat of a heart that should never have to feel the bitter touch of anguish.

We watched. We assessed. And then a predatory curiosity prickled at our skull. A sound we did not remember ever making drummed to life in our chest, harsh with disuse, sharp with possession, warm with the blue fire of our inter-woven souls.

Troubled, I pushed the cold presence back and focused on comforting the sad female.

"It is," Hope cried, turning her face into my body. It was disturbing how much pleasure I drew from her trust, how well her tiny frame fit in my lap. "He said . . . he s-said he was d-done."

A flash of anger tightened my shoulders.

Breathe. Find your center.

In control of my emotions—and my body—once again, I dared to glance down. Hope's lips were white with tension, her eyes welling with misery and heart-ache. Every so often she would rock herself, drawing arms and legs as close to herself as possible, using the natural motion to bring her hair forward and blocking her face from my sight.

Signs of shame.

I knew them only too well.

"I am sure he did not mean that he was done with you, *banajaanh*." I pulled her hair aside, crushing the impulse to wrap it around my wrist, pull her head back, and mark her neck. "Tell me what happened."

She blanched. "It was my fault."

"What was your fault?"

"I . . . I didn't tell him. Didn't trust him enough." Her breath hitched. "When he left . . . the look on his face . . ."

Oh, my sweet, little human.

She trusted Ruarc. I had seen them together often enough to be sure. It was not Ruarc she did not trust, but herself.

Of course, my self-loathing brother would not see it that way. He would have been tormented by his perceived failure, torturing himself with all the ways he might lose her should he fail again—to protect her, to hunt down those responsible for putting nightmares in her eyes. Whatever Hope thought she had seen on his face would have been nothing more than a reflection of his feelings for himself.

I took a few deep breaths—forcing the cold intellect of the predator further away in favor of the warmth of the earth, of nature—and reflected on the situation. Ruarc would no doubt sort everything out when he was back. Meanwhile Hope would hurt. There was no way around it. No matter how much I wanted to take away her pain, our best chance to keep her—

When had I decided to keep her?

At once my skin tightened and my gums itched. A fiery storm brewed in my center, forcing me to push aside thoughts of letting her go before my control snapped.

Am I even capable of caring for yet another person? To be responsible for their wellbeing and safety?

I had failed so many times in the past. In fact, my biggest failure had cost me everything. Even myself. The thought of watching another person slip through my fingers sent daggers of dread scraping over old wounds and sparked a fury I could not afford to let loose.

"Whatever you saw, Hope, was not aimed at you," I finally said, tucking the hair she kept bringing forward behind her ear. "Ruarc, he . . . struggles." I paused, searching for the right words. "I know he told you about his past, but did you know you are the only one he has ever told—except me?"

Wide eyes grew impossibly wider. "Really?"

I nodded. "He only told me because it is necessary for a pack to know each other's weaknesses, especially a pack as small as ours. He gave me his permission to tell the others, but has never talked about it with anyone else. The fact that he told you speaks volumes."

Her lush lower lip wobbled. "I still hurt him," she said quietly. "He doesn't want me anymore."

Sudden violent wrath rose on wings tipped with claws. They beat at my ribs, fighting against the tight bonds I forced upon them. The churning, chilled anger made my eye twitch.

A misunderstanding. Only a misunderstanding.

I looked down at the female in my arms. At that moment she seemed so young. Too young to have experienced all the horrible things she kept locked inside her mind. There was so much she needed to know. Her life had barely begun and lacked in vital experiences.

Who were we to want her as our mate when she had yet to live? To unequivocally bind her life to ours until the day we died would be the height of unfairness.

Of cruelty.

But despite all that, the thought of forcing her away never entered my mind.

It was hard to concentrate with her body pressed up against mine like this, with vulnerability shining in her beautiful, brown eyes. But the sadness I felt radiating off her in waves was more disturbing than any thought I could conjure. So I tilted her chin up to meet my gaze and attempted to make her understand. "Ruarc believes himself to be unworthy."

An indignant gasp let me know Hope did not agree. Before she could protest, I held up a hand. "We both know that's not the case, but in this instance it only matters what Ruarc believes. You have seen him angry, you know he has a volatile temper, and that, coupled with his sheer size and intimidating looks, has scared away more people than you would believe."

She rubbed the heel of her hand against her chest, a pained expression painting her face sallow. I could no more stop my arms from tightening around her than I could cease my next heartbeat. The urge to rub my scent over every inch of exposed—and clothed—skin pushed against my carefully contained control. It had been years since I was this close to breaking.

To letting go.

Shaking my head, I settled for drawing her scent as far into my lungs as I could. "It is likely Ruarc thinks he has failed you." I struggled to keep my voice even. "That, in you not trusting him, he has proven himself unable to take care of you."

"But . . . that's not true," she cried, pushing against my chest until she could see my face. "He must know that isn't true!"

"I know that, and you know that. He does not."

"H-how do I fix it?"

"You wait," I replied. "Wait for him to calm down, and then you can talk. About everything."

A tear trailed down her cheek, stabbing at my chest. "O-okay."

"Between you and me," I started, hugging her closer, "I believe he may fear becoming like his sire."

"That's absurd! His . . . his *sire* was an evil tyrant. Ruarc is kind and protective and gentle!"

I smiled. "You are right."

Some of the tension seeped out of her, and she slumped against me. Once or twice, she peeked up, sorrow and confusion occasionally receding to give way to a curiosity, a warmth that I prayed would grow for her as it had grown for me.

I spent the next few minutes concentrating on soothing her sorrow when it rose, and encouraging her curiosity when the sorrow ebbed. Her gaze was often drawn to my face, and by pretending I did not notice, she allowed it to linger.

Once she had looked her fill, I stroked a finger across her cheekbones, following the lines of her heart-shaped face down to her pointed chin—she had taken to sticking it out in a stubborn manner, mimicking Ruarc, when she felt particularly strongly about something—and across her full lips.

Her scent, the scent I could never truly escape, filled me with every breath.

It was almost . . . peaceful.

For a moment in time, all of the heavy responsibilities that weighed me down felt somehow lighter. The ever-present hollowness in my gut filled with her light. Her energy. The very essence that was Hope.

Hope. What a fitting name.

I closed my eyes and looked inward; to the burnt pile of ashes that was the man I used to be. There, buried under the crumbled coals, I noticed something new. A tiny, green plant sprouting up from the charred wasteland, reaching for the sky.

It was terrifying.

Opening my heart meant risking everything I had built. It

meant putting everyone's lives in danger. If I dared to take the bird with the broken wings as my mate and someone tried to take her from me . . .

I would unleash my beast upon the world and break the promise I had made on that fateful day I became the monster my mother's people had accused me of being.

And this time, there would be no coming back.

53

RUARC

MY WORLD HAD NARROWED DOWN TO TWO PINPRICKS OF BLACK light. Everything was gray. Gray and desolate and tinged with a dangerous, reddish hue.

I raced down the stairs, jumping the last three and rushing outside.

My skin crawled with the need to Change. To run. To fight. To fucking hunch over and clutch at the shredded remains of my heart.

Claws punched out from the tip of my fingers.

The door rattled on the hinges behind me from the force I'd used to slam it shut.

Not enough.

Aggression bled through the pain slashing at my insides.

Fangs exploded from my gums.

The look on my female's face . . .

I closed my eyes.

Pure devastation.

My claws dug into any flesh it could find. My thighs, my palms, my biceps.

Blood slipped down my arms.

Wanted to go to her. Comfort her. But what peace could I give her when she didn't trust me?

Not good enough for her.

I stumbled away from the driveway, cut across the front lawn, and headed toward the forest.

Couldn't help her. Couldn't ward off her demons or slay her enemies. Whoever hunted her, if they found her . . .

"God-fucking-dammit!" I roared to the sky and took off into the woods.

Felt unstable. Like the world had gone sideways and I no longer knew which side was up.

Helpless.

The grueling pace made stealth impossible, and several critters fled in my wake. Needed my body to hurt. To match the cracks in my heart and the misery reflected in Hope's wounded eyes.

I'd hurt her. I'd fucking hurt her.

My hands curled until my claws tore deep gouges into my palm.

Yeah, I'd been angry, and yeah, I'd been short. But hadn't been cruel. Hadn't said anything to count for her expression of anguish.

Why'd *she* looked so sad? *I* was the one who'd left with knives stabbing at my chest. *I* was the male unable to garner his female's trust. I'd failed her.

Was she scared of me? Was that it?

All females are scared of you, you big brute.

Wanted to protect her. Love her. Keep her safe.

Slay her enemies, torture her tormentors, utterly destroy anyone who's ever hurt her by ripping them apart, small piece by small piece.

Disgusted, kicked at the nearest tree.

The thick trunk fractured, tilting to the side with a groan, then thundering into the earth with a devastating *crack*.

Can't even control your temper.

No wonder she feared me.

A howl of challenge pierced through the thick night. I veered to the right. Stopped. Tipped my head to the side. Listened.

Another howl.

A sliver of moonlight peeked from behind stormy clouds, casting shadows off the gnarled oak trees separating me from a good fight.

Throwing my head back, I roared a challenge of my own.

The forest went utterly quiet, critters hiding and insects reeling.

I spun around and headed back the direction I'd come, knocking down smaller trees and using my claw-tipped fingers to destroy any obstacles in my way.

Hope's teary eyes flashed through my mind.

I slashed at a nearby tree.

The urge to go to her, to soothe her, crashed against my fury like unrelenting waves of thunder.

Lightning sparked, and my jaw elongated to make room for all the big, sharp teeth shooting from my gums.

Have to go to her!

Can't. She doesn't trust you. Doesn't want you there.

When I finally spotted the wolf who dared challenge me, I didn't hesitate. I ripped off my clothes while the ground sped closer, changing shapes as easily as I changed a shirt.

Once I was down on all fours, standing on paws instead of feet, I bared my teeth at the wolf facing me.

His lips peeled back, a snarl tearing through the small space between.

It was all I needed.

I threw myself at him, catching a tuft of gray and brown fur between my teeth.

He danced away. I followed. He turned. I lunged.

Teeth and claws flashed. Dark growls and furious snarls rent the air. Speckles of bright-red blood glinted in the few beams of moonlight penetrating the thick canopy of leaves above us.

After several minutes, we broke apart. Circled.

Jason's ears lay flat against his skull, offering no tell to reveal his next move.

I watched. Waited. There. A slight tension in his hind-leg.

Got you.

I turned, prepared for the attack. We collided with a boom of sound. Would've been deafening if my ears hadn't been pounding with the roar of savage rage.

Jason *dared* attack me. *Dared* challenge me for what was mine?

A savage snarl ripped loose, and I threw my whole body forward. His jaw snapped closed, inches from my throat, and I saw red.

Seconds later, I had him pinned on his back, my jaws clamped around his neck.

A searing pain in my side told me his back claws had found purchase against my ribs.

I gave him a violent shake. He lost his grip. I squeezed harder. He whined.

The fight was over.

Too damned fast!

I shook with unleashed violence, barely able to pry my jaws apart long enough to let him go. While he stumbled away—shaking his head and sneezing twice—I changed back into my human skin and waited for him to do the same.

Not patiently. Seething.

"You shithead," Jason snarled. He'd clamped a hand over the bleeding in his neck. "Do you know what you did?"

Instead of making me angry, his accusation slumped my shoulders. "Doesn't trust me, Jason. Won't tell me anything."

"So you break her heart?" he yelled.

My eyes narrowed. "Break *her* heart?"

Jason lifted his hand, cursed at the blood still flowing, and glared at me. "Telling her you are done with her has that effect," he snapped.

I stilled. "What?"

He shot me a suspicious glare. "You told her you were done. She's crying her eyes out right now. Grieving." He began pacing. "Probably wondering what this means with her position with the rest of us."

While I tried to digest that ridiculous claim—Jason pointed a shaking finger at me, ignoring the blood pouring from his wound. "If she leaves because of this, I *will* follow her."

My temper ignited. "Leave?" I hissed. My hand shot out, grabbed Jason by the neck, and squeezed. "Explain."

Even though I was cutting off his air supply, the pup had the nerve to frown at me. "You dumped her, Ruarc. She thinks you are over."

Suddenly my world went red. My vision swam, no longer gray but bathed in the color of warm, wet blood.

Done with her? She thinks we are over?

I threw Jason to the ground.

Twisted rage prodded at my beast. It came, ready to battle, but there was no one to fight.

Nothing made sense. Everything burned. Burned with a white hot rage. Burned with a soul-tearing pain.

Not only didn't she trust me, she didn't want to be with me?

She wants to leave?

"Tough shit," I snarled and stalked away.

Jason's strangled voice yelled something, but I was too far gone to make sense of the words.

I ignored the agony piercing my heart and focused on the anger. She thought she could get rid of me?

Never!

Once I got my hands on her she would never doubt she belonged to anyone but me ever again.

HOPE

After I finally pulled myself back together, I became acutely aware of where I was sitting.

"Uhm, Ash?"

"Mhm?"

"You can let me up now."

Ash captured me with his gaze, and I . . . I froze. The look in his intense, blue eyes stopped my heart between one beat and the next. Fear and heat mixed in my chest like the finest powder, leaving me unable to tell one from the other.

I had no words for the cold intellect watching me from Ash's eyes. It was him, but still . . . not.

Lethal.

Violent.

Inflexible.

I knew then that I was seeing the part of him he kept locked away from the world. The part that was responsible for the tightly reined control, the leashed danger, the deceptive *stillness* that always accompanying the quiet male.

Terror beat against my chest while the coldly calculating predator looked down at me. The fear was as old as time itself; instinctual and immediate. But the attraction flaring to life inside me was anything but.

It was like that deadly presence spoke to the monster inside me, stroked its hide in a way *I* could feel. As though we were one.

And as quickly as that ancient power had appeared, it vanished. And only Ash remained.

I shuddered, flashes of heat and ice stroking up my sides.

Ash didn't seem to notice. "Yes." He shook his head and flashed a wry smile. "I apologize."

The change from terrifying predator to quiet, serious man would have been hard enough, but when you threw in a smile as well?

I couldn't look away. When he smiled he seemed so much younger. Freer. Like whatever heavy burdens he carried were brushed off and just floated away.

He caught me staring and my cheeks heated under his scrutiny, those piercing eyes seeing too much.

"You don't have to apologize," I murmured, using my hair to shield my face from his assessing gaze. "You were wonderful. And I repaid you by crying all over your nice shirt."

Ash rose and helped me to my feet. "Any time, *banajaanh*," he said, the endearment sweeping through me like a warm summer breeze. "Although I should hope you have no more occasions to cry."

"Me too." But if I couldn't fix things with Ruarc, I knew I would be crying my eyes out for days to come.

You have to tell him. Ruarc deserves to know. He deserves to have your trust.

There was no longer any choice. I couldn't let him believe those terrible things. Couldn't let him think he was anything like his father when he was the most affectionate, gentle, furiously protective man I'd ever known.

And I'd already lost him. He would stay lost unless he knew the truth.

And probably once he does, too, but what choice do I have?

It wasn't as though I could lose him twice.

"Hope!" A bellow so loud it vibrated beneath my feet.

My eyes widened with shock—and maybe a hint of fear—and darted to Ash. "But . . ." What was I trying to say?

Ash glanced from the door to my face. "I think it is time for you and Ruarc to have that talk." His eyes darkened until they resembled the stormy blue of a tempest sea. "If he scares you tell him to back off. If you need help, call out. One of us will be there."

Then he left.

A few seconds later, the door flew open and bounced against the wall with a loud crack.

"Hope." A growl, a warning, a snarl—all rolled up into one, ominous admonishment.

He stalked across the room. The glow in his silver eyes turned nearly incandescent. Flecks of red dust, almost like paint, flaked off his arms and drifted to the floor. His chest was bare, a solid wall of muscle, of smooth flesh marred only by a few raised scars.

My mouth went dry.

A creak sounded in the hall, and Ruarc spun around and threw himself at the door, closing it with so much force a piece of wood splintered off.

I stared at the sliver of wood, unable to tear my eyes away. In the back of my mind I was aware of Ruarc's raging presence, his fury like a cape billowing behind his body as he moved. But that sliver of wood . . .

It reminded me of the feeling I'd gotten when Ruarc had dumped me. Only instead of a sliver, it had felt like half my heart had fallen away.

While I was blinking down at the stupid piece of ruined door, my feet left the floor, and the woodsy smell of pine cones and warm, angry male surrounded me. Strong hands were wrapped around my ribs, holding me effortlessly in the air and reminding me once again how very strong Ruarc was. His furious, silver eyes bored into me, black slashing brows lowered in an impressive scowl.

I understood his anger. I'd been wrong to hide from him, to withhold my trust. My only excuse was fear.

Fear of seeing caring turn to contempt.

Fear of seeing desire turn to disgust.

Fear of seeing my reflection in his eyes and knowing he hated me as much as I hated myself.

I wanted him back, and to have any hope of achieving that, maybe I had to trust him enough to believe he wouldn't go charging into the Hunters' lair half-cocked, but instead listen to me when I told him it couldn't be done. Not by him—never by him, never by any of them, if I had anything to say about it.

And if he doesn't listen, I'll just not tell him where they are. Or what they call themselves.

Hoping confessing my secrets would bring him back to me, I opened my mouth. "Ruarc, I—"

"Not another word," he interrupted in a voice made of gravel and rough leather.

His head shot forward and his lips captured mine in a desperate kiss. No, not a kiss, a mash of lips, teeth and tongue. A war where victory came hard won, pleasure the ultimate price.

I moaned, dragging an answering groan from Ruarc's chest.

Liquid fire flowed through my veins. Burning.

My toes curled.

Rough, so rough, he grabbed my hair and dragged my head back, exposing the long line of my neck to his mercy.

A nest of fluttering birds danced in my stomach, batting their wings and making me soar. My sex clenched in response to the delicious waves of heat rushing from my neck down my chest, swirling in my belly before traveling down my inner thighs.

No thoughts crossed my mind save the feelings he tore from me with his frantic assault.

Whisker rubbed over my skin. Teeth nipped at warm flesh. His mouth found mine, our tongues battling.

I grabbed his shoulders and dug my nails into hard muscle.

When he walked us backward and fell down on the bed, twisting in the air so I landed on his chest, nothing but pleasure flooded my body. When his hot mouth moved to my chin, his tongue darting lower to lick over my pulse, I felt like I was coming out of my skin.

I writhed above him, wild with the frenzy building in my core.

A sharp pain woke my drugged mind. I noted the achy spot between my neck and shoulder, the slight sting where his teeth had marked me. But as soon as his tongue came out to soothe the abused flesh, dazed pleasure swamped my senses and left my brain muddled.

"My Hope, *mo chridhe*, my heart," he growled, the possessive sound muffled against my neck. With a quick twist I was beneath him. The soft mattress cradled my back while Ruarc hovered above me, using his elbows to hold most of his weight.

My arms snaked around his neck, pulling him down so I could taste his lips again. I wanted more of his drugging kisses. More of the ferocious need I could feel clawing at my skin.

I needed.

I ached.

I burned.

And his taste . . . warm, spicy, male.

Angry. Fiery. Possessive.

Another groan tore from his throat, this time accompanied by a growl that sounded half feral. He attacked my lips with renewed vigor, until every nerve in my body was on fire. Every muscle tense with anticipation, with want.

"Mine," he growled and bit the other side of my neck.

This time there was no pain, only a soaring elation that swept through my soul, soothing ragged wounds and plugging the holes that had been cut out by past trauma.

Something inside me perked up. A whispering, dark voice

floating through my head, purring words like 'mate' and 'worthy male' and 'want. Always *want*.

My lower body arched up, a whimper leaving me as I felt the hard, hot length of him against my center.

Ruarc tore his mouth away, silver eyes flashing. "Too soon." The statement was a hoarse, growl, dragging over my skin in a fervent caress.

Too soon?

The words made no sense to my befuddled mind. I had waited so long for this. For a male like Ruarc.

Shaking my head, I arched my spine and rubbed myself against the delicious hardness in his pants.

A feverish snarl reverberated in my skull, and the Ruarc's big palm cupped my sex. "This what you want?" he growled. He firmed his hold, pressing the heel of his palm against me, branding me with his touch.

My voice deserted me. All I could do was nod as I stared up at him.

Ruarc. *My* Ruarc.

The possessive thoughts must have shown in my eyes— Ruarc's gaze darkened and his lips drew back in a feral smile. "*Mine*!" He stared me into submission, then used his claws to rip my shirt, to tear my pants and underwear. Leaving me bare.

This time there was no shame. His eyes remained locked on mine, never dipping down to glance at the vulnerable flesh he'd exposed.

I couldn't look away. His face was a stark mask of need, of want, a furious, barren landscape where the only softness was his lips.

They trailed down my body. Teeth nipped at the lower curve of my breast.

I gasped.

A dark growl, his tongue curling around my nipple. Licking. Sucking. Creating a burning line of pleasure that shot from the hardened tip down to my core.

His teeth scraped over it.

My breath got trapped in the vicinity of my throat.

Every tug, every lick, every bite caused an answering spasm between my legs, until I felt lightheaded from the delicious sensations.

He left my breasts and dragged the bristles on his jaw down my body. His tongue dipped into the indentation of my navel, startling a breathless giggle out of me.

His head shot up with a darkly satisfied expression.

That image burned into my soul; the beauty of my wild, untamed Ruarc—his shoulder-length black hair falling around his face like a dark, fallen angel, teeth bared in a feral grimace of want and need, looking so handsome and possessive and *wild*.

A moan slipped between my parted lips, and Ruarc answered with a sound I'd never heard before; part snarl, part groan—dark and violent and so arousing I squirmed.

He moved, mouth fastening on the flesh right above my pelvis.

"Oh!" My hips jerked off the bed. I couldn't speak, couldn't think, couldn't *exist* a second longer without Ruarc's hard body sliding against me.

I wanted to ask him what he was doing—why his mouth was so close to *there*—but before I could, his hand was back on my naked sex, cupping, his thumb spreading the lips and—

My mind went blank.

"So hot," he growled, feral need ablaze in an ocean of silver.

I couldn't answer.

"Gonna taste you. Not stopping until you scream for me."

The muscles in my thighs tried to squeeze together, but Ruarc was between them.

All I could do was feel. Feel as he moved his hands under my thighs. Feel as he spread my legs and leaned in, warm breath making me moan. Feel as he pressed a hot, open-mouthed kiss to the most private part of me.

My stomach contracted with shock and pleasure, his tongue sweeping across my aching flesh. My world shrank and the edges of my vision swam as Ruarc ignited a firestorm of dark, insatiable *need*.

My hands shot forward of their own volition, grabbing two chunks of Ruarc's silky hair.

At my touch, a savage growl erupted from the big male, the vibrations against my core twisting me until I thought I would implode.

"Mine!" he snarled, then his lips closed around a hard pebble of flesh—flesh I'd never been aware of before this moment—and I almost shot off the bed. He tongued the hard nub, used his lips around it, on it, everywhere.

I grabbed on to his shoulders, raking my nails down the hard muscle, catching at his biceps.

It was too much. His mouth . . . dear god, his mouth . . .

He devoured me.

There was no finesse to his attack, no carefully constructed plan. He licked, sucked and nibbled on every part of me, hungrily attacking my core with a desperate savagery that was beautiful in its own way. One moment he licked around the center, teasing that hard pebble that suddenly ruled my universe. The next, he sucked one of my inner lips all the way into his mouth, groaning when my body clenched around the finger he used to tease my opening. The finger plunged deeper inside, hitting a spot that made me see stars.

Then he removed his finger and replace it with his tongue, thrusting in an age-old rhythm my body recognized, one that set fire to every nerve.

His tongue stayed inside me, licking and licking until I

wondered if his goal was simply to taste as much of me as he could.

"So fucking sweet," he groaned and plunged his tongue back into my core.

My hips jerked, my mouth opened on a long, loud wail.

Ruarc replaced his tongue with a thick finger and used his mouth to torture the hard pebble of flesh that made my legs shoot off the bed and my back arch as though I was a puppet on a taut, enrapturing string.

Gasps and moans tore out of my throat, making me hoarse with the pleasure I was voicing.

Ruarc sucked, and I cried out.

He licked, and I threw my head back and nearly wept.

He stroked and nibbled and ate, and I was dying, dying dying . . .

Tight. My stomach was so tight. Alive with excitement. Pleasure.

My legs started to shake, my nails dug into Ruarc's skin, my lungs contracted. I couldn't breathe, couldn't speak, couldn't give sound to the screams trapped deep inside.

I looked down at Ruarc, his face buried between my legs while his molten, silver eyes were fixed on me. The ferocious intent written on his face, the wildness burning in his eyes, the way his finger rubbed at the spot inside me, his mouth sucking on that hard nub, his claws digging into my hip, the savage growl vibrating against me . . .

Everything clenched. Deep. Hard. Unforgiving.

My heart stopped. Restarted. Raced. And finally my lungs filled with air.

I couldn't stop the scream that ripped from somewhere deep within when Ruarc once again concentrated on the little piece of flesh between my legs. He sucked it into his mouth and grazing it with his teeth.

I convulsed, arms and legs shaking with bone-deep pleasure. It streamed through my body, pulsating out from the place Ruarc was *still* licking.

Everything went dark.

Once it was over, after I'd experienced every color in the rainbow like a physical caress, I collapsed against the mattress.

My eyes felt so heavy. I couldn't open them. Couldn't even blink when Ruarc's powerful body landed next to me. Or when his arms came around me, pulling me into his warmth, cocooning me in safety as my sated body was pulled down into the dark abyss of sleep.

The last thing I heard was a deep, satisfied growl, "*Mine.*"

I slept.

54

HOPE

The first few minutes after I woke up from my pleasure-induced sleep were filled with blushes, stammers and general awkwardness.

By me, not by Ruarc.

Ruarc looked as comfortable as he could possibly be. One muscular arm supported his weight as he leaned over me, a lazy, self-satisfied smile peeling his lips back from his teeth.

My breath caught.

"Sleep well?" he asked in a rough, gravelly voice, sending shivers of remembered pleasure down my spine.

"No more running away," he growled, chin lowered to his chest. Glaring.

My mouth dropped open. "But . . ." Then my jaw clenched as indignant anger flared to life. "*You* left *me!*"

Ruarc pounced. He caged me beneath him, lowering his head until our noses brushed. "*Never!*" he snarled.

"But you did! Y-you said you were d-done—" My voice broke.

A large hand cupped my chin. "*Mo chridhe*, my heart," Ruarc muttered. He looked at me with such a tender expression it brought tears to my eyes. "Didn't mean it like that. Could never be done with *you*."

I sniffled. "Then what did you mean?"

He shook his head, a thousand emotions glittering in his eyes. "Meant the conversation. I was done with it. Too angry." He stared down at me, trailing a finger after the tear that escaped. Frowned. "Never meant to hurt you. Not good with words." His frown deepened, and then he leaned down and kissed away another stray tear. "I'm sorry."

"I'm sorry too, Ruarc. I should have told you what you wanted to know. In fact . . ." I took a deep breath, steeling myself for what was to come. "I want to tell you everything. I trust you, Ruarc and I—"

He swooped down and captured me in a hard kiss. For a moment, he was all I could feel, his scent all I could smell, the possessive snarls spilling out of him all I could hear. And then his lips gentled, pressed to the corner of my mouth, my cheek, brushing across my eyelids.

When he pulled back and gazed down at me, his eyes shone with emotions I couldn't read, but I found myself wishing with my whole heart that one of them was love. I wanted him to love me the way I loved him. Thoroughly, and without restraint.

I didn't even know when I'd started loving him, but I knew it was a feeling that would never go away.

"All that I am is yours," he whispered against my lips, a quiet intensity to his words.

As if pulled from the deepest recesses of my soul, the urge to answer in kind pushed at my throat. Only I didn't know the correct words, so I settled for a simple, "And I'm yours."

The beginning of something, the first flutters of a connection, clicked into place. A bond. Held together by a couple of fragile, silver threads. Instinctively, I knew they could become so much more; a bond that could never be broken.

649

Unless it was torn apart before it fully formed.

Ruarc squeezed his eyes closed. When he opened them again, the joy I saw made my heart skip a beat. He spun us around so I was on top and hugged me with arms that shook, fierce words of possession and affection tumbling from his lips.

I hugged him back as hard as I could and basked in his closeness. My Ruarc. My protector. My warrior. My love.

We lay like that for at least thirty minutes. The steady beat of his heart pulled me further down into his embrace. He couldn't stop touching me, sweeping a palm from my shoulders down to the curve of my back, rubbing his nose against my neck, burying his hands in my hair.

And I touched him right back. He was so strong, my Ruarc. Hard all over. Strength in every line of his body, in his wide chest and broad shoulders, in the arms that held me so tightly, in the hands that touched me so gently.

I felt safe. Safe and loved.

But of course, he couldn't love me until he knew who I really was.

I had to tell him about my past.

Sensing the moment had come, Ruarc cupped my face and brushed his thumb over my lips. Then he lay back down and waited.

"I . . . I don't really know where to start," I began, "but I guess it started when—"

Banging at the door interrupted my confession.

Ruarc glared at the sound, looking like he wanted nothing more than to finish the job he started last night when a piece of the door had splintered under the force of his anger. Grumbling under his breath, he made sure the blanket covered all of me and muttered a dark, "Come."

Ash walked in. His long, black hair was pulled back, intricate braids following the lines of his temple all the way back to the leather throng holding the silky mass. One of the braids ended in a silver ring, another had a feather woven into the knot.

He looked like a warrior prepared for battle.

He cleared his throat, drawing my eyes to his face. Tension surrounded the grim line of his mouth and his eyes were shuttered. "We have a problem."

Ruarc sat up and pulled me between his legs, careful to keep me covered. "What is it?"

"We have been called to the assembly." Ash's sharp gaze turned to me. "Hope is to join us."

To be continued

GLOSSARY

<u>Scottish Gaelic</u>

- *A chuisle* - The endearment has grown to mean my dear/my love. But it comes from *mo chuisle* which directly translated means "my pulse." The thing that keeps my blood flowing through my veins, keeps me alive.
- *mo chridhe* - my heart
- *m'eudail* - my darling, my dear

<u>Ojibwe/Ojibwa</u>

- *Niijikiwenh* - brother
- *Banajaanh* - little bird/baby bird/fledgling

<u>Fae</u>

- *Lithbhár* - directly translated it means 'blodless' - It's a harsh insult among lycans and have evolved to mean someone who is the worst sort of coward.
- *Dè cháiní Bháan Mahír* - Children of the white wolf

653

Want more backstory on the guys?

Become part of my Elite Readers Newsletter and receive a secret scene from Ash's youth!

As a member of my Elite Readers Newsletter, you will be notified of my new releases, be the first to see cover reveals, and you'll get snippets and excerpts from works in progress as well as deleted scenes sent straight to your inbox!

Type this link into your internet browser to sign up:
https://www.subscribepage.com/ascension

Enjoy this book? You can make a big difference

Reviews are one of the most important things for an author. They help get attention for our books, and often a review can be the reason why a reader decides to give an author a chance or not. Being a brand new author, I depend on reviews and word of mouth to get my book-baby out there, and though I don't have the power of a publishing house behind me, I have something much better…

You!

A reader who made it to the end of this long, loooong book, committing time and energy to live, for a moment, in Hope's world—even though there are so many other amazing books out there, so many other worlds to explore.

It would mean the world to me if you could spend just a few minutes leaving a review (it can be as short as you want, even one sentence makes a difference) on this book's Amazon page.

Thank you very much!

.

ACKNOWLEDGMENTS

Are you still reading? If you are, then I dedicate my first acknowledgment to you, my reader. Without you, my story would be hidden away in some drawer (and on multiple hard drives because I'm an anxious stressmuffin—according to my hubs) never to see the light of day. I'd still write—for how could I stop?—but it would never be more than a hobby, something I'd do for myself in the few minutes I manage scrape together ever day. But with more people like you, the one who reads to the end, not wanting to miss a single word, I may one day be able to write full time and share with you all the stories waiting to be put to paper. So thank you, dear reader. From the bottom of my heart, thank you for reading my book.

And to the rest of people who made this book possible . . .

First, my mom. You instilled a love of reading in me from a very young age. You read hundreds of books to me, and when your voice grew hoarse and you couldn't go on, you encouraged me to learn to read so that I wouldn't have to wait for you to recover.

So I did.

Your unwavering love, support, and encouragement helped me get where I am today. Without you, I would not be an author, I would barely even be a person. So thank you for everything, and thank you for always telling me to follow my dreams.

Besse, I wish you were still here. I can never thank you enough for everything you've done for me, everything you've brought into my life. Not a day goes by where I don't miss you.

Thank you Sarah, my best friend, my sister in all ways that counts. You introduced me to paranormal romance, and I've been hooked ever since. Thank you for being there for me, always, and for flying out this summer when grief kept me from reaching out. You'll never know what it meant to me.

Serena and Reggie… I don't know what to say other than thank you. You're amazing, and I wouldn't be here without your love and support and amazing ability to turn my full on sob-fest into laughter. I never get tired of talking to you guys, and you're basically stuck with me for life. I'm a barnacle and you've been barnacled. Ericacled? Anyway, you're both too talented for your own good and I can't wait to see where this journey takes you both!

Penelope, you kicked my ass! Seriously, your (occasionally) snarky feedback and blunt advice made me a better writer (though probably not as good as you'd like). Your friendship has made me laugh more times than I can count, and though you often need a good slap (which I'm always happy to provide), you're a great friend and an amazing writer! Can't wait for your book to be done!

Maya, thank you for your friendship, laughs, the peens, and my first ever swag pack! You rock and your books rock too! Waiting quite impatiently for the next one to come out…

And my lovely betas…

Without you, this book would probably be a hot mess! Charlotte, Leanne R, Leopardwolf, Lori, Lesley, Katy K, Katy J, Kelly, Mikayla, Leanne A, and Hannah… Thank you! Not only did you help me improve my book, you helped me keep going when I felt like quitting. Your encouragement, friendship, and the way you rooted for me are all huge reasons this book made it off my harddrive and onto Amazon. Seriously, you guys are amazing and I couldn't have done it without you!

Thank you to my cover artist, Ravenborn Design, for designing a cover I fell in love with, and for being patient, talented, and just an overall gem!

And Candice, you were the first to welcome me into the author world. You helped me start a group, you answered all my inane questions, and you were so kind and supportive and encouraging that, for the first time, I thought 'I can do this'. Thank you for your support and friendship—you've made a difference.

Michelle at Rascon Revisions, thank you for answering all my questions and your help with a few of the more unruly scenes!

And last but never least, my husband. Thank you for your relentless support, your never-ending quest to take care of me and make sure I'm happy, for all the dinners you've cooked, all the love you've given me, all the massages, all the kisses and hugs and snuggles. And thank you for always thinking I'm the best, even when I'm clearly a lunatic, haha! Without you, this book would never have happened.

I love you.

ABOUT THE AUTHOR

Erica Woods is an animal loving, coffee-addicted, chocoholic who lives in Norway with two fur babies of the purring variety and a hubs of the supporting, slightly growly variety.

When she's not writing (which is seldom) she can be found clinging to her hubby like a koala bear (yes, she's needy) with a book in one hand and some kind of snack (most likely chocolate) in the other.

Besides being crazy about animals and obsessed with all things romance, Erica likes to be near the ocean, draw, fantasize about life on foreign planets, and tease her hubby until he chases her around the house while she squeals.

Fun times.

Want to know more about Erica? Visit her website or join her reader group!

Website: Ericawoods.net

Reader group: Into the Woods - An Erica Woods Reader Group

Made in the USA
Coppell, TX
09 April 2021

53153801R00388